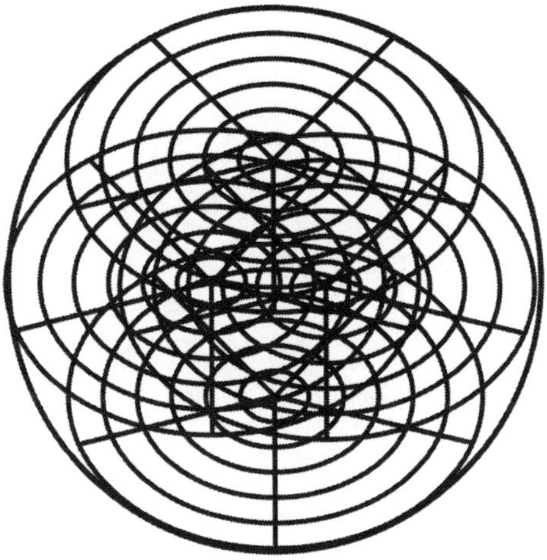

The Furies' Bog

DEBORAH JACKSON

The Furies' Bog

Published by Deborah Jackson

Cover Design and Illustrations by Jessica Jackson

This book is a work of fiction. Any references to historical events, real people, or real locales are used fictitiously. Other names, characters, places and incidents are products of the author's imagination, and any resemblance to actual events or locales or persons, living or dead, is entirely coincidental.

Library and Archives Canada Cataloguing in Publication

Jackson, Deborah, author.
The furies' bog / Deborah Jackson.
Edited by Rachel Eugster.

Includes bibliographical references.
Issued in print and electronic formats.

ISBN 978-1-5239-8596-8 (paperback).--ISBN 978-0-9878833-6-0 (html)

I.Eugster, Rachel, editor II.Title.

PS8619.A2422F87 2016 C813'.6 C2016-901151-8
C2016-901152-6

Printed and bound in the United States

ALSO BY DEBORAH JACKSON

Ice Tomb
Sinkhole
Time Meddlers
Time Meddlers Undercover
Time Meddlers on the Nile
Mosaic

CONTENTS

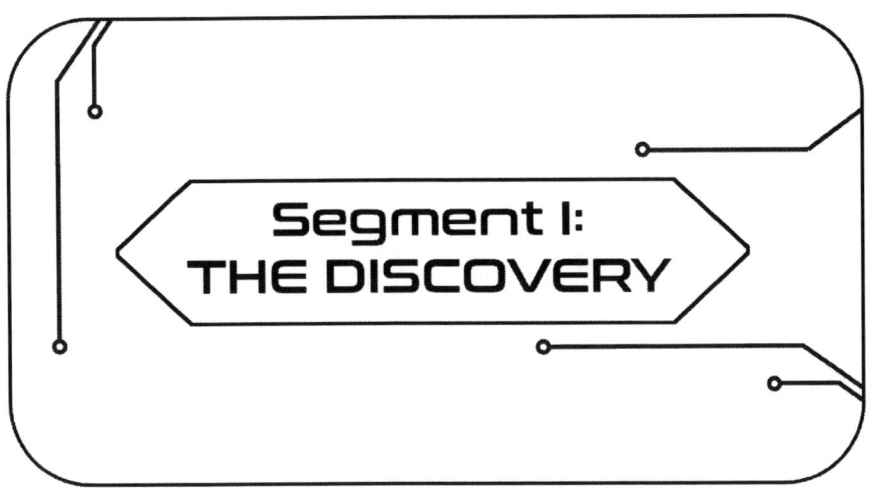

Segment I: THE DISCOVERY

TERESUS (KING OF the Thracians) came to Pandion's aid and smashed the enemy armies, thus winning a great renown for his glorious victory. Pandion, impressed by his wealth, the number of his retainers, and his glorious ancestry (which he traced back to Mars himself), gave him Procnê as wife. But Juno, patron of wedlock avoided the feast. . . . No Graces attended their marriage. Only the Furies were there, with torches snatched from a tomb.

—Ovid, *Metamorphoses* 6.424-431

Scanning...

Located: Chapter 1

BARUTI CRINGED AS a gust of polar wind swept through the inadequately insulated helicopter and swirled eddies of crisp, bracing air around his face. He breathed out. Ghostly white. He shivered and leaned subtly toward his companion, another perhaps more sane biologist.

Shaun Wilson, a tall ropy fellow with uncannily green eyes and a flop of blond hair reaching nearly to his nose, looked up from his perusal of his GPS, aimed a somewhat wicked smile at him, and crooned through the mic, "A little cold, my friend?"

"You call this summer?" Baruti grunted.

"Still wavering on spring, but yes, it can feel like the dead of winter. Especially if you're from Botswana." He added a sly wink.

Baruti suppressed another shiver and slunk even deeper into his thin layer of fleece.

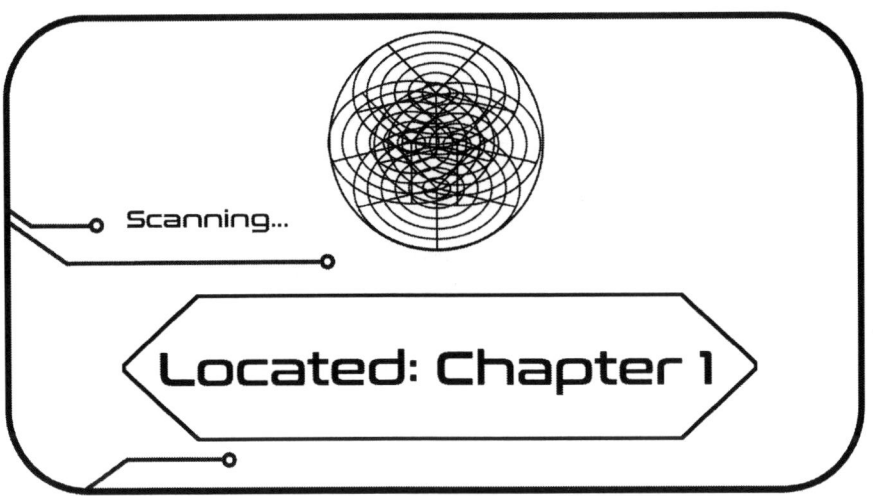

"Honestly, I don't know why a man would leave his perfectly comfortable life studying the wildlife of the Okavango Delta and come here." His hand swept the view outside the window, the miles of stunted black spruce bordering on vast polygons of vegetation surrounding syrupy brown water. Miles of unchecked bog—lichen and moss the predominant plant life—a good place to sink and disappear. Yet there was something so calm about it. So . . . unmolested.

Colors blossomed in the gray dawn. Fringes of sunlight tickled the many ponds, transforming the melting ice into a kaleidoscope of green, yellow, turquoise, even rust. A migrating herd of caribou raised their great antlers as the aircraft sped past, pausing in their search for a spikelet of sedge to crop. Small birds flapped in the air, and one grand creature with a six-foot wingspan hovered off the coast. An eagle, perhaps?

"Yes, it does seem odd," said the pilot, a thickset, black-bearded Canadian of undoubtedly Italian origin. DeLuca was his name. Wilson said he doubled as a geologist, in a rather sneering manner. Wilson liked to sneer, Baruti noted. And joke. And wink.

Obviously he took no delight in inorganic substances.

"Too dry and dusty at times. Too *moleto*. Hot. I needed a change."

"One extreme to the other, though, man," said DeLuca. "Why didn't you choose something moderate? South of France. Now that would be the ticket."

"And what would I study there?" asked Baruti. "Sunbathers?"

"Sun worshipers. In bikinis." He looked back and winked; the helicopter shimmied and dropped a few sickening yards.

Baruti clutched the seat cushion, his heartbeat matching the thumping of the rotors. "Dr. DeLuca . . ."

"Tony," he replied, swerving and swaying the craft back to level. "And no, Baruti. I'm not going to crash us . . . today."

A strong gust of wind begged to differ as it grabbed the craft and shook its threadbare aluminum frame, rattling every loose component and sending the helicopter into a miniature rotation. Tony fought the controls and barely averted a death spiral.

Bile filled Baruti's throat. What had possessed him to pursue . . . no, to take this course of action as a biologist in the extreme north of Canada?

Watch your words, even in thought. It's easy to let thoughts slip into speech.

Wouldn't it have been simpler to follow the demise of the declining populations of ostriches or wildebeest in the Delta? Or even to have resumed his studies of the gorilla in the Congo? And if he must come to this bone-withering, frost-bitten land, why not study the woodland fox or the dwindling packs of wolves near the southern border? Why Polar Bear Provincial Park? Why polar bears?

It was the only option. Yes, of course, the only option . . . for an insane man on an insane mission.

"There," shouted Wilson, completely oblivious—or at least he seemed that way—to the buffeting wind and the looping path of the helicopter. A bare speck of white loped across the tundra, not particularly intimidating from this height.

The helicopter swung around and angled downward. The speck grew substantially, like a snowball accumulating mass as it hurtles down a slope. Longer, wider, heftier, gorilla-sized, and bigger, but without the gorilla's shy aspect. It looked up and watched the helicopter's approach with borderline disdain, its lips curled to expose teeth. DeLuca hovered above, but tilted to the left—to the Baruti Mbeki side, of course—while Wilson leaned over and shoved open the door.

Wind thrust through the opening—biting, snarling wind that threatened to flash-freeze Baruti's eyeballs—as DeLuca tipped the helicopter toward the bear.

"Are you trying to send me into the beast's jaws?" asked Baruti. A cowardly question, he knew, but surely the pilot could hold the craft level.

"The closer, the better shot," said Tony. "You're strapped in, aren't you?"

"Yes," he replied, eyeing the thin straps that held him above the now growling specimen a few mere feet below.

Wilson fumbled a dart into the tranquilizer gun, trying to aim at the creature's back from the jittering vehicle, with the gun slung across Baruti's legs.

"Hold still," he muttered. "I've almost got him."

Hold still?

DeLuca tipped; Baruti slid; Wilson fired.

The bear growled, groaned, and then collapsed. His long glistening snout of sleek cream-colored fur tipped with a black knob of a nose crashed to the arctic tundra. His massive body, weighing likely 1,000 pounds—beginning to thin through the summer but still notably rotund—sprayed jets of water as it hit the spongy earth. His monstrous paws, with their equally monstrous claws, fell limply to the side.

Wilson retracted the gun and slapped Baruti on the back. "Now we just have to tag him, my friend. The bears are adapting to global warming, their numbers growing steadily, according to the Inuit. We just need to substantiate their claim. Amazing how animals adapt."

"Does that mean I will adjust to this cold?" he shivered out.

"Only if you accumulate more blubber," said Tony, smacking a hand on the inner tube that encircled his belly as he gently set the aircraft on the ground. The ground slurped greedily at the skids, insisting they settle a foot deeper than the surface appeared to be.

"Is this location stable enough?" asked Baruti, picturing the bog gobbling up the helicopter just like Skywalker's unfortunate fighter in the classic film *The Empire Strikes Back*.

"As stable as it's going to get here," said DeLuca. "This is a shelf—a raised gravel beach that provides a path through the bog. It's narrow, but I can see its outline delineated by the black spruce. It's solid enough or we'd be sinking right now. But be careful of the surrounding mire. A few shelves, many sinks."

"Well, tranquilizer's a-wastin'," said Wilson. "Let's measure, tag, and skedaddle before the brute wakes up."

He kept a firm grasp on his tranquilizer gun as he gingerly stepped from the helicopter. DeLuca snatched a revolver from his backpack and hopped out the other side. He took two steps, rotated on his heel, and beckoned Baruti with a slight jerk of his head.

Time to get *leswe*.

Baruti fumbled with the buckle, taking a bit too long, which drew a hooked eyebrow from Wilson. Released, he swung feet first toward the gaping exit, the cold drilling into his exposed face, threatening to expose even more of his inadequacy to the task at hand, or to the greater task.

"Wait," Wilson warned before he could jump down. "Watch where you walk. There are certain pathways through the bog with thick enough moss to support your weight. The rest is, well, bog. Follow my footsteps."

Baruti nodded, jumped from the craft an inch to the right of where the Canadian biologist had landed, and sank, deeply and firmly, into the mud.

"Are you serious?" he asked no one in particular, since Wilson was already trotting down the path and DeLuca was circling the helicopter several feet away. When Wilson had said "follow my footsteps" Baruti had assumed this meant "basically," as in "as close as possible," not "in the very cradle of each print," as if they were entering a minefield.

Luckily, the skids of the aircraft were still within reach. Baruti clutched the metal appendage and yanked himself loose.

"Hurry," yelled Wilson from beside the mound of polar bear. "If you want to lay a hand on the gorgeous creature before he bites your hand off."

"Fell in the mud," Baruti tried to explain, then thought better of it since it would make him look even more incompetent, and strode forward on the definitive path of footprints, not deviating a fraction.

The sun shot pale beams through the clouds, tracing the outline of the stout geologist and the tall biologist as mere hills beside what could only be described as the Everest of bears. Baruti trudged toward them as they threw their measuring tapes around his girth, tackled his massive paws to get a scraping from his claws, and as Wilson drew blood in ample vials.

"Here. Tag his ear," said Wilson, tossing the glue-on satellite tag over to him.

Baruti spent an extra minute admiring, one more stroking the pearl-white fur as the bear lazily drew breath, then another minute to set the tag and tack it to the beast's fuzzy ear.

"Magnificent, isn't he?" said Wilson, no longer scornful or teasing. Baruti gazed over the expanding and retracting ribcage to meet the biologist's eyes. The man's apple-green irises had taken on a gleam, a sparkle that only a biologist could summon as he gazed at the king of species.

"I would not like to encounter his teeth or his claws on any occasion when he wasn't dosed with adequate tranquilizer but, yes, what a remarkable creature. The lion is also remarkable and one to be wary of, but certainly not capable of thriving in this climate."

Wilson met his eyes. "I once visited your country, with all its diverse species, my friend, before the widespread extinction event. I prefer my object of study, but I certainly appreciate yours."

A desperate yearning crept into the biologist's eyes that Baruti couldn't fathom. Or maybe he understood it all too well.

A soft moan emerged from the bear's mouth, enough to give Baruti a start, especially while leaning against its foreleg next to the massive snout.

"Tranq's wearing off," said Wilson, snapping out of his own spell. "Just a few more things . . ." He rustled out tweezers and a swab from his sample case, plucked assorted hairs from the bear's chest, then forced open its lax jaw and stroked the interior of its cheek with the swab. He collected these samples in standard specimen jars and tucked them securely in a sealed plastic bag.

"Do you suspect him of a crime?" Baruti remarked.

"Only the crime of not surviving into the next century. I know the species is rebounding, but it's still endangered, and it wouldn't take much to tip it near the brink again. I'd like to keep DNA on file, in case we need to reconstruct."

"Fair enough," Baruti replied. "Although cloning the species won't restore its habitat."

Wilson's gaze clashed with Baruti's again, and he maintained eye contact for an uncomfortably long time. Too long, considering the bear was snorting in air, reviving.

"Too true," he finally muttered. "Well, I think that about covers it, anyway. Give him a kiss and we're out of here."

Baruti frowned.

"Kidding," Wilson clarified.

Would he ever adapt to this man's bizarre sense of humor?

"A hug will suffice."

That said, he wrapped his rather lengthy arms around a quarter of the bear's belly and squeezed it tenderly.

"I think I'll skip the hug," said DeLuca, slinging his backpack over his shoulder and striding toward the path. Wilson shrugged and motioned for Baruti to walk in front of him. No doubt he'd noticed Baruti's embarrassing exit from the aircraft.

"Remember—"

"Keep in DeLuca's tracks. I know."

The plush carpet of lichen and moss squelched beneath his boots as he tramped after the geologist, rapidly catching up to him and hugging his shadow, each footstep conforming to the leading man's print. He felt immeasurable sadness and immeasurable relief to be leaving the bear behind. He appreciated close encounters with such magnificent creatures, but he also respected their instinctual and sometimes unpredictable nature, and bore the scars of too cavalier an attitude toward leopards, hippos, and even an annoyed ostrich. Lions, not so much. Lions respected him.

The bear grunted and sputtered, gradually regaining consciousness. Perhaps DeLuca should pick up the pace. Wilson, the seemingly calm and collected bear specialist was spurring Baruti on by occasionally clipping his heels.

Another snort and a canyon-deep growl burst from the bench of moss and gravel where the bear lay slumped. Wilson rotated on his heel, impelling Baruti and DeLuca to turn in unison. The bear was no longer stretched across the tundra completely doped, but was half sprawled, half struggling to get up, as he aimed his bobbing, disoriented head in their direction.

DeLuca pivoted back toward the helicopter and proceeded to hop-sprint down the spongy path. Baruti followed in his tracks, or close to his tracks, but his tracks were becoming increasingly haphazard. Then DeLuca's ended, as he sank into a deep morass. Baruti skidded to a stop, but not quickly enough. His feet slipped off the edge of the flimsy moss path and into the swamp and thick mud that surrounded it.

"No!" he yelped, as he struggled and sank. He clawed at the moss, a thick overlay that might offer a lifeline, but the spongy quilt tore and fragmented in his hands. He sank through a cushion of peat until his boots crunched on something solid. The bottom of the quagmire had an oddly brittle quality. It felt as if his boot were clutched in an actual claw.

"Give me your hand," said Wilson, extending his arm, a look of urgency in his eyes. "It's not very deep, just disgusting and muddy. But our friend is definitely awake, and we need to haul ass."

Baruti reached for and clutched Wilson's hand, and pulled with equal urgency, but his feet were still clamped in the jaws of some persistent swamp beast.

"I'm caught in something at the bottom," he tried to explain, as his wrenching, tugging effort merely moved him a fraction. Wilson dug his boots into the gravel, venturing only as near to the fragile boundary as he dared, and gave a ferocious yank. Baruti pulled free, or the snag pulled with him, and he tumbled onto the shelf.

"Oh crap!" said Wilson, blinking at Baruti's feet.

Baruti twisted around and found that his boots had acquired a most bizarre attachment. A horribly crumpled, mangled, human-shaped mud-creature. He'd broken through what was apparently the ribcage. He could distinguish no features in the misshapen face, but reddish mud-caked hair was clinging to a typical human skull. Obviously not the remains of a polar bear.

"Oh," said DeLuca, from his slogging approach in the bog. "That's interesting."

He advanced toward the path, but stumbled before he reached it. Fishing in the molasses-like water, he discovered another limb, which was attached to another ribcage, and another skull.

"More than one, too."

"Cree?" asked Wilson, casting a backward glance.

"Possibly. But I don't think this is Cree." He tugged a chain with a circle-shaped pendant from the grip of tissue and gristle near the creature's skull. He polished it on the least mud-offended sliver of his shirt and unveiled a grayish tint.

"Silver, I believe," he said.

Wilson grew pale, and a soul-clutching shiver engulfed his entire body. But he dismissed their discovery in an anxious tone as he helped DeLuca from the bog and practically pushed him toward the helicopter.

"Whoever they were and whatever that is, it can wait. We have a polar bear to consider."

A thunderous roar punctuated his remark. The men carefully dashed along the path, angling for the helicopter, but DeLuca still held the chain up to the light in fascination.

It didn't fascinate Baruti, though. Now, if the body had possessed distinctive African features and the chain had glittered with diamonds, he'd have trouble disguising his joy.

Scanning...

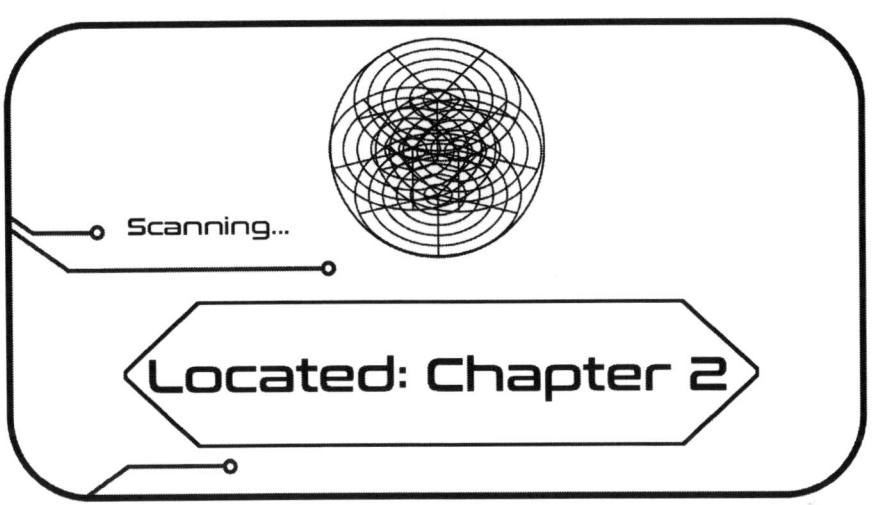

Located: Chapter 2

COULD THERE BE *a more mud-choked, fetid, abominable place in the world?*

Felicity gritted her teeth as mud coiled around her boots, slopped over her gloves, and dripped into her hair. Dr. Jan Vandermeer leaped from the ridge of peat that teetered on the edge of the swamp and into the hollowed bowl they'd scooped out with the slowly sinking excavator. He landed in the soupy water at the bottom and splattered more mud in all directions, particularly Felicity's way, adding to the stripes on her face. Soon she'd resemble the body that was wedged in the peat in front of her.

"Could you not do that?" she snapped before she could stop herself. She wiped her face with a badly soiled sleeve that did nothing more than smear the muck.

He grinned, of course.

"Does it really matter, my dear?" he asked. "We will all need showers at the end of the day. But look at our find!"

"Not exactly *our* find," she muttered. "The dairy farmer's find, when he decided to mine peat for fertilizer near the edge of the swamp. And not exactly unique anymore, either."

"But still fascinating."

He winked, his topaz eyes brimming with glee, his teeth flashing within the neatly trimmed oval of his bronze goatee, his sunburned face flushed an even deeper red. For a minute, she could forget he was fifteen years older than she. For a minute, she could forget he was an archaeologist. For a minute . . .

"Well, shall we examine our delicious discovery before we extract it?" he said, in his gruff Dutch-accented voice, rubbing his hands together.

Felicity cringed. He noted it with a grunt of insight that quickly dissolved his ecstatic smile. His glow became a glower that withered her shoulders in shame.

Why did she have to be so squeamish?

"This is an honor, as you should know."

And now the lecture begins.

"To find the remains of our predecessors that tell us extraordinary details about our past. To find them virtually intact. To be the first to look upon their faces after 2,000 years of hibernation. My father was there, at the site, when they extracted the Yde girl—a graduate student such as you. What a day that was. When he told me the story, it ignited my passion for archaeology, particularly since it shed some light on the history of the people in this region. He could immediately see that she was a child. As they plucked the mud from her body, they observed an odd glint of color in her hair—a red tint that bore no similarity to her original shade, but rather was due to an alteration in chemical composition imparted by the acidity of the bog. But how glorious that the hair, the face, the brain still existed, so well preserved.

"Can't you feel it, Felicity? The momentousness of this discovery? Does it not whisper to you as if these prehistorical people are reaching out across the centuries to finally reveal their secrets?"

Felicity nodded and tried to mold a grin on her tight face.

"Nothing like it," she muttered. Nothing like standing knee-deep in sludge, sloshing through miles of soggy bog, examining withered corpses, and attempting to interpret their stories of pain, terror, and violent death through skin scrapings and intestinal extracts. Nothing like it.

Jan . . . Dr. Vandermeer—better not to think of him as Jan—scraped away a gummy clod of mud from the body in an almost tender fashion. A face emerged—

compressed, distorted, but obviously human, with eyes, a nose, and definite plaits of hair twisted up in the strange Suebian knots that were the typical style worn by Iron Age men in this part of Europe.

"Look at this," said the good doctor, grabbing her arm.

A shiver ran through her at his unexpected touch, then another, deeper one as he gently placed her fingers on the sagging scalp.

"Of course you know, if you've studied the bog people at all, that the bones are generally dissolved in this nutrient-poor, acid-rich peatland after such a long period of . . . embalming, shall we say? But we might find an intact brain just as preserved as the scalp and this lovely plait of hair. Can you feel something else?"

He grinned again, his expression practically beatific. How could anyone grin while touching a corpse? How could any man find joy and such supreme satisfaction from digging up fossilized bones and decrepit mummies? She could easily understand feeling pulse-throbbing exhilaration while feasting your eyes on the golden treasures of Tutankhamen, or the magnificent silver horde at Hildesheim. When she'd first laid eyes on the Roman Minerva Bowl in the Altes Museum in Berlin, drunk in the depiction of the goddess seated in full battle headgear upon her rock throne, she'd nearly fainted at the thrill. Not only was the artifact exquisite, an artistic masterpiece, but she represented everything Felicity aspired to become but felt was inevitably beyond her reach. How she longed to be powerful, noble, and yet compassionate and creative, just like Minerva—or, as the Greeks called her, Athena—the goddess of wisdom and war, medicine and art.

A chapter in her archaeology textbook. But to Felicity, archaeology was art and mythology her alternate reality.

She shook her head—imperceptibly, so Vandermeer wouldn't see.

But not *this*.

Yes, she could scrutinize Van Gogh's ominous painting of the bog boat, feel drawn to the boldness of his brush strokes and the mystery of an intangible past, with a passion approaching Dr. Vandermeer's. But to actually touch a bog body, to follow the contours of slimy, tanned flesh that was millennia old, and let her trembling fingers wander over the crumpled features . . .

What? Now that was interesting.

"He has a hole in his head," she said, probing gently. An obvious depression lay in the already dissolving and misshapen skull.

"Yes, my dearrr." He rolled his r's pleasantly and nodded. "Probably where they bashed in his head."

Felicity gulped and retracted her hand.

"Why?" she whispered.

She'd studied the archaeological evidence, but she still couldn't understand—didn't *want* to understand.

"An offering, a sacrifice. We've often found that bog remains have head injuries along with— Oh, yes. There it is. A cord around his neck. His attackers clubbed him on the head first, undoubtedly so he wouldn't have to consciously suffer through the strangulation."

"Or they didn't want him to struggle. Or they just wanted to ensure he was dead," she added. "But that still doesn't tell me why."

"Perhaps they sacrificed him for some evil deed, or some 'perceived' evil deed."

Felicity shivered and, naturally, the ubiquitous mist that constantly draped this region in Holland drifted over their site at the same instant, dusting her skin with icy droplets.

"They cast him into Hell," she remarked.

"Or what they perceived as Hell—the entrance to the Underworld."

"I'm starting to understand why they felt that way."

The mist swirled around her, dotting her face with dew, scattering moisture over her arms, and raising goosebumps on her skin. She shuffled a step away from the body.

The archaeologist raised his eyebrows, his mouth betraying a twitch. Was he finding her too hesitant?

"I recall other eerie images and folktales derived from beliefs of the Bronze Age that persisted into the Medieval Age. Evil spirits dancing over the bogs as jack-o'-lanterns—the swamp-gas flames. A hollow-eyed creature, mud-cloaked, with a blanket of greens, that rose out of the swamp disguised as a beautiful woman and lured her victim with siren songs."

"Sounds like a scene from *The Lord of the Rings*."

"Well, Mr. Tolkien did adore his mythology. Another story tells of how the gas could paralyze a person passing by. Do you feel sluggish, my dear? Are you having trouble moving?"

"You're enjoying this, aren't you?"

"Tremendously."

"We're in the middle of a densely populated country, even if it doesn't seem that way right now. I don't scare that easily."

"Yes, you do," he said. "I've given up on lecturing you. If you want to make this into a chore, I'll try to make it a nightmare."

Felicity was taken aback. "I'm sorry, Dr. Vandermeer. It's not that I'm not interested . . ."

"I've never met a student like you," he said. "Oh, the casual archaeology undergrads I understand. But at your level, I expect a little enthusiasm." He grasped her by both arms as if to shake some sense into her.

She cringed, but she still felt a flutter in her belly. She couldn't help but admire him, even when he was brusquely stern, dripping with mud, and fondling a corpse.

"Tell me why you're here."

"I—I . . . Dr. Vandermeer, I do like archaeology, sometimes. I took a double major as an undergrad. Art. In particular sculpting—especially forensic sculpting—because my father thought I'd be more likely to secure a job, you know, in this economic climate, if I could do something practical. But there were no jobs, or at least no one would hire me. I adore art—my focus has always been on classical Roman and Greek art. But no university would offer me a scholarship to continue my studies in art, just like no one offered me a job. I—I guess I wasn't good enough. But I achieved high marks in archaeology. I thrived on a dig in Greece. And several universities, including Harvard, offered me a scholarship to pursue my master's degree. I had to keep studying something that might actually lead to a career. I do love artifacts. Just not bodies . . . very much."

Jan Vandermeer released her arms and dropped his hands. He scratched his head, even though he was trickling dirt and possibly mummy residue into his hair.

"You shine on paper," he said. "That's why I accepted you for this project. I had no idea. . . . I can't employ a student who won't even get dirty."

"I could reconstruct him," she said enthusiastically.

She envisioned the indelicate measuring of shrunken tissue, the tedious reassembly of soft bone fragments, but resisted the urge to shiver.

"I could help you determine facial features, do body measurements, perform MRI scans to define the basic contours of his face. Then I could create a mold and, in all but true animation, bring him back to life."

The professor nodded warily. "I suppose you have some passion for the ancients, regardless of your queasiness over fieldwork." A tentative smile crept onto his face. "Back to life. I'd love to hear his story."

Felicity contemplated the bog people's stories, none of them pleasant.

"Maybe he has a deformity. Maybe they executed him because he wasn't perfect."

She sighed, thinking of the pronounced limp to her left leg from the fractured bones and torn ligaments she'd suffered in a car accident. If she'd lived in the days of the bog people, she'd have been bludgeoned, strangled, and hurled into a swamp, too.

"Well," said the archaeologist. "I suppose I could free you from the fieldwork and set you up in the lab."

Felicity released a silent sigh. It would be such a relief to get back to the laboratory, back to the reconstruction she preferred. The mist swirled around her, continuing to probe her thin sweater, but she didn't feel quite as cold.

"Doctor, I would be happy to assist you in the lab," she said.

"Good. When we're finished here today, you'll be finished here on site. Now, let's see if we can snap some decent photographs. . . ."

The phone—that swank sliver of microchips in her pocket, carefully sheltered from the mud and moisture—sang out at that moment, interrupting him. Felicity wiped and wiped her hands until they were reasonably gunge-free, then answered, stepping away from Dr. Vandermeer.

A holographic representation of the thin blotchy face and bony frame of Frank Campo, another grad student under the tutelage of the eminent Professor Lugan and a bonified jerk, lit up in midair.

"Hey there, doll." He winked. "Lugan has another job for you."

"I'm busy enough here," she said. "Why would she pull me away from a dig?"

"Maybe because she knows you don't like to get your hands dirty," he said, his voice dripping with smug satisfaction. Nothing would give her greater pleasure than to stretch her dirty hands around his wiry throat and squeeze. Unfortunately, that possibility was removed by an ocean—a fact of which he was well aware, as he sat cradled in a comfortable chair in the lounge of the Harvard Peabody Museum of Archaeology and Ethnology, grinning obnoxiously.

"Right," she said. "And this isn't enough? What does she have in mind?"

"Well, you're now considered the bog expert, and they've made another astounding bog discovery. So you're to get neck-deep in mud again, my gal."

"I'm not 'your gal,'" she snapped. "Where does she want me to go? Denmark? Britain?"

"Oh no," he practically drooled. "This is so much better than Europe. You're to get on a plane, and then on a train, and possibly a float plane, and maybe even a canoe."

How could a man grin so widely that his teeth filled half the virtual screen? Or in his case, a boy in the body of a man. A little puny boy with a little puny brain.

"Where!"

"Place called Polar Bear Provincial Park, in Northern Ontario."

"And where will you be?"

"I'll be in Athens, my gal, dusting off the Parthenon, and then digging through the Alepotrypa cave in southern Greece. Sweet heavenly assignment."

"Greece? I thought you were the African expert?"

"New area of study. Better surroundings." He smirked. "Enjoy the mosquitoes."

Felicity turned off the phone with a definitive blink. She looked up into the clever blue eyes of the Dutch archaeologist, who was clearly observing and analyzing her from his position beside the body.

"She's snatching you away from me," he said, as she approached.

She nodded. "She's sending me to another bog."

He raised his eyebrows and almost smiled. Why did everyone revel in her misery?

"Where?"

"That's the weird part."

She paused. And shook her head. And slipped a muddy hand through her hair before she realized what she was doing and whipped it out again.

"In Canada."

His eyebrows arched even higher, and his quizzical smile withered into a puzzled frown. She knew exactly what he was thinking.

Who ever heard of bog bodies in Canada?

Scanning...

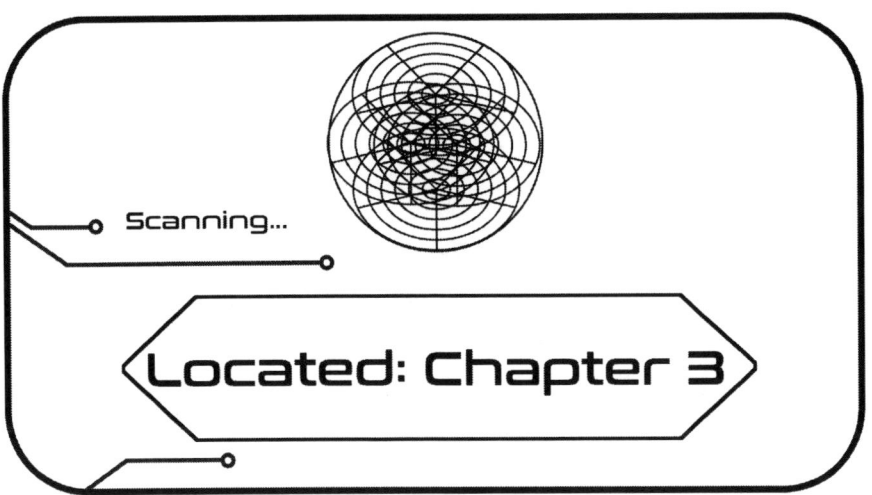

Located: Chapter 3

THE DOOR SLAMMED in a tiny breach, supposedly a door, in the teepee-shaped airport terminal, as a baggage handler carted away three—yes, only three—suitcases. Felicity switched on her tablet, hoping—no, praying—that she'd finally find Wi-Fi or a cell tower and get a signal, after all the hours of civilization-free train travel from Cochrane, a town at the outer limits of Ontario's roadways. In a conveyance quaintly labeled the Polar Bear Express, she'd rocked for hours through dense forest with only the clickety-clack of wheels tapping rail assailing her ears, and the lovely view of treetops and more treetops—Douglas fir and black balsam—obscuring anything beyond. If there was anything beyond. Even that view had been tarnished by streaks of rain, which blurred the landscape from mundane to excruciatingly dull. To top it off, her infrequent trips to the restroom were nothing less than a wind-blast to the bum, with all human excrement delightfully deposited on the train tracks for the bears and chipmunks to sniff at. Or more likely to groan at and flee from in disgust.

But she'd finally arrived at the airport—this one-room structure—and was now waiting for the float plane to pick her up and deposit her on the Winisk

River in Peawanuck. She was to be escorted by the brilliant scientists who'd uncovered bog bodies in Polar Bear Provincial Park. She wondered if there were actually polar bears there—not really a stretch—and whether they found petite archaeology grad students tasty. Most likely they did.

The Internet blinked on. She sucked in a breath, exhaled, and logged onto her email.

Had Professor Lugan finally answered her questions? There it was. A response.

> Glad to hear you're on your way. I know I'm asking a great deal of you, Felicity, but with your exceptional eye for detail, you have so much promise. You just need to get your feet wet with the fieldwork.

Yeah, right. More like I'll let you drown for a while before I reel you back in.

> Since you've been introduced to the bog people—rather splendid, aren't they?—

Splendid? Blackened, shriveled corpses?

> —I've chosen you to initiate the investigation of these bodies. They are in a rather remote location, as you've already gathered,—

Remote? Timbuktu would be more populated.

> —and I'm sure you're wondering whether they're simply remains from ancient Cree burial grounds,—

Which we shouldn't desecrate.

> —but something unusual has been discovered with the bodies. An artifact.

Felicity suddenly perked up. *Likely an arrowhead or a bead necklace.*

> My dear Felicity, this is right up your alley. Something of a classical nature that is out of place in the cradle of Cree and Inuit territory.

Felicity held her breath.

> I'm not going to tell you.

Are you kidding me?

> It would spoil the surprise. But I need you to investigate, authenticate—

Okay.

> —and examine the bodies.

Of course. She groaned under her breath.

> This could be one of the greatest discoveries of the 21st century, or it could be a hoax. My guess is a hoax. But that doesn't preclude the fact that these are bog bodies, nor that they might provide us with valuable insight into the First Nations' past.

Yes, the lovely bog bodies. Felicity, we don't want to wallow in mud, so you do it!

She sighed and closed the mail. Then she opened a new window and tapped off a quick note to her parents on the virtual keyboard, rather than sending them a video note that might reveal too clearly her mood. Right now, her dad was likely acquiring another Picasso for his collection in the museum, and her mom would be adding a dash of the dramatic to her latest abstract painting. Artists, art collectors, art enthusiasts.

And she was the failed sculptor-turned-bog-body-specialist.
She wrote:

> I'm alive.

Scratch that.

> I've just traveled through tunnels of trees that would make Tom Thompson drool, and it was so boring.

No, scratch that, too.

> I absolutely love my job, especially when I have to grope through mud and fondle corpses.

Okay, they'll think I'm a coward and feel guilty at the same time.

> I'm on the most exciting adventure to the North.

Better.

> I miss you, and . . .

And I'm feeling faint.

Crap. She hadn't eaten much of anything since she'd left Amsterdam, mainly because there wasn't anything to eat, or at least nothing that appealed to her. Just tasteless ham sandwiches and chicken noodle soup. *Idiot!*

She rose, then staggered, as her weak leg rebelled.

"Ma'am, are you okay?" asked a tall guy in a flannel shirt and ripped blue jeans who had just sauntered in through the door. He whipped out a hand to steady her.

"I'm fine," she said. "Just famished. I didn't eat on the train, so I guess my blood sugar is a bit low."

He held her arm another second before letting go, then gave her an understanding smile.

"Nothing too appetizing on the train, I know. But the coffee shop here has a few decent treats."

He beckoned her with a jerk of his head, then strode to the counter across the room. Although she felt like she had little choice, it was obviously the best course of action, so she followed, doing her best to disguise the limp. But she still wobbled as her head swam obnoxiously.

He eyed her unsteadiness, poised to help again if need be.

At the counter, she ordered an egg sandwich and coffee, for long-term energy and a quick burst of vigor.

The coffee was served instantly. Felicity spiked the cup with a teaspoon of sugar, and took several gulps of the strong brew.

"Are you sure you're okay?" the man asked.

"Yes. Feeling better already," she said, trying to avoid his inquisitive look.

The server handed the egg sandwich over the counter. Felicity grabbed it. She staggered to a bench, opened the container, and began to munch on her meal, slurping her coffee between bites.

The tall stranger followed and lowered himself down beside her. She gave him a furtive glance, which did nothing to settle her nerves or ease her embarrassment.

He was quite attractive, with honey-blond hair that rippled over his ears and keen green eyes. His strong jaw showed the shadow of a beard.

"Not many new folks make the trek up here, unless it's midsummer," he said. "Where're you heading?"

"I'm supposed to catch a flight to Winisk River. I guess I didn't count on the delay and forgot to eat enough."

"Winisk River?" he said. "You wouldn't happen to be an archaeologist?"

Felicity caught her breath. *Small town, news travels fast. Especially in the remote north.*

"Grad student, but, yes, in archaeology."

"Well," he said. "What a coincidence. I was sent down here, along with my trusted pilot, to collect you. But you're younger than I expected. Name's Shaun. Shaun Wilson. I'm the resident biologist."

He held out his hand. She shakily grasped it, her pulse rate climbing at the touch of rough but surprisingly gentle fingers. It spiked even higher when she realized how clumsy and stupid she'd appeared in front of the scientist who was also her escort.

"Felicity Cratchett."

"Felicity? Well, you don't look too happy at the moment, but that's understandable."

He smiled, exposing gleaming, perfectly even teeth. Damn, she should at least have brushed hers. They were probably still streaked with mud.

"Hey, Tony," he called to a short, husky fellow with an exuberant potbelly who was just emerging from the portal to the runway, and letting in a rush of unseasonably cold air—or unseasonable for Boston or Holland, at least. "I found our passenger."

The pilot swaggered toward them, his hands thrust in his pockets, his lips gradually curling.

"Hello," he said, shaking a hand free. "I'm Tony. Tony DeLuca."

"This is Felicity," Shaun introduced her. "She was a little faint from hunger, so I had to introduce her to our less-than-gourmet airport food." He grinned.

Tony's smile dragged down a notch.

"You seem kind of young for an archaeologist," he remarked.

"She's a grad student," said Shaun.

Tony's smile disappeared altogether.

"I was under the impression that Harvard was sending a bog body expert. A Dr. Lugan?"

"That's my faculty adviser. She sent me because I guess I'm the expert she can spare." Felicity smiled as sweetly as she could. "I just came from the Netherlands, investigating other bog bodies. I'm the man for the job, so to speak."

She kept her smile pasted on, but doubted it was very convincing, especially to these seasoned field men.

"Right," said Tony, frowning and meeting Shaun's eyes. "Working in the park is not exactly a picnic, though. We just have tents; no hotels."

"I can do tents," she said.

"Great," said Tony, although he didn't look like he was buying it. He gave her a level look. "Right then. The plane is waiting." He waved to the back of the building.

Felicity nodded, polished off her sandwich, and gulped the last dregs of her coffee. She pushed to her feet, ignoring Shaun's proffered arm. He wasn't deterred, though. He continued to hover like a doting mother bird. Not that she didn't appreciate his protective presence, or even just his presence. But she needed to be tough. She needed to exhibit the qualities she most admired—the Minerva qualities. She could no longer cower at mud and bodies, and she definitely should follow in the wise footsteps of the goddess and stay as fit and healthy as possible. She'd already shown these men that she'd been less than sensible.

"L— lead on," she stammered, cursing under her breath.

Tony sighed, turned, and marched toward the door—because there was no ramp, no neatly enclosed walkway to the airplane. Felicity trailed him, with Shaun at her side. When her limp became apparent, he gently took her arm.

"I'm really fine," she said, attempting to pull away.

"Yes. Absolutely," he said, and tightened his grip.

They tramped onto the tarmac, the wind slapping at their coats, the concrete icy beneath their boots. The men drew her to a jeep, not a plane because, of course, they were using a float plane and were still a slight distance from water. The jeep sped for several miles to an isolated dock on the Moose River, where the plane bobbed in the agitated waves. The sky was gray. The waves were gray. The pint-sized plane was a pale wintry white.

Shaun helped her into the back of the plane. Shaun buckled her in. Shaun brushed his hand against her belly.

She wished that he would stop touching her. She wished he'd never seen her falter. She didn't want to be his next conquest. And she wasn't a seal pup he had to rescue. She had a job to do. She was the expert they'd called in. It didn't matter that it was another bog job. This time, she couldn't fail.

The plane sputtered and roared, spinning waves in its wake as it soared into the gray sky. Below, there was nothing but stunted black trees and wind-punished bushes groping for nearly non-existent soil. Beyond that, bog.

Scanning...

Located: Chapter 4

MARS. COULD THERE be any bleaker destination? Any vaster, emptier world where only the savage wind blows? Canyons and craters filled with dust. Pebbled, marbled, lifeless terrain draped with dust. Rust-colored dust that peppers the horizon. Blazing dust. Boring dust. Soul-sucking dust.

How does one alter this cold, lifeless planet into a habitable Eden? Hurl water at it? Bombard it with asteroids? Release stored energy and greenhouse gas components to blanket the atmosphere and restart a dead engine?

Bold, but brilliant. *Eventually, we can jump-start evolution.*

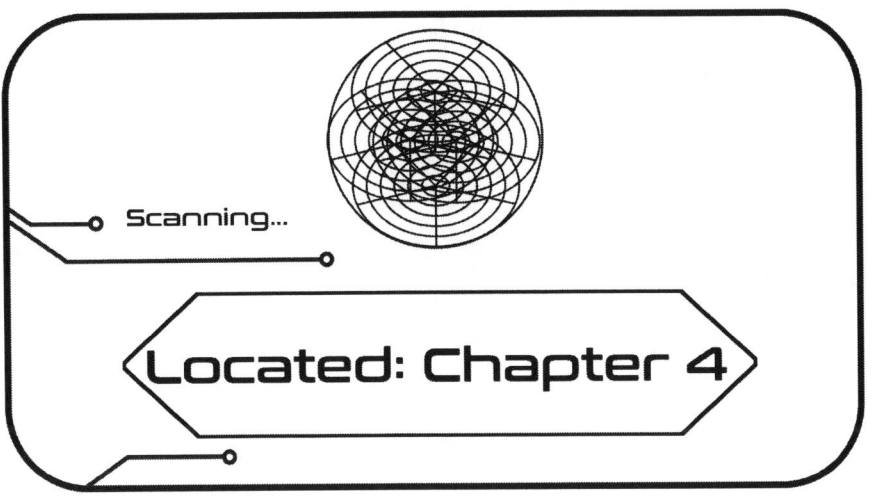

Lucas assumed a wintry smile, as cold as a Martian night, as he peered at the russet ball through the thin shield of his helmet. They were outside the VASIMR-powered *Phoenix*—their Variable Specific Impulse Magnetoplasma Rocket–powered spacecraft—drifting along in space during an EVA, a spacewalk. Both astronauts were clipped to a safety tether, as they scooted down a telescopic boom toward the robotic spacecraft and the mechanism towing the comet. The robotic spacecraft—the Asteroid/Comet Redirect Vehicle, or ACREV—had remotely captured the comet on its orbit near Jupiter from the Kuiper Belt and towed it over a period of several months toward Mars. On this EVA, they must first ascertain that the capture bag had remained tightly cinched since ACREV had snagged the comet, and also that it was still prepped for a spring release when they altered the comet's current trajectory and aimed it at the red planet.

Lucas pulled himself forward, his body floating outward from the boom. It was a simple process, and coupling the slow-motion movement with the buoyancy of zero gravity had become second nature to him after the six-week journey to intercept the robotic spacecraft with its precious captive. The *Phoenix's* plasma/ion engine, the latest in high-speed technology developed for interplanetary travel, utilized a nuclear generator. It was working efficiently with relatively few hiccups and had reduced what would typically have been a six-month journey to six weeks. However, Lucas did notice a slight quiver in his muscles, alerting him that they had become weakened even after such a short flight, despite his superior DNA and the added component of having had artificial gravity for part of the journey. Once the team settled on Mars, they would be blessed with continual gravity. It would only be one-third as strong as Earth's, so their muscle mass would still diminish, but not to such an extreme extent. Their bodies would adapt. Terraforming Mars was Step One. Mars altering their own genetic code would be Step Two.

Step Two was several centuries away from becoming reality. Perhaps.

Lucas inched along the end of the boom, gradually scaling the capture bag, which hugged the jagged body of the ammonia-rich comet. Ammonia and carbon dioxide would be the primary gases they were about to introduce into Mars's atmosphere. This process would thicken the atmosphere and contribute to a runaway greenhouse effect—the very feedback loop that had been wreaking havoc on Earth for decades.

The International Space Agency and Galactic Resources, the mining company funding the terraforming process, had been moderately successful with the first few waves of bombardment, as they flung small asteroids and comets at the planet. They'd also landed remote ships on some of the bigger asteroids to alter their orbits and send them crashing into Mars. As these "space rocks" approached the red planet, most of the gases peeled off into the atmosphere, while widespread detonations occurred on the surface, melting the CO_2-rich permafrost and releasing additional greenhouse gases. Through these efforts, the average temperature at the south pole had been raised by 8° F, globally increasing temperatures by at least 10° and altering the 6-millibar pressure to hundreds of millibars.

A rather remarkable achievement, if Lucas did say so himself, since his role in the terraforming experiment was, and continued to be, instrumental. When the colonists finally arrived, they wouldn't need bulky spacesuits and extreme-weather gear to survive on the surface. But the problem still remained of creating an ozone layer to protect any introduced flora or organisms from the harsh UV and cosmic rays that assailed Mars. And they would also need to build up the concentration of oxygen in the atmosphere to mammal-friendly proportions with hardy oxygen-generating plant life.

Bacteria and other microorganisms were the answer. The second task in their EVA: drill a hole deep into the comet's icy shell and seed it with dormant, genetically-modified and -enhanced cyanobacteria and archaea—wonderful little oxygen and methane generators designed to withstand the heat of impact. The comet would pulverize rock on the planet's surface and create hollowed bowls simmering with water where the bacteria could flourish.

These bowls would eventually nurture other plants, such as sphagnum moss and ericaceous shrubs. These bowls would become bogs.

A bog produces methane and feeds an expanding variety of plants. A bog creates soil, a rich black peat. A bog might be Earth's undoing, but a bog was a gift to Mars.

"Hey there, Luke. How's it going?" asked Gita Alatas, an astrobiologist and the commander of their fourteen-week mission.

"Almost to the soft site."

This was the ideal location to commence drilling, a weak zone in the icy material that had been recently exposed to roiling heat as the comet flew by the sun.

"Jolson's right behind me."

Not that he wanted to mention his co-driller, Astronaut Bob Jolson, an astrogeologist and the least hardy member of their team. Bob had become ill en route, probably from a virus he'd picked up before leaving Earth. Although he'd assured them he had completely recovered, he was already breathing heavily into the comm from this minor exertion. Quirky, happy-go-lucky Bob had also been responsible for their having nearly missed their comet rendezvous, by applying the trajectory-altering burn a little too long when they'd experienced a computer malfunction. Then, to top that off, blaming the recent solar flare—which had only added about 5 rem to their radiation level—and deteriorating vision, which he claimed was from their zero gravity stopover on the Lunar Space Station, he'd almost botched the capture of ACREV. Gita had been monitoring with the camera and readjusted their aim just in time, or they might have buckled their ninety-three-billion-dollar spacecraft. But somehow, despite Bob's failings, they'd captured the vehicle, towed the comet into low orbit above Mars, and were now seeding and prepping for the release of another bacterial insemination.

The universe would be better without Bobs.

Lucas cast Bob a scowl as he cut a square in the capture bag, while Gita suspended the massive drill of the mechanical space arm above their target.

It would be better without Jennifers who dump toxic pesticides into pristine streams; and Hadjis who transport giant hogweed, which is known to cause blindness, from Asia to North America to feather out their gardens; or Borises who release their pet anacondas into the Florida ecosystem where they seem quite content to kill all the native species, including alligators. The universe would be much improved if it dumped certain DNA from the evolutionary chain.

"Almost there," said Bob, as the boom shivered along its length. Not a good sign.

Bob was having trouble maintaining a solid grasp on the boom. His muscles were rebelling because he hadn't adhered to the ISA's strict regimen of exercise while he was ill.

Lucas ignored Bob and helped guide the laser drill onto the selected site, attaching braces and punching in bolts to keep it secure.

"Bob, your heart rate's accelerating," said Gita. "We have a good two hours of drilling to do. You sure you're up to it?"

"I'm fine," said Bob, floating around the boom and coming level with Lucas. Lucas glanced quickly through Bob's faceplate. He was flushed, and his face glistened with perspiration. Bob was either going to pass out or drop the precious packets of bacteria and send them sailing off into space where they might, eventually, thousands of years later, seed *another* planet.

"Breathe, Bob," Lucas said patiently, even though he felt like throttling the weakling.

Bob nodded and proceeded to take deep whiffling breaths.

"Now fasten your tether to the boom so we don't lose you."

Or the bacteria. Nothing would make him happier than to lose Bob. But the astronaut was already tethered to the hatch of the *Phoenix*, so there was no real hope of that. However, if he lost his grip on the boom he might sail several feet away, and Lucas would be required to expend extra effort to haul him back.

Bob stopped breathing—unfortunately it was only momentary—and clipped his tether to the end of the boom.

"Ready when you are," he said, with a wink.

"Sure," said Lucas.

Weak, clumsy, a waste of good oxygen. And not ready by a long shot.

"Except we need the shield."

"Oh. Right," said Bob.

He released his hold on the boom and fumbled with the belt and link with which he'd attached the shield to his suit. The Kevlar in their suits would protect them from micrometeorites in space, but if the drill blasted ice particles toward them at this proximity, the projectiles might puncture the material, and then they'd lose pressure and be exposed to the vacuum of space.

Bob released the drill shield and nearly failed to recapture it, his hands having an epileptic fit of trembling. Damn Bob.

Lucas reacted as quickly as zero gravity allowed, seizing the thick Plexiglas sheet and positioning it between their bodies and the drill. He anchored it to the capture bag with grappling hooks. Then he flipped the switch, triggering the laser. A beam shot from the nozzle and sliced into the frozen shell of the comet, melting and vaporizing the ice, and also deflecting multiple droplets into space. They refroze instantly, resembling a still-shot image of a geyser. The initiation sequence complete, all they needed to do now was to monitor the drilling process and finally, when they'd penetrated as deep as was required, lower the bacterial specimens into the comet.

Lucas kept one eye on the beam intensity and the integrity of the drill position and the other on the red planet. It drifted below his suspended body, a mosaic of bronze, tan, salmon, and charcoal mountains and valleys, extinct volcanoes, and intricately carved canyons. Craters pocked the entire surface, most of them millions of years in age. But now, rather than the ubiquitous dust, daring curlicues of cloud streaked the atmosphere, trapping moisture and creating ozone.

What a thrill to be part of this renewal process, even though he wouldn't get the chance to explore the surface. He recalled the first human explorers who'd set foot on Mars years ago and discovered remnants of bacteria and a wealth of precursor molecules that proved without a doubt that this planet had once harbored life.

Yes, Mars had once flourished! And asteroids had been crucial in creating a viable planet, he'd learned through his studies of planetary geology. During what was classified as the *Noachian* period, 4.1 to 3.7 billion years ago, which started with the formation of the Hellas impact basin—the second largest impact zone on Mars—an age of warm temperatures and abundant water began. Asteroid impacts had introduced energy and volatile gas, just as the comets would do now. Carbon dioxide and nitrogen from the atmosphere had bound readily with magnesium, iron, or sodium in the minerals on the planet's surface to form carbonates and nitrates. Volcanoes like the enormous Olympus Mons—a shield volcano three times the height of Mount Everest and with six times the base diameter of Mauna Kea—had recycled these elements by boiling nitrogen and carbon dioxide out of the minerals and reintroducing them into the atmosphere.

What a wondrous sight it must have been—this active planet bubbling with life and awash in shallow oceans. But the volcanoes had died and Mars had reabsorbed its atmosphere. Mars, without a vital core of circulating magma and therefore without an electromagnetic field, no longer had the ability to shield the surface from the charged particles of the solar wind. Even with all humanity's efforts at terraforming, the absence of a circulatory system would continue to plague them. The upper atmosphere and the ozone layer would be vulnerable to the particles carried by the solar wind and, once stripped away, would no longer block the UV radiation that nothing, including extremophiles, could survive. But with the ozone up and running, they would have centuries to consider the problem. Maybe they'd have to tow a few asteroids into orbit and combine them to create an artificial moon. Mars did have moons—Phobos and Deimos—but neither one had enough mass to promote circulation and an EM field.

That's why the Gilgamesh Movement is proceeding too quickly. Let the scientists contemplate this issue further, before they are of no more use. After all, they aren't all Bobs. The Movement should look at them as resources that needn't be squandered prematurely, especially since the terraforming may take another century to prepare Mars for permanent settlement.

The laser beam's progress suddenly stalled, and a warning light flashed on the drill monitor, indicating that they might have encountered an obstruction—most likely a rock buried in the comet. But they'd already tunneled 500 feet. He stopped drilling to temporarily adjust the laser to a higher setting before restarting it and pulverizing the stubborn rock. Soon they would be approaching the ideal depth—800 feet into the comet's interior.

"Pretty amazing, isn't it?" said Bob, pointing at the Martian surface, barely paying attention to their expensive hardware. "I wish they'd let us land."

"Good idea," said Lucas, tempted to swat the man's head. "Land on the most unstable planet in the solar system, right after we've kick-started its volcanoes and generated massive earthquakes with our comet and asteroid bombardment. And if we don't think that's a great enough challenge, I'd love to set down in the middle of one of those dust storms, just to see if we can crash the MADVEC."

"Well," said Bob. "I'd be willing to take the risk. It may be dangerous but, hell, space is dangerous. After all, we won't live long enough to see it when it's finally ready to settle."

You won't, anyway. Which will be a blessing.

Longevity or cloning might give Lucas the opportunity, though.

"Even if it were a possibility, we'd be wasting valuable fuel and we could miss the targeted fuel depot and become stranded. We need to stick to the mission assigned us."

"Are you really such an obedient drone?" asked Bob, eyeing him through his long Bambi lashes. "You ignored Mission Control when they instructed you to review the mission details regarding the previous asteroid capture and tow around the moon. Instead, you kept checking engine control systems as if

Geneva doesn't monitor them 24/7. And when you did finally scan through the document, you spent an awfully long time recalculating, as if you didn't trust the genius minds behind the mission."

Lucas bristled. If there was anyone he didn't trust . . . But maybe Bob was more observant than he'd realized. Gita usually left Lucas to his own devices, confident he'd follow procedure and make accurate calculations in case of computer malfunction, since he was the designated flight engineer and copilot. But Bob had always been nosy. Lucas had assumed, from Bob's obvious uncertainty and dubious abilities, that this was his way of double-checking his own work—looking over Lucas's shoulder to extract information that he might be lacking, and probing Lucas with questions to ensure that he performed his own operations correctly. But maybe Bob wasn't as bumbling as he seemed.

"We won't always have those genius minds to rely on, as you should know."

"I know. I know. I nearly goofed. I guess I depend too religiously on the computer, and I didn't realize it had jumbled all the data. But if we'd missed that comet it wouldn't have had the same repercussions as redirecting our homeward-bound asteroid."

"Which is why I was recalculating. But you're wrong about the repercussions. Any delay in the terraforming could mean disaster on Earth, too. We only have finite time to make Mars habitable before our overburdened planet dies."

"I guess," said Bob. "Which is why I'd like to help you in the Near-Earth Asteroid Capture and Retrieval Mission. Just to have, you know, an extra pair of hands, in case there's trouble."

"There's no drilling involved in that one," said Lucas, trying to keep his voice level. "It's just a matter of relocating the asteroid to a location that is accessible for the mining crews near the moon. It doesn't require an astrogeologist."

The last thing he needed was a bloody buffoon like Bob peering over his shoulder, interfering in his work. He'd busted his ass for this assignment. He'd mortgaged his life to get through graduate school and astronaut training, scored brownie points with the ISA for his Mars seeding proposal, then tripled his score with a moon mission that proved he was equipped to handle space travel. He'd never experienced a touch of space sickness, had maintained his muscle mass like an Olympian and, despite a double dose of radiation exposure because of back-to-back missions, showed not a hint of genetic aberrations nor any deterioration of his vision. He was the ideal man for this mission, with the ideal brain. Someone like Bob shouldn't even be allowed to approach his corner of the spacecraft, let alone intrude on his work.

"You may not require it, but it always pays to have someone double-check your work."

"After what happened with your last assignment, docking with ACREV . . ."

Bob flicked his finger at the drill unit. He tilted his head and followed up with a wave of his hand.

Lucas returned his focus to the unit, noting the signature depth.

"Don't you think it's time to switch off?"

"Yes, Bob. I think it's time to switch off."

He switched off the laser, instantly erasing the intense beam, which temporarily played havoc with his vision. When his pupils finally adjusted to the blackness of space, he motioned to Bob.

"Time to place the specimens."

"Undoubtedly," said Bob.

Lucas eyed the man again. Had he known all along that they were approaching the ideal depth? Was Bob playing a game with him, acting the fool to keep him complacent while at the same time attempting to make him seem incompetent? Did Bob, perhaps, know about the Movement? Was he thinking of sabotaging Lucas's career because of his involvement with them? But no one knew of their plan except insiders, and who among them would leak . . . No. Not his brother. He might be an aggravating oppositionalist, but he wouldn't have gone that far.

"Yes, we're ready," said Lucas. He detached the drill from the comet's surface, yanking out bolts, then informed Gita that she needed to retract the space arm.

"Very good, Lucas," said Gita. "And I'd keep the arguments to a minimum, guys. I know we might be getting on each other's nerves after living in such close quarters, even if it was a short hop, but an EVA is not the time to let off steam. I don't want to see any mishaps out there, especially considering the cost if we fail on this mission."

"Not a chance," said Bob. "We're not arguing, are we, Lucas?"

Did Bob just grin through his contoured space helmet? Lucas gritted his teeth, but Gita's command required a response.

"No. No arguments. We're bosom buddies out here. Mission almost completed."

Bob fumbled with his pack—or was he fake-fumbling?—and finally extracted the capsules of bacteria. With the capsules neatly tethered in a tensile net, the whole assemblage resembled a massive condom. In the meantime, Gita had extended the opposite arm with a telescoping pole and a strong, thin cable. Lucas clipped the samples to the cable, and they began the tedious process of ever-so-gently lowering the bundle of bacteria into the comet. Since there was no gravity, the cable had to be powered to force the bundle into the cavity and to the proper depth.

This was a twenty-minute procedure, but eventually Lucas released the bundle, and the cable was carefully withdrawn from the deep pocket in the comet. As Gita retracted the arm, the men's last task was to return to the capsule, working their way hand over hand along the boom. Bob's breathing rasped through the comm like a whistling tornado; his arms continued to tremble with every grip and release. Since contracting the virus, he'd become physically ill-equipped for this mission. But was he mentally competent? Or maybe even canny?

As they approached the hatch, a nagging thought badgered Lucas. Bob blotted his view like a bloated wall, blocking any glimpse of Mars or the hatch or even the vast emptiness of space. Bob should be dismantled, blasted apart, dismembered. Bob stood—or floated—solidly in his way.

He ripped open his Velcro pocket with eager fingers, tunneling toward the cushioned utility knife at the bottom—the tool he'd used to cut into the comet's capture bag, and a necessity in case their tethers became tangled and kept them from returning to the hatch. Now he could sever a tether for another reason. Of course, it would require a solid push to get Bob beyond the short flight distance the fuel in their jetpack allowed.

Lucas's fingers hovered over the thick cord of Bob's tether which, as Bob climbed closer to the hatch, dangled back toward him and constantly flicked against his helmet. He raised the knife, poised to slice.

"Bob, do you really want to visit Mars?"

"Yes. Absolutely. I dream of it." He didn't look back or give any indication he found Lucas's question disturbing.

Lucas hesitated, the temptation so excruciating his head throbbed. But in the final instant he retracted the blade.

I wish I could make your dream come true, Bob.

He re-sheathed the knife in his pouch.

But I may need you just a little longer.

Bob sailed in through the hatch, totally oblivious, as Lucas gazed one last time at Mars—a russet and butterscotch orb cupped in the void of space. He had an inexplicable ache in his belly.

And you don't deserve Mars, even as a corpse.

Scanning...

Located: Chapter 5

BARUTI SHIVERED AS he wobbled over a patch of exposed rocks on the riverbank. A massive cow with an intimidating rack of palmate antlers—a moose, perhaps?—raised its snout from the rippling waves, where it was delicately sipping the frigid water. It was still several feet away and not as threatening a sight as the polar bear, but it paid to be cautious. These creatures were also known to charge.

At least that's what he'd read in his swift absorption of all things Canadian.

His companions had offered to drop him off in the pleasant village of Peawanuck, where he would be surrounded by the friendly Cree. There he could tuck into his sleeping bag in the reasonably warm Catholic church and sip heavenly hot chocolate that would thaw his nose and fingers. But he'd declined. He would wait for them at the helicopter on the Winisk River, and search the roadway and the air for that odd accumulation of traffic in this remote region.

"Miners," Wilson had replied in their tent the night before, when Baruti had asked about the trucks and excavators he'd seen parading through Peawanuck on his way to Polar Bear Park. "They've found another deposit of diamonds."

DeLuca, the geologist, had snorted.

"They *think* they've found another deposit of diamonds. But if you look at the composition of the rock,"—and he'd actually opened a virtual map from his tablet—"you'll see that the kimberlite intrusion,"—he tapped a glistening shaft of rock—"is well to the south of us, in Attawapiskat, where the South Africans set up shop years ago."

"Kimberlite?" Baruti feigned ignorance.

"A volcanic pipe, an intrusion into the bedrock from an earlier active age that often contains diamonds. Did you know that some of the rocks, particularly in the northern region of Hudson Bay, are the oldest intact rocks found on Earth—some 4.28 billion years old?"

"Really," said Baruti. "And that has to do with diamonds how?"

"It doesn't have anything to do with diamonds," said DeLuca, a gleam in his eye. "I just threw that in because it's cool, and we're all scientists."

Wilson had grunted, which drew an evil eye from the geologist.

"Rocks tell us as much about our planet as polar bears," he'd snapped.

"Yes. So let's gouge them out of the earth, strip mine, blast, pummel, and smash them, and send clouds of soot into the air so the polar bears, and we, for that matter, can't breathe without coughing, can't traipse across the earth without tripping, and—"

"Unfortunately, we do need resources to survive, especially since our population has grown in explosive increments, the last few years."

"We don't need diamonds!" Wilson had practically shouted.

"Yes, we do. We need them for lasers, for X-ray machines, for that bloody laptop from the dinosaur age you insist on carrying around, along with our latest quantum computers. How can you track your polar bears without rocks? What a complete ass," he'd added under his breath.

Baruti had looked away, at the tent bowing in from the wind, at the half-empty beer bottles sitting on the nylon floor, at the partially consumed stew growing more glutinous by the second. It was an old argument, not worthy of comment. No doubt these men usually worked together quite harmoniously, but the bodies had spooked them nearly as much as they'd spooked him—although they weren't about to admit it. DeLuca and Wilson kept insisting that the bodies were an archaeological find, but he worried—he even suspected—that they weren't.

"I miss the rhinos," he'd said to the wind.

"Excuse me?"

Wilson had suddenly deflated like a punctured tire. He'd known exactly what Baruti was talking about.

"They were never beautiful creatures. They never evoked the same reverence and admiration in the general public as the polar bear. But where the bear can adapt because he can alter his patterns to suit the environment, the rhino was simply slaughtered. Where the industry is justified, we sigh in resignation at the destruction it renders. Where was the justification in that?" *And which species would be next?* he'd wondered silently.

No one had answered. The two others had just stared solemnly at their half-eaten meal.

Baruti had shuffled out of the tent afterward, leaving his beer and his congealing stew behind. He'd gazed across the tundra to the mysterious bog, which was acquiring a violet hue as twilight merged with dawn. Was he up to this job? Had they recruited the right man? He'd killed a man before. It had taken more than a greedy poacher sawing off a bloody horn to spur him to action, but he'd not balked at the task. Could he do it again?

He'd shaken his head, shivered. The shadows had rapidly retreated as the sun shuffled cautiously over the horizon.

It was frigid here, but not empty, not without austere beauty. Even in the early dawn, lavender blooms of heather blushed in the sun, and myriad white geese fluttered down to the small bog hillocks and the polygons of drying mud like gentle snowflakes. A herd of shy caribou was crossing acres of sparse forest to venture near the shoreline, a tawny rippling blanket with jagged loose threads where their horns projected from the mass. He could even see the hump of a white whale emerging from the cobalt waves of Hudson Bay.

That was this morning, a few hours ago, before the scientists had hauled their sleep-weary bodies out of camp to usher in another expert—an archaeologist. The group was growing, which would make his task more complicated.

Baruti heard the sputter of an engine in the distance. He aimed the telephoto lens of his camera at the moose, angling ever so slightly to the right, to the road. A massive semi jounced over the ice-cracked pavement, two men hunched behind the dash, a pudgy middle-aged Caucasian man with frizzy ash-blond hair and a taller scarred man with, possibly, Shona features. Baruti tapped the trigger, his camera shuddering through repeated clicks. *Snap. Snap. Snap.* What were they transporting? Diamonds? Raw slag? Mining equipment? Samples? Death?

Were they going to venture into the scientists' camp and begin posturing, promising to preserve the land and wildlife while their actions inferred quite the opposite? What were they up to now? What had prompted them to aim their devious eyes at the Canadian North?

The pictures would be meaningless without a peek in the back of one of those trucks. But it was too soon for that. He'd wait for the archaeologist. If this expert revealed what he suspected, then he'd have something more to go on, proof that their operations were merely a front and something sinister was afoot. And if he had proof, this time . . . there'd be no escape for them.

A buzzing sound from the air alerted him to the scientists' possible approach. He spotted the distant speck in the sky to the south, a gnat that gradually swelled in size and began angling for the river. But DeLuca didn't sweep around for a northerly landing. What was he doing? He was heading right for the massive limestone cliffs that rose eighty feet above the river, where the banks were tidily carved into a canyon. Was he insane?

Then Baruti remembered the man nearly tipping him out of the helicopter. Yes, he was insane.

DeLuca waggled his wings and lowered the plane precisely between the cliffs, the wings nearly clipping both sides as the plane descended. He sloped downward precipitously and bounced onto the river with an echoing slap of floats against waves. The engine powered down, and the plane began skidding to a halt, tilted precariously forward.

Baruti backed away.

The plane shivered another ten feet, danced for a few seconds high on the tips of its floats, then slammed back onto the water, upright. A breeze washed over Baruti, chilling his already frozen face. He said a silent prayer of thanks that the aircraft hadn't tumbled nose-over-floats, and he didn't need to dive into the bone-chilling water to rescue the idiot scientists. He was also extremely relieved that he hadn't decided to accompany them.

The door to the plane snapped open. DeLuca skipped out with an unsettling clownish smile on his face. Baruti met his grin with an eye roll, as the crazy geologist gathered up a rope and tossed it to him.

"Tie me up, will you, buddy?" he called.

Baruti caught the rope and spiraled it around an aluminum post jammed into the muddy bank that would act as the dock in this secluded spot. He hauled gently on the rope and anchored the plane to the post. DeLuca leaped out and steadied the float against the makeshift dock.

"There you go, Wilson. You can help our guest out."

Wilson popped his head out from the back of the plane, bobbled out the door, and presented his hand to someone in the back. Baruti could hardly contain his surprise when a petite, wafer-thin woman with thick auburn hair and waif-like eyes draped her slender leg over the edge of the craft and teetered on the float. She jumped from the float to the bank, ignoring Wilson's proffered hand.

When she staggered onto the bank, she turned and scowled at DeLuca.

"Did you really have to land between cliffs?"

DeLuca shrugged. "Hey, we made it. And we're not even wet. I thought you were the man for the job."

Was there a sneer in DeLuca's voice? What had the lovely lady done?

"Felicity," said Wilson, jumping to the bank beside her, with his usual grace and agility. "This is our other resident biologist, Baruti Mbeki. Baruti, Felicity Cratchett, archaeologist-cum–grad student."

"Pleased to meet you," said Baruti.

Grad student? Now that explained the tender age. And perhaps a bit of DeLuca's disdain. He'd expected an expert.

Baruti held out his hand, the customary greeting here, and she shyly shook.

"You have quite an accent. Are you from around here?" she asked.

"I hail from Botswana, but I had this nagging desire to study creatures from other regions. Think of me as an exchange student." He smiled.

She nodded and staggered again, her balance obviously upset by the extreme flight. Wilson reached out to steady her, but she flinched away. Strange.

"Are you all right?" Baruti asked. "I believe DeLuca has kamikaze tendencies. I nearly fell out of his helicopter yesterday."

"Helicopter?" she said, her eyes growing enormous. Unusual eyes they were, too. Thick-lashed and haunting like the antelope, but colored like the gray dawn streaked with flecks of lavender.

"Ah, they didn't tell you. The site where we discovered the bodies is still several miles away, in an area without roads and no channels for a boat or Jet Ski. I'm sorry to say you will have to camp on the tundra with us until you've extracted them. But I would be happy to help, no matter how cold and miserable the job."

She blinked and eyed Wilson with a pinched forehead, almost as if she were angry at him.

"I expected a tent, but not a helicopter," she muttered.

"Sorry," said Wilson. "Another ride. But at least we have plenty to eat."

Now that was an odd statement. Was he afraid the girl would wither away? She was thin, but not, as far as he could determine, starving.

"I can handle a helicopter. As long as the pilot knows what he's doing," she added softly.

"And I can deal with a student," said DeLuca in a much louder tone. "As long as she's halfway competent and knows enough to eat sufficiently on the job."

Suddenly Baruti understood, at least partially. The girl had already proved to be unreliable or foolish in some respect. Perhaps she hadn't taken the time to eat a substantial meal on her way north and was feeling the effects. And she was angry at Wilson because he was treating her like a child in need of a guiding hand, and even more angry at DeLuca, whom she simply ignored, because *he* was treating her like a liability.

Regardless, she was the expert the powers that be had sent to investigate. He would trust their judgment and hope she would provide him with more information. Maybe enough to confirm his suspicions. He trotted past the two men and beckoned her down the path to the helicopter.

"I think you'll do fine," he said. "I've adjusted to DeLuca's piloting quirks. I've even adapted to the climate, although I still shiver uncontrollably at times."

He slipped her an encouraging smile.

She returned his smile and hurried behind him on the trail, her step marked by a pronounced limp. Not only young, and in DeLuca's mind of questionable competence, but a tad lame. He felt warmth flood through him, a flaring of compassion. Not a good thing. Chase it away. Tromp on it. He would not succumb to it again. It might tear him from the path he'd chosen. It might cause him to waver. He'd thought it had been trained out of him. He'd thought he would no longer be tormented, but would simply mark his passage with suitable revenge.

He decided then and there: If she stumbled, he would reach out to help her. If she shivered in the dark, he would keep her warm. If she balked at any creature, he would snatch her away from danger. He would be Wilson. He would make her hate him.

After . . . he got what he needed.

Felicity wobbled as her toe grazed a surface root, and grabbed a branch to steady herself. Baruti noted the stumble out the corner of his eye, but he didn't turn around, nor did he slow his steps to match her stride. When he reached the helicopter, he turned back and found she'd nearly kept up, and was limping forward decisively just beyond the tip of the rotor. He opened the door and hopped in, not even offering her a hand. When she slung herself in, she shot him a broad smile, until Wilson swung in beside her and gave her a boost.

Baruti shook his head.

Wilson, you can't read people at all, can you? Do you really think we like to be reminded of our weaknesses? Do you really think she will thank you for hovering like an overprotective parent? Maybe DeLuca is right. You are a complete ass.

Just to make it absolutely undeniable, Wilson knelt down, tenderly draped the seatbelt over the girl, and snapped it home.

Scanning...

Located: Chapter 6

"CAN I SEE the artifact?" asked Felicity, when they'd finally reached the puppet-sized tent that hugged the ground on the scrub grass near the coast. Shaun had explained that it had to be erected with a low apex and fastened tight to the ground, or the persistent wind off the bay would likely topple it or bell it out and rip the stakes from the soft earth, sending it hurtling into a polar bear den. He'd grinned when he'd said it.

"I thought you might want to see the bodies first," said DeLuca, his voice a wintry monotone. Well, at least he wasn't snarling anymore.

Felicity had tried to question them in the plane and the helicopter, but they'd refused to answer. Even the friendly Botswanan biologist hadn't offered any details. They'd simply said that they couldn't speculate. She was the expert, so they'd leave the interpretations to her.

She looked at the three of them now and silently classified them: Shaun—honey-blond, classically handsome, overly friendly, and too nurturing; Baruti—dark, rugged, with intense, intelligent eyes and a disposition that was oddly warm and politely cool at the same time; and last and hopefully least, Tony—bulky, brittle, potentially a bastard.

No prejudging now, she chastised herself.

"No. The artifact is why I was called in to consult. I need to know what you found."

Shaun nodded and groped in his backpack, producing one of his T-shirts wadded up in a ball. He carefully unfolded the bundle and removed a chain of conjoined elliptical links, with a circular pendant swinging from it. A cloak of tarnish left it blackened with a speckled hue of gray.

"Silver?" she wondered aloud, holding it up to the light.

Shaun shrugged, but DeLuca nodded, albeit reluctantly.

"I believe so. Which would be unusual but not fantastic in this location, except for the markings. It's nothing a Cree would have produced or even traded for, in the past. Maybe the person in the bog died fairly recently and bought this on eBay, but, well, he . . . she . . . the body . . . . looked old."

Felicity fetched a tissue from her purse, wet it with a squirt from her water bottle, and scrubbed ever so gently at the residual mud and tarnish. The pendant still appeared mottled, but she was certain. The size was that of a denarius, the face none other than the emperor Vespasian; it was a Roman coin. Even the etchings, although barely legible, could be distinguished as COS III, indicating the third time the emperor held the consulship, around 71 or 72 AD.

"Oh, my God!" she said.

"Do you think it's real?" asked Baruti, crowding closer.

"I can't be sure. It could be a fake. But this certainly looks like a Roman coin."

DeLuca snorted. "So you think our body on the Hudson Bay coast is *Roman*?"

"I didn't say that," said Felicity. "I couldn't say that with any certainty until I've examined it in a lab. And frankly, I doubt it."

"Then how would you explain this?" asked Baruti, his eyes strangely lit up.

"I can't. An artifact of this age and origin shouldn't be here. Sometimes Europeans wore Roman coins as pendants, but there weren't any explorers this far north. Well, not many, anyway."

"D'you think we've finally found Henry Hudson?" said Shaun, with an uncertain grin.

Felicity shrugged. Could this be the lost explorer who was abandoned by his crew in the upper region of James Bay, near the belly of Hudson Bay and the present-day Polar Bear Provincial Park? That would be an extraordinary find, something to trigger a cascade of excitement among historians and archaeologists. But she was transfixed by the impossible. Rome. She shook her head. eBay, where hundreds of Roman coins were passed on to collectors on a daily basis, was the most likely answer. If that were the case, they'd need a medical examiner for this body, not an archaeology student.

"Well," she said, shaking off the spell. Gently, she folded the coin and its chain back into Shaun's shirt—which seemed a far too intimate gesture. "Shall we look at the bodies?" They had arrived at the moment she dreaded.

Shaun nodded, but the cords in his neck stiffened. Her own muscles were absolutely taut, but she imagined a biologist would be accustomed to the autopsy and dissection of corpses, at least of the animal variety. DeLuca shrugged and barely batted an eye as he slipped out of the tent, which didn't surprise her considering how he handled aircraft. But Baruti, who appeared to be the least hardy in this environment and who was still shivering in the brisk wind, grinned and beamed a radiant smile at her.

"I was rather alarmed by them, at first," he said. "But this is a mystery far more fascinating than polar bears."

"Nothing is more fascinating than polar bears," said Shaun. "But the site's a few miles from here. It's not easy traveling, so we'll be riding the helicopter again. DeLuca picked up some stretchers in Peawanuck to transport the bodies, but we're not sure how many are buried in the bog. It might take a few trips to collect them all."

Felicity felt a familiar lump develop in her throat, and followed by a few scattered knots throughout her abdomen. *Several* bodies. She'd had enough trouble dealing with one.

"I guess we have work to do, then," she said, grinning with an expression that she hoped exuded enthusiasm.

Baruti's eyes crimped, apparently unconvinced. She scrambled to her feet and rushed out of the tent, her bum leg dragging and snagging a guy line, nearly tripping her. Shaun instantly shot out his arm and steadied her, while Baruti, following closely behind, continued to gaze out over the bristly terrain as if nothing had occurred. He might have even let her fall and get up again on her own. It seemed so un-gallant, yet it was exactly what she needed. Someone who'd encourage her Minerva fantasy, even if she doubted it herself.

"Are there polar bears at the site?" she asked, trying to maintain an even tone.

"We tranquilized one there," said Shaun. "But he's probably moved on by now. We'll keep an eye out and our tranquilizer guns at the ready."

He patted her arm with his free hand, while maintaining his grip with the other.

"I'm all right, you know," she assured him. "Just an old injury to my leg, but it doesn't affect me much."

"Right," he said. "But I don't mind lending my support *at all.*"

He winked suggestively, and she couldn't deny that she enjoyed his touch and was captivated by his arresting green eyes, which were imbued with a tint of catlike amber, but his manner implied that she needed a crutch.

She patted his hand, smiled, and forcibly extracted her arm.

"That's nice, but I can stand on my own just fine."

She hobbled after Baruti, who was already halfway across the field to the helicopter. Blue-green lichens brushed against her boots, which began to accumulate a lingering crust of ice from some soggy patches. A seal rose out of the rippling waters of the bay and snorted, shocking her as it flopped onto the shore and eyed her with an X-ray stare. She stopped for a moment, mesmerized by this novel communication, but then she snapped the spell and moved on.

Her gaze wandered over the pancake-flat horizon. Rhododendron, crowberry, and mountain cranberry lent an early summer blush to the emerald and black land, which stretched to distant peaks of straggly forest. After living in densely populated cities and working in small, neatly-worked plots in the Netherlands, this view seemed limitless and eternal. Of course, that was an illusion. Even the Arctic was suffering the creep of human invasion, and the frigid temperatures were yielding to the warmer breeze of a man-made greenhouse.

The ice-melt was inevitable, although it had been briefly subdued by a staggered scientific effort. She knew that eventually this flat plain would flood, unless the Canadian government could erect dikes and reclaim land like the Dutch. Hardly likely. There would be thousands of miles to rescue, and that wouldn't save coastal cities, or Holland, for that matter. As the oceans encroached on more and more land, and mankind kept breeding, every isolated region would be inundated with either water or human development. The irony lay in that, while they were losing Earth to greenhouse gases, they required them to terraform Mars.

She turned to face the gyrating rotors, her stomach churning at the thought of DeLuca's flying habits. He might think of them as carefree—she would call them extreme and reckless. But something caught her notice out the corner of her eye. Another plane, and then another, soaring over the pristine landscape—a parade of planes that seemed better suited to a New York City airport or a military base than the Canadian North.

She hurried to catch up with Baruti.

"Why all the planes?" she asked the biologist. "Almost looks like a squadron. Are there military camps around here?"

Baruti shook his head. "I don't think so. I think they're the miners."

"Miners? What are they mining?"

"They're prospecting for diamonds. Maybe even found some already," said Shaun, hovering again, although now his face was flushed from chasing after her. "Always invading the bears' space, and the caribou's, and the birds'; digging out and destroying their habitat for sparkly little rocks for women to wear on their fingers. Why? Most people don't even get married anymore."

Felicity flinched. She nonchalantly slid the birthday gift from her father—a diamond and ruby ring—around her finger, so the stones faced her palm.

"Some people still like to adorn themselves," said Baruti. "Or make trinkets or icons. But there are a few other uses for diamonds. Miners are not necessarily monsters."

He said this with a straight face, without inflection in his voice. Why did she sense that it was an act, a speech a politician would make to justify something he knew was absolute hokum?

"But you don't believe that."

He looked down at her, narrowing his eyes; but not in an angry way, just with apparent surprise.

"DeLuca believes it," he said. "And I suppose he has some valid points. I've met miners, and I've met monsters, and they aren't *always* the same beast."

Felicity caught her breath. What did he mean? Was he talking about blood diamonds? The miners and even children who'd been exploited for so many years in various countries in Africa? She opened her mouth to inquire, but he spun away and dashed for the helicopter.

"Baruti has this way of speaking bluntly," said Shaun. "Sometimes you know exactly where he's coming from. Sometimes it leaves you totally bewildered. I think he's had a hell of a life."

Felicity nodded and followed the biologist, Shaun nearly hugging her side. Why did everything on this side of the world seem so complicated? For a minute, she longed to be back on the other side of the Atlantic, digging up simple, sad European sacrifices.

FELICITY HEAVED ON the humongous drysuit, shaking her head at its ridiculous proportions. No one had imagined a petite woman archaeologist would be joining their excavation, so no one—meaning DeLuca, who was in charge of supplies—had thought to select a smaller drysuit. She hadn't considered that the bog where they'd be extracting the bodies wouldn't have been partially drained to give her better access, so she hadn't brought one along, either.

The suit flopped around her arms and dragged at her legs, but it would have to do. At least the gloves were more elastic and were one-size-fits-all, she noted as she tugged them on. Baruti and Shaun were also donning drysuits and gloves, while DeLuca maintained his usual attire—jeans and a flannel shirt—since they needed to station one assistant on the gravel ridge above the water to remove the bodies, once they were liberated from the mud. Apparently the ridge was the only solid path through this saturated land—a crest of pebbled and crushed rock deposited by wave action through the millennia.

Felicity looked out over the bog. The cloying smell of rotting plant material rose from the brackish water and assaulted her senses. Small squalls of mosquitoes swept in and hovered like mist over the dozens of ponds. She swatted at them and dabbed extra repellent on her face.

"Be very careful where you step," she said. "You can't see anything in this water."

"Looks and feels like molasses," said Shaun. "Baruti and Tony already crunched through a couple of your bodies. Sorry about that."

"You shouldn't really be sorry," said Baruti. "Otherwise we wouldn't have found them. But at the time, I was sorry to have found them." He shuddered. "Nightmare creatures."

Felicity couldn't agree more. She'd handled and photographed enough skulls in her sculpting classes. She'd even helped to arrange a mummy exhibit at the Boston Museum. Those were no problem—sanitized, ready for public viewing. But, here at the source, these slimy boneless bodies still curdled her coffee.

She lowered her legs into the motionless water, sending it jostling from side to side between the compact peat hummocks. Slithering down deeper, her feet brushed something spongy that didn't feel like mud. She shifted her boot and settled her foot in something nearly as spongy, but which felt less gelatinous and more like pudding.

"It looks like this might be a . . . corpse-free place to stand."

Felicity shifted a few inches backward, then a few more, finding a relatively open path. She dipped her gloved hands into the water, seeking the jelly-like material. Shaun splashed in beside her, near enough to be her shadow. He shuffled even closer—far too close for comfort—prompting her to edge sideways until her boot nudged the pliable mass. Baruti entered the pool directly behind Shaun.

Well, it was now or never. Time to get totally dirty and absolutely grossed out.

Felicity leaned into the water, her nose brushing the surface as she groped underneath and finally discovered the mound at the bottom. She whispered her hands over its breadth, estimating dimensions. She stretched her arms, measuring height, shuffled sideways, and added another three feet to her calculations. The body was significantly above average height for a typical man from an earlier age—over six feet. It seemed slightly swollen in the torso, so a little broader than Shaun through the chest, although that could be attributed to gases within the tissue as it decomposed. The canvas tarps they'd carried along from camp should suffice to lift and remove the bodies, if they were all a comparable size. DeLuca had also obtained over-sized body bags to protect the remains once they were extracted.

"Can you hand me a tarp?" she asked DeLuca.

He shook out a folded beige rectangle of canvas and placed it in her outstretched hands.

"I want you two to roll the body," she instructed the biologists, "cradling it along its length *really carefully* so I can tuck this underneath. Then we lift it all at once, but almost in slow motion. The tissue might fragment or the legs and arms could fall off. You hold the legs, Baruti, and we'll roll together, so hopefully we can pull him out in one piece."

Shaun grimaced, but Baruti didn't bat an eye. Just a tiny twitch in his lips suggested he might find the job distasteful. She took a deep breath, searching for inner strength. Somehow she must adopt the same kind of poker-face.

She rolled up the tarp to halfway across its width and slipped it along the edge of the body. The men shuffled alongside her and groped in the water, digging their fingers under the fleshy mound.

"Okay. On three," she said. She counted it out, and at "three," they turned, and she shoved the rolled-up edge underneath. She sighed when she felt them gently lower the body back onto the tarp.

"That only gets us halfway," said Shaun.

"Now we have to repeat the process on the other side, and I'll pull the rolled section of the tarp out straight. Just like transferring an immobile patient in a hospital from a stretcher to a bed."

Hopefully, they'd watched a few hospital dramas, but by their squinting expressions she doubted it. This wasn't a standard method of bog body extraction. This was something she'd improvised from her high school volunteer days at the Boston General.

They shuffled one by one around the body until they'd reached the opposite side and repeated the procedure. Felicity detected a tear in the corpse's lower limb at pelvis-level, but she could excuse whatever damage was done. They weren't exactly supplied with modern tools in a dredged pond. When the tarp was properly aligned, she instructed Shaun to shuffle back to the other side and Baruti to remain beside her—a much better arrangement, since they kept jostling each other and touching far too frequently, drysuit or no drysuit.

"Now we lift," she said. "At a snail's pace," she added.

Baruti seemed comfortable with this tedious, meticulous rate of extraction, but Shaun seemed antsy, as if he'd like to wash his hands of cuddling corpses as soon as possible. And who could blame him? But she needed him to reel back the adrenaline or, when they were through, the body would be nothing but scraps of flesh and curdled cartilage, and potentially a head so crumpled it would resemble a deflated soccer ball.

"No quick jolts. Try to watch each other and work in synchronicity."

Shaun grunted his agreement. Baruti smiled as if he gloried in the grotesque. She wished she could feel the same.

They bent their knees, clutched the edges of the tarp—their faces dipping in and out of the muddy water—and lifted, gradually straightening their legs. The tarp rose inch by inch and, as it gained the surface, water streamed off the gelatinous mound. A head appeared, with clumps of stringy hair. A body came next, stippled with mud and cloaked in remnants of disintegrating clothing. All three excavators shuffled, grunted, shifted, and turned, until DeLuca could grab the tarp and assist from the ridge. He had a stretcher ready, draped with a body bag that was unzipped and spread wide. So as to avoid too many transfers, they raised the tarp right over the stretcher and laid the corpse within the body bag.

"Next," said Shaun, obviously anxious to escape the flesh-tainted waters of the swamp.

Felicity nodded, but the fully revealed body held her gaze. A drooping brown mass surrounded the torso. It could be a cloak, or it could be a coat. Sopping furry leggings enfolded the feet and lower legs—possibly wool, but more likely fox fur or some equivalent. But the remaining garb, the wide skirt that circled the waist and sagged over the legs, could not be any modern-day clothing. It didn't resemble an explorer's outfit from the seventeenth century either—leather breeches and a waistcoat.

"What do you think?" asked Baruti. "Is this an ancient or a fresh corpse?"

"I don't know," said Felicity, still mesmerized by the irrefutable evidence.

"Of course you don't," he said. "But you suspect something."

"What I suspect," she said finally, looking up and meeting his searching gaze, "is impossible. So we'll wait and do a full examination at camp, and then, once he's been transferred to a lab, I'll take a peek under the surface. We won't make assumptions. We'll gather proof."

There, that sounded like a professional archaeologist, didn't it? No one would ever suspect that her knees were nearly crumpling and her tummy was a tightly-clenched ball. And yet, a flutter of curiosity brushed away the revulsion. Maybe she was no longer the artist but was becoming the investigator—the puzzler who could piece together clues from the past and revel in the story they told. Maybe, if she could believe in herself as much as Professor Lugan did, she could still transform into a worthy expert.

"Are we going to finish this?" asked Shaun. Poor mud-draped, miserable Shaun, who kept wrinkling his nose and visibly suppressing the urge to vomit. He didn't hover anymore. Maybe he sensed her newfound strength.

"Sure thing," she said, and swung around, dragging her boots through the tangled roots and spongy earth until she found the next heap of withered flesh. "We'll get this finished before you pass out," she couldn't help but say.

Scanning...

Located: Chapter 7

"I DOUBT WE can finish this today," said Felicity. "I'm starting to think there are dozens."

"Or at least ten," said Baruti, his hands scooping into the mud again and shifting their eighth body.

Five had been carefully wrapped by DeLuca and strapped to the stretchers. He'd already conducted two flights with two bodies each to their camp and was now preparing to deliver the fifth and sixth. Not all of the remains were intact. Several had detached arms and legs; one had misplaced its head. None of the subsequent bodies wore the same clothing as the first—although all were swaddled in a knee-length garment resembling a tunic—which was ridiculous.

The three scientists now worked in unison, avoiding all jerks or wobbles that might destroy tissue, although Felicity noticed that Shaun's face still looked a tad green. They raised the eighth corpse, water bubbling and splashing as it coursed off the leathery specimen and sought to return to its undisturbed state in the ripple-free bog beyond. But as discernible features emerged and clothing sprang free of the mud, Felicity gasped and nearly dropped the bundle.

"It doesn't look like the others, does it?" said Baruti, his face pressing closer, even more engrossed with this one.

A thicker thatch of hair clung to the scalp, worked into a silky black plait that sloughed off the mud easily. The face still retained shape and bold angles. Were the bones intact? A coarse material was wrapped around the legs, the color bright, even through the muddy overlay; it looked like blue denim. A stretchy fabric with lettering across its width covered the torso. Not Roman numerals or Latin. She deciphered it, but could hardly believe her eyes. It read *Roughriders.*

"Correct me if I'm wrong," said DeLuca, "but this guy looks like he's wearing jeans and a sweatshirt."

"Not exactly Roman," said Baruti. "Not exactly old."

Shaun didn't utter a word, but his face had grown slack and turned ashen.

"I guess we should call the medical examiner," Felicity said, her voice shivery again—no longer a voice to inspire confidence. For a minute she couldn't move, either.

"Coroner," grunted DeLuca.

"Well, we'd better get him to the path," said Baruti, taking charge without hesitation. He didn't seem even remotely shaken, while Shaun looked weak and wobbly.

"One step at a time, as we've been doing. This one is no different, no matter how he ended up here. We can't leave him buried in the mud. It's probably more important that we rescue him than the others."

"But w—we might be disturbing a crime scene," said Felicity.

DeLuca chuckled and shook his head. The laughter was derisive, rather than being provoked by anything funny about this situation, because there was absolutely nothing funny about this situation.

"Do you really think that a crack team of forensic investigators will come rushing to the middle of a bog along Hudson Bay to investigate? One RCMP officer, maybe, if this is some scientist or miner. If Cree, one low level detective."

"Seriously?" said Felicity. "That level of prejudice still exists here?"

"Seriously," said DeLuca. "That level of prejudice still exists everywhere."

They hoisted the new, definitely contemporary body onto the recently vacated stretcher that the geologist had brought back. More mud sloughed from the face, revealing a flared nose and rounded cheeks. It was hard to determine skin tone, but with the rich ebony hair, this person was looking more and more Cree.

"We probably shouldn't extract any more bodies until the police have determined if there was foul play involved, and have had a chance to do a thorough search of the area," said Felicity.

"Well, I think you have enough to go on," said Shaun. "More than enough to go on."

"Should we take this body to camp along with the others?" Felicity asked.

She grappled at the side of the ridge and tried to bounce out of the cavity. But her foot stayed lodged in the mud—her weaker foot—and she wobbled backward, tumbling into the soupy water they'd stirred up, complete with floating tissue and body parts. As she plunged underwater, disembodied fingers caught in her hair, and a bloated sac of indeterminate flesh smacked against her cheek. She scrambled to get up but couldn't get her feet under her, the muscles in her weak leg flinching and rebelling. Before she could manage a grip on the spongy ground, a hand snatched her from the watery graveyard and hoisted her up, her head clunking against someone's chest. Shaun, she expected. But when she wiped off the mud and no doubt some clinging tissue—*Oh God, could anything be more disgusting?*—she beheld Baruti's calm face and mildly shocked expression. He seemed as surprised as she was that he'd lent a hand.

He quickly released her and mumbled an apology.

"I would have been fine," she sputtered. "But I didn't want to dive into that, so . . . thanks."

She looked up to witness Shaun vomiting on the gravel beside their most recently recovered corpse. No wonder he hadn't come to her rescue. But really, it should be she retching and throwing up, and it wasn't. Amazing.

"Are you okay?" asked DeLuca, scowling at her and Shaun, both.

"Absolutely." She scowled back. "Even though I'm the one who took a nose dive into a cesspool of body parts, I'm not the one puking."

"Great," he said, hardly sounding impressed but not scowling quite as much, at her.

"To answer your question: Yes, we might as well bring him along. Since he was dumped into the bog along with a whole heap of likely unrelated bodies, it's going to take weeks to sort out whose DNA belongs to whom. I don't envy the sorting process."

Felicity winced. Undoubtedly, she'd be part of the sorting team. Which meant she might be stuck here, or be required to travel back and forth from this location to a lab for quite some time.

Surprisingly, DeLuca offered her a hand out of the water which she surprised herself by accepting. How could it be considered cowardly to want to escape this nightmarish bog? He couldn't think any less of her, anyway. Or maybe he could, but at this point she didn't care.

Baruti gladly accepted the geologist's assistance, although he still didn't seem as shaken as anyone else. He squatted down beside their most recently rescued body, squinting at it and nearly touching it.

"What are you doing?" she said. "You can't touch it anymore. The police—"

"I suppose you're the expert," said Baruti. "But do you honestly think in the mix of other bodies and tissue I'll be disturbing evidence if I look for a bullet hole?"

DeLuca tilted his head, and even Shaun looked up from his hunched position, wiping his mouth. They were probably all thinking the same thing.

"Why do you think he was shot?"

Baruti shrugged noncommittally, as he crept closer to scrutinize an area on the corpse's skull with a sunken, fragmented appearance. After a moment, he said, "Looks like a head shot. Probably from a high powered rifle. Like the poachers used to wipe out the rhinos at home."

Felicity caught her breath. Baruti was suggesting murder, which was enough to send shivers through her body despite the drysuit. But it was the image he evoked of the *extinction event* that chilled her even more deeply.

"Or hunters for elk and caribou. Even seals," said Shaun. "It could have been an accident."

DeLuca looked skeptical. Baruti even smiled.

"Yes, I suppose it could have been," he said, his long face twitching with amusement. "Does the thought of a murder disturb you, Shaun?"

"I just can't see any reason for it. Here," he said, swallowing repeatedly and taking deep breaths. Obviously he was still being hit by waves of nausea. "If we have any murders in this area, they're usually due to domestic issues and not usually covered up."

Baruti shrugged. "Maybe it has to do with the Romans, or whoever they are. Don't you think it's rather coincidental that this person ended up in the same bog? Maybe he discovered the bodies first and someone didn't want him to."

Cold sweat streamed from Felicity's pores at Baruti's suggestion.

"Why would anyone want this site covered up? Especially enough to kill someone? Even if these remains have been here for centuries, it only has archaeological significance. We didn't find gold or priceless artifacts. Just bodies."

"Hmm," said DeLuca. "But weren't mummies sold for profit for years in Egypt, even in ancient times?"

"These aren't mummies," Felicity clarified. "They're bog bodies—very hard to preserve once you remove them from the bog. And I haven't heard of a black market for these. It doesn't make sense."

"Neither does a mining company digging for diamonds where there are no kimberlite pipes," said DeLuca. "Where two unrelated things don't add up in the same location, they're usually related."

His statement hung in the air, rife with implications. Felicity hugged her arms to her chest. Was something sinister happening in this remote region of Canada? Could they have stumbled onto a mystery that might put their own lives at risk? And why was Baruti smiling?

She might as well ask.

"Baruti, why are you smiling?"

He eyed DeLuca, then shrugged, a grin still perched on his face.

"Our geologist, who has spent the last three days defending the mining operations in the North, has just suggested the miners are monsters."

"No," DeLuca replied, his expression a hash of emotions. "What I've just suggested is that the miners aren't miners. And maybe the time is ripe for a mining inspector."

"Right," said Felicity. "Good idea. Let's call in the police and other experts. I also need to transport the bodies back to a lab as soon as possible, before they start disintegrating from exposure to air. For safety's sake, we won't breathe a word of this to anyone."

And I need to get out of here as soon as possible. I didn't sign on for a murder investigation.

"But you're the archaeology consultant," said DeLuca. "If the miners aren't miners but have some association with these supposedly ancient bodies, the police might need your expert opinion."

Felicity met his gaze. His hard, penetrating, critical gaze.

"You are the man for the job, right?"

"Stop it, Tony," said Shaun. "She's young. We might be talking murder here. Give her a break."

Baruti didn't say anything. He didn't nod to agree with Shaun, but his eyes swept over her, evaluating her in a disquieting way. Why did it matter what he thought of her?

She knelt beside the bodies, once again analyzing. Along with those who resembled each other in appearance and dress but didn't look particularly Roman, there was one who wore ancient attire that suggested a Roman legionnaire, and one who was undoubtedly Canadian and definitely not ancient at all. She owed it to all of them to find out why they'd died. She'd been delegated the responsibility. If she left now, she'd be abandoning them, even if she accompanied them to a lab. If the authorities needed her to investigate and interpret archaeological findings in a mining operation, then that's exactly what she'd do, with a police escort. Young, foolish, inadequate—they could call her what they liked. But she hadn't felt queasy since she'd arrived, she hadn't thrown up despite the stew of body parts, and she wasn't about to cower away from another, potentially more dangerous, assignment.

"I am the *person* for the job," she said, straightening, standing, and briskly shedding her drysuit. "I can tell you right now that we have one man who seems to be wearing Roman apparel, and several men and women who appear ancient, but have some other cultural affiliation. And we have a *woman* from the current age," she emphasized, "probably from the Cree nation."

Their eyes snapped wide at her assessment, suddenly realizing what they'd overlooked in the mud-enshrouded corpse.

"I'd like to examine them in a little more detail at camp before we organize transport. I think we will definitely need a police escort, but with their help I think it's time to check out the diamond mine for diamonds and whatever else they're cooking. Agreed?"

"Agreed," said DeLuca.

He gave her a stiff nod, clearly the most she could expect from him. Baruti saluted, which almost made her laugh. But Shaun looked forlorn, as if she'd just signed on for a one-way expedition to Hell. Why would he be so concerned for her? And why did it still make her angry?

She could picture her father hovering over her in the hospital after her car accident. Her aunt whispering to her cousin, "She's such a fragile thing, poor darling. Be surprised if she lives through this." Her painful tears as she struggled through yet another round of physiotherapy.

And then there was Professor Davies, her mentor, the man she idolized, scrutinizing her sculptures and shaking his head. "I'd like to, Felicity. I know it's your passion. But you just don't have enough talent. I can't recommend you for a scholarship. You might be able to do forensic work, but I really think you should pursue a career in archaeology. It's not second best if you throw your heart into it."

No, it wasn't second best, bog bodies and gross assignments aside. And *she* wasn't second best. She wasn't as seasoned as Professor Lugan, but she was becoming quite skilled at discerning detail, at detective work, at analyzing a decayed or glutinous mass and deciphering the clues it provided. She could stand on her own two feet. She didn't need a crutch.

She met all their eyes and even managed to summon a smile.

"Then let's get to work," she said.

Scanning...

Located: Chapter 8

"I DON'T UNDERSTAND your objections," snapped Bob, who had strapped himself firmly to the dinner table so as to avoid floating through the capsule while he sipped at his coffee from a capillary flow cup. Bob was a conventional fellow who couldn't seem to dispense with mealtime etiquette and allow himself to float serenely in midair while eating or taking a coffee break.

"You don't strike me as a man who always obeys the rules."

Lucas fought to contain his emotions. That was far too intuitive of Bob.

"They monitor the MADVEC from Earth. They'll know if we abscond with it within minutes—they still monitor it around the clock, and a laser signal will be transmitted the second it fires up. Besides, even if I did want to directly disobey our instructions, the surface is so unstable right now, the risk—"

"You know we can land in the northern hemisphere, a considerable distance from the last bombardment, before we release this comet. We're creating an ocean there. Don't you want to see it, in reality rather than virtually? With your level of radiation exposure they may never let you fly here again."

And with your level of incompetence, they'll certainly never let you, Bob. Was that what this ridiculous scheme was all about? Bob seizing his last opportunity for exploration?

Gita, who'd been unusually quiet throughout their exchange, twirling her glossy teak-colored hair around her finger and studying her coffee, suddenly piped up.

"It's worth considering. In terms of exploration, we're given considerable leeway, as long as we don't waste fuel and jeopardize future missions, or miss the ideal return window to Earth. We're no longer hampered by as tight a return window to Earth with an EPR engine anyway. A few days of exploration would not be out of the question."

Were they both insane? Of course, despite the International Space Agency's rigorous selection process, they were the same as every other astronaut—IQs off the chart (although Bob might be an exception), easily capable of lying to the psychologists during their screening interviews, extremely arrogant with self-centered objectives. Those objectives inevitably were: escaping the confines of an overly-crowded planet; traveling in space and exploring the universe, particularly to another planet; and then gaining glory upon their return.

Astronauts were the equivalent of pop stars, only their stars would shine far more brightly and for a longer period of time than any other, especially if they had PR skills. There was little glory to be gained in rerouting an asteroid or comet anymore. It was old hat. Even setting foot on Mars had been achieved several years ago. But not setting foot on a wet Mars, an algae-speckled Mars growing gradually greener, a Mars that had acquired enough of an atmosphere for them to dispense with pressurized suits and simply substitute elasticized jumpsuits, face masks, and a tank of air each, to walk freely on the surface. On the other hand, Mars was active now, with volcanoes bubbling lava, and expanding sub-terranean aquifers created by warming, and even the occasional earthquake that could easily fracture the ground where they proposed to set down a spacecraft. And where it wasn't wet enough yet, the dust storms persisted. What Bob was proposing was extremely hazardous.

And it would delay another crucial step in the Movement's plan.

"I can't—"

"You don't have to," said Bob. "You can scooch down in your bunk and read a novel while Gita and I explore the planet. If something happens, you can detail all your objections in the log and distance yourself from any responsibility. But is that what you really want? Do you want to tell your grandchildren 'I brought Mars back to life, but they wouldn't allow me to explore it. I had the chance to walk on its surface once, if I'd been only slightly rebellious, but I didn't take it.'"

So easy, isn't it, Bob? To play upon my ego. It may be as gargantuan as yours, but it's not the same. I would rather not harm Mars-in-the-making, because I see my future in it. Your future is blurred, and may even end before this mission is complete.

But it was clear to Lucas that they'd made up their minds, and he would either have to stay behind and let them trouble the terraforming, or accompany them in order to monitor them on the surface. Either way, he couldn't stop them unless he killed them—not an entirely unpleasant thought, particularly when it came to Bob—but that might jeopardize the return mission.

"Fine," he said bluntly. "I'll join your little adventure. Two days, three at the most, considering the conditions. We snap a few photos, we walk along the shore of the ocean, we collect samples, to see how the terraforming is progressing and at least have a partial excuse for having made a side trip. You want your minute of fame, I'll give it to you." *And then some.* "But for God's sake, don't do anything reckless."

"Yes, Mother," said Bob with a smirk. Man, Lucas wanted to slap him. What an obnoxious bastard.

But Gita smiled and patted his shoulder, surprising him with her touch.

"Of course we won't. This is very exciting, but we will treat it as any planetary mission."

Lucas experienced a flutter of arousal at her touch. Not enough to prompt action, mind you. He wasn't about to risk botching the mission for a quick roll in . . . midair, since they'd deactivated the artificial gravity. He wasn't as weak as his brother. Shaun's passion for polar bears was nothing compared to his passion for women, especially since his divorce. And he had behaved so recklessly and emotionally lately, Lucas feared he was becoming unstable. But Shaun was still his brother. Lucas would continue to defend him, especially to the men and women in the Movement who argued for his removal. As few enough people existed with their family's exceptional "qualities," to speak of getting rid of Shaun was preposterous. Besides, Shaun would never betray them.

Lucas missed his brother. They'd grown apart because of Shaun's objections to Gilgamesh. The Movement's plan fully supported his ideals, but unfortunately Shaun's empathy extended beyond polar bears and other rapidly disappearing creatures on Earth. Shaun thought that reintroducing them on Mars would be enough, and that any harsher measures would be unnecessary.

Which reminded him—bringing his thoughts back to the present—that he should ensure he was involved in the choice of landing site. Preferably a good distance from any recent excursions. It wouldn't do for them to stumble upon "buried treasure," especially with Bob along. As innocent and bumbling as the astronaut seemed, something more devious dwelt in his heart; Lucas was sure of it now. A something that would revel in bringing Lucas down. He wasn't a total idiot, either. He had somehow obtained an advanced degree—albeit in space rocks—and survived astronaut training—no small feat.

"I'll prep the *Phoenix* for docking with the MADVEC," said Gita, breaking into Lucas's thoughts. "We'll decouple from the ACREV and leave it and the comet in orbit until we've completed our tour of Mars."

Lucas nodded, but a shiver rippled through him, nonetheless. They were actually going through with this risky business. They were going to defy orders and descend to Mars.

"I'll plot our descent vector to ensure we land on the safest site," he replied.

"Sounds good," Gita replied, as she pulled herself out through the doorway and into the corridor toward the *Phoenix's* docking hatch.

Lucas coasted to the main console and pulled up a map of Mars.

The last two landings had been on the Tempe Terra, a vast smooth plain of higher elevation in the northern hemisphere near the Kasei Valles. Kasei was a dry river valley and an outflow channel that originated in the two- to three-mile-deep Echus Chasma just north of the massive canyon system, Valles Marineris.

But the planet had been considerably altered since those landings. The parabolic mirror that had been erected ten years ago was in orbit, where it redirected and focused the sun's rays at the north polar region, the location of the majority of the ice and carbonic snow. Ever since its deployment, this mirror had been melting the crust of ice and permafrost and consequently flooding the Vastitas Borealis, a basin that had held an ocean 3.8 billion years ago. Enough ice had been melted or vaporized, uniting with the vapor produced from melted comets in the atmosphere, to create clouds and, by extension, even occasional rainfall. This condensation and ice melt had succeeded in filling a considerable portion of the basin. Even the canyon of the Valles Marineris, located near reactivated volcanoes, had been partially recharged with water as the planet warmed and melted the sediment-laced ice.

With all this activity, the Tempe Terra base would undoubtedly be unstable, even though it was located several thousands of miles from the volcanic mountain chain, as it was still within an area that could be inundated with seeping magma and heating geothermal aquifers.

So, in order to avoid that area, for this reason and others, he would have to plot another descent vector for the Mars injection. Perhaps they should set the capsule down on Arabia Terra, another ridged plain like Tempe Terra, but sufficiently distanced from it by an area of lower elevation, the Chryse Planitia basin. It was near an ocean fill zone, which might please Bob, who wanted to dip his fingers into an ocean. And another automated fuel factory had been set down in the region, essential for resupplying their ferry, the MADVEC, with methane for rocket fuel. These factories absorbed carbon dioxide from the atmosphere—since Martian air was 95% CO_2—and combined it with hydrogen that had been transported from Earth. The ISA had remote-piloted the factories to Mars prior to the initiation of dozens of manned missions to the planet. There would be plenty of fuel for the MADVEC to re-achieve orbit and dock with the *Phoenix*.

Bob finished his coffee, released himself from the table tether, and drifted toward Lucas.

"Looking for a landing site?"

"Obviously," Lucas said.

"I wouldn't mind setting down in the same area as the last crew. Great view, near a canyon." He winked. "It even has caves, especially Vitalis, where they discovered the first Martian archaea and biological precursor molecules."

"It's unstable, Bob. And Vitalis is still quite a hike, near Mawrth Vallis." Where had the committee found this guy? "The Mars Global Surveyor detected multiple tremors in the Tempe Terra zone recently. We don't want to damage the MADVEC. We don't have any other way to get off-planet."

"But they've only delivered five fuel factories, two of which are in the southern hemisphere. We don't have many choices."

"Arabia Terra should do fine. It might even have an ocean view by now."

"But not quite as dramatic," said Bob. "Rather boring. A few craters and dunes, but very few canyons or caves."

"It's Mars. Honestly, what do you want? The planet is still a dead rock; no fish in the sea, just a few flecks of algae here and there where we planted them. Yes, it's an alien planet. So anywhere we set down should be a thrill, for what it's worth. But are you really willing to risk becoming stranded there with limited oxygen and only emergency rations? The next scheduled flight is several months away on the books, and any damage to our HAB or the flight vehicle might put us in extreme jeopardy."

"Being strapped to the EPR engine on the *Phoenix* puts us in extreme jeopardy every day. Okay, so they upgraded the safety features since the first two exploded on the way to Mars, but nothing can save us if we have a reactor leak or the magnetic shield fails, or if a spark ignites our multiple tanks of hydrogen propellant. I'd be willing to take a chance on a slightly less stable location on my one and only visit to Mars to see some of its spectacular features."

Lucas sighed internally. This man was determined to set their expiration date.

"Well, I'm not. You're too much of a risk-taker, Bob. I don't know how you passed the psych evaluations. When we transfer to the MADVEC, I'm plugging in the coordinates for Arabia Terra."

Bob glared at him, clearly not willing to back down. But surprisingly he said, "Fine. We'll play it safe. At least we'll see the ocean and witness how the terraforming is progressing. We'll be able to test the air quality too, see if we can start introducing subarctic plant life—something other than cyanobacteria and genetically engineered lichens."

Bob leaped into midair and pushed off toward the storage bay to gather the laser spectrometer and other instruments and equipment to take measurements and collect samples when they landed. Lucas practically sighed aloud. Now that he'd selected an appropriate landing site, he might actually enjoy this excursion.

Yes, it wasn't part of the plan. And yes, it would delay their return to Earth. But he had to admit, nothing could be more thrilling than touching down on Mars, a planet that would seed a new generation and hopefully leave behind the parasites who now inhabited Earth. He'd never dreamed that he would get the chance, not for several years, and perhaps never. But maybe having Bob along wasn't the worst situation, despite his irritating comments and constant hovering. Once in a while, in a world gone to hell, rebellion was just what was needed.

Scanning...

Located: Chapter 9

BARUTI CRAWLED OUT of the tent the next morning, the bite in the air wrenching the drowsiness from him in an instant. More effective than a double espresso. The wind swirled around him, peppering him with ice particles and frosting his eyebrows. In the distance, the granite columns of Sutton Ridge jutted from the surrounding sink of bogs and stunted trees like an alien castle, its battlements withstanding bone-stripping wind and the constant assault of ice and snow. So odd that this feature existed in the soggy wetlands and frozen ponds of the tundra. No doubt it was the product of a volcanic intrusion, like the kimberlite pipes farther to the south, but not of the same composition, according to DeLuca.

Baruti had studied the geology of diamond formation before. He understood that kimberlite pipes are volcanic channels that develop deep in the Earth's crust due to a sudden, violent eruption of magma that explodes upward. When the magma reaches the Earth's surface it can pool in a circular shape, forming something like a maar, but surface remnants are rarely seen, since the eruption site is usually swathed in vegetation in the years that follow. These pipes serve as carriers for diamonds.

Yes, he likely knew as much about diamonds as DeLuca. Not that he was particularly interested in diamonds. Just diamond miners. Or diamond mines that served as fronts for other operations.

Movement caught his eye beyond the grass field that extended in front of him, amongst the patches of rocks and lichen in the bog. A white shape that streaked across the emerald and cerulean background. A polar bear?

No, too small. Could be an arctic fox or wolf. He didn't feel particularly alarmed, but it would be wise to be cautious. The wild dogs and hyenas he was familiar with in the Okavango were nothing to sneer at, particularly as human expansion pushed them out of their habitat and jammed them up against civilization.

"What do you see?"

The voice startled him. It was the young archaeologist—Felicity. He found her hunched over one of the bodies they'd extracted, probing it ever so gently. The sight of her triggered a wave of melancholy. He nearly sighed, and kicked himself besides. He should have insisted that she abandon her investigation—even of the older corpses—when they'd discovered what was in all probability a murder. He was less affected by the thought of the two men, particularly the idiot Shaun, getting caught in this web of murder and deceit, although they had done nothing to deserve it either. But he would be more distraught if Felicity were killed.

"A fox, I think. A well-defined white creature leaping over the tundra."

"Or a polar bear?" she asked, her voice betraying a ripple of nerves.

"I don't think so. Not massive enough."

He squatted beside her, eyeing the tweezers in her hand, the threads of material she had separated from the corpse, and the tarnished metal object that rested on the ground.

"What have you found?"

"Just a silver bracelet."

She pointed at the object with a corkscrew twist that could circle a wrist.

"Origin?"

She smiled shyly. "You really want me to stake my reputation on a cursory examination?"

He leaned forward and whispered, "You're a student. You need to establish a reputation. Why not begin here?"

She looked into his eyes, not fearful, so trusting.

"All right. The bracelet could be Roman, but I don't think it is."

"Why?"

"Because of the big picture. This man is bearded. That's rarely seen in Romans, although he's a long way from home and it might not have been easy to shave in this environment. But even more extraordinary is the way the beard is teased into curls at the tips. And he's wearing what looks like a mantle over his shoulders, not a typical tunic. I found a cap on one of the others, too. Shaped like a helmet, but gathered into a top knot."

"Meaning . . . ?"

"Phoenician."

"The sailors?" said Baruti.

"Yes. But there is absolutely no evidence that the Phoenicians ever sailed farther than the Mediterranean or the northern coast of Africa, let alone to this remote area in North America."

"Isn't there?" he asked.

Should I tell her?

"No," she said. "Unless you have information I don't."

People rarely solved puzzles when missing so many pieces. If she was exactly who she claimed to be—the expert and not the wavering child—she was exactly the person he might need. But the deeper he pulled her into the mire, the more likely it was that she would never escape.

"Perhaps I do," he said.

He was still wrestling with whether he should show it to her when the throb of a helicopter interrupted him. The aircraft was approaching their camp. At first, it appeared to be the size of a mosquito, but gradually it assumed more daunting proportions. It descended and hovered for a few seconds, seeking a solid patch of gravel to set down upon.

DeLuca flipped open the flap of the tent, massaging his temple in an attempt to prod his sleep-drugged brain out of its coma.

"Police?" asked Baruti.

"Not yet," said DeLuca.

Which undoubtedly meant the miners. How easy it would be for them to make four scientists disappear, although that would not be a brilliant move, at this stage of the game. Even so, Baruti reached into his pocket and gripped the compact pistol, one of two he'd procured when he'd landed in Toronto.

The helicopter settled on the ground, rotors thumping. The downdraft shattered ice crystals, sending showers of them hurtling toward the camp. Felicity quickly zipped up the body bags and covered them with a tarp that was tied to sturdy pegs.

"Idiots," she muttered.

But the miners could hardly have heard of their discovery, unless they'd been apprised through some official channel. Indeed, Baruti wouldn't be surprised if some officials were woven into the fabric.

As the engine died down, two men jumped from the back of the helicopter. They were tightly wrapped in parkas and woolen hats, but Baruti recognized one of them from the truck he'd photographed. The first was stocky and deeply tanned, with bottle-green eyes and ash-blond hair. The other—the man he recognized—was slimmer, with darker skin tones and possibly Shona features, although both men had squat foreheads and pronounced chins. They crunched over the crust of frost that covered the moss and blades of grass, their gazes traveling to the array of tarps on the ground.

As the first man strode forward with eager steps, the other paused and looked at Felicity. Baruti saw lust and violence in his eyes, although the other scientists probably wouldn't interpret it as such. She returned his look with equal intensity. Brave girl.

"Hello, there," said the blond man, sweeping each scientist with an exhaustive look, even Wilson, who'd finally emerged from the tent and stood scratching his head. "We are your next-door neighbors, so I thought it appropriate that we meet. Gerald Hunter." He extended his hand to Baruti first.

"Baruti Mbeki," he muttered.

The man smiled, shook, discarded his hand quickly, and moved on. He shook DeLuca's and Wilson's hands, then, as Felicity got to her feet, gave her small fingers an extended shake. Bastard. No doubt he was assessing her as not much of a threat.

"This is my assistant, Hondo Nsogwa. Hondo and I are from the African continent, which I've surmised that you are as well, . . . Baruti, is it? Our company works predominantly in Africa, but we're looking to expand."

"Are you prospecting for diamonds?" asked DeLuca.

The man displayed a plastic smile. Nothing of his soul touched it.

"Yes. I'm sure you've heard of our operation by now. Huge territory, small world. Especially in the North." He paused. "We're not affiliated with the Attawapiskat operation. We're a start-up company. No blood diamonds to scar our records, I swear."

"Never occurred to me," said Tony dryly. "You are a long way from Africa."

"Yes, well . . . I admit, the Grosbeek operation turned our sights this way. I believe every metal and mineral has been excavated in Zimbabwe. Still some virgin territory up here." He winked. "We do have permits."

"Never doubted it," said DeLuca.

"And I was told you were tagging polar bears. What do you have under the tarps? Seals to snag them with?" He chuckled and directed a pointed look at Felicity.

Baruti rolled his eyes. The man's performance was as thin as a worn pair of boxer shorts.

"They're just . . . We've found . . ."

Please lie, he begged her silently. Not that these guys weren't already fully aware. Why else would they have flown here at the break of dawn? But to admit anything would be to invite scrutiny.

"Samples," said DeLuca. "Biological samples that shouldn't be disturbed. We're conducting some experiments in the field. Very sensitive."

Hunter swept the tarps with a penetrating gaze, and gave a terse nod.

"I understand. Wouldn't want to muddle your research. Just, as a scientist—not always a business man, mind you—couldn't help but be curious. I'd love to learn about your discoveries. Particularly regarding the rebounding polar bears. Is it true?" He turned to Baruti.

"Looks promising," he responded. *Unlike the elephants and rhinos, as you well know.*

"Rather odd that you've come all this way to study Arctic creatures. You know, they even talk about you in the village—in Peawanuck. The biologist from Botswana. So why polar bears, my friend?"

Baruti's gut clenched at the term. As if they could ever be *friends.*

"I've studied enough animals on their way to extinction. I wanted to investigate a species with hope of recovery. If we can understand how this species adapts, maybe we can save the few that remain."

There, you marago. *See if you can make me stumble.*

"I imagine you don't care for miners," said Nsogwa, speaking up for the first time. "You think we disrupt the environment too significantly, and disturb the creatures within it."

He'd stepped closer to Baruti, but still slanted glances toward Felicity. Was he the henchman, or the leader? Often quieter men harbored more secrets.

"I have nothing against carefully conducted mining operations," replied Baruti. "As long as you're respectful, we'll respect you. And Dr. DeLuca, here, is a geologist. He's likely a fan." He tried to smile, but his lips felt like stone.

"Really?" said Hunter. "A geologist who chases polar bears?"

"Actually," said DeLuca, "a geologist who flies helicopters and float planes for poor pathetic biologists who have no other means of transportation. But in fact, I wouldn't mind having a look at your samples."

"We've only just begun to prospect," said Hunter. "Not much to show yet; just setting up operations. But if you have a nose for diamonds, I would welcome your input."

DeLuca pressed his lips together. No doubt he wanted to point out that the warehouse he'd noticed from the air, the fleet of trucks, excavation equipment, and cargo planes, hardly seemed like a small-scale prospecting endeavor. But that would invite a raid on their camp, possibly even an assassination attempt.

"No nose, really," he said. "I'm more interested in Sutton Ridge and studying the rock formations for the Canadian Geological Survey. When I don't have to fly these junior scientists."

Hunter and Nsogwa looked startled, but immediately reset their impassive expressions. Perhaps they were worried that DeLuca would, while conducting his survey, detect something fishy at their site near Sutton Ridge.

"Junior?" Wilson finally spoke up. "Just because I can't fly doesn't mean I haven't been hiking, canoeing, and traveling through the North for years while I studied the wildlife."

He didn't mention Felicity, but Hunter's gaze now settled on her. Nsogwa's eyes were already fixed on her.

"Guilty as charged," she said. Her voice jangled a bit, but she met their scrutiny without flushing. "Grad student. And not quite accustomed to the environment. But these men are breaking me in."

"I imagine they are," said Hunter.

Nsogwa leered. For the first time Baruti noticed his unusual eyes, a deep shade of olive, rather than mahogany, something like his own mother's. Maybe they had similar ancestry.

"I—I didn't mean . . ."

"Of course not, my dear."

Baruti gritted his teeth. So patronizing.

Felicity bristled, but remained quiet. Little did she know, these men put *some* people in a category below the dirt they trampled on, if what Baruti suspected was true. For a moment, they became more and *less* than men. For a moment, they grew horns and reptilian tails. Baruti shook his head, and the vision cleared.

"I'm just getting my feet wet," Felicity tried to clarify. "Getting experience in the field."

Baruti suppressed a smile. She'd gotten more than her feet wet. Swimming in body parts.

"Which reminds me," said DeLuca, cutting into the conversation. "We have a great deal of work to do today. I'm sorry to be abrupt, but maybe we could chat again in Peawanuck at a later date. Our experiments are time-dependent."

"Certainly," said Hunter. "Didn't mean to interrupt your very important work. I wouldn't mind a drink around the fire in that quaint little village. Gets awfully chilly here. And I'd love to learn more about your research."

"Yes," said Baruti. "As we would yours." He couldn't help himself.

The men gazed at him, obviously taking more from his comment than a superficial meaning. It was stupid, really, to encourage more scrutiny. But he imagined his cover had already been blown. And these men knew exactly what lay beneath the tarps. They also knew that the bodies had been reported to the police, and that they could hardly charge in, rake down a number of scientists, and do a complete mop-up afterward without triggering an RCMP investigation.

"I'm sure our work would bore you to tears," said Hunter. "Just digging in the dirt."

"Digging for diamonds," said Baruti. "Not really a profit in it, though, if all you find is dirt."

"Oh, we usually find something," said Nsogwa. "Something worth *madi*," he added in Setswana.

He nodded, the movement so brittle his neck looked like it would snap, then pivoted toward the helicopter in a brisk military-like maneuver. Hunter now sported a huge grin, displaying a row of glistening ivory teeth that seemed to overwhelm his mouth. He patted Felicity on the shoulder as if she were a dog, and tromped after his companion.

The scientists watched the copter as it took off, spraying them with swirling grass and pellets of ice. They shielded their eyes, and kept watching the aircraft shrink in the sky until it finally disappeared. Wilson swiped a trembling hand through his hair, DeLuca curled his hands into fists, but Felicity stood without a wobble, her hands pressed to her lips, as if she were deep in thought.

She turned to Baruti, her eyes locking with his.

"What did he say? *Madi?* What does that mean?" she queried.

Baruti hesitated. "Money," he finally said.

He shifted on the grass and tore his gaze away from her. He couldn't tell her. He couldn't tell any of them. Yes, *madi* meant money in Setswana, but it also meant blood.

Scanning...

Located: Chapter 10

DAYNA LUGAN TOOK a long, delectable drag on her cigarette, as she propped her feet up on the scuffed oak coffee table in her office and closed her eyes, drinking in the silence. After a minute of happy indulgence, she opened her eyes and examined her desk, which was appropriately festooned with artifacts and facsimiles. She reached out and touched the plastic-wrapped Mayan codex, then gently tapped her fingers on the fake Medieval goblet, which was filled to the brim with wine. Early in the day to start, she knew, but after a three-hour lecture for summer students and four intensive hours spent in translating the codex, she deserved a break, didn't she? Especially after her husband had mistakenly texted her instead of his mistress last night—*Hey sweetness. Are you in town yet? I can't stand another night with the nagging professor or another dull monologue about her brilliant grad students. Not to mention the grisly details of her latest excavation of bog bodies.*—she definitely deserved the sweet syrup of the gods, or a toke from the stash of one of her students.

Bastard!

As if she didn't have enough to deal with, starting with her attempts to ignite enthusiasm in her fresh undergrad chicklings over what several of them had termed "dusty relics." They were obviously only taking archaeology to fulfill their course requirements. At the same time, she had to keep track of her grad students who, parceled out to various countries, were either putting her reputation as a teacher into jeopardy or ramping it up a few notches. Now what? Nasty arguments, separation, divorce?

She had to admit, it had been a long time coming. In recent years, she'd welcomed her annual summer break—although she'd had to forego it this year to cover lectures for an ill colleague—and especially the year of sabbatical she'd taken to study the European bog bodies—her specialty. She'd reveled in the freedom—the opportunity to traipse through the Netherlands, Germany, and England, and to get her hands dirty in the field while leaving her lawyerly husband to his corporate shenanigans. After he'd washed his hands of pro bono work for the poor, the disadvantaged, the outcasts who often needed an inclined ear, he had started defending banks, the double-dealing executives of high tech companies, and even the odd client who emitted a whiff of Mafia. Just touching him made her feel dirty, something she'd never experienced even while nose-deep in mud-entombed corpses.

He hadn't failed to notice that she shrank from his touch more and more every day. She hadn't failed to notice his quick recovery from her aversion.

Perhaps she deserved some of the blame. Perhaps she'd driven him away when she'd failed again and again to conceive, when she'd fallen into a depression after the one daughter she'd managed to carry to term had died shortly after birth, and especially when she began casting accusing glances at him after the birth mother of their adopted son had challenged Evan's every legal maneuver and managed to reclaim her child. She'd tried to control the unfair feelings of blame and had only looked at him that way when he shouldn't have been aware. One thing about Evan, though: He was constantly aware of everything. A lawyer's habit.

She'd have to tell him it was over today. She'd have to call. . . . No, text first. Then a face-to-face.

Dayna drew up her contact list on her cell phone and accessed Evan's name. *Need to talk. Can we meet for lunch?* she texted.

The next second, a video call request appeared on her interface. Felicity, patching in via satellite from the Canadian North. Fabulous. At least she'd have a distraction for a few minutes, something to keep her mind off the inevitable. She opened up the link on her virtual computer.

"Felicity?"

The girl's pale freckled face and auburn hair, bordered by blue-green lichens and a bone-colored canvas tent flapping in the wind, filled the space above her desk.

"Hello, Professor Lugan. I hope I haven't interrupted your work. But I've made some . . . discoveries I thought you should know about."

"The artifact?"

"Is definitely Roman. It looks authentic."

Dayna blinked, still confused by this finding. She'd been sure it was a hoax, which was why she'd sent a grad student, rather than investigating herself.

"Are you sure?"

Felicity's face fell, her eyes fluttering in that nervous habit of hers. What a stupid thing to say. The girl, despite her proclivity for self-doubt, was quite astute.

"Of course you're sure. It's just so . . . incredible. A plant, perhaps?"

"I don't think so. There's more—"

Dayna's cell phone jangled in her fist; she was still clutching it after sending off the fateful text. She glimpsed the caller ID and, yes, inevitably, it was Evan. For some reason, he hadn't selected video call.

"Excuse me, Felicity. I have to take this call. I'll just mute the sound for a minute."

She tried to summon a reassuring smile, but she knew it could hardly be more brittle.

"Evan?"

"Hey, Day."

She rolled her eyes. She used to find his corny nicknames charming, but not any longer.

"What's up? I have a meeting over lunch, so I can't make it. I'll probably be working late, too. But if it's something serious . . . I can talk now."

Now? Well, was there any point in putting it off?

"I know about your affair."

Blank silence. She looked up and found Felicity watching her with those enormous gray eyes. Unfortunately, as innocent as they looked, they were also extremely keen and connected to a whip-smart mind.

"Day? I don't know what you're talking about."

"Honestly? I wonder if you sent that text on purpose."

"Text?"

More silence. No doubt he was scrolling through the list, then slapping his forehead.

"I really don't think we should do this on the phone. I think we should meet . . ."

"Do . . . this?"

Felicity tilted her head and coiled a strand of hair around her finger. Dayna turned away from her, but now she was facing the door to her office, and it sprang open without even a knock. Rejik Maesterzoon, her colleague in anthropology, barreled through the door. In his pale blue pinstripe suit and white tie, with his fluffy white hair and overly bleached teeth, he was a startling sight.

"How many emails do I have to send? Dayna . . . Oh, you're on the phone." He looked behind her. "And also on the phone."

"Yes, Rejik. I'm in the middle of something . . ."

"Middle, schmiddle. It will all have to wait. They've found another mysterious artifact."

"Artifact? Where? What?"

"Day, sweetheart. You're misreading it. I was meeting with a client, and we tend to joke about our wives." Evan's voice had a crooning quality.

"Evan, hold on a second." She stared at Rejik. "Well?"

"Something from a Florida bog that isn't quite Everglades material, or even Native American."

"Yes?"

Did he not see every pronounced tendon in her neck, or the bounding pulse in her forehead?

"Beads. African beads, created from ostrich eggshells." He grinned. "Oh yes, and more bog bodies."

"Day!" she heard Evan nearly shout from the phone. "I think I can make lunch."

"They'll need you to authenticate," said Rejik. "I can find a replacement for your lectures for a few days."

The video feed from the Arctic flickered, and Felicity began to wave frantically.

"Just a minute," she said to her cell. "Just a minute," she said to Rejik.

She pounced on the audio icon and looked at the wind swirling strands of the girl's hair high into the air, at her wide eyes. The camera seemed shaky.

"Felicity?"

"There's something weird going on here. We just felt a rumble—the ground shaking. It felt like an earthquake, but I wouldn't be surprised if it was a bomb. There are strange people hanging out here and something that looks like a murder. Most of the bodies are wearing Phoenician clothes, except for the one that's distinctly Roman, but there's also a Cree woman wearing a Roughriders jersey. The biologist thinks she was shot in the head. I know I'm rambling, but I don't know how long this connection—"

The holographic image vanished.

Dayna attempted to trigger the video icon. She tried to reestablish the link, but one line kept repeating: *Unable to connect.*

What the hell was going on in the Canadian North? Phoenicians? Romans? And now an African ornament turns up in a Florida bog? And why was the ground shaking in the North? But one thing the girl had said rattled her even more. *A murder victim*, right alongside those ancient bodies.

"Day? Day?"

She glared at her phone. Finally she jammed it to her ear.

"Evan, I want a divorce."

She hung up before he could make another plea.

"Rejik, forget Florida. I need you to get me on a plane to Polar Bear Provincial Park."

"Are you kidding? This discovery—"

"This is my student, my responsibility. If any harm comes to her . . . Get Frank to look into this Florida artifact. I'm sure someone just tossed a trinket they picked up on an African safari into the mud. But I'm not leaving anything to chance."

"You sent Frank to Greece."

"Well, recall him."

"You know, I really don't like that student of yours. He's much too smug for my tastes. He'll be giving an earful to the dean, and his wealthy parents will be threatening to withdraw their generous donations to the university, just because we hauled him back for a less-than-ideal assignment. Particularly one that isn't within the parameters of his thesis studies."

"Ask me if I care," she snapped. "Frank has extensive experience with African relics, or I wouldn't even suggest him. He is my best expert for a preliminary analysis, regardless of his manners. Felicity is my Roman expert, and she guarantees me that her relic is Roman. But, despite the wild implications of a Roman relic sitting on the far shores of Hudson Bay, what scares me is having it mixed up with a potentially recent murder. I need to get her out of there until we can be sure there is no risk involved."

Rejik nodded. "You go pack some polar fleece. I'll try to book the flights. It's probably not the easiest destination to reach in a short period of time."

"Do your best."

She grabbed her purse and, *what the hell*, gulped down a last mouthful of her wine.

Rejik peaked one eyebrow. But he didn't say a word, not until she reached the doorway.

"Um, Dayna. I know you have a dozen other things on your mind, but . . . when you get your divorce, would you consider going out on a date with me?"

She glanced back at his entirely-too-bright smile. Of all the insane, inappropriate . . . But why the hell not?

"Maybe," she threw over her shoulder, and dashed down the hall.

Scanning...

Located: Chapter 11

THE NEXT DAY—after the visit from the miners and the subsequent earthquakes—Tony DeLuca placed a semi-automatic pistol into Shaun's hands, astonishing everyone, as he slung a Winchester rifle over his own shoulder.

"I'm going bear hunting," he said. "You guard the camp, buddy."

"What the hell are you talking about?" Shaun snapped.

"Closer look. I take the helicopter; you wait for the cops. If those men are diamond prospectors, then I'm the local shock jock."

"Well, you do irritate the crap out of me," said Shaun. "But if they have no problem killing a Cree woman, what makes you think they'll hesitate to take you out? Besides, the police should be here by early afternoon. Let *them* investigate these miners."

"There might not be any bodies left to investigate, if we have another one of those 'quakes,'" said DeLuca.

Felicity shivered. She could still feel the vibrations juddering through her body and hear the ice cracking along the shoreline: *snap, snap, whoosh*. But even more alarming was the sound of crisp popping, like carbonated bubbles from a gigantic soft drink, as gas escaped the adjoining bog.

"Do you think they're setting off explosives?" she asked.

DeLuca looked at her, and then through her—his mind obviously racing through possibilities.

"I don't want to speculate. I just know earthquakes rarely happen up here. And your bog bodies won't stay *cohesive* for long, now that they're exposed to the air, especially with the added component of tremblers. And I don't like what the bog is doing."

"I'll join you," said Felicity.

"No," said Shaun. "You stay here with Baruti, and I'll go with Tony."

"Absolutely not," said Tony. "You guard the camp and the bodies. Baruti can join me."

"No objection," said the African biologist, hastening inside the tent.

Shaun glared at DeLuca, but the geologist stood his ground. This might become a long pissing match, one she didn't quite understand. She knew Shaun was somewhat soft, at least around corpses. But that didn't mean he couldn't handle himself in other situations, or at least manage to sleuth around a mining camp. After all, he'd been monitoring and handling polar bears for years.

"They might be back, and I need *you* to stand guard," Tony snapped. His eyes bored into Shaun's for a brief but intense moment before he turned away.

Felicity caught the look. *Did he not trust Baruti?*

Well, it *was* strange that an African biologist had arrived to investigate polar bears just after an African contingent of miners had decided to prospect in the same region. But while Baruti had displayed an odd glee when she'd revealed the potential ancient origins of the bodies, and his comments always seemed to allude to something deeper than the subject matter, she hadn't detected the same ruthlessness, conceit, and arrogance in him as seemed to exist in the two men who'd visited their camp. He'd been about to share something with her—something she imagined was extraordinary—before the miners had dropped by, but he hadn't mentioned it since then. He was obviously withholding information, but she doubted he was an actual threat.

"All the more reason for you to stay put. And I would rather you not get shot before the police arrive. A few more hours, man," said Shaun. "Then at least you'll have a police escort, *if* they let you get involved."

"A few hours is all it might take for those men to shut down operations and create a smoke screen," said DeLuca. "I need to know what the hell they're doing over there. If they're killing Cree and . . . messing with the environment . . . whatever the hell they're doing isn't in our best interests, I'm sure."

Shaun sidled closer to the geologist. "Tony," he whispered. "If you have to do this, I would be the better person to help investigate. I don't trust the African."

"Really? And you want to leave him alone with Felicity?"

Shaun looked at her, and a warm flush invaded his cheeks.

"Felicity can take care of herself," she said.

"Of course she can," said Tony snidely. "Felicity is bullet-proof and a marksman, no doubt. The man for the job."

What an egotistical, chauvinistic . . .

"If you're worried about me, then take me along. Who is better qualified, if the girl's death does have to do with ancient bodies or artifacts?" *Certainly not you, jackass.* "And weren't you rather insistent I remain here to investigate that angle?"

Tony snorted. "Yes, you are absolutely qualified, and likely to pass out without sufficient food on hand. Sorry, sweetheart. To find anything before they cover it up, we'll have to hike in. I think I'll be better off with Baruti," he said, as the biologist wriggled out of the tent. "We can take photos for you to examine when we get back, if we find something there that is within your area of expertise. I'm not in the mood to hold your hand."

Felicity had a deep desire to lob something at him, something that would result in seeing him curled up on the grass and heaving, the way Shaun had done earlier. Something like . . . a detached, mushy, half-collapsed head. But she could never dishonor the head that way.

Baruti busied himself with strapping on his pack, but he seemed antsy—smoothing out his jacket, giving the zipper of his windbreaker an extra tug. His gaze flitted over to her and then to the others—as if he'd overheard their argument and was bothered by it. Finally, he fumbled at his belt, and then, astonishingly, withdrew a pistol from beneath his jacket.

"Why are you carrying that?" asked Shaun, stepping backward.

Baruti ignored him and turned to Felicity.

"I'm not entirely comfortable leaving you with the bodies. They are most likely the target of these men, and possibly others. And I'm certainly not comfortable leaving you without a means of protection."

He stepped up to her and pushed the pistol into her hand.

"Just flick the safety off, point, and shoot. Don't shoot unless you are certain, because there's no second chance. But if you are certain, don't hesitate, either." He leaned toward her. "You are the man for the job."

Felicity gazed at the weapon, absolutely stunned. The cold steel mold, the deadly trigger; it felt completely foreign in her hand. Her parents had always been proponents of gun control and had refused to keep one in their house.

"Where did you get that?" asked Shaun. "You wouldn't have made it through airport security . . ."

"We were hunting for polar bears, am I not correct?" said Baruti.

"Well, yes, but . . ."

"Polar bears are not benign creatures, am I not correct?"

"Well, yes, but . . . they rarely—"

"I am not an idiot," said Baruti. "Are you ready to leave, Tony?"

DeLuca nodded, his lips curved in an amused smile.

"Make sure you don't shoot Shaun," he threw in Felicity's direction. "Unless he deserves it."

Her fingers tightened around the grip of the gun, and she shivered slightly. This, beyond everything else, spoke to her of their potential peril. Baruti, the coolest man in the group, the man who "must have had a hell of a life," as Shaun had put it and who, as a biologist in Botswana, had undoubtedly spent much of his time defending wildlife from ruthless poachers, believed she needed a gun.

"You really should warm up inside. You're shivering," said Shaun, casting an enormous shadow over her as she documented the clothing, the helmet, the odd Phoenician beard of the body she'd prosaically labelled Body #3. She meticulously recorded every detail on her tablet.

The brisk wind from the bay penetrated her ski jacket and probed every chilled nook and cranny of her body.

Better to be cold than dead.

Her hand crept to the gun sitting next to the body bag, in a cradle of bristly lichen. This weapon in her possession was a bizarre anomaly, like these bodies in the pristine, unsullied north.

"No one in sight," said Shaun, resting a comforting hand on her shoulder. "No need for a gun. If it makes you feel better, keep it close, but at least take a break and eat something."

Yes, Mother, she felt like saying. But when she looked up into his warm willow-green eyes and her gaze followed the line of his impudent jaw, she didn't think anything like *mother*.

No, she admonished herself. *You are Minerva, Athena, product of Zeus and Zeus alone. You will not fold at the sight of a gorgeous man. You are the goddess of war and wisdom, not sex.*

"I guess I am hungry," she muttered, avoiding his gaze.

She shouldn't be alone with this man. He was a menace. Not because he presented any danger to her, but because he reminded her of a Greek hero. Of course, the Greek hero was predominantly a dimwit, and he often experienced the odd psychotic break, as well. She should take that lesson from mythology, if nothing else. She'd fallen for the hero once, on last year's overseas dig. He was a tall, confident mountain-climbing grad student, with the daring (and temper) of Achilles. But she soon found that he resembled his predecessors too closely. Like the Greek hero, he was never capable of sharing more than a sliver of his shadow.

Besides, this man wasn't giving her enough room to become her own hero.

"I cooked up some stew," he said.

Certainly, she'd noticed the aroma, and the man puttering over the camp stove while fussing with his satellite phone. Certainly, she'd done her best to ignore him.

"Not the most appetizing, but it's hearty." He cautiously trapped her hand, and she allowed it to be trapped.

He guided her to the collapsible table beside the tent, where he'd swaddled two bowls in tea cozies. The sweet scent of mingled beef, carrots, and potatoes emanated from the bowls and fluttered under her nose, stirring the juices in her stomach. She was hungry. She was hungry for food and nothing else.

"I kept it warm for you," he said, slipping the tea cozy off one of the bowls.

"Thanks," she said, trying to avoid his intense gaze. Her heart fluttered as she felt his eyes travel down her body.

She had to admit she was tempted.

Then she remembered the steel weapon in her hand and the man who'd placed it there. As Felicity slid into the chair, she set the gun beside the bowl, within easy reach.

She looked up at Shaun and saw that his eyes had strayed to the gun, too. His facial muscles twitched as if something was troubling him. Was it the gun, or Baruti?

She dipped her spoon into the rich concoction, stirred it, and brought it to her lips.

"Is it warm enough?" he asked. "Are you feeling warmer?"

"Yes, it's quite warm."

"Not too hot, though?"

"Just right," she muttered. "I'm not Goldilocks, by the way."

"No, you're not. But your locks are quite lovely. Copper. Like a rich sunset."

He didn't give up easily, did he? She touched the gun, to remind herself of Baruti again, but suddenly realized she didn't need it.

"Thanks. But you know, compliments will get you nowhere."

She sent him a sharp look, then dipped her spoon into the stew again.

"I wasn't thinking of getting any— Well, maybe I was. I can't help but find you attractive."

"But I'm not," she stated flatly. "I was in a car accident a few years ago, and I have scars up and down my body, not just my leg."

He smiled, as if not offended in the least. She hoped her resistance and the thought of her scarred body would make him back away, stop pressing, but instead, he said, "We all have scars. Want to see mine?" And he took off his shirt.

A puckered stripe wandered over his right pectoral, ending at the nipple.

You bastard!

"Polar bear," he stated blandly.

"Look. *Dr.* Wilson—"

"Shaun."

"Dr. Wilson. Please put your shirt back on. I'm really not interested."

"But you are. I can see it in your eyes." He grinned as he balled up the shirt in his hands. Gooseflesh was popping up all over his skin as the brisk wind whipped around him, but he made no move to put it back on. "What's the harm in a little fun?"

"The harm?" she asked. "When there may be men coming to kill us? And honestly, *I'm just not that into you*," she insisted.

The grin on his face collapsed. "Oh. Okay." He casually pulled his shirt over his head and slipped it around his chest. "I thought you might . . . I guess I was wrong."

Felicity heaved a sigh of relief. She'd been wondering if she'd need to use the gun to make him back off. He obviously wasn't accustomed to rejection. She hated that he'd made such a bold attempt, because it altered their relationship—taking it from overprotective but still respectful to totally unprofessional. How could she prove herself, if these scientists couldn't take her seriously?

"Sorry," he said, and began to eat his own stew. "I can be an idiot sometimes."

Now came the awkwardness. He would stop hovering and instead avoid her, which might make her time here strained and uncomfortable.

Oh, why did men have to make life so complicated? Why must they so often cross boundaries uninvited? Although she'd done nothing to entice him, she would now have to soothe his bruised ego to restore their relationship as fellow scientists.

"I guess you misread my signals. I am grateful for your help with the bodies," she said. "Nothing more, nothing less. And I appreciate your cooking." She smiled.

"Thanks," he replied, not looking up. "Story of my life. Always misreading, until it's too late."

She wondered what he meant. Was he really talking about sex and relationships? Somehow it seemed like a deeper statement—one he might want her to probe. But she really didn't want to, for fear of what it might unearth. She opened her mouth to say something casual, but before she could utter a word, a figure appeared on the horizon, and then another, the crunch of their footsteps snapping through the air. Felicity instantly dismissed Shaun's statement, snatched up the gun, and aimed it at the intruders, reciting Baruti's instructions in her head. *If you are certain, don't hesitate.*

Scanning...

Located: Chapter 12

FRANK CAMPO FONDLED the bubble-wrapped package, which he had placed with great care beside him in the battered Mazda rental car, as he sped over blistering asphalt in Florida's southwestern interior. He should be approaching the Panther Wildlife Refuge soon. Then he would only need to travel another few miles to the border of the Everglades. The site, Dr. Maesterzoon had explained, was just south of Interstate 41—Alligator Alley. Didn't that sound precious?

How he longed to return to his dig in the Alepotrypa cave, the Hades cave on the Mani Peninsula of Greece. Five years ago, the archaeologist in charge of the site had released his sole jurisdiction over this spectacular cave, which was crammed with tools, pottery, and even silver and copper artifacts dating back to the Neolithic age, to allow examination and study by other archaeologists and their crews of student assistants. Five thousand years ago, the entrance had collapsed, preserving everything inside, including ritual burial plots. The presence of the burial plots had led to speculation that the cave had once been considered an actual entrance to Hades, the Greek underworld, in ancient times.

But what was even more intriguing to Frank was the terracotta jar and the artifact he'd recently unearthed, which displayed striking similarities to the Qumran Hills discovery in Israel, one hundred twenty-five years ago. Alepotrypa's location on the southern tip of Greece would have provided easy access for sea traffic in antiquity, and Jeb Walters, an archaeologist from California, had recently exposed a side passage that ancient Greeks had dug over 2,000 years ago. He'd verified the approximate date by using the carbon-14 method on fragments of wineskin and antiquated digging implements like mattocks found near the entrance. Frank had suspected the existence of the passage for two years now, since receiving his Bachelor of Arts and Science in Archaeology degree and moving on to graduate school, since the summer he'd sidestepped his African studies for a brief foray into the translation of Hebrew artifacts and documents. He'd directed Jeb to the location and, naturally, Jeb had taken all the credit for the discovery.

Yes, Frank felt snubbed and unappreciated. Yes, Frank was breaking every rule that pertained to a guest invitation to study an archaeological site. And yes, he didn't care. What could they do to him? Bar him from any more Greek digs? He'd rather be stationed on the Nile anyway, or searching for Solomon's lost treasure in Israel, or elsewhere, following the clues of the copper Dead Sea Scroll that were linked to this new artifact. Wouldn't solving this mystery lead to the ultimate Howard Carter moment?

He eyed the prized parcel reposing beside him. He'd never have stolen the artifact if Professor Lugan hadn't pulled him off his dig. Pulled him to, of all places, the Florida Everglades. Despite the air conditioner blasting brisk, cool air over his face, a bead of sweat trickled down his back. Bog bodies. He shuddered. Why couldn't she recall Felicity from her arctic adventure, since bog mummies had now become her specialty? Felicity. He ground his teeth at the thought of the girl who was theoretically his rival. Pale, petite, feeble. She couldn't get through the day without tripping and nearly knocking over an artifact. And rather than simply admiring and interpreting ancient art, as was the mandate of archaeologists, she clung to hopes of achieving her own DaVinci moment.

Yet he'd still hit on her, because . . . well, because she was attractive and within easy reach. And she'd bitten his hand before he could even pet her, the bitch. How he wished he could see her now, knee-deep in bog mud, fumbling through a stew of corpses, and no doubt being groped by a fifty-year-old bush pilot. Then he wouldn't look so bad, would he?

Of course soon *he* would be fumbling through bog mud and corpses, too.

The parallel chain-link fences of the wildlife refuge came into view—a tall, bold network of ash-colored steel that sandwiched the road, along with scalloped ditches of earth-brown water that flickered with life—alligator life, no doubt. Beyond the barriers, bristly Florida pine jabbed at the sky, and swatches of palm trees swayed in the breeze. This was the habitat of the elusive panther, who could be brooding on a branch and peering over the roadway, wondering if he should leap the fence and tackle the lone car that had disturbed his morning snooze. What bothered Frank more than the thought of a surprise attack—he was perfectly sheltered in his car, after all—was the eerie quality of this lonely stretch of road, which was completely stripped of traffic. Florida—at least the Florida of his vacation days—usually swarmed with human activity: tourists, honking vehicles, jostling trucks, all adding to air that construction had rendered barely breathable. This interior route was obviously unpopular among motorists, but it had been recommended by the rental car agent to avoid a two or three-hour delay on a major roadway.

And, as if to add to his agitation, around the bend he suddenly came upon a crew of highway workers clearing off the smeared remnants of road kill, chopping back vegetation, and repainting the faded passing lines on the pavement—a chain-gang road crew with bright orange vests that shouted *Prisoners at Work*—and with less than vigilant guards, since they seemed to be spaced several yards apart. Just as he decelerated, obeying the skinny dude covered in tattoos who was holding a sign that read *Slow Down* and *Keep to the Left*, the engine hiccupped, then burped and chugged but, thankfully, the clunker kept moving through the maze of workers.

One of the prisoners—a bald man with a bulky build, a wealth of scars criss-crossing his face, and deep-set surly eyes—scowled at him, as he steered the vehicle around the man's heap of palm fronds and seared grass, which awaited pick-up by the truck that lagged well behind the crew. Frank shrank down in the cracked leather seat until he was barely able to peer over the dashboard, and focused on gripping the wheel. It seemed the guards doubted these prisoners would even attempt an escape, on account of both the natural deterrents and the manmade ones: the twenty-foot-high fences topped with barbed wire, beyond which panthers hunted, and the moats alongside the road (between the asphalt and the fences, of course), which were home to more than a few hungry alligators.

Frank shook his head. Not a good spot for the car to break down.

"Turn right at the next intersection," said the sexy digital voice on his GPS unit.

About time. Finally past the last member of the gang, he slithered upright, scanned the map, and noted he had only another five miles to travel. At least that would put five miles between him and the prisoners. But he doubted it would take him any farther from the alligators.

Frank increased his speed until he reached Interstate 41, where he was told to turn right. Here traffic became somewhat denser; two cars actually passed by on the highway before he could make the turn. No doubt, traffic was thin because it was June, not exactly the peak season in Florida. He swung onto the main road, surprised at how clear his view immediately became. No high ridges, wooded regions, or fences existed on this stretch of highway. Nothing but broad ditches of swamp-green water, bordered by clusters of tall saw grass, extended to the horizon. He could easily scope the waterways for alligators, and he was instantly rewarded with the sight of cruising, sunning, grinning reptiles that, if they weren't snoozing, seemed to be eyeing his passing car with interest. Funny how the birds—ivory-feathered ibises or roseate spoonbills—perched daringly close to those toothy snouts, not in the least ruffled by their presence.

"Turn right 200 feet ahead," said Madame GPS.

A slight gap in the billowing grass fields appeared up ahead, beyond which stretched a lush forest of tropical trees and plants that, like everywhere in the Everglades region, was crisscrossed with streams, ditches, and swamps. A short bridge connecting to a gravel road pushed through the gap.

Frank veered to the right and bobbled over the rutted road, which traveled beside a creek. To his left, saw palmettos, royal palms encircled by strangler figs, and various ferns and cacti fringed the road. To his right, standing, staring, squawking birds of brilliant sapphire, white, and yellow plumage, along with cruising, partially submerged alligators, filled the murky green water.

"You have reached your destination," the GPS said.

Frank stopped.

"Thank you, darling. Except, where is it?"

The gravel road continued into the far reaches of the Florida backwaters, but an inkling of a path poked through the ferns and grass to the left. A mud-streaked SUV was parked here, beside the creek.

"Yes, Frank. You must now hack your way through the jungle."

He shook his head. How he missed the beautiful rolling countryside and innumerable bays of Greece. What he wouldn't give to be perched cliffside watching the sailboats cruise the turquoise Aegean. Yeah, he even missed Greece itself, with its plodding pace and its surprisingly chilly swimming pools.

He flicked off the engine and nudged open the door. The outside air flooded over him and tucked in close—a limp blanket of humidity that challenged his asthma-inflicted lungs. He coughed, sucked in a deep breath, marshaled his courage, and trudged toward the path. There was barely enough room to maneuver around the grasping branches, but here and there he came upon swaths of clear-cut sections where the verdant growth hadn't yet rebounded. Obviously, a futile attempt to clear the land and dredge the swamp. He rolled his eyes. Any first-year geology student would know that this soil would yield only a decade or two of crops before it could no longer renew itself, since the richness of the Everglades loam depended on the replenishing properties of indigenous flora that would be wiped out by modern-day farming and non-native crops.

"Mr. Campo?" a voice called from beyond the trunk of a royal palm, several feet ahead.

"Yes, I'm making my way . . ."

A short, purple-cheeked, ebony-haired fellow came thrusting through the fuzzy ferns, wiping mud-streaked palms on his Florida Panthers T-shirt, all the while.

"Right this way. Right this way."

The man strode toward Frank.

"Hi. I'm Ali Farid, from Southwestern U. I'm an undergrad, so I'm not allowed to touch anything, you know. The rest of the crew left for a few days, since they weren't prepared to extract the bodies yet, and they were waiting for Dr. Lugan's—well, *your* assessment. It's just over here. Amazing discovery. Keep coming. Oh." He stopped.

Oh? Frank halted in midstep. *Oh, what?*

"Hold it right there, Mr. Campo. Right in front of you. Little diamondback rattler. Might want to let it move on first."

Frank stopped right there. He gazed at the "little" eight-foot specimen. It was a bronze and cream, diamond-patterned snake neatly disguised amongst the decaying vegetation and surrounding mud, and it was slinking forward in the standard S pattern just three feet in front of him. Damn snakes. He'd encountered a cobra once on the dusty plateau in the Valley of the Kings—a hooded, hissing reptile that provided plenty of warning and allowed him ample time to back away and give it a wide berth. But that had been enough to shake him up for hours.

The rattler crept closer, making it more and more difficult for Frank to breathe, especially when his lungs were already feeling challenged by the clouds of humidity. Then, a sharp-edged rattle like hail on a tin roof chattered through the air.

"Is he, like, going to strike?" asked Frank, his voice annoyingly weak.

"No, I don't think so," said Ali. "He's not posturing, just telling you to back off."

"Well, I'm listening," said Frank, stepping ever so cautiously backward, as the snake slunk ever so determinedly forward.

"Is there a reason he has to come this way?"

"Only because it's the path he has chosen, I imagine. You just happen to be in his way. But obviously that doesn't bother him." Ali chuckled.

"Oh, yeah."

Frank chuckled too, only nervously and with undisguised irritation. He reversed a step. The snake pushed forward.

"Well, fine," he snapped. He turned and walked quickly back down the path that he'd just negotiated, whipping the branches aside, as he practically raced to the gravel road.

"Mr. Campo," came a fervent shout from Ali. "He just left the path. You should be all right, now."

"All right," said Frank. "Sure." He eyed the alligator that had ventured out of the creek and was nosing and possibly contemplating puncturing the tire of his car with its serrated teeth. "Not sure that's possible in this godforsaken swamp."

****

THREE HOURS LATER, Frank was slowly sinking in bog mud. Mosquitoes buzzed near his ears, nipped at his neck, swarmed around his head. He swatted frantically at the pests, but merely succeeded in flicking mud all over his hair.

"There. You see the body?" Ali said with glee.

How could anyone be this enthusiastic while extracting bog bodies? He was beginning to envy Felicity. At least her bog bodies weren't surrounded by snakes and alligators.

Frank examined the twisted corpse, which was arranged in a flexed position and staked down with teepee-like wooden shafts that were bundled and tied at their central convergence point. The whole arrangement brought to mind the Windover bog bodies found on the northeastern side of Florida near Cape Canaveral in 1982. There had to be a connection. But those bodies had been discovered in a pond where the water had a near-neutral pH, which kept them somewhat preserved, even in this warm climate. This location would likely have a very high acidity level that would have dissolved the tissue, if it was of any substantial age. Bog bodies were preserved in the North because . . . they were in the North. And it is cold—freezing, actually—in the North. Yet these corpses couldn't be remains from a modern era either, not staked down in this ritual manner, not in this remote location, covered in layers of peat.

After three hours in the steamy swamp, Frank had uncovered three bodies, which resembled the two that had already been exposed when the farmer had dredged this pond and removed the soggy soil. Despite the recent excavation, water was already seeping back into the hollow, leaving Frank trudging through knee-deep soupy sludge that reminded him of the garbage masher in the classic *Star Wars* movie. No doubt a Jedi-eating monster lurked beneath this putrid water, too.

Or Frank-eating.

"There it is. There's another necklace," shouted Ali. He pointed trembling fingers at the beads looped around the sunken throat. "Ebony-and-tan painted ostrich eggshells, threaded together with sinew, perhaps? That's what the first one is, according to the small sample Dr. Winston extracted."

"You're sure?" said Frank, unable to fathom this.

"Tested, triple tested, undeniable. They're still working on carbon-14 dating. We should have the results later this afternoon."

"But these bodies are very similar to the Windover bodies. And if they are from the same tribal group, that means they could be 7,000 years old. How in the hell would they have ostrich eggshell beads, like . . . like those the Bushman people created?"

"Bushman people?" asked Ali, his thick eyebrows crushed together.

"Yes. They lived—and a few still do, although they're virtually extinct—in the Kalahari Desert and the Okavango Delta region in southern Africa. They were primarily hunters, but many were artists, too. Some of the Bushmen cave paintings date back to 70,000 years—the oldest cave art ever discovered. But they certainly never possessed the skill or equipment to cross the Atlantic."

"It does sound ridiculous," said Ali. "But, you know, we've found some nonsensical things lately, haven't we? How about the *female* gladiator bust discovered in Germany? Or the ruins in Wales that predate the pyramids? Or even more bizarre, the pyramid in Indonesia that some claim is 13,000 years old, with stone-age tools beside it. Contradictory evidence.

"We keep constructing theories that we think explain human evolution and cultural development," he continued. "But they're often debunked, or at least considered questionable, as new discoveries come to light. We don't know anything for sure, even with modern scientific methods of investigation, because we don't have accurate records that go back to the dawn of humanity, and the records that exist are sketchy, or are skewed by the historian's prejudices and background. You can even look at *today's* record-keeping and find it's based on media-bias—that is, limited to what the media feels is worthy of attention. And you might say that everyone owns a camera now, so there can be no confusion. But brief clips don't convey the total picture. How many social media entries are cleverly disguised propaganda, or the work of hysteria-mongering conspiracy theorists?"

Frank eyed Ali with new respect. Undergrad or not, the guy certainly possessed some insight into the microscopic view that most people in the world maintain. It was so much easier to process little dribbles of information than to collate them, piece together a puzzle, and develop a comprehensive theory. Of course, his own microscopic view was more concerned with a certain copper artifact than an anomalous string of beads. But that would have to wait until he performed further analysis of his treasured relic.

He removed a wooden tongue depressor from his pocket and gently feathered away the mud from the corpse's neck. His hope was to extract the entire body as a unit to preserve the necklace and continue his analysis in a more luxurious environment. But this discovery went beyond mere bog bodies or even textiles. The burial shrouds adhering to the withered flesh of these bodies appeared to be of sophisticated weave. That once again suggested Windover, where the loom-woven shrouds had revealed that the ancient people discovered there were far more advanced than had been previously thought. Controversy still existed regarding their unusual DNA, which was unique to the North American haplogroup. But this, if it was authentic, would top anything found at Windover. Ancient African beads in a Florida bog?

"I need to detach this necklace from the flesh and examine it in detail. It might take an hour or so."

He paused and slapped his neck, as another bloodthirsty mosquito dove into his exposed skin.

"Damn. I think my bug spray is wearing off. Can you toss me the can?"

Ali picked up the small pump-action can of repellent, shook it, and then shook his head.

"Think it's empty. Did you shower with this?"

"It's an old can I brought with me to the cave in Greece. I guess I should have stopped on the way down to buy a refill."

"Your water bottle is empty. So is mine. Plus, I'm starving. Want to stop for a while, grab something to eat in Everglades City, and restock supplies?"

Frank's stomach churned and ached at the thought of food. The physical challenge was sapping his energy and leaving him dehydrated, too. But he was also lathered in mud, and he just wanted to retrieve the artifact and continue his work in an air-conditioned lab or, better yet, check in at his swanky hotel and kick back for a while. He couldn't rush the process and damage the relic—Professor Lugan would kill him—but he had no desire to spend any more time out here in rattlesnake country than was absolutely necessary.

"Um, Ali. Since you're not as dirty as I am, maybe you can make a run for supplies and pick up lunch. I'd like to keep at it, at least until I can remove the strand of beads."

Ali nodded. "If you really love the job . . ." He grinned.

Frank grimaced. Even to this undergrad, it was apparently obvious that Frank didn't love the job—at least not this part of it.

"I shouldn't be longer than an hour."

Ali departed, as Frank continued burrowing around the corpse. Possibly a female, it had long braids and the most obnoxious way of staring right through him, from the obsidian bowls of its sunken eye sockets. Despite the oppressive heat, a chill seeped into his flesh. At the same time, a ruthless cloud of mosquitoes commenced stabbing his neck and arms with renewed vigor. And the Greeks thought their benign cave with a few spiders and bats was the entrance to Hades! Obviously they'd never been to Florida in June.

But . . . He stopped his work for a moment and gazed at the beads. *Someone has. Someone, or several someones, who shouldn't have been capable of a trans-Atlantic voyage.*

As Frank chipped at and flicked away the mud, and strove to ignore the biting insects, a splash sounded at the far side of the hollow. He jerked his head up and peered at the turbid water, noting that its surface was disturbed by small successive circles of ripples.

His first thought was *alligator!* But the water was too shallow; the plated hide of an alligator would be easy to spot jutting above the surface. Probably just a frog or salamander. Rattlesnakes didn't like to swim, did they?

The ripples subsided, and he turned back to his tedious excavation. Dollop by dollop, he removed the clinging mud that encircled the woman's throat. Gradually, he excavated a groove around the precious necklace. He had just whipped another chunk of mud behind him, when . . . *What was that?* He leaped backward, nearly toppling into the water.

Something had brushed past his leg. Something sinuous and scaly. Something very long, very big, and very muscular.

His gaze flitted around the pond, searching for movement and a clear path, while at the same time he instinctively scanned for the best exit strategy. Ripples to the left, climbable bank to the right. No time to consider. He launched himself to the right and scrabbled at the slippery mud, grabbing for roots to hoist himself out of the pit.

One backward glance as he was mounting the steep bank told him it was too late. A supple, substantial snake with splotchy tan and brown patterns was speeding through the water. It whipped out at him, mouth gaping, and clamped enormous jaws onto his hip. A bolt of pain shot through his abdomen as the creature coiled around his legs and midriff, its pulsating muscles constricting.

Son of bitch. He was going to die. This was no rattler. This was a *Burmese python!*

He collapsed into the roiling water, as the snake wrapped its impossibly long body around him in multiple circuits and applied crushing force. Frank pushed, grasped, scrabbled, tore at the creature, but couldn't peel it off, couldn't loosen the squeezing mass, couldn't detach the monstrous jaw.

"Help!" he screamed, although who could hear him in this remote region? And who would be willing to tackle a snake?

"Help!" he begged, although he was rapidly losing his breath, or even the capacity to breathe, as the snake crushed his ribcage and pulled him under the shallow water.

This was it. Who would have thought he'd be safer in Egypt, with its cobras and scorpions, malaria-carrying mosquitoes, and its many terrorists. He yelled one more time, forcing his scant remaining air out over his vocal cords. These would be his last feeble words in an empty jungle, before he'd ever had a chance to etch his name in the history books. What memorable words they were.

"Fucking snake!"

Scanning...

Located: Chapter 13

BARUTI SWABBED AT his neck. He felt quite warm, for a change, no doubt due to the five-mile hike through twisting gravel paths in the bog, and the squeeze-and-stumble through thorny scrub and over broad heaps of dead trees. Right now, he and DeLuca were negotiating thickets of dwarf birch and black spruce, where stunted saplings battled for life in the nutrient-poor soil and punishing winds. DeLuca had tucked the helicopter behind a beach ridge, far enough from the miners' camp to block the sound and sight of their approach.

As they crept increasingly closer to the camp, massive slabs of pink granite rose from the surrounding flatland, a citadel towering over the groveling kingdom below. Sutton Ridge, as DeLuca had explained earlier, was an outcropping of volcanic bedrock completely alien to the peat bogs and gravel ridges that dominated this region. Three miles north of this monolithic geological feature, a sprawl of tents and Quonset huts interrupted the landscape, along with a gunmetal gray warehouse.

As a flash of light burst from the edge of the compound, DeLuca ducked behind a shrub. Now within a mile of the mining camp, they had reached a transitional zone between the undersized trees of the boreal forest and an open expanse of level grassland and bog that was characteristic of the tundra—an area where two men strolling through the territory would stand out like boulders on a beach.

"What was that?" asked Baruti. "Binoculars?"

"Or possibly a rifle scope," said DeLuca, screwing his own high-powered scope to the mount on his Winchester. "If they're up to something—something Machiavellian enough to kill to protect—then they probably have guards stationed around the perimeter of their site."

Baruti crouched down beside DeLuca and peered briefly over the tips of the scrub. A tower of some sort jutted from the flatland—a giant spike of orange metal.

"Is that a drill rig?"

DeLuca nosed his rifle through the ferny branch and placed his eye to the scope.

"Could be. But it looks odd. Taller than your average drill rig. And if they're just scouting for minerals or diamonds, as they claim, they'd be most likely to use a mobile platform. That looks more permanent."

Another flash leaped from the same general location. Baruti fumbled the binoculars from his pack and zeroed in on the source. Several men were scrambling beside reflective metal instruments and covering them with canvas tarps.

"What are they covering? Solar panels?"

"Too small. They look like seismometers. Very strange."

"Whatever they're doing, it doesn't seem to be related to archaeology. I see no evidence that they're excavating the surrounding bog. And they do appear to be conducting a mining operation of some sort."

"I don't understand this," said DeLuca. "It's unlikely they would unearth diamonds here; any decent geologist would point that out. Why select such an unpromising location? What is there about this stretch of no-man's land that would attract their attention?"

"Are there any faults near here?"

DeLuca tilted an eyebrow. Maybe Baruti shouldn't have spoken up.

"Just the Winisk River Fault. Why?"

Well, it wouldn't hurt to impart some information. Enough to spur the geologist onward in his investigation.

"I've heard of this company, DITEK, in my country. They are said to be conducting experimental mining techniques. As you may know, the Okavango Delta is an extension of the Great Rift Valley. We have several faults there, and often experience earthquakes. But it seems that wherever this company conducts their experiments, the earthquakes increase in intensity, duration, and frequency."

DeLuca's tilted eyebrow became peaked, and he turned to look directly at Baruti. *Now perhaps he will understand the gravity of the situation.* By revealing this information, Baruti had pitched this enterprise beyond that of a sleazy mining company attempting to sidestep environmental issues, or a band of treasure hunters digging for archaeological relics and selling them to the highest bidder. Way beyond.

"That's insane," DeLuca said. "Why on Earth . . . How . . . ?"

Baruti shrugged. "I don't know why, but maybe that"—he pointed at the gigantic rig—"has something to do with the how."

DeLuca lowered his rifle and slumped on the ground, his brow etched with furrows. For several minutes, he studied the moss-speckled earth in front of him. Finally he breathed out, "Geothermal drilling can trigger earthquakes. Certainly, in the Okavango region, there'd be heat energy close enough to the surface to attempt that type of drilling. But here, in the Arctic—?" He paused, the furrows disappearing one by one.

"We've had some anomalies, over the last hundred years."

"Anomalies?" asked Baruti. Now he might finally get some answers.

"Unusual earthquakes. In 1989, one rocked the middle of the Ungava Peninsula. For this part of the world, it registered an unprecedented magnitude of 6 on the Richter scale, and its orientation was contrary to the direction that would be consistent with seafloor spreading in the Atlantic. Strong earthquakes occur, and volcanoes erupt, near tectonic plate boundaries, like portions of the Ring of Fire in the Pacific, along the mid-Atlantic ridge where the seafloor is spreading, in areas like Iceland, and in the Great Rift Valley. But they rarely occur in the middle of the North American continent. The kimberlite intrusions are over 500 million years old, dating from the Proterozoic era. They developed when the North American continent was situated over the mid-Atlantic rift, but it has drifted to the west, since then. No volcanic activity has occurred in this region since that time. But the odd 1989 earthquake I mentioned resulted in surface faulting and lifted the shorelines of some lakes, causing the sediments to change the water's color to turquoise. And we've had a number of smaller quakes since then. None of them follow the predicted pattern."

"Are you thinking they're man-made?" asked Baruti.

"No," DeLuca said instantly. "I'm suggesting that, maybe, a new mantle plume is developing. If that were the case, it would create a hotspot closer to the surface—something that would imbue the rocks with heat and could be tapped for geothermal energy."

"Plume?" asked Baruti. He'd studied some geology in university, but it had been a long time since then.

"A theory that suggests that regional hotspots that can also trigger earthquakes and volcanoes can exist far from plate boundaries. Areas where the Earth's crust is thinner, like the Hawaiian Islands and the flood basalts in Siberia. But it's far easier to transport and utilize geothermal energy when it's found a little closer to civilization. This kind of operation wouldn't pay for itself. And if it *is* geothermal drilling they're doing, why all the secrecy? It's not new technology."

"And it doesn't sound like anything worth committing murder to protect," said Baruti.

DeLuca slipped his hand through his coarse, unruly hair and rolled his eyes skyward, apparently as perplexed as Baruti. He placed his eye to the scope again and gradually shifted the rifle through several mechanical sweeps. Baruti followed his example with his binoculars, but could see nothing unusual except for . . . Hmm. Were those sentries? One man and one woman were walking along the outskirts of camp in opposite directions, with rifles dangling from their hands. Perhaps one of those rifles was the source of the flash. To the right of the rig, an asphalt strip had been laid down that was obviously a runway for airplanes. It looked like a plane had just landed—a fat-bellied cargo plane—and several men were offloading supplies. Some packaged material was heading for the warehouse, while a forklift full of boxes was loaded onto the aircraft, in exchange.

Baruti swung his binoculars over to survey the area beside the runway, and spotted the helicopter Hunter and Nsogwa had flown to visit their camp.

Hunter stood by the chopper's cabin door, his tanned face and jutting chin just visible under the broad brim of his taupe safari hat. He was consulting a tablet with another man, as workers loaded the helicopter with what were clearly scientific instruments, and something that looked like a radar antenna. But another image tugged at Baruti's peripheral vision. A lean, well-proportioned, arrogant figure with distinctive Shona features bobbled into view. A man he knew intimately, although they'd never met before their brief encounter at the scientists' camp. A man whose soul was as hollow as his conscience. Hondo Nsogwa.

Nsogwa appeared to be arguing with the male sentry, flinging his arms at the swampy fields and scraggly forest surrounding the site. He grabbed the man's rifle, shouldered it, and jammed his eye to the scope. With crisp precision, as though he'd zeroed in on and flushed out prey many a time in this fashion, he swept the weapon systematically over the terrain. There was no suggestion of hesitation while the rifle was leveled in their direction, but Baruti felt a tingling in his throat, nonetheless. It buzzed and stung as if he had a knife poised at his carotid. And the echo of the words of a dying friend whispered in his ear: */Xuri kxaosi*, meaning "tricksters," in the *!Kung* language.

"I need to get a closer look," muttered DeLuca, retracting his rifle and shouldering his pack. He lifted his water bottle, took a slug, and eyed Baruti solemnly. "It's best if you hang back, in case I get caught."

"And do what if that should happen? I have never flown a helicopter, and I do believe we're some distance from our own camp, or Peawanuck, if I were to eventually manage to locate them after a grueling hike that could take days. No, I will accompany you. I understand the risks." *Believe me, I do.*

DeLuca grunted. Baruti wasn't sure it indicated assent, but there was a veiled undertone of approval in his voice. Perhaps he was coming to respect Baruti and trust him, to a certain extent.

Not a wise decision, my friend. I will do what my heart demands. No more. No less. You are of little consequence.

He uncapped his own water bottle, gulped half the contents, then replaced it in his backpack.

DeLuca rose, half-crouched, and said, "Keep low and follow me. There isn't much cover between here and the camp. We'll try to zigzag and dive to the ground every twenty-five feet or so. Hopefully, we won't be too obvious."

He didn't wait for a reply, but instantly scooted forward, dodging deadfall and brackish pools, launching himself onto crisp patches of lichen and spongy moss. Baruti trailed him easily, risking a peek at the sentries at every "diving station." No sign that any of them were on high alert. And Nsogwa had disappeared.

Halfway across the soggy field, DeLuca signaled to him to hold up. A gaggle of Canadian geese blocked their path, honking, waddling, and flapping at each other like a cluster of children jostling for a soccer ball.

"We don't want to spook them and have them take to the sky," he whispered.

They sank down on the moss and waited. But the birds seemed content to drink, shower, and argue, without any indication they'd been disturbed. The two men would have to circle around the flock in a wide arc to avoid startling them. But just as they crept to their feet, a throbbing noise filled the sky. The helicopter had taken off and was angling toward them. Both Baruti and DeLuca flung themselves to the ground and burrowed into the sedge. The geese squawked and huddled together as the rotors generated a downdraft, ruffling their feathers and flattening the grass around the two men, likely leaving them fully exposed. Had they been detected? But the aircraft moved on and flew at very low altitude, the sound fading ever so slightly, but then holding steady—a continuous motorized pulse bleeding into the air just to the south.

Baruti raised his head and surveyed the sky, spotting the helicopter where it hovered over the granite bulwarks of Sutton Ridge, its radar antenna pointed at the ground. Hunter leaned out the cabin door, ensured the device was securely fastened to the fuselage, then nodded to the pilot. The helicopter set off in an easterly direction, possibly to take topographic measurements. How odd. Baruti looked back at DeLuca, eyebrows raised.

"I have no idea," muttered the geologist. "Could be remote sensing. But this might be a good time to make a run for the warehouse, while the geese are scattering and noisy as hell."

Baruti nodded, noting the disturbed group launching into the sky on widespread black-tipped wings, or waddling closer to the camp, honking their displeasure. Keeping in tight formation with the birds, the men jumped up, crouch-walked forward, and ducked down again. By now they were within fifty feet of the warehouse and still remained undetected in open country. Miraculous.

Baruti scanned the area between the enormous rig—or whatever it was—and the warehouse, searching for the circulating sentries, but they seemed to have vanished. Maybe they were taking a coffee break, although it was unlikely Nsogwa would have dismissed both of them. What did that mean?

He tapped DeLuca on the shoulder and shook his head, signaling the easy access. Suspiciously easy. DeLuca leaned toward his ear and whispered, "I'm never one to turn down an invitation."

Leaping up, he raced over the last stretch of open ground, fleet as a gazelle and uncommonly graceful for such a large man. Well, no doubt they were already caught in the poacher's trap, so why not at least make a courageous last stand? Baruti dashed to the side of the warehouse, quickly catching up to DeLuca, and pressed his back to the rippled sheets of steel. Sweat erupted from his pores as he contemplated their next move. They edged around the corner of the building, but didn't spot a miner, prospector, or supervisor strolling outside the warehouse. The workers must have retreated inside, or to the huts scattered throughout the area. DeLuca pushed onward, aiming for the partially open sliding door, while he gripped his rifle nervously. He poked his head through the doorway, but immediately retracted it, eyes wide.

"Gentlemen, come in. Come in. I've been expecting you," boomed a voice from the interior. Nsogwa's voice; no mistaking it.

Baruti met DeLuca's eyes. What a hopeless mission. They weren't exactly 007 material, despite his training. And fleeing now would accomplish nothing. There was no escaping these men, who were so well stocked with guns and vehicles, so perhaps it was time to end this game once and for all.

Baruti slipped around DeLuca and strode through the door, head held high. He expected a number of men to surround him, tightening the noose. He expected the muzzle of a gun to be jammed against his head. But instead a warm mug was pressed into his hands.

"Coffee?" said Nsogwa.

Scanning...

Located: Chapter 14

FRANK'S MOUTH AND nose plunged underwater, but his ears didn't. He heard something impossible, but teasingly hopeful.

On the heels of his last words, he heard a reply.

"They are a damn nuisance, aren't they? Well, I could let you die, man, but I hate snakes too."

Suddenly the coils loosened, as a flurry of movement and frantic splashing erupted. Frank raised his head and sucked in a sweet, life-restoring breath. The tension oozed from his body as the living ropes fell away, although he wondered if his bones had been snapped. He pushed up tentatively, poking his head out of the water and fumbling on weak hands and knees. Above him stood a hulking man, hacking and snipping at the muscular body of the snake with what appeared to be garden shears. Segments of snake were scattered throughout the partially dredged pool, rubbery fragments that seeped blood. Finally the man cast aside the shears and seized the snake's head, which was still clamped to Frank's hip. He pried apart the massive jaws, releasing the tortured flesh.

Frank flipped over and sat up, shivering, his legs enveloped in soft mud. He looked up and gazed in absolute adoration at his rescuer. Then he took in the neon-orange prison coveralls and recognized his rescuer—the bald, bulky, menacing guy from the chain gang.

"You okay there, man?" the prisoner asked.

"A— alive, I think," said Frank. "What the hell? A p— python. What is a python doing here?"

The man cocked his head, scanning Frank with vague interest.

"You must be a stranger to these parts. Otherwise you'd realize we're swarmin' with pythons. Some idiots bought them as pets years ago, found out they were too hot to handle, and chucked them out in the Everglades. And they bred and bred and bred. Thousands of them now."

"Oh, yeah," said Frank. "Now I remember. Another sign of the world gone haywire. I—I don't know what to say. Thanks."

"*De nada.*"

Frank's savior nodded and grinned, exposing a crooked row of tobacco-stained teeth. He stuck out his hand, and Frank didn't hesitate, criminal or no criminal. He grasped the scabbed, work-roughened fingers and was instantly hoisted onto his feet.

"Whatcha doing out here, anyway?" the guy asked.

"Archaeology," said Frank, gesturing toward the corpses across the pool, which was now littered in snake parts. "We found what appear to be ancient bodies, probably buried here in the distant past. I'm Frank, by the way."

"Pedro," the man replied. "Fun job." He winked.

"Hardly," said Frank. "Especially where snakes and alligators hang out."

"Well, I used to think hackin' weeds and squeegeeing armadillo guts off the road sucked more than anything in the world. But, man, I think you've got it worse."

"No arguments here. Hey, is your crew nearby?"

They must have moved along quickly to have reached this road. And why would they have even bothered with *this* road?

"No, man. Still working by the panther refuge. I climbed the fence, crossed the refuge, climbed the fence."

"Oh," said Frank.

This man was no longer a prisoner. He was a fugitive. An hour ago, that thought would have sent icy currents through his guts; but his guts were aflame right now and only just intact because of this man.

Without warning, his muscles rebelled, and he staggered. Pedro grabbed his arm to steady him.

"So," said the big man. "You gonna turn me in after I saved ya from the snake?"

He was still gripping Frank's arm, but with only moderate pressure to maintain his support, so Frank didn't sense any threat.

"No," said Frank. "That would be . . . rude."

He slapped on a tentative grin, but it was quickly erased as a bolt of pain shot through his abdomen, accompanied by a series of spasms in his legs. He trembled and wobbled and barely suppressed a scream.

"Maybe you need to see a doctor," said Pedro. "But I can't stick around for some ambulance to come getcha."

"I don't think I need an ambulance. But I could use a driver."

He met Pedro's eyes.

"You sayin' what I think you're sayin'?" Pedro asked, a hesitant fire igniting in his gaze.

Frank sighed. "I need—" He grimaced, absorbing another blitzkrieg of pain, then continued. "N— need to free that damned necklace from that damned corpse, and then I'm getting the hell out of here. But I'm not sure I can drive. My whole body feels like it's on fire."

"Sure, man. Then you got yourself a driver. But what necklace are you talkin' 'bout? I know a thing or two 'bout necklaces."

"You *do*?" said Frank, his voice hitching upward on the last word.

"Helped myself to one too many. How I ended up in orange coveralls." He donned an unabashed grin.

Ah. Now he understood. "Jewel thief." At least it wasn't "ax murderer." "Well, I doubt you'd care too much for this particular piece of jewelry. Just an old bead necklace. Not valuable at all, except to dudes like me. It just . . . doesn't belong where we found it."

Pedro eyed him crookedly, nursing a shrewd smirk. "You need some help liftin' it?"

"Yeah," said Frank. "But it's a delicate job. I'm not sure . . ."

Another wave of pain rolled through him, triggering spikes and needles and gut-clenching stabs.

"Oh, who gives a damn! Can you help me over to the bodies?"

"Sure, man."

Pedro clutched his shoulders as he limped, juddered, and splashed across the pit, parting a sea of creamy snake flesh, scaly skin, and shredded serpentine internal organs.

"Just stand by, in case I fall over," said Frank.

Pedro hovered, while Frank fumbled in his pocket for his tongue depressor. Of course it was gone. He'd dropped it the instant the snake had attacked. But—what the hell . . . He burrowed his fingers into the corpse's ropy flesh and ripped a healthy portion right off. The necklace was embedded in the fibrous gristle.

"My boss should forgive me if she thinks I did this while a snake was attacking me."

Pedro chortled. "Hey, I'd be your alibi. But . . . how 'bout I support you and you keep holdin' onto the . . . mummy meat? It's kinda gross, man, and . . . I'd rather touch a snake."

"Yeah, it is disgusting," said Frank, cradling the flesh and necklace combination nonetheless. "Hard to believe this is my bread and butter. Now, let's get the hell out of here."

"I'm with you, man."

Pedro wrapped an arm around Frank's shoulders, practically holding him up, as Frank hobbled to the steep bank that bordered the pit. Pedro left Frank propped against the mud wall while he climbed to the rim, then offered him a hand to muscle him over the bank. Frank handed him the necklace first, which Pedro reluctantly captured with an obvious revulsion. After setting it gently on an exposed root, he turned and hoisted Frank up and out of the real entrance to Hell.

Pedro continued to lend Frank solid support, at times completely carrying him, until they reached the gravel road. Alligators scrutinized them from the nearby creek, but made no move to intercept them. They probably smelled python.

Frank halted near the rental car, as an alarming thought struck him. What about Ali? He'd have to text him and describe the attack so the student would know why he'd bolted. He'd have to somehow explain how he'd chopped up a snake single-handedly, maybe using archaeological tools he'd stashed in his trunk. How could he make this plausible?

"We're almost there," said Pedro, squeezing his shoulders in encouragement. "Just a few more steps."

But after Step One and before Step Two, they heard the rumble of a car engine and the crunch of tires on gravel. Ali must be returning. Or . . . a police car was investigating this isolated lane sweetly situated next to a panther refuge. Either way, they were screwed, or at least Pedro was.

Frank hopped the final two steps, wrenched open the car door, and popped the trunk.

"Get in," he hissed at Pedro, waving at the trunk.

ALI'S SUV ROLLED to a stop just behind Frank's rental car while Frank was still leaning against the open front door. Ali turned off the engine and stepped out, carrying a plastic cup of iced tea in one hand and a grease-soaked paper-wrapped burger in the other.

"I wasn't sure what you felt like eating . . . What the hell happened to you, Frank? I thought it was just mud, but you look . . . bloody." He swished his hand over the stains on Frank's pants and the large crimson splotch on his T-shirt. "You okay?"

Frank stumbled against the side of the car, gripping the doorframe to regain his balance.

"No. Not great. I was attacked . . . by a snake."

Ali's rich olive skin paled to the color of toasted wheat.

"Have you been bitten? Was it the rattler?"

Frank shook his head.

"Python. Huge sucker. I went back to the car to see if I could find some better tools to strip away the mud. All I found was garden shears."

Ali raised an eyebrow.

"I brought it back to the pit, thinking I could wedge it behind the corpse's neck and approach the beads from that angle. That's when the fucking snake attacked. I . . . you guys are going to kill me, but I ended up hacking away part of the neck because, you know, I was dying." He pointed to the flesh-enfolded necklace that he'd quickly tucked into a plastic specimen bag and tossed on the leather seat. "But it was damned lucky I had the shears. The python coiled around me and started to squeeze, but I snipped him off."

"You're . . . kidding," said Ali, his face twisting in a way that looked uncomfortable.

"Do I look like I'm fucking kidding?! The snake guts are all over the site. And the shears are somewhere in the water."

Frank stumbled again, and—that did it!—he just couldn't stand up anymore. He eased himself onto the cushioned comfort of the front seat, shuddered, and tipped his head against the steering wheel.

Ali dashed quickly to his side, setting the drink and burger on the car roof.

"I think you need an ambulance, Frank."

"No!" Frank snapped. Too forcefully, he imagined. "I'm just . . . shaken up. The bleeding's stopped and I'm bruised, but that's it. No broken bones. I'm going to rest here for a few minutes, then head to the hotel in Naples. I'll examine the beads there before I transport them to the university, if that's okay. After I clean up and maybe nap first. Takes the steam out of a guy, wrestling a snake."

"No doubt," said Ali. "But . . . are you sure you're okay to drive?"

"Yeah. I can manage."

Ali stayed wedged in the car door, apparently reluctant to let Frank leave. Frank didn't know if he was worried or, just as likely, didn't buy his story.

"Well, at least relax for a minute and drink something."

He handed Frank the cup of iced tea, obliging him to take it.

"Thanks," he muttered, clasping the cool drink, which was dripping with condensation. He wondered if he'd vomit the minute he took a sip.

"Okay, you have me totally curious," said the skeptical undergrad. "I must see this snake."

He pivoted and trotted toward the path, turning back once, maybe to see if Frank would object.

Be my guest, buddy. You're going to find solid evidence of my snake story. But maybe you'll notice two sets of footprints instead of one, the second set belonging to pretty big feet. That would invite questions.

Time to leave. Especially since the sweltering heat rising from the interior of the car was like a sauna, and Pedro might be suffocating in his compact trunk.

Frank yanked the keys out of his pocket—still there, thank Zeus—and tossed them onto the seat beside the necklace. He eased the door closed so as not to alert Ali, and started the car, which might alert him anyway. Then he swung in a U-turn onto the road, veering around Ali's SUV and almost into the mesh of tropical plants and boggy vehicle-gobbling ground on the side of the road. He swerved back, a little too sharply, and almost ended up in the alligator-infested people-gobbling creek on the other side.

Man, he was in no shape to drive. But it was all good. Before he reached the main highway he'd pull over and let Pedro out so he could drive. As long as they could avoid any encounters with police, they should be able to reach his hotel safely, where he could collapse and recuperate. Of course, he might have to field questions when he delivered the necklace to the university, but that should be easier once he'd had time to collect himself.

After all, he didn't intend to steal this necklace. Once they had it back in their hands, why would they care about a second set of footprints? And the snake story? That might even get him a few pity dates.

A grin made its way onto his face, but it was quickly replaced with a severe wince.

Scanning...

Located: Chapter 15

DAYNA HEAVED A sigh of relief, as the captain of the jet boat throttled back the rpm's and brought the vessel to a gentle glide, coasting through the ice-encrusted inlet of James Bay, the last nauseating leg of her journey to Polar Bear Provincial Park. Despite a view that boasted nothing but bleak ridges fringed with frost and a desolate, treeless, flat-textured plain, she found it somewhat soothing that her gaze could extend over vast distances unobstructed. She experienced a mild shiver at the nippy temperature, and a more pronounced one from a glimpse of ranging polar bears, but her Cree guide from Windy Tours reassured her with a smile, as he aimed the boat at a pebble-strewn beach.

Here at last. Whoever imagined in the current age that travel could still be so tedious?

She recalled the many hops this journey had required, simply to reach the scientists' camp. Boston to Toronto was a simple matter. But Toronto to Timmins? A five-hour delay. Then another two hours to connect with the next float plane, which didn't bundle the trip into one continuous flight, but forced her to endure a series of jouncing, breath-snatching takeoffs and landings, with stopovers in

Moosonee, Fort Albany, Kashetchewan, and Attawaspiskat, before she finally arrived in Peawanuck. From there, she'd procured a tour guide, Jim Sâkêwêw, from the Cree company Windy Tours—the only transport available to convey her farther, via jet boat. Nor had she realized that there was no direct route to the camp. They had to travel twenty miles north, up the Winisk River to Hudson Bay, then follow the coastline south for another thirty miles. Since Jim had promised her a timely arrival, she'd had to curb her objections when he accelerated to blistering speeds, chopping through the waves with spine-crunching jolts and driving a face-slapping airstream over the windshield.

"The camp is another mile over that ridge and along a gravel path," Jim informed her. "But the ground is primarily bog, so I'll lead you. You wouldn't want to wander off the path, never mind accidentally slipping into a bog and getting very wet! Still pretty cold this time of year, for you southerners, anyway."

She eyed the guide, a trim, fit fellow, approximately forty years old, whose face was permanently creased with laugh-lines, as if he were constantly amused. Instead of the polar fleece that she'd sensibly adopted for this trip, he was wearing a windbreaker that was flapping open over a faded blue T-shirt. She supposed Boston would put her in the southerner classification in his mind, since he probably found the biting wind balmy.

"Thanks," she said. "I've seen my fair share of bogs, so I know what to be mindful of. It's really the presence of bears that I find unsettling."

He smiled and shrugged, but didn't utter any reassurances. All the nature films depicted polar bears as handsome, misunderstood creatures whose environment had been defiled by humans which positioned them as victims. But they were still wild animals—one-thousand-pound animals with razor-edged claws and bone-breaking jaws and teeth. Obviously, Jim agreed with this assessment since, after cutting the engine, he removed a tranquilizer gun from a storage berth, and then extracted a rifle, too.

Dayna gripped the rail and began clambering over the side, but Jim tapped her arm.

"Hold on a second till I beach us good and solid."

He splashed down into the water and grabbed the tow line, dragging the bow of the boat onto shore. After ensuring that it was secure, he offered her a hand, while she leaped from the deck and landed on the crunchy, glittery surface of the beach, which was obviously embedded with ice crystals. At least she'd had the foresight, in the flurry of preparation, to include sturdy hiking boots with good grips.

Dayna staggered and paused, taking a moment to shed her sea-legs, which seemed determined to rock her back and forth.

"You good?" asked Jim.

"I'm fine," she shouted, then lowered her voice when she realized she no longer had to compete with the engine. "Not accustomed to boat travel, or the shimmying of small planes, either. But a hike is more my speed, so let's continue." She pasted on a stiff smile, to project a semblance of strength.

Jim gave her a nod and began tramping across the rocky beach, at a leisurely pace. Dayna followed, stepping cautiously until she felt reasonably balanced. Then she raised her head high to view and admire the landscape, to breathe in the crisp, fresh air, and to keep an eye peeled for polar bears.

The endless expanse of stunted, olive- and emerald-colored bushes and ground-hugging lichen interspersed with occasional murky ponds—the total absence of bulges and folds in the terrain—now seemed oddly disquieting. She spotted a sweep of ivory to the south that disrupted the green carpet like a spilled can of paint, but then, in a synchronous flapping of wings, it burst into the sky. Nothing but a flock of geese. Dayna heaved a sigh and tried to shake off her fears. Besides, there might be far more dangerous activities occurring in this region than random polar bear attacks. Activities that precipitated murder.

But her information was sketchy, at best. A fleeting comment on a virtual screen. But perhaps this guide could contribute additional details.

"Jim," she began tentatively.

"Yes, Ms. Lugan?"

"Dayna, please."

He turned to her, sporting an amused smile.

"Dayna, then. Don't worry. I can deal with the bears. But they usually keep their distance, anyway."

"I'm not really worried about that."

The crinkles deepened around his eyes.

"I had a feeling there was something else, since you're in such a hurry to reach your student."

"I was wondering . . . Has anyone in your town gone missing recently?"

He looked startled.

"Well, yes. Somewhat recently—a number of months ago. A friend of my daughter's. Donna Kimiwan. Her family reported her absence to the police, and they searched the town and the surrounding area, but didn't find her. She did tend to canoe and hike on her own, though. We thought she might have been attacked by a bear, or slipped into a river or bog and drowned. There are many ways to disappear in the North, and it's unlikely anyone will find what's left of you. Wolves can even make your bones disappear."

Dayna shivered.

The Cree guide shrugged. "It's the sad truth, but the way of nature. If it happens, at least we nourish the earth."

"Did . . . Donna, is it? Did she mention to your daughter any unusual activity, or something sinister she might have witnessed before she disappeared? Is it possible that her disappearance wasn't an accident?"

"Donna had a lot of problems," said Jim with a sigh. "She drank too much; she sometimes did drugs. She slept with too many men. Even one of the scientists at your camp, I think. Tony DeLuca we've known for many years, but it was the other one, the newer one, that she dated. Wilson, I believe he's called. The biologist and tracker of polar bears. She was such a wreck, I didn't believe half of the things she said. She probably got drunk one night and drowned."

Or saw or overheard something she shouldn't have and was eliminated.

"What did she say that you didn't think was credible?"

Jim stopped in his tracks, just as a couple of low-domed apricot-colored tents came into view along the horizon. He faced her fully, all traces of amusement gone.

"Why are you so interested? How do you even know that someone has disappeared?"

"I—I . . ."

How could she explain without disclosing sensitive information? A charge zapped through her nerves at another terrifying thought. What if Jim was involved in this girl's murder?

But she didn't need to utter a word.

"They've found her, haven't they? The scientists? Your student? They've recovered her body."

Dayna looked down at the soggy ground. Had she just hampered a police investigation? Or . . . maybe she'd just jeopardized her own safety.

He clutched her arm, demanding that she meet his gaze. Despite his angry tone, his eyes radiated warmth like the welcome rays of the spring sun.

"It's okay," he said. "I understand that you can't elaborate. I will tell you what I know."

Dayna licked her lips and nodded, anticipation and dread building within her.

"She spoke utter nonsense. She said things like, 'The gods have arrived.' 'The Earth is doomed.' She declared that the earthquakes were only the beginning. 'We will burn up in volcanic ash or drown, as the oceans rise and inundate the land.' 'People have angered the spirits of the Earth, and they are rising up, prepared to destroy us and cleanse the world of the human infestation.'

"Does that make any sense to you?" Jim asked. "Doomsday prophecies? If they've found her body, my guess is that she killed herself."

Dayna sagged, feeling completely out of her depth. She was not a police detective. Yes, she certainly solved puzzles and investigated mysteries, but only those of the past. Even if she played amateur sleuth, nothing Jim had said would explain why this girl might have been murdered. If the victim was this girl. Perhaps she *had* killed herself. She certainly sounded unstable. Or, another thought within the realm of possibility, a cult that enjoyed brainwashing young minds had seized control of her. But that still suggested suicide.

But one piece of this puzzle didn't fit within the paradigm of cultish behavior. Donna had apparently been dating, or simply having casual sex with, one of the scientists at Felicity's camp. Not many scientists would encourage or indulge cult predictions and hysteria.

"The scientist she might have been sleeping with . . . Do you know anything about him?"

Jim shrugged. "Attractive, for sure. We're wary of newcomers, but he seemed all right. Really concerned about the environment. But I guess he has a taste for young girls, too. Donna was the second one he slept with."

Dayna broke eye contact with Jim, her skin prickling with unease. He must have sensed it, because he quickly changed the subject.

"We're almost to the camp. You'll find out for yourself, soon enough."

That didn't make her any less concerned. But at least she'd finally reach Felicity, and hopefully find her still in one piece.

"Right. Thanks. I'm really worried about my grad student, especially since you've been experiencing earthquakes."

Jim didn't respond, other than to turn and tramp forward.

"You have been experiencing earthquakes, I've noticed, according to the USGS data. Just like Donna said."

Jim still maintained his silence.

"What do you think of the earthquakes?"

"I don't like them," he finally said. "They don't belong here. But I don't think it means the end of the world."

She chuckled. "No, I don't either."

They continued the final trek without further conversation. Dayna found it odd that she'd somehow struck a nerve with a benign question about earthquakes. His comment that they "didn't belong here" seemed without foundation. Surely earthquakes were a natural phenomenon, with the potential to occur nearly anywhere in the world.

They were now approaching a wide gravel- and scrub-covered area—a sizable, solid platform within the bog that accommodated a camp and the helicopter pad. The compact tents became vivid tangerine humps projecting from the ground, and to the east Dayna noticed several tarps staked down and covering a substantial segment of the field. She understood their significance instantly. Protective shrouds for the mysterious bog bodies, no doubt rapidly decaying, now that they'd been extracted from the preservative anaerobic layers of peat. And among them would be the additional corpse, a possible victim of foul play.

She spotted two people sitting at a table just outside the tent. One stood up, highlighted by the sun, and seemed to be pointing a . . . gun.

Dayna froze, but as she squinted and stared, trying to determine who was threatening them, Jim grabbed his own rifle. He pumped a shell into the chamber and raised it to shoulder level.

As his finger twitched near the trigger, it dawned on Dayna who the petite figure was.

"No," she cried, pushing the barrel down. "That's my student!

"Felicity!" she called. "It's me. Dr. Lugan. What are you doing?"

The girl gradually lowered the weapon. "Dr. Lugan?"

Dayna marched forward until she could see both people clearly. It was undoubtedly Felicity, with her vibrant red hair and, beside her, an attractive blond man in his late thirties. Was he the last man to "date" Donna Kimiwan? She suppressed a shiver.

"What are you doing with a gun?" she asked.

Before she could say another word, a series of five musical notes within the tent announced a call of some sort. The man grinned sheepishly, and ducked back inside.

"Well, hell," he exclaimed immediately.

"Who is it?" asked Felicity, setting the gun down on the table.

The man reappeared, gripping a laptop. "I guess communications have been reestablished. Long distance communications, too." He smiled effusively and stretched his hand toward Dayna. "Shaun Wilson."

"Dayna Lugan," she replied, grasping his hand limply.

"Felicity's faculty adviser, am I correct? I imagine she spooked you with our news and the sudden loss of communications. Well, I'll let you get up to speed with your student while I take this call, since I don't want to miss it."

Felicity raised her eyebrows.

"It's from Mars," he explained.

Scanning...

Located: Chapter 16

BARUTI GRIPPED THE warm cup, unable to fathom the sloshing black liquid it contained, or to process the grinning face of his enemy meeting his narrowed gaze with a wink. The jagged edge from a chip in the ceramic mug pierced his index finger, deeply enough to draw blood, but that hardly qualified as a vicious attack. Nsogwa swept another cup from a nearby counter, where several mugs and an industrial size coffeemaker were arrayed. He placed it in DeLuca's hand, forcing him to release a double grip on his rifle.

Not exactly the pounce of a murderous thug, but that would be foolish and cowardly, wouldn't it? These men had always been suspicious, but never stupid. Until . . . they killed a Cree woman.

Well, now that he and DeLuca had been warmly welcomed into the establishment, why not look around? Baruti surveyed the interior of the warehouse. Hydraulic gadgets, barrels of fuel, and—there they were—the mysterious boxes the crew of workers had transported from the cargo plane. Two employees were even now ripping off packing tape, prying open the cardboard lids, and removing . . . Hmm. Interesting. Portable containers labeled "cryocoolers." And in the adjacent boxes? Lab equipment and liquid nitrogen cylinders. A woman in head-to-toe lab-issue protective gear and gloves grabbed a cylinder and a cryocooler and transported them to a partitioned section at the back of the warehouse.

"Now, gentlemen," said Nsogwa. "Now that you're warming up, you can put away your guns, join me in my office, and we can have a little chat."

He smiled graciously, his arms spread wide in such a sickly display of *djinn*-like subservience that Baruti nearly choked on his coffee. How he wished he could jam his gun into the vicious man's mouth and pull the trigger.

But DeLuca, realizing Nsogwa wasn't about to kill him—at least not yet, anyway—slung his rifle over his shoulder and gave a brisk nod. Baruti's gun was concealed, so he just shrugged and displayed his empty hands, hoping Nsogwa would not dare to frisk him.

"Very good," said Nsogwa. "No bears in here that you need to worry about."

Baruti raised his eyebrows. *Except the one right in front of us.* He sipped his coffee to disguise his distrust. The brew was ridiculously thick, as if it had sat so long in the coffeemaker it had congealed. It was also extremely strong and bitter, but at least it was hot.

The tall Zimbabwean ushered them into an office that was segregated from the rest of the warehouse with Plexiglas windows perched on a half-wall. He gestured to some serviceable wooden chairs and settled into the plush leather swivel seat in front of a holographic computer. The accommodations, the high-priced and advanced technological equipment, seemed overly luxurious for mining prospectors in a remote location. And cryocoolers? What would they use them for?

"Welcome to our humble operation," Nsogwa said. "I know we extended the invitation, but I didn't expect you'd take us up on it so soon."

"Well," said DeLuca, seating himself stiffly in one of the chairs. "It's a small world up here, in northern Canada. And I'm a geologist, so you piqued my curiosity. Although when we first set out, we were simply scouting for bears for Baruti's research. And I wanted to hike up to Sutton Ridge, too. Love that anomalous hunk of granite in the middle of bog country."

"Well, we're always happy to receive fellow scientists. I'm sure you've already determined that this isn't your standard prospecting operation."

DeLuca took a moment to collect himself. He sipped from his mug to buy more time, then said, "That's a massive rig you have out there."

"Yes," said Nsogwa. "Geothermal drilling rig."

Baruti blinked, shocked that he would immediately admit to subterfuge. He accidentally slurped his coffee.

"We've been studying this region for some time. We think it would be an ideal location to set up a facility, and we certainly require energy for that. We suspect there might be a mantle plume in this region; perhaps we could also supply the northland with sufficient energy to offset any damage we might do to the environment through mining."

"What makes you think there's a plume?" asked DeLuca.

Nsogwa squinted at him, looking genuinely surprised.

"Surely you, as a geologist, already suspect that it might be possible, since this region has experienced so many unusual earthquakes and episodes of uplifting. But we're also conducting additional studies. We're performing SAR interferometry remote sensing to determine if the landmass is bulging. We're also conducting seismic topography measurements, to detect variations in wave speed. As you know, Dr. DeLuca, lower wave speeds are potential evidence of the presence of hot mantle material which is, of course, richer in iron."

"If there is a plume—the existence of which is still just a theory—tapping it might release more heat into the environment and increase the effects of global warming," said DeLuca.

"We'd do our best to contain that. We want to collect the energy, not release it."

"And are you also releasing shock waves? Earthquakes?" asked DeLuca.

Baruti frowned at him. Surely he should know better than to provoke potential killers.

Nsogwa's eyes creased momentarily, but he exhibited no other reaction.

"Well, as you undoubtedly know, earthquakes are a side effect of geothermal drilling. But they're not on such a massive scale as to cause significant damage. Our mission is to save and protect the environment, not destroy it. As you should already know," he said, looking directly at Baruti, "since we've taken extraordinary measures to protect the declining wildlife in the Okavango Delta."

DeLuca turned to Baruti, eyebrows raised. "Measures? What measures?"

Baruti kept his gaze steady, although his gut was churning with fury. He hated to admit these people were involved in any charitable activity, when he knew the other half of the equation.

"They're attempting to reintroduce the rhinoceros into the Delta. They fund a cloning company that aims to revive extinct animals."

For a moment, he was blinded by visions. Heaps of blood-stained tusks and a distraught, scarified man who lay sobbing beside them, stroking their pearly tips. The vision altered, and this same man appeared, trembling as he painted animals on the rock walls of a cave—bronze, ebony, silver, maroon—as he stroked wavy lines upward from the elephant, the gazelle, the hyena, to represent their life forces drifting away. And each spirit toppled another in a horrific domino effect. And then the final scene. This man he knew so well, sprawled on the ground, panting, bleeding from several bullet holes, and beating his fist upon the overlapping boot prints that surrounded his body. The blood spread in an ever-widening pool.

Baruti ricocheted back to the present, to complete attentiveness. He regarded Nsogwa with barely-disguised loathing.

"That's interesting," said DeLuca, stroking his chin. "So you're like that soft-drink company."

Nsogwa's eyes widened. "Pardon me?"

"Protect the polar bears. An altruistic company. Profit is only secondary, right?" He swallowed the last dregs of his coffee and set the cup on the gleaming glass desk.

Did Nsogwa's lips betray the slightest quiver? "For a company to thrive, it must earn money. But it must also feed its employees, promote industry and innovation and, if it earns enough, return to the Earth what it has taken by restoring and nourishing it. If a company has no money, it has no means to perform this last great and difficult task." He paused. Then he added, "Our conflict of interest is the opposite of what you think. We care more for the Earth and its biological heritage than for profit. The cloning industry is extremely expensive. It might eventually rob our company of sustainability."

"As will mining for diamonds where there are no diamonds," muttered DeLuca, under his breath. He obviously believed, as Baruti did, that Nsogwa was draping silk over a dung heap.

"Gentlemen," Nsogwa responded, pushing his chair back brusquely and standing up. "I'm sure this may be difficult for you to understand—a corporation that is truly concerned about our fragile Earth. And I'm sure you'd like to see proof that we aren't simply here to rape the Arctic region and destroy what's left of this delicate habitat. So I'm going to show you that proof."

He strode to the door and beckoned them to follow. Baruti took a final sip from his cup, then set it on the man's desk, while DeLuca bounced up, unable to contain his eagerness to explore. They joined Nsogwa as he whisked them across the warehouse to the partitioned section at the opposite end.

"This might be a tad cold," he warned.

Baruti was not surprised. They'd just transported cryocoolers and liquid nitrogen into the room. But a niggling worry leaped into his mind. Should they enter? Was this Nsogwa's method of disposing of them? It would be easy to eliminate them with a direct, concentrated spray of liquid nitrogen. Instant freeze-ray; probably instant death. Then all he'd have to do is toss them into a bog. If their bodies were ever found, it would be assumed they'd fallen in, couldn't escape the mud and tangle of roots, and died of exposure. No proof of foul play, this time. No gunshot wound.

But he couldn't deny that he was extremely curious about the cryocoolers.

Nsogwa opened the door, releasing a wave of cool air. He stepped inside and looked back at them expectantly.

DeLuca tossed an uneasy glance at Baruti, obviously nursing the same misgivings. Regardless, he shuffled through the entrance, turning a wary eye on Nsogwa, his hand twitching near his rifle. Baruti followed, slipping his fingers closer to the concealed weapon in his jacket.

The open door emitted a cloud of vapor, as the warmer air from the warehouse collided with the cooler air inside, although it was hardly as cold as a freezer. The woman who'd removed the cryocooler was hovering over sample jars and transferring what was evidently biological material to vacuum-sealed flasks. She looked up when they entered. Although she was gowned and masked, wisps of blond hair escaped the puffy surgical hairnet. Her eyes were an unusual amber color.

She paused when she noticed Baruti. It was as if she recognized him, and he felt a tingling of familiarity too.

Briskly, she returned to her task. She loaded flasks into the portable coolers and injected a layer of liquid nitrogen into the bottom compartment to preserve the specimens. The transfer of gas to the compartment resulted in an occasional spill, which created the flowing vapor they'd noticed upon entering and dropped the temperature in the room.

Nsogwa approached a prepared cryocooler on one of the tables and pulled on insulated gloves from a nearby trolley. He handed identical gloves to Baruti and DeLuca. With extreme delicacy, he lifted the lid, removed a vacuum-sealed flask from where it was tucked into the upper tray of the cryocooler, along with several others, and handed it to Baruti. The label on the glass exterior read *Ursus maritimus*, the Latin name for polar bear.

Baruti donned the pair of gloves and accepted the flask, although he bobbled it at first with clumsy ineptitude, much to his annoyance. Inside, he could distinguish several stiff white hairs.

"DNA samples?" he asked.

Nsogwa nodded. "No rhinoceroses up here. But we collect samples wherever we prospect—complete cryogenic zoos. Obviously, we won't need to clone the polar bear, since it's rebounding from near-extinction. But, just to err on the side of caution, we're collecting the DNA of various species that are on the brink of extinction or were in danger of collapse in the past. The specimens, obviously, must be kept frozen. We are in the process of setting up a laboratory here, but in the meantime we will be transferring most of them to our lab in Zimbabwe, where our scientists are perfecting the cloning technique. So far, we've been unable to reintroduce the rhinoceros because the issues of cloning continue: shortened telomeres and birth defects."

DeLuca massaged the bridge of his nose as if he were developing a migraine.

A wisp of a smile perched on Nsogwa's lips, but then he took pity on DeLuca. "I'm not the best person to explain, since I'm not a scientist, but a businessman. Reena!" He called to the woman still actively transferring specimens. "Would you care to enlighten our guests on the problems of cloning?"

She replaced the sample, while muttering under her breath, then turned and graced them with a brittle smile. "I would be happy to," she said, in a tone that clearly suggested the opposite.

"Reena is our Canadian geneticist," Nsogwa said proudly, as if this alone would impress DeLuca.

He looked unimpressed.

"Nice to meet you," he said. "Strange that you're working for a Zimbabwean company."

"Not really," she said. "DITEK recruits scientists from all over the world, and since they decided to come here . . . Besides, I like their philosophy. Preserve, replace, renew."

And massacre, if that doesn't work, thought Baruti. Why did she look so familiar if she was Canadian?

"You'd be surprised at how many scientists appreciate our work," Nsogwa remarked, looking pointedly at Baruti. "Regardless, I was attempting to explain our unfortunate failures with cloning, but I think I'm a failure at that, as well. Can you take over for me, Dr. Wilson?"

Baruti started, but he instantly masked his surprise. DeLuca's impassive expression remained unchanged. Perhaps it was a common name.

"Certainly," she replied. "Clones are often subject to premature aging. One reason for this phenomenon is that the DNA is usually extracted from an older specimen to begin with. Another is that in order to clone an individual we have to replicate their cells many times over. The telomeres, which are the tips of the chromosomes, become too short—a product of the aging process due to repeated episodes of replication via mitosis. They're also often missing the enzyme telomerase, which can repair telomeres and rejuvenate an individual, to a certain extent. It's an ongoing issue with cloning, but we're close to an answer."

DeLuca nodded repeatedly, as if he understood, then said, "Really not my area of expertise." But he did wriggle his hands into the gloves Nsogwa had dispensed, and he accepted the flask from Baruti and scrutinized the sample that was no different from those in Wilson's collection—that is, the Dr. Wilson who resided in their camp.

Nsogwa chuckled, as he looked sidelong at his colleague with a barely noticeable eye roll. "I'm sure *you* grasp the process and our difficulties, Dr. Mbeki," he prompted.

"I do," said Baruti. "I just don't understand what cloning has to do with diamond prospecting."

"Absolutely nothing," Nsogwa replied. "We happened to be searching for diamonds, then discovered what might be a mantle plume, and changed our business strategy. Cloning extinct animals is our primary goal, but there's no profit in it, so we decided to pursue a secondary angle to fund it."

Nsogwa retrieved the sample from DeLuca and reinserted it into the cryo-cooler tray. He regarded Dr. Wilson for a brief moment, as if conveying a non-verbal message, then closed the lid, removed his gloves, and tossed them onto the table.

"There really is nothing more to see, gentlemen," said Nsogwa, in the process of dismissing them.

But Dr. Wilson interrupted him. "What is your specialty, Dr . . .?" She was gazing directly at Baruti.

"Mbeki," he supplied. "Mammalian adaptation to extreme climate alterations. Particularly the larger species who seem to have the most difficulty."

"Hmm," she said. "Maybe in another life we might have worked together." Her lips trembled ever so slightly.

"Our lives aren't over yet," he said. He didn't know why he said it. She was extremely attractive and seemed to have a passion for reviving extinct species, but he sensed an underlying coldness. Yet . . . Perhaps he was just too lonely.

"I know another Dr. Wilson," he added. "Someone who studies and appreciates polar bears as much as I adore elephants and rhinoceroses."

"You do?" she replied, pressing her lips together.

"He works with me, here in the North. Maybe you know him. His first name is Shaun."

She blinked, but her expression didn't alter. "Never heard of him," she said. "But Wilson is a common name, even among scientists. I may have read a paper by him, though. Polar bears? It rings a bell. Or he could be the scientist who was mauled by a polar bear a few years ago. I heard that on the news. Never can be too careful."

Had she just delivered a threat, or was that a benign comment on a news item? He met her eyes, and she donned an unconvincing smile.

"Well," she said. "I have reams of work to do. Very nice to meet you both." She swiveled abruptly and bustled across the room, returning to the table where she'd been working initially.

"I believe it is time for me to return to my duties as well," said Nsogwa. "I would love to give you a tour of our lab when it's complete, but that will have to wait for another day."

"Well, thank you for showing us your . . . specimens," said DeLuca. "Although I was hoping to see some raw ore."

DeLuca peeled off his gloves in an oddly pretentious manner. He turned and stepped toward Nsogwa, as if to block the man's view of Baruti, and flicked a hand behind him at the cryocooler tray on the opposite table.

Baruti smirked, suddenly feeling deliciously devious. Obviously DeLuca believed little of Nsogwa's and Dr. Wilson's explanations.

Actually, it was likely that half his account was true. Certainly the science behind the subterfuge was accurate. But the benevolent part was too farfetched to accept. And it certainly didn't explain the dead body.

Baruti snatched the portable cryocooler from the table and slipped it into his pack. He re-shouldered the pack just as Nsogwa brushed past DeLuca and motioned for them to exit.

As they followed the Zimbabwean, Baruti delivered a quick nod to DeLuca. Mission accomplished. Nsogwa maintained a brisk pace, marching them through the main body of the building and toward the sliding doors where they'd entered, as if eager to dispense with them now that he'd concluded his performance.

"Perhaps you understand our objectives, now," he spoke over his shoulder. "I welcome any further questions you might have, and I would be happy to provide a tour of our geothermal rig, upon your return."

Nsogwa stopped at the door and shook their hands. He waited expectantly for them to exit.

"One more question before we go, if you would be so kind," said Baruti. "I fully support cloning, as long as the replicated animals are respected and returned to their natural habitat, or what remains of it. As long as the restoration of extinct animal species to their former state is the objective of the research. Is DITEK concerned with any other aspect of genetic engineering?"

Nsogwa smiled, but it was hardly a warm gesture, since his jaw clenched.

"Are you referring to DNA tampering? Creating new biological species through recombinant methods that might heighten human health, or even lengthen life, and thereby provide our company with another source of profit? Like . . . the Frankenstein experiments performed several years ago that created misshapen, tortured creatures it was a mercy to put to death?

"No, Dr. Mbeki. We have nothing like that in mind, I assure you."

"That's good," said Baruti. "I'm very glad that you haven't violated international law."

Nsogwa's eyes narrowed just enough to alarm DeLuca, whose hand slipped onto the stock of his gun.

"Really appreciate the tour," he said, and edged toward the exit.

But before they could escape, Nsogwa stepped to within a handspan of Baruti's face and grabbed his arm.

"You, of all people, should understand why we're doing this. You've witnessed an extinction event. You know exactly what is happening to our planet." He paused, then added, "We have the same objectives, even though you seem blind to the fact. We're . . . conservationists. We believe in preserving the deserving."

Baruti gritted his teeth, but nodded as Nsogwa, much to his relief, released his arm.

"Before they're all dead," he said, and walked out of the warehouse without a backward glance. He strode at DeLuca's side, as calm and composed as if he hadn't just pulled off a heist. As he proceeded through the navigable portions of the bog and toward Sutton Ridge, he did his best to ignore the prickly sensation induced by visions of men with guns tracking his movement.

But he couldn't suppress a shiver as Nsogwa's words echoed in his mind, speaking the volumes that their little tour had not.

Preserving the deserving.

Scanning...

Located: Chapter 17

LUCAS CLOSED HIS eyes as the MADVEC shuddered through the ionized atmosphere. Friction boiled beneath the heat shield, while the bullet-shaped capsule plunged toward Mars and decelerated from 10,000 feet per second to 1,000 feet per second. His heart always skipped a few beats during descent, as they were trapped in this claustrophobic cabin while their capsule cut through the atmosphere like a jagged blade blundering through tough steak.

"Woo hoo," shouted Bob, obviously energized by the freefall. "Do you feel it? Thicker atmosphere. Becoming similar to Earth's."

"But still deficient in oxygen," Lucas managed to gasp out, as the vehicle rocked from side to side and performed an awkward bounce.

"Well, that should change, once we've finished introducing the oxygen-generating cyanobacteria and scattering the lichen over the rocks. Eventually, when we establish forests, we'll be able to stroll on the surface without elastic suits, tanks, or masks."

"That will be exciting," said Gita. "But I prefer to see Mars before it resembles Earth in every way. I'd like to experience the desolate Mars, the alien planet, still coated in red dust."

Lucas, puzzled by her comment, turned toward her, although even cranking his head a few degrees was a challenge in the staggering g's.

"We've established that it's hardly alien, since bacteria has been bouncing back and forth between our planets in meteorites for millennia, and since we discovered the precursor molecules to our bacteria of origin. We are more likely descended from Martians than from a distinctly Terran evolutionary path."

"But, in our evolutionary bodies, we are unique to Mars. And Mars essentially died, long ago. So it is predominately alien, especially before we began meddling with its atmosphere, and heating the surface, and injecting biological entities."

The vehicle passed through the fire of rapid entry and deceleration and began a calmer descent, causing the nauseating vibrations to abate. But just as the bubbling in Lucas's stomach subsided, the capsule lurched, as the computer engaged the retrorockets.

"Yes, we have approach!" shouted Bob, pumping his fist. Lucas wondered when he would start giggling and bouncing up and down in his seat, heedless of the fact that he was strapped in and engulfed in his pressurized suit.

The spacecraft tufted clouds of exhaust as it braked and gradually drifted down to the planet's surface. Multiple craters appeared on the laser remote sensing or lidar screen, along with a sculpted canyon resembling a creosote ribbon. . . . Wait a minute. It looked like they were approaching the Kasei Valles—the steep-walled gully to the north of the Valles Marineris and the Tharsis Mountains—and the Tempe Terra region, the highland plain fringing the canyon. The exact location he and Bob had disagreed about, and which he had rejected as a suitable place to land. What the hell . . . ?

"Bob, did you reprogram the MADVEC? Did you change my coordinates?"

Bob didn't answer. He gazed with full focus at the lidar screen. The visual representation of the landscape usually had near-photographic similarity to the real thing, but for some reason it appeared blurry.

Gita pressed her eyebrows together as she eyed each of the others in turn. "But I thought you had approved this landing site. Kasei embodies the essence of both the original Mars and a newly terraformed Mars. It has an expanse of dusty, boulder-filled craters and ridges on the plateau. But it also sits next to the

Kasei Valles, a three-billion-year-old canyon carved by a deluge of water, no less. And it's somewhat near Vitalis, the cave where our first explorers discovered the precursor molecules. What location could be more panoramic or give us more wide-ranging features to explore?"

"But it's unstable," said Lucas. Was he surrounded by morons?

The capsule braked again with a bile-launching jerk, and cruised ever closer to the peppered regolith on the Tempe Terra.

"Is this really how it works, Bob?" Lucas said, with a half-snarl. A boiling wave of fury surged through his veins. "We discuss; you agree to my suggestions; then you renege on the agreement and do whatever you want, anyway?"

"You're not one to discuss, Lucas," said Bob, still goggling at the screen. But his eagerness was now tempered by a tautness in his voice. "Besides, we're already disregarding several orders just by commandeering the MADVEC and embarking on this excursion."

Lucas examined Bob's face through the curvature of his helmet. It looked distorted, but he could still see pinched brows and a rising flush in the astronaut's cheeks.

"Be that as it may," he said, "that doesn't mean we have to be suicidal. And what do you mean—'I'm not one to discuss?'"

"Tell him, Gita."

"Do we have to get into this *now*?" asked Gita, her jaw flexing as she faced the padded nosecone.

"Now would be a better time than when you give a crucial command and he ignores it. Lucas, you are not the leader on this mission, as you well know. Yet you question Gita's orders far too frequently. And you don't seem to value our opinions, when we discuss an issue. You grind your teeth and argue as if we aren't every bit as qualified for this mission as you are. No, Gita, it's time he learned the truth. She doesn't confront you about it, because she's worried about your temper. 'It's not worth it,' she says. And living in a confined module in the black of space can 'do things to people.' But both Gita and I decided at the outset that the Kasei Valles/Tempe Terra site was ideal for our purposes, and since you would have tried to overrule us and possibly inform the ISA, if Gita put her foot down, I didn't tell you."

Before Lucas could respond, the craft jolted to the ground, robbing him of breath. At least, he told himself it was the landing.

Bob released his belts and began poring over the monitors, examining the data for all the crucial systems. He also glanced at the lidar screen, to ensure the capsule had parked on stable ground.

"It looks like we're good. All systems nominal," he added.

"*Good?*" said Lucas, finally catching his breath. "In refusing to divulge your plans, you've basically kidnapped me and will be subjecting me to all the hazards of this location that may threaten my survival. How can that be *good*?"

"I think I see the propellant plant and the rover. We've set down fairly close. Excellent navigation, Gita."

She grunted, "Thanks." Then she turned to Lucas with a wavering smile. "I'm sorry Bob lied to you, Lucas, but he must have felt it was necessary. If you hadn't agreed to the landing site and informed the ISA of our plans before we coupled with the MADVEC, they might have remotely disabled it, removing any chance we would have had to explore this planet. I know you're worried about the area, but what is life without risk? We've risked exposure to high doses of radiation and several space hazards just to get here. And this region—including the Vitalis Cave and all it signifies—well, it's every astronaut's—probably every human being's—dream to visit. You must feel some excitement, too."

He wanted to shout at her, "How much is a dream worth?" But he knew his companions were far too stubborn to immediately refuel and jet back up to the *Phoenix*. He'd lost control of the situation, but not entirely. He could still direct the excursion covertly, and keep them restricted to the regions he specified.

"All right," he said. "We're here, regardless. Might as well make the best of it. It might even be warm enough to discover some liquid water."

It was summer in the northern hemisphere and, with the terraforming efforts, temperatures could sometimes reach as high as 40°F. At night, it would still dip to well below freezing, but at least the planet no longer experienced extreme temperature variations—from +50°F at the equator to -110°F—and one could now draw similarities to Earth's polar regions.

Gita's eyes lit up—a quiet dance of fire that belied her outward calm. She chucked off her belts and clapped him on the shoulder, shocking him into speechlessness. She certainly didn't seem as angry at him as Bob had suggested.

"Shall we disembark?" Her grin was infectious.

"Maybe we should change into something a little lighter, first."

He was already experiencing a sensation of added weight, which was compounded by the enormously bulky suit—a product of Mars's gravity, although, of course, Mars's gravity was only 0.38 that of Earth's. At least they now had the option of lighter, elasticized outfits that prevented the swelling or tissue bruising that could be induced by Mars's still too-thin atmosphere.

Originally, the air pressure on the red planet was between six and eight millibars. Terraforming had transformed it, elevating it to nearly 200 millibars. The top of Mount Everest boasts a 300 millibar pressure, which often leads climbers to become short of breath, as they have trouble absorbing oxygen in their lungs, and overcompensate by hyperventilating. Sometimes this leads to cerebral or pulmonary edema—a swelling of the brain or lung tissue caused by excess fluid. The air of Mars, with its overabundance of CO_2 and lack of O_2, wasn't breathable anyway, so they would need to rely on their rebreather tanks and masks, at all times. The pressure was now at a safe enough level that they could probably dispense with the elasticized suits, if they were willing to take the risk.

Gita, still feeling the aftereffects of extreme g's, fumbled awkwardly with her helmet and finally detached it. Tossing it on the seat, she stepped drunkenly to the rear compartment, where the bodysuits, tanks, and masks were stored. Lucas unlocked his restraints and removed his spacesuit, although with considerably less enthusiasm and a great deal more finesse. He padded to the rear of the capsule and accepted a tensile bodysuit and a light jacket from Gita. Bob performed the same procedure and followed Lucas a mere two steps behind, adhering to him, as always, like electrostatically charged dust.

Ten minutes later, they were prepped for egress, having topped off the cool-weather gear with snug cotton caps and facial masks attached to rebreathing units. Gita inadvertently bumped into Lucas in the confined space, while Bob kept jostling him to the point of irritation. At some point, punching Bob might be in order.

They moved into the airlock, sealed the inner hatch, then opened the outer hatch. A haze surrounded the spacecraft, blurring the rosy Martian ground and distorting the distant suggestion of a sun into a violet blotch in the sky. Lucas gazed at the landscape with wonder. He felt suspended in time, as if the airlock divided him from all things earthly and alien, present and past. He felt as if stepping from the capsule would take him into a world with billions of years of alternative history.

Bob advanced onto the platform and slid the ladder to the ground. But Lucas wasn't about to give Bob first contact with Mars. "How about you let Gita go first?" he said.

Bob eyed him with a hard gaze, but he couldn't object to Lucas's suggestion without looking petty. "Sure," he said, and stepped aside for his commander.

Gita smiled, ignoring the tension between the two, and swung out onto the ladder. As she descended, Lucas took the opportunity to follow immediately, leaving Bob in the rear.

Gita murmured in wonder as she set foot on Mars. It was so eerily quiet. The haze drifted around her, with the wind subdued, for some reason, as if it had temporarily revoked all claims to a devilish nature.

Lucas swiftly stepped down beside her, summoning a mild crunch from the regolith and shifting the rock and sand beneath his boot. With an exaggerated stamp, he planted the other boot, establishing a stable footing in the uneven soil. The mysterious fog swirled past him in meandering currents like a gentle stream. He stepped forward blindly but, just as his eyes suddenly adapted to the mirage-like world, he caught sight of the silver wall of the propellant plant, the glittery curve of the human habitation module, and beyond it, a ridge—most likely the edge of an impact crater.

How extraordinary to actually have an uninterrupted view of this world and to look upon it with his own eyes, rather than through the isolated images he'd studied most of his life. He'd have to send another message to Shaun once they'd finished exploring, to try to describe this moment. He'd whisked off a video message last night, just in case they didn't survive the descent—something he always worried about. He'd not disclosed their plans, in case Mission Control monitored his messages, but he had informed Shaun they were orbiting Mars and about to do something noteworthy, which the Flight Director could easily equate with their comet release. Even though he and Shaun were at odds about

Gilgamesh and so many other things, he still felt closer to his brother than anyone else. Perhaps that was because they'd shared the same pain at the death of their father. Perhaps it was because they had been selected for a higher purpose. Or, most likely, it was simply because they were siblings. Whatever the reason, he wished he could share this experience with his brother rather than his current companions. Particularly one.

"We're really here," he said, as Bob joined him on the rocky surface and nudged his arm none too kindly.

"Rather momentous, isn't it? And you didn't want to come," said Bob.

"It truly is spectacular," said Gita. "Can you feel the g's? I would love to find a crater and race down the slope in the red soil, feeling like a kid again. But even better, I'd like to hike into the canyon and maybe explore a cave. A place where life might have thrived at one time. To think that this was the birthplace of life on our planet, and that it will be our next home planet."

"Our next home planet," Lucas echoed. But for whom? For rabid human beings to abuse once again? Or for wise men and women to nurture and respect? But he knew he couldn't give voice to these thoughts.

"A planet of possibilities," he said, instead. "But also an unpredictable planet, since we've awakened the sleeping volcanoes. So let's . . . watch where we step, so we don't fall and puncture our air tubing. Let's wait for the mist to clear before we race down a slope to the bottom of a crater. Even the canyon may be more unpredictable with the added moisture. Possibly prone to landslides."

"Killjoy," said Gita, in a mildly admonishing tone. "We will explore with the utmost caution, of course." She eyed him sternly through the transparent arc of her face shield.

Lucas shrugged off the tone and strode toward the propellant plant, ignoring his own advice. The mist was nearly impenetrable. He peered through it as if through a thick veil, yet each step landed firmly on the ground, creating barely a shift in the rocky rubble.

First, they must determine if the telemetry was correct and the factory was fully stocked with propellant—so they would have enough fuel to return to the *Phoenix*. After that—after the mist cleared—they could explore all they wanted, as long as they adhered to his itinerary. Bob and Gita's desire to see the Vitalis

Cave might present a problem, but it was still a good day's travel by rover, and he could probably prevent that excursion. Running down the slope of a crater hardly seemed like the best use of oxygen, but rovering to the Chryse Planitia to witness the extent of the newly developing ocean, or inspecting the channel in the Kasei Valles, to determine if water had entered the chasm—since the ISA had detected a trace farther south on satellite imagery—those would be worthwhile treks.

As he plunged forward a few more steps, a casual gust of wind speared a gap in the mist. The silvery titanium shell of the propellant plant loomed in front of him—a squat silo-sized capsule that housed reactors and various components for gas conversion. Beside it, he glimpsed the wheels and chassis of the rover. Lucas paused. Why was he looking at the underside of the vehicle? It must have tipped over on its side. But . . . was Martian wind strong enough to do that? The winds on this planet were notoriously high-velocity, with storms registering speeds of 30 to 60 miles per hour, but they generally died down during the summer. Furthermore, given the planet's thin atmosphere, a 60-mile-per-hour Martian wind was only equivalent in strength to a 6-mile-per-hour breeze on Earth. But they'd been toying with the atmosphere and climate, recharging the wispy clouds with moisture from the melted comets. Could the winds have now become strong enough to flip a rover?

"What do you make of that?" he asked his fellow astronauts.

"Wind must be picking up. I haven't noticed any tornadoes on the satellite sweeps, though," said Bob.

"Well, as long as it's not damaged," said Gita. "There's certainly not even a breeze at the moment." She paused a few steps behind him and shrugged. "We should be able to tip it right-side up, especially in this low gravity."

He nodded, but that wasn't what worried him. He had no desire to be swept off a cliff, if they started exploring and the wind decided to surge again.

"I'm not sure we should—"

But his statement was cut off as the ground sagged beneath him, then exploded, and launched him high into the air. He could only think of two words from the immortal lyrics of his favorite classic song as he jetted upward.

Rocket man.

Scanning...

Located: Chapter 18

"I HAVE RESERVATIONS," said Frank.

The concierge eyed his muddy, bloody clothes.

"Okay, so you really need to know, don't you?" And he told the story of the snake.

FRANK OGLED THE parcel, a snugly wrapped box that sat beguilingly on his bedside table at the Sandstone Inn in Naples. His gaze drifted to the plastic bag that contained the mélange of corpse gristle and—was that a curd of brain?—encircled by an oddly displaced necklace.

Two archaeological treasures, he said to himself, mainly to keep his mind occupied while Pedro splashed iodine on his wounds and patched him up with gauze and bandages. *Both with secrets that might shake the world on its foundations.* Would this discovery, and the inevitable sensation it created, be enough to make his parents proud? He doubted it. Even though he'd achieved two prestigious degrees at Harvard, and had impressed countless professors with his affinity for accurately dating and classifying cave paintings and *!Kung* artifacts in Africa, he would always be considered the runt of the litter next to his sister, the neurosurgeon, and his brother, the astrophysicist.

"Ouch," he yelled, as Pedro attacked the wide gash in his abdomen, where the python had chomped through his skin and the underlying layers of tissue, with aggressive soaking and patting.

"Hold still, ya big baby," said Pedro, in a tone that suggested he was only half-joking. "This snake doesn't pack any venom, but he could still give you a nasty infection, 'specially in *that* water."

"Don't I know it," Frank muttered.

"Anyway, I'm almost done. What then?" Pedro asked, looking up shyly from beneath his lashes. "I should be on my way 'cause, you know, I'm a fugitive, and I don't fancy goin' back to jail. Will you be okay on your own? I know I owe ya . . ."

"Not as much as I owe you," said Frank. "But I was thinking . . . You're familiar with jewels and fencing and other shit. And I might need a partner."

Pedro cast him a sidelong glance, as he taped the last square segment of gauze over Frank's wound.

"Partner? You're a mummy collector with one of those fancy degrees. I'm a . . . well, you know."

Frank shifted and winced as waves of pain pulsed through him.

"My work is not all above-board, if you know what I mean. Let's just say I'm an archaeologist with a taste for treasure. And I will never be a mummy collector." He grimaced. *Leave that to Felicity and Dr. Lugan.* "I've . . . acquired something in Greece that might lead me to a hoard of treasure, if I translate the language correctly and if I can decipher the clues. And I could use an assistant who has ties to . . . let's just call it 'the underworld.'"

Pedro gripped the side of the bed and stood up awkwardly, sporting a look of mild astonishment. The lines in his forehead deepened, as if he were considering Frank's proposal from every angle.

"I shoulda figured . . . But your buddy at the mummy pit. He woulda seen my footprints, if he checked out the snake story. And I'm pretty sure he did. No one tells a story like that without callin' to folks."

Frank had been thinking the same thing on the seemingly endless drive to the hotel. He'd been constantly checking the rear-view mirror and expecting the blare of sirens at any minute.

"I'm not totally sure about Ali. But he seemed like a decent guy. I don't think he would have been too concerned that someone helped me survive a snake attack. I would hope he'd be grateful he didn't find my body beside the mummies instead."

"So . . . ya think I'm safe here for now," said Pedro. "But what about that hunk of meat and necklace? Don't ya have ta bring it somewhere? Or were you thinkin' of fencing it? I don't think anyone would want to buy those silly beads."

"No, not that. But I do have to examine it at the university here, since archaeology departments get jurisdictional, and I'll have to write up a report for my professor. I need to investigate this artifact for a few days just to make everything look satisfactory. But after that, I can start deciphering this." He pointed to the bubble-wrapped package. "It's a copper scroll that has similarities to another relic some archaeologists discovered in Israel in 1952. It could be a map. Are you interested in searching for buried treasure?"

"Jewels and gold and shit?" asked Pedro, his eyes glistening.

"And shit," said Frank. He'd pegged the man quite well—the Sundance Kid to his Butch Cassidy. And he owed him jewels and gold and shit, anyway. Otherwise he would have been python food.

"I'm not sure, man. You really want to work with . . . me?" He sounded suspicious, although the notion of treasure hunting clearly appealed to him.

"Yes!" Frank practically shouted. "Don't you understand? You saved my life! And I think we have a lot in common. We both want more than the shoddy deal we have. You may think I'm a lot different, but honestly, I don't see myself teaching or sitting behind a desk or digging up mummies for the rest of my life."

Pedro grimaced and briefly nodded, as if he could certainly relate to Frank's last comment.

"Say I agree," he said. "Does that mean we have to go to Greece? I don't have a passport, man, and if I did, they probably have my name, photo, and prints on file at every airport. I'd never make it through security."

"We might have to travel there, or to Israel, or somewhere else. Wherever the clues lead. Don't you know a forger who can doctor a passport and create fingerprint adhesives? I'm willing to pay. You could work on that while I assemble the puzzle, hopefully before anyone figures out I boosted this bit of the Codex. We'll stay in the U.S. till I have coordinates. Do we have a deal?" He held out his hand.

Pedro scratched his head doubtfully, but his eyes held a contrasting gleam.

"Wellll," he said, stringing out the word as if it were linked to a long train of thought. "You had me at 'partner.'" He shook.

IN THE SLUMBERING silence of the science lab at Florida's Southwestern University, Frank delicately plied the fragile beads from the strangling grip of blackened tissue. Summer had left this lab virtually deserted. A forlorn row of computer monitors and 3D simulators stared blankly at him, thermal cyclers for DNA analysis sat at a standstill, stacks of sterilized beakers were packed in a corner, and not a student or even an extra-diligent researcher was in sight. Since the lab was used by several disciplines—environmental science, bioarchaeology, biology, geochemistry, and a long list of others—the room contained a sprawling assortment of equipment, from gel electrophoresis apparatus to gas chromatographs, from electron microscopes to X-ray diffractometers and centrifuges. Ali had arranged his access to the equipment, particularly the microscopes, so he could perform his examination of the necklace and utilize the thermal cycler to create a polymerase chain reaction map of the ancient DNA.

Frank would proceed with the DNA analysis of the tissue he'd extracted—well, torn away—after a thorough examination of the necklace. Much to Pedro's disgust, Frank had kept the remains cool in the miniature refrigerator of his hotel room, and then transported them to the university in a cooler, carefully cushioned in ice packs.

Now, he gently tipped the tissue and what appeared to be a globule of brain onto a sterile tray for examination. Plucking delicately with tweezers and slicing stubborn fibers with a scalpel, he released the string of beads, and tenderly slipped a segment under the scanning electron microscope. Blasting the artifact with electrons caused a holographic image to appear in the air. The distinctively pitted external layer of calcium carbonate instantly identified the beads as pure ostrich eggshell, and also revealed criss-cross patterns that he recognized. These patterns, along with the shape and quality of the strokes, suggested the imprecise but rather ingenious technique the *!Kung* employed in refining the shell into distinctive circular shapes, possibly using a springbok horn, and punching holes in the middle with a hand-drill, followed by the final step of polishing the beads with a whetstone. He was ninety-nine percent certain this was *!Kung* workmanship. Once Ali obtained the date, he could add another percentage point. Although he'd examined enough of these artifacts to be certain, he proceeded with the final step of authenticating relics by comparing it with photographs he'd taken in southern Africa.

He set the digital photos side by side on his screen with a detailed and enlarged image of the actual piece.

Yes, it was clearly the same.

So the necklace was an authentic African artifact, incredible as that seemed. But he supposed anything was possible, especially now that he had survived a python attack in the Everglades.

So next, he must attempt DNA analysis of the tissue. If it was, indeed, intact brain tissue, he might get some useful data that would help identify whether this mummy belonged to the North American haplogroup or, by some miracle, was a direct descendant of the African group.

He gently excised the contorted tissue, which resembled a cheese curd, placed it under a UV light to decontaminate it, and then teased it into a flask. He added detergent and placed the material into an ultrasonic bath, to remove any external contamination. The next step was to extract DNA by adding organic chemicals that would separate the DNA from other biological molecules, like proteins, and spin it in a centrifuge, delivering the genetic material to the top organic layer. Now came the tricky part—amplifying the strands by triggering the polymerase chain reaction.

To create repeated sections of a chromosome, he would first need to separate the DNA double helix by heating it in the thermal cycler. This would liberate template strands. Using an enzyme that copies the existing DNA molecule, he would then create a new DNA strand. This duplicating would be repeated several times, theoretically doubling the amount of DNA with each cycle. At the end of the PCR process, millions of copies of the original targeted DNA segment should be present, thus making it easier to identify base pairs and perform sequencing.

This was the ideal method when working with a limited or degraded sample, since it would allow specific strands and segments to be targeted and compared to sequenced genomes. It was not foolproof, but if contamination had occurred, they could certainly distinguish human from mouse and bacteria. Once they'd sorted out human, they might gather enough information to identify specific haplogroups.

Now he had nothing left to do but wait the necessary two hours for the cycler to run, transfer the copies of DNA to a sequencer, and begin analysis. He laced his hands behind his head and sat back in the ergonomic office chair, which was obviously not designed for students. He tried to ignore the stabs of pain in every muscle and joint, particularly in his wounded abdomen. His thoughts drifted to the copper scroll secreted in his hotel room, under the diligent guard of a fugitive jewel thief. Perhaps he should worry that Pedro would steal his stolen artifact, but he doubted it. Greed for the treasure that the scroll might lead to would likely keep him from absconding with it. If only Frank didn't have to waste time doing mundane analysis for Professor Lugan, he would already be deciphering the Codex. He sank deeper into contemplation, transferred the DNA to a sequencer in a quasi-dream state, and eventually began snoring, after resuming relaxing in his chair.

"Hey, Frank," said a distant voice, startling him awake and making him jolt the chair backward to a precarious angle. He blinked and saw a blurry Ali striding across the room.

"Hey," he replied. "I—I was just finishing the DNA analysis. I think we found some intact brain tissue."

"Cool," said Ali. "But the program's almost finished," he said, indicating the blinking screen. "I guess you've been snoozing for a while."

"Oh," said Frank. "It's really quiet in here."

"You don't have explain, Frank. You were attacked by a python, for God's sake. You really should have stayed in bed."

"I'm okay," he replied. "Just tired and sore. I wanted to finish the work here, so I could head back home soon. You're right. I could really use my *own* bed."

Ali nodded, then spun a chair beside Frank, facing the virtual screen.

"Well, let's see what we have."

As he pulled up the data, he casually commented, "It's good you escaped that snake, Frank. Miraculous, really."

Frank eyed him sideways and murmured his agreement.

"No one would think less of you if you had some help, though. I'm grateful, as are other members of the Archaeology Department, that you survived."

"Thanks, Ali. So am I," said Frank, trying to keep his voice even.

"So many students are tracking through there today, to start the general extraction process, that it will be a muddy mess. But there are even more volunteers just to see evidence of your snake attack. You're a celebrity."

Ali smiled, then activated the comparison program that would align the bog body PCR segments alongside standard DNA from various species with parallel chromosomes.

Frank practically sighed in relief. Ali knew he'd been helped, possibly by a convict, but Ali wasn't going to talk. And no telltale footprints would be noticeable after today.

The computer performed the requested operation and flashed up its results.

Ali frowned at the screen. Frank leaned forward. Where were the linked genes and images of comparable DNA?

"This can't be right," Frank said.

"Not exactly *!Kung*," said Ali.

"Nor is it North American."

"Or even *Neanderthal* or *Denisova*."

The computer read-out was strung before their eyes, along with words that hardly seemed possible. "Unknown hominin species."

A burst of adrenaline surged through Frank's veins, but at the same time, his guts sagged in disappointment. So much for the Codex. This wasn't a Howard Carter moment, but a Senut and Pickford one. Less glorious, but likely much more significant, requiring months, if not years, of additional painstaking study. They'd just discovered *another* extinct hominin species.

Scanning...

Located: Chapter 19

FELICITY CRINGED INWARDLY, as her professor eyed Shaun and the gun with equal intensity, while she, her guide, and Shaun, who was engrossed in his laptop and listening to his message with earphones, clustered around the camp table and sipped at bitter instant coffee from plastic cups. She could understand her professor's aversion to the weapon, since she had shared it most of her life, but why was the same stern expression directed at the biologist? Had she witnessed the pass he'd made at Felicity? Had she misinterpreted Felicity's response? Not that it would be any of her business one way or the other. Felicity took another gulp of her disgusting coffee, still pondering what to say to the teacher who'd come racing to the North after their brief conversation.

She made an attempt.

"I'm sorry I pointed a gun at you."

Professor Lugan waved away her words. "I understand," she replied. "If you believed there was a murder . . . But I thought you were a strong supporter of gun control." She swept a hand through her hair—a hand that appeared to be taut with suppressed emotion.

"I am, usually. But after finding someone with a bullet hole in their head, and then after hearing explosions . . . Well . . . it changes your perspective." She looked down, feeling a wave of shame, but not entirely convinced she was wrong. Firm beliefs sometimes only stayed firm until they were tested in extreme circumstances. Now, she was a firm believer in exceptions to the rule. "I should catch you up on what we've discovered. One of the bodies we found among the Roman and possibly *Phoenician* mummies"—she paused as Dr. Lugan's eyebrows drew upward—"was probably a Cree woman—murdered, most likely. Something very suspicious is happening here. The other scientists went to investigate a new prospecting operation nearby, and I decided I should stay and help, because they thought this company's presence might be related to the bog bodies and they might need to consult with me again."

Dr. Lugan shook her head. "Clearly, this is a matter for the police, Felicity. All you needed to do was arrange transport for the bodies, once the authorities were finished here. You should have left immediately."

"I don't think I'm in any danger," she replied, looking beyond her professor to Shaun. "There are two of us, and two other scientists." Her adviser looked less than pleased with the direction of her gaze, and the hint of a scowl touched her lips.

As if he could sense they were paying attention to him, Shaun looked up and pulled out an earphone.

"Sorry. Did I miss something?"

"No," said Dr. Lugan. "Felicity was just explaining how she wasn't in any danger. I didn't exactly get that impression, though, when she brandished a gun."

Shaun tapped off his computer and turned to face her.

"Our colleague, Dr. Mbeki, may have spooked Felicity with his assessment of the body," he explained. "And he gave her the gun. I assure you, Dr . . . Lugan, is it? . . . that I wouldn't have let her come to any harm."

Dr. Lugan pursed her lips, as if she were analyzing Shaun's words and doubted he was telling the truth. As if she thought Shaun . . . How crazy was that? If her adviser only knew how overprotective he was . . .

"Can I see the body?" asked the Cree guide, a man Dr. Lugan had introduced as Jim Sâkêwêw. He'd been silently sipping his brew without comment, without eye contact, with a distant expression on his face. But now, as sharpness reawakened in his eyes, he turned to her.

Felicity sucked in her breath, because he was looking to her, not Shaun or Dr. Lugan, to make this call. Why wasn't he asking Shaun, who was obviously the leader in the camp at the moment? But Shaun hadn't led the bog body extraction, Shaun wasn't an expert in human remains, and maybe this man found Shaun suspicious, too.

"I'm not sure I should let anyone see her until the police arrive."

"Why haven't the police come yet?" asked Dr. Lugan, a question they all should have been asking.

Felicity shrugged, while Shaun sighed and donned an apologetic smile.

"They're usually slow to respond in this part of the world. Too few officers to handle too many adverse situations, and they have to travel such long distances. But I think Dr. DeLuca called the RCMP when he reported the murder. They could be wrangling over jurisdiction."

"What does it matter if the police are around?" said the guide. "It's possible that I can identify her. I promise I won't touch anything. I really don't even want to go near the bodies. But if this is the girl who disappeared recently from our community, her family has a right to know."

"In her . . . present condition, I doubt you'd recognize her," Shaun said immediately. "She's wearing a Roughriders sweatshirt, but her facial features have deteriorated from being immersed in the bog."

"I thought the bog preserves bodies," said Jim, ignoring Shaun and looking directly at Felicity again.

She cleared her throat. "It preserves tissue, particularly if sediment has covered it quickly, but it eats away at calcium—bone—and her skull is losing its original shape. A good forensic sculptor"—she cast a quick glance at Dr. Lugan—"could probably reconstruct her face to look more natural. But that would have to take place in a lab, with proper measurements and tests."

"I'm sure once that happens," said Shaun, "or if a forensic team can compare DNA samples, the police will inform her family—if she is the missing girl you're talking about."

Jim Sâkêwêw finally looked at Shaun, so caustically and with such a tightly clenched jaw that the biologist jerked backward. The man's hand twitched on the barrel of his rifle.

"If she is the girl I'm talking about, *you* should know."

Shaun glanced down, played skittish fingers over the case of his laptop, and didn't answer.

Felicity's chest tightened until it had become difficult to breathe. *Why doesn't he answer?* Of course she knew. He was more than likely the type of man she'd suspected along, which is why he'd seemed so sure of conquest of her. The Greek hero. But that didn't mean he'd killed the girl. He wasn't a psycho, was he?

"Should you know?" asked Dr. Lugan, gripping her cup with taut fingers, as if Shaun might leap over the table and strangle her.

Shaun gulped down his last swallows of coffee, grimaced, and wiped his mouth.

"If you're talking about Donna, I dated her briefly. She was a sweet kid, but too young for me, and I would never have hurt her. I don't know if that's she. She did like to wear sports T-shirts and sweatshirts, although she swapped them for sexier clothes when we . . . went out. I think she was addicted to meth, and I wasn't into drugs, *ever*," he said emphatically. "It ended—I ended it—six months ago, long before she disappeared."

He turned to Felicity. "You don't believe that I . . ."

"No," she said. "I don't believe you're *deranged*." She tipped him a reassuring smile.

Wouldn't she know it, feel it, if he were a monster?

But had their breakup driven the poor girl, Donna, into some sort of spiraling depression? Had she done something crazy, or approached the wrong people? Had he inadvertently caused her death?

"Felicity," said Dr. Lugan, her voice tapping an unusually high note. "I think it's time you showed me the bog bodies—not the girl, mind you. Then we'll return to Peawanuck with Jim. Your safety is my responsibility, and I won't be comfortable until I've extracted you from this mess. If the police want to contact us, they can find us in Peawanuck, while I arrange our flights back to Boston."

Felicity stared openly at her professor. She understood Dr. Lugan's anxiety, but she'd made a promise to these men. And Baruti . . . Baruti had faith in her.

"Dr. Lugan, I'll show you the bodies, but I'm not leaving yet. We've found ancient people who don't belong in this part of the world. It's more puzzling than anything I've ever encountered, and I have a responsibility to them, too. I need to determine why they're here, in this remote, illogical location, and what their secret is. Why someone might even kill to keep it. This girl may have nothing to do with the other bodies, but maybe she's the key to this entire mystery."

Dr. Lugan's eyes flashed. "It's the *ancient* puzzle that you and I have the authority to deal with," she said. "We're better equipped to investigate that in our laboratory at Harvard. Transportation—"

"Might take days," Felicity said. "If you're worried, you can stay with me until then. In the meantime, why don't you have a look? You might have some ideas about how the two puzzles might be connected."

Felicity rose, gestured to Dr. Lugan to follow, and strode toward the tarps. She flipped a corner to reveal the shriveled remains of a Phoenician sailor with a tattered cloak and a teased beard. His sagging face gave the impression that he was discouraged and haunted in his weary life.

"This isn't Henry Hudson. These aren't the remains of a Cree burial site. This is someone who might have navigated around northern Africa in the days of Herodotus, but never left a hint behind that he might be setting out for an arctic destination. Why has no one ever heard of a Roman-chartered expedition in this direction or even to the legendary Thule? And why would anyone kill to cover it up?"

Dr. Lugan moved toward the tarps and crouched down beside Felicity, her eyes crinkled in deep thought.

"I don't see how a young girl from the Cree community could be connected to these bodies. From what Jim was telling me, it sounds as though the missing girl might have been susceptible to the seduction of a cult. After all, she was spouting doomsday prophecies. But sacrificing people to the bog is an ancient ritual, not something adopted by cults, at least not any I've heard of. How could Roman and Phoenician explorers, or whatever they were, be linked to a modern-day cult?"

"Doomsday prophecies?" said Shaun who, despite severe looks from Dr. Lugan and Jim, had risen from the table and followed them to the tarps. "I don't remember her saying anything that odd."

"She spouted a lot of crazy things before she disappeared. Like 'the gods are taking revenge and cleansing the Earth of the human infestation.' She mentioned imminent catastrophes," said Jim, eyeing Shaun for any reaction.

And strangely, he did react. He stiffened. He frowned. He gazed at the laptop still clutched in his hand.

"Stop looking at me like that," he snapped. "I'm a biologist who studies polar bears. I would never have anything to do with a cult."

"What's on the computer?" asked Jim.

"Excuse me?"

"You looked at it when I mentioned the supposed prophecies. Were you chatting with someone who might say those things?"

"No!" said Shaun. "I was listening to a video message from *my brother*. He just happens to be an astronaut on a terraforming mission to Mars."

"Mars?" said Dr. Lugan. "Well, we're straying farther and farther from ancient Phoenicians and Romans. Although Mars was the Roman god of war," she said, with a twitch to her lips. "I suppose we shouldn't make accusations without any real evidence. We don't even know if the body you found belongs to this girl."

Before she'd finished speaking, the repeated chop-chop of a helicopter's rotors reached their ears.

"That's likely the other guys returning," said Shaun. "They might have found some answers . . ." His words petered out, and he stared at his laptop again. "All I know is that when you chase mysteries and murders, you often find yourself in a world of hate. I turned my back on that world long ago. I try my best to protect the defenseless, like the polar bears and other endangered creatures of the North, and avoid the Hatfields and McCoys. But I guess even here it's nearly impossible to escape the crossfire."

If there was ever a suspicion—and there was none in Felicity's mind—that Shaun had committed this vile act, his words should have erased that idea. Shaun was the epitome of human compassion; he was the Earth Mother tending her garden. But as she weighed his words, she wondered what he was really trying to escape.

"Well," said Dr. Lugan, raising her voice as the helicopter's incessant throbbing grew louder. "Let's hope this girl's murder isn't connected to a never-ending feud. But whatever the case, I think it prudent for my student," she looked at Felicity, "to be far removed from this site and whatever mysteries and dangers it holds."

Her gaze traveled back to Shaun. Obviously she still didn't trust him.

The gyrating rotors blasted lichen and grass into their faces as the helicopter touched down. Baruti looked through the windshield and grinned, but his expression instantly transformed into a frown when he noticed Dr. Lugan and the guide. Felicity wondered if they'd unearthed any more artifacts in the miners' camp, or if they'd detected diamonds, or if they'd exposed more bodies. She wondered if she could somehow convince Dr. Lugan to let her stay in the camp a little longer, not just to learn more about ancient remains, but to discover why she was so drawn to Baruti.

And she wondered if Shaun was right.

Hate, greed, and jealousy were often at the root of every evil deed. Would pursuit of this mystery lead her to a world better left untouched? Would it sink her deeper into the bog?

Segment II:
THE SERPENT STRIKES

AN ANCIENT grove lay nearby, untouched by hatchet or billhook. Within, half-hidden in bushes, there opened the mouth of a cavern, a shallow arch, supported by rough fitted pieces of stone.

Plenty of water poured out—but within lurked a terrible serpent, sacred to Mars. Its head bore a crest resplendent and golden. Fire shot from its eyes. Its body was puffy with venom. Triple its tongue, and triple the line of its snapping teeth.

—Ovid, *Metamorphoses* 3.30–37

Scanning...

Located: Chapter 20

BRIGHT FLASHES AND streams of color, like a fiery aurora borealis, blitzed Lucas's brain. He vaguely remembered flailing upward as sand, ice, and dust peppered his suit. Despite the loud pop of the explosion, a dim part of his mind registered an immediate hiss, as if his oxygen tubing had been punctured. Then the brisk launch skyward ended, the lift beneath his body yielded to gravity, and he experienced a nauseating plunge toward the carpet of steam and, beneath, red rocks and inflexible soil.

Crunch. Pain ripped through his legs, back, neck, and skull. He was a cracked egg, leaking milky innards. But even that seemed like nothing compared to the desperate in-drawing of his chest, as his body searched for breathable air and received only gulps of poisonous carbon dioxide. He gasped and clutched the ground, the life pouring out of him. It seemed Mars held no love for him, not in this germinating stage of its existence.

As he continued to struggle, feeling his efforts diminish as he sank into weaker and weaker grapplings for oxygen, a squeak and an exclamation filtered through his comm.

"Bob, don't!"

His mask was violently ripped from his head. Cold, thin, misty air rushed into the gap and stung his exposed skin. Was Bob accelerating the process? But another mask immediately engulfed his face, cinched briskly to a tight seal. He gasped, drawing the critical blend into his lungs. Oxygen, more precious than gold on this planet, permeated his air sacs, replacing the overabundance of carbon dioxide. But he still felt so groggy, so oxygen-depleted that he couldn't move, could do nothing but wheeze and suck at the finally breathable air.

"Bob, hold on!" he heard Gita yell.

Somewhere, as if through the sonic streams of a horror film, he registered pounding footsteps on the ground, exhausted puffs of strained breathing, *whumps* as an airlock opened and closed, then Gita's soothing murmurs.

"Breathe, Bob. You're okay. It's all right. You're going to make it. I'll crank up the oxygen in the capsule."

You're going to make it, Bob? *That's great. Just great. I'm still lying on a bed of rocks, beaten to a bloody pulp, struggling with oxygen starvation, and you're worried about* Bob? *And by the way, Bob, what the hell was that explosion?*

He drew in a shuddering breath, then realized he hadn't said a word, which was probably a blessing, since Bob might have just saved his life.

"H— hello," he said through the comm, following the word with a series of gasps and a prolonged sigh. "Does— does anyone hear me?"

"Lucas," said Gita. "Just sit tight, okay? We're coming. We had to return to the MADVEC to replenish Bob's air supply, since he gave you his mask and tank and he's become hypoxic. We also needed to rustle up a stretcher to carry you. Your tubes were torn, when . . . when you were tossed upward. I think volcanism is warming the ground in pockets under the ice and causing sporadic outgassing."

Lucas paused, remembering that outgassing of carbon dioxide from beneath the ice could be explosive—propulsion that could reach a speed upward of 100 miles per hour. No wonder he felt like he'd just been ejected from a Thunderbolt and landed without a parachute. But if outgassing had occurred, and if it had flipped the rover, it probably wasn't finished yet. Lying here, sprawled on the rough rock, he felt so helpless, so fragile and exposed. He'd never experienced such devastating weakness and pain before. But he had to move.

Lucas groped the pebbled surface at his side and tried to roll over, but spikes of agony drove into his legs and arms, the muscles along his spine spasmed in protest, and his guts quivered and melted like roasted marshmallow.

"Ahh," he yelled. "I need to move! Can't . . . Can't . . ."

But the pain overwhelmed him. He slumped backward and lay still.

"Stay . . . right . . . there," gasped Bob, obviously regaining strength and overcoming his oxygen deficit. "We'll . . . come . . . get . . . you."

"Will that be before or after the next geyser?" he moaned, but immediately regretted it. His life depended on his fellow astronauts. Sarcasm wasn't going to further motivate them. "Sorry," he muttered. "Sorry."

"Lucas," said Bob, gasping again. "You're . . . an ass. But I'm not . . . going to let you die down here. Got . . . that?"

"Thanks," said Lucas, shivering as the pain retreated and a bitter chill replaced it. "You're an ass too, Bob," he couldn't help but add.

Bob chuckled, an oddly comforting sound that suffused his frigid body like the gentle wash of a warm wave. He settled back to wait, his eyes fluttering as he was jolted by jab after jab of pain. Above his head, through the protective Plexiglas of his face shield, ice particles drifted down in the aftermath of the eruption—a wondrous world asparkle with amber fairy lights. The fog stubbornly lingered, a thick wall to either side, permitting him no view beyond. Maybe he was falling into a stupor, his body desperate to escape the omnipresent pain. Could Bob and Gita even locate him in this stew of fog, or would they wander right past, missing him by inches on pass after pass until they finally gave up the search? Would he die on Mars and add new material to the carpet of organics?

Minutes dragged by. Or was it hours? He became miserably conscious of his rasping breathing, the pressing weight of his muscular pecs, the pulsing of his heart, the nagging squeeze of his spandex clothing, and the loud buzzing of white noise in his ears. But all this he would welcome, if it would replace the stabbing pain that gutted him again and again.

"I'm dying," he groaned, gripped in a sudden burst of panic.

"No, you're not," said Bob sternly, with no pause or hesitation, with no hint of his earlier struggle to breathe. "We're going to roll you over, Lucas, and slip the stretcher underneath your back. It's going to hurt like hell, but you're a tough asshole, right?"

Bob's voice didn't sound any louder than when he'd been recovering in the MADVEC, but when Lucas opened his eyes, a shadow was blocking the light, interrupting the constantly streaming mist. Lucas blinked, trying to wipe away the blur, and the shadow adopted Bob's disproportionate features. He had never felt so happy to see that lopsided, irritating face. Beside Bob in the wispy orange nebula floated Gita, appearing as ethereal as the conditions around her. She smiled and stroked his head.

"You're going to be fine, Lucas. I promise."

He wanted to believe her, but his pain receptors told him otherwise.

"Okay, on three."

Bob counted as he and Gita burrowed their arms underneath Lucas. "Three," echoed in his mind as they gripped and rotated his body, causing every tormented muscle, punctured portion of flesh, and fractured bone to scream. But he didn't scream. He bit through his lower lip and tears escaped his eyes, but he didn't scream.

Gita or Bob must have finessed the stretcher underneath him, but he hardly noticed. They lowered him onto it gently, Gita crooning in his ear and, as they released him, he felt as if he were bathed in sparks. Either Gita or Bob, he couldn't remember which one, possessed more than basic first aid training, so the possibility existed that he would survive. But at the moment, he wished Bob would boot him in the head and knock him unconscious.

"You okay there, Lucas?" asked Bob, probing at his throat for a pulse.

"Alive," he gasped. "Tough asshole."

Unexpectedly, Bob gently squeezed his shoulder—the one part of his body that was apparently undamaged.

"Damn right," he said. "Now we're going to lift you and carry you to the HAB. We'll try not to jostle you too much, but you're a big boy, Lucas, and we have puny little muscles. And don't even think of reminding me of my less-than-ideal physical condition. We can't do a damn thing about it right now, but I can manage. So you keep being a tough asshole, and I'll reward you with a well-deserved shot of morphine when we get inside. Deal?"

"Deal," Lucas muttered. "But . . ." He clenched Bob's forearm. "Only if you finally admit I was right."

Bob looked confused. "Of course you're right. About what?"

"A— about this," he stammered. "A— about Mars being a cauldron, not a v— vacation paradise. About this . . . trip being a mistake."

"Lucas," said Bob, leaning over him. "I'm sorry I talked you into this. I'm sorry you're in pain. And about setting down in this location, you were definitely right. But, Lucas, we're not finished with Mars yet. So no matter how hard it gets, we'd better learn to live with him."

A crashing wave of pain temporarily blinded Lucas. And he did scream. And he did moan. And he wasn't a tough asshole, as Gita and Bob hefted the stretcher and plodded over the rough terrain, jiggling and shifting him and triggering every pain receptor in his body. But despite the flood of agony, his tormented mind couldn't dismiss Bob's words. What could he possibly mean, they weren't finished with Mars? Were they stranded on Ares rock?

MINUTES PASSED, HOURS, days. Who could tell? Lucas was blessed with the balm of sedation and painkillers while Bob, the medic, set his fractured leg, washed out his wounds and padded them with bandages, jabbed him with needles and flushed his body with antibiotics. He made groggy attempts to ask for more information, but Bob refused to answer, or if he answered, Lucas couldn't understand, through the distorted waves of sound and his minimal state of consciousness.

In his dream state, Lucas traveled back to his childhood, to skipping stones with his brother beside a babbling brook, to chasing swallowtails in the meadow near their log cabin, to the pure scent of pine and balsam while hiking beneath the tall trees of the forest. He thought of his mother, a broad-boned, brusque woman with olive-green eyes and a tendency to contradict herself, and a conversation he'd had with her on one of their frequent excursions in a secluded national park.

"Why can't we live here in the woods?" he'd asked. "Far from people who want to hurt us."

"No place is far enough," she said, ignoring the fact that their community still tended to group in farming enclaves like the Amish, only sending the odd bright student out into the world to learn all the latest advances in science and install themself in a position where they could protect their people. "Instead, we must hide in plain sight."

"Why do they want to hurt us?" he asked, ever inquisitive.

"Because we're different," she said, and patted his head. "Because, with our background and beliefs, we cannot mix with them, and they find that suspicious. Because they are primitive."

Lucas's ten-year-old brain had no trouble understanding suspicion and hate, since he found it so often within his own community. No matter how often his mother reiterated the rhetoric of "them versus us," he knew that the people of his community were no strangers to jealousy, lust, anger, and violence, just as they were equally capable of love and compassion. But he heeded her words and avoided other groups, until he and Shaun were selected to become educated outside their network so they could fulfill the Gilgamesh Movement's mission.

Shaun, however, didn't share his brother's or his mother's distrust, which irked the leaders of the Movement to no end. He'd acquired his father's curiosity and empathy; he adored the Earth and all her creatures. But he hadn't been there, a witness to the brutality of the outsiders, the day his father had died. He hadn't seen how they slaughtered on a pretext; how they gorged on violence; how they eradicated anyone whom they perceived as a threat or even a nuisance. His father had been trampled, not by the mentally unstable or a random violent faction, but by a crowd of supposedly sane consumers—product-hungry people fighting to obtain the next crumb of technology.

His father, who had always excused every offense and extolled every innovation, had died for nothing but a new virtual simulator of the planets.

Lucas had accompanied him that day, eager to acquire this educational toy, so he might eventually be accepted into the ISA program. When the staff announced that only one hundred simulators remained, the swarm of people stirred worriedly and elbowed each other in an attempt to surge forward. A look of alarm had crossed his dad's face. After all, most of these people were the outsiders, unpredictable and often violent. His father had swept Lucas from their path and shoved him against the wall. But when his father had stepped back into the line, one man thought he'd butted in and punched him. His father easily wrestled this man to the ground, but others joined in, pounding and kicking, until even mighty Zeus would have crashed to the street. But did anyone think to whisk his bleeding body aside when the doors opened to allow consumers in? Lucas had tried to reach his father, but wave after wave of shoving humans pulsed past, thrusting him backward, stomping over what remained of his father with no thought given to what they were walking on.

Now he despised the outsiders as his mother did. But he also knew it was only a matter of time before some clever person stumbled upon the disguised community that sheltered his family. It was only a matter of time before the carefully concealed research and the underlying network were exposed. Even as he faked camaraderie with his fellow astronauts, he suspected they perceived his rage. No doubt that was why they often shied away from any close relations.

But he sometimes wondered if he truly had the guts to carry out his orders—if he had the "right stuff."

EVENTUALLY THE DREAMS, the persistent memories that evoked terror and rage, subsided. Eventually a day arrived when he awoke and his vision seemed clearer, his mind more grounded, his senses restored. He could focus on the metal-framed bunk, the narrow weave of his woolen blanket, the stark white cabinets filled with survival staples above his head. Nearby, brushing her rich bronze hair and gazing at a read-out on her tablet, sat Gita. The movement of her eyes while she focused on the screen triggered various windows to open on the HAB's wall—a miniature holographic representation of the Martian landscape. Bob was nowhere in sight.

"Shouldn't we return to the *Phoenix* before one of these explosions damages our MADVEC?" he asked.

Gita looked up and set down her brush and tablet. "You're awake?" she said, sounding surprised. She leaned over and scanned his face, no doubt trying to determine how lucid he really was.

"Bob's been slipping you horse tranquilizers, so I didn't think you'd be conscious yet. But I guess he should have given you an elephant's dose."

"Very funny," said Lucas. "I'm not that gargantuan, am I?"

"A Titan," she smiled.

He shifted uncomfortably at the description and felt a cascade of sparks tumble through his side. But the pain seemed surprisingly tolerable.

"How bad is it?" he asked, since she hadn't answered his question. She could interpret that any way she wanted. How bad was their situation? How bad were his injuries? All he required were crumbs of information. He obviously wasn't dead; that was a good sign. But he could become so at any minute if they didn't leave this unstable planet.

"You have a fractured tibia, a dislocated right shoulder that has been reset, some puncture wounds from the rock shrapnel that also caused intestinal damage, and a mild concussion. Bob performed surgery on your belly and removed a small section of bowel. Unfortunately, we have nothing but an antiquated 3D printer here, so he couldn't replace the tissue. Once he permits it, you can begin ingesting some liquid meals. But you're healing nicely, Lucas. Bob says it's because you're in such great shape and you're pigheaded—too stubborn to die." She winked.

"He would say that."

Lucas considered his situation. In his condition, there was no way he could pilot the *Phoenix* back to Earth.

"How long before I'm ready to work?" he asked, dreading the answer.

"You don't need to push it, Lucas. Just rest and allow your body to heal. I'm sure Bob will start you on a regimen of short walks soon, although you can't walk very far in these tight quarters. We don't want any setbacks, so you have to take your time."

"But shouldn't we have left Mars by now? I can heal just as quickly on the *Phoenix*, on our way back to Earth."

Gita's eyes drifted to the side. She smoothed her hair awkwardly.

"Well, you see, Lucas, we can't return to the *Phoenix* immediately. The, uh, the outgassing eruptions damaged the propellant factory, and it will take some time to repair. Two reactors were damaged and several cryogenic tanks ruptured, spilling most of the methane and venting it into the atmosphere, so we don't have enough for launch. Luckily the oxygen tanks are still intact, so we have an adequate supply for the HAB."

"Oh, damn," he muttered.

He should have suspected something this catastrophic. But some good might come of it. If they could survive until the factory was repaired and had produced sufficient fuel, that would give him more time to heal and regain enough strength to assume his duties once again. But that was nothing they could count on, with the volatile state of Mars at the moment. A more likely scenario was that another eruption would damage the MADVEC or the ISPP, possibly irreparably. Or their HAB would be destroyed. Or Bob or Gita would become injured, as well.

Oh, why hadn't he fought harder to stop this insane excursion to begin with? Or why hadn't he let them explore without him? But either way, he would need at least one other astronaut to pilot the *Phoenix* if her computer malfunctioned again. So even if he'd refused to participate and had stayed behind, that could have left them just as stranded.

Another problem scratched at his mind. What if the other astronauts decided to explore on their own now? He was in no shape to redirect or stop them. Bob could even now be—

"Where's Bob?" he asked, suddenly feeling short of breath.

Gita sighed. "Bob is assessing the damage to the propellant plant. I've already tallied our losses, which are considerable, but he's determining the extent of the damage to the components and reactors and whether we have enough material to repair them. We might have to do a rover run to another plant to collect supplies or even fuel, depending on his assessment."

"Oh," said Lucas, trying to disguise his relief. Repair of the fuel factory would keep them busy and a rover excursion would carry them far from any sensitive areas. "That bad, eh?"

"Well, yes. But we have to focus on the positive. You survived a CO_2 burst, and you're healing well. We didn't lose you." Her smile was painfully pleasant, as if she really cared. "The MADVEC has sustained no damage so far, and we have a well-stocked HAB where we can live for several weeks while we effect repairs. The rover, from what we've determined, will only need minor repairs to make it fully operational. It could have been much worse."

She touched his arm, her fingers lightly smoothing his sleeve below the sling, perhaps to soothe him.

"We'll get through this, and then we'll fly home. If you hadn't been hurt, I would welcome the opportunity to become the first settlers on Mars."

She would feel that way, wouldn't she? It couldn't have worked out better for her and Bob, getting an unprecedented opportunity to explore the planet. They weren't suffering any pain or experiencing any disabilities.

Well, there was nothing he could do but make the best of it. If he healed fast enough, he could hasten the process by adding his expertise and muscle to the task of repairing the factory.

"I suppose I need to thank Bob," he said.

"Is that really so difficult? You guys just rub each other the wrong way. But he didn't hesitate, when it came to saving your life."

Lucas felt a ripple of unease—a ripple that triggered new pain pathways throughout his body. He grimaced, then worrying she'd misinterpret it, he said, "Just the pain." He gritted his teeth, rode out the assault, then gathered his thoughts. "I guess I wouldn't, either."

She smiled, which helped him relax momentarily.

Wouldn't he, though? Or would he have watched Bob suffocate, revelling in his struggle? Did he share any of his brother's empathy, or was he ruled by community fervor? Perhaps he was inflamed by an image he couldn't erase.

"Well, I hope you never get the chance to return the favor," said Gita. "But at least we're a team when the going gets tough. We can easily transcend all the petty arguments."

"Easily," said Lucas, emphasizing the empty word.

Scanning...

Located: Chapter 21

DAYNA RERAN the DNA analysis and comparison on the Phoenician bodies, which weren't exactly Phoenician bodies, while still refusing to come to terms with the startling results. Around her in the lab in the Peabody Museum of Archaeology and Ethnology was a strange group.

Felicity, who was a familiar sight in this workspace, had parked herself nearest the digital display terminal, her posture wooden and her eyes skittish. Hovering at her shoulder, restlessly tapping the cryocooler in his lap, sat the biologist from Botswana, Baruti Mbeki. For some reason, he had insisted on joining them in their investigation rather than staying on to track polar bears. He was the man who'd triggered Felicity's paranoia, but he also seemed to admire her abilities and, by association, transferred some of that admiration to Dayna. Usually she wouldn't allow someone without archaeological expertise in the lab, but when he'd produced the samples he'd "borrowed" from the prospectors—who were obviously genetic engineers—and issued a heartfelt request to run them through her lab instead of going through proper channels, like the police, she'd immediately granted him access. Proper channels were often closed down when someone applied enough money or political pressure, and the "borrowing" aspect made involving the police a troubling proposition. It was a risk, but casual genetic engineers made her nervous.

The other predictable figure was Frank Campo. He was leaning back in a chair, his feet propped up on a nearby desk in his usual relaxed manner. The instant he'd returned from Florida, he'd sprung his own unfathomable news on her, while flashing his sample and results. Beside Frank sat a mysterious stranger—Hispanic, heavily muscled, dressed in a scruffy T-shirt and ripped jeans—a man Frank had introduced as a friend, fellow student, and expert in snake removal. Frank said they had driven from Florida rather than fly and had taken a slight detour to New York to drop something off at the man's father's place. What that was had not been specified. Frank had then related the story of Man versus Python, and even displayed his scars, chilling Dayna and simultaneously making her flush with guilt.

How could she possibly have conceived . . . ? Yet her concern for Frank had always been underwhelming, and for Felicity, likely because of her small stature and health issues, well above that for other students. She'd rushed north at the first inkling of danger, although the girl had come through the situation virtually unscathed, while Frank, in Florida at her behest, had nearly died. Her guilt was probably the only reason why she'd allowed his "friend," who hardly looked like a student, to remain in the lab.

Although Felicity had objected, Dayna had persuaded her to leave the site at Polar Bear Provincial Park after the police had finished questioning her. The two RCMP officers had retrieved the Cree girl's body and allowed Dayna to convey the first bog bodies to her lab, arranging transportation via helicopter and cargo plane out of Peawanuck. Since Baruti had insisted on joining them, it had taken less inducement to get Felicity to leave, and the three of them had accompanied the bodies to Boston.

Now, after the first labor-intensive examinations and biological tests, they were all waiting breathlessly. The DNA results flickered into the air in holographic presentation, blips and spikes scrolling through the space surrounding their heads, displaying the same incredible results.

"They match," Dayna said, looking at Frank. "We've discovered another hominin species that outlived *Neanderthal* and *Denisova*, and originated even later."

"A different species?" asked Dr. Mbeki.

"Yes, though definitely hominin. It appears to be *Homo sapiens*, but not completely *Homo sapiens sapiens*. We know that the chimpanzee differs from us by 1,465 nucleotide positions in its DNA, *Denisova* by 385, and *Neanderthal* by 202. This new species has only 175 position alterations, so it certainly is related to us, and the split must have occurred after *Neanderthal*.

"Chimpanzees and humans diverged six million years ago," she continued, getting into her professorial mode. "Humans and *Denisova* 1,040,900 years ago, and humans and *Neanderthal* 465,000. We must assume this species developed later, and is closer to us on the evolutionary scale. But it still has enough variances to make it quite unique molecularly, which could make it appear physically different as well. This is something Felicity and I can explore in the lab when we examine the bodies. We'll zero in on specific genes, like THADA, which is related to energy metabolism, or DRG3 isoforms, which affect neurodevelopmental pathways. We'll see if this species has some of the same selective sweeps in the RUNX2 gene, which would mean more human features than *Neanderthal*, especially in regards to skeletal and cranial structures. Are you sure about the beads, Frank?"

"They match *!Kung* work to a tee."

"Very odd. We'll have to consider dates and see when your Florida . . . "

"Python people," Frank supplied.

"Python people," she said with a wince, "might have lived in North America, and if there's any connection to your . . ." She looked at Felicity.

The girl shrugged.

"Polar bear people?" suggested Baruti.

"But they're clearly Phoenician, with maybe one Roman," Felicity objected.

"And yet they're not," said Dayna. "We've now cataloged the genome of every ancient haplogroup that we were aware of, particularly the Romans and Phoenicians. These people were decidedly different."

"The Bushmen people, particularly the *!Kung* in the Tsodilo Hills, worshipped the python many years ago," said Baruti. "According to their creation myth, mankind descended from the python, and the original streambeds around those hills were the work of an enormous python as it roved the territory, circling the hills in search of water. So perhaps there was a reason the python protected your mummies," he said to Frank. "And perhaps the polar bear who was patrolling near the bog where we discovered the others—or someone else—was protecting the . . . Phoenicians—or travelers, if you will."

"You believe that animals are spiritually connected to people more than through our DNA?" asked Felicity.

"I don't know," he said, with a hint of mournfulness. "I believe, to a certain extent, what a *!Kung* man told me a few years ago. He said, 'when all the animals die, then we will die.' The *!Kung* believed that animals were once people, which in a sense is true. We descended from apes. Our connection to the animal world is intimate. The *!Kung* were definitely dying, as the human world encroached on the Kalahari and the animals began their spiral toward extinction. In the last hundred years, most of the *!Kung* abandoned hunting and gathering and became ranchers. But when they were hunters, they would only kill what they needed to survive, and they would often put themselves in harm's way to protect the animals from poachers. Although they were losing their identity, like so many of native peoples, a few retained smatterings of their cultural habits and beliefs—especially those who still lived in the Kalahari or Okavango region. They felt their spirits wither with every new extinction."

"But we still have domesticated animals," Felicity objected. "Not all the animals will die, nor will all the people. The *!Kung* were referring to themselves because they put themselves into dicey positions, and possibly because they refused to adapt to change. Even so, you said some of them are now ranchers, so they, themselves, are domesticating animals and preventing some extinctions."

A wavering smile, secretive and somewhat patronizing, flitted across Baruti's face.

"Sometimes we should look backward as well as forward. In the past, the *!Kung* felt the death of every animal they killed. The hunter, when he returned to the community after shooting an animal with a poisoned arrow, would enact a ritualistic representation of its passing, before retrieving its body the next day. They appreciated the sacrifice and respected the animal's gift toward their survival. In their shamanic journeys to the spirit world, they would take on the form of various animals, particularly the eland, and they would ask permission to kill, rather than seeing it as their right.

"We don't feel the deaths of the animals we slaughter. We don't view it as a sacrifice. We bend animals to our will when we domesticate them. Some people, like these prospectors"—he said the word through gritted teeth, as if they were responsible for the extinction of all species—"think that simply cloning and reintroducing extinct creatures will somehow replace everything that's been lost. But if clones are introduced into a controlled environment, that doesn't restore balance, particularly if they are studied and manipulated, as the woolly mammoth was. The free spirit of the animal is gone. We continue to survive, it's true. But sometimes I wonder if we're really living or if we died a long time ago."

A pall of silence hung over the room, a funereal atmosphere that seemed to match the biologist's words. Of course, as archaeologists, Dayna and her students clung to the past. The scientific underpinnings made it respectable, but Dayna spent her days digging up relics and exploring evaporated cultures because of a deep longing for a way of life that had long since passed. She traveled each day from her sterile lab to her robotic vehicle to her 800-square-foot apartment, barely touching a blade of grass. When required to do field work, to slog through mud in thigh-high boots and collect the fragile remains of corpses, to fly over the brackish elliptical ponds blanketed with emerald algae in the Arctic, or explore the dusty desert tombs in Egypt, she didn't hesitate: She gathered her wings and flew.

"Well," said Frank. "I suppose it is sad that we've lost so many animals as our population grows. But I for one still feel alive. And I'm glad that my buddy here didn't pause to say a prayer before he chopped that python to bits."

"It didn't look like he was protectin' anybody to me," said Pedro. "He just wanted a meal, and Frank looked juicier than an egret or a rabbit."

Dr. Mbeki studied Frank and his friend with a strained intensity.

"Yet the python would rarely bother with a human in its own environment. It would seek out wild pigs, antelope, rodents, birds. But in the Everglades it has no natural predators to keep its proliferation in check, and it's eating through the available food sources. Crocodiles, lions, tigers, puma, even eagles—which no longer exist—all these creatures would feed on the python. Alligators aren't quite large enough to tackle a full-grown specimen. Humans removed the python from its natural habitat. When, as usual, they grew bored with their pet or found it beyond their capacity to handle, they gave it the perfect habitat to destroy. No matter how you slice it, humans either ruthlessly hunt a species to extinction or cause its overgrowth, which has a domino effect of extinction events on others. I understand your feelings, Mr. Campo, but I still pity the python. It's really just another victim of abuse."

He paused, winced, then took a deep breath and rubbed his forehead.

"Well, we definitely are responsible for a number of ailments in the world," said Dayna, thinking Dr. Mbeki was being too vehement, and could be a radical environmentalist who would think the eradication of the human species was well justified. She should have insisted that security search him thoroughly before letting him into Harvard's treasury of archaeological relics. "But we aren't all to blame for the acts of a few stupid or ignorant human beings. And I'm certainly glad you're still alive, Frank."

"Thanks, Dr. Lugan. I wasn't particularly fond of the python when it was squeezing me to death."

"Maybe we should concentrate on our discovery. A new species of *Homo sapiens* that might have survived into the Roman era. Is their presence in the same bog in any way linked to the girl who was murdered? And if so, how? We've made other discoveries of various closely-linked species, like *Denisova,* that are astounding, but certainly don't provide a reason to kill. It's no longer news that several splits occurred in humanity's evolution since the ape. But we can't rule out that the murder was totally unrelated. Maybe even something personal." She looked at Felicity.

The girl fidgeted, but thrust out her chin.

"Do you still suspect Sh— Dr. Wilson? I think you're way off base. He's a scientist who cares about animals. There's nothing violent about him."

"He's a scientist who also seems to have a propensity for sleeping with young girls," said Dayna.

Felicity's gaze shied away from Dayna's. So he may have at least tried to seduce her.

"Maybe he began an affair with the murdered girl and lost interest in her. Maybe he formed a new relationship, which made her jealous. She might have threatened the new relationship, or even threatened him. Murders are often personal, and this young girl has no association with archaeology or the science community that we know of, except for Dr. Wilson."

"Hmm," said Frank. "If he liked to murder girls, Felicity, it's good you didn't stick around. He might have been tempted, you know, if you brushed him off . . ." His eyes were bright as if he were joking, but Dayna detected some underlying pain there, too.

Felicity glared at him, her jaw rigid.

"Frank, this isn't a joke," Dayna said sternly. "Anyway, we'll let the police pursue that angle. But I can't allow you to return to the site while the possibility exists that Dr. Wilson was involved. And if the murder does have to do with the bog bodies, the other question we need to ask is who would want to keep the existence of this species a secret?"

"An anthropologist who has his or her eye on a Nobel prize when the information is released," suggested Felicity, eager to shift the suspicion from Dr. Wilson.

"Maybe a treasure hunter," said Frank, massaging his jaw. His eyes flicked to Pedro, then skittered away. "You said Felicity discovered a coin pendant attached to one of the bodies. Maybe there are more. Or maybe this species fled Rome or the Canaanite coast with a hoard of treasure that belonged to the Roman Empire. If someone discovered a reference to these bodies in an ancient text that gave their possible destination, they might be searching. They might even have no qualms about killing to keep their existence a secret until they recover the potential cache. Greed is a common motive."

"Or maybe," said Dr. Mbeki, "some prospectors found the bodies near a site they wanted to exploit—to liberate diamonds or mine a mantle plume for energy, or . . . something more sinister. But a Cree girl discovered them also, and was about to tell the world. An archaeological find of this significance would bring hordes of scientists to the North, enough to threaten discovery of their plans and halt any more prospecting in the area. It would be a simple matter to drug her, feed her cultish nonsense to make her seem unstable, and then dispose of her without triggering a major investigation. Depression, psychosis, disappearance, suicide. Easy to dismiss."

"You talk as if you know these people," said Dayna.

"I know *of* these people, Dr. Lugan. As much as they spout conservationist philosophy, I suspect them of gross misconduct in the Okavango, and possibly even murder there, as well. My friends, the last of the *!Kung* clansmen to still maintain a traditional lifestyle, even though their spirits had already been broken, were hunted and massacred two years ago by a party unknown."

Frank looked startled, then quickly frowned.

"The genocide," Dr. Mbeki continued, "was blamed on poachers, but this company that has set up operations in the Hudson Bay region was 'prospecting' in various districts in the Delta and desert at the time."

He paused and winced again, squeezing his eyes shut for a moment.

"Could I trouble you for some pain reliever?" he asked. "I seem to have developed a terrible headache."

"Of course," said Dayna, grabbing her purse, rummaging through the contents, and extracting a headache remedy. Baruti dry-swallowed two tablets before he continued.

"When Dr. Deluca and I investigated the prospectors' camp, they admitted to tapping a mantle plume for energy. I don't know exactly what their agenda is, but I think we might find more answers if we examine these samples."

He unlocked the portable cryocooler in his lap, displaying a triple tier of flasks.

"Do you have a biohazard bag?"

She nodded and provided him with a transparent bag. Donning gloves, he gathered the receptacles and deposited the sealed specimens inside, releasing a trail of vapor as the liquid nitrogen evaporated. Several containers clattered mildly when they struck the table top through the protective plastic. Baruti spread them side by side to allow for a proper view. Adhesive labels were fastened to the flasks, but all that was typed there were numbers.

"Why don't we see what these people are cloning?" he said. "The flask Hondo Nsogwa showed me was labeled *Ursus maritimus* for polar bear. But these samples have no clear designation." He stripped off his gloves and placed them into another biohazard bag that Dayna handed him. "I can't help but wonder what kind of genetic manipulation they're really attempting."

Suddenly, Baruti's implications were clear. A *frisson* swept through Dayna that seemed every bit as numbing as the liquid nitrogen.

"Viruses?" she whispered. "Biological weapons?"

Baruti shrugged. "There's only one way to find out."

Scanning...

Located: Chapter 22

After Dr. Lugan had prepared the DNA samples—having donned the highest level of protective gear against pathogens, and after insisting that everyone else clear the clean room—she initiated the process of DNA sequencing and identification. Now, all that remained was to wait for results—something that would take approximately twenty minutes. Felicity, Baruti, Frank, and his friend Pedro had crossed the campus, making their way between vintage buildings. Passing classic constructions like Weld Hall, an 1872 red-brick dorm bracketed by two tall towers, and Emerson Hall, a 1905 pillared block-style building named after Ralph Waldo Emerson that resembled a courthouse, they eventually reached the communal hall that contained fast food kiosks and a standard cafeteria—a glass and steel confection that stood in contrast to its more venerable companions. They'd been instructed to take their time and enjoy an extended lunch, while Dr. Lugan headed to her car. She had a meeting to attend off-campus, and since rumors suggested she was getting a divorce, it might involve a lawyer.

Felicity quickly grabbed a sub at a nearby kiosk. Although Baruti frowned at her choice, he trailed her to the same counter and ordered a salad and milk, tossing a longing glance at the Thai food stand across the room. Frank opted for the hamburger stand, his hulking companion clinging to his shadow like a sticky web. Good. She could at least escape his obnoxious comments for a while.

For some reason, Baruti seemed annoyed with her. He made that abundantly clear when he tried to carry her tray.

"You might drop it," he said.

"I've got it," she snapped, yanking it from his grasp.

"Have you? Are you really capable of taking care of yourself? You seemed ready to trust Shaun Wilson, when there are questions about his involvement with the murder."

"You've spent more time with him than me. Do you think he killed that girl?" she asked, scanning the crowd and finally locating a free table. She collapsed into the rigid plastic chair, as Baruti slid into the one facing her. He didn't look at his food, but kept his unwavering focus on her.

"I don't know. He cares deeply for the polar bears, but that doesn't mean he isn't capable of anger and jealousy, or violent behavior. I do think he is hiding something."

"Well, most people have something to hide. But murder? Seriously? He just seems too . . . kind," she said. "There's nothing evil about him."

"Perhaps," he replied.

Baruti jabbed a tomato with his fork and jammed it into his mouth, chewing aggressively, as if he were trying to make her uncomfortable. Why? Was he jealous? Did he think she was defending Shaun because she had romantic feelings for him? Nothing could be further from the truth. She didn't even like him very much, especially after the way he had kept hovering and then had actually hit on her without any encouragement. But the fact that he was so inclined to protect her spoke volumes about his character. And she just hated to see innocent people drown under false accusations.

She bit gently into her sub, nibbling at the bread and trying not to look at the trickle of tomato juice running down Baruti's chin.

"I'm sorry about your friends," she mumbled through her mouthful.

He looked startled. "My friends?"

"The *!Kung* people. The ones who were killed."

Baruti swallowed the remains of his tomato in one big gulp and stabbed at his lettuce, but suddenly threw down the fork in disgust.

"They were more than my friends," he said harshly. "They were the original people, as you should know. As your friend," he commented, waving his hand at Frank Campo, who was even now threading through the throng of students toward them as if he intended *(dear God!)* to sit with them, "should know, since he has studied their art and artifacts."

"'Original people?' Do you mean the L0 haplogroup?" Frank asked.

"Yes. The first migration, 150,000 years ago, from Central and Eastern Africa. The first people to produce cave drawings 70,000 years ago."

"The first evidence of ritual," said Frank, smiling and taking a seat beside Felicity. He tossed his tray onto the table, while his friend circled to the other side and slammed his large frame into the weak plastic chair, threatening to crumple it. Frank, smirking obnoxiously, shifted the chair closer to her.

"Not that you would know anything about it, my gal, what with all your sculpting and bog work."

"Don't call me that!" she snapped.

"What? 'My gal'? Just an expression. 'Course you're not my gal. You're obviously Professor Lugan's gal, since she went charging off to the Arctic to rescue you."

"Frank, get lost," she said, curbing the desire to toss her sub in his face.

Baruti eyed Frank, but instead of supporting her, he offered Frank a smile.

"Not yet," said Frank. "We were discussing the cave paintings discovered in the Tsodilo Hills as evidence of the first rituals ever conducted. The primary archaeologist to study that region stumbled upon them about seventy years ago. She found rock spearheads that had been transported from somewhere much farther afield, clearly brought to the hills for a specific purpose. The *!Kung* people burned the spearheads, but only the red, more colorful ones. Clear evidence of a ritual and the beginning of abstract thought. It's where we all began, Felicity. Where intelligence was wrought."

Intelligence? Somehow it must have skipped a generation or two, in your family, she felt like saying, but she gnawed on her sandwich instead.

"So what happens when we obliterate our beginnings?" asked Baruti.

Frank shrugged, although his chin quivered slightly. "It is sad to think that most of them are gone. But the remaining *!Kung* were only faint reflections of the first people."

Felicity realized instantly that Frank was being far too dismissive. "What happens?" she asked.

"The roots die," said Baruti. "The trees have no more grip and can find no sustenance. The trees die; the earth becomes bald, dry, eroded. The earth crumbles, the winds carry it away, the rain washes it to sea. Nothing remains but a barren world. What occurs is an ever-widening domino effect of disintegration."

"As Felicity said before," Frank replied, "*we're* not dead. The Earth hasn't crumbled away. We still have more than enough resources to sustain us. And eventually we'll have another world to inhabit in Mars. The loss of people and traditional cultures is a tragedy, but we can still learn about our past from the artifacts they left behind."

Baruti sighed. "Does your interest in archaeology really just amount to objects and treasure? The *!Kung's* respect for the natural world lies in their culture, and relics and the odd written account won't transmit those values to scientists. And too often, the scientist's views are projected onto the object of study, not the other way around. The *!Kung* were the seeds of all *Homo sapiens*."

Frank looked startled. Felicity wondered why, but after considering the way his area of study had shifted from the *!Kung* and other Bushmen clans to the Dead Sea scrolls and Greek tombs, she suspected he'd lost interest in humanity's origins and become more fascinated with her creations.

"No," said Frank. "Artifacts aren't my sole pursuit. In fact I was quite interested in anthropology a few years ago. When I interviewed the *!Kung*, I found their beliefs and way of life fascinating. And their paintings, going back 70,000 years, were phenomenal. And if they were the seeds for all of us . . ."

"They didn't live like us, did they?" asked Pedro, who'd been quietly observing the others, while shoveling food into his mouth. Creases lined his forehead. "These *!Kung* people. They didn't want or need many things."

"How did you figure that out?" asked Frank.

"Well, all you've been lookin' at or talkin' about is beads made from eggshells and paintings in a cave. Then you, Mr. Mbeki, went on about hunting and animals. If they didn't want things, man, other than a few beads that they made themselves, then they probably didn't steal. They probably never got all googly-eyed over gold or diamonds."

"Actually," said Frank, "they didn't care about all the things we find valuable, but they were still similar to us. The best hunter usually got the most attractive wife, or sometimes two wives—at least among those who still lived in the traditional way. They were generally peaceful, but quite human. Which brings us back to our incredible discovery. Not-quite-human people wearing *!Kung* beads. Not-quite-human people in a subpolar bog. How long do you think"—he looked at Felicity—"it will take us to study the bodies, excavate the Florida remains, and process the study with Dr. Lugan? A year?" He asked as if the time focused on one of the most incredible discoveries of the century would be a waste of his time, as if he had something far better on his agenda.

"Probably longer," she said. "We'll first have to date the remains and see if we can establish a link between the two. Since these bodies exist, there are likely others buried or preserved in obscure locations that no one has stumbled upon yet. I'd still like to travel back to Northern Ontario and see if we can discover any more bodies or artifacts in that location. I'd also like to sculpt reproductions of some of those we unearthed, to fill in more details and develop a clearer picture of their physical appearance. There's so much to do. But before we return there, we have to be positive they aren't connected with the murder."

"I get why these dudes, these miners, would want to hide what they're doin' if they're makin' weapons," said Pedro. "But I don't get why they'd kill these *!Kung* people."

The others turned to him in surprise. Felicity didn't believe for a second he was a student, but he seemed to be pondering this mystery just as deeply as they were.

"Well," he shrugged. "What would they have to gain? Wiping out a harmless bunch of natives in Africa who didn't own much of anything other than beads and huts."

"Maybe, like this Cree girl, they discovered something they shouldn't have," said Baruti.

"Like what? Would they even understand all that energy mumbo jumbo? Or germ warfare?"

Baruti sighed. "Probably not. Those who had become ranchers, possibly. But they lived farther afield and managed to survive the slaughter. Most of those killed still believed in evil spirits. I don't think they would have challenged the miners. But maybe they just got in their way, interrupted their 'prospecting.'"

For a minute, no one spoke. It seemed so tragic that people could be murdered just for being in the wrong place at the wrong time.

Pedro shook his head. "No. I doubt it. You keep talkin' about how important these *!Kung* people were, and how they've been there from the beginning. Now you find other people with a long history in the Everglades, wearin' beads from the same place in Africa, and some in the North where these same miners show up. So maybe it isn't what the *!Kung* people found out or where they were that put them on the hit list, but *what they knew*.

"It's like Mr. Mbeki said, 'we shouldn't forget our beginnin's,' not just for all the fancy philosophy reasons, but for all the clues that lead back there. Were these miners makin' weapons? Why would the *!Kung* people care about that? Were they poachin' animals for their experiments? The *!Kung* people might not like that, but how could they be a threat to somethin' that's been happening for centuries without any real checks? None of it makes sense. At least not yet. But I think you two"—he pointed at Baruti and Frank —"can figure it out."

Frank raised his eyebrows.

Baruti's face crushed into a frown.

"The two of us?" he asked.

"You both seem to be experts on these people, even though you . . . think differently. If you put your heads together, you might come up with somethin'." He pointed at Felicity. "And Frank said you know about these bog bodies. So maybe there's a connection there, too."

Felicity grimaced. Why was she always called upon when it came to grisly remains, required to tinker in human flesh? Why couldn't her job be to investigate the Roman or Phoenician link?

"Bonus," she said.

But Baruti's eyes lit up.

"And we need a thinker," he said. "A man who can connect the dots."

He directed his gaze at Frank's friend, who had indeed proved he had remarkable gray matter. But she still couldn't imagine what these original people knew that was so threatening they needed to be silenced.

"So let's make it official," said Baruti, looking at Frank and Felicity, in particular. "We become a collective; we share information; we work as a team.

"Well, if it gets us to answers faster . . ." said Frank.

Felicity turned to him, still nursing her suspicions. "So . . . what?"

"So, we can . . . solve the mystery," he said, patronizingly.

"So . . . you can return to Greece?" she asked.

"Greece is nice," he said. "I like Greece. But, of course, I have a job to do."

"Yes, you do, Frank. I don't get you at all. This discovery could land you a Nobel prize, but you don't seem to care."

"It will probably land Dr. Lugan a Nobel Prize. You and I will get a scrawled acknowledgment in the back of her published study."

Felicity rolled her eyes. "What about the murders? What if they're really significant? Don't you think that's more important than Greece?"

Frank sighed. "Felicity, I once tried to tell you what was important to me, but you didn't care to listen. Even when we *had* to do a project or a dig together, your eyes kept wandering when I talked, like nothing in front of you was as interesting as what you could conjure up in your imagination. You understand what I'm talking about, don't you, Dr. Mbeki?"

Baruti looked startled, but quickly shrugged.

"He does, you know," Frank answered for him. "People like you, sweetheart, but only for a short while. They quickly wise up. Especially when you don that helpless female act and suck up to the faculty so they can't resist coddling you. I was surprised when Dr. Lugan finally sent you on a more grungy assignment. So don't you dare lecture me about my ethics or my priorities." He narrowed his gaze as if he'd like to throttle her. "I'll work with you because I have no choice. But I won't listen to you, until you get off your high horse and say something worth listening to."

Felicity's ire grew with every word he said, but the tightening in her chest doubled at the same time. He was a greedy bastard, always angling for the choicest assignment no matter whom he had to trample to get it. Yet here he sat, figuratively slapping her for—basically—being a little dreamy and, the odd time, gaining some favor among the faculty. She didn't deserve the abuse, at least not to this extent. But she couldn't refute him, either, since she knew she did wander off point sometimes. She understood that he felt slighted because he'd been attracted to her and she'd repeatedly rejected him. But he was reducing her to such small proportions in front of Baruti, a man whose opinion she did care about, that it practically brought her to tears.

"I think we all need to calm down and take this off a personal level," said Baruti. For some reason, he looked at her warmly. "None of us is perfect, and we might be able to help each other if we can keep a professional distance and learn to work together. I've observed your performance in the field, Felicity, and I believe you have talent and excellent assessment skills. Mr. Campo, Dr. Lugan can't speak highly enough of your African studies, so even though you'd rather be somewhere else and work with someone else, I think you will be invaluable to this team. Pedro, is it? You've more than impressed me with your observations and conclusions. We don't have to like each other to be effective and . . . maybe even brilliant." He grinned.

"The fellowship of the ring," Felicity mumbled.

"Are you calling me a hobbit?" asked Frank, but surprisingly the tension had left his voice.

"No, I wouldn't give you that much credit," she said. "But if we need to solve this mystery, which seems to become more and more tangled the deeper we explore, I'm hoping that you'll turn out to be a wizard."

Scanning...

Located: Chapter 23

DAYNA EXITED HER robotic Mazda, wishing she could slam the door rather than watch it glide shut behind her. The Peabody Museum had an older entranceway, without automated sensors, but if she slammed that one into its frame she might actually crack or shatter the vintage glass, and that would make her the enemy of every archaeologist on staff. If only she could focus solely on the new discoveries, and empty her mind of all the arguments and pain in her personal life.

The meeting between Evan, his lawyer, and hers had taken two hours—well past the completion of the DNA sequencing. Two hours that had been emotionally draining and filled with arguments and accusations.

"I needed a wife," said Evan. "I needed someone who enjoyed my touch and didn't keep pining over the kids we'd lost. I needed someone who wasn't so involved in her digs and her students' lives that she could barely spare a moment to talk to me."

"Don't," she'd snuffled. The pain was still fresh, after all these years. "You don't understand, because you barely held her; you didn't feel her heartbeat stop. And Thomas was just another acquisition to you. With all your expertise, you couldn't even prevent the birth mother from reclaiming him."

"That's not fair," he snarled. "I did everything I could. Don't you dare suggest I didn't love him as deeply as you did. But I moved on. I had to. You just keep burying yourself in this hole of sorrow that you've dug, and you blame me for trying to be happy again. But even so, I didn't ask for this divorce. I grabbed happiness where I could, and I stood by your side. There are different ways to be faithful."

"I may not have been the sunniest wife, but how can you call what you've been doing fidelity? You glory in money and sex; you think that will ease the pain, without even considering that it would cause *me* pain. You used to be concerned for the underdog, but now you support billionaire corporations and defend their corrupt practices. You attend every slutty office party. Even when I was with you, you flirted with other women. But you refuse to even stop by for a moment at my faculty festivities or to meet my grad students—to understand why I care for these bright young people. You have not the slightest interest in my work anymore, even though our human origins and the European bog bodies used to fascinate you. At least you'd listen as attentively as I would when you'd discuss a case. I may be stagnating in pain, but you're flying into the sun, Icarus."

And so the mud-slinging continued, until the lawyers broke it up. Evan definitely could assert claim to the bulk of their estate, but the arguments resumed when they began discussing splitting their possessions. Dayna had no interest in bilking Evan of his millions simply as payback for the pain he'd caused her, but she couldn't part with the precious photographs of their adopted child, or the perfect sculpture they'd spent days searching for to adorn their foyer. She didn't have a profligate lifestyle, so money wasn't the issue. Still, it seemed he wanted to argue over savings accounts and investments. Maybe he couldn't accept that it was over, yet. Maybe he still loved her, in a weird, twisted way. She knew she still treasured certain memories.

They swamped her, suddenly making her pause midstride. She caught her breath and leaned against the wall.

She could see the two of them, hunched over beneath the murky light of a streetlight, sopping wet, sharing a laughing fit when they'd missed their taxi after a dinner date and ended up umbrella-less in a downpour. She could feel the tender kiss he often bestowed on the inside of her elbow, something that always made her quiver. She adored the mischievous smirk that played at the corners of his lips when he'd tease her about her job. One Christmas, the year she'd received a grant to take her explorations of the European bogs further, he'd even presented her with a ridiculous dive suit.

Despite the teasing, he'd respected her work then, and she'd respected his. And they'd both been passionate about their careers. His eyes would often glow with a deep internal fire when he talked about the people he would rescue from an unjust system. He couldn't stop chattering about one case in particular—a homeless client who'd tried to save a woman who'd been mugged and shot but instead, with her blood on his hands, had been accused of murder. And how despondent he'd become when he'd lost the case and the man had been sent to death row.

"Evan, what happened to you?" she whispered under her breath. Tears threatened to spill down her cheeks, but she couldn't let them escape. Not here. Not now. She missed him terribly, the man she'd fallen in love with, and despised the vacuum he'd left inside her.

"Dr. Lugan," said Felicity, grasping her arm to steady her. The girl's companions trailed far behind, as if she'd sprinted ahead of them. "Are you okay?"

Dayna sniffed and straightened her sweater, backhanded a tear from her cheek.

"Yes," she said, trying to control her voice. "It's just been a difficult day."

"Do you want to talk about it? We can wait for the results, if you'd like to talk."

She faced Felicity and squeezed her arm in appreciation.

"No, dear. I don't want to talk. I want to forget about it and get back to work."

"I guess it helps," Felicity said, "if you love your work. It can help you forget almost anything."

Dayna squinted at her, noting a longing in her eyes that seemed to be a permanent fixture.

"I know you would love to sculpt your own masterpieces, much more than examining DNA or digging for corpses in the dirt. But you have a great analytical mind, Felicity. Maybe one day you'll discover you love what your mind can do as fervently as what your hands can create."

"I think that man, Pedro, has one of those minds, too," Felicity said. "Better than mine."

Dayna tried to camouflage her surprise, but Felicity must have seen it flicker in her eyes.

"He doesn't think the murder of the Cree girl and the murders of the *!Kung* people have anything to do with a biological weapon. He thinks there might be a motive we haven't even considered."

She went on to explain their conversation over lunch.

"It seems far-fetched," Dayna said. "And yet somewhat logical. We'll see in a few minutes. At least we'll know what these people are cooking."

She turned and strode forward, feeling slightly more stable. A purpose, a mystery, and a group of intelligent, fascinating people to explore it with—that would all help distract her from the emotional carnage of the past week. Felicity followed, and the others quickly caught up. En masse, they trooped up the stairs and surged expectantly into the lab.

Dayna gazed at the blinking light on the virtual monitor that indicated the sequencing was complete for the various strands of DNA. She signaled the processor to display the results.

"Here we go," she said with bated breath.

The findings scrolled across the room in midair, highlighting gene matches and sorting them into species. Not a virus among them. The results displayed common mammals and even some insects, which corresponded to the numbered flasks.

135 *Rangifer tarandus* (caribou)

129 *Oreamnos americanus* (mountain goat)

143 *Lepus arcticus* (Arctic hare)

101 *Bombus polaris* (bumblebee)

115 *Somateria mollissima* (eider duck)

150 *Salvelinus alpinus* (Arctic char)

Altogether, fifty species were listed.

"This is strange," said Dayna. "No viruses, thank God. But I don't see any extinct species, either."

"The majority of them are northern hemisphere–based," said Dr. Mbeki.

"There are even fish. It doesn't make sense. And it certainly doesn't match their explanation."

"But it doesn't look like anything worth killing over, either," said Felicity. "It's like a bank of cold weather creatures."

"Why collect species that aren't even endangered?" said Frank.

"Unless they plan on killin' them and then bringin' them back to life," said Pedro. "You know, somethin' like the Bible story—Noah's ark—where Noah saved a male and female of each species but God killed the rest."

Dayna stared at Pedro, feeling as unsettled as when Baruti had suggested biological weapons. Felicity was right about this man. He wasn't exactly polished, but he seemed to have a knack for making connections.

"Are you suggesting," said Frank, "that they're transporting these species elsewhere because they're planning to do something very destructive in the North? Something that might have cataclysmic consequences?"

Pedro looked confused.

"Boom," Frank explained, flipping his hands outward. "Atomic?"

"Why there?" asked Dayna. "It's the least populated area on the planet, besides Antarctica. What would they gain by destroying a few acres of tundra?"

"Bog," said Felicity. "Many acres of bog and permafrost. All they'd be doing, if we're talking about some nuclear explosions, is warming things up and melting the snow and ice, which is already melting rapidly anyway, what with climate change. And contaminating a pristine environment. What would be the point?" With a little gasp, she rushed on. "Maybe it has to do with the Cree. Maybe they want to kill them for some reason, just like they exterminated most of the *!Kung*."

"They could easily do that without destroying the wildlife," said Dr. Mbeki.

"Just a minute," said Dayna. "We're making a lot of assumptions here that may be way off base. If they're collecting these samples and experimenting with cloning, then they're geneticists, not miners or nuclear physicists. Although they may be terrorists, we can't be sure of that, either, without further proof. It could be that they're simply scientists experimenting with various genes to determine a solution to the telomere problem in order to restore viable extinct species, as this Dr. Nsogwa told you, Dr. Mbeki. Or they could be collecting genetic material for any number of other purposes."

"So what do you suggest?" asked Dr. Mbeki. "We knock on their doors and ask?"

"That would be one way to go about it," said Dayna. "Rather than storm their camp with guns drawn."

The biologist smiled. "You forget, I visited their camp and they led me to the samples—exactly the samples they wanted me to see. Not these. You also forget that shortly after they arrived in the North, the Cree girl was murdered. A pattern that has followed them from Africa."

"But none of these incidents are proof. They're entirely circumstantial," snapped Dayna, tired of the fear mongering. Solid evidence is what they needed, not this toxic speculation.

Dr. Mbeki bared his teeth in agitation.

"If a man pulls out a gun on an innocent group of students," he said, pulling out a gun, "does he need to pull the trigger for you to suspect him of evil intent?"

Dayna's chest locked. Her heart thumped wildly.

But Dr. Mbeki merely opened the chamber to show her it was unloaded, then replaced the weapon in his belt beneath his jacket.

"D— Dr. Mbeki. Why are you carrying a pistol around in Harvard?"

The others stared at him, wide-eyed.

"Only because I have a feeling these men might get a little suspicious when they discover I stole their vials. But I'm an expert with weapons so, as I demonstrated, I didn't carry it loaded into your school. But I can load it quickly, if it turns out we were followed."

"Expert?" asked Frank. "As in . . . military?"

"No, Frank," he said. "Expert as in . . . that's classified. I'm sorry to be so blunt, but I needed to illustrate my point. These people have already pulled the trigger. We just didn't witness it. But should we wait until they launch a rocket before we act? Should we plod at the pace of science before the prospect of imminent destruction? Or should we move in, silently and quickly, to snare them? I need answers, and I need your brains to find them."

"Dr. Mbeki? Are you really a biologist?" asked Dayna. She had to know what they were getting into.

"Absolutely. A biologist who is very worried about our planet and the potential dangers this group represents. But I do have connections to some high-ranking individuals who are also worried. You must grasp the urgency. We don't know what their true agenda is, but we can safely assume it's destructive in nature."

"If these people are terrorists, as you're insinuating, then it is a case best left to the CIA or Interpol." She narrowed her eyes at him just enough to let him know she thought he was associated with one of these groups. "I have no intention of putting my students at risk."

"They may be terrorists, but they're also scientists. So we can't discern their motives without the cooperation of other scientific minds."

He reached into his backpack, and Dayna felt a resurgence of panic. She shuffled Felicity and Frank behind her, interposing her body between them and the biologist, or whatever he was. But instead of pulling out a gun this time, he gently brought out an ivory object encased in plastic. Mud partially obscured the bony cap, and fragments had broken off, leaving sizable gaps, but it could only be a skull. He smiled as he handed it to her, apparently amused at her protective stance.

"The *!Kung* kept this skull concealed in a cave, protected, but not revered. They feared the spirits of the dead more than anything in this world, and I always wondered why. My friend, Tsosa, once showed me the cave—a place where they had danced and performed rituals, in the past—and I noticed the skull, but he wouldn't speak of it. The *!Kung* never spoke of the dead. And draped over the skull was an artifact."

He removed another item from his pack and set it beside the Roman coin on Dayna's desk. It was an intricately carved golden bracelet with a winged scarab filigreed in the center.

"Phoenician," gasped Felicity.

"Possibly," Baruti replied. "When I discovered the *!Kung's* murdered bodies, I remembered these carefully cached items, and I went to retrieve them. I think of them as the only memorials of a noble tribe, or perhaps a deadly secret. But I suspect they have significance that only an anthropologist or archaeologist could readily discover. You would experience no real risk simply investigating in your lab the bodies you discovered, these genetic samples I've provided you with, and this skull and artifact, now, would you?"

Dayna eyed the skull, intrigued, despite herself.

"No, I suppose not."

"However, I do think I would be better equipped to solve this mystery if Frank would accompany me to Africa. Together, we might discover whether the *!Kung* hold the key to the devil's fortress. Or, I would welcome Pedro as a bodyguard, if you prefer."

"No," said Dayna. Was the biologist mad? To think that she'd put her student, who'd already nearly died from a snake attack, into the hands of a man she knew nothing about, who was an expert with weapons and sounded like a spy!

He turned to Felicity, eyebrows raised.

She shrugged. "I'd go," she said. "But I don't have Frank's expertise."

"No," said Dayna. "Absolutely not."

"Why don't we ask Frank?" Baruti asked.

Frank calmly returned Baruti's gaze, although he leaned against the desk for support. "I don't know." He looked at Dayna, and she shook her head adamantly. "We have a lot of work to do here, and I'm not exactly at one hundred percent right now. I know Pedro suggested we put our heads together, but I wasn't thinking Africa."

"There. That settles it," said Dayna. "We'll examine your skull and artifact, Dr. Mbeki, but beyond that, you're on your own."

Dr. Mbeki sighed. "Well, then, I suppose that whatever happens next is on your heads."

Without another word, he spun on his heel and walked out.

Scanning...

Located: Chapter 24

BARUTI SLAMMED THE door of his hotel room, a budget-conscious choice on the outskirts of Boston. A threadbare comforter in a faded floral pattern swaddled the bed, a battered wooden dresser crowded the opposite wall, and dusty windows looked out over a parking lot. He swept his backpack from his shoulder and tossed it on the mattress, then whipped out his gun and threw it into the middle of the bed. The lavender polyester folds enveloped the damned weapon, creating a ludicrous nest for it.

"Idiot!" he snarled.

How could he have lost his temper and alarmed the people he needed the most? Sometimes he felt blinded by rage, and sometimes he simply felt blind. Why was it that with every passing day his sharp focus deteriorated, blurring his thoughts and producing a throbbing pain at the back of his head? Now, the symptoms seemed to be escalating, the headache becoming more severe and disturbing his rationality. And why were the muscles in his arm twitching? He sighed and collapsed into the scuffed wooden chair beside the window.

"We are all dying," he heard the scrape of Tsosa's voice in his ear. He remembered this conversation, from after his friend had left the ranch and returned to a traditional *!Kung* lifestyle. There was a man who had always been more philosopher than rancher. "Since we've been swallowed by modern culture, we've lost our sense of community; the individual is valued the most, and not the group. And individual pursuits, even when taken up by a group, are divisive, leading to arguments, scuffles, and wars. The things that bound us—our sense of humor, our undistorted view of the world and its creatures, our joy in each other's accomplishments rather than simply our own, and the sharing of all necessities—are fading from our existence. But I will not feel rage. Rage is the most destructive force on our planet. It has been with us throughout the ages. It is with us now, slipping between the shadows, crawling down our throats while we sleep, crushing our last hope. It is the deadly lion we used to worship, but eventually cast out for its wickedness."

Baruti felt its grip now, binding his chest, as he grieved over a village of dead friends. But he'd always wondered at Tsosa's words. Was it possible that *!Kung* beliefs had become muddled with the Biblical story of the garden of Eden—the lion simply replacing the snake? There was no way to know whether the tribe had been overly influenced by missionaries over the centuries, or if the story was a pure retelling, with an ancient mythological significance. Now, after Pedro's suggestion, he wondered if there was even more to it.

But he'd likely ruined his chance to find out, with the help of a few academic minds. Of course, most of them were young, untried minds without the wisdom that came from years of study. But that could have been an asset, considering what he'd observed of academics like Dr. Lugan. Often, older scientists had preconceived ideas that clouded their judgment. He needed a team with crisp, open minds to unravel this mystery, since he'd lost his edge, and he wasn't an anthropologist or archaeologist, and he knew that something disastrous was pending.

Well, he supposed he should start packing and head back to Botswana in the morning. He'd have to keep digging for clues, and he'd probably wind up dead, if he kept digging in Canada. Dragging himself to his feet, he opened the top drawer of the dresser and tossed assorted pants, underwear, and button-down cotton shirts into his sports bag, along with the few polar fleece items he'd purchased for his northern excursion. But he paused mid-toss as his mind drifted again, hovering over the delicate cheekbones, freckled skin, and pronounced limp of the girl, Felicity. He'd been drawn to her from the beginning, even though he'd vowed since his wife's betrayal and the deaths of his friends that there would be no more close ties, particularly with women.

But he could sense that the girl, despite her physical disability, her ambivalence, and her occasional squeamishness, had some underlying strength and an extraordinary brain. She displayed an odd reverence for the dead people she fished out of the bog, and seemed passionate about determining their history. He could see her fitting pieces together, even as she located body parts. She might be the crucial mind that would sort through all the disparate fragments of this mystery and connect the relevant pieces. But he'd also noticed a dreamy aspect to her personality. Her brain devoted half its neurons to a fantasy life. Perhaps she had one foot always planted in the classical world of her studies and her artistic yearnings. Maybe that's why she so adamantly defended Shaun Wilson, a man whose face and physique resembled the marble deities in a Greek garden.

But Shaun looked like a man with many secrets. Despite his passion for polar bears, he didn't seem to belong in northern Canada, unlike DeLuca. DeLuca was a man so organic to the North he was similar to the bedrock he studied, whereas there was nothing rugged or hardy about Shaun. He probably hadn't murdered the Cree girl, but he had known her. The shock in his expression and the retching afterward had nothing to do with squeamishness over bog bodies. And maybe he had some idea about why she'd been murdered but had kept it to himself, which raised Baruti's hackles and his suspicions.

He shook his head and cast another crumpled garment into his bag. Before he could grab the next, though, a quiet knock came at his door. Startled, he reached for his gun. Had Hondo and his associates already discovered their samples were missing?

Tap, tap.

More knocks, this time louder.

He sidled up to the door and peered through the peep hole. There she stood—the girl he couldn't stop thinking about. He lowered the gun, then tossed it back on the bed. If he'd had time, he would have concealed it, but if he delayed opening the door any longer she might think he wasn't there and leave.

He threw the door open, shocking Felicity into stepping backward. Frank and Pedro stood behind her.

"Baruti," she said, wide-eyed, her hand flying to her chest. "I was beginning to think you'd already left."

"Not yet," he said. "But I was packing. Come in."

He swept his hand to the side and backed into the room, leaving them enough space to enter.

They tromped in, Frank eyeing him uncomfortably, Pedro scanning the room and immediately spotting the gun, and Felicity limping past with a tentative look that grazed his jaw and his shoulder and came to rest on his hand.

"It's on the bed," he said, pointing out the weapon enfolded by the floral-patterned comforter. "I know it was a stupid move, showing it to your professor just to demonstrate the danger these people represent. I just became . . . frustrated. I didn't mean to alarm anyone."

"I know," said Felicity. "You handed me a gun before. It was shocking, but it helped me understand. I just keep wondering, though. How do you get through airport security with all your weapons?"

"I don't," he said. "I pick them up in every country we land in. Connections. When you're dealing with killers . . ." He shrugged.

"I get it," said Frank. "Which is why I'm still nervous about going with you to Africa."

"You're considering it?" asked Baruti.

"I never said no." Frank dropped his slim body into the wobbly wooden chair by the window.

"You said we were a team," Felicity began. "That if we put our heads together we might stop something . . . bad, maybe even catastrophic, from happening. Mysteries intrigue me, but I wouldn't have considered collaborating, especially with Frank"—she tossed him a frown—"just to solve a mystery. If these people are planning to tamper with the environment or the creatures in it, or maybe even kill people, I can't stand by and just let it happen, if there's something I can do to prevent it."

"So you are all thinking of joining me in Africa?" asked Baruti. "If you accompany us, Felicity, who will examine the bog bodies and decipher the DNA here?"

Felicity took a deep breath and looked at Frank, who shrugged, then nodded.

"Dr. Lugan can examine the bodies and assess the DNA. And hopefully your skull too. We want to help find out what the *!Kung* knew."

Baruti scratched his head and studied each of their faces in turn: Felicity's twitchy, but with a firm set to her jaw; Frank's tight with lips compressed, but calm; Pedro's completely relaxed and angling a sly glance at him.

"I don't imagine I'll be able to finish retrieving and examining every body from the Everglades particularly quickly," said Frank. "That will take at least a few years. And the *!Kung* are my area of expertise—or at least they were—and I'd much rather traipse around the Okavango or the Kalahari than juggle body parts in that python-infested swamp."

"There are pythons in the Okavango," said Baruti, unable to disguise a smug note in his voice.

"I know," said Frank. "And black mamba, and lions, and the odd hungry crocodile. I've been there before. But Pedro will be joining me as my *bodyguard*."

The way he emphasized the last word suggested to Baruti that he would be guarding against more than wild animals.

"And did Dr. Lugan agree to this excursion?"

He knew the answer, but he had to ascertain what their mutiny would entail.

"No, of course not," said Felicity. "She'd never agree to our going AWOL and leaving her with the task of excavating this new species and doing all the tests and preservation work that will require. Plus, she'd be worried. She's like a mother hen. Sometimes she shoos us out of the roost, but she never stops clucking over us. After Frank was bitten and nearly strangled by the python"—her eyes seemed to say, "and I wish he'd been swallowed, too" —"she probably won't even permit us to take part in a dig again. But we're her students, not her children. It may delay our graduation, and she might not welcome us back, but I think solving this mystery is more important than her reaction. I don't even know if we can help you, but we'll do all we can."

"I understand your willingness to help, Felicity, since you discovered the dead girl. But I'm a little puzzled by you, Frank. It's obvious you still don't trust me. You're still recovering from a recent injury, caused by a wild animal, no less. The Okavango has its share of wild animals, although they are fewer every day.

Are you sure you want to join us?"

Frank hesitated, then shrugged. "Okay, I admit I'm a little nervous about this trip. But I'm also curious. I'm curious why anyone would want to exterminate the *!Kung*. They were harmless people, happy people, when I met and interviewed some of them three years ago. They had few possessions, and they weren't clamoring for more. I found that hard to fathom, but also refreshing. They loved one another unconditionally, placed no unreasonable demands on tribe members' shoulders, didn't categorize people by status, worked for survival but never for greed, laughed all the time—my God how they loved to laugh. It doesn't make any sense to kill them." He paused.

"So, yes, I didn't like it when you pulled out a gun. But if you knew these people and someone massacred them, then I understand why you're upset. I'm not much of a gunslinger or a sheriff who tries to bring people to justice. I don't think I'll ever be a wizard." He looked at Felicity. "But I do know the *!Kung*," he said, turning back to Baruti. "I know their traditions, their art, their mythology. You know them personally. I know them professionally. Maybe together we can save the remaining few or uncover a clue that will explain why these bastards killed them. Maybe I'm a little angry too. And maybe I wouldn't stop you if you pulled out that gun again . . . on the right people."

Baruti leaned against the wall, still processing, surprised by Frank's words. Curiosity made sense as a motivator, but he hadn't expected this man to have feelings for the *!Kung* people, much less be outraged by their murder. Maybe there was more to him than Felicity had implied. Or perhaps his professor had cultivated compassion as well as curiosity in her students. He lifted a hand to his forehead and massaged his temple. This was good, wasn't it? He'd now assembled a team—a willing, passionate, motivated team. But why was the throbbing behind his eyes intensifying? Why did he feel the need to vomit?

He remembered his father's words, when he had demanded to know how their cherished dog, Zumbai, had died. Zumbai, his childhood companion. He couldn't accept that his pet had died of natural causes, when they'd buried him quickly in the night, before Baruti could see his body.

"Do you really need to know?" asked his father. "Do you think it will bring you comfort? Do you wish to know how deeply a man suffers before he dies?

The pain that crackles and erupts in every nerve? Or is it better to assume he drifts into a peaceful slumber? Would you rather know that hell is a description of our world, which is so often bathed in fire and the blood of war, and not an alternate reality that we can escape at the end of our lives?"

Tears had filled Baruti's eyes, because the answer had to be more terrible than the abominable wisdom his father had just imparted. But he couldn't walk away. "Yes. I must know."

"Well, then," said his father. "I will tell you. He was barking too loudly—a tender insult to the ears, nothing more—and your mother slit his throat."

Scanning...

Located: Chapter 25

LUCAS AWOKE TO myriad crashes and bangs loud enough to yank him from sleep and trigger a stab of pain in his abdomen.

"Wh— what?" He blinked several times to gain focus, then looked across the HAB to locate the source of the disturbance.

Bob, of course.

Bob had emptied several shelves of freeze-dried food and was stuffing them into two iron-gray backpacks on the narrow twin bed.

"What are you doing?" he asked. "Moving?"

Wouldn't that be nice? Maybe Bob had found a convenient cave with a miraculous airlock and a large oxygen reservoir.

"Getting prepped for a rover excursion. She's all fixed," said Bob, not even bothering to look up and make eye contact. "The explosion punctured the titanium sheeting, disrupting the air seal, but I welded a new sheet in place. The seal is intact now. The only issue is the radar navigation system. Only the lidar is online, but that may only tell us the thickness of the mist and may not detect obstacles." He continued packing ruthlessly.

Lucas grunted and rolled on his side, slithering his legs over the edge of the bed and pushing his torso upward at the same time, to propel his body into sitting position all in one move. This he'd learned from Bob was the least painful mode of transition from lying down, to sitting, to eventually standing upright and walking. No twisting of his wounds was involved in this move.

"Shouldn't be an issue if you take it slow. And the fuel cell?"

"Functional."

"Great," said Lucas. "When do we leave?"

Bob shoved one more packet into the bag, then turned and faced him, his bristly eyebrows raised. Or maybe his entire expression was bristly.

"*We* aren't leaving. *Gita and I* are leaving, and *you* will continue healing."

Lucas grasped the bar beside his head—a patient-assist device recently installed—and wrenched his body upward, bringing his face level with Bob's. Well, not level. The top of his head was actually a handspan above Bob's.

"And when was this decided?"

"Lucas." Bob placed his hand on Lucas's back as if he needed either support or a gentle nudge. "Just sit down and relax."

"I've had a good week to heal," Lucas said. "Which I tend to do quickly, especially with that extra fracture sealant you injected. And I may be an asset if the rover breaks down en route. I can't spend the week it will take you to travel to the next propellant plant and back just lying around like a slug doing nothing."

Bob sighed. "I understand your frustration, Lucas, but you're not ready. Even with the rover's cushioning suspension, the trip would bounce you around too much. After all the progress we've made getting you back in shape, I don't want to see that incision reopen."

"I'm willing to take the risk," said Lucas. He'd had enough of being cooped up in this tin can, sipping pea soup and listening to dramatic Beethoven recordings—the ISA's idea of relaxation therapy.

"Well, I'm n—"

The door to the restroom, if one could call a closet that, creaked open, and Gita stumbled into the main salon of the HAB, straightening her jumpsuit. She halted mid-step and eyed the two men with an intuitive tilt of her head.

"What's going on?"

Bob sighed again, which seemed to be all he did lately.

"Lucas wants to accompany us to the Arabia Terra factory. He doesn't seem to realize that he can barely stand."

Gita arched her eyebrows, sweeping his body with probing eyes that were likely noting the wobble in his knees, and the twitch of his usually solid abs.

"Why not?" she said, shocking everyone. "He looks fine to me."

"Are you kidding?" asked Bob, swinging toward her with a sharp, accusatory glare.

"Okay," she said. "If you want the truth, he looks terrible. But I can imagine his behavior after we leave, and it isn't pretty. He'll get so bored he'll probably head out of the airlock and inadvertently injure himself again. Seriously. And nobody will be here to patch him up. At least in the rover we can keep an eye on him and ensure he gets enough rest and proper nutrition. It's just a HAB away from home, anyway."

Bob rolled his eyes and sighed again, a long drawn-out exhalation.

"It's going to be tight, three of us packed in like chickens in a factory farm for as many as ten days of travel. Not to mention the extra food and medical supplies we'll need."

"Bob," said Lucas. "It's not that I don't appreciate what you've done for me." *But sometimes I don't.* "And I don't like to remind you every minute that it was your idea to descend to the planet." *When every other minute will do.* "But since I'm here, in this state, I don't think it's fair to groan about the extra burden I'll place on your expedition. Instead, you should embrace what I'm willing to offer, slightly disabled or not. I have special skills, which were of no use on the *Phoenix* but will definitely come in handy in our current situation. I have intimate knowledge of the ISPP structure, components, and function. I've also studied the northern terrain for years, in preparation for possible early colonization."

Bob looked surprised.

"Yes, I was selected before they canned that enterprise and opted for aggressive terraforming, after all the natural disasters on Earth and the rapid depletion of resources. I probably know every bump in the road."

"And you'll also *feel* every bump in the road," Bob felt the need to point out.

"No doubt," Lucas replied. "But we still have plenty of painkillers. I'll just grit my teeth and suffer through it. It's still better than twiddling my thumbs here and watching the dust or, since it seems more prevalent in the landscape, *fog* blow past."

Bob expelled a chest-emptying sigh, signaling reluctant acquiescence.

"Fine," he said. "Try not to be too much of a pain in the ass. And if you try to lay the guilt-trip on me one more time . . ."

"I'm done," said Lucas, holding up his hands, and wobbling, and nearly falling backward.

"Do you think you can pack your own clothes and your ration of food and water? The recycler on the rover is twitchy, so we'll need to carry more drinking water, along with the required amount for the fuel cell."

"I'll do my part," he replied. "Is the electrolysis unit for the fuel cell still working properly?"

Bob closed his eyes for a moment, as if he didn't believe that Lucas would do anything but weigh him down, or as if the answer to his question was a weight in itself.

"Barely," he finally said. "I loaded extra hydrogen and oxygen on board, just in case. That will get us to the site. But if it malfunctions, there won't be enough to get us back. So we'd better pray that the factory is still operational. All our telemetry suggests that it is, but that doesn't mean something can't happen to it before we get there. This is our only hope, so *please*, Lucas, stay off my back until we arrive on site. I need full focus."

Hmm, Lucas wondered. Had he been that ornery a patient? He hadn't even considered the stress Bob was under, and that he might be so badgered by guilt that Lucas's comments were adding to the strain. That could lead to more mistakes—something they couldn't afford, if they wanted to get off this rock.

"Bob." He reached out to touch the man's shoulder in a gesture of truce, but instead wound up grasping it—painfully, by the look on Bob's face—to avoid falling over. "I'm sorry. I'm a lousy patient, and you're a fantastic doctor." The words felt like sandpaper in his mouth. "But, really, you're an even better technician and rover expert, and you'll get us there and back without a hitch. I promise I won't cause any more trouble, and I'll do my best to help. I'll even take shifts driving."

Bob snorted. "No, you won't."

"I can help."

"You can drive us over a cliff since you're still on painkillers."

"I'll stop."

"You will not."

"Why do you have to be so stubborn?"

"Why will you not listen to me when I tell you you're not ready? I may be letting you come along, but I'm not backing down on your treatment plan, Lucas. Because I'm your doctor. I'm determined to keep you alive, and the rest of us, too. So there's no way in hell you're driving, you're taking the medicine I prescribe, and unless you can offer useful advice, you'll keep your mouth shut, sit back, and enjoy the ride. *Capiche*?"

Lucas mumbled, "Fine."

"Lucas will behave," said Gita sternly. The look in her eyes was a warning that he'd better comply with her orders this time.

Bob nodded stiffly, zipped his pack closed, and shuffled to the front of the HAB to retrieve another pack from the storage compartment.

Gita slipped closer to Lucas and whispered in his ear. "You understand that Bob's the leader on this expedition, right? And the success of it is so vital we can't afford a mistake. I know you're frustrated with the healing process, and ticked off that you were injured in the first place, and I don't blame you. But if you need a voodoo doll to shove pins into, use me, because you don't need me to repair the factory. I'm not familiar with it. I'm not as essential as Bob for this particular operation, and I deserve some of the jabbing, too."

He looked into her eyes and noticed strain. Both she and Bob were wrung out, not just with the business of survival and repair, but with guilt over his injuries and the team's situation. He did still blame them, but no doubt his injury would be inconsequential in the long run. And so would they. But for some reason, his heart quivered in his chest. And he nodded obediently. And he even smiled and said, "I don't hate you."

She drew herself up and met his gaze with a brief nod.

Then Bob looked in their direction, taking everything in with a scowl. He was probably interpreting their intimate conversation incorrectly, so Lucas added in a louder voice, "I don't hate you either, Bob."

****

THE ROVER BOBBLED along the rocky terrain, shuddering over crusty red rocks and hard sepia soil blistered with pockets of carbon dioxide. Bob had swung a wide loop around the most active area, which still erupted from time to time with a crisp pop and a rusty plume of sand and pebbles.

A lightweight elliptical vehicle composed of carbon fiber and titanium, the Mars rover was essentially a sealed, pressurized motor home. Originally designed for the planet before terraforming had begun, it contained an airlock—a two-man compartment in the back where astronauts could don their spacesuits and then depressurize before venturing out into Mars's thin atmosphere. The atmospheric pressure on Mars was now sufficient to eliminate this step, except they would still need to maintain the seal to keep the required oxygen/nitrogen blend contained within the cabin, and protocol dictated they always leave one person within the safety of its walls during any sortie on the planet's surface.

The rover now angled downward on a thirty-degree slope, threatening to flip nose over rear end and tumble to the bottom of the Kasei Valles. Unfortunately, this was the only route that wouldn't take them hundreds of miles out of their way to get to the Arabia Terra base—a route that demanded they descend into the chasm and then enter the south and still dry portion of the languidly filling seabed on the Chryse Planitia. At this bearing, they'd traverse the shallowest grade, several miles north of the most treacherous region where cliffs plunged downward into a trench as deep as the Grand Canyon, but at a much steeper angle. They'd also avoid water and ice flows, since the sea hadn't extended this far south yet. But the imaging satellite had detected the first sign of liquid water in the Vastitas Borealis, and it extended into the Acidalia Planitia and the northern stretch of the Chryse Planitia.

A gritty layer of fog still hung in the air, obscuring their view through the windshield, which made traveling even more touchy, despite the assistance of automated lidar navigation. The fog and dust might camouflage some objects, such as boulders, from laser detection. The boulders in this region could reach a diameter of up to six feet, and if the rover were to ram into one of those, it could be damaged beyond repair.

"Maybe we should scout ahead," said Lucas.

Bob frowned, but kept his focus on the terrain.

"You know, because of the fog and our angle of descent. If we nick a boulder or skid on loose gravel, we might lose our grip."

Bob's frown deepened. A bead of sweat trickled down his face, winding through a forest of stubble, since he'd been far too busy and preoccupied to shave.

"Lucas has a point," said Gita, gripping the armrests of her seat. "*I* should scout ahead. This slope is far too tricky to leave anything to chance, especially with this perpetual mist."

"It's also risky to walk in this location," said Bob. "If we should experience another CO_2 burst . . ."

"If we lose the rover, it would be far worse," said Gita. "Then we all die. Stop for a minute and let me get prepped."

"I could—" Lucas clamped his mouth shut when Bob shot a supremely frustrated look at him. He stopped the rover, though, and didn't offer any further objections.

Well, at least he'd made an attempt. Lucas shuffled out of his seat and replaced Gita in the navigation chair. He was in no condition to act as guide, anyway. Every fiber in his body throbbed, and every bounce over the ripples in the gradient triggered severe spasms in his belly that made him clench his teeth. Bob and Gita couldn't help but notice how sweat tracked the contours of his jaw and how he strained to keep the nausea at bay, taking an occasional quick gulp of air like a dolphin after an extended dive.

Gita finished squeezing into her elasticized jumpsuit and hiking boots. After threading her arms through the straps of her rebreathing tank, she clamped on the mask and face shield. She stepped through the back door of the crew cabin into the airlock compartment, adding a thumbs-up gesture just as the door thumped closed.

Lucas clipped the mic to his ear and spoke softly. "Be careful."

"Mars demands it," she replied. "I'll be fine."

Bob sat disconsolately in the driver's seat. His hands clasped the wheel tightly. The veins showed through his skin like a leaf stained with methylene blue for inspection under a microscope. His eyes were creased uncomfortably and a peculiar paisley pattern crisscrossed his skin—or at least it looked that way to Lucas, through his opiate-clouded perception. For the first time since the explosion he actually felt sorry for Bob.

Gita's lithe body appeared in front of the rover, looking insubstantial as the mist shimmered in the headlights and swirled around her. She seemed to be floating on cloud. Eventually, the mist swallowed her completely, pinching off the gap she'd nicked in its stream.

"Okay, Bob," she spoke through the mic. "Keep coming. No obstructions here. Some talus, but nothing too loose or unstable."

Bob shifted into gear and eased the vehicle forward, its wire mesh wheels crunching over the duricrust—the salt-hardened surface—and the encrustation of pebbles on the ground. Lucas gripped the armrests of his seat as the jiggling motion ricocheted through his body, particularly his sensitive belly. Damn, this was going to be a long, excruciating trek.

"Stop," said Gita. "There's one monster of a boulder directly in our path. Loop around to your left to avoid it."

Bob swung the steering wheel to the left and crept forward again, the mist still a virtual wall in front of the rover. They proceeded in this halting fashion for the next hour, as they descended the two-mile-long slope. Lucas, when his vision wasn't clouded with pain, noticed the stiffness of Bob's shoulders, the iron grip he maintained on the wheel, the constant flexing of his jaw. Bob was a nervous wreck.

Several times, Lucas was tempted to offer his services as driver. Several times, he chewed on the words and refrained. Another solution would be for Gita and Bob to swap tasks, to at least give them a different perspective and alter the burden of tension. But if he suggested it, it might come across as an order, which he knew they wouldn't appreciate.

But when Bob began swiping sweat from his brow, he couldn't keep quiet any longer.

"Maybe we should stop and rest," he said. "This canyon slope is a hell of a challenge, and you guys must be tired."

Surprisingly, Bob stopped the vehicle and looked over at him, not with annoyance but with a timid grin that was possibly saying thanks.

"Good idea," he said. "This is unquestionably the most challenging terrain on our course. A rest is definitely in order. How about it, Gita?"

"Sure," she gasped. Obviously the slope, the poor visibility, and the exercise itself were taking its toll. Her drooping frame suddenly emerged from the salmon-tinted mist directly outside the windshield. She circled around to the airlock and five minutes later tromped in through the crew cabin. With a long gusty sigh, she collapsed into the seat behind Lucas.

"You okay?" he asked, swiveling around to look at her.

"Fine," she replied. "Just not accustomed to walking downhill for that length of time, especially while watching every step for stability and barely seeing beyond my nose. Brutal challenge."

"Maybe you could take a turn driving." He delivered the suggestion with utmost caution.

Bob glanced at him, his lips twitching, but he remained silent.

But Gita shook her head adamantly. "Not yet." She wrenched open a cupboard at her side, poured water into a mug, and guzzled it in two gulps. "When we get to a fairly level driving situation, I'd happily swap duties. On my feet out there, if I take a tumble I might injure myself, but that would be just another glitch for us. But if I tumble the rover, our chances of survival are practically nil. Bob is the better driver, according to our logged rover training sessions. That's why he hasn't suggested relieving me outside. And I might be in better shape physically," she added tentatively.

She smiled at Bob, and he floated her a feeble grin. He agreed with her on both counts—one which made him seem competent, the other weak.

They sat in silence for the next half hour, Gita and Bob devouring energy bars and swigging high-calorie protein drinks, Lucas trying to nibble and sip his own allotment of food and drink, but still fighting the surges of nausea and pain. Finally, Gita grunted and thrust herself from her seat, wobbling determinedly toward the airlock on stiff legs. Nobody said a word. It required all their energy to focus once again on achieving the bottom of the chasm and hopefully the more benign effluvial outflow channel of the Kasei Valles.

A few minutes later, Gita trudged around the rover and slipped into the impenetrable folds of unrelenting fog. She began calling out instructions, and

Bob guided the vehicle forward, sideways, around, and down, with deft though exhausted hands.

Two hours later, they reached the channel without a scratch on the rover's body, after only one controlled skid, and without a hitch in the vehicle's controls or engine. So far, so good.

"Are you ready to do the driving?" Bob asked Gita. "You've been out there a long time, and this fog isn't showing any signs of dissipating."

"Soon," said Gita. "I'd like to explore the channel down here first. There's a considerable bed of rocks on this side. Must be the outward bend in a meander that deposited debris. And the duricrust isn't very level, either. I'm discovering ripples or bulges, likely from past currents when water flowed through the canyon. Then there's—"

A resounding pop and hiss interrupted her.

"Gita?" asked Lucas. "Are you all right?" He knew that sound . . . intimately.

"Yes, Lucas. I'm fine. I imagine you guessed that was another CO_2 burst. I felt a slight gush of wind and some grit peppered my suit, but nothing too serious. But . . . that's interesting. My feet are cold. Something is rushing along the ground. I'm just going to investi— Hmm. Water? I think there's water seeping into the channel."

Bob stopped the rover, his entire body locked with tension, while Lucas felt a concentrated flush in his chest.

"Maybe seeping isn't the right word. Flowing might be. It's come up to my knees now. I'm heading back, guys." The note of fright in her voice couldn't be mistaken. "Back up the rover."

Bob cranked the vehicle in reverse and ground the tires into dirt. The rover burrowed deeply as it climbed backward and upward. Lucas's heart fluttered frantically in his chest as Gita's gasps and pants carried through the comm. She was obviously sprinting toward the rover. Then he heard an *oomph*, followed by a muffled scream.

"Dammit. Fucking Mars," he heard himself say. But his mind was spinning so frenetically he didn't even realize he'd spoken. He whipped off his safety belt, grabbed a jumpsuit from a nearby drawer, and wriggled into it as quickly as he could manage. Without pausing to catch his breath, he dashed through the crew cabin to the airlock door.

"Lucas," yelled Bob, still grinding the rover backward. "What the hell are you doing?"

Lucas slapped on a mask and face shield at the same time as he jabbed the switch to seal the airlock.

"What do you think I'm doing, Bob?" he asked. "The same thing you did, once. Taking one for the team."

Scanning...

Located: Chapter 26

WALK, DAMMIT, WALK.

Pebbles, cobbles, rocks rolled beneath his feet. Knives, scissors, scalpels of pain sliced into his flesh. Ice, frost, rippling impenetrable fog seeped around him.

Water covered his boots, nipped at his ankles, and triggered prickling sensations up and down his legs. It was liquid, but incredibly cold and frosting into the air as it mixed with dry ice, creating an even thicker blanket of fog.

"Gita," he called. "Where are you?"

"Lucas?" she gasped. "I managed to grab a boulder, and I'm standing on it. But the water is rising, and I don't know in which direction to swim for the rover. Where are you and Bob? Give me a directional sound. I think my GPS has gone haywire from the soaking. God, it's cold." Her teeth clacked through the comm.

"I'll give you a sound to orient by," said Bob. "And Lucas, get back in here! Gita can swim. You can barely walk."

"'Get back in here?'" said Gita, aghast. "Lucas, don't be ridiculous. You're in no shape to rescue me."

A long, strident honk resounded in the chasm, but despite its hollow quality

Lucas could certainly determine its direction. Which gave him an idea.

"Gita," he said. "Can you toss some rocks into the water? I might be able to find you if I hear the splashes."

"No, Lucas. I'm swimming toward the rover now. Keep sounding off every thirty seconds, Bob. Lucas, for God's sake, return to the rover."

A distinctive plop sounded nearby—to his left and downstream. Well, that would work too. He angled in her direction, wading into ever deeper water.

The water resembled tomato soup, dyed the color of the iron-rich rock and dust, stirred with a concoction of sand and ice. As the new flow disrupted the dry soil and the solidified CO_2—dry ice—in the channel, it boiled away the top layer, churned up mud, and increased the liquid's viscosity enough that it battered his legs and threatened to sweep his feet out from under him. But even with the roar and chatter of the gushing water, he heard desperate efforts to swim—strokes and splashes, gasps and moans.

Could Gita really contend with this aggressive flow? Would he be able to reach her? Would he be swept away soon, too, leaving Bob to fend for himself on Mars with limited oxygen and supplies and an impossible route to navigate, with only a small likelihood of survival?

What had he been thinking, plunging recklessly out of the hatch to save a woman he barely knew and shouldn't give a damn about, anyway?

Maybe it was simply a matter of survival. He plodded forward, the pain nagging at his belly, the cold numbing his damaged legs. If he let her die, he would have one less specialist, one less body, one less extra pair of hands to fix all their broken parts and launch them back toward Earth. One less meant less chance of success.

But he knew it was more than that.

He charged through the current, prying each foot from the mud and placing it awkwardly onto the next unstable surface—sometimes this was sagging gravel, sometimes ankle-twisting rocks, sometimes sinking sand or spongy mud. He was rapidly losing feeling in his legs, but he continued to force them woodenly onward.

The splashing teased his ears, sounding ever closer.

"Gita," he said. "I can hear you. You're right in front of me. Keep coming."

He waved his arms, and the steam in his path parted momentarily. The electric blue shimmer of her jumpsuit reflected into his eyes, merely six feet away. But she was flailing as if she was losing strength. She was sputtering helplessly into her mask. The water seemed to be driving her backward the same distance she was able to advance with her weak strokes.

Even though he was nearly spent—his body screamed at him from the exertion and from the torque on his fragile muscles and injured flesh—he leaped through the discharge and grabbed her arm. But now he found himself in a deeper segment of the channel, and he could no longer stand.

Well, it was either swim or die.

Maintaining his grip on Gita's arm, Lucas kicked and stroked with his free arm as Gita stretched and burrowed the gloved fingers of her opposite hand into his suit. She wound herself around him, her arms circling his neck and shaking loose his grip to free his other arm. She added desperate kicks to keep them afloat.

Lucas kept swimming, plunging his arms into the coarse stream, kicking frantically, as he applied his internal direction-finding radar to each blare of Bob's horn. *To the left, to the left, to the left.* With each stroke, he could feel the throb of his pulse bounding in his ears, as the cold and toil sapped his strength, bitter length by bitter length. The water around him leaped and splashed in chaotic joy, rounding bends and boulders, steaming into frost, crystallizing into ice, chilling him to the bone.

"Don't give up," gasped Gita, as if sensing that he was weakening.

She kicked and gripped, her body shuddering against his.

He wouldn't. He couldn't. He was a god, compared to her. A tower. A pyramid of ancient stone. An immovable obelisk. He could withstand the pulse of a growing flood.

Then a monstrous wave splashed over him, and he sank below the surface. Luckily, their tanks were lightweight and filled with gas, so they bobbed up again. He kicked once more, kicked and stroked and chopped through the wave. A shock ran through him when his feet tapped the ground. He scrabbled and found purchase.

Gita still clung to him, so he hoisted her up, even though the effort threatened to topple him over. Plodding forward, he plowed through the current, shivering, and dragging Gita along until she found footing that allowed her to keep her head above water. But he didn't release her yet. He unclasped her hands from his neck, simply so he could breathe more easily, and seized her arm once again.

"Keep . . . walking," he sputtered. "To the left."

She nodded and clutched his arm, giving it a squeeze that was both an answer and a gesture of warmth and gratitude.

And so the monumental effort continued. They walked, splashed, contended with floating debris, shivered, shuddered, tripped and fell, plucked themselves from the stream, discovered shallower water, stumbled forward, felt their clothes crystallize, muttered, gasped, nearly cried—in fact he was sure Gita was crying—staggered, encountered a slow rise beneath their feet, kept listening to the beacon—Bob's beacon—crunched onto solid ground, parted the mist, located a twinkling light, spotted the anomalous emerald of the rover's paint, groped toward it, opened the hatch, collapsed inside.

As soon as the airlock seal had engaged, the rover's motor turned over. Its wheels ground into the rock, as they felt it toddling upward in a slow, steady creep. Lucas and Gita stared wordlessly at each other, too exhausted, cold, and miserable to move, even to remove their wet, frozen bodysuits. The rover finally came to a halt, but before they could utter a word, Bob opened the inner hatch and swooped down on them, his arms laden with blankets.

"You'll have to strip out of the suits," he instructed, as they shivered and shivered.

His voice became a constant drone in their ears.

"Oh, for God's sake. Lucas, you've reopened your wound."

"Gita, drink some hot chocolate. Attagirl."

"Let me towel you off."

"Hold still, dammit. I need to stitch that closed."

"I must say, I'm glad you're alive, but that was a stupid stunt."

"Do you need a shot for the pain?"

"I'm tempted to pump warmed IV solution into you guys. Hypothermia's a bitch."

"Soup. It's soup, Lucas. Not motor oil. Sip as much as you can."

This went on until the adrenaline wore off, and Lucas was finally able to ignore all the prickling and zapping sensations of his chilled, pain-riddled body. A soft oblivion enveloped him, as he sank into a delicious coma. It was strange, though. Just before he fell asleep, he caught a glimpse of Gita staring at him, her steady, clever eyes evaluating him with a depth she rarely turned his way.

A RUMBLE EVENTUALLY penetrated Lucas's narcotics-numbed hearing. It shimmied through his body, igniting a series of sparks. His eyes fluttered open, as he nudged himself toward consciousness, revealing the tight confines of the rover, which wobbled this way and that. He shifted, attempting to roll over, but something gripped his chest and legs, halting any movement. He looked down. Ah, they'd belted him in, to keep him from rolling out of the bunk.

Fumbling with stiff, cold-reddened fingers, he finally managed to unbuckle the top belt. The one around his legs required considerable abdominal effort, which nearly wrung a yelp from him as he bent and hunched and jerked at the metal latch.

"What are you doing, Lucas?" asked Gita. Her voice blared down on him from above.

As he looked up, she crouched beside the bunk, coming to eye level with him.

"We have to travel quickly because the water level is rising. Bob is sure we'll get ahead of the flow if it isn't too substantial, and that's the only way we'll make it to the Arabia Terra base. But you need to rest and recover, so you're better off staying in the bunk for now."

She tapped his shoulder, casting him a flinty look.

"I don't want to lie down anymore," he grumbled. "I need to change position, and . . . and I'm thirsty. I'm not a child. Let me sit up, at least."

Gita glanced toward the cockpit and met Bob's eyes in the mirror. He shrugged and sighed.

"Okay," she said, through a wan smile.

She released the buckle around his legs and laced her arms around him, tilting him upright as he shuffled his legs over the edge of the mattress. He grunted as a burst of pain radiated from his belly; but he gritted his teeth and took deep, guarded breaths until it subsided.

"Are you all right?" he asked, as much to redirect the focus from himself as to inquire, since she was clearly in better shape than he was.

"Can't seem to shake the chills," she said. "Otherwise I'm doing quite well, thanks to you."

She placed her hand on his shoulder, igniting a medley of strange and wondrous sensations. Not arousal; this was something new. He'd acted totally selfless and contrary to his core beliefs to save this woman. Now she believed him to be something other than what he truly was—a knight of some sort. She had faith in him. She thought he'd acted out of compassion. Had he? Could he possibly value her beyond the skills she could contribute to their survival? It was a frightening thought. He couldn't afford deep feelings, least of all for these people.

"I—" he said, words forming knots in his throat. "We need you to pilot the *Phoenix*. I couldn't allow—"

"Yes. Of course," she said. "In your condition only adrenaline made it possible. But what caused the adrenaline?"

"Survival instincts," he muttered.

"Right."

"Can we really out-pace the discharge of the river? I'm guessing volcanic activity has thawed frozen aquifers underground and opened channels into the canyon. Most of the CO_2 will probably bubble out of the soil as vapor, and some of the water droplets will freeze immediately, but if it doesn't slow down it will eventually become a steady stream, and there may be no way around it."

"Raft?" she suggested, with a mirthless chuckle.

He shook his head and gazed through the windshield. Puffs of fog still blotted the landscape, although enough breaks had developed to allow fairly effective visual and lidar scanning. Bob abruptly pivoted the rover to avoid striking a three-foot-wide boulder in their path.

"Well, you didn't risk your life to rescue Gita just to give up now, did you, Lucas?" asked Bob. His shirt-back was drenched with sweat, and he didn't chance a peek over his shoulder, but he'd obviously been following their conversation. "We'll keep trying to advance to the base until we run out of options."

"We don't have enough water for the fuel cell to get beyond the Arabia Terra base, do we?" asked Lucas, thinking that if they headed back, perhaps over the

Tempe Terra to the Alba Patera base, they would encounter another propellant plant while traveling over easier terrain, although it might bring them frighteningly close to the Tharsis volcanic mountain chain, which was becoming uncomfortably active.

"No," said Bob succinctly. "It's Arabia or nothing."

Lucas nodded and lost his balance as another burst of pain shot through him. Gita instantly clutched his shoulder and steadied him.

"Well then, let's hope there's an end to this surge. If we were back in the *Phoenix*, gazing down from a safe distance, we'd be eyeing this with wonder. A spontaneous river on Mars. A new source of nourishment for the algae blooms, and soon, hopefully, more sophisticated plant life. Another sign of the planet's rebirth."

"I *was* eyeing it with wonder," said Gita, "until it nearly swept me away. But this planet is volatile right now, and not exactly kind to our species yet, particularly when we have to rely on manufactured oxygen supplies and limited fuel production plants. I just wish we'd"—her voice dropped decibels—"listened to you. But then," she whispered, "we'd never have gotten to know you. Not really."

Lucas felt a new kind of pain erupt. But it wasn't physical.

"I'm an ass," he whispered back. "Just like Bob said. Don't ever forget that."

Gita shook her head.

"No, you're not. Irritating? Yes. Pigheaded? Absolutely. But also brilliant and bold and . . . tender in here." She patted his chest.

Before he could protest, she pivoted and headed back to the cockpit. She didn't know him. She had no idea what he was capable of. She'd placed him on a pedestal, and he didn't belong there. He wasn't worthy of her faith. And, in all truth, he was the devil that Mars harbored. If they were to survive this situation and escape the planet, he would quickly lose his shine and be forever tarnished in her eyes.

Scanning...

Located: Chapter 27

FRANK STUMBLED OUT of his open-air bedroom—essentially a canvas-covered frame on a raised wooden platform—in the safari lodge north of Maun on the southern edge of the Okavango Delta. It was early July, before the annual river floods, and it would soon be winter. Although the rains had not yet begun to roll in from the Angola highlands, the air was nippy and a brisk wind blew from the south, carrying with it a little dust from the Kalahari desert. Frank headed over to the lodge's restaurant, and settled into the wicker chair on the veranda. From here, he could survey the eastern tip of the island—a dry kidney-shaped patch of land surrounded by wetlands—as a waiter served him *rooibos* tea. The warmth was welcome, but unfortunately, he craved the caffeine that the redbush tea lacked. He blinked bleary eyes and ducked automatically as a baboon swung over his head, leaping from the dark, dense crown of a nearby mangosteen tree.

"You want breakfast?" asked the waiter, a short, muscular man with tight ringlets of mauve-dyed hair and a sullen tilt to his chin.

"What's on the menu?" asked Frank, remembering discovering on his last trip to the Okavango two years before that the people often snacked on mopane worms—sundried moth caterpillars that tasted like a savory blend of salt and dirt. His mouth didn't water at the prospect.

"Chicken necks with fat cakes, or *motogo*."

"*Motogo* it is, then," said Frank.

Sorghum porridge certainly sounded more appealing to his unsettled stomach than chicken necks.

The wind ruffled the parched grass around the lodge and bent the tall stalks of papyrus that marched along the water's edge and a short way into the swamp. The water level was low at this time of year, as moisture evaporated or was siphoned off by the thirsty Kalahari. Before the rains in Angola swelled the river, the edges of the Kalahari Desert would encroach on the Delta, greedily devouring the fingers of water that meandered in channels between palm islands. A *!Kung* Bushman had once told him that as the water drained, bottlenecks would develop and concentrate the number of fish. This, in turn, would attract toothy tigerfish—large predators. As these creatures became crazed by the surfeit of prey, a feeding frenzy would ensue. Sometimes people would be caught in the middle of the frenzy and would also be consumed. Frank shuddered. It was best to avoid the channels at this time of year, but, of course, Baruti knew of a *!Kung* clansman who might still be living centrally in the Delta and had suggested they begin their search there.

A grunt interrupted Frank's thoughts. He looked up to see Pedro easing his bulky frame into the reedy chair opposite him, which produced an alarming creak. It had been both comforting and annoying to have Pedro along. Luckily, they'd managed to procure a reasonably priced fake passport in New York on their way to Boston, and had triggered no alarms while passing through Customs on the series of flights to this distant tip of Africa. But since they'd arrived, Frank had been forced to share a room with Pedro, since the lodge had very few rooms and was fully booked. Frank had gotten little sleep, between the man's blustery snores and the shrieking of the monkeys and baboons outside.

"Noisy freakin' place, ain't it?" said Pedro, releasing a deep sigh and setting his chin in his palm. "Whatch'ou got there? Tea? I could use a coffee or, even better, a beer."

"I know what you mean," said Frank. "And if the noise weren't enough, it's the damn mosquitoes buzzing around your head all night." *And the snoring snorts that could put a hippo to shame.*

The waiter silently materialized again, beside their table, and deposited another cup of raspberry-tinted tea in front of Pedro.

"Breakfast?" he asked, in a reproachful tone.

"Sure. You got some eggs?"

The waiter shook his head.

"Cereal? Toast?"

"We have porridge," said the waiter. "Or chicken necks with fat cakes."

A devilish smirk touched the corners of his lips. He must revel in the grimaces his American and European guests displayed at their menu options, which explained why he emphasized that particular dish. Furthermore, he looked like he'd rather dump the food on their heads than serve it to them.

"Seriously?" said Pedro. "Before coffee? Porridge, then."

The waiter nodded and slipped away as silently as he'd appeared.

"I'm not sure I can get into the food here, man. I don't—damn!"

The same baboon that had swung onto the rafters of the veranda earlier—a lean, ropy fellow with a melancholy face—now swung back, even lower, brushing Pedro's head with his robust butt before grasping hold of a branch of the mangosteen tree and leaping away from the lodge.

Frank chuckled. "And you thought the Everglades was a jungle," he said. "At least he hasn't tossed shit at you, yet."

Pedro raised his eyebrows with a look of disgust that was priceless for such a worldly guy. "He would do that?"

"He's an animal, man. He would do just about anything. But at least he wouldn't wrap himself around you and squeeze the life out of you."

"I guess I can take a bit of shit," said Pedro, the revulsion dissolving into a grin. "Now, Frank. I wanted to talk to you without the others around. And since the African guy and the girl ain't up yet, this might be as good a time as any."

"Sure," said Frank.

Pedro snatched his cup from the wooden table and took a generous gulp. He smacked his lips in a confused manner, and shrugged noncommittally. An acquired taste, this *rooibos* tea. Frank didn't mind it himself, but it had taken a few days to get accustomed to it on his last trip to the Okavango.

"Is there something here besides beads that you're really interested in?"

"Answers," said Frank.

Pedro shook his head. "Not good enough. What are those answers worth to you, man? Do you think these miners are sittin' on diamonds, whatever other shit they're up to?"

Frank felt the tea bubbling in his gut. "So you don't believe that I'm pissed off about the killings? You think, just like Felicity, that it's all about the money. You, yourself, said the murders probably weren't about money, mining, or weapons. Yes, you and I have a deal, and it involves a treasure hunt. And yes, I think there are probably a few pockets of diamonds scattered around this territory that haven't been found, despite centuries of digging. But I have no interest in mining gems and all the blood that has been spilled for them on this continent. This place, the artifacts, the people; it gets into your blood. The *!Kung* rituals, their pageantry, their rhythm; it taps something in your soul. I can't stand the thought that someone just . . . *iced* these people. People I studied. People I . . ." He couldn't express the strange love affair he'd had with the *!Kung* over the years. Something his father had scorned, of course.

Pedro sloshed the tea around in his cup and sipped at it, his forehead profoundly creased.

"I never heard any of those science guys talk about a soul before."

"Well, that's because it would make them look extreme, biased, and illogical. Science must always be objective. Religion, and by extension the belief in the soul, demands that we connect *specific beliefs* to our spirituality. And there are so many specific and disparate beliefs in this world that it's easy to get confused and frustrated.

"Religious stories are often based on mythology; but the foundations are ignored because it might contradict the core beliefs of the religion. But if you keep working your way backward, you find that people have functioned in the same way since the dawn of time. Even in primoridial times, a song could transform mood. A dance or a ritual could cleanse guilt. A painting could soften the harsh lines of the world. These people had it all, even at the beginning—art, music, religious rituals. I think they had more than we have now. I still want my treasure, but when Baruti told me these people were gone, I felt like smashing my scroll to pieces."

"What scroll?" chimed a distinctly feminine voice from right behind his chair.

Damn. Couldn't Pedro have warned him? But the man still seemed absorbed in Frank's words, his Sasquatch hand scratching his bald pate.

"Nothing," he muttered, as Felicity ducked under another low-hanging baboon and sat beside him at the table.

"Did you find something besides beads in Florida that you didn't tell Dr. Lugan about?"

"No, Felicity. Bodies and beads were all that I found. Oh yeah. And a big snake."

The girl tossed windblown strands of auburn hair out of her eyes and glared at him.

"Don't keep playing the sympathy card, Frank. It might work with everyone else, but it doesn't work with me."

Tea suddenly appeared in front of her, and the breakfast options were recited. Felicity passed on the chicken necks, too.

"What does work with you?" he asked. "Oh, I forgot. Greek gods and their counterparts. Like that guy you dated in Greece last summer."

Felicity paused in sipping her tea, a warm blush feathering through her skin. For a moment, Frank thought she was going to chuck the steaming contents in his face.

"I know what you're doing," she said, tamping down her rage. "But I'm not biting this time. You were talking about a scroll and treasure as if you were Long John Silver and somewhere on your person had secreted a map."

"I was talking about how devastated I was to learn of the loss of the *!Kung*."

"So devastated you wanted to 'smash your scroll to pieces.' Not rip, but *smash*. There are very few scrolls in the world that you could smash."

"Trip of the tongue. I meant rip. And it was just a scroll I found in Egypt last year that I've finally gotten around to examining lately. Worth a lot, but not worth anything when you compare it to these people."

"Uh huh," she said, sipping her tea. Before she could probe any further,

Baruti swung around the corner of his camp-style room and entered the dining area on the veranda. He smiled broadly at them.

"Good. You're all up," he said. "We have a long journey ahead of us today, by *mokoro*, so I suggest you eat hearty."

"*Mokoro*?" asked Felicity.

"Hand-carved dug-out boat, something like a canoe. It's just a short hike to the nearest channel, which is our access point to the main channels in the Delta."

He strode around the table and settled comfortably in a chair across from Felicity.

"Um, aren't there crocodiles in the channels?" she asked, a quiver in her voice. This was the first time she'd shown any trepidation about their excursion.

"Yes, of course. Hippos, too. But we can usually keep the crocs at bay, and if we run into hippos, well . . ." He shrugged.

"Well?"

"We'll have to backtrack and detour around them," said Frank, remembering his one and only encounter with hippos. They weren't exactly obliging, and they weren't exactly friendly. The Great Wall of China would be easier to bust through, and safer, even if guarded by Qin Shihuang's army.

"I see," she said, stroking her teacup.

The waiter appeared and plopped steaming bowls of *motogo* on the table, then slapped a plate full of chicken necks and fat cakes in front of Baruti. The waiter hadn't even taken Baruti's order, but maybe he didn't have to. All the men at the lodge seemed quite familiar with the biologist. Baruti grunted his thanks in Setswana, eyeing the plate in delight, as if he found the meal genuinely appetizing.

As he dug in, though, and began devouring the fat cakes, he stopped chewing momentarily and returned Frank's stare. Frank lowered his eyes and dipped his spoon into the porridge.

"It tastes far better than your hamburgers," he said.

"I'm sure it does," said Frank, dipping, slurping, and swallowing. "I had my share of the local food on my last trip here. I can't say I love all the dishes, but I can't say I hate them, either."

Baruti grunted, gnawed, then bit off a substantial chunk of chicken. But instead of looking at Felicity—who kept throwing him odd fluttery glances—or eyeing Pedro—who was searching for the sugar pot—he keep angling his head and his overly intense gaze toward Frank.

"What was your least favorite dish?" he asked.

"Um, I don't know," said Frank. He didn't want to appear rude, but Baruti was forcing the issue.

"Let me guess."

The African ground the chicken between his molars with extreme gusto, then threw out the question that Frank had known would come.

"Mopane worms?"

Baruti grinned a merciless, unholy grin.

"Worms?" said Felicity, swallowing her porridge audibly.

"Actually, they're moth caterpillars," said Frank. "And they're delicious." He hoped Baruti understood sarcasm.

Baruti chuckled. "They're not so bad, especially when they're cooked with tomatoes, onions, and garlic. And they're chock full of protein, iron, and calcium. Very nutritious. And they taste, well . . ."

"Memorable," said Frank.

"Will we have to eat these memorable worms?" asked Pedro, obviously not enthused.

"Well, they are great snacks for when you're on a trek. Something like trail mix." He smiled. "We'll need sufficient calories and protein to keep up our energy level."

"Yes, we will. Why not trail mix?" said Frank, regretting not having packed every nonperishable item in his cupboard for this trip.

"Sorry," said Baruti. "They don't carry it here. You'll have to make do with the local cuisine."

He gripped his tea cup and slurped appreciatively. But before he set it down, a spasm ran through his arm, causing him to splash some of the steaming liquid onto the table. Baruti frowned, set the cup down, and continued.

"Or would you rather I killed a python and roasted it over a fire?"

Frank didn't know how to read Baruti's teasing. *Is he gauging my stability?* he wondered.

"I don't know if I'd want to eat the thing, but I wouldn't mind seeing it dead. I don't think I'll ever look at a snake the same way again."

"And did you adore snakes before the attack?" asked Felicity, joining in the ribbing.

"No, I suppose not. I never really did get into the snake worship thing when I studied in Egypt. But I'd rather not cross paths with a snake at all, this time around. You'd better keep your shears handy," he said to Pedro.

The man sipped his tea and grinned.

Despite his snake experience and the trauma it had inflicted, Frank found that he felt quite at peace venturing into snake territory with a local man who was handy with guns like Baruti, and a snake snipper with a well-conditioned body like Pedro. Or maybe he was just being blissfully ignorant.

"Well, I can't imagine the same"—something nudged his shoulder. Probably the baboon again—"thing can"—it touched his neck—" happen to a guy"—it whipped around his head and blinded him—"tw— What the hell?" he yelped, leaping to his feet.

The serpentine *thing* fell away as soon as he left his chair. He turned while backing up, astonished that no one was reacting in any way, except with . . . laughter.

The long, gray, snake-like thing bopped him in the nose. It was attached to a long gray face with enormous floppy ears, one of which had a jagged rip in it, as if a hungry crocodile or belligerent hippo had torn off a healthy chunk. The enormous beast placed a gigantic circular foot on the flimsy wooden veranda, causing it to groan, and tore a mangosteen fruit from the tree branch that waved above Frank's head.

"I see you've met Gertrude," said the waiter, smiling maliciously as Frank was showered with leaves. "She's a bit of a nuisance, but rather harmless. We tell people who complain that the animals were here first. If you can't live with them, you shouldn't have come for the 'safari experience.'"

Baruti murmured his agreement, while gazing at the elephant with an adoring look on his face.

"I didn't really come for the 'safari experience,'" said Frank, picking leaves from his hair. "And the *!Kung* were here almost as long as the animals. But I can live with Gertrude."

The waiter, who'd probably expected him to say something quite different, tilted his head and examined Frank thoroughly before giving a considered, protracted nod. Then he grabbed a broom and shooed the elephant away.

Scanning...

Located: Chapter 28

FELICITY WAS CAREFUL not to rock the boat. The *mokoro* sat so low in the water, and the green and golden papyrus reeds reached so high above her head, that it seemed she was gliding through the channel at the same level as the multiple crocodiles she'd spotted since they'd left dry land. Eye to eye, close enough to rub noses or compare cavities. Far too often the creatures had brazenly cruised right up to their boat, but their guide at the helm, Kelong, quickly swatted them away, as if they were annoying flies. He dipped his paddle into the water now, serenely, majestically, standing in the hand-crafted canoe with extraordinary balance. The reeds slipped silently past, but the chirp, mutter, and caw of a thousand birds rang out throughout the Delta, the boat's passage sometimes spurring a burst of feather and wing as white pelicans or orange-beaked skimmers or the occasional woodland kingfisher with brilliant powder-blue plumage took to the sky.

"Are we nearly there?" she asked Baruti for probably the fifth time, sounding like a child but unable to curb her impatience, particularly when another crocodile peered through the reeds.

"Not yet," he replied, his voice grinding down on the words out of sheer exasperation with her, she imagined. "Why don't you try to relax and admire the view? We have the crocodile situation under control. See those islands that rise between the channels? Some of the small ones are actually termitaria—termite mounds."

Felicity wrinkled her nose, but didn't turn to face Baruti, in case he noticed her distaste.

"And will we be walking on these termite mounds?" The thought of crunching over hills of insects held little appeal.

"No. We're looking for a larger island where Kwi might still be living with a few family and group members. They move their *scherms*—improvised huts—from island to island, depending on where they find the best hunting grounds during the changing seasons. But they should be in this general vicinity. They inhabited shanties on the outskirts of Maun several years ago, but were so discouraged with the forced relocation, the unsanitary living conditions, and the shame that modern society heaped on their shoulders for their primitive lifestyle in ages past, they couldn't continue. It was existence, not living. Finally, as filmmakers and writers began to produce more insightful material about them and their origins, and people in archaeological circles began to show them respect, they came to admire their ancestors and decided to return to the old ways. They make themselves scarce and don't welcome intruders, but I got to know them in my surveys of the animal populations in the Okavango region. They trust me, or at least they did before the massacre. If word of the massacre has reached them, they might not welcome a visit, and they might try to hide. We need to catch them before they decamp."

"Don't you think the people you suspect of the massacre might have heard of them too? Maybe they are also searching for them to finish what they started. Maybe they've even found them."

Baruti touched her arm, causing her to swivel her upper body to look at him.

"It's possible. But not many people knew about this particular group, so I'm certain they're still alive and well."

His touch was obviously meant to reassure her, perhaps to communicate that she would be safe, perhaps to keep her from dwelling on what they might discover on this island. It wasn't a typical Baruti gesture, at least in respect to her. He was more likely to hand her a gun, either literally or figuratively, and say, "Deal with it, whatever may come." But maybe he just wanted to touch her. The notion made her a little uncomfortable. She liked him—more than anyone she'd ever met—but she wasn't certain that she desired him.

She was tempted to slip out of his touch, but she let his hand stay there, gently grazing her elbow, until it was calmly retracted to his lap.

"I hope so," she said.

"Wow," said Frank as his *mokoro* skimmed alongside theirs, a slim sweep of battered wood that now matched their speed prow for prow. "You guys look intense. Worried about the crocs?"

"Not at all," Felicity replied, eyeing another scaly log drifting among the reeds. "They seem to have enough antelope to eat."

She waved at the small herd of sitatunga, tawny creatures that were partially striped and partially spotted. They splashed through the shallows amid the water berries in quick hops, scattering dragonflies, then dashed onto a nearby island.

"The crocs won't bother you in the boat, unless they're full-size adults with big appetites," said Baruti. "But if you fall in and actively splash and kick, they might decide you'd be an easy meal. So whatever you do, don't splash and create a ruckus if you fall in. Some people have lost limbs in the Okavango before they could be rescued."

No longer reassuring, are you, Baruti?

They rounded a bend in the channel and entered a narrowing passage that erupted with miniature fountains. Small fish leaped out of the stream, silver scales glinting in the bright sunlight. One even landed in their canoe, flopping about before the guide scooped it up with his paddle and tossed it back in.

Kelong, their stoic guide, looked nervous for the first time since they'd set out. He mumbled something to Baruti in Setswana. With a subtle twist of the paddle, he redirected the *mokoro* toward the nearest island—a lump of grassy land dotted with squat phoenix palm trees and a few thorny acacia and scrub bushes.

"Are we at a potential rendezvous location?" Felicity asked, since they were obviously landing.

"Possibly. But most likely not," said Baruti. "Kelong would rather not take the boat through the feeding area."

"Feeding area? *Crocodile* feeding area?"

"No," said Frank, leaping out of his own *mokoro* and onto the shallow, muddy bank. "Tigerfish."

"Tigerfish?" She pictured tangerine beasts with black stripes that were twice her size and had enormous spike-toothed jaws. "Never heard of them."

"They only live in certain areas of Africa," said Frank, now playing the expert. That annoyed her. "The Zambezi and here. The goliath tigerfish are even bigger, but they're farther north."

"How big?" she asked, not really wanting to know.

"Three feet, at most," said Baruti. "The Congo specimens can grow as large as five feet, but they never get that big here. They aren't that dangerous, either, except at this time of year, when the fish are forced into smaller and smaller channels as the water recedes. At bottlenecks like this, the abundance of readily available food triggers a feeding frenzy in the tigerfish, and they act in some respects like piranha. They can be so violent as they gorge themselves that they could tip the boat. And they won't distinguish between the fish and you, so we'd rather not guide the boat through the middle of their feast and provide them with a smorgasbord."

Felicity gulped and quickly abandoned the *mokoro*. Kelong dragged the boat over the mud and between the tufts of grass on the island, just as another fish flipped onto the shore and flopped among the reeds.

Pedro had joined Frank on dry land, but he kept gazing at the roiling water, thoroughly intrigued.

"I bet they're goin' to feel very sick after today," he said, chuckling.

"Plump and groaning," said Baruti, flashing a smile.

"I wouldn't mind seein' one," Pedro said.

"We're not here to fish," said Baruti, obviously not in the mood for a delay in their search.

But Kelong, ever the accommodating guide, snatched the flip-flopping fish from the grass, hooked it to a fishing pole he pulled out of the canoe, and tossed it into the water.

Within seconds, the line jerked and stiffened. He reeled and tugged until he had wrenched a two-foot tigerfish out of the water. The fish floundered and gasped, but continued to chomp on the bait with glistening, spiky, quarter-inch teeth.

Felicity shuddered. The silvery fish was indeed lined with several black stripes that resembled its namesake. And no doubt it could inflict serious damage with its needle-sharp teeth. The predator kept scissoring its jaw, before the guide chucked it back into the water.

"Sideshow over?" asked Baruti, sending Kelong a castigating glare. "We probably have many more miles to travel before nightfall. I'd like to at least scout a safe island where we can sleep, if we don't find Kwi."

"We're sleeping out here?" asked Felicity, feeling uncomfortable again. With crocodiles, tigerfish, maybe even some lions in the neighborhood, she didn't relish the thought of sleeping outdoors. Plus, it was considerably colder than she thought it would be in Africa. But the real reason was something she'd rather not dwell on. She'd be sleeping near Baruti again, just as in those first few days in Ontario. And although she felt safe in his presence, or at least *safer*, she also felt awkward because she hadn't determined her feelings for him yet.

"Yes," said Baruti. "Surely you realized that. Surely it can be no more challenging than sleeping in the bitter north of Canada. And it certainly will be warmer."

"Brutal," said Frank, smiling obnoxiously. "Maybe we can find some bodies for you to dig up, just so you'll feel more at home."

She scowled at him. Why did he always have to bait her? Then it occurred to her she'd be sleeping next to him, too, as well as his buddy, whom she found slightly creepy. The fact that he'd saved Frank was small comfort, since she and Frank were constantly butting heads. Her choices were limited, with only three small tents between them. Maybe a shaggy wildebeest would be just the ticket.

Kelong shouldered the *mokoro*, and Frank's guide, Dave, hoisted the other canoe. Both men easily supported the weight as they headed across the island. They followed a well-worn path, which was likely an animal track that had been trampled and furrowed by the passage of elephants or hippos or possibly even rhinos. A few amber birds flitted out from beneath the blanket of grass. A speckled monitor lizard scampered away as they disturbed a hidden nest. The frenetic splashing of the fish faded into the distance.

Felicity followed Baruti, his broad shoulders obliterating any view ahead on the trail. Frank trod close behind her, his asthmatic breath occasionally gusting against her neck. Once she stumbled, her weak leg dragging and catching a stone. To her irritation, Frank leaped forward and caught her before she fell. He juggled her in his spindly arms for a few seconds, then stood her upright again.

"I would have been fine," she snapped, prompting Baruti to turn around.

"Yeah," said Frank.

"I trip once in a while. It happens. You don't have to catch me."

"Sure," said Frank.

"I'm strong enough to do anything you guys can do."

"Right," said Frank.

"I wasn't the one who was nearly eaten by a python."

Frank narrowed his eyes. "Lucky you," he said.

"Frank," said Baruti. "I know it's no imposition to catch a falling person when you're trotting right behind her, but next time, let her fall."

Frank smiled triumphantly. Felicity glanced back at Baruti and saw that his face had cracked into a grin, too.

"I guess I'm something of a joke to all of you, aren't I? The bog excavator. The go-to girl, whenever they unearth a mummy. The pathetic kid who can barely walk."

Baruti sighed and shook his head. "You are both pathetic kids," he said, "because you underestimate yourselves and are on the defensive all the time. Does it make you feeble, a liability, the fact that you have a few disabilities? Actually, I think it makes you stronger than most people, because you have adapted and overcome, prevailing in a difficult field despite your limitations. Would you have hurt yourself if you had fallen? Probably not, because the mud is soft. Was Frank actually being kind by catching you and preventing a possible injury? Yes, especially since he doesn't like you very much. Was he being overprotective or offending you in some way by his attention? No. It appeared to be nothing more than an involuntary reaction. And Frank, no one could have survived that python attack unaided. Your only weakness is your inability to laugh at yourselves."

With that, he turned and strode after the disappearing guides, accelerating the pace, which made Felicity stumble more than once. This time Frank didn't even raise a hand to steady her.

But he did mutter something at her back that she did her best to ignore.

"Hopefully next time you'll fall in a pile of elephant dung. Then I'll laugh. I'll laugh longer and louder than you've ever heard anyone laugh before."

AN HOUR LATER, they reached the other side of the island. Baruti explained that the islands were usually much smaller—a few dozen feet across—but with the drop in water level at this time of year, they could expand to several square miles. But there was no sign of Kwi and his clan on this island. They'd have to travel deeper into the Okavango.

The guides slid their *mokoros* back into the water—which was now placid and thankfully crocodile- and tigerfish-free—and they began paddling through the channel again. Felicity wondered why she seemed destined to explore murky, muddy water and, more often than not, liberate corpses from said water and mud. Was it because she'd first tasted freedom when she began handling mud, cradling it in her palms and fashioning discernible shapes? Was it because those shapes were crude, without structure or expression, but instead resembled the crumpled, boneless mummies in the bog?

She feathered her hand through the water, stroking aimlessly, forgetting what might be lurking beneath the surface.

Baruti, who'd switched places with her in the *mokoro*, noticed her gliding pathway of bubbles. He studied it, the creases slashing through his forehead just visible in his profile as he gazed into the water. He sucked in a chest-full of air, then gradually released it into the papyrus maze around them—a long, satisfied sigh. Then he dipped his hand into the tea-colored water just ahead of hers, breaking in a new thoroughfare, laying a flutter of bubbles behind him that collided intimately with and often mingled with her own.

Felicity's heart slammed against her chest. She nearly gasped, but held herself in check just in time. Her mind swirled with a sudden surge of blood. Was it all denial? Or was she suddenly seeing the light? She didn't just want him; she wanted everything about him. She craved his virile power that was ten times stronger than Ben's, her Greek fling, or Shaun's, for that matter. She yearned for the kindness and compassion that shone from him even when he waved a gun around. This was a man who chastised her for not realizing her own strength.

Who dared to laugh at her, and encouraged her to laugh at herself. How she admired his insight, his imagination, his intimacy with animals. Even though he seldom touched the creatures, his eyes followed them with adoration and respect. He never touched them unless they wanted to be touched. But he'd touched her.

Had he known before she did?

She took a deep breath and slid her hand closer to his trail of bubbles, close enough that the bubbles blended frantically and happily.

Baruti looked down at the patterns their hands made in the water. He looked back at her with a puzzled frown. He opened his mouth, and she waited for him to say something momentous.

He said, "I'm not feeling very well."

His lips quivered, and he pitched forward. She reached for him, but it was too late. He fell right into the water and slipped underneath in a stew of bubbles.

Scanning...

Located: Chapter 29

"I DON'T BELIEVE you've heard a word I've said. *Dayna.*"

Rejik snapped his fingers in her direction across the battered wooden table in DiMaggio's, the campus's conventional Italian restaurant.

"Y— yes?" She blinked and took a long savory sip of her coffee, trying to focus on their conversation, which of course centered on her spectacular discovery. She was having trouble concentrating, though.

"I understand this is a difficult time for you," he muttered. "But don't you think you're better off without a philandering husband? You can devote more time and energy to this project and to people who share the same passion for anthropology and archaeology."

Dayna pinched the cup with her fingers, nearly breaking it.

"You know, I haven't thought of Evan in days. At least not at work."

"Then what is occupying your mind, my dear?"

"My students," she said, gritting her teeth.

"Ah, yes. The wayward students. Very disobedient lot you've acquired recently. Where did they toddle off to this time?"

"Botswana," she said. *With a possible lunatic*, she wanted to add, but thought better of it. She hadn't determined which was the actual threat: Dr. Mbeki or the people he was investigating. Either way, disclosing too much information might get her students, or even herself, killed. Besides that, the sensitive material that filled her lab—unique bodies, genetic samples, and a mysterious skull—might also attract nefarious characters.

"I'm surprised you're not chasing after them, as you did when you flew off to the Arctic after that Felicity girl." Rejik scratched his scalp, raising copious strands of fluffy white hair. "And why on Earth would they abandon this discovery, which could net them a prestigious job on the faculty, once they graduate?"

"They heard there might be another body in Botswana, like the Florida and Ontario specimens. They're investigating on their own, since I didn't give them permission to leave. I'm angry, but I have no intention of pursuing them." *Besides, I have no idea where I would even begin to search, in that immense territory. Dr. Mbeki could be taking them anywhere in the Desert or the Delta to search for* !Kung *survivors, if that's what he's really doing.*

Rejik shook his head, a disbelieving frown creasing his face.

"I've never heard of graduate students jeopardizing their careers so recklessly before. Do they think another extraordinary discovery will negate their insubordination? And now you're left without assistance in your own examination of this species. Would you like my help?" His eyes glittered; his lips trembled.

Greed had already replaced the wonder. Not surprising, really. Who wouldn't salivate at the chance to chew on another piece of the evolutionary pie, or explore a unique branch of the phylogenetic-splitting tree?

"No, Rejik. I appreciate the offer, but I have chosen some of my junior students to assist me. I'm sure we can manage."

His eyelashes fluttered downward in dejection. His shoulders sagged slightly.

"Well, if you would at least permit me to release you from the constant toil for a few hours, my dear. Another date, perhaps? The opera? Dinner at The Capitol? You can't keep working 24/7."

Dayna recalled his sloppy kiss on their first date the night before: his lips peeled back from his pearl-white teeth, the wreath of snowy hair surrounding her face like an over-sized cotton ball, then a smack as he thoroughly devoured her mouth. She liked him as a colleague, but she just couldn't get past his awkwardness, his quirks, and his Einsteinian looks.

"I don't think so, Rejik. Not now, anyway. I'm not really over Evan yet, and I need to focus on this extraordinary find. It's kind of you to offer, though."

He looked even more deflated, and for a moment she sympathized. He was obviously lonely. His wife had left him several years ago for a younger man—a less accomplished but wealthier and more attractive man. He must have been devastated. But she just couldn't muster any passion for him. She wished he'd never suggested the date, and that she'd never accepted. Then perhaps she could have shared all the madness surrounding these bodies with him, and her fear for Felicity and Frank. He was an intelligent, principled man who was dedicated to the study of anthropology and had a gift for teaching. She wished she could tap his mind and his empathy regarding all her troubles. But it wasn't to be.

Dayna tossed back the last dregs of her coffee and pushed her chair out from the table, scraping the floor with a cringe-inducing screech.

"It was a lovely lunch, Rejik. Thanks for rescuing me from the lab for an hour. I needed the break. But I must get back to work."

He fondled his own cup forlornly and nodded. "I know you must. Again, if there's anything you need help with . . ."

"I know where your office is."

She smiled, slipped her purse over her shoulder, and headed for the door. The heels of her aging leather pumps clicked on the worn hardwood, and a few faculty members turned their heads, acknowledging her with smiles that were nevertheless solemn. Undoubtedly, they'd heard of her impending divorce. She jammed through the doorway as quickly as she could and nearly sprinted across campus, sad relief spreading through her like a balm. In minutes, she reached the Peabody building and hustled toward the archaeology lab.

As Dayna entered through the pressure-sealed door, Gloria Tenant, a first-year graduate student in the master's program, immediately corralled her. "I'm glad you're back, Dr. Lugan. I'm worried about tissue degradation. I think it's happening already."

"Please keep the body in cold storage and only remove it when it's necessary to extract another sample. Did you spray it with ionized water?"

Gloria nodded and briskly began swathing the body—a male with a teased beard in the Phoenician style—in nonadhesive plastic wrap, zipping closed the body bag around it and trundling the stretcher back to the cooler. Stavros, a second-year graduate student, had photographed the corpse and was examining his digital prints in a corner of the room. Next, he would proceed with an MRI scan, followed by a selective autopsy.

Dayna would pursue the DNA analysis, comparing every body they'd retrieved with the genome of standard samples of *Denisova* and *Neanderthal* and, of course, human and other animals. So far this species was quite unique, matching the other bodies and the Florida samples, but still clearly a distant cousin to *Homo sapiens sapiens*.

She was itching to examine the skull Dr. Mbeki had transported from Botswana. It was fossilized, and therefore very old, but she needed to apply a more technical description than "archaic." She'd already tested a sample to date it, and was awaiting results. But a DNA examination was essential to establish the haplogroup.

First she'd better check her email, though, just to be certain Felicity or Frank hadn't transmitted their location, or sent a red flag. Her eyes still burned when she thought of the note they'd left to explain their absence.

Dear Dr. Lugan,

We're sorry to leave you at such a crucial time, considering our discoveries and the assessment and preservation work that needs to be performed on the remains, but we can't dismiss Dr. Mbeki's suspicions. Frank, his friend Pedro, and I have decided to accompany Dr. Mbeki to Botswana. We will spend a few weeks searching for clues regarding the *!Kung* people and their part in this mystery, particularly the reason why they were executed.

I'm sure you understand the importance of this endeavor. I know that you don't trust Dr. Mbeki after his passionate outburst, and you may not trust my judgment, either, since I still believe Dr. Wilson is innocent of any wrongdoing. But you often trust Frank's judgment because he rarely makes mistakes. Frank is the one who seems most adamant that we embark on this investigation. Even though he's been through that snake attack in Florida, he still insists. I hope you will trust him this time.

Trust him? I trust him to respect and secure artifacts, not cross swords with a maniac or, more likely, a spy.

As for the work, we plan to put in double-time when we return. The bodies should keep, since they have for two thousand years or more. But know that I would never leave you in this predicament if I didn't feel it was necessary.

Keep? They were in a bog, my dear, unexposed to our corrosive air. But you know that.

You might be a little worried about Dr. Mbeki.

A little?

He is very passionate about the *!Kung* people and the animals that are becoming extinct. I'm sure he would never have pulled such a crazy stunt if he weren't desperate to find answers and seek justice for those killed. And I agree. We simply can't sit back and let this nightmare of violence and murder continue. I know that he would never hurt us. We will be quite safe with him.

Like you were safe in Northern Ontario or the Everglades?

I promise we will return as soon as we have explored the situation in Botswana. Again, I apologize.

My best regards,
Felicity

Dayna opened her mailbox, once again spotting the galling letter. No other note from her rebellious students appeared in the email column, even though she'd sent them countless queries. Their silence was unnerving and extremely frustrating. But . . . this was interesting. She'd received a number of videoconference requests over the past hour from Dr. DeLuca, the Canadian geologist in Northern Ontario. Why would he call her, rather than send an email? She was tempted to immediately return the call, but that would delay her examination of Dr. Mbeki's precious skull. She'd booked the thermal cycler for the next two hours to perform a PCR assay on samples of the fossilized bone. Its shape suggested that it might belong to the Khoisan haplogroup, and be simply a *!Kung* ancestor, but the proportions differed from the average Bushman skull. If the fossil was in any way connected to her bog bodies, she had to know. And the Phoenician artifact concealed within the same cave could be a coincidence, but it screamed *link*.

Dayna abandoned her virtual display and opened the locked cabinet in her office. She hadn't trusted this fossil to the open lab, where her students might discover it. She stared for several seconds at the unusual specimen: the short forehead, the chipped jaw, the honeycombed rock within the skull cavity. The supraorbital ridge was no more pronounced than that of *Homo sapiens sapiens*, and far less so than *Neanderthal*. But the jaw seemed more elongated than the average modern human, and the width an inch or so broader. A *Neanderthal*-like bulge existed at the back of the skull—occipital bunning. She removed the skull from the cabinet and set it on her desk, unable to shake scattered pinpricks of unease down her spine.

Had Dr. Mbeki placed an infected specimen in her hands? But if that were really his intention, he would have used the first specimens he'd delivered as his vector. Perhaps she was getting too paranoid.

In this position, her virtual display hovered above the skull—a shimmer of highlighted emails. Then a jangling of climbing notes startled her—the melodic tones of the videophone. The sound rang right through her core. She glanced at the display and saw an odd address blinking in harsh blue letters: Moosonee, Ontario.

What did he want? Maybe it would only take a minute.

But she needed to get the sample processed. And it was essential that she initiate the PCR copying in the thermal cycler, or her DNA tests would be delayed at least another week. The entire science department stood in queue for their turn at the cycler.

No, Dr. DeLuca. You'll have to wait.

She opened her sampling kit and extracted a miniature chisel and tweezers, along with a test tube and bottles of solutions. Switching on the ultraviolet light on her desk to kill any contaminant bacteria, she tapped as deep as she dared into the skull. From there she chipped at the interior aspect of the fossilized bone from the posterior curve, allowing the powder to fall onto a sterilized cloth on her desk. Repeating the process, she extracted five samples from various locations on the specimen, to increase the chance of obtaining at least one or two samples that were uncontaminated with bacteria or with the DNA of some other animal or hominin. Each sample of bone powder she sifted into an extraction buffer solution that would melt the bone and collagen and release the DNA .

The video call had long since stopped ringing but, as she worked, she couldn't help but wonder what could possibly be so urgent.

Once Dayna had retrieved sufficient samples, she headed out the door, the tubes carefully tucked into a cushioned container. Gloria eyed Dayna's bag, as she tinkered with her own specimens, and curiosity seemed to get the better of her.

"What are you working on, Dr. Lugan?" she asked.

"Some samples from a colleague that I've neglected lately, but had promised to inspect. I must clear my desk so our specimens can receive my full attention. It's nothing very interesting, Gloria. Keep working on the Arctic bodies."

"Yes, Professor." Gloria's furrowed forehead suggested she didn't believe a word. And Dayna understood. The discovery of another hominin species would make even the most anal archaeologist drop everything on their desk, regardless of past promises.

"I'll be across campus in the Bauer Core lab."

Now Gloria's eyebrows were reaching for her hairline. Only the most advanced thermal cycler was located at the Bauer lab, and only a priority sample like their new species would warrant a slot in that machine.

"Will you be long?" she asked.

"An hour to prep the samples and initiate the cycle. The lab techs will transfer the copies to a sequencer for me and send the results here, so I shouldn't be longer. Contact me if you hear from Felicity or Frank. No other interruptions though, please."

"Sure thing. I was wondering, where did you send Felicity and Frank? I mean, if they had a chance to work on these—"

"It's none of your concern," Dayna snapped, but immediately regretted her abruptness. "I mean, they would be here, but we may have discovered more of these unusual bodies, so I sent them to investigate."

"Where?" Gloria asked, her eyes suddenly gleaming with eagerness.

"I can't reveal that yet."

The gleam disappeared and the suspicion returned. Gloria was still a neophyte, but she was also very bright.

"Just let me know if they call."

"Yes, Dr. Lugan."

Dayna rushed out of the building, her heels clacking on the pavement and echoing between the old stone libraries, historic halls, and modern concrete-and-glass dormitories on the Harvard campus. She reached the Bauer building in ten minutes, threading her way through the mass of science students wandering in and out of the robotics and instrumentation labs, and hurried into the Bauer Core lab, hoping she hadn't cut the time too short by indulging in an overly long lunch. She began the process of preparing the specimens, performing a silica extraction—using tiny glass particles that attach to DNA—and then spinning the solution in a centrifuge so the glass particles would collect into a pellet. Finally, she could extract the DNA using a wash solution. She had the extracts nearly ready when her cell phone rang. She stripped off one glove, reached into her pocket, and checked the caller ID.

Gloria.

A tremendous rush of hope flooded through her. Frank or Felicity?

She tapped the phone and opened the video link. "Yes?"

"Hi, Dr. Lugan. I know you said not to disturb you until you were finished with the cycler, but this guy's been calling the lab. He says he needs to talk to you, urgently."

"Let me guess. Dr. DeLuca."

"Yeah. That's him. Blond guy, great-looking."

Dayna frowned and couldn't help but glare at the vials on the rack, at her hand gripping the phone right above them.

"He says it's a matter of life or death. I mean he was pretty frantic. I really wouldn't interrupt . . ."

"Just send me his link," Dayna said. "I'm going to initiate the PCR process, and then I'll talk to him. If he calls back, tell him I'll just be a few more minutes."

Dayna tapped her phone to disconnect and slipped her hand into a new sterile glove. She dribbled primer and polymerase solution—which held snippets of DNA code that would copy the original sample—into a number of vials, added the controls to double-check the process, then slid them into the cycler.

"There," she sighed, removing her gloves and instructing the cycler to begin the procedure.

"Now, Dr. DeLuca. What do you want?"

Fumbling her phone from her pocket, Dayna opened the latest contacts and touched the link Gloria had added. The phone tinkled twice, then the link opened up and the long face, arresting catlike eyes, and incredibly well-proportioned features of Shaun Wilson appeared.

"Dr. Lugan. Thank God."

"Dr. *DeLuca*," she said, with disgust.

"I'm sorry. I didn't think you'd return *my* call."

He looked down for a minute, but Dayna sensed an underlying arrogance that suggested he wasn't ashamed at all of borrowing his colleague's name.

"Really? Well it crossed my mind that it was you, when my student described you, but I returned your call anyway."

"I thank you for that," he said. "This is of vital importance. Dr. DeLuca is ill—seriously ill—and I think it might be related to the samples Dr. Mbeki . . . appropriated, or to the visit the team made to the miners. I had to make you aware, so you could assess Dr. Mbeki and maybe quarantine him. Felicity, is she . . . ?"

Dayna leaned against the wall. Her breath . . . She couldn't catch her breath.

"What are his symptoms?" she managed to puff out.

"He was experiencing headaches, the last two days. Then this morning, he came down with a fever, his muscles became spastic, and finally he started screaming in pain. We flew him to Moosonee, but the doctors can't seem to determine the cause or prevent his condition from worsening. They're convinced it's a biological agent, but any treatment they've attempted has been ineffective. He's becoming paralyzed, and if it continues it might arrest his breathing. I—I don't think he's going to make it. Has Dr. Mbeki shown any symptoms? Or Felicity?"

Dayna gripped the cycler, still straining to breathe. The samples Mbeki had brought to the lab . . . Could they still contain a biological weapon, even though nothing had been detected? Could the skull or even something the men had touched be contaminated? She hadn't noticed any signs of illness or odd symptoms in the biologist, except . . . a headache. But then she recalled the quivering of his arm after he'd tucked the gun back into his belt, something she'd associated with nerves. And perhaps his ill-considered behavior was due to this . . . sickness, too.

"Dr. Lugan?" he said, deep concern evident on his face.

"Felicity was all right the last time I saw her. Dr. Mbeki was experiencing headaches. They both left for Botswana yesterday."

"What? Why? What could possess her . . . ? Can you reach them?"

"I've tried, but they don't answer my emails or my calls."

He grimaced, and his image went fuzzy, as if his hand was trembling.

"Then I'll have to go there in person," he said. "I don't know how infectious this is. Where are they?"

"That's just it. I don't know. Both my students left without my permission, against my wishes, so they don't want me to contact them or come after them. All I know is that they're looking for *!Kung* people and artifacts somewhere in the Okavango."

Should she be telling him this? But he was obviously worried, even frantic, and that certainly wasn't the behavior of a killer.

"There must be some way to trace them. I'll fly to Botswana and start searching there. They would need accommodations and flights. And I don't think there are many towns in the Okavango, so that might reduce the search. I should be able to find them, hopefully before anyone else falls ill."

"I'll join you," said Dayna. "This is getting too dangerous for my students."

"Dr. Lugan, I'm not sure—"

"I'm going with you, Dr. Wilson, whether you like it or not."

"Okay, fine. We'll meet at an airport en route and continue together. Since you're an archaeologist, you might have a better idea where we should search, anyway. I just wish I didn't have to leave Tony. But he can't hear me anymore. I think . . . he's already gone." The biologist swallowed a sob.

"I'm sorry," said Dayna, her chest constricting in ever tightening bands.

"He was my friend. Sure, we had our arguments, but he didn't deserve this. You don't believe I'm a killer now, do you, Dr. Lugan?"

She shook her head. The emotions were too genuine.

"I can't let this go any further," he muttered. "I can't let anyone else die." The connection snapped off.

Dayna stared for a long time at her phone, tamping down fear and terror, zeroing in on his last words.

"Let *what* go any further, Dr. Wilson?"

Scanning...

Located: Chapter 30

LUCAS CRADLED A cup of tea in his hand as he rechecked the coordinates on the Mars GPS from his position in the copilot seat beside Gita, who was now the driver. A flutter of unease brushed his belly as the rover skirted the rim of the crater Oxus Patera. Their coordinates were 0 degrees E, 38.5 degrees N, several miles northeast of Mawrth Vallis and the Vitalis Cave, and if their situation weren't so desperate they'd probably stop for a sightseeing tour. But that wasn't the only thing that evoked the sensation of skittering spiders in his stomach. The scientific community had concluded that Oxus Patera and nearby Ismenia Patera exhibited all the features of an ancient supervolcano: scalloped, breached rims composed of multilayered igneous material on low relief. They'd concluded that these features were large collapse structures due to resurgent pyroclastic and lava eruptions.

What had occurred in the past could happen again, particularly since the sleeping volcanoes had now been reawakened.

So far everything looked quiet, though. The fog had lifted; the rippling, pock-marked terrain extended before them in a dusky apricot hue; the slope to their right descended at a moderate angle that posed no real threat to the vehicle, even if it drifted over the edge, something Gita had no intention of letting happen.

They could hear no rumble of unstable ground, no pop and hiss of CO_2 bursts, no rush of unexpected rivers. But fluffy billows of burgundy-tinted cloud hovered to the east, hinting at rain. What an odd circumstance. Rain. On Mars. Odd, but absolutely within the realm of possibility, with all the melted ice and scattered liquid pools on the surface.

"It's so peaceful," said Gita. She turned to him and smiled.

He returned her smile, although his own felt tight. He still wasn't entirely comfortable with the more relaxed relationship she seemed to be cultivating. During the two days it had taken to reach Oxus Patera—twice as long as originally hoped, because of the detour—Gita had smiled at him more often than frowned, her demeanor was far less brusque, and she had included him in every discussion of routes.

He sipped his tea before he replied. "For now."

"Let's hear some optimism, for a change. We didn't think we'd make it this far, after the whitewater channel eruptions. Now we're just one day out from the Arabia Terra base; just one day away from almost assured escape."

Lucas shook his head. "One day's travel to the propellant plant. But we still have to return to the MADVEC, or we'll never escape. And with this treacherous flood extending farther north as long as the aquifer keeps discharging, we might have to take an even longer detour. That is, assuming the plant is still operational and has produced enough fuel for liftoff to orbital rendezvous."

"Killjoy," she remarked. But she slipped him a sidelong look, since no doubt she was well aware of all the ifs and buts in their quest.

"I wish we could stop off at the Vitalis Cave," said Bob, depositing snacks—dried fruit and nuts—beside the mugs of tea he'd prepared, then sitting in the additional seat slightly behind them but within easy view when Lucas swiveled his seat around.

"Haven't we been delayed enough? Aren't there sufficient hazards on this planet without asking for another one by leaving the safety of the rover for a frivolous sightseeing tour? In a cave, no less?"

"The rover isn't *that* safe," said Bob. "But I wasn't suggesting we go spelunking. God knows we've been through enough." He cast a timid glance at Lucas as if he were actually saying, "God knows *you've* been through enough," in the form of an apology.

"Of course," said Lucas. "I should have known you weren't suggesting it."

He'd heard enough apologies, and he preferred Bob to be his usual cocky, irritating self. Lucas had to admit, albeit grudgingly, that Bob had more than made up for his error, in saving Lucas's life, in repairing the rover, in captaining this mission with extraordinary stamina. A small part of him had even come to admire Bob.

"I'd love to see it, too," said Gita, keeping her gaze fixed on the terrain. "I'd love to glide down the slope of Oxus Patera and sample the soil. I'd love to experience the marvels of Mars and forget the horrors. But it's far from sensible right now."

"And our number one priority is to reach the Arabia Terra base," said Lucas, "since we have no idea if the magma channels are also active in this region and are building for a blow from Oxus, here."

"Bite your tongue," said Bob. "Every time you suggest something bad might happen, something worse does." He grinned at Lucas, the first time in days that the threads and creases through his face were not from tension. It was doing him a world of good to relax for a change and let Gita assume driving duty. But now Gita's shoulders were slumping with fatigue, so maybe it was time for her to take a break, as well.

"Do you want me to drive for a while?" Lucas asked. He slurped at his tea, savoring the flavor of soothing, though stimulating, mint. Bob had been experimenting with flavors to make their bland food and refreshments more tasty.

"I suppose you could take a turn," said Bob, "considering you swam an Olympic trial the other day with no severe setback in your condition. Rather remarkable, actually. You really are in peak condition. I have no objection, as long as your head is clear." He peered into Lucas's eyes, assessing the degree of focus.

"Been off the pain meds for a full twenty-four hours. I'm very sharp," said Lucas.

"Well, then. How about it, Gita?"

"I suppose," she said, looking far more concerned than Bob. But she braked the rover, nonetheless, and jammed it into park. She hopped out of the driver's seat and gestured with a flourish.

"Captain?"

"Oh captain, my captain," Bob added.

"Walt Whitman," said Lucas, trying to interpret Bob's grin. "Did you ever read the poem?"

"Well, I . . . heard the expression in a movie, years ago."

"*But O heart! heart! heart! O the bleeding drops of red, Where on the deck my Captain lies, Fallen cold and dead.*"

"Oh," said Bob, momentarily flustered. "I wouldn't . . . I mean, I didn't realize . . ."

"Obviously," said Lucas. "No inferences taken." He stood and clapped Bob on the back, before easing himself down into the "captain's" chair. "Take a nap, Bob. Gita and I can handle this. You've done most of the driving, to date."

"Well, I thought I'd navigate—"

"You've really foregone far too much rest, Bob," said Gita, sliding into the copilot seat. "Lucas will be fine—I'll keep an eye on him—and you deserve a nap. Go on."

Bob pursed his lips, then reluctantly agreed. But before he shuffled toward his bunk, he placed a hand on Lucas's shoulder. "Take it easy. Respect your limits."

"Yes, Doc," said Lucas with a smile, finding Bob's hand strangely comforting. Although it had been induced by extreme adversity, maybe they were finally becoming a team.

An hour later, they'd trundled well past Oxus Patera and were skirting the Mamers Valles. The entire time, Gita had nattered on about trivial matters, avoiding intense technical material and never broaching more intimate topics. Obviously, she didn't want to distract him on his first responsible job since his injury.

In the back, Bob's snores blended with the gentle purr of the motor. More of the soft cumulus clouds to the east had congregated in burly clumps, and a deeper tinge of indigo tainted the orange hue. A brisk wind was stirring up dust, and the occasional swirl fashioned a dust devil.

"I think we're in for a storm," said Gita. "Time to let me drive again."

"I'm perfectly fine to keep going."

"But I don't want to risk it, since you're still recovering. I'll make it an order, if need be."

"Honestly, I can handle this. If it gets bad enough, I'll stop. I'd rather we seek cover on the leeward side of a hill if the wind speed increases, though," he said, trying to change the subject so she would consider their predicament and leave him at the wheel.

"We could descend into a crater to escape the wind."

"Where the rain could accumulate? After our last experience with flood water, I'd rather not. Hey, that dust devil—"

He broke off, as pebbles and fine particulate matter spat at the windshield. The wind rocked the rover as if it were a cradle.

"—looks quite nasty," he finished, as the devil whipped past. "I know we're trying to revive Mars, but sometimes I prefer the low atmospheric pressure of the old Mars, where the devils hardly carried a punch. Where it was dry and docile and perfectly predictable."

"Would you prefer it if everything were predictable?" Gita asked. "If everything and everyone followed expected patterns and rules and never stepped out of line? Wouldn't that be boring? And if that were the case, wouldn't I be dead?"

He stared with intense concentration at the ink-stained horizon. The first drops of rain pecked at the window.

"Is it anathema to speak of it?"

"It is when a storm is brewing and I'm trying to drive without distractions."

"Point taken. Which is why I should drive. We should discuss this before you bury it, though."

The drops multiplied, blurring the view ahead and distorting the image on the screen along with it. The flimsy windshield wipers couldn't handle the sudden downpour. Lucas decided to stop the vehicle.

"You'd think they'd have installed better windshield wipers on the rover, if they had any foresight."

"They designed and constructed it before the ISA decided to jumpstart terraforming so far ahead of schedule. And I believe the next generation will have more than these token strips of plastic, when the colonists arrive."

She paused, gazing at the rain as it streamed down the window. Lucas braced for it. He knew what was coming next.

"Are you through with brooding? Will you at least admit that you're a better person than you would have anyone believe? That you aren't a robot roped to protocol? Can you acknowledge that despite being injured and landing where you didn't want to go, and even striving for survival, that you're happier now?"

A stern gust of wind battered the side of the rover, as rain peppered the windshield and clattered against the titanium shell. Bob had stopped snoring. He was probably awake.

Lucas gripped the steering wheel and turned to look at Gita. Her eyes held a tender quality that sparked an internal shiver.

"What do you want from me?" he asked quietly, words that were casually swallowed by the wind. But she heard them.

"I have always admired your skills and intelligence, Lucas. God knows I had reason to be frustrated as well. Your ego has often gotten in the way of any team operations. You were so rigid and distant. At one point, I thought you hated us. But when Bob saved your life, you began to change. It was as if you didn't expect him to, which is ridiculous. I would have done the same thing, but Bob acted first. Then *you* did something you didn't expect to do either, didn't you? We are bound to each other, not just for survival. . . . You may refuse to admit it, but you're not so different from us. You need us as much as we need you."

"Of course I need you," he pronounced, through slightly gritted teeth. "We are a team. We rely on each other."

"You're not listening," she said sternly, almost angrily.

"Yes, I am," he replied. "I need you to make me . . . human. I'm not a . . . *robot* anymore." He crunched down on the word as if it were bone.

"Oh, that's not what I meant. Please don't look so hurt. I guess I'm not expressing myself very well. I don't know how to say how . . . wonderful you are."

"Now," he clarified.

"Excuse me?"

"How wonderful I am *now*. You think it's because I've changed. That I've never done anything unselfish before. That the decision to save you was predicated on Bob's sacrifice."

"No, that's not it at all."

"Sure it is."

"Stop being so pigheaded."

"So now I'm pigheaded, as well as bland and robotic and selfish. As well as a total ass."

"Well, you got the last part right," said Bob, standing up beside his bunk, then grabbing the frame as a blast of wind rattled the rover.

"Stay out of this, Bob. I was talking to Gita."

Bob tramped through the narrow path in the crew cabin to the drive station cockpit. He glared at Lucas as if he wanted to throttle him. "You always try to twist everything we say into an assault on you—on your skills, your integrity, your behavior. And I admit, I did doubt you at first, which is part of what precipitated our many arguments before we landed here. But we're not at war, Lucas. We're not spies dancing around each other from opposite sides. Gita is trying to tell you something, but you select one word to home in on and ignore the rest."

"What is she trying to tell me, Bob?" Lucas asked, his jaw clenched so tight he could barely spit out the words.

"Well, it's actually pretty obvious. If we could choose only one man to be marooned with on this bloody red rock, one man to rely on above all others, it would be you, you miserable, fucking asshole." Bob swatted him brusquely on the shoulder.

Then a screeching, swirling wind devil blindsided them and knocked the rover clean on its side. Its three occupants were thrown into a heap, Lucas on top of Gita and Bob, a tangle of legs and arms and aching ribs.

"I'd choose you, too," he whispered, waiting for the hiss of an airlock breach.

Scanning...

Located: Chapter 31

BEING FLIPPED ONTO its side had dented the rover, but hadn't punctured the precious balloon of breathable air. No oxygen loss occurred, and they had merely to don their elasticized suits and oxygen masks and tip the rover right side up again to make it serviceable. Easier said than done.

Bob said he'd packed a hydraulic jack in the outside storage compartment, for just such a disaster. If they could get the vehicle raised to a forty-five degree angle, it should tip back onto its stout wheels with just a few extra shoves. It also helped that gravity on Mars was much weaker than on Earth. They still had to wait until the rain stopped and the ferocious wind subsided, which meant two hours spent twiddling their thumbs and worrying that they'd missed identifying a leak that could be insidiously draining their life support.

When the rain tapered off, it took another hour of superhuman effort—of heaves and groans and exhausting maneuvers—but finally they stood the rover upright and rendered it operational again. After a series of systems checks, they were back on their way.

The next four hours, thank goodness, were uneventful, and at times the general mood in the rover was even jovial. Since Bob had made his strangely sentimental statement, the tension between them had evaporated. Lucas could forget who he was and the complications his involvement in the Movement would entail, and simply enjoy the company of fellow survivors and Mars explorers. He could chat unreservedly with Bob and Gita about terraforming and plasma engines. He could enjoy the rocky, ruddy landscape. And when the distant glitter of ocean water and spectacular ice peaks beckoned on the horizon, he actually suggested a slight detour.

Why not? They were past the problematic area. They had enough fuel for an unscheduled excursion for a few hours, and despite constant instructions from the ISA—issued in bitter tones—to adhere to the straightest course possible, since their survival was paramount and they must complete their mission—although their rebellion was unforgiven and unforgivable—he was struck by an urge to break protocol.

"Seriously?" said Bob from the pilot seat. "*You* want to make a detour?"

"It's an ocean," said Lucas, on navigation duty once again. "On Mars." He directed a blithe grin at Bob, feeling giddy, for maybe the first time in his life. "You know we'll never return here. They'll never let us near a spacecraft again. We'll be grounded and probably prosecuted. They might have overlooked the joyride if our temporary mutiny had only been for two or three days without incident, but not weeks, not after I was injured, not with all the stability issues on the planet and the potential for damage to the MADVEC. I know I objected to any deviations in our course to begin with, but the surface here seems reasonably stable. And I think we'll regret it if we don't take a few minutes to consider how far we've traveled, how incredible it is that we survived two disastrous events, and how glorious this transformation of the planet is."

"And it might even be beautiful," said Gita, strolling in from the lavatory in the crew cabin.

"And there's that," he agreed.

"Let's do it then," said Bob, twisting the steering wheel and altering the rover's easterly course to a northerly one.

Only two miles later, the flat stretches of barren ground with erratic red boulders interspersed with crater gouges, buttes, and ridges, along with the odd wind-sculpted dune of fine sand, came to an abrupt end. An ocean tinted faintly blue, and flecked with pearl and cinnamon icebergs, stretched to the horizon. A delicate fog clung to the surface—evidence of the evaporation that continued farther north, as the space mirrors reflected the sun's rays onto the polar region—but there was enough liquid to lap against the fine sand.

Bob continued driving until he reached a hillock near the shoreline, then parked the vehicle and shut down the engine.

"Anyone for a day at the beach?" he asked.

Gita beamed, her lovely Latin features absolutely radiant. "I'll just change into a bikini and grab a beach blanket." She hustled to the storage compartment and whipped out their suits and rebreather tanks and masks, as if they were truly beach apparel.

"We'll need sun block."

"Sun visors, anyway," said Lucas, crowding close to her and accepting his own oversized jumpsuit.

"And a thermos of lemonade."

"Coffee," he corrected, slipping out of his clothes and squeezing his thighs into the spandex legs of the suit.

"Some lawn chairs," said Bob, wading into the conversation.

"I think we'll have to make do with a rock."

"And a picnic basket full of goodies," added Gita.

"Or a rack full of specimen jars," said Lucas.

"Ah, Lucas. You take all the fun out it," Gita replied good-humoredly. "This isn't a work vacation."

"But would you forgive yourself if you didn't test the salinity of the water, and the sedimentation and temperature, to see if we could introduce arctic char in the future? If you didn't scoop up the first evidence of a liquid ocean and transport it home to all the oo's and ah's of our colleagues? We are, and will always be, first and foremost, scientists."

Gita sighed. "Yes, I suppose. I just wanted to imagine we were taking time off."

"It is time off from driving," said Bob, "and repair work and pumping fuel and analyzing instrumentation. It is time off from stitching closed Lucas's wounds. Don't look at me like that. I had to do it twice, you know. It's time off from worrying about survival, because we need to stop worrying and start living. This is living, on Mars." He grinned, hitched his rebreather tank higher on his back, and slipped the mask over his face, topping everything off with a tight-fitting cotton cap.

Now thoroughly outfitted, the three companions exited the rover through the airlock and plunged through drifts of powdery sand flecked with ice crystals. They drew nearer the gentle wash of waves, which rippled over the surface of the planet but were not tugged by the small moons to produce any significant tide. The ocean contained larger ice floes and bergs, along with muddy-looking fragments, but determined channels of liquid pierced the crystallized chunks.

"Beyond breathtaking," said Gita, through the comm. She bounded up to the icy border between land and ocean and crouched down, dabbling her gloved fingers in the briny water. This would be the moment in any science fiction movie where a creature from the depths—a creature that had defied all odds and survived underground for eons in the Martian desert—would leap out of the water, seize her arm, and whisk her under. Lucas's throat constricted, despite how ridiculous the idea was. He'd grown up reading science fiction that had little to do with science.

"Hmm, isn't this interesting?" said Gita, winding the noose ever tighter. "I think some of our algae has already seeded."

She grabbed her pack and extracted the sampling kit. Then she scooped a sterile container into the melted ice. Holding it up to the light, Lucas could spy emerald specks dancing on the liquid surface.

"Rather far from the comet injection sites, isn't it?" asked Bob. He leaned closer and squinted into the jar.

"Mars is blooming," said Gita, with an ecstatic grin.

Now would be the instant when the algae would suddenly multiply to such a degree that it would fracture the container, pierce Gita's suit, and infect him and Bob by proximity, causing their agonizing deaths.

It floated serenely.

"Why are you looking so pale?" asked Gita.

"I guess whenever something amazing happens, I still expect the worst. Like a CO_2 burst. Or an aquifer eruption."

Gita patted his arm and said soothingly, "They're just benign little organisms, bioengineered to survive in this climate. They're resistant to cold and UV radiation, they have extraordinary salt tolerance, they have little need of oxygen, and they don't mind propagating on bare rock and soil. But I imagine they prefer the moisture we've stirred up and released; and that's why they're flourishing. By kickstarting the planet early, it's possible we could introduce more complex plant life sooner than expected, which will eventually make the air breathable. This isn't a time for fear. It's a magical moment."

"Agreed," said Bob. "But allow Lucas his PTSD. If anyone has the right to an anxiety attack, you do, buddy. I do think, though, that we've finally hit upon a good thing."

He gripped Lucas's shoulders firmly, as if to hold him up in case his knees buckled. "Let me know if you're feeling short of breath," Bob whispered, as if Gita wouldn't hear if he lowered his voice.

"I'm good," said Lucas. "It's remarkable—the organism's exponential growth. Mars might actually be ready for colonists in twenty years. Not that *we'll* ever see this planet again."

"Would you want to live here?" asked Gita, her eyebrows flexed with curiosity.

"Who wouldn't?" said Bob. "Despite the volatility, there's space—endless, magnificent space. No crowding. No pollution. We're fostering the proliferation of life rather than snuffing it out. And the neighbors are fabulous." He eased his hands off Lucas's shoulders, still eyeing the steadiness of his knees. "We could set up our trailers right next to each other." He winked. "Go for jogs. Explore the Vitalis Cave."

Just as the knots loosened, Bob's words wrenched them tight again. "This was a minor risk, but if you're suggesting we detour to the cave . . ."

"I'm not, Lucas. Relax. That we'll save for another day. And I think you're wrong about our chances of returning here. I know we'll be barred from space travel for a period of time, but we are the first people to set foot on a newly terraformed Mars. That will count for something in the history books. I think we'll be coming back someday, maybe to settle on the planet. We could even be part of the same colony. You and your partners, me and Rossi, my girl," he smiled. "We'll set up the neighborhood pub."

Gita smiled and stroked the specimen jar. "Colonizing," she murmured. "Exactly what the algae is doing. I hope you're right, Bob. I hope we get the chance. But I would still like to keep some regions human-free, in a zone that still resembles pre-terraformed Mars."

A crack stung the air, like a gunshot. Then an ample slice of a nearby iceberg calved into the ocean, distributing choppy ripples. Lucas noticed more and more flecks of blue-green algae dotting the water. Twenty years. It would take several more to carry out every nuance of the Movement's plan, and Bob and Gita wouldn't view him in such a neighborly fashion once he set things in motion. But why should it matter to him what they thought? Yes, they'd become friendly. Even friends. Yes, working side by side with these people he could forget that he'd lived a separate life, that he'd been fed propaganda with occasional grains of truth. But could he forget what had happened to his father?

And regarding Mars . . . Surely Bob and Gita were not oblivious. They should realize that the human pattern of consumption and destruction would follow them to other planets, regardless of anyone's good intentions.

"I could use a drink right now," said Lucas.

"Good idea, once we get back to the rover. A toast to our survival and future return," said Bob.

"Do you think colonized Mars will be any different from Earth?" Lucas asked, scrutinizing Bob's face.

Gita frowned and nestled the sample into her case, turning away as if she knew the true essence of his question and didn't want to add her thoughts.

"Of course it will," said Bob. "Fewer people means fewer squabbles."

"That depends on who the people are and whether they nibble or devour. How do you screen for that?"

Bob looked out over the sea—a vast glutinous mass of ice and water—shading his eyes, even though his face shield should protect them well enough. "I didn't know we were going to get into a deep philosophical discussion, Lucas. I thought we were on vacation."

"I would be happy if we could simply stay here. You, me, and Gita. Never to return, if that were possible. Blow up the *Phoenix*. Sabotage future excursions. Keep this planet to ourselves."

"Now who's being greedy?" asked Bob.

"You know it will become another Earth. The differences will crop up as soon as they land. The first pioneers will struggle to establish housing and introduce basic farming, so there will be minimal squabbles until the matter of survival is firmly addressed. But eventually this planet with newly established life will begin to flounder under the weight of petty emotions. And the appetites will grow. They always do."

"Maybe we won't live to see that day," said Bob. "Maybe we won't even get off this planet. You may get your wish, but the only way we could stay here with the present limited resources is as corpses."

Gita sighed—an exasperated sigh that whistled harshly through the comm. "Will you guys stop discussing such morbid topics? And sharing your pessimism," she added, glaring at Lucas. "We're explorers and scientists, not statesmen. And we can't solve the problems of human nature. We can only try to do better, especially when we start over, here. Hopefully our history lessons will come into play. What we're doing is converting this planet into a Garden of Eden. We can't worry about snakes yet."

"Agreed," said Bob.

"Fine," said Lucas. "Dismiss it. Avoid it. Dance around it. The fat cat funded our expeditions and the terraforming," he said, referring to Galactic Resources. "The fat cat will want bonus food for his efforts. The snake is already in the garden—pardon my mixed metaphor."

"Lucas, we feed at the fat cat's trough, to further mix your metaphor," said Bob. "There's nothing we can do to prevent him from devouring resources. We can formally object, but that would look hypocritical. We can suggest a slow, measured pace to terraforming, and put forward the idea of parks to preserve some uniquely Martian territory," he added, with a nod to Gita, "but we have no authority to control what occurs. When you accepted this job, you knew full well who was funding it. Regrets are understandable, particularly after everything you've been through. But I think this discussion isn't helpful at the moment when our focus should be on survival and maybe even getting some enjoyment out of this trip."

"Enjoyment," Lucas muttered. *Is that the best you can do, Bob?* He was so discouraged he felt like collapsing on the sand. He had so hoped that Bob, who had become considerably elevated in his mind since their flight on the *Phoenix*, would take a stronger position, would champion the protection of Mars and display some backbone. Or that Gita—who seemed most enamored of the original Mars—would. Was Lucas the only astronaut who wasn't crouched under the knee of the corporation? But he was crouched under another knee. He wondered, when the time came, whether he could stand on his own, free and clear.

Scanning...

Located: Chapter 32

FELICITY FROZE, FOR a moment too stunned to move or even comprehend. The next second she acted, because no one else did. She dove into the cloudy water, caring little if it disguised crocodiles or snakes or hungry hippos. She swished around in the channel, blinking stinging eyes, and tried to find Baruti's sinking body. She searched and searched underwater, suspended particles nipping at her corneas, then finally spied him. He was floundering, but not kicking or making any attempt to swim upward and seek air. She dove straight for him, snatched his suspended arm, and tugged him toward the surface, astonished at how limply his body hung from her hands. The only movements she sensed were a series of convulsions transmitted from his muscles to her hands like an electrical current.

Above water, he gasped, then sputtered out tea-colored liquid, coughing repeatedly until he had emptied his lungs. The shivering continued, making it difficult for her to maintain her grasp and keep him afloat. Just as his flailing arm slipped from her fingers, someone bumped against her side and grabbed hold of him to keep his head from going under.

Felicity reacquired Baruti's arm before she glanced to her side to see who'd come to her aid. She expected Kelong or Pedro, and was shocked to find Frank bobbing in the gentle current, his arms supporting the biologist around his chest and under his shoulder blade, while tipping him backward so his face wouldn't flop into the water.

"You okay?" he asked.

She nodded, suddenly realizing she'd been sputtering, too.

"Hey," he called to Kelong. "Can you bring the *mokoro* alongside? We'll push him from the bottom while you pull him out of the water."

The guide responded, but slowly. Why had he done absolutely nothing to help when Baruti had fallen? Maybe he wasn't too keen on swimming in these waters—which was understandable—but considering that Baruti was running and funding this expedition, shouldn't he or Dave at least have tried to rescue their client?

Kelong paddled back through the current until he reached them, then guided the boat the last few strokes before casting the paddle into the hull. His main issue would be keeping the boat steady while he hauled Baruti over the side.

"Ready?" asked Frank, eyeing her keenly. Was he noting her own rapid breathing, which was as much from worry as the rescue swim and her struggles to keep Baruti from drowning?

"Yes," she blurted out. "Let's do this."

"On three."

He counted, as Felicity fumbled her way down Baruti's taut belly to find his thigh with her other hand. At three, they heaved, while Kelong grabbed hold of Baruti's arms and tugged him into the *mokoro*. Baruti flopped down on the rough boards, his body still convulsing and his feet dangling over the side. Frank nudged his left leg into the boat while Felicity lifted his right. When she released him, she splashed backward and plunged under the water, unable to stay afloat. Frank whipped his hand out and yanked her to the surface again, before she could sink too deep.

She didn't want to be grateful to Frank for anything, but she didn't react in a surly manner this time. How could she? She cast him a wintry smile—the best she could muster at the moment—then even accepted his help to board the *mokoro* herself, allowing him to support her bottom with his hand.

Once safely out of the water, her priority was to attend to Baruti, who just kept shivering and shivering, his teeth clacking and clattering like maracas. But she had to take a few moments to breathe, and shiver herself, and try not to cry. What was wrong with him? What the hell was happening? What should she do?

She looked across the little gap of water between the canoes, searching for Frank, whom Pedro was hoisting back into their own craft. She looked to Frank for guidance, but Frank was taking his own time to breathe and shake off water. He wasn't uttering a word. Pedro sent her a puzzled and helpless expression, equally speechless.

Baruti's shuddering subsided, but he didn't open his eyes. He was breathing in short, shallow bursts, his skin the color of bleached mahogany.

"Baruti," she said, leaning down and tracing her fingers over his face. "Tell me what's happening. Are you in pain? Do you think you have a fever?"

His eyelids fluttered. "Sick," he said. "Feeling pain."

"Where?"

"Everywhere," he muttered. Then a stream of unintelligible words bubbled from his lips, with forceful vowels and rolling r's, most likely in Setswana.

Since Frank still sat quietly in the boat, staring at her but not commenting, Felicity knew that she must take charge, that she had to act. No one else seemed inclined to do anything but cast her anxious glances.

"We need to get back to the lodge," she said to Kelong.

He stared at her too, for a painfully long time. "No," he said. "It's nearly nightfall. We can't make it back before dark. And once it's dark, the channels are far too dangerous. We must camp on an island for the night."

"But . . . Baruti needs medical care. He needs a hospital. Could we possibly call for a helicopter to land on one of these islands?"

Kelong shook his head. "No cell towers here," he said. "Everywhere else, but not this deep in the Okavango. No connection, no calls, no rescue. We camp for the night, and take him back with the boat tomorrow."

Felicity was on the verge of tears or hysteria, one or the other. He'd voiced their only choice, but what if it was too late by tomorrow, after the long *mokoro* ride back to the lodge? What if Baruti was so ill that he wouldn't last the night? It seemed ridiculous that he'd switched from perfect health—or nearly perfect health, considering his apparent headaches—to extreme illness in almost an instant. But one look at him, at the streams of sweat that rolled off his brow and the erratic quality of his breathing, was enough to convince her his situation was dire. This could hardly be a cold or flu. He'd passed out and fallen right into the water—a seasoned biologist who was well adapted to African ailments and must have acquired a robust immune system. It was beyond comprehension that their strongest member was now the weakest.

"I guess we have no choice," she said, the fear and fatigue bleating in her voice. "We find an island, set up camp, and wait for dawn. Maybe Baruti will even recover overnight and we'll have nothing to worry about."

Kelong nodded and shrugged—agreement with her first statement, doubting her last. He turned and slipped his paddle into the water, churning determinedly through the channel, examining islands cloaked with Phoenix palms and acacia and bristly with bushes. But whenever Felicity pointed to one he shook his head.

"Too small. Crocodiles will find us."

She gulped and didn't question his judgment. The idea of spending a few nights on the Delta with a strong Baruti by her side had been disturbing enough. But without his confidence and knowledge, his keen eye for danger and his tender relationship with the animals, she felt completely overwhelmed.

And what if he didn't recover? What would that mean to them, to her, to everything they were trying to accomplish? Would they have to give up? And if they did abandon the chase and these killers carried out their plans, would that torment her conscience forever?

But something less important to the group but far more vital to her, personally, plucked at her mind. What would it mean to lose Baruti just when she'd found him?

She stroked his cheek. He shuddered again, and moaned, as if to match her spiritual heartache with his physical pain. She curled her fingers around his sweaty palm and gently squeezed. She murmured soothing nonsense to him, anything to ease his misery.

Then realizing they would both freeze in their wet clothes, she stripped him of his clinging muddy shirt and soaked pants, then wrapped a blanket around him. She sorted through her own pack to liberate a dry sweater and jeans and, as discreetly as possible, shed her clothes and replaced them, even though the men's eyes strayed toward her as she changed. Frank made no attempt to disguise his own change of clothing, shivering as he went.

As the sun slowly descended into the trees, creating an eerie monochrome world, Kelong stopped paddling and pointed at the murky shape of a substantial island—a dry oasis in the liquid desert.

"Good size," he said. "We should find a place to camp that's far enough from the channels to sleep safely."

"Okay," said Felicity. "Let's land and hurry, before it gets too dark."

Kelong and Dave beached the *mokoros* and dragged them farther up between the reeds and grass until they were satisfied they wouldn't float out into the channel, should the deluge from the highlands begin flooding the Delta. Then they gathered provisions—pup tents and backpacks filled with food and camping equipment—distributing some packets to her, others to Frank, while Pedro helped them carry the *mokoro* with Baruti still inside as if it were a travois. They tramped for several yards until they reached a colossal tree—a baobab with a trunk that split into several bulbous sections, capped with spiny branches that stretched sideways bracketing a great overhang of leaves. Kelong grunted and set the *mokoro* down, prompting Pedro and Dave to do the same.

"Is this where—" Felicity queried, but Kelong held up his hand.

He scanned the tree in the semi-dark, walking around it and probing every branch. Finally he nodded. "No leopards," he remarked, chilling Felicity all over again.

"We make camp here. Eat supper," he continued.

Felicity had no objection, assuming there really were no leopards. Or other predators. She was bone-weary from anxiety and from rescuing Baruti in the water, and her belly was aching with hunger. She assisted the men in setting up the tents, while Kelong started a fire to boil water and cook spaghetti and vegetables from their provisions. Once the tents were erected and the sleeping bags had been rolled out on their waterproof floors, Frank and Pedro transported Baruti to the nearest one and tucked him within the insulated padding of a sleeping bag. He groaned and flailed as if insects were chewing on his organs and fire was burning through his veins.

Felicity sat just outside the tent, accepting a bowl of spaghetti topped with soggy asparagus from Kelong. The others gathered around her and silently spooned the noodles into their mouths, too tired and miserable to speak but still prompted to eat by deep pangs of hunger. Even if the guides' only food had been mopane worms, Felicity would probably have devoured them, if they could somehow supply her with enough energy to help Baruti.

When they'd eaten their fill, the guides gathered the dishes and carried them a short distance away to wash out the residue. Frank shifted closer to her around the fire, beckoning Pedro to join them in a huddle.

"What do you think is wrong with him?" He gestured to the tent where Baruti still lay twitching and groaning. "It came on so suddenly."

"I don't have a clue," said Felicity.

"I have a clue," said Pedro. "Either food poisoning or Ebola."

"Seriously?" she whispered.

"Well, he was handling what he thought might be biological weapons," said Frank. "Maybe he did bring something back with him from Northern Ontario."

"But the samples weren't anything of the sort," said Felicity. "Food poisoning would be more likely, since we didn't eat the same thing at breakfast. The chicken necks?"

"It's possible," said Frank. "But he's not shitting his breakfast in streams, if you'll excuse my description. He's having severe muscle spasms."

"It could be anything," said Felicity.

"It could be anything, but the guides didn't help at all when he fell in. Maybe they poisoned the food."

"No," said Pedro, unexpectedly. "They were scared. They look superstitious, and they might think o' this type of thing as black magic. Or they've seen enough Ebola or other diseases to make them jittery. They probably didn't want to touch him."

Felicity nodded. It made sense, and she hoped he was right. She didn't want to think of the implications if the guides had had something to do with Baruti's illness.

"I'm going to try to give him some water. He's burning up, and we don't have an IV or any useful medical supplies. Just bandages and topical antibiotics.

A first aid kit is useless for anything internal."

"Good idea," said Frank. "We need to bring his fever down somehow. I have a bottle of acetaminophen in my pack, but I doubt he'll be able to swallow it. But be careful not to *force* fluids or pills into him, or he might aspirate and die all the sooner."

Felicity snapped him a reproachful look. "He's not going to die."

Frank raised his hands. "'Course not. I just meant . . ."

"I know. But we have to stay positive. Baruti is strong, and he's going to fight this, whatever it is. I'll be careful."

For some reason Frank reached out and patted her arm—an unusually warm gesture for him. "I know you will."

The guides sauntered back into camp, muttering to themselves and flicking their eyes at the path and the tree. They'd suggested the tents be erected on the far side of the tree, away from the path. Felicity guessed that animals employed this path to travel across the island, and that they'd best not tempt their curiosity.

She sorted through the food supplies until she unearthed a canteen of water and a cloth to moisten and apply to Baruti's lips, if that was the only way to rehydrate him. She also discovered a flashlight that, thankfully, projected a strong, steady beam when she flicked it on. Frank offered her his stock of acetaminophen, which she accepted with a grateful nod. Then she rose and tramped quickly over the brush and grass to Baruti's two-man tent. Felicity crouched down and crawled into the confined space.

Casting the yellow beam of the flashlight over Baruti, Felicity was disturbed at what it revealed. Baruti was shivering and muttering, a sheen of sweat glistening on his brow. She set the light on the floor and crawled closer. With a deep sigh, she nudged him with her hand.

"Baruti," she said in a hoarse voice.

No conscious response. He thrashed and lay still. He thrashed again, struck her a firm blow on the knee, and then lay still.

"Please, Baruti . . ."

His eyes fluttered open and he gazed right at her, and *through* her. His eyes made her think of lasers that could slice through steel, but they seemed totally unaware.

"It's okay," she said softly, stroking his brow. "Try to drink something. I'll bet you're thirsty."

She held the canteen to his mouth. He blinked, and for a moment she thought he was becoming coherent. But then his lips quivered and he sank his teeth into the spout.

"What's happening?" she asked. "Was it something you ate? How can I help you?"

"They knew," he muttered, startling her. "They knew."

"Who knew what?" she asked, cold sweat cropping up on her skin.

"They recognized me. C— c— coffee."

"Do you want coffee? I don't think that will help."

"C— c— coffee," he yelled. "I drank coffee!"

Felicity sat back on her heels, blinking away tears. She understood. She knew what was happening to Baruti. And it wasn't an illness or injury he'd suffered, but a deliberate assault. The men whom Baruti suspected of foul play and had investigated in their mining camp had recognized him, or at least recognized the threat he posed to their operations.

"Poi-son," she whispered, her voice cracking on the word. "They poisoned your coffee?"

He blinked and met her eyes, his expression calm and rational for the first time in hours. Then he confirmed her guess with just two words. And ignited another desperate concern.

"And DeLuca's."

Scanning...

Located: Chapter 33

"PLEASE, HAVE YOU seen this man?" asked Shaun, displaying a photo of Baruti to the concierge, a portly, gray-bearded man standing pompously behind the dust-speckled desk in the third shabby hotel in Maun that they'd visited. "It's very important we find him. Or this woman?" He displayed a stunning capture of Felicity, which showed her smiling shyly with her sweet dimpled face and arresting gray eyes.

Dayna did her best to corral her temper every time he flashed the photo. Why had he photographed Felicity? Was she another young girl he'd developed an interest in?

The concierge raised his eyebrows curiously at the first photo and looked amused by the second. He muttered something in Setswana, then beckoned a bellhop, who strode casually toward the desk. The concierge asked permission, then turned the phone in Shaun's hand and presented the picture. The man nodded and chattered away, indicating the photo with a tilt of his head. Dayna caught the word "Mbeki" and her heart thumped with resurrected hope.

After hours of flights and transfers through New York, Johannesburg, and now Maun—the springboard to the Okavango Delta, which was the area Dr.

Mbeki had contemplated searching—and skipping from hotel to hotel in this dry, dusty town on the edge of the Kalahari desert, they might finally have discovered a real lead.

"Yes," said the concierge, skimming through his log of guests. "Dr. Mbeki did check in two days ago. It was only for one night, and then we helped him book a lodge in the Okavango—Raintree Lodge. But you need to fly there, as with most camps in the Delta. I can arrange your transportation, if you must reach him as soon as possible. Air Okavango usually flies out in the morning, but if you charter a private plane they'll leave whenever you like."

Dayna grimaced. Her credit card debt was mounting exponentially—flights to Africa were hardly cheap—and a private charter . . . ? Even Shaun seemed to balk, but only for a second.

"Fine. Book it. But we'd like to try to reach them first. Can you give me the link to the lodge?"

"Certainly." A smirk appeared on the man's face. Obviously, he would receive kickbacks for the charter. He displayed a link for Shaun to copy, then tapped away on his antiquated computer, making the required entries while asking their names and passport numbers.

"Dr. . . . Lugan?" the concierge queried Dayna as he entered her information.

"Yes?"

"You are a medical doctor?" he continued.

"An academic one," she replied. When he stopped typing and questioned her silently, she added, "I have a Ph.D. in Archaeology."

"Hmm," he said. "Interesting. And Dr. Wilson?"

"Biology, I believe."

Shaun confirmed with a nod of his head, although he had turned away and was attempting to establish a video connection with the lodge. He spoke for several minutes with the host at the facility. Dayna, looking over his shoulder, felt a surge of hope at finally making contact, but it was immediately dashed when the man explained that, yes, Dr. Mbeki had checked in, but he and his party had departed for a few days with canoes and guides. They were camping out on the Delta.

"There. Your flight will leave at 2:00 p.m." The concierge beamed, entirely too entertained by the idea. And he studied Shaun's face for a long time, which was equally suspicious.

Two o'clock in the afternoon. She glanced at her watch. It was 10:00 a.m. now, so they'd have four hours to kill. They could wander through town and look for a restaurant to have lunch—something that served fare a little better than what passed for food at airports and on planes. But a disturbing thought tickled at the back of her mind. She still knew next to nothing about Baruti, the gun-toting biologist.

"Do you know Dr. Mbeki at all?" she asked the concierge. "I mean, he must travel through here periodically, since he inventories the animals in the Delta. Have you ever met him before?"

Shaun peaked his eyebrow curiously, but didn't comment.

"Yes," the man replied. "Although I've never seen him with the girl before, and I wasn't on duty when he checked in. He rarely stays at the hotel because his father lives in town now. But I suppose he didn't want to burden his father with so many guests. He booked four rooms, one for each of two men, one for the girl and, of course, his own."

"His father?"

"An old man," he responded. "Not too fond of house guests anymore. A little senile."

"Where might his father live? I would like to visit him before we fly to the lodge. I'm a friend of Dr. Mbeki's, and I should pay my respects."

At first, the concierge hedged. He frowned and scratched his head. He studied both of them in turn, as if assessing their motives. But he must have found them sufficiently benign, because he finally gave her the address and even supplied directions. Baruti's father's house was simply six blocks from the hotel. They could easily walk there and still make their flight in plenty of time.

Dayna thanked the concierge, and beckoned Shaun to leave. But as they reached the door, she heard the man babble urgently in the Setswana language, and she also heard a click as if he'd taken their picture. Flipping a glance over her shoulder, she noticed he was making a phone call and was holding the device up to his face. But when he discerned her interest, he lowered the phone and beamed another greasy smile her way.

The arrival of two scientists—who were actively chasing other scientists—would be fuel for gossip, she imagined. And people were snapping pictures all the time to update their social media status. Perhaps this was a particularly dull day in Maun. Perhaps.

As they strode back onto the street, and once they were well out of earshot of hotel employees, Shaun tugged on her arm and stopped her on the narrow walkway of cracked concrete.

"What is this all about? Baruti may be dying. Felicity and the others too. And you want to visit his *father*? How could he help in any way?"

"To be honest, I don't trust Baruti, even if he is ill," she replied. *I don't trust you, either.* "He wielded a gun in my lab at Harvard. It was unloaded and he said it was just to make a point, but he insinuated that he had extensive training with firearms. I want to find out everything I can about him before we track him down. If someone poisoned him and DeLuca, then we should find him in terrible shape. But if we don't, then maybe *he* poisoned DeLuca. We can't rule that out. And that puts Felicity and Frank in even greater danger. I'd like to be well apprised of the situation before we walk into it, in order to protect my students. An addled father may be a better informant than a clear-headed one. He might provide us with background details without even intending to."

Shaun released her arm and nodded, apparently satisfied. At least he didn't seem alarmed. And he wasn't armed, either, which gave her some confidence that he wasn't homicidal.

"He seemed quite harmless when we tagged the polar bears. I'm surprised he pulled a stunt like that. Although he did carry a gun, he seemed more concerned for Felicity and the state of the environment than he seemed a man with an evil agenda. I'm glad you told me. I'll be a little more wary of him, too."

You'll be wary of *him*? How strange and twisted those words sounded, coming from a man who apparently had intimate knowledge of secrets and schemes that involved murder.

"I have no intention of letting Felicity or *you*, Dr. Lugan, come to any harm," said Shaun, staring deeply into her eyes like a hypnotist. How magnetic he was. And how attractive, with his strong cheekbones and beautifully proportioned forehead, which was brushed lightly by glossy golden hair. He reminded her of a Greek effigy, a statue of the god Apollo with classic features and perfect form. He reminded her of something else, too, but she couldn't place it.

"Well, that's nice to know," she said. "But I think I can look after myself."

"Of course," said Shaun, dropping his gaze. He was certainly well aware of his allure, and quite disappointed when it failed to captivate. "I suppose we should get on with the visit."

"As quickly as possible, since we have a flight to catch."

TWENTY MINUTES LATER, Dayna and Shaun were trudging down Moremi Street to the location their GPS had directed them. She tugged her jacket around her shoulders, surprised at the cool temperatures on the border of the Kalahari, especially during the day. But it *was* winter in this country, and the thermometer could dip below zero, freezing some of the shallower waterways. She rechecked the address and stopped in front of the first brick-and-mortar house on the street, a far cry from the thatch huts two blocks back but considerably more modest than some of the colossal estates she'd spied bordering the river. Dr. Mbeki's father lived in an average bungalow on an average street that wouldn't look out of place in Boston or Chicago, although the acacia thorn trees and the occasional encounter with a donkey—here came one now, casually sauntering down the street untethered, with no apparent owner—certainly wasn't typical in the States.

"Well," she said. "Here we are."

Without further ado, she stepped up to the door and knocked. Shaun inspected the neighborhood before joining her. He seemed satisfied that they were safe.

"I'm comin'. I'm comin'," they heard a voice inside mutter. A few seconds later, the door swung inward, revealing a compact, emaciated, grizzly-cheeked man with salted hair. He blinked twice, then narrowed his eyes.

"Haven't you milked me dry yet? No more taxes." He waved his arm as if to dismiss them, and was about to close the door.

"We're not tax collectors," said Dayna, trapping the door handle in her hand and embarking on a battle of arm strength, the old man shoving while she pushed back. And she was losing, until Shaun added half a hand to the task. "We're friends of Dr. . . . of Baruti's, your son's."

The man suddenly released the door and backed up, sending Dayna flying into the room. She nearly toppled over, but regained her balance just in time.

"Baruti," he said. "Where is he? Always traveling, traveling, traveling. Never see him. Is he with you?"

He looked around her, behind her, frowned for a particularly long time at Shaun, then shoved him aside to look out the door.

"Baruti!" he called. "Baruti." He turned around and grabbed her by the arms. "Is he dead?"

"No. Of course not," said Dayna, trying to reassure him. She smiled and shook her head, disguising as best she could the fact that he might be. "Why would you think that?"

"Why? *Why?* Because two strangers show up at my door. Americans?" He released her and stepped back, his eyes raking her up and down.

"One Canadian," Shaun felt the need to amend.

"He is always goading strangers. And putting himself in danger! Hunting down poachers, arguing with diamond miners, standing at the forefront to oppose powerful men, all to protect a helpless band of *!Kung*, one small boy, and a few measly animals. Someone—someone like you or the other man—will bring him to my door one day, butchered."

"The other man?" asked Dayna, still pondering the "one small boy" remark.

"I suppose you want tea."

"I could use a cup," said Shaun, nudging Dayna with his elbow—a warning to proceed cautiously.

"Certainly," she obliged. "I would love some tea."

The man ushered them farther into the house—a house adorned with tiles in rustic earth tones and swirling patterns, and shelves upon shelves of animal figurines. Giraffes, elephants, baboons, even a gorilla, balanced on wooden ledges. The room immediately opposite the door was a cozy sitting room, simply but tastefully furnished with beige armchairs surrounding a wicker coffee table. On the table sat a majestic ceramic lion with a flowing golden mane, its face frozen in a silent warning snarl.

"Sit. Sit," the old man urged, and shuffled on his bony legs to the kitchen. He puttered about, hurling clanks and clicks to their ears, along with the hiss of a steaming kettle. Ten minutes later, he emerged with a tray, teetering and tottering until Dayna was tempted to leap up and help him, before the tray clattered to the floor. But that might shame him and end their conversation prematurely.

Clank. He lowered the tray, complete with teapot and three royal blue cups, to the coffee table, nearly bowling over the lion.

"Tea, tea, tea," he muttered. "Always tea."

He poured red-tinted liquid into the cups one by one, spattering a few drops onto the table, as his hands shook. Then he shoved a cup in Dayna's direction, which she quickly grasped before he could drop it. "Cups are from the Queen of England," he informed her.

Dayna did her best to keep a straight face. "What a lovely gift."

"Ha! You think I joke. Not about tea. The Englishman brought them: those and the guns."

He grabbed at the other cup and thrust it at Shaun.

"Guns?" said Shaun, accepting the tea from the gnarly, knobby fingers.

"Guns, yes, guns. Unquestionably guns. 'To protect your Baruti,' he said. The spies never do their own work. They always recruit, recruit, recruit. 'My son is a scientist, not a spy,' I told him. 'He is neutral.' But he laughed at me. He laughed and laughed. 'No one is ever neutral,' he said."

Dayna sipped her tea, a rooibos blend, she noted. Shaun sipped his tea, one eyebrow peaked.

"'I do not want a dead son,' I said. But you know what he said to me?"

Dayna shook her head and sipped.

The old man eased his arthritic body onto the chair opposite. He grasped his own cup and slurped his tea, dribbles escaping his mouth. He fondled the cup and stared at it, as if mesmerized by the sloshing liquid, forgetting he was in the middle of a conversation.

"What did he say?" Dayna prompted.

"Who?" asked the old man, breaking the tea's overpowering spell and gazing across the table at them. "My, you have lovely eyes." He was looking at Shaun.

Dayna suppressed a chuckle, although she also felt mildly insulted. Yes, he did have beautiful eyes but . . . did she look so shabby beside him?

"The Englishman," she added. If only he would reestablish the connection.

"The Englishman?"

"With the guns," said Shaun. "Did he put your son in danger?"

"He sent him away. He even sent him to Canada. Can you believe that? Always trying to save the world, even the polar bears."

"They're well worth saving," said Shaun.

"And you are another one. I should have known." The old man frowned at Shaun, a chastising look like he might give his son if he were embarking on a ridiculous crusade, or had spilled a drink on the floor. "You stand in front of them, to protect them, and they will rake their claws through your back. And those who would kill them will send their bullets through your chest. Standing in the middle is where you die."

Dayna shuddered. How true those words seemed, although she had no idea what they were standing in the middle of.

"Did he ever say who was on the other side? Who was carrying the gun? And what they were trying to do?" asked Dayna.

"Well, if he knew that, he wouldn't need a spy, would he?" asked Mr. Mbeki.

Dayna sighed, becoming frustrated. It was obvious this man knew as much as they did: That there was a conspiracy that involved some very dangerous people.

"Did the man—the Englishman—have a name? What did Baruti call him?"

"John, Joe, Jim. Jim, that was it."

"Jim . . .?"

"Well, Bond, of course."

Dayna rolled her eyes and met Shaun's glance. He looked as frustrated as she felt. "Of course."

"Well, he wouldn't use his real name, would he?" said the old man, slurping his tea, then slamming the cup onto the table. "You think I'm a fool, don't you? That I believed he was that movie character. He was nothing like him. Scarred, olive skin, short and stocky. And he looked like he loved the beer." He extended his hand from his belly to suggest a substantial paunch.

"And what did he say," Dayna tried again, "when you told him you didn't want a dead son?"

"He said exactly what a spy would say, because he knew everything about my son. Everything! He said . . ." He lowered his voice, as if to speak the words in anything but hushed tones would be to grant them more credence. "He said, 'Give him the chance to defend our troubled world from more terror and violence. Let him to do something of consequence . . . before he eventually goes mad, like his mother. Then he will be worse than dead.'"

A tear trickled down the old man's cheek, the last remnants of a river.

Scanning...

Located: Chapter 34

IT WAS IMPOSSIBLE to sleep.

Felicity lay on her back in the tight confines of the sleeping bag, as Baruti tossed and turned, groaned and twitched. She'd managed, through a great deal of coaxing on her part and coughing on Baruti's, to get some crushed tablets of acetaminophen and water into him, but the fever refused to be suppressed. If he'd ingested poison, she imagined the antipyretic drugs would do absolutely nothing. What he needed was an antidote.

When Baruti did quiet down for the odd few minutes, she heard the wailing, shrieking, and crashing of Delta creatures outside their tent. It sounded as if they were clustered around the baobab tree, circling and preparing to pounce. Then a thumping and a pounding came from the direction of the path and shook the ground beneath her. Unable to stem her curiosity, and terror, she peered out the nylon window of the tent. The gibbous moon illuminated the island in swaths, through rips in the clouds, and it lit up the enormous rump and hind feet of a hippopotamus, as it swayed and clumped past their encampment. And then another. And then another.

Luckily, the hippos had no interest in swerving off the path to investigate tiny pup tents. Or in stomping the intruders to smithereens beneath their sizable feet. Or in slicing through them with their sharp, powerful teeth.

Felicity slithered back into the tent and remained sitting upright, her spine rigid, her teeth clenched in near panic. She watched Baruti, as he was shaken with waves of spasms that ran through various limbs and muscle groups. But when he looked about to cry out, she covered his mouth.

Finally, the pounding subsided, returning the island to a merely mildly disturbing domain of indeterminate rustles and squeaks. Felicity eased her hand from Baruti's mouth and found his eyes wide open and desperate to meet hers. He grabbed her arm and held on.

"Be careful," he said. "They'll stop at nothing."

"We already know that," she whispered.

"When I'm dead—"

"Hush. We'll get you to a hospital tomorrow. You're going to be fine."

"When I'm dead," he insisted, sounding completely lucid for a change, "you and Frank need to be careful. Find James Gerard of the World Environmental Protection Agency. It's a front for Interpol agents. He has harbored suspicions about this company for some time, but now he'll know for certain that I'm on to something. He'll protect you, I hope. Tell him everything, except . . ."

He shivered and moaned, released her arm and clutched his belly. Felicity muffled a cry, feeling his pain as if it were her own. She huddled closer to him and wrapped her arms around him.

"I wish I could help . . ."

He shuddered. He gritted his teeth. He straightened and touched her hair.

"Except," he continued, "don't mention there might be a connection to the *!Kung*. Find it yourselves. You, Frank, and Pedro. I don't trust him that far. I don't know who to trust, except you."

Tears glittered in his eyes, not just from pain, she imagined, but a telltale sign of his desperation and despair.

Why did this have to happen to him? Why now, when she'd finally realized how much he meant to her? She kissed his cheek, touched his lips.

"Don't. What if—"

"Poison isn't infectious," she said.

"But I'm not sure . . ."

"Yes, you are. And we're going to find an antidote."

"A long shot," he muttered.

"Why did you drink the coffee?"

"I expected a bullet, not a beverage. And I was cold. Stupid, too. I'm sure they didn't miss that I stole those samples."

She stiffened. "Dr. Lugan. Do you think . . .?"

"They might go after her, yes. Warn her."

"As soon as I can."

He grimaced and groaned again, clenching his jaw. He reached around her back, returning her embrace and possibly seeking comfort for his excruciating pain. If only she could swipe it away, delete it, rewind time to those moments before he and DeLuca flew to the miner's camp, before he placed the gun in her hand.

"I made a mistake," she confessed.

"You too?" he said, chuckling absurdly.

"With you. I waited too long to let you know I care. Frank is right. I'm always looking for the fantasy."

"Life is whatever you make it. You don't need to bury yourself in fantasies."

"Sometimes it's easier that way."

"That's everyone's problem. Always looking for the *easy* way. When I die, I want you to grieve for me." He gripped her back, placing a demanding hold on her.

"Of course. . . . But you're not going to die."

"Don't take the easy path. Let yourself feel. Even pain is better than nothing."

"I'll never stop crying," she whispered.

"No. Eventually you will. But you need to start."

He shifted, although it was obviously painful, since he tensed and cringed as he moved. Then he kissed her, fully and deeply, completely unrestrained. He could only manage a few seconds, but those seconds were unbearably sweet.

He rolled back, his arms flopping to the side. "I—I can't feel my legs," he muttered.

His breathing quickened, and he gradually faded from consciousness. But something even more terrifying struck her. His muscles weren't twitching anymore. In fact, he was hardly moving at all.

She lay beside him and held him, already grieving, because he *was* dying. Eventually she drifted into a light, troubled sleep, waking every time he cried out. As the night wore on, she sank deeper into a subconscious realm, becoming more oblivious to his struggles until . . . she started awake. It was still dark outside—with just the creeping fingers of dawn touching the sky—and so quiet. Was it a sound, or the lack of sound, that had startled her?

She blinked, trying to focus her eyes and rouse her foggy mind. She looked with rising anxiety at Baruti's deathly still body. Then, he murmured and released a stuttering breath. Still alive, thank God.

But then a shadow fell over her, blocking the dim light through the . . . *un-zippered* . . . mesh of the door. Someone was crouching over Baruti. Someone who gazed at him with unwavering intensity. Someone who clutched a knife.

FRANK WRIGGLED OUT of his tent, stood, and stretched, the pale light of dawn trickling through the dense leaves, branches, and broad array of baobab roots, and touching the dry, crisp ground in clusters and starbursts. He was thirsty, and he needed to take a piss, but before he could shuffle two steps, he sensed movement on the path and between their tents. He blinked his bleary eyes, but the steady, deliberate, and cautious movement toward their camp was certainly not made by local wildlife.

He counted three—no, four—skinny men with dark, curly hair. Two wore loincloths, the other two light cotton cargo pants with no shirts. It was cold to be parading around shirtless, but it didn't seem to bother the intruders. One man with a swirling design of scars on his chest noticed him standing under the tree, stopped, and regarded him for several seconds with a hooded, thoughtful gaze as if he recognized him, but then continued to slink toward Baruti's tent. In his hand, he clutched a knife, the dull, scratched blade undoubtedly still lethal if he wanted it to be. But the weapon was held in a casual way, as if incidental.

Frank, although not alarmed, retrieved his own knife from his bag, just in case. He thought of waking Pedro, but he imagined the big man's looming presence might startle and chase away the very people they wished to speak with. He was sure they'd approached their camp because of Baruti. Maybe they'd recognized his voice, when he'd muttered and cried out in his delirium.

Frank tucked the knife into his pocket and stood again, ever so cautiously. Another man drew closer to him, ducking beneath the branches—a man with prominent cheekbones, several chipped teeth, and a close-shaven head. He examined Frank through sun-crinkled eyes and halted his advance.

"*Tshjamm,*" Frank said, a *!Kung* greeting.

"Hello," the man returned. Naturally this *!Kung* man knew the English language, and Setswana too, no doubt. He might have returned to the old ways, but he was not oblivious of other cultures, although still clearly wary. The *!Kung* had always been wary of strangers. Now they had good reason for their suspicions.

"We have an ill fellow," Frank said. "Someone you may know. Baruti Mbeki?"

"Yes," the man responded as if that was obvious. "He bleats and makes the whole Delta aware of his presence. He will probably attract lions."

"What does the old man want?" Frank asked, pointing at the scarred *!Kung*. Frank sidled as casually as possible toward Baruti's tent, but he wasn't quick enough to prevent the man from ducking inside.

"He means no harm. He is our shaman, and although Baruti might be better served in a hospital, the old man thinks he can help." Strangely, the *!Kung* man chuckled as if he weren't quite convinced. "Besides, he's a long way from a hospital."

"That's where we're heading this morning. Back to our lodge, and then hopefully we can grab a flight to the nearest hospital."

"Do you think he will live that long?" The man didn't look him in the eye. While this was considered good manners among the *!Kung*, an effort to avoid offense, Frank thought the real reason was that he didn't expect the biologist to live another hour.

"I hope so. It's a strange illness, and it came on suddenly. I was just getting to know him, and to respect him, too. His death would be a blow to us, and even more to you. Because he came here to help and protect you."

The man raised his eyebrows.

A stir came from Frank's tent. The flap opened, and Pedro stumbled out, tensing in alarm and triggering the same response in the small cluster of *!Kung* men.

"It's okay, Pedro. All is good. My name is Frank," he said to the fellow beside him. "My colleague is Pedro, and he saved my life, even though he didn't know me at the time. He may look threatening, but he's a very good man."

The *!Kung* visitor nodded, assuming a more relaxed posture. "My name is Kushe. The old man is Kwi. These are Toma and Noma," he said, introducing the other men. They gathered around, offering shy nods.

Before Frank could respond, a stifled shriek came from Baruti's tent. Felicity must have been startled to find the old man hovering over her. He'd better calm her down before she did something stupid.

"He's not here to hurt you, Felicity," he pitched his voice toward her tent. "He's a *!Kung* man, and he came to help."

"Oh," she said. "Can you help? I—I think he's dying."

Kwi muttered, "*Gaua*," spooking Frank, even though he didn't believe in such things. He knew a little of the *!Kung* language, particularly the words that referred to their beliefs and mythology. A *gaua* was a spirit of the dead that could bring disease and illness or good fortune to its chosen subject, according to the great god's whim.

Felicity fumbled with the flap, then leaned out of the tent, catching Frank's eye. Her hair was tangled around her face, her makeup smeared and blotchy. But she still looked presentable, even attractive, which ignited that burning irritation in his gut again.

"Baruti thinks he was poisoned," she said, "when he drank coffee offered to him at the miners' camp. But he has no idea what the poison is. We need an antidote."

Frank shook off his irritation and concentrated on the problem at hand. "Maybe the shaman has an herbal remedy, but I'd rather trust this to a hospital. It's too late to pump his stomach, though."

Kwi shook a rattle in the tent and mumbled a stream of words in the *!Kung* language—words that Frank couldn't interpret. Frank crouched down and peered into the small cavity where Felicity, Baruti, and the shaman were squeezed together. He observed the man gazing into Baruti's eyes, examining his tongue, shaking the rattle—which was constructed of dry cocoons strung together and undoubtedly filled with chips of ostrich eggs—over his head and torso.

"What is he saying?" he asked Kushe.

"He thinks he knows this poison," said the Bushman, a question in his voice as if he, himself, was startled by the shaman's words.

"What is it? If we know its name, we might obtain an antidote and save him." Felicity looked up at Kushe with pleading eyes.

He avoided their gaze and dug his ragged sneaker into the crusty earth beneath the tree. "There is no antidote to this poison. No cure."

Frank's chest tightened, and pain rippled through him where the bands of muscles pulled on his lacerations and bruises. He wobbled, but Kushe caught him before he could fall.

"Have you been poisoned, too?" he asked.

"No. I don't think so," said Frank. "Just an old injury kicking in. What kind of poison has no cure?"

This couldn't possibly be an indigenous substance, because Baruti had been in the Arctic. But then again he'd been dealing with African men. . . .

"The grub from the chrysomelid beetles. In the past we used it to hunt. Still do sometimes. It kills fairly quickly, in a day or two, when introduced into the bloodstream on the tips of arrows."

"Death is certain?"

Kushe shrugged. "I have never seen an animal survive who has tasted its bitter sting. We are very, very careful when we harvest it."

Felicity wrenched herself from the tent, an obstinate look in her eyes.

"You can't be sure. You can't be sure this is even the same poison. We need to leave, *immediately*. We need to get him to a hospital, and they will damned well cure him."

"Or maybe we should stay," said Frank, although he knew he should brace for war with the girl. "And do what we came here to do. We may never get this chance again."

"Are you insane?" she snapped. "We're not going to sit around and chat while he dies. Baruti is—"

"Paralyzed," said Kwi, in perfect English.

Scanning...

Located: Chapter 35

THE ARABIA TERRA In Situ Propellant Plant peered over the horizon, a squat, gunmetal gray silo shimmering in and out of view through silken sheets of mist.

"We have arrived," said Bob, grinning unreservedly.

Gita cheered, teetered forward from the crew cabin of the rover as it bumped over the stubbly ground, and entered the cockpit. Lucas was still navigating, a position he preferred to sitting in the back and monitoring atmospheric conditions.

"And the plant looks intact," he mentioned, cautiously. "Although we can't be sure it's working properly and has created enough methane until we check out the cryogenic coolers."

Bob aimed the rover for the sealed door in the compact titanium shell of the ISPP, and the last few minutes of steady climbing, with occasional dips in the cratered and cobbled terrain, dragged out as if they were hours. Finally, he parked the vehicle and switched off the engine.

"So," he said, before anyone moved. "Let's hope it's functional, has not leaked any fuel since it was activated, and that the last mission specialists left us a trailer to carry the fuel back to our launch site."

He stood and stretched before strolling to the crew cabin as if he weren't nearly bursting with frantic energy. Lucas met Gita's eyes, reading impatience and fear there that was equal to his own. They trailed after Bob to the rear storage compartment and donned their tensile suits and oxygen masks, all too aware that the oxygen reserves they'd been bleeding from the tanks were almost depleted, given their limited water supplies, and the fact that the water in the ocean was too briny to use.

The plant held their only hope of continued survival on the planet, let alone of their ability to return home, because the plant produced oxygen for life support, in addition to methane for rocket propellant, and the rover's electrolysis unit could only supply enough oxygen for short excursions.

Within minutes, they'd exited the rover through the airlock compartment and stood before the plant door. Bob broke the seal, which was only there to protect the components from Martian dust, not to create an oxygen-rich environment. They would need to keep their masks on and tanks operating while in the plant.

Bob held the door open for Lucas, and Lucas stepped through, followed by Gita. Bob tramped in behind them, shutting the door with a mild clank. They now stood in an anteroom that resembled an airlock, only this room was designed to minimize dust contamination. Bob activated the magnetic scrubbers, which attracted the iron-rich dust and swept it from their clothes, although, since the atmosphere was becoming increasingly saturated, their outerwear was more damp than dusty. Once they looked sufficiently clean, Lucas opened the inner door.

The entrance was near the reactors, far from the CO_2 intake ducts and the compressor, once again to minimize contamination. The ISPP plant functioned through two primary subsystems: a thermochemical compressor and catalytic reactors. Since the Martian atmosphere was composed of 95.5% carbon dioxide, 2.7% nitrogen, and 1.6% argon, with traces of other gases, even for the first human missions NASA and other space agencies decided to use the resources available on Mars to produce fuel for the return flights to Earth. Now that they had developed an EPR engine, as was installed in the *Phoenix*, they no longer needed methane in chemical rockets for the return trip. But it was still required for liftoff from the planet to orbital rendezvous.

The plant worked in four steps: first, resource collection and conditioning; second, chemical conversions; third, separations, recycling, and product purification; and fourth, storage.

Converting carbon dioxide to methane and oxygen demanded two reactors, a Sabatier reaction unit and a Reverse Water/Gas Shift unit. The Sabatier reaction ($CO_2 + 4H_2 \rightarrow CH_4 + 2H_2O$) produced the methane and water and the RWGS reaction ($CO_2 + H_2 \rightarrow CO + H_2O$) produced carbon monoxide and water. Hydrogen had been transported from Earth, although it could now be collected on the planet through the available water sources and electrolyzed, once the settlers arrived. But initially, one of the key steps in producing oxygen after carbon dioxide had been fed through the RWGS reactor was electrolysis, to separate the hydrogen and oxygen and reuse the hydrogen for both reactors.

The RWGS and Sabatier reactors worked in tandem with heat exchangers to conserve heat and energy.

"The reactors look intact," said Lucas. The hum and rattle of circuits, valves, pumps, and blowers evidenced ongoing activity within the plant. "I'm going to walk through and do a visual inspection. Why don't you check the numbers for each station on the monitor, Bob?"

"I'll check for leaks of water or gas," said Gita. "We need to be certain the fuel and oxygen is pure."

"Listen, too," said Lucas. "A hiss could mean a broken seal."

Gita nodded and began to walk and crawl around the CO_2 sorption pump, Sabatier reactor, RWGS reactor, phase separators, electrolysis unit, and downstream gas separation system. Lucas did the same, in the opposite direction. First, he inspected the compressor that collected the Martian air and heated it, using temperature swing adsorption—adsorbing the CO_2 in microchannels via a catalyst, then heating the gas to compress it and desorb it downstream, thereby collecting a pure product. He could see nothing amiss—no cracks in the titanium-plastic composite that housed the microchannels.

He strode past the reactors and the recuperators, eyed the electrolysis unit, which seemed to be in order, then proceeded to the cryogenic coolers. All the systems seemed nominal, the cooler sensors indicating that the reservoir was half full of methane, clearly enough to fill the MADVEC tanks that stood against the wall. The oxygen tanks were also near capacity. They should have more than enough for the return trip in the rover, and enough to restock the HAB, if need be.

Pivoting on his heel, he marched back into the operations section of the plant, where Bob stood before a terminal, swiping through the logs on the mainframe.

"Everything good?" he asked.

"I'm seeing poor performance in the system, and some alarming numbers, but I think that's because of the higher atmospheric air pressure that exists now. They designed this for a pressure of 0.8 kPa, not 20, so the temperature gradient is skewed and the pressure is too high at the top end, exceeding optimal values. But at least it hasn't blown. How is the holding tank?"

"Half full. And the oxygen tank is nearly full. It doesn't matter if it blows now, as long as we retrieve the fuel first."

"I'm going to shut it down then, just to be on the safe side."

Lucas agreed. The last thing they needed was another explosion, this one potentially robbing them of their last chance to leave the planet.

Bob typed instructions into the antiquated computer system, and the hum, buzz, and minor pops that marked the opening and closing of valves immediately ceased.

"Um, *guys*. What was that?" Gita asked from beyond the Sabatier reactor.

"No worries," said Bob. "We have enough fuel. I'm just shutting the plant down, as a precaution."

"Oh. Okay," she said, in a more relaxed tone. "I don't see any leaks." She stepped around the reactor and strode toward the two men. "I'll look for a trailer in the storage room, while you guys begin filling the tanks."

"Call when you need help hitching it to the rover," said Lucas.

If looks could burn . . . "I won't need help," Gita replied.

Lucas and Bob headed to the south side of the building, where the cryogenic coolers were located. This portion of the plant was segregated, with a clean room protected from dust contamination by an inner and outer hatch. Spare tanks were stored in a corner of the room. The men rolled the tanks to ports in the methane and oxygen cryocoolers and filled them one by one, the rocket fuel first, then the oxygen. Ten minutes, later Gita opened the inner hatch to assist in loading. She'd discovered a trailer of the appropriate size, which she'd coupled to the rover and backed into position as if up to a loading dock. That was welcome, since the full tanks of cryogenic fuel were now extremely heavy. Bob and Lucas lugged them through the clean room and hatches, and then all three astronauts heaved the tanks onto the trailer. The oxygen tanks were smaller and lightweight, and could be carried between the two men by hand.

"I can't believe it," said Gita. "We're finally having some good luck."

"Well, this portion of the planet does appear to be more stable," said Lucas. "But with all the radical alterations we've introduced through terraforming, even a usually reliable fuel plant like this one will experience hiccups. GALRES designed all the original hardware for a thin atmosphere with dry air, not for higher pressure and the water vapor that's pervasive now. We'll have to inform the scientists when we contact Earth, so they can alter the design and fashion new components, if necessary. Or to send in a decent 3D printer to reconstruct pieces here. And I'm sure we could convert the existing water to oxygen using electrolysis now, without transporting additional hydrogen from Earth."

"That will certainly help support a small colony," said Bob.

"Yeah. I suppose so," said Lucas, wishing he'd filtered his words. "But as long as Mars keeps experiencing CO_2 bursts and exploding aquifers, they should hold off on permanent settlements. I have a feeling a flood of volcanic eruptions will be the next consequence of the bombardment."

"As long as *we* don't see them," said Gita. "Up close and personal."

"We're a long way from Oympus Mons," said Bob, in an attempt to be reassuring. "But I suppose we should start heading back to the Kasei base, as soon as possible." He finished strapping the last cylinder to the trailer bed, carefully cushioning it with blankets from the rover to avoid excess jostling.

Satisfied, they piled into the vehicle, and ten minutes later they were under way. All the rover systems appeared to be operating smoothly, although Bob drove at a much slower speed to accommodate the trailer full of compressed rocket fuel.

They proceeded over gritty red hillocks and threaded through boulder-strewn mazes. They swung around steep-sided craters that dipped unexpectedly into view, apparently obscured from the lidar sensors by the ever-present mist.

Bob avoided a perilously deep chasm just in the nick of time, when he caught sight of the hidden rim just as it began crumbling away from the edge of the rover's wheels.

"Do you want me to drive?" asked Lucas, a fluttering sensation reawakening in his belly at their near tumble into a ravine. Why, ever since their arrival on this planet, had he felt that they were doomed? Why did it seem, despite the upswing in their luck, that they would never escape? Why did he still have the desire to throttle Bob, even though they had developed a singular trust? Maybe because he knew that it was weak to trust another fellow, that such a bond was easily shattered by facts and human frailty. Maybe because it was rendering *him* weak and more apt to doubt his capacity to carry out his own mission, and even to question the integrity of the mission itself.

"If I get tired, I'll stop or let you or Gita take over," said Bob. "But at this snail's pace, I doubt we'll have any mishaps. Don't worry."

"That was a close call," said Lucas, feeling the need to point it out, since Bob was in denial.

"Do you think you could do any better?" asked Bob, obviously irritated. "The mist scatters the light to the lidar sensors, creating an imprecise view of the topography ahead. Since the radar is out of commission, I have to rely on my vision, just as you would if you took my place. But I haven't driven us over a cliff."

"Yet," Lucas muttered.

"Seriously? After all we've been through, now that we're finally on the home stretch, you're going to start arguing—"

The rover jounced into a deep rut that snapped Lucas up and down in his seat, the movement ricocheting through his belly and stabbing him in his wound.

"Watch the road," snapped Gita. "Lucas, shut up!"

"Sorry," he mumbled. "I'm just getting a bad feeling."

"You don't usually act on or even mention feelings." She obviously couldn't help herself. "Bob was doing a fine job, as always, until this nonsense began."

"The mist is extremely dense in this oceanfront zone. Maybe we should wait for it to clear before we continue."

As if to emphasize his point, a massive cloud enveloped them, so impenetrable to the naked eye that it was like being wrapped in a mummy's shroud. The lidar went haywire, its screen showing only a rusty haze and indeterminate blobs, a featureless soup of pixels. Bob reduced the rover's speed, to the point that it was barely inching forward.

"Maybe we *should* stop for a few hours," said Bob. "But I don't want to risk waiting too long, in case we run into more difficulties swinging around the discharging aquifer. If it extends too far into the Chryse Planitia, it will eventually unite with the sea, and then we're screwed."

"Point acknowledged," said Lucas. "I don't mean to be . . ."

Bob eyed him.

"Well, you know."

Bob cast him a brittle smile.

At the same instant, a pronounced shudder ran through the vehicle, as it was wrenched to the side and halted, even though Lucas could feel the tires spinning, seeking traction.

"What the hell?" said Bob. "The terrain is flat here, I swear."

"But the trailer might have tilted into a sizable rut," said Lucas. "Or it's slipping over the rim of a crater."

"I'll take a look out the back window," said Gita.

"Good idea." Lucas leaped from his seat and scrambled to follow her to the rear airlock. But as they desperately scanned through the shatterproof glass, nothing was revealed in the opaque fog.

"Can't see a thing," he yelled to Bob. "I'll jump out and see if I can spot the problem on the ground. Maybe it just needs a push."

"I'll go too," said Gita. As they donned their outdoor apparel, she cast him frequent glances, a worried crease lining her forehead.

Once outside, Lucas understood their dilemma even before his eyes could penetrate the mist as far as the trailer. As soon as he struck the ground, his boots sank solidly into tangerine muck. He heard the slurp of suction as he yanked them free. Gita yelped in disgust, as she leaped out of the rover and plunged into the same gluey substance.

"I guess the trailer's stuck," she said.

But as Lucas plodded toward its murky outline, he realized it was something more alarming. The ground itself sagged, slumping under the weight of melted permafrost and the newly introduced rain that the parched soil couldn't absorb. It was also possible that a spring or discharging aquifer had sent a creeping tide down the slope into an adjacent crater. This slow landslide—thick as trickling syrup—had snared the trailer, while the rover had managed to win through to more stable ground. He stared at the trailer, feeling befuddled for a second or two, before he came to a decision—one that his companions would undoubtedly hate. He seized the hitch, pivoted the lock, and ejected the spring-loaded pins.

"Lucas, what are you doing?" snapped Gita, although she made no move to stop him.

The trailer, now released from the hitch, began sliding backward. Lucas vaulted away from it, but not far enough from the path of the rotating boom. Gita launched forward and slammed him to the ground. They lay engulfed in mud and watched with rising tension as the trailer loaded with their very precious cargo tilted, tumbled, and bobbled down the slope, as the booms and roars and scrapes of repeated impact filled the air.

"I HAD TO do it," said Lucas, leaning against the shattered frame of the trailer, as Bob flung his hands up, gripped his head, and gazed furiously at the dented and punctured tanks, along with one that had ruptured explosively, spraying fragments into the others.

"Not one," he whimpered. "Not even one left intact."

"We'll head back," said Gita. "We'll restart the reactors and refill the cryo-coolers."

"If I hadn't detached the trailer, it would have dragged the rover into the gully with it. The rover wouldn't have survived a tumble like that; and even if it had, the tanks would have bombarded it with shrapnel."

"Not even one," Bob moaned.

"We're still alive," said Lucas.

Bob finally stopped examining the wreckage, looked up, and sharply met his gaze. "Are we, Lucas? How many additional tanks did we leave in the ISPP? How many?"

Lucas shrugged.

"You know there was only one extra methane tank. And one oxygen tank.

Not enough, by any account, for liftoff. Not even enough for life support in the HAB until the ISA can dispatch a rescue team."

"We repair the tanks," said Gita, her eyes shifting back and forth between the two of them, her mind scrambling for solutions where none existed. "We return to the ISPP, repair the tanks, refill them . . ."

"Have you looked at them?" barked Bob, plucking a snarl of silvery white metal from the scattered fragments that resembled the broken skeleton of a downed aircraft. "We're not equipped to repair this amount of damage. We'd have to rebuild it completely, which we could do if we had a decent 3D printer, but we didn't bring one down from the *Phoenix*. Even if we did magically find a printer, we don't have the time. We don't have enough water to continue generating oxygen in the rover for more than a few days."

"Then we collect it," said Gita. "There's water in the air, in case you didn't notice. We'll design a moisture trap, distill the water, and live in the rover until we can repair the tanks or our rescue ship arrives."

"The scrubbers," said Lucas. "The CO_2 scrubbers aren't designed for long term use in the rover. Not months or the year it will undoubtedly take them to arrive. We'd need replacement cartridges, which we don't have. And I'm sure the ISA won't be risking the other EPR spacecraft since this . . . disaster was due to our own disobedience."

"So what then? We just give up?"

Bob turned to Lucas, his eyes twitching as if he were experiencing a short in his nervous system. "Couldn't you have wedged something solid under the wheels, given them grip?"

"No," said Gita, stepping between them and raising her arms. "Stop the blame game. I was there. Remember? We had no time. It was a mudslide, for God's sake. The sliding soil was dragging the rover down with it. We had no choice. Lucas made the only logical decision in that split second, or we'd all be dead now. Not in a few weeks or months. Now. He provided us with time to improvise a solution. And we're too goddamned bright not to figure this out."

Bob narrowed his eyes, the twitching showing no sign of abating. He looked around Gita to zero in on Lucas again.

"Lucas is too goddamned bright not to realize that we're screwed. That's why he hasn't suggested any brilliant solutions, only pointed out problems. He bought us time, I'll give you that. But only that."

"Well I, for one, am glad we have more time. And you would have probably died in the wreckage, so you should be grateful for it, too."

"We don't have to give up yet," said Lucas softly.

"Or maybe the weight of the rover would have curtailed the skid and prevented the trailer from tumbling," snapped Bob. "Maybe we'd still have intact tanks, if he'd left the trailer attached and let the rover go. The risk to me would have been worth it."

"You would have died," Lucas said softly, again. "It was a sure thing if I'd let it go."

"What did you say?" asked Gita, turning to face Lucas as if delayed signals to her brain had finally connected.

"Bob would have died."

"Not that. Before that."

He took a deep breath, gulping air from his mask. "We don't . . . have to give up . . . yet."

"Of course we don't," she said, enveloping him in a warm smile. "But you have an idea, don't you?"

"Not so much an idea as a possible destination. A place where I think there might be supplies. Tanks, food stocks, perhaps stored fuel."

"What place?" asked Bob. "The nearest alternate base is beyond our range now."

"Not a base. Just a storage depot. Near the Vitalis Cave."

"Storage depot? How is it that Gita and I never heard of this depot?" said Bob, his voice crisp with doubt and sharp with anger.

"That's because you didn't read the source material. I did. Our mission had nothing to do with landing on Mars. And all the distributed mission-required reading didn't include it because it's merely a storage cache. I just came across it because I tend to be thorough."

"Then why didn't you think to mention it before?" asked Bob. "If it's near the Vitalis Cave, it's closer to the MADVEC than the Arabia Terra base. We could have headed there first."

"I didn't because . . . because I couldn't be positive. And I didn't know if it would be well enough stocked with fuel, or that the fuel was even viable. And finding out will require cave exploration and extraction, which will be hazardous as well. But when it came down to letting the rover—and *you*—go, or keeping our one and only source of life support—and *you* —intact while we investigated this other possibility, I chose the rover—and *you*. It may be a longshot, but it's better than nothing. I made a decision quickly, but not mindlessly."

Bob stood rigidly, in ponderous silence, continuing to glare at Lucas as he mulled over his explanation. The tension, the hopelessness he'd been experiencing seemed to be cycling through a feedback loop that he was having trouble escaping. But there was obviously more to this heavy silence, a deception Lucas had long suspected.

"I nearly died after the explosion," said Lucas. "But you saved me, through an astonishingly selfless act, and I now trust you with my life. In this instance, whether you will admit it or not, I've returned the favor. But I still don't think you trust me. Not for a minute. Not beyond your line of sight. You never did, and I don't think you ever will, no matter what you said yesterday."

"I . . ." said Bob, but his words trailed off into the hiss of his rebreather. He couldn't deny it.

Gita looked stricken, but she didn't defend Bob. In the back of her mind, she must have been aware of his pretense, too.

"But whether you trust me or not, I'm going to get us off this goddamned planet. And if you don't survive, it will be your own damned fault, not mine."

He turned and stomped up the slope, wondering why he felt so angry, so bitter, and so drained. Why should it matter what Bob thought at all?

Scanning...

Located: Chapter 36

“IS THIS THE island where you have your *werf*?” Frank asked Kushe, using the *!Kung* word for “village.” Kushe looked away. Kwi continued to shake his rattle over Baruti’s head and motionless body where he lay in his tent, while the group sat around the fire and watched.

“This is pointless,” said Felicity, still sitting vigil beside Baruti. “Kelong, Dave, we need to leave, now!”

“No. Not here,” Kushe finally answered Frank. “And we move around a lot.”

The guides were indifferent to Felicity’s plea. They looked at Frank and Pedro, in that order. Her pale face flushed, but everyone continued to ignore her.

“That’s good,” said Frank. “Because someone means you harm. That’s why Baruti was poisoned. He was tracking the people who . . .” He paused and wondered whether he should continue. Did these people know what had happened to the other *!Kung*?

“Killed my brothers and sisters? Yes, I know. I don’t know why, but I know someone wants us eliminated.”

“Does anyone care that Baruti is paralyzed? That he’s *dying*?” asked Felicity.

“I care,” said Kwi, and he tapped her forehead with his rattle. “Don’t you see my efforts? Do they mean nothing to you?"

"But they're . . . ineffective," she muttered.

"They may be the only thing that *is* effective. But I don't understand how he is paralyzed by drinking the poison. It doesn't work that way. It enters the blood, but not the meat. Animals have swallowed the poison with no ill effect."

"That's right," said Kushe. "I read about it once when we lived in Maun. I read about the poison's action in the body on my brother's computer when I was studying our heritage. It works through the blood. It destroys hemoglobin. It doesn't work through . . . digestion."

"Then this isn't the same poison," said Felicity. "There's still hope, if we get him to a hospital."

"But it *is* the same," said Kwi, dropping his rattle beside Baruti and snatching Felicity's flashlight from the tent floor. He flicked on the light and aimed it at the biologist's face, then scanned down his neck and chest, pushing aside the fabric of his shirt. Working outward, he eventually began to examine Baruti's arms and hands and fingers.

"Aha!" he exclaimed, pointing to Baruti's index finger. "A cut! A small nick in the skin. Not made by an arrow, but it follows the same principle. He didn't swallow it. They knew how to kill him."

"He's not dead," screamed Felicity, nearly hysterical.

Frank sighed in resignation. He'd have to deal with this girl whom he despised, before he and the *!Kung* could exchange any useful information. And he'd have to deal with her in a gentle manner. He excused himself, and got up from the fire, moving in Felicity's direction. When he reached Felicity, he knelt down beside her and plucked her hand from her side, cradling the rough, cold-cracked fingers in his own. She stared at him defiantly, as if she wanted to scratch his eyes out.

"I believe them," he said. "I know it's hard to hear, but Baruti knew that he'd been poisoned, and by the very miners who'd been active in this region—the same people who might have murdered the other *!Kung*. Sometimes evil people and psychopaths are amused by irony. They employed the *!Kung* poison, even though they are obviously enemies of the *!Kung*. Baruti is paralyzed; he's dying. This poison has no cure. But we've made contact just as we set out to do. If we leave now, we might never discover what makes these people a target. We might be handing them over to be slaughtered, too. And maybe many others, depending on the scope of this conspiracy. It's imperative that we discover the miners' plans before any more people die. It's too late for Baruti. I don't think the medical community can help."

Tears gathered at the corners of Felicity's eyes. She'd tried so hard to hold them in, to appear strong and rational. For once, he felt sorry for her. Did she really care this deeply for the biologist? It seemed like more than infatuation.

"You don't know that for sure," she whispered. "A few hours might make all the difference. Why won't you give him at least that much time? We can return here and talk with these people later."

He leaned toward her ear and whispered, "Can we? Will they still be here, or will they clear out? That's the smart thing to do, when you know someone is hunting you."

"Hours . . ." Kwi mused. "How many hours since Baruti encountered these men?"

"Three days," said Felicity. "They were in the North, in Canada."

"Hmm. Too long. Then he should already be dead."

Her eyes snapped wider, no longer appealing to Frank but demanding that he listen. "Then it isn't the same poison. He still has a chance."

"It might be the amount," said Kushe. "A pinprick to the finger would deliver far less poison than arrows that are liberally smeared with it. Perhaps death isn't certain."

Kwi raised his eyebrows and shook his head. "Delayed, perhaps. But soon, he will no longer draw breath. His heart will freeze like his other muscles. He fights it. Maybe he will win. If I reach into the spirit world, I will know for sure. I need to see him. I see nothing but lions around him now."

Kushe shuddered.

"What does that mean?" asked Felicity.

"*!Kung* believe," said Frank, "that certain famous sorcerers, formerly medicine men who chose to be poisoners and evil magicians instead of healers, have taken the form of certain lions. He is equating the miners with these sorcerer-lions."

"Do you really still believe this?" Felicity asked Kushe, her voice grating on every word. "You've been introduced to the world of science. Surely you know that they're human, not mystical beings linked to animals."

"I believe that humans can have mystical qualities. I believe we are all linked to animals. And who knows what happens to the spirit once we die? I've been taught to doubt. Doubt has been demanded of you. But is doubt really what Baruti needs?"

"Kwi might be able to help," said Frank. "He may reveal something that might help." When would she wake up and realize that the beliefs and knowledge of these people could be the key to the revelations they were seeking, to the *!Kung's* survival? And maybe even to their own, since the miners probably wouldn't stop at killing them, too?

"Baruti is already overdue in dying, so maybe he will survive. But you can't extract a poison that has already been well distributed. I think that only his own body can fight it and repair itself, especially if it was a weak dose."

"A hospital could provide him with life support as he fights it," said Felicity.

"Or Kwi will give him a reason to live, which is sometimes as effective as medical intervention. Another hour, Felicity. I don't think it will make a difference. It's a long way back to the lodge, and then who knows how long it will be before we can fly Baruti to Maun? But that hour could make all the difference to his survival and others'. We've got to give Kwi this chance. If Baruti dies for nothing, you won't forgive yourself, either."

"What do you think we can learn from this hocus-pocus?"

"The purpose of this hocus-pocus," he said.

FELICITY AGREED, BUT only because she had no choice. Ridiculously, the guides were looking to Frank for leadership and instructions, and Frank seemed to care little for Baruti's life. Baruti had drawn the gun earlier, but Frank had turned it around on him and now seemed determined to pull the trigger. He could rationalize it all he wanted, but it made no sense to delay treatment for a shamanic ceremony.

Kwi commanded his small group of men to collect more firewood and feed a new fire, which he'd started a good distance from the baobab tree. He added crisp, dry branches and leaves until the fire licked the sky in lustrous flames. Then, he asked Frank and Pedro to retrieve Baruti from the tent and bring him near the fire. Baruti didn't cry out anymore, or even open his eyes. His body hung limply from Frank's and Pedro's arms as they trundled him, sleeping bag and all, closer to the crackling flames. Felicity tried to settle on the ground close by, but Kwi denied her this proximity, waving her back with a fierce gesture. But he did this from a distance, displaying a strange combination of dominance and timidity.

"He sees you as a potential barrier," said Frank, sitting next to her cross-legged, his knee brushing hers. "And also as a stranger. The *!Kung* have always feared strangers. He doesn't know how to control you."

"Why should he need to control me?"

"Because you don't trust him. And you might interfere. We need to study the process, Felicity. We need to find out what they know. Sit back and be a scientist. Set aside your emotions, for Baruti's sake, as well as for these people."

How completely uncharacteristic of Frank. Yes, he was holding Baruti for ransom, but his objectives, although cloaked in scientific objectivity, seemed entirely personal and focused on the *!Kung*. She had never thought he cared for anyone besides himself.

"I won't interfere," she said, shifting to the side so her knee no longer touched his. "As long as he doesn't endanger Baruti further. But I still don't think creating a log of shamanic practices will result in some revelation about these killers."

"Observation is only the first step, as you well know," Frank whispered, as Kwi extracted crushed leaves from his pouch and sifted them onto the fire, generating a dense cloud of gray smoke. Kwi murmured and chanted, his eyes rolling back in his head. Then he drank the smoke, breathing in a great gulp; but he didn't cough or sputter, suggesting that he was immune to its particulates and toxins.

He called out in a hushed whisper, "*Haishi, Gao ha, Nao, Gara.*"

"Those are names," said Frank, recording every nuance of the ceremony with his phone. "Different names that belong to their great god."

Felicity tried not to roll her eyes. Would lightning stream down from the sky? Would a disembodied voice call from the clouds?

Kwi continued entreating the gods, chanting their names over and over for several minutes. But then he grew silent, maintaining a breathless pause that made even Felicity hold her breath. She was familiar with this type of ritual, through her many anthropology classes. Kwi was falling into a trance, undoubtedly provoked by the substance in the smoke or some other hallucinogen he'd ingested.

Suddenly, Kwi shuddered and shrieked; his eyes rolled so far back in his head that all that remained were the whites, leaving a sightless stare as if his eyes were windows shuttered with blinds. Reading up on these practices had not prepared Felicity for witnessing one. Prickles of unease like the jabs of tiny needles raced up and down her body. For some reason, she shifted closer to Frank until her knee rested against his again.

He didn't seem to notice, he was so engrossed in the scene.

Kwi fell forward, right into the fire. Felicity yelped and jerked in his direction, but Frank locked a grip on her arm and held her back.

Astonishingly, the man raked his fingers through the glowing coals on the outer edge of the ring, seemingly oblivious to pain, and—horror of horrors—began to wash his face in the coals.

After seconds that seemed like hours, he stood up, his face ash-covered and soot-blackened, but Felicity couldn't spot reddened or seared flesh. She frowned and looked at Frank. How?

"Watch and listen," said Frank, keeping his phone steady.

Kwi walked over to Baruti with innate vision, his pupils still hidden. He knelt beside him, his hands fluttering like erratic monarch butterflies, tracing a path over his face, down the contours of his body, over the gash of his wound. Baruti yelled. Kwi shrieked. Kwi tossed his hands into the air, as if he'd gripped an evil entity and was hurling it into the sky.

Then he fell to the ground beside Baruti and lay still.

"WHAT JUST HAPPENED?" asked Felicity, still feeling shaken as if a lightning bolt had blitzed the earth right beside her and sent static electricity sizzling through her body.

Frank swiped off his phone and turned to her. "Kwi drew out the sickness and shrieked it into the air, flinging it back to the evil spirits who'd brought it."

"Right," said Felicity. "Sure."

A tight smile tugged at the corners of Frank's thin lips. He leaned toward her, and she thought he might add a more scientific observation, but instead, he kissed her on the cheek and whispered, "I appreciate your reluctance, but I still hate you, darling."

She bristled and was about to slap him, but he was already bouncing up and heading toward the shaman. As he crouched down beside Kwi, Kushe and the other men gathered in a tight circle around the man. Kwi opened his eyes, his irises fully restored to their original position. He nodded at Frank.

"He is strong," the man said, shuddering. "I always knew there was a thread, but never suspected it was so woven into him." He sat up and met Frank's eyes.

Felicity scrambled to the circle and squeezed between the men. She knelt beside Baruti, examining his ashen face for some sign of revival, despite common sense dictating that any expectation of improvement was ridiculous. He lay still, his only movement the barely perceptible rise and fall of his chest.

"What is so woven into him?" asked Frank.

"The lion," replied the shaman.

Frank frowned. "I thought the lions were the poisoners."

"And so they are. Lions will hunt. It is their nature. From the dawn of time, the *!Kung* have had to trick the lion, for he was always stronger and would sometimes kill us. But at some point, we became friends and began to . . ."—he searched for the word in English—". . . cooperate with each other. Since we were greater in number, we would drive the antelope to him, he would kill it, and then we would share the kill. But eventually we learned how to survive without his strength, through our own . . . resourcefulness. When we discovered the poison to hunt, it became an easier task to kill the antelope, while the lion continued to rely on his power and nothing else. We surpassed him and he grew angry. Eventually, frustrated and dispirited, he left us. But he left behind remnants of his soul. He left swatches and threads among the children of the jungle as he wandered farther north. Baruti has within him flickers of the lion's fierceness, and he has carried some of his arrogance, too. If the poisoning lions had recognized these remnants in him, they might not have tried to kill him. Or they recognized them and decided to kill him just the same, for he is but a faint reflection. But it is the lion in him that keeps him alive."

"What are you saying?" Felicity couldn't help but interject. "That Baruti is in some way connected to these poisoners? I don't understand."

Frank sat back on his heels, his face creased and cluttered with his evaluating thoughts. How could he make anything out of this mumbo jumbo? Felicity wondered. The whole idea that Baruti was associated with the men he was chasing seemed ludicrous, particularly since they'd tried to murder him. She could be way off base, but what she could make of the tale was that the poisoners might have known the *!Kung* sometime in the past. She knew from her readings that in some cultures information of historical significance was passed down in metaphorical tales. So, according to Kwi, the poisoners, or *lions*, had first shared a bond with the *!Kung*, as they hunted together. But, eventually, the *!Kung* had outfoxed them and outdistanced them through . . . *innovation*? But was that a reason to dispose of them permanently? Particularly in modern times? The *!Kung* might have been innovative in hunting and gathering, but that was tens of thousands of years ago, and once agriculture had reared its head they were left far behind. This story of first cooperation, then competition and ingenuity, explained absolutely nothing.

Like who these poisoners were. And what they planned to do in the present.

"The lion keeps him alive," murmured Frank. "He is, after all, a biologist."

"You're not talking about animal spirits?"

"No, Felicity. I'm talking about science. Something you're ignoring altogether, even though I advised you to take notes."

Now he'd lost her completely. Was he referring to an aspect of Baruti's biological make-up that was keeping him alive? Something that a lion possessed, too?

"Frank—" She stared at him, but then noticed something behind him—something sinuous and slithery—slinking toward him. "Frank!" she yelled, pointing a trembling finger.

"Felicity, now don't get upset. I'm just asking you to think."

Well, there was one way to get his attention quickly. "Frank, is . . . is that a *python*?"

Frank jumped up and whirled around, nearly stumbling into the fire. He stepped backward, and Pedro stepped forward like a shield.

But it wasn't Frank who answered.

"No," said Kushe, backing up and looking equally flustered. "That's a black mamba."

Scanning...

Located: Chapter 37

DAYNA SLUMPED ONTO the firm mattress of the four-poster bed, exhausted from traveling, but even more so from how heart-sick she felt after the unintentional revelations from Baruti's father. If Baruti wasn't dead or dying, he could be involved in some sort of spy game, investigating an international conspiracy, or . . . he might be mentally ill. Any or all of these possibilities could place her students in extreme jeopardy.

She stared at the walls of her room, which were nothing more than flimsy canvas barriers against the outdoors—an outdoors that teemed with wildlife. Her first encounter with the locals had been upon arrival at the door to her room, which was basically a tent on a raised wooden platform designed to keep the shelter above ground-level and, no doubt, snake-level. Shuffling across the dusty boards of the porch came a troupe of bustling and rather opinionated banded mongooses, wearing their striped prison attire. They tramped in front of her, around her, beside her, and they just kept coming and coming and coming. There must have been at least fifty. They muttered amongst themselves; several eyed her with casual curiosity and muttered to her as they nosed past. They seemed not the least bit shy.

As the crew finally disappeared into the underbrush, weaving between the prickly clumps of grass, Dayna heard a soul-chilling hoot. She set her bag on the ground and gazed up into the tall sheltering branches of the adjacent mopane tree. Perched on a lower limb, gazing at her speculatively, was the most enormous owl she'd ever seen—two feet tall, with ginger-speckled plumage and oil-black eyes. If it weren't for that glassy obsidian stare, this plump feather giant would look as huggable as a stuffed animal in the window of a toy store. No doubt he was not benign, but she felt comforted by his presence, considering that rats, lizards, and snakes were likely on the giant-owl menu. After Frank's near-fatal encounter with a deadly reptile, Dayna was feeling particularly sensitive about snakes. She and the owl continued to contemplate each other in a silent exchange full of wonder and wariness, until a baboon swung down from a higher branch, bobbled around the owl, and showered him with cat calls, prompting him to move on. Spreading his magnificent wings, he darkened the sky, then flapped over the scrub-covered islands and sparkling channels of the Okavango.

These encounters were stimulating, to say the least. But Dayna had a feeling the animals in the Okavango were the least of her worries.

As she lay back on the bed, she examined her surroundings. The room was functional, with a small wooden dresser with an oval mirror, a card table supporting a lush drapery of potted ferns, a plain double bed shrouded in a beige bedspread, and canvas walls with screen windows that still hadn't managed to fend off a scattered orchestra of bugs. But the bugs, primarily mosquitoes, didn't disturb her nearly as much as the fact that Felicity had slept in this same bed two nights ago, and Felicity hadn't returned.

And Frank? Poor wounded Frank, whose intelligence and tenacity she often admired but just as often ignored. Was that because he had a tendency to be steady and reliable, and was therefore easily overlooked? Was Frank dying now too? Had he been rescued only to fall into Baruti's trap?

A knock came at her door, startling Dayna from her thoughts.

"Dr. Lugan?"

"Yes, Dr. Wilson. Come in."

She would have preferred to speak to him in the lounge or somewhere outdoors, but he obviously wasn't willing to wait for her to settle in.

He opened the door and stepped inside, nudging another pesky mongoose out of the way.

"I must say, I love the surroundings. I wish we were here for a different reason." His face was slumped with seriousness, yet a gleam shone in his eyes.

Dayna pushed herself to sitting position, then reluctantly offered him a seat on her bed.

"I'm not surprised that you would love the surroundings. Bustling with biological gems, despite the continuing depletion of the diversity of species on our planet. I just saw a gigantic owl."

As he sat down opposite her, tilting the mattress in his direction, she described it, and his face lit up with instant recognition.

"Pel's fishing owl. Definitely a rare species."

Dispensing with small talk, Dayna got to the point.

"Did you have any luck with the manager? Is there a way to catch up to them?"

He sighed. "Doubtful. He knew the direction they'd headed, but there are countless channels they could have explored, and innumerable islands where they might have camped. We'd get hopelessly lost looking for them. I think we'll just have to wait till they return. If Baruti is ill, I'm sure they'll about-face and head back immediately. Especially if he has the same symptoms as DeLuca."

"I'm not a very patient person. And after speaking with Baruti's father . . ."

"Why don't we go for a walk?" suggested Shaun. "Rather than speculate about horrible things and just get more and more anxious, we could explore the paths around the lodge. I'm sure we'll be rewarded with an incredible view and some more unique animal encounters. It might help us to forget our worries for a few minutes."

His eyes had grown dimmer and more creased as he spoke. She realized he was at least as worried as she was, and needed to escape his spiraling thoughts.

"Sure," she said. "You're right. I've never been on a safari. Most of my excursions have taken place in populated regions and have involved dead specimens more than living. This should be refreshing."

She smiled, but her face felt brittle with the effort. He nodded, grabbed her hand, and tugged her to the door with a reenergized grin—another example of his boyish charm. Despite the fact that he was likely her age, he often acted so young. He could switch his mood in an instant. He seemed to be constantly brimming with energy. He regarded the world around him with wonder, but nothing held his attention for too long—particularly women, she imagined, since he was still single. She could see how Felicity would swear by his innocence—of murder, anyway. He exuded innocence.

And yet . . . he knew something he wasn't telling her. The words echoed in her head: *I can't let this go any further. I can't let anyone else die.*

Shaun released her hand as soon as they reached the main path, perhaps realizing it was inappropriate. Part of the path was a raised boardwalk on the same level as the lodge. It circled the six rooms and connected to the central front desk and eastern dining area, with several ramps leading away from the structures like bicycle spokes. From there, certain paths ended abruptly to the north and south in one of the two lagoons that narrowed the center of the grounds like an hourglass, while others plunged deeper into the tree-filled wilderness to the east and west. But all were curbed by wetlands and open water, giving the impression that the lodge was located on an island. One could conceivably wade to the next protrusion of dry land, but it would be far safer to travel by boat, especially considering there were crocodiles in the water.

As they strolled down the nearest ramp, the path became a stretch of dusty, dry ground, with a layer of gravel and sand that distinguished it from the grass and scrubland on either side. The murky border of the wetlands that transitioned to open channels of water lay just beyond.

"Do we need to worry about snakes, Dr. Wilson?"

"Shaun," he said with a smile. "And I'm sure you have a first name. You can maintain your professional distance if you like, but the formal titles become tedious after a while."

"Dayna," she said.

"Of course we have to worry about snakes, Dayna. And I'm sure they're worried about us. So watch where you step, and be polite."

She couldn't help but smile. "I appreciate your honesty," she said. At least he wasn't being obnoxiously reassuring or overstating his expertise.

They continued to walk along the path, through a cluster of palms that shortly gave way to an open expanse of papyrus-rich marshland.

"Hold," said Shaun, grabbing her arm.

She froze, her stomach knotting at the thought of a potential fatal encounter. He pointed and, lo and behold, a train of majestic elephants splashed through the water and parted the reeds not fifty paces from the path. Dayna heaved a sigh of relief and watched the hypnotic scene. Calves nudged the huge hind legs of their mothers while adult males plodded in the rear of the procession, every trunk swinging in synchrony as if to an imaginary beat. It was an extraordinary sight, embroidered with black and white storks soaring above the water and an endless emerald-and-tan carpet of bristly stalks and reeds. Shaggy wildebeest foraged in the distance, brisk brush-strokes of brown. It was as if she'd stepped into an artist's dream, where wildlife of all shapes and sizes and colors abounded, where the sharp angles of modern architecture in bland gray steel and reflective glass no longer existed, where every snapshot wasn't marred with the too-familiar human frame. Here contours were more random, and fleshy sags and bulges, frothy bubbles and jagged edges prevailed. Nothing was precise or predictable.

"Stunning, isn't it?" Shaun obviously wasn't referring to just the elephants, although they were stunning.

"I think I've lived too long in a dead place."

"The Arctic is like this, only colder," he smiled.

"I can see why you chose to live there, besides the dictates of your career. It's very . . . refreshing. Far from human entanglements, too."

"Not far enough," he muttered.

"I guess we've all experienced those problems," she said as innocuously as possible. "I . . . well, I'm in the midst of a divorce."

He shifted his gaze toward her, fine lines whispering through his face. "I'm sorry. I was married once, too. It didn't work out. She was too . . . fanatical." His eyes wandered back to the elephants.

"I see. It can be so hard to realize that you've made a mistake. We experienced some painful events," she said, thinking of her lost children, "and I guess we couldn't get past them."

"That happens sometimes, I imagine. There are certain things that you never recover from."

"Yes. And then we grew apart. I turned to work for solace and he turned to

. . . other women." She shuddered, suddenly swamped in pain. Why was she revealing so many intimate details of her personal life? Did she really need to, just to draw information from him?

"I suppose . . . men sometimes do that when they're hurting."

"Understandable, but not forgivable," she said.

He didn't respond.

"I really did love him, though."

He watched the elephants, presenting his shoulder to her.

Say something!

Finally he did, in the softest tones. "She believed in a religion, a cult, I guess you could call it. I was part of it too, to a certain extent—till I went away to school and broadened my horizons. The more I read and researched, the more I analyzed the extraordinary connections we all have, *all of us*, biologically—genetically—but even psychologically and culturally, the more I felt alienated by their beliefs. It's incredible to me that we can change our genetic codes with bacteria or viruses—that's how intricately we're linked to all life on Earth. And now even to Mars, and probably the rest of the universe. I couldn't accept their fears. I couldn't accept their choices."

"What were their beliefs?" asked Dayna, holding her breath.

A wintry smile touched his face. And he did turn to her. "Do you believe in competition, Dayna?" he asked. "Do you believe in Cain and Abel?"

"The story of Cain and Abel is one of a competition for affection—an unhealthy although understandable competition between brothers for a father's love, which seems to take place in every family. But Cain took extreme measures to win the competition, and ultimately he lost."

His face grew pale. "Yes. He did."

"Is this cult in the habit of murdering people?" she asked. She had to.

He blinked several times. An elephant trumpeted nearby. He swept his eyes downward and opened his mouth as if he couldn't find words.

"They . . ." His phone jangled in his pocket—a piercing sound in the calm air. He pulled it out, swiped it on, and answered. The conversation consisted of mostly limited responses on his part: "Yes. I see. No. Thank you for letting me know. 'Bye."

He slid the device back into his jeans before meeting her eyes. She realized he wasn't going to answer her question. He wouldn't indict his ex-wife. But he did have some other grave news that was answer enough.

"DeLuca is dead," he said.

"THE BLACK MAMBA is the deadliest snake in Africa," Kushe explained, pushing Felicity farther back from the slithering gray-green creature. "But they're usually quite shy. It's odd that it seems to be so interested in Frank."

"Maybe it smells python on him," said Pedro, quickly recounting the incident in Florida.

"Perhaps the snake is his animal spirit," said Kwi, grinning as if he were joking.

"Lucky me," said Frank.

But the snake who'd seemed so intent on joining the discussion veered away from the fire and instead shot toward Baruti, winding through the dirt at tremendous speed.

"Baruti," Felicity yelped, leaping to his side, only to be hauled back by Pedro. His burly arms pressed her tightly to his chest, nearly choking her.

"Let me go," she yelled, as the snake nudged the outside of Baruti's sleeping bag.

"What are you goin' to do?" he asked. "Jump in front of it? Offer it your leg to snack on? Don't be stupid. It probably won't bite if he don't move. And he ain't movin'."

As the snake slid over Baruti's legs, so poorly protected by the down-filled sack, Baruti moved. His eyelids twitched. His lips smacked. His left arm shifted an inch to the right.

"Oh my God!" yelled Felicity, still struggling in Pedro's grip. For just a minute, she'd like Baruti to stay paralyzed. For just another minute or two. "Baruti, don't move," she called.

Baruti's eyelashes fluttered. "Felee—icity?" he said, in a semblance of consciousness, but not alert enough to fathom the danger.

The snake paused, flicked a tongue at the material, then turned and slunk away through the seared bristles of grass on the other side of the sleeping bag.

The entire group collectively sighed. Pedro released Felicity from his arms, and she sprang to Baruti's side, kneeling in the dirt. She stroked his forehead and he looked up at her—he actually looked *at* her and not *through* her.

"Why's it called a black mamba?" asked Pedro. "It ain't black."

"If you're about to die, you'll know why it's called that," said Kushe. "The inside of its mouth is black."

"Ah," said the big man. "I'm glad we didn't see it, then."

"It didn't appear to be in attack mode," said Kushe, "although you never can tell with that snake. Too unpredictable."

"It seemed to be fleeing," said Kwi, scratching his head. "It is a timid snake, despite how toxic its bite."

Felicity ignored the conversation. All they could talk about was the darn snake, when Baruti was regaining consciousness.

"How are you feeling?" she asked.

"Weak," he replied. "Sore. Strange."

"Getting better," she said sternly.

"I dreamed," he said. "I dreamed of polar bears and corpses and a mud-covered girl." He smiled, his eyes sparkling with memory.

She gripped his hand, giving it a tender squeeze and receiving a weak response.

"I dreamed of caves filled with mounds of skulls."

She frowned.

"I dreamed of friends gathered tight around me. Friends with copper skin and inquisitive eyes. Friends with pale skin and terrified eyes. Friends with reptilian skin and perceptive eyes—but I'm not sure *they* were actually my friends."

Still delirious, she decided.

"I dreamed of lions."

"Of course you did," she whispered. That much he'd obviously overheard while he was semiconscious.

"Lions with lustrous manes in menacing poses. Lions with dubious spirits. Lions who stand on the edge of the path and don't skulk away or dodge into the field, as most lions typically do, when confronted with humans. Lions like that one."

He raised a trembling hand with hers still attached and pointed.

At once it was obvious what had frightened the snake. At the edge of the path, peering through the mesh of scrub bushes and grass, was a lion.

Dayna staggered. Even though she'd expected the news, she'd still hoped . . . that he wouldn't die, that there was no poison, no conspiracy, no danger to her students.

Shaun caught her in a firm grip before she could fall, although she probably wouldn't have fallen. He raised her up, although her rubbery knees could still perform the same function. He held her close, and she let him, even though she should beat him off with a stick.

"I feel like we should hunt them down, find them, somehow. We can't just wait here until . . . they die."

"I feel just as helpless as you," said Shaun. "But it's the only thing we can do. I'm hoping the autopsy report will give us answers, but that will take hours, even though they'll speed it up, since they're worried he contracted something infectious."

"I hardly knew him, but *you* must be devastated." She looked into his unusual eyes, searching for a sign of suffering, and spotted the veiled glitter of tears.

"He was . . . a good friend. For the most part, we got on well. He was a rock hound. You know how they are."

"Not really. I never mixed with the geology department. People sometimes call geologists oddballs, but I've always been fascinated with ancient bone and dead tissue, so I shouldn't be one to judge, either."

"I find that hard to picture," he said. "You and . . . the dead. I've seen Felicity neck-deep in mud and floating tissue, but you seem too . . . elegant for that type of work."

Maybe it was time to extract herself from his arms. Flattery would not get him anywhere.

She tried to push gently against his chest, and for a moment he tightened his grip instead of letting go. Then he released her so suddenly she staggered again.

He caught her elbow to steady her, then snapped his arm away and turned toward the lodge.

"I suppose we could have some tea."

"Yes, it would be something to do."

He looked at her with a concentrated squint that said he could think of *other* things to do, and she wanted to slap him. Why was he behaving this way? His friend had just died. And wasn't he concerned about Baruti and Felicity? Wasn't that the whole point of this trip?

They walked along the path, and Dayna was no longer distracted by the musical serenade of the animals and birds; she was no longer flabbergasted by the ecstatic bursts of color and activity. All she could think of was tea. Yes, that sweet, berry-colored tea. She could drink a whole pot.

Forty minutes later, she was on her third cup, sitting on a porch overlooking the lagoon on the southern side of the lodge—an area attached to a dock where tours departed—when two *mokoros* landed, the guides jumped out, and tied off the vessels. Dayna stood, stared, strained her eyes, examined the passengers.

"It's not them," said Shaun.

"How can you tell? They're at least fifty feet away. We should walk down and take a look . . . ."

"I have excellent eyesight. It's not them."

Dayna lowered herself to her chair, still eyeing the small group intently. But he was right. There were two girls, and none of them were as petite and skinny as Felicity, the men were far taller than Frank or Baruti, and all of them chattered away in Italian. She slumped in her chair and cupped the mug in her hands, seeking its warmth, comfort, and distraction.

Shaun raised one eyebrow. "You're going to get tea-logged."

"Maybe I should go for another walk. Alone," she added.

"I wouldn't advise it. Those pesky snakes are still about. And crocodiles. And hippos."

Her shoulders sagged. "Then there's work. I can do work. At least I have my tablet in my room."

"Can you? I suppose you can try."

"Do you have a better suggestion?" Stupid. Why open that door?

"Not a one," he said.

"So," she said, standing. "I'll leave you for now and sift through some data in my room. You'll let me know if you hear anything? Or if they return?"

"Of course I will. Good luck with your work." He remained slouched in his chair and sipped at his own brew, which had switched from tea to beer.

She practically ran back to her room, dodging the new guests and a trio of vervet monkeys trying to steal figs from a food service cart. Why was he affecting her this way? She'd met her fair share of attractive men, but she'd never been so compelled to . . . But she'd never been free like this before, either. Maybe that was it. And he seemed to exude sensuality, as if his pheromones were tuned to her frequency. But he should be grieving for his friend. And she should be worried about her students.

She opened her tablet and stared at the screen. She looked at and finally began flicking through email messages, many of them congratulatory notes from colleagues. Gloria had also sent her the latest results from the tissue analysis of the Phoenician mummy. The DNA wasn't identical to the others, but incorporated all the variations of the same unique species.

Gloria had also forwarded the results from the Bauer Core lab. There were several repeats from the PCR process, but two sequences in particular had been copied several times and identified as belonging to unique specimens. One, she was certain, belonged to the skull, and it correlated with the DNA from Felicity and Frank's discoveries: the PBPP—Polar Bear Provincial Park—species, for lack of a better label.

So there was definitely a *!Kung* link to an extinct species. That didn't really surprise her, since the *!Kung* belonged to one of the oldest known haplogroups on Earth. If this species had developed before modern *Homo sapiens*, then, like *Neanderthal* and *Denisova*, it had probably followed the same out-of-Africa migration. But it also might have migrated to or even developed in southern Africa.

The other distinct DNA sequence was labeled as a contaminant.

Obviously, Gloria had perused the results. In her email, along with the data, she'd added a comment: "The DNA from your "backlogged" work contains base pair sequences identical to the unknown species or PBPP genome. But I think you should look at the contaminant and consider re-running the sequence with another specimen. Also, the C-14 dating results place it at 70,000 years old!"

Dayna paused, astounded. Then it didn't match the 2,000-year-old Phoenician artifact at all—its presence was a coincidence, for sure—but it did suggest a place of origin for this species. But the contaminant bothered her. She scanned through the markers, her eyesight blurring, then clearing, then blurring. The sequences in total had the human number of base pairs with human matches, so it certainly wasn't bacterial. A human contaminant, probably her own, even though she'd been very careful while handling the skull for the most part. If it wasn't her DNA, it must be Baruti's or one of the *!Kung's*. But the base pair matches were skewed, with some unique genes present, such as PRR20, a *Neanderthal* and PBPP gene that encoded for a proline-rich protein of unknown function. Additionally, some typical genes were abnormally coded, such as TRPM1. This was usually a defunct gene, but here the start codon was present, which made no sense.

"Damn." She threw the tablet aside. She just couldn't focus.

Then a knock came at her door. Not a pounding but a subtle tap.

She took a deep breath, prepared to meet whatever news had arrived, but not really prepared to open the door.

She cracked it. He was leaning against the frame.

"I thought ten minutes would suffice."

"I don't . . ."

He attacked her with his lips and hands. She should have attacked back—to defend herself—but she collapsed. Dammit, she was so weak.

He shoved her into the room. He slammed the door shut. He threw her onto the bed.

In seconds, they were disrobed and locked together and forgetting all about . . . what was her name?

Scanning...

Located: Chapter 38

FELICITY, WHO NEVER seemed to Frank to live up to her name, caught Frank's attention with a squeak of fear. Frank turned and stared at the poised creature, his heart pounding. He wondered what it was contemplating. It was a male lion with a fluffy mane, a muscular tawny torso, and twitching whiskers that could indicate that it found the humans interesting or, more likely, appetizing. He didn't really give much credence to the animal spirit concept. He knew that the *!Kung*, like many aboriginal cultures, told of otherworldly experiences they had while under the influence of mind-altering or psychotropic drugs, but they weren't to be taken literally. He also knew that shrieking a patient's illness into the air was most effective with what the *!Kung* called "star sickness,"—stars being the eyes of dead people. It's possible this was what was diagnosed by Western medicine as depression. The *!Kung* also passed down ancestral memories in the form of spiritual beliefs and fables. And they might have a sixth sense while dealing with something they recognized, like this poison.

So he didn't find it significant that a lion was at this moment standing on the fringe of their camp watching them, although it was alarming. But he did find it noteworthy that Kwi had connected Baruti to the lions, and that lions, having once been their allies, now seemed to be their mortal enemies. The *!Kung* had always regarded lions as strong, brutal, and fierce. The heroes of their legends were often small jackals who tricked, lied, and narrowly escaped, rather than larger, bolder creatures such as lions. Nothing gave them more pleasure than to tell a tale of a lion being scalded, singed, duped, cuckolded, or killed.

"Your kindred spirit watches over you, Baruti," said Kwi, looking disconcerted by the new arrival. "He even chases the snakes away." He eyed Frank, which triggered a flush of annoyance.

"I'm not going anywhere, and I'm not a snake. In case you didn't understand the story, I'll try to make this clear. The snake tried to *eat* me."

"But instead you ate him."

"Pedro ate him. Or, rather, hacked him to pieces."

"Makes no difference," said Kwi. "Pedro is your guardian."

"Is there something we can do about this lion?" asked Felicity, who didn't know there was nothing they could do about the lion, unless one of their guides managed to swipe a gun out of his pack, or one of the *!Kung* managed to grab a spear from the ground. But an attack with either weapon would probably just piss him off.

"Stand boldly and hope he is well fed," said Kushe. "He is not stalking us, but he also shows no fear."

"He has great power," said Kwi. "As does Baruti, to overcome the poison. He wonders whether he must fight him or bow down to him."

"Can't we just shoot him?" asked Felicity, ignoring Kwi's comments.

"He'd be on us before I could reach a gun," said Kelong. "If I move suddenly, it could provoke him to attack. Let him decide the first move. Since we aren't running in fear, he may become unnerved."

The lion shook his mane as if befuddled, and placed one paw forward. At first his gaze seemed locked on Baruti, but now he turned toward Frank.

Why me? Is there something about me that screams "food"?

"Obviously, he's flustered," said Baruti, surprising everyone. "They're so transparent. Lions live to eat, sleep, and lord it over the other beasts. Usually they don't approach humans, but occasionally you'll find one that's bold enough or hungry enough. He finds it annoying that we're not showing any fear. If one of us should run, he'd bound after us and pounce."

Baruti paused and sucked in a breath, as if he'd become winded. But he pushed himself up to a sitting position on trembling hands.

"I think he had his eye on me, since I look the most vulnerable, but he also smells your injuries, Frank. We're the weakest right now, so we need to exhibit strength. Turn and face him. Look him in the eye. The only creature we really need to worry about is the one who poisoned me."

Doubt rippled through him, but Frank decided that if he should trust anyone's instincts regarding wild animals, it would be the biologist who dwelt in this region. He turned and eyed the creature, teasing a scowl from its lips. His internal organs quivered like mice under a cat's paw, but he disguised his fear as best he could. He spread his legs to achieve a solid stance and narrowed his eyes, looking deeply into those gilded irises, which were so enormous and so reflective that one could almost believe the lion was supernatural. The lion bared his teeth but, incredibly, he retracted his paw.

"Take a step toward him, Frank," said Baruti.

"Really?" said Frank. He wanted to ask Pedro to do the posturing for him, but he knew that wouldn't save him if the lion returned later to stalk the weak. Besides, it would look even more cowardly to . . . It would just look cowardly.

"Fine," he muttered.

He shuffled his foot through the rustling grass, then placed it decisively in the lion's direction.

The beast regarded him, twitching its whiskers.

"Felicity," whispered Baruti. "Support me with your hand, but don't make it too obvious. Otherwise I'm going to fall backward at the worst possible moment."

Out of the corner of his eye, Frank saw Felicity wind her arm behind the man's back, laying down a support beam for his quivering muscles.

The lion kept watching Frank. It didn't notice the clandestine movements of its alternate prey. Obviously, one step wasn't going to be enough. Frank took another, and another.

"Don't push it," said Baruti. "You may force his hand."

Certainly he should stop while he was ahead and follow the biologist's instructions. But he seemed to have no will of his own, now that he'd begun moving forward. The principle of inertia took over. He stepped agilely and resoundingly, stomping the brittle grass in a series of crackles, leaving deep bootprints behind where he had stepped, animating the ground as well as his own body. By God, he was not going to let another creature crush him in its jaws. He was the king and not the other way around.

"Snarl all you want," he snapped. "Extend your claws. Bare your teeth. I can still beat you. I will beat you back into the bush where you came from!"

"Frank," said Baruti. "I didn't say challenge him."

But Frank hardly heard him. All he could hear was a great splash in the water, all he could see was a whisper of sly, sinuous movement, all he could feel was an explosion of pain and the rapidly pulsing cords around his body.

Never again!

"You think I'll let you bite me! You think I'll let you squeeze the life out of me! You think I need somebody to rescue me again! I'll snip you to pieces this time, you bloody snake!"

A flash of fear or surprise or total bewilderment crossed the lion's face. His snarl faded and transformed into a slack jaw and a shaking of his head, accompanied by an odd blubbering snort. He backed another pace or two away, as Frank advanced like an army of one. He was nearly upon the lion. Frank's imaginings became reality. He felt the solid wooden handles of garden shears in his hands. He was prepared to snip the head right off the huge creature.

Before he reached him, though, the lion turned and bounded away across the grass, veering around the palms and mopane trees, dodging bushes, fleeing in terror as if pursued by a raging twister or a stronger lion.

Baruti sighed. Felicity sighed. Kushe smiled and Kwi danced, while the guides and other *!Kung* stood silently with mouths wide open.

"Lower me down," said Baruti to Felicity. "Then go help Frank."

Felicity lowered him down, but she didn't move. "Frank doesn't need any help, apparently. Although I think he's gone crazy."

"The best defense, I suppose," said Baruti. "Animals fear the madman, or the maddened creature. I know that well."

Frank shook his head and nearly collapsed. He didn't like what he was hearing, but he could see clearly again. He could see clearly enough to realize he hadn't confronted a snake.

"What are you saying . . .? That I'm . . . mad?"

"No," he replied. "You're not mad, Frank. But you had a moment of madness in you, as we all have sometimes. And it was a well-timed moment. So let's appreciate occasional madness, rather than scorn it. Only if it's permanent and untreatable do you need to worry."

Frank squeezed his eyes shut, then opened them and gazed at his hands. "I'm not actually carrying shears. I was going to attack him with my bare hands. I really am crazy."

"You might have won," said Pedro. "Or, at the least, you would have given us the time to grab our own weapons and fight him too. Maybe the snake did give you more guts," he said, with a broad grin.

"How are you feeling?" Felicity asked Baruti, dismissing the lion, now that it was no longer a threat and turning all their thoughts back to the original and pressing issue of the attack on Baruti and his still questionable health.

"I have a headache," said Baruti. "But I don't know if it's the usual migraine or a residual effect of the poison. The good news is that I'm still alive."

"The great news," said Felicity, bestowing a dazzling smile on him. Frank felt the familiar ache return to his belly. For a brief, petty moment, he wondered why Felicity couldn't have been the one the lion had attacked.

"You defeated the poison," said Kwi, squatting beside him. "It was our grub poison, I am certain of it."

"How?" asked Baruti, his forehead creased. Kwi pointed at his hand, and a dawning comprehension entered Baruti's eyes, as he turned it this way and that. "Of course. How crafty. Even if we didn't drink it, it would still affect us. All we had to do was grab the cup, which he made sure we did. And it would be untraceable, unless the medical staff who ended up treating us knew of its origins."

"Baruti," said Frank, trying to shake off the effects of his blind moment of madness—or courage—and get his mind to focus on the most important aspect of this poisoning. "Kwi thinks you have glimmers of the lion in you, and that's why you defeated the poison. I know it's rather far-fetched, but I was wondering if these geneticists, as Dr. Lugan seemed to think them, have contrived some sort of immune system booster, or—if it's even remotely possible—have somehow altered their DNA to withstand this poison, and whether you might have been exposed to the virus or whatever vector they used to reprogram their genes? You did meet them in the Okavango, you said."

Baruti frowned. He smoothed the rumpled material of his sleeping bag with jittery fingers. "It's hard to say what I've been exposed to, but yes, I did visit their camp here clandestinely, which is when I began to suspect them of foul play. Or there could have been something attached to the samples I retrieved. But I don't understand why they'd bother to develop genetic resistance to this specific poison. If they have been altering codes, they may just be making the cells more resilient—doing something general, not specific. It certainly would explain why I survived this usually lethal poison.

"You sense we have something akin, the poisoners and me?" he asked Kwi.

"Yes," Kwi said. He looked at Kushe for a moment as if he was reluctant to speak further. They chatted back and forth and, by the few words Frank could decipher, he realized Kushe was explaining to his elder what Frank had suggested in lay terminology—that Baruti might have touched something that had altered his body's makeup.

"No," said Kwi. "Not new. The lion is not new to you, Baruti." He looked to the heavens for a moment, as if he could trace the paths of the invisible stars. "It has come to you from the beginning. And it is very old: truly, as old as the *!Kung*."

THREE TIMES. DAYNA couldn't believe it. How many years since she'd had so much sex in such a short period of time? And so intensely, frantically, and joyously? This man seemed absolutely devoted to giving her pleasure, worshipping her body, but she knew it could hardly last. He adored all creatures and, among those of the human persuasion, women in particular. But in a way, it seemed like predation. It was as if he needed to devour her to sustain himself, but as with a meal, the sustenance was only temporary.

The first time, the omission was forgivable. She'd simply forgotten. She was too involved.

The second time, she'd nearly gotten the words out, but he'd kissed them away.

The third time, she'd asked, although she knew it was a little late. "Maybe we should use a condom?"

He'd ignored her. It couldn't be deliberate, could it? He wasn't that devoid of common sense. He couldn't know that she was basically infertile, either. He was simply too passionate, his blood had been diverted from his brain, he was hearing impaired.

But it was during the third time when the answer to the question still niggling at the back of her mind suddenly came clear. The results—laid out in front of her like a photograph in her head, even as her body threw out spasm after spasm. The odd result from the contaminant DNA wasn't an error in the PCR or sequencing process. It wasn't due to misread base pairs. The contaminant DNA was a *mixture* of human and PBPP extinct species—a hybrid. Perhaps the PBPP species had cross-bred with *Homo sapiens sapiens* to a small extent like *Neanderthal*, although this wasn't a minute gene admixture. Or . . . perhaps PBPP wasn't extinct.

Scanning...

Located: Chapter 39

A FULL DAY'S journey over the Martian terrain, which alternated between frosty, crackling soil, resilient volcanic bedrock, and sagging mud crisscrossed by the occasional stream, brought the team to the edge of the Vitalis Cave and the shattered crust in a lava tube just beyond it. The cave bordered the deep gully of the Mawrth Vallis, an unusual channel because it contained no terrain made chaotic with fractures and pits, and because it was partially filled by an ancient lava flow in the upper region. A faint sparkle projecting through breaks in the mist suggested that it could also be experiencing a discharge of water from an underground source.

"Oh, how I wish I could explore the Vitalis Cave," said Gita.

Lucas aimed a questioning look at her, hoping that would suffice as a reminder of their agreement.

"I know. We need someone to man the loading of fuel topside, and I assumed that task because I don't have caving experience. I have no issue with that, and I'm not reckless enough to go exploring on my own. But we still have your injury to consider."

"Injury or not, I'm still in peak physical condition, as Bob said. And I've explored some pretty deep caves in Mexico. Plus, I know what we're looking for."

"Right. At least Bob will be monitoring your condition. But I'm still confused. Why would GALRES situate a storage depot in such an inaccessible location? I can see the sense in having emergency supplies buried in deep protective cover while the planet is undergoing rebirth, but it seems a rather challenging location from which to extract fuel, and therefore illogical."

"I have no idea why they chose this location. I found a tangential reference to it in an obscure file, so I could be entirely wrong about this. But at the moment, it's our best hope," said Lucas.

Bob shrugged. His affect had been flat, his responses subdued, during the entire trek, and he had refused to engage in conversation with Lucas other than the necessary discussion regarding their mission, probably because he could sense Lucas's fury. But since Bob had some caving experience and Gita none, Lucas had no alternative but to accept his assistance in the fuel-retrieval mission.

They had salvaged what they could from the trailer wreckage and constructed a sledge from the flatbed that they could use to carry the tanks that were supposedly stocked in this cave. The trailer's wheels had been irreparably damaged, so once the sledge was loaded, they would have to drag it very carefully behind the rover, across the rough and potentially explosive terrain.

As Lucas guided the rover forward, the Vitalis Cave yawned from the wall of a large crater that resembled a collapsed caldera. This region was entirely of volcanic origin, and possibly becoming unstable too. Lucas skirted the rim and finessed the vehicle to within a reasonably safe distance of a wide black chasm that gaped open in the ground before them. The radar proximity alarm, which had suddenly become active, chimed with irritating frequency until Gita switched it off. Lucas was relieved to see that the fog obscured any surface evidence of the cave's true purpose.

"Well, let's hope this will be our liberation," said Bob, uncoupling his safety belt and striding toward the airlock. He quickly changed into his gear, while Lucas took his time, happy to make Bob wait.

"Be careful," said Gita. "I know I don't have to say this, but spelunking on Mars is far more risky than doing it on Earth."

"Yes, of course," said Lucas, trying to keep the sarcasm from his voice. "We'll take our time and double-check our bolts and links."

The two astronauts spent the next thirty minutes rigging for the rappel and securing a series of bolts to the solid rock that bordered the cave. They also suspended a cable across the width of the sinkhole, feeding it through a pulley with a remote locking mechanism that could be activated in the center when they hoisted the tanks up with the assistance of the rover's electric winch, or unlocked and rolled to the side, where Gita could guide the tanks over the lip of the cave and drag them onto the flatbed.

A nagging fear flogged Lucas, as he drew near the edge and attached himself to the rope. He had no real fear of rappelling; he'd scaled enough mountains and explored enough depths in the years before he'd engaged in space travel. But special items lay sheltered within this cave, and he didn't know the exact layout. Could he keep Bob away from the sensitive material? And could he field questions from this pertinacious man who still didn't trust him? This man who, admittedly, had saved his life, but who was also a nagging blister on his heel that kept scabbing over and reopening?

"How deep, do you think?" asked Bob, peering over the edge.

"Three hundred feet is my best guess," Lucas said, backing toward the precipice. "Keep sharp."

He flicked on his helmet light and jumped off, reeling down the rope, then squeezing the brake and swinging suspended over the black throat of the hole. Immediately, he released the clamp to sail downward again. The attenuated neck of the sinkhole bowed out near the bottom and curved into the shape of a bell, as the impenetrable blackness of the cave swallowed the dim light from above.

"Gita? Probably going to lose comms soon."

"I hear you," she said. "Stay safe."

Abruptly, Gita's comm cut out as she continued to prep the rover's winch beyond the reach of the signal, but Bob's remained operational, since he stood within a direct line of transmission.

"Near bottom yet?" he asked.

Lucas tipped his head and swept the light underneath him. A solid floor of glistening charcoal met his beam, accentuated by bulging boulders and chunks of breakdown from the collapse.

"Almost," he replied.

Within seconds, he touched the bottom at speed, the abrupt stop jolting his legs and jarring his spine. He wobbled sickeningly, then regained his balance and unclipped his carabiner from the rope assembly.

"Off rope," he stated. "You can begin your descent, Bob."

As a whirring, whizzing sound echoed in the chamber, Lucas stepped away from the dangling rope and probed the darkness with the cold beam of his helmet light. From his perusal of certain classified maps, he knew that if they proceeded southeast, following the natural slope of the lava tube, they should find the now-vital storage depot. But the ground displayed by the beam had a crumbly appearance. Slabs of fractured rock, scattered pebbles, and a glittery pale dust that had undoubtedly rained down from above lay strewn all around, creating heaps and knobs that might be a challenge to negotiate with a load. Then, he noticed a path hugging the cave wall that looked spacious enough to transport tanks.

He looked up, contemplating. Bob's headlamp, originally a pinpoint of light, grew steadily larger like an oncoming train. Ever bumbling, yet still somehow competent. Getting the job done while playing a bullshit brotherly role. Lucas stepped away from the opening and followed the narrow furrow through the breakdown boulders.

"Lucas, am I getting close?" asked Bob.

Lucas didn't answer. He might as well give Bob the same silent treatment that Bob had given him for hours.

"Come on, man. Let's stop with the pettiness."

Lucas didn't offer a grunt.

Bob slammed onto the bottom of the cave, triggering a *crack* that echoed briefly like a gunshot.

"Crap. Thanks for all your help, Luke."

"Did you really need help, Bob?" he couldn't help but respond.

Bob snapped off-rope, his light drifting slowly around the cave—no doubt seeking Lucas while also surveying the surrounding hollow space.

"I'm sorry," he said. "How many times do I have to apologize? You saved my life. I was acting like an ungrateful idiot. Can we move past it now?"

"Take the path to your right," said Lucas. "Head to the wall. I think the supplies are this way."

"Great. So we can't move past it," said Bob, his light ricocheting off the wall and scattering among the piles of rock as he advanced. "Do you know how dangerous that is in our present situation?"

"I know exactly how dangerous when you can't trust someone who's supposed to have your back."

"Look, I lost my head . . ." Bob rounded the nearest obsidian slab and speared Lucas with his light. "Oh, there you are. I'm glad you waited for me."

"Sure. Like it makes all kinds of sense for me to leave you behind," Lucas snapped, although it did, which begged the question of why he'd waited. Probably because Bob would undoubtedly discover the path just as efficiently as Lucas had and follow him anyway, which would, once they arrived on site, demand more explanations and amplify his current difficulties.

"Lucas," said Bob, stepping to his side and reaching tentatively to touch his arm. "You had more information than I did. I overreacted, but it was a volatile situation. I do trust you. I've come to respect you. Now can we work together again, effectively, as a team, and find a way to get off this planet?"

"Fine," said Lucas. "There's no sense in holding grudges, is there?"

"Absolutely none," said Bob. "That's essentially why we have too many wars on Earth. Let's not make the same mistake here."

Lucas nodded and strode forward, edging away the darkness with his flashlight, trying to find it within himself to forgive. The mounds of rock blocked any view of the depot, which was neatly cached in the farthest coils of the sinuous arms of this cave. After twenty minutes of plodding and crunching over volcanic litter and winding around the odd boulder, they came upon an area that was completely filled with breakdown, except for a roofed-over tunnel immediately in front of the path where they walked.

Well, at least there was still a path. Hunching down, they squeezed through the claustrophobic tunnel single-file until, several paces farther, the wall of breakdown ended and they stepped into a small domed cavern the size of a killer whale's aquarium at Sea World. In the center of the cavern sat a glittering oval pond fed by drops of water that seeped through seams in the ceiling above and dribbled into the hollowed rock. On the surface of the water, an emerald skin of algae and lily pads drifted and bobbed along with the faint ripples. Even more extraordinary, though not entirely unexpected for Lucas, plants also crowded the ground along the edge of the pond, extending outward in a thick carpet. Arctic plants, like mountain crowberry, with its spiny leaves, and long jade strands of polar grass.

"Holy crap," said Bob, his momentum momentarily suspended. He blinked and gawked, his mind twirling through suppositions that Lucas would now have to redirect.

"Those plants require oxygen."

"The algae must be providing a sufficient quantity in this protected environment. The atmospheric pressure is high enough now, too, to support hardy plant life."

"But they require sunlight for photosynthesis," said Bob.

Lucas shrugged. "Natural light is seeping in from above."

"From . . ." said Bob, angling his head and eyeing the rock ceiling, ". . . windows?"

"Genius," said Lucas. "I guess this is an experiment that they wanted to keep a lid on, in case it failed. The UV rays would still penetrate the windows, so they had to engineer plants that are tolerant of high radiation levels."

Bob slanted a look at Lucas that he couldn't interpret. Well, no matter. This much he was bound to discover. Hopefully the urgency of their situation would curb his appetite to explore further.

"I wish we had time to document this at length, or the capacity to retrieve samples. But we didn't exactly bring along specimen jars. Let's look for those tanks."

He skirted the edge of the pond and tramped farther into the cavern, into a niche that reflected their helmet lights with a muted glow. Eventually, Lucas's beam displayed the source of the reflection—a series of stacked shelves that extended deep into the alcove, fading at the limits of the beam's projection. On the first shelf sat the bulging aluminum cylinders they coveted. Lucas practically leaped on them, checking the sleek metal for the prominent labels of CH_4 and O_2.

"There's enough," he said, patting them, tempted to kiss them. "It will take a few trips back and forth, but we should be able to haul these out."

"I still have doubts about our makeshift trailer," said Bob. "If these get jostled too much . . ."

"It'll work," said Lucas. "Just as long as we drive at a slow, steady pace and place one spotter outside, when we encounter rough terrain. Let's get these lugged to the cable."

Bob didn't move, but looked to either side, sliding his light along the stacked shelves until it couldn't penetrate any farther.

"This is a hell of lot more than 'a few supplies.' What do we have here?" He stepped along the aisle, crowding closer to colorfully labeled plastic boxes and titanium cases. "Freeze-dried food. Water. Medical supplies. Solar panels. Heating units. The payload alone, to carry all this to Mars, let alone transport it to a remote cave . . . Why have I never heard of this depot?"

"The ISA doesn't tell us everything, Bob. GALRES is even more tight-lipped about its plans for this planet. Can we get started? Transporting the fuel will require all your energy and focus."

Bob aimed his light deeper into the alcove, illuminating a seemingly endless row of shelves that looked like nothing so much as government archives.

"Sure," he said, and turned back.

Lucas released a silent sigh as Bob crouched down beside him. While Bob grabbed the top of the cylinder, Lucas heaved up the bottom. He tucked the tank onto his shoulder and helped Bob adjust his excruciating load. Unfortunately, the cylinder was angled downward toward Bob and the ground because of Lucas's exceptional height, so Lucas would have to keep a solid grasp on it, to prevent it from slipping forward. In this fashion, they trundled the tank over the uneven surface of the cavern, and then the constricted tunnel, stepping carefully. The only sounds that disturbed the hollow space were the grunts of their efforts bounding off the cave walls.

After at least forty minutes of carrying this extremely heavy burden, they reached the dangling rope and cable suspended from above. Lucas and Bob worked together, rolling the tank onto a tarp, tying it securely in the center, then triggering the winch to raise the cable. Hopefully Gita would be observing the cable and would exit the rover at the appropriate time to retrieve the cylinder.

Lucas watched the cable ascend, then brake at the top, waiting for Gita's arrival. Suddenly her voice chimed over the comm, as she unlocked the pulley and slid the entire contraption to the rim of the sinkhole. They chatted for several seconds, until the tank had been safely guided to solid ground, and then he trudged back along the path with Bob as his shadow. Twinges of pain nipped at his spine, but Bob seemed in worse shape, his shoulders drooping in exhaustion.

Nonetheless, Bob didn't complain as they proceeded with the next tedious extraction. But when they reached the sinkhole, Bob staggered under the weight of the fuel cylinder, and wobbled precariously.

"That's the worst of it," said Lucas, as he tucked the tank into the tarp-and-cable assembly. "Why don't you sit out the next haul, Bob? I can handle the O_2 tanks, myself."

"Wouldn't hear of it," said Bob. He whirled around and stumped toward the path, ignoring Lucas's protests.

Now he was being unreasonable. His shirt-back was soaked with perspiration; he could hardly catch his breath; he stumbled more than walked. He was in no condition to transport another tank. Maybe this obstinacy stemmed from their argument. Bob was determined to prove that he was a loyal team member, someone Lucas could count on. Or maybe he was just an idiot, although Lucas no longer believed that.

But when they approached the pond for the third time, even Bob couldn't deny his own fatigue.

"I—I think I've had it, Lucas. You're right. I need a rest."

He slumped to the ground near the miracle pool, stretching his weary body alongside the unlikely greenery and vibrant blossoms. Fumbling through his pack, he retrieved a water bottle and attached it to the straw with an incorporated gate valve that hung from his mask. He bit down on the valve to open the tube, and began to drink through the straw. He sipped gratefully at the life-restoring fluid, sighing between gulps. Lucas seized the opportunity to rehydrate, as well.

Even though the next tank was a much smaller oxygen tank, he would need additional fluid to complete the task of carrying it solo, since Bob was unable to assist.

"Well, I guess I'll finish the job," said Lucas, although a voice in his head screamed at him not to leave Bob unattended. "But I really don't feel comfortable leaving you alone here, Bob. If we experience a collapse, or . . ."

Bob relaxed his posture, sprawled comfortably on the ground, and closed his eyes. "Seriously, Lucas. I'll be fine. The cave seems relatively stable. When you return for the last tank, I should be able to assist you."

Lucas stood rigidly beside the shelf, indecisive, unable to move, as if his feet were bound to the solidified lava. Bob appeared to be totally relaxed and not interested in moving. His eyelids fluttered and tucked in against his cheeks. His facial features slouched appreciably. Even his muscles and joints sank toward the ground, as if they'd lost all tension. As long as he stayed that way . . .

What could Lucas do that would not arouse suspicion but proceed with the task? He heaved the oxygen tank onto his shoulder and hurried down the path, weaving and winding, climbing the occasional obstructing boulder, skirting projecting knobs and spears, eventually securing the next load.

"Hey. How's it going?" asked Gita, as he activated the hoist. She must have been awaiting their return at the edge of the sinkhole, since her voice projected clearly through the comm.

"Nearly done," said Lucas. "Bob's sitting out this haul. He's exhausted."

"No wonder," she replied. "Maybe you should take a break, too."

"I'm fine. Just getting a few muscle aches. Nothing that a good bath won't cure."

Gita chuckled. "I wish. I think rain is in the forecast, though, so you'll have to settle for a shower, or possibly a mud bath. Seriously, though. Don't push too hard."

"Wouldn't dream of it. Watch for any weak patches in the ground around the sinkhole, if it starts raining."

"You do realize who you're talking to?" said Gita, with a hint of annoyance in her voice.

"Sorry. Insufferable again, I know. It's just that this entire planet is like quicksand, especially since we began saturating the atmosphere. But at least this tank should be easier for you to manage. I'll be back soon."

"Roger that. Look after Bob."

Lucas caught his lip between his teeth and glanced up at the spillage of light from the cavern's mouth. He could not discern the outline of Gita's body from this distance, but her presence radiated down on him, as if it wasn't a casual comment. She was reminding him of his responsibilities despite the fracture in his and Bob's relationship.

"Roger that," he said, wanting to add that Bob could damned well look after himself.

He stomped over the rocks, crushing powdery flakes of basalt beneath his feet. It boggled his mind that she could torment him so easily with a few simple words flung down a sinkhole. Why would he even give it more than a minute's thought? Something was happening to him. A transformation that was liable to rip him apart.

He turned the last corner of the path that led into the cavern, then halted. As he realized what he was seeing, or *wasn't* seeing, his heart thumped savagely against his chest as if demanding to be released. Bob was no longer lying on the ground near the pond. Bob's light was flickering deep in the alcove.

"Hello, Lucas," he said, his voice low-pitched and ominous, almost purring.

"Bob?"

Lucas slunk forward. He rounded the borders of the emerald pond and crept down the corridor between the stacks, chasing Bob's flashing light—a bright, pupil-contracting beam replaced by sudden darkness as the man looked up at him, then returned his attention to the items on the shelves.

"Tell me something," he said as Lucas approached. "Why do we need goats and water fowl on Mars? Why do we need arctic char? Why do we need . . . mammoths?" He pointed at the containers aligned along one shelf, undoubtedly genetic material labeled with the species he'd just mentioned.

"I have no idea," said Lucas.

"DNA," said Bob. "That's what this is. A cryogenic zoo of DNA, and a botanical garden, too. I imagine we'll eventually reseed this planet and establish some hardy wildlife and feed stock. But why store it here . . . now?"

"Seems rather premature."

Lucas settled his hand on the shelf beside him, propping up his weakening body. His heart refused to return to beating at a calmer pace, and he could feel a revealing flush creep up his throat. He let his eyes drift, rising and falling over the endless variety of specimens. Eventually they came to rest on a box of syringes. There was no label on this box, though it had been deliberately marked with unusually curved X's.

"It's as if this is a reservoir of earthly species; there are thousands of specimens on these racks. How did you know about this place, Lucas, when Gita and I had no idea? What is this place, really?"

"A storage depot. That's all I read." He stepped closer to Bob, while reaching behind his back with one hand, teasing open the box, and removing a syringe.

"You may wonder why I don't trust you, Lucas. It's because I know you're hiding something. And this . . . reservoir is right in the middle of your . . . subterfuge, isn't it? That's why you clamored against any thought of visiting the Vitalis Cave."

"I'm only concerned with our survival," said Lucas.

"Our survival," mused Bob. "Does this . . . fountainhead in the middle of a dead planet have to do with *our* survival? Or does it have to do with a radical faction that wants to annex Mars and take possession of it for their exclusive use?"

"I don't know what . . . you're . . . talking . . . Oh, this is useless. You've known all along. You've been spying on me, haven't you? You couldn't be sure, so you forced me onto the planet to test your theories. I could have killed you, Bob. I could have killed you at any time. But I didn't. I saved you."

"I saved you too, Lucas."

"You did. But why? Just to determine what I knew about this planet? Because I couldn't lead you here if I were dead?"

"No. That wasn't it at all. It wasn't in me to . . . just let you die. I'm not that callous. Although I knew you hated me. After your . . . accident, it's never been about this."

"Until now."

"I can't unsee it."

"No, you can't," said Lucas, uncapping the needle on the syringe. "So that leaves me with a dilemma."

Bob looked so cocksure. "What? You're going to kill me now? After I saved you? After I worked my ass off to keep you alive? I don't think you have it in you, either."

"Right," said Lucas. "Not at all."

He swung his arm around and plunged the needle into Bob's exposed neck in the gap between his tensile suit and face mask. Bob groped at it, but his pathetic defensive grapplings were too late. The fluid had been flushed into his system. Lucas nonchalantly removed the needle and tossed the empty syringe onto the shelf.

Bob staggered backward and pawed at his neck.

"What . . . *What the hell did you do?* What *was* that?"

His knees buckled, and Lucas caught him in his arms. He gently lowered him to the ground.

"You're feeling a little weak, no doubt. I think there's a sedative in the mix."

Bob kept blinking and looking up at him with wounded, terrified eyes.

"You know what, Bob? You're right. I don't have it in me. I'm not entirely cold and calculating. I'm not a robot, as Gita has suggested I once was. And you're wrong if you think I hate you. That's the problem. I should, but I don't. It's so messed up. You and I, well, there were moments when I thought we'd tuned in to a corresponding frequency. We'd established this connection, since you mended my body and brought me back from near death. You gained my respect. And I thought you might actually care about Mars, too. Too bad I was wrong. Too bad the connection has been severed."

"Luke . . ." Bob's words were garbled, but he spewed out a plea. "Don't . . . le— eave me."

"I have to, Bob." Lucas stood and took several strides away before turning back. "I can't trust you to keep quiet about this cave and all the treasures it contains. I can't trust you to preserve Mars for the real Martians."

Bob raised a twitching hand, then lowered it.

"You'll be okay, though. I guarantee it. After all, you're in the Genesis Cave."

Segment III: GENESIS

THE QUEEN GOES out of her house, dressed for the Bacchic orgy. She bears the signals of madness: a vine-leaf crown on her head, a fawn skin hangs from a shoulder, a javelin rests on the other.

So Procnê with her mad crew run screaming over the woodland, a terrible vision to see. Bacchus, she feigns, is her master; in fact, it is you, O Furies of pain, who drive her along.

—Ovid, *Metamorphoses* 6.533–538

Scanning...

Located: Chapter 40

PAIN. STABBING AT his throat, clutching at his chest, prickling through his skin. Hard to breathe. Impossible to move.

Rest. Sleep. Dream.

Escape the pain.

But he couldn't escape the dreams, the images of his "friend" smiling at him, leaning over him protectively, then stabbing him in the back, in the neck, in the heart.

Was blood pouring from his veins? Was poison coursing through his body, corroding tissue and damaging organs? Why did he feel as if he were on fire?

A surge of fear rushed through him, but then a languid, unfeeling, uncaring state slackened his pace, entered his mind, and carried him back into a dream state.

Nothing existed here but memories and half-baked theories.

A man with livid facial scars, wearing cut-off jeans and a safari hat, meeting him on the dark roadway outside Johnson Space Center.

A map of Mars with a red circle around the Vitalis Cave.

Accounts that displayed long, endless columns of numbers and dollar signs funneled into something called the Genesis Program.

A picture of . . . Lucas. *That was his name. With a gun-range target on his head.*

Words that were meant for someone else, someone that he couldn't be . . . "If he does anything suspicious, kill him."

And his protests . . . "But I'm an astronaut, not an assassin. I can't kill . . ."

But the man—the spy, that's what he was—beat back his protests. "What do you think the terrorist will do? Do you think he can gain control of Mars without killing a few people along the way? Watch him, be wary of him, and wheedle out his agenda. If it comes down to it, you will act in the best interests of Earth and the ISA."

The memories flashed forward to his opportunity, when he'd discovered the contents of the cave. The moment he should have acted—killed Lucas.

But he'd been incapable of completing his task.

And Lucas had killed him.

Not dead! his mind cried, as a thousand insects chewed on his flesh and a thousand needles pierced his skin. *Why can't I wake up?*

A bleeping sound penetrated the fog.

He tried to force his eyes open, but they remained stubbornly resistant.

Must regain consciousness. Air will eventually run out. Must replace . . .

Finally, his eyes flickered open. The light from the windows set into the cave ceiling had dimmed; several hours must have passed. His rebreather should have at least a two days' supply of breathable air, so he would be okay. He would be fine.

Except . . . that bleeping sound still pulsed in his ears.

He shifted, but even that small movement triggered spasms in his muscles. And breathing was a tortured affair, causing gurgling sounds to escape his lips. He felt as if he were choking to death, drowning. What had Lucas injected into him? What kind of poison?

He had to move. He had to catch up to Lucas in the cave, before he departed with the rover. Maybe he still had a chance.

He pushed his tormented body upward, and finally managed to sit up. His flashlight lay beside him, strobing a weak light along the aisle and shelves.

He clutched the cylinder and tilted it toward his tank apparatus, where he could view his oxygen gauge. He checked the level. And rechecked it. And checked again.

The needle had slipped into the red zone. Almost empty. And a warning light was flashing, along with the bleeping sound that blared like a foghorn in his strangely sensitive ears.

No. It couldn't be. Two days?

I'm dead, then. He began to slouch down, to curl up on the ground, to surrender.

But . . . there were oxygen tanks in the cave. On one of the shelves. Somewhere near the pond.

I can get there. I'm alive. He didn't kill me. He said he didn't kill me.

Bob clipped his flashlight to his belt, then groped at the solid shelving unit, clutching the brackets, hoisting himself up. He staggered upright and lurched forward, his heart pounding ferociously, sweat erupting from his pores.

He should be cold in this frigid cave, but he was burning up.

Suddenly the intermittent alarm became a steady alarm. The tank was empty. The gentle breath of air no longer drifted over his face. His only hope was that the plants of that tiny burgeoning ecosystem were generating enough oxygen in the cave to sustain him until he could reach the tanks. He whipped off the mask and kept struggling along the shelves with their heavy load of supplies, gripping the aluminum supports to keep upright. He struggled and gasped, but he didn't collapse and die. Not yet, anyway.

Finally he saw it, like a beacon in a lonely sea. The ivory gleam of a portable tank, captured in the bobbling beam from his flashlight. He was nearly there. He was going to make it.

But with only two more steps to take, his knees buckled and he fell to the rock floor. He whimpered and collapsed on the ground. His breathing stuttered, and he felt the darkness seep into his mind again.

HOURS PASSED, OR eons. Who could tell? Especially if you're nothing more than a fading dream.

Am I dead now?

Bob opened his eyes.

Pain still flickered in just about every muscle in his body, but it was subdued. He was still hot and breathing fire, but not unendurably so. His body prickled and itched but, even though no mask was attached to his face, his lungs still somehow captured air, although with great laborious heaves.

It was dark—a blank, ebony emptiness. But maybe that was because—he groped at his belt and found the cylinder. He tapped it, flicked it on and off, but no light appeared.

"Battery's empty," he said to himself, his voice hoarse.

But he'd stashed extra batteries in his utility belt. Always be prepared in a cave. He fumbled one out, sprang the latch on the bottom of the flashlight, ejected the spent battery, and reinserted the fresh energy source.

Now . . .

The cave lit up, displaying the stacks beside him, the glittering pond in front of him, and a substantial amount of survival staples behind him. He was sprawled on the floor, but still alive, still breathing.

He took several deep breaths, filling his chest excruciatingly each time, then exhaling in whistling puffs. On his fifth deep breath, however, he felt dizzy and nearly passed out.

He took a shallow breath.

Could the plants be supplying enough oxygen? But . . . the air was thin on Mars. Too thin to breathe without adverse effects like pulmonary edema. Better not tempt fate.

He hoisted himself up by grasping the shelves and played his light over the stacked cylinders. When he found a small excursion tank, he swapped it for his empty one and programmed the oxygen/nitrogen blend. He expected to breathe more easily when he reattached the mask, but for some reason his chest still ached and his head still swam. He kept gasping, too, as if his lungs couldn't fathom what to do with the air.

Bob sank down to the ground again and rested another hour, trying to catch his breath and stem a swirling cyclone of dizziness. Finally, he decided he needed food and water, probably desperately, before he began his pursuit of Lucas and Gita. He staggered to his feet and rummaged through the shelves until he found a stock of energy bars and water bottles. Taking what time he must, he nibbled at the bars and gulped the water, experiencing intermittent waves of nausea, but thankfully keeping the nourishment down.

The next step was to test his condition. Whatever Lucas had administered, it hadn't killed him. So maybe it wasn't poison but simply a sedative. If that were the case, he would eventually recover, and could potentially even contact the rover before it passed beyond the horizon and the range of radio contact. Doubtful, but possible.

Not if you've really been out of commission for two days, a voice whispered in his mind, but he ignored it.

Bob heaved to his feet and began the long trek through the cave to the sinkhole entranceway. If the route had seemed interminable when they'd first traversed it, it was doubly so now, with the added tremors in his legs and the uneven pace of his breathing and the strange sense of overwhelming weakness in his body. If what Lucas had stabbed him with was a sedative, it was a potent one.

Eventually, a sullen wash of light appeared, dense and weary, tinted a sad, murky coral color like the first light of dawn probing through thick cloud. He looked up to where the wide circular opening beckoned, and saw that the rope still dangled along the side of the rock like an invitation. Lucas had not retracted it.

Why?

Was Lucas actually waiting for him on the rim of the sinkhole, his conscience having gotten the better of him? Doubtful. Or was this simply a tease? A way to torment Bob further?

Bob approached the rope with caution, fully expecting it to be a mirage. He would touch the shimmering lifeline, and it would dissolve. But it didn't. He touched it, he tugged on it, and it appeared to be secure.

Bob linked his ascender to the rope and began the long tedious climb upward. His arms rebelled every few feet, and he stopped frequently to hang suspended from the clip, winded, waiting to reacquire energy. But each time, he resumed the climb, and two hours later he scrambled over the rim and collapsed onto solid Martian ground. The area was still bathed in fog, but was infused with a pearly light that indicated the sun had risen.

He lay sprawled on the ground for several minutes, puffing and wheezing. But there wasn't time to rest. He had to activate his comm unit and try to establish contact with Lucas or Gita. Hopefully Gita.

He switched on the unit and spoke into the mic, his voice still croaking pathetically.

"Gita? Gita? Do you read? Gita?"

No response.

Well, if Lucas was monitoring comms there wouldn't be a response, would there? But he had to at least try to change the stubborn man's mind.

"Lucas? Lucas, whatever you're caught up in, I know you're a good man. Don't leave me here to die. You know I can't survive here. There aren't many tanks left. I could never make it to the HAB, and if I did, there wouldn't be enough oxygen in reserve for me to survive until the ISA sent an extraction team. Lucas, you might as well have killed me."

No response.

"Lucas," he pleaded.

He rolled over and sat up, near tears. He scanned the terrain, but there was no sign of the rover, just a track laid down by the flatbed—a thick rectangular gouge in the russet soil.

How could Lucas have convinced Gita to abandon him? But she trusted him to a degree that Bob had never been capable of. Maybe if he had, if he'd simply ignored the enticing secret of the cave, he'd be on that rover right now.

The fog rolled back from around him, revealing more of the barren volcanic talus, but then he noticed something on the ground near the piton where the rope was attached.

It was a single square black case. It was partly camouflaged by the reddish mud that spattered it, but a corner projected enticingly from the soil. He crawled to the case and zipped it open.

Inside, carefully cushioned between the padded partitions, sat a tablet.

Bob extracted the device gingerly and swiped it on. The screen flickered to life, revealing a long series of indented paragraphs and an attached document.

A message from Lucas . . .

Bob,

If you've made it this far, I imagine you've realized that you won't die. I didn't kill you. You were right. You made it impossible for me to do what I should have.

But you think I've sentenced you to death anyway.

Yes, I'm leaving you on Mars. Yes, you have limited supplies. But you will have enough. Enough to last you for years.

Your first thought, as mine would be, is the limited oxygen supply. The stores are inadequate for an extended period of time. You're right about that. There's hardly enough for a few days, since we extracted the rest. But oxygen is being generated in the cave by the bioengineered plant life, and the algae we deposited on the planet is generating oxygen as well. But what's even better in your case is that you don't require the same concentration anymore.

I've given you all you need to survive. I've given you a fighting chance. You wanted to be a Martian? Guess what, buddy? You are one.

Read this publication (which was never published where you could have seen it) and you will understand what I've gifted you with—a blessing, not a curse. You will be the first Martian resident. And your name will live forever. Enjoy.

Your friend and enemy,
Lucas

Bob gazed at the document in horror and fascination, captivated by the title: Human Artificial Chromosome MarsChr47. He tapped the screen, opened the document, and began to read.

Human Artificial Chromosome (MarsChr47) [1]
An Adaptation Chromosome Designed for Mars Homo Sapiens 1 Colonists

Adrian Hunter, Chatiwa Mbeki, and D. J. Jackson

Keywords

hypoxia, adaptation, radiation, Human Artificial Chromosomes or HACs, genetic engineering

Abstract

The concept of altering the human genome to facilitate colonizing Mars has been under consideration for decades, but ethical constraints have stymied research in this area. Also, difficulties in designing a cell line that is universal and not genome-specific and fraught with failure due to immune system response have delayed progress. Human Artificial Chromosome (HAC) MarsChr47 will be successful where others have failed, although we have yet to test it on Mars. In this review, we describe the design and construction of the chromosome, identifying the exact genes that were altered or redesigned to meet the demands of the current and future Mars environment. Since this environment is in the process of being terraformed, it has low oxygen and high radiation levels currently, a foremost consideration. In our discussion, we include the method of introduction into the host genome.

Initial Design and Construction

---

1 *This document contains a variety of technical terms that may be confusing to the average reader. Feel free to skip over it, if you find it tedious. Some explanations will follow. The main ideas are highlighted in bold font.*

We began by converting somatic cells to stem cells according to the Sommer et al. procedure—harvesting and culturing somatic cells, introducing a stem cell cassette of the four genes required to reprogram the cell—Oct4, Klf4, Sox2, and cMyc—via a nonintegrating lentiviral vector, thereby converting them to pluripotent (iPS) stem cells. The lentiviral vector causes only the transient expression of the four genes, since these particular genes are potential oncogenes, and if they were permanently integrated into the genome could cause cancer. **In this manner, we changed skin cells into stem cells that could develop into any type of tissue or organ.**

Our main construct was the HAC we are calling MarsChr47. Since Mars currently has an atmospheric pressure of 200 mb (150 mmHg), despite the fact that our micro-biosphere in the Genesis Cave has transformed the air from a mixture that is predominantly CO_2 to an oxygen/nitrogen blend that is equivalent to that on Earth, the low pressure only delivers 20% of Earth's oxygen at sea level, about the same as the amount at a height of ~ 4,000 m above Mount Everest. We believe that even with vigorous terraforming efforts the air will always be thin on Mars, and that not only is it possible but it will require less energy to adapt organisms to the environment rather than to alter the environment sufficiently to accommodate Earth-based organisms. **The challenge was to remodel specific genes to allow for high-altitude survival at low-oxygen levels, particularly those genes that can be adapted to mitigate against *hypoxia*, or insufficient oxygen in the blood.**

After consulting several studies that examined the evolutionary adaptation of certain high-altitude dwellers to hypoxia, we determined the essential genes that needed to be modified or knocked out. Some of these genes are involved in glycolysis and the TCA cycle of metabolism, and are downregulated in populations that live in the Ethiopian highlands, the Andes, and the Himalayas. **A particular 208-kb gene-rich region on Chromosome 19 has a number of genes involved in hypoxia adaptation.** We will provide a summary of all the genes incorporated into MarsChr47 at the end of the review. In this section, we will provide a sketch of the three main genes that were modified, and examine one in greater detail.

CIC
Capricua transcriptional repressor
Location: Chromosome 19
Coordinates: 42,284,582..42,295,797

When there is a demand for increased O_2, this gene, which represses the continuation of the cell cycle and inhibits cell proliferation, is downregulated. Since gene knockout is difficult in vivo, we established the DNA sequence alterations in our HAC that result in gene suppression and silencing of the original gene on Chromosome 19. Splicing and removing this gene from Chromosome 19 itself, along with all its introns might result in dysfunctional transcription factors for other purposes that we have not yet determined, or interference in micro-RNA machinery. Transcription of an antisense RNA sequence will result in a mating with the original transcript and deactivate it, preventing translation and the production of repressor molecules.

CIC is involved in the repression of the EGFR cell signaling pathway that regulates cell proliferation. **The targeted cells are alveolar cells in the lung, which when activated contribute to remodeling and creating greater surface area, in order to extract the maximum amount of oxygen from the environment.** Removing the effects of this repressor gene fosters the generation of adapted alveolar cells.

PAFAH1B3
Platelet-activating factor acetylhydrolase1b, catalytic subunit 3
Location: Chromosome 19
Coordinates: 42,297,033..42,302,800

When there is a demand for increased O_2, this gene is downregulated. As indicated with CIC, we decided to incorporate the altered gene—to facilitate downregulation and signal its suppression to other factors and pathways—along with an antisense RNA silencing mechanism for the original gene on Chromosome 19. We will explain this in greater detail in the section entitled HAC Construction.

Although this gene was labeled according to its role in hemostasis and platelet aggregation, and admittedly has a small role in hypoxia situations, as it induces platelet aggregation in pulmonary microcirculation, we believe its suppression in low-oxygen environments is primarily **neuroprotective. In other words, knocking out this gene will protect the brain from oxygen starvation and cell death.**

In low-oxygen conditions, the cells become deprived of oxygen, their primary energy source. This stimulates a signal within the cells to break down lipids to obtain energy, thereby mobilizing fats as additional energy sources. PAF is an enzyme that can cleave oxidized lipids in the *sn*-2 position up to 9 carbons long and thereby release unesterified fatty acids and form lysophospholipids. **These fatty acids and their metabolic products are important for normal brain function.**

Docosahexaenoic acid (DHA) and arachidonic acid (AA) are found in brain cell membranes. Depolarization during cerebral ischemia—brain oxygen starvation—leads to the opening of voltage-gated Ca^{2+} channels and a flood of neurotransmitters. Stimulated by this process, both AA and DHA are released, but whereas DHA is neuroprotective, AA induces prostaglandin production and may skew fine-tuned neurological functions. When the metabolism of AA is altered, it has been implicated in neuronal death. AA responds to $cPLA_2$ (Ca^{2+}-dependent phospholipase A_2), a group within which PAFAH1B3 is classified, whereas DHA responds to $iPLA_2$ (Ca^{2+}-independent phospholipase A_2), an alternate enzyme activated by an alternate gene.

We believe that downregulation of PAFAH1B3 will **protect the brain from neuronal misfiring, inflammation, and plaque formation** resulting from the excessive release of AA, while it will not interfere with the release of DHA, which mitigates neuronal pathological reactions.

LIPE
Hormone Sensitive Lipase
Location: Chromosome 19
Coordinates: 42,401,507..42,427,426

This gene encodes a protein in both a long and a short form, which is produced by alternative translational start codons—a triplet of amino acids that signal where to begin translating the code into a protein. The long form is expressed in tissues such as testis, where it is involved in steroid hormone production. The short form is expressed in adipose tissue, among other tissues, where it hydrolyzes stored triglycerides to free fatty acids for energy.

This gene is suppressed by the incorporation of two missense mutations in the exons that result in a dysfunctional version of the enzyme lipase (see Appendix A). We were primarily concerned with its short form, as **inhibiting it reduces lipid/fat metabolism as an option in low-oxygen environments.** An organism with this alteration preferentially metabolizes glucose, but at a slower rate of consumption and via a subdued glycolysis pathway, which prevents the build-up of lactic acid. **Lipid metabolism is less efficient than glucose metabolism in terms of O_2 consumption.** For every mole of O_2 consumed, the production of 53.7% more energy in the form of high-energy phosphate bonds is achieved from the metabolism of glucose over lipids.

We designed the gene from the top down, coding the normal gene, then excising the sections indicated for alteration with restriction enzymes that cut the DNA at the appropriate sequence, and replacing it with a sequence of DNA constructed of matching oligonucleotides that implanted the mutation. The DNA was introduced through the recombination of altered CIC, LIPE, PAFAH1B3, and others, with sequences that match many on Chromosome 19.

The other crucial genes for hypoxia tolerance were assembled in the same fashion. In addition to the hypoxia adaptation genes, we embedded a sequence for the activator of the CAT (catalase) gene, **a key antioxidant enzyme** in the body's defense against oxidative stress. Since Mars colonists will be exposed to **high levels of ionizing radiation, this enzyme will help mitigate the damaging effects of hydrogen peroxide**, although we suggest that all colonists take additional protective measures.

HAC Construction

The human artificial chromosome (HAC) is a microchromosome of approximately 10 Mbp (mega base pairs).

The HAC was initially assembled with bacterial artificial chromosomes (BACs) containing large arrays of cloned or synthetic alphoid DNA repeats from Chromosomes 5, 13/21, 14/22, 17, 18, and X.

HACs contain regions of both euchromatin and heterochromatin and thereby allow for the transcription of active genes, while less essential DNA remains dormant.

In addition to the repeats and altered genes, we added RNA silencers to inhibit the normal genes from functioning in their corresponding chromosomes without inhibiting microRNA and other DNA coding sections. For this we utilized antisense RNA technology. A sequence for each gene was constructed in an antisense orientation with respect to the promoter. Hence it was transcribed in **reverse orientation**, allowing it to link with the template strand of the mRNA and **cancel it out**. Therefore, **the new gene will effectively take over for the old**. In the case of LIPE it will create a dysfunctional gene, to subvert the pathway to lipid metabolism and trigger various signaling cascades of its suppression, which will stimulate the consumption of glucose as a primary energy source. Simply utilizing an antisense RNA sequence to subvert the pathway on the original chromosome would not be sufficient, since it wouldn't signal the cell of the metabolic alteration.

Once the HACs were assembled, they were introduced into a stem cell culture after the somatic cells had been converted to stem cells, as discussed above, and the cells were allowed to replicate.

These cells, grown no larger than 1 micron in size in order to diffuse through the capillary walls, will be injected into the bloodstream, which allows them to disperse everywhere in the body, but **must only become functional with respect to the specific cell environment that activates the corresponding genes**. Therefore, it was essential that we find a mechanism that would **bind the introduced cells** to the cell membranes of the appropriate tissues—muscle, brain, heart, lungs, adipose tissue—in order to establish a "garden," so to speak, of introduced stem cells that will replicate rapidly. We have been fairly successful in utilizing genes from *Yersinia pseudotuberculosis*. Within the HACs, we encoded genes from this organism for **virulence and cell adhesion, along with the suppression of the immune system**. This will allow the stem cell injections with HAC to be universal, eliminating the need to acquire cells specific to the recipient's genome.

The Yop gene from *Yersinia pseudotuberculosis* (Ypt) resists internalization by immune system cells and eludes the bactericidal actions of neutrophils and macrophages. Yop undermines the host cell's immune response by disrupting signal cascades and preventing T cell and B cell responses to antigen-binding. Yop also secretes a transmembrane protein, *invasin*, which binds to the host cell integrins. The chromosomal invasin gene **promotes the attachment of the invasive cells**, much like natural substrates such as fibronectin, but with a stronger bond and an optimized surface.

We also encoded ligand production for specific receptors to guide the cells to the appropriate tissues. This will direct the cells **to seek out specific tissues, where they will bind and begin reproducing**.

The final component in the construction of the HAC that we had to address was a **shut-down switch for the cells to prevent over-replication, which might lead to cancer**. We inserted a coding section for density receptors that would sense overcrowding and transcribe a repressor of growth factors. Hence the cell cycle would reroute to G_0. This was a delicate mechanism, as we had to balance the scale of cells necessary to initiate a complete incorporation of the HAC into the specific tissues of the organism that needed to be altered, yet to stop the replication before it would become lethal.

List of Genes Altered and Incorporated in the HAC MarsChr47

CIC (Capricua transcriptional repressor)
Location: Chromosome 19
Coordinates: 42,284,582..42,295,797
Alveolar reconstruction

PAFAH1B3 (platelet-activating factor acetylhydrolase1b, catalytic subunit 3)
Location: Chromosome 19
Coordinates: 42,297,033..42,302,800
Neuroprotection

LIPE (hormone sensitive lipase)
Location: Chromosome 19
Coordinates: 42,401,507..42,427,426
Metabolic pathway alteration

PRR19 (proline-rich 19)
Location: Chromosome 19
Coordinates: 42,302,132..42,310,821
Proline-rich proteins inactivate tannins considerably more effectively than do dietary proteins, resulting in reduced fecal nitrogen losses.
Conservation

TMEM145 (transmembrane protein 145)
Location: Chromosome 19
Coordinates: 42,313,325..42,325,062

Transmembrane proteins pass through the lipid membrane one or more times and consist of a section translocated into the endoplasmic reticulum and a section exposed to the cytosol. Transmembrane protein 145 is involved in a G-coupled receptor signaling pathway. The ligands that bind and activate G-coupled receptors include light-sensitive compounds, odors, pheromones, hormones, and neurotransmitters.

Signaling and Neuroprotection

MEGF8 (multiple EGF–like domains 8)

Location: Chromosome 19

Coordinates: 42,325,609..42,378,769

MEGF8 is a single-pass type I membrane protein that contains several EGF–like domains. Epidermal growth factor or EGF promotes cell growth, proliferation, and differentiation by binding to its receptor EGFR.

Cell growth and differentiation

CXCL17 (chemokine [C-X-C motif] ligand 17)

Location: Chromosome 19

Coordinates: 42,428,543..42,442,984

CXCL17 is a homeostatic, mucosa-linked signaling protein. It is associated with the innate immunity and/or sterility of the mucosa and is primarily expressed in bronchi.

Respiratory tract protection and preservation

CAT (catalase)

Location: Chromosome 11

Coordinates : 34,438,925..34,472,060

Catalase, an antioxidant enzyme converts hydrogen peroxide to water and oxygen, reducing the toxic effects of hydrogen peroxide on the body due to ionizing radiation. Ionizing radiation has been shown to destabilize chromosomes and increase genetic mutation.

Radiation protection

HIF1A (hypoxia inducible factor 1, alpha subunit)
Location: Chromosome 14
Coordinates: 61,695,401..61,748,259
HIF1A is the alpha subunit of the transcription factor hypoxia-inducible factor-1 (HIF-1), which is a heterodimer composed of an alpha and a beta subunit. HIF-1 operates as a master regulator of the body's homeostatic response to hypoxia—both cellular and systemic—by activating the transcription of several genes, such as those that affect energy metabolism, angiogenesis, and apoptosis. It also mobilizes other genes whose protein products increase oxygen delivery or promote metabolic adaptation to hypoxia.
Metabolism, hypoxia adaptive transcription factor

AGO1 (argonaute 1)
Location: Chromosome 1
Coordinates: 35,883,209..35,929,610
AGO1 is a member of the Argonaute family of proteins involved in RNA interference, which may include small interfering RNA-mediated gene silencing. This microRNA machinery is necessary for HIF-dependent transcriptions and cell viability under hypoxic conditions.
Hypoxia adaptive transcription mediation

HES2 (hes family bHLH transcription factor 2)
Location: Chromosome 1
Coordinates: 6,415,232..6,419,919
HES2 is a homologue of *Drosophila* hairy and Enhancer of split proteins. It reduces the expression of TCA cycle genes under hypoxic conditions.
Metabolism, TCA cycle reduction

Glossary of Terms:

alphoid DNA repeats: Centromeric alphoid DNA in primates represents a class of evolving repeat DNA. In humans, chromosomes 13 and 21 share one subfamily of alphoid DNA, while chromosomes 14 and 22 share another subfamily.

alveolar cells: Pneumonocyte (of the lung); any cell of the walls of the pulmonary alveoli; often restricted to the cells of the alveolar epithelium (squamous alveolar cells and great alveolar cells) and alveolar phagocytes.

amino acid: An organic compound containing at least one amino group and one carboxyl group. In the amino acids, there are monomers for building proteins. These monomers consist of an amino group and carboxyl group that are linked to a central carbon atom, the α carbon, and to which a variable side chain is attached.

antigen: Any material (usually foreign) that elicits an immune response. For B cells, an antigen elicits the formation of an antibody that specifically binds to the same antigen; for T cells, an antigen elicits a proliferative response, followed by the production of cytokines or the activation of cytotoxic activity.

antisense RNA: An RNA sequence that is complementary to all or part of a functional RNA.

ATP: Adenosine triphosphate is a molecular unit of currency. It is used to transport chemical energy within cells for metabolism.

B cell: A lymphocyte that matures in the bone marrow and has antigen-specific receptors. After interacting with an antigen (a foreign substance) a B cell proliferates and differentiates into antibody-secreting plasma cells (blood cells).

base pairs (bp): The association of two complementary nucleotides in a DNA or RNA molecule, stabilized by hydrogen bonding between their base components. Adenine pairs with thymine or uracil (A–T, A–U) and guanine pairs with cytosine (G-C).

cell cycle/G_0: The cell cycle is the ordered sequence of events in which a eukaryotic cell duplicates its chromosomes and divides into two. The cell cycle consists of four phases: G_1 before DNA synthesis occurs; S when DNA replication occurs; G_2 after DNA synthesis; and M when cell division occurs. Under certain conditions cells exit the cell cycle during G_1 and remain in the G_0 state as nondividing cells.

chromatin: The complex of DNA, histones, and nonhistone proteins from which eukaryotic chromosomes are formed.

chromosome: A discrete unit of the genome carrying many genes and made up of a single molecule of DNA.

codon: A triplet sequence in DNA or mRNA that specifies a particular amino acid during protein synthesis. Of the 64 possible codons, three are stop codons, which do not specify amino acids but rather cause the termination of synthesis.

depolarization: A decrease in the cytosolic-face negative electric potential that normally exists across the plasma membrane of a cell at rest, resulting in a reduced inside-negative or inside-positive membrane potential. This results in an action potential and the transmission of a signal in the nervous system.

DNA (deoxyribonucleic acid): A long linear polymer, composed of four kinds of deoxyribose nucleotides, that carries genetic information.

EGFR cell signaling: The signaling initiated by the epidermal growth factor (via a cell-surface receptor bound by tyrosine kinases) stimulates cell proliferation.

endoplasmic reticulum (ER): A network of interconnected membranous structures within the cytoplasm of eukaryotic cells. The rough ER is associated with ribosomes and functions in the synthesis and processing of proteins; the smooth ER, which lacks ribosomes, functions in lipid synthesis.

epidermal growth factor: One of a family of secreted signaling proteins that is used in the development of most tissues in most animals.

euchromatin: Comprises all of the genome in the interphase nucleus except for the heterochromatin. The euchromatin is less tightly coiled than heterochromatin, and contains the active and potentially active genes.

eukaryotic: A class of multicellular organisms whose cells contain membrane-bound organelles and a nucleus in which the genetic information is stored.

exon: The segment of a eukaryotic gene that codes for a protein.

fatty acid: A carboxylic acid that consists of a hydrocarbon chain and a terminal carboxyl group, especially any of those occurring as esters in fats and oils. They can be either saturated or unsaturated and are usually derived from triglycerides or phospholipids.

gene: The physical and functional unit of heredity that carries information from one generation to the next. In molecular terms, it is the entire DNA sequence, including the exons, introns, and transcription-control regions necessary for the production of a functional polypeptide or RNA.

genome: The total genetic information carried by a cell or organism.

glycolysis: The metabolic pathway in which sugars are degraded anaerobically into lactate or pyruvate in the cytosol, with the production of ATP.

hemostasis: The stoppage of bleeding or hemorrhage.

heterochromatin: A region of chromatin that remains highly condensed and transcriptionally inactive during interphase.

hypoxia: Insufficient levels of oxygen in blood or tissue.

integrins: A large family of heterodimeric transmembrane proteins that function as adhesion receptors to promote cell-matrix adhesion, or as cell-adhesion molecules to promote cell-cell adhesions.

intron: Part of a primary transcript (or the DNA encoding it) that is removed by splicing during RNA processing and which is not included in the mature, functional mRNA, rRNA, or tRNA.

ligand: Any molecule other than an enzyme substrate that binds tightly and specifically to a macromolecule, usually a protein, to form a macromolecule-ligand complex.

lysophospholipid: A partially digested phospholipid (a lipid with a phosphate group) that lacks a fatty acid chain.

macrophage: A phagocytic leukocyte (white blood cell) that can detect broad patterns of pathogen markers. They function as professional antigen-presenting cells.

micro-RNA (miRNA): A very short RNA molecule in eukaryotic cells that can regulate gene expression.

missense mutations: A mutation in which a base change or substitution results in a codon that causes the insertion of a different amino acid into the growing polypeptide chain, giving rise to an altered protein.

neuro: Relating to the brain.

neurotransmitter: An extracellular signaling molecule that is released by the presynaptic neuron (nerve cell) at a chemical synapse (junction) and relays that signal to the postsynaptic cell.

neutrophil: A phagocytic leukocyte that is attracted to sites of tissue damage and migrate into the tissue. Once activated, neutrophils secrete various chemokines, cytokines, bacteria-destroying enzymes, and other products that help clear invading pathogens.

nucleotide: A building block of nucleic acids composed of a pentose sugar, a nitrogenous base, and one or more phosphate groups.

oligonucleotide (oligodeoxyribonucleotide or oligomer): A short molecule of single-stranded DNA.

pluripotent: Capable of developing into any type of cell or tissue, except those that form a placenta or embryo.

polyunsaturated fatty acid: *Polyunsaturated* refers to a compound in which two or more of the carbon-carbon bonds are double or triple bonds. A *fatty acid* is any long hydrocarbon chain that has a carboxyl group on one end. Polyunsaturated fatty acids are a major source of energy during metabolism and are a precursor for the synthesis of phospholipids, triglycerides, and cholesteryl esters.

prostaglandin: Any of a class of unsaturated fatty acids that are involved in the contraction of smooth muscle, the control of inflammation and body temperature, and many other physiological functions.

restriction enzyme (endonuclease): An enzyme that recognizes a specific duplex DNA sequence and cleaves phosphodiester bonds on both strands, between specific nucleotides.

RNA (ribonucleic acid); mRNA, tRNA, rRNA: A linear, single-stranded polymer, composed of ribose nucleotides. mRNA (messenger RNA), tRNA (transfer RNA) and rRNA (ribosomal RNA) play different roles in protein synthesis.

single nucleotide polymorphism (SNP): A variation in sequence between individuals of the same species caused by a change in a single nucleotide; responsible for most variation between individuals.

somatic cell: Any plant or animal cell other than a germ cell.

stem cell: A self-renewing cell that can either divide symmetrically, to give rise to two daughter cells whose developmental potential is identical to that of the parental stem cell, or asymmetrically, to generate daughter cells with different developmental potentials.

TCA cycle (tricarboxylic acid cycle or citric acid cycle): A stage of tissue respiration that involves a series of biochemical reactions occurring in the mitochondria in the presence of oxygen, by which acetate, which is derived from the breakdown of foodstuffs, is converted into carbon dioxide and water with the release of energy.

T cell: A lymphocyte that matures in the thymus and has antigen-specific receptors that bind antigenic peptides. Cytotoxic T cells kill virus-infected cells and tumor cells, while helper T cells are required for the activation of B cells.

transcription factor (TF): The general term for any protein, other than RNA polymerase, that is required to initiate or regulate transcription of eukaryotic cells. General factors, which are required for the transcription of all genes, participate in the formation of the transcription-preinitiation complex near the start site. Activator transcription factors stimulate while repressor transcription factors inhibit the transcription of particular genes by binding to their regulatory sequences.

transcriptional repressor: A protein that inhibits the transcription of a particular gene.

unesterified fatty acid: A fatty acid molecule lacking an ester group. Esters are chemical compounds consisting of a carbonyl adjacent to an ether linkage.

voltage-gated Ca^{2+} channels: Transmembrane proteins that form ion channels in the membranes of excitable cells (*e.g.*, muscle cells, glial cells, neurons, etc.) that are permeable to the calcium ion Ca^{2+}. Activation allows Ca^{2+} to rush into the cell which, depending on the cell type, results in the activation of calcium-sensitive potassium channels, muscular contraction, the excitation of neurons, the up-regulation of gene expression, or the release of hormones or neurotransmitters.

Bob closed the document, his lips trembling. He looked up at his surroundings. The fog had dissipated, leaving a clear view of the barren ground, the scattered craters, and the scalloped canyon in the distance. The russet tint of iron oxide shaded everything, from the plateaus to the valleys to the alien clouds. The planet that had looked so beautiful, so captivating, a few weeks ago had acquired a taint, as if the addition of moisture had deepened the color and weakened the appeal. This moisture, which should have made it glisten, had tarnished it instead.

But no, the altered atmosphere hadn't tarnished it. The letter had. And the changes within him, no doubt.

Was it a gift? This additional chromosome incorporated into various tissues in his body? The stem cells that were breeding new cells? His body would now tolerate the pervasive low oxygen levels and low pressure. He could breathe on

Mars, or at least in the cave, without a tank. His body would be radiation resistant, enduring the brutal assault of UV radiation without shielding, and even without needing the addition of a moon to create an EM field that would protect the germinating ozone layer. His lungs had been altered and reconstructed, his metabolic pathways rearranged. Some transformation had even been wrought in his normal neural response, to protect his brain in low oxygen conditions. But with all these changes, would he be able to return to Earth? Or was he becoming someone or something else? Obviously, they'd adopted another person's DNA to create these stem cells, and then tricked his immune system with additional genetic variations derived from *Yersinia pseudotuberculosis*—bacteria, no less. Would the DNA change him in some fundamental way other than adaptation, even if the cell alterations were limited to specific tissues?

What have you done to me, Lucas? You've altered my genes? You've made me an organism that can survive on Mars and may only be capable of surviving on Mars.

This time, the tears seeped out and he didn't suppress them. There was no one to see them, anyway. No one to care. Lucas had done something far worse than killing him. He'd sentenced him to live out his life on Mars—something he'd always desired, but never like this. He would not be a colonist among other colonists, but rather a hermit, whiling away his days in absolute solitude, as he became a new organism. A Martian.

THE ROVER CRAWLED over the rock-studded ground, the slowest pace Lucas could endure and still maintain his sanity. He stared straight ahead, only flicking his eyes back and forth from the view ahead to the navigational screen, avoiding Gita's penetrating and undoubtedly accusatory gaze. They were cruising along the rim of the Mawrth Vallis, traveling beside a sheer drop into the enormous chasm now bubbling and frothing with eruptions of brassy water and jam-packed with ice floes. In the distance, they could see the vigorous geyser shooting up from the confines of the river valley and spilling into the Chryse Planitia. If this canyon looked impossible to cross—and it did—would they be able to circumnavigate the discharge on the plain? And even if they did, could they get ahead of the Kasei deluge, or would the entire Chryse basin soon be flooded?

"I know I promised not to talk about it anymore," Gita muttered.

"You did."

"But I just don't understand how he could be so careless."

"I did everything I could, but he ignored my warnings not to stray off the path."

"I don't doubt you, Lucas. And he could be a klutz sometimes. I know that exploring caves can be hazardous—as hazardous as space travel—but . . . to fall into a shaft so deep you couldn't rappel down and at least retrieve his body . . . ? Why didn't he see it? What was he doing? Why wasn't he probing every step with his flashlight? And . . . how can you be sure he's dead? How could you . . . ?"

"Desert him? I went after him, Gita, as I've explained over and over again. I rappelled as deep as I dared, as far down as the rope extended. I still couldn't see him. I couldn't hear him. There's no way he could have survived that long a fall. I did everything I could. Don't you think this is tearing me up inside?"

And it was. He wasn't lying.

"You were angry at him."

"Really? You would actually think . . ." He dared to eye her, if only momentarily. Her hair hung lank around her face, an oily mass of tangles, and her eyes were red-rimmed and tear-brimmed. She looked worse than he did, which was sickly and pale, he imagined, with the added irritation of his hands shaking uncontrollably every so often, as he clutched the wheel.

"No, I'm sorry. I can't imagine anyone would be that angry, especially at the person who'd saved their life."

He gritted his teeth. He knew exactly what she was doing—extending her claws and plunging them into his wounds.

"Do you want me to go back? Do you want me to search depths that are beyond my reach, in a hopeless quest just to get some closure? To bury him? Do you want me to die too? Do you want to die?"

Surely she realized that if they kept delaying their departure, the flood would eventually meet a second body of water: the Acidalia Planitia Ocean, and they would be cut off. Their window of survival was very small, if it existed at all.

"No," she sniffled. "No," she said. "He's dead. I have to accept that, just like you have."

"Okay," he muttered and gripped the wheel in a desperate attempt to still the shakes.

They continued to creep forward. Lucas scanned the horizon, seeking an end to the unrestrained discharge. A trickling. A calm death. But the flow continued as far as the eye could see, or at least to where its horizon flickered into a cloud of mist.

Unexpectedly, the rover bounced and tilted, jamming Lucas's teeth into his lower lip. As it landed level again, he stopped the vehicle and went to look out the back window at the condition of the flatbed. The tanks were still there on the titanium planks, still tightly secured, thank goodness. None had been dislodged or damaged.

"Damn," he said, as he slid back into his seat. "I should have seen that rock. Or the radar should have. I guess it's malfunctioning again. Maybe I should go outside and navigate, just to be sure we don't hit another obstacle."

"It was my fault," mumbled Gita. "I'll go."

Before he could protest, she scurried out of the cockpit and toward the airlock in the back. She wanted to escape him. She was no longer being kind and supportive. Somehow, she knew he was lying. It couldn't have been more obvious, when he'd told her of Bob's fate after climbing out of the sinkhole. She'd spent a day—a day—calling to Bob on the comm, ignoring Lucas's protests, sitting beside the drop and simply staring into the abyss. She'd wasted precious time, but he'd allowed her her grief, because he was wrapped up in his own. Because he couldn't convince her. Because he needed to convince himself.

But finally, he'd pulled her away from the cave and prodded her to consider her own survival, and his. When he'd mentioned his own death, she'd awoken from her stupor. She was still in charge, still responsible for Lucas's life, in her own mind. She would try to focus on their escape from the planet, even though she was bewildered and angry and probably didn't trust him anymore, either.

Lucas waited for Gita to exit the rover, then placed the vehicle in gear again and pushed on. She trudged through the diaphanous curtains of mist, the only sounds filtering through her microphone the grunts of her exertion. She zigzagged around the volcanic rubble, barking directions here and there, hugging the rim of the canyon far too often, which triggered spasms of anxiety in his gut.

"Angle to the left," she snapped. "Boulder."

He complied.

"To the right."

He veered back.

A few minutes passed with steady, uninterrupted progress.

"To the left."

And . . .

"To the left."

And . . .

"To the left."

"Off the cliff?" he asked.

For a minute, she didn't respond. Then she said, "Oh. Better swing way right then."

He swung right and bounced over scattered egg-sized rocks, barely missing the boulder she'd advised him to detour around.

"Subconsciously, you'd prefer I turned left, though."

"Don't be silly."

"I cared for him too."

"You hated him."

"I was angry at him. There's a difference."

"Of course there is. I'm sorry. I'm just . . . still in shock. I know we're supposed to have the 'right stuff,' so we can weather any crisis and still do the job. You do. You climbed out of that dark pit and carried on as if he never existed."

"Not true." *So not true.*

"Turn right. Another whopper."

He angled to the right and followed her trudging stoop-shouldered form.

"I just don't understand how you could give up so quickly. You charged after me in a maelstrom, risking everything to save me. Even if you were angry, why did you only try for two hours?"

"Dead is dead, Gita. Even if I'd tried for two days, even if I could have reached him, he'd still be dead. I gave up because I thought about it logically, not emotionally. I considered the length of the drop, the gravitational forces at play—even if Mars's gravity is less than Earth's, it's still strong enough to cause significant acceleration in his fall—and his rocky landing. It would have shattered every bone in his body. I didn't hear him groan or scream. I didn't hear his breathing over the comm. I analyzed everything as I was trained to do, because . . . because I didn't want to think about anything else. I didn't want to feel. I still don't. So can we focus on the task at hand? Can we stop talking about him? It won't change anything.

"I did what I had to," he added, mostly to himself.

"I thought there was more to you than that. That you weren't just a cold analyst."

"Well, maybe there isn't," he said. "Maybe you should accept that. Maybe that's what will keep us alive and get us back home in one piece."

Gita stumbled, just as he snapped out the last word. She wobbled and then plopped to the ground, head in hands. She gasped in his ears and sobbed once or twice. Damned emotional woman! Lucas stopped the rover and set the brake, gripping the wheel as his hands quivered again.

"I don't think we're going to make it, Lucas."

"Don't say that. Of course we are."

"Not if Mars keeps picking us off one by one."

"Now you're sounding superstitious, which is totally illogical. I told you that Mars would be hazardous, although of course you knew that. You can't reanimate a planet in a few decades without significant atmospheric and surface disruptions that make human exploration extremely hazardous. But Mars is not out to get us. It's not an entity with the thoughts and intentions the ancient Romans liked to confer on it. And we have the means to reach the MADVEC. If you give up now, Bob's sacrifice will be for nothing."

Gita raised her head and looked squarely at the windshield of the rover. "You make it sound as if he did something noble. But it was just an accident, wasn't it?"

"Yes. Absolutely. But he did do something noble. He helped us retrieve more fuel. He saved my life to get us this far." *He's testing our Mars adaptation treatment to see if it's effective.* Cold, man, cold. But he had to be cold—icy to the core. Once again, Lucas willed his hands to stop their quivering.

"He deserves a hero's funeral and an extended grieving period. I'm sorry we can't give him that, but we have to keep moving. When we're back on the

Phoenix, we can cry and write eulogies and experience the full extent of our pain, but not now. Not while the Chryse basin fills up with water and ice until a crossing becomes impossible. Please get up and keep walking. Or exchange tasks with me, and I'll scout for the next few hours. You can kick me and punch me all you want, because it was my fault for not watching over him better, but don't stop moving."

Gita shifted her gaze to look out over the canyon, following the ripples and the jagged outlines of the tarry ice floes. She slapped the ground, but immediately pushed herself upward and stumbled to her feet. With exaggerated movements, she turned away from him and faced the nebulous horizon, then walked forward with weary but determined steps. And she didn't say a word. Not a murmur. Not a sigh. No additional accusations or far-too-intuitive reasoning. Just one breath. And then another. And another. And this painful, plodding silence was even more effective at deepening his guilt and tormenting his mind. But at least it put Bob farther and farther out of reach.

Scanning...

Located: Chapter 41

BARUTI WIGGLED HIS toes, then shifted his leg to the side. He still felt incredibly weak, with the effort of making simple movements a brutal challenge to muscles that felt as if they were bound to weights. A persistent metallic taste lingered on his tongue, a residue of the poison. But he could move; he could swallow; he could smile at Felicity, who hovered over him faithfully, like a devoted nun.

Kwi sat across from him and watched his struggles, examined his body, and intermittently shook a rattle over his head, while Kushe leaned toward Frank and chattered about inane things. They'd remained on the little island for three days now—three days devoted to Baruti's recovery and the further investigation of *!Kung* beliefs. Two women had joined them—Nhwakwe and Kutera—worried when the hunters had not returned to their village. They seemed fascinated with Baruti, whom Kwi firmly believed shared roots with the poisoners.

How could that be? Hunter and Nsogwa clearly came from different ethnic backgrounds—Hunter South African and Nsogwa from the Shona tribe. Or did they? Hunter's skin tone was darker than a typical southern African of European origin, and his nose was less pronounced. Nsogwa's skin color was definitely darker than his companion's, but something about it seemed anomalous, like an afterthought, and his eyes were the color of wet moss. And although Baruti would love to deny it, he did share several unique features with these men: a jutting chin, lighter pigment in his irises, and a truncated forehead. Plus they had characteristic bulges at the back of their heads. His mother had the same skull shape, which he'd always attributed to her genetic ancestry. Could he be related to these men? And if so, was there a mutation in their ancestors' DNA that Baruti shared? A beneficial mutation that gave his cells the ability to *eventually* recognize and eliminate the poison?

This poison, diamphotoxin, was hemolytic—it destroyed red blood cells, thereby reducing the amount of oxygen or nutrients that could be distributed to the rest of the body's cells, causing muscle paralysis, organ failure, and eventually death. It was a single-chain polypeptide that would bind to a protein that prevented its deactivation. Perhaps his immune system had recognized the toxin and switched on genes with the unique ability to produce a competitor. This competitor would have to alter the configuration of the protein to force the toxin's release, which would allow the greater immune system to eliminate it entirely. It could explain why he'd first succumbed to the poison's effects, but later recovered.

But was Nsogwa also immune to this poison? And how did Kwi recognize "the lion" in him? Facial and bodily features? Could he tell by looking at the spacing of his eyes, the length of his arms, the crevices in his palm, like geneticists who can identify a genetic disorder by these simple observations? They could often spot conditions like Marfan syndrome, a genetic disorder of the connective tissue, where a person with this condition would have arachnodactyly—excessively long fingers. Kwi could be a geneticist, without access to the libraries of scientific study but with his own observational and traditional skills.

As Baruti continued to flex his muscles and test his limits, he listened in on the conversation between Frank and Kushe. Today, Frank was asking the obvious questions. He'd backtracked from delving into shamanic rituals and *!Kung* fables and had begun probing into more basic information. Who were the *!Kung* and why were they so important? What made them important enough to eradicate?

"You had all the modern conveniences on your ranches outside Maun. Why did you return to this kind of lifestyle, barely scratching a living from the Delta and the surrounding desert?" asked Frank.

"Modern conveniences," said Kushe. "Yes. Too many. Too many things. And some would have more. And some would have less. One man's cattle would die, and he would have no possessions, and his neighbor's cattle would thrive, and he would have many. And what he would have in overabundance he would give to his neighbor, as is only fair. But the others, the people of the modern world, would scorn him for squandering his wealth. They placed value upon him for his things. When all things were equal, he had no value. That is not the way of the *!Kung*.

"The best hunter would always share with the weaker or the less skilled. He would rather share than be begrudged. The modern world is so clever, and yet it wages endless wars. Is this so difficult a concept to grasp?"

Frank looked at Felicity, for some reason. A stygian darkness crept into his eyes. "Difficult only because it goes against our nature," he said. "We always want more. We are rarely satisfied with an equal portion. Not that we ever get one. And those who have more wealth than they could spend in a hundred lifetimes often end up killing themselves. Go figure."

"They become buried beneath their possessions. They are too heavy. We are happy with simple things," said Kushe. "A shelter, a wife or husband, children, and occasionally a full belly. The sky, the earth, and laughter."

"The lion rarely laughs," said Kwi. "He just roars."

"Who is the lion?" asked Felicity. "Is he someone, or a group of people, that you're familiar with?"

"Yes," said Kwi. "But surely you know him, too. He bore the first grudge. You made him into a human in your stories, but he is all the same. He came before us, but when he fell out of favor with the great god, he killed his rivals. He will do it again. He sits on his rock and watches. He watches the hyenas fight with the jackals, who in turn bicker with the wild dogs. They share the same mother, but yet they invent differences to justify their divisions, even when they have a fair allotment of meat. The lion finds us disturbing. The lion fears and envies us. He is weak in numbers, and he knows that, despite his physical strength, we will destroy him if we band together—if we can ever band together. And so he hides in the murky branches of the thorn tree until the day when we will each become isolated, and then he will pounce."

"You speak of myths, stories of jealousy and power, like the story of the Egyptian god Set, who longed to usurp the throne of his brother Osirus, and so eventually killed him. Similar stories have been passed on in different forms in different cultures, but probably date back to the dawn of human speech and storytelling. The lion is the jealous brother. But do you know his face, today?" asked Frank, mild exasperation evident in his voice.

"His face," said Kwi. "He has many faces. Even Baruti shares half his face."

Baruti blinked and traced the contours of his cheekbones. Half his face. His mother's face. And he had great height, too. He had towered over his father from an early age. Was it his mother who was genetically linked to the miners?

He looked up as he felt eyes boring into him—Frank's and Felicity's, in particular. Pedro was frowning and looking off into the distance. Pondering the riddle with his sharp mind.

The *!Kung* women studied him too, crinkling their noses and pursing their lips. "He is fierce," said Kutera. "But not cruel. I remember when you came to the bush, Baruti, and defended a baby elephant that poachers had left to die. I remember you. You chased away the lions."

Baruti nodded, containing the tears that threatened to spill from his eyes, reminded once again of the slaughter. "And I have no interest in killing you," he said. "Quite the opposite."

"No, Baruti," said Kwi. "You do not share the lion's fear. You have no knowledge of it. But you are a result of it."

Baruti shook his head, totally bewildered. "I am . . ."

"Connected to them," said Felicity, her voice strangely resonant. "You're . . . a Phoenician, but not a Phoenician."

"Or a Florida bog body," said Frank.

"The link," said Pedro, "'tween a newer people and an older one."

"You're saying the miners were not just experimenting with genetics, but are genetically unique themselves? That they are the species we discovered in the North? But that still doesn't explain what they're doing in that region. Since the bodies were discovered after their arrival, it couldn't be a matter of simply digging them up and disposing of them, if what worries them is being exposed. Maybe they were searching for their ancestors, but the other biological samples point to something quite different. And why remain hidden at all? I know you mentioned their fear of us, Kwi, but modern humans aren't going to wage war on them. Scientists would be fascinated. . . ."

"Yes, they would," said Felicity. "They'd put them through rigorous testing. They'd be testing everyone worldwide to see if anyone shared their unique genetic signature. They'd set them apart. And they'd list them as an ancient species, maybe view them as less evolved. When we looked at the bodies, we saw immediately that they are less compact than most people are. Every one in that camp seemed rather tall, with a big bone structure—somewhat like you, Baruti. Isn't that where the jealous brother comes in? Division and classification? And isn't 'Neanderthal' often used as a derisive term? Maybe their fear is justified."

"So that's why they're killing your people," said Frank. "Because you, through your ancestral stories and familiarity with them, know who they are. They want to maintain their masks."

"They keep their masks by burning their bones," said Kwi. "They have been digging them up for the last century throughout the Okavango and burning them to ash. But we have hidden the bones our ancestors protected. My people feared the burning. If you disturb the dead, the spirits will torment you. We have many, many bones, some from the very beginning. Perhaps the lion should fear you most of all, Frank Campo. After all, the snake is the strongest of all creatures, even though it crawls on the ground. A mother adder even killed the god Pishiboro when he laughed at her babies, and left his body to decay in the rank corners of the Delta. Now, the water that flows in the rivers of the North and the pools that have formed in the land here are the rottenness of Pishiboro as his body decomposed."

"They should be afraid of *me*?" said Frank, choking on his own incredulity. "What threat do I pose?"

But it made perfect sense to Baruti. "You found the beads. You've studied the *!Kung*. Now you're searching for a connection. You have access to modern tools of genetic analysis, and you're also an anthropologist. You and Pedro brought us back here, suggesting that the *!Kung* are the key to this mystery. And you're dogged, determined to find answers to the massacre that has left you deeply affronted. If they fear discovery, before they do whatever they're planning, then once they learn of your existence, you are their greatest worry."

"But what are they planning?" asked Felicity.

Baruti shrugged. "What can we determine from their activities? They are gathering a Noah's ark's worth of genetic material."

"You're still thinking destruction, some sort of terrorist action?" asked Frank. "But maybe they're more concerned with staying hidden. It all points to repopulation, not annihilation. Yes, they've killed, but only to keep their secret."

"There's no place on Earth to hide anymore. There isn't a niche that hasn't been inhabited where they could start over," said Felicity.

They pondered the enigma for a while. They fidgeted and scratched the sand. Then Pedro's eyes opened wide as if he'd discovered the god particle, and he looked up at the sky.

"That's right," he said. "There's no place on Earth."

How much information should she share?

Dayna cast an awkward glance at Shaun, who lay sprawled on the bed beside her. She followed the contours of his chest as it rhythmically rose and fell and curved down gracefully to his flat belly. The sheet now covered his lower body, but after having spent three days with him, she now knew every part of him, every curve and hollow, intimately. What had come over her? It was as if he were a drug and she'd become instantly addicted.

But she'd insisted on protection after the first day, and he had reluctantly acquiesced, although it was probably too late if he was diseased. *But there is no hint of disease.* She'd visually inspected him in the shower and on the bed before and after their escapades, and could find no aberrations on his skin or elsewhere. At first he'd looked offended, discerning the scientific approach in her behavior, but eventually he'd reveled in her audacity.

It was strange to spend three days with someone in such close contact and still know next to nothing about him. And still worry about sharing information with him. There was no trust at all in this relationship, or whatever it was. She still didn't know whether he'd played a role in the murder of his friend, nor what association he had, if any, with the people Baruti was investigating. Or that his wife had. She was reluctant to tell him about the new species, particularly her revelation regarding the contaminant in her sample of the skull.

Even more worrisome was the fact that Felicity and Frank had not returned. That could mean Baruti had never become ill and they were still investigating the *!Kung*. Or—a terrifying thought—they were *all* in trouble. How significant was it that Baruti might be some sort of hybrid between modern humans and the new species they'd unearthed? If he'd discovered his genetic mutations, it made sense that he would be driven to exhume more details. That he'd seek out every connection. But he'd seemed more convinced that the geneticists or genetic engineers in the Canadian North were devising some catastrophe. In fact, by his obscure explanation, it sounded like he'd been recruited to follow them by a spy, which didn't suggest a personal connection at all. Could it be a coincidence?

Baruti, of course, came from Africa. If this species had originated in there alongside the *!Kung*, it certainly was possible there had been interbreeding in the region, which would have led to the development of hybrids. After all, *Neanderthals* had interbred with *Homo sapiens* in the Middle East and northern Europe. But since genetic testing was rarely done in this country, Baruti might not have known. There were still so many questions regarding this bizarre conspiracy, like what connection existed between the bodies and the killers. She still couldn't fathom it, other than a link to genetics.

"You're deep in thought," said Shaun, shocking her by his sudden wakefulness. His head was turned toward her, and he shifted his body so he could prop his head on his elbow and gaze at her more fully. "Are you thinking of me?"

"How egoistic," she said. "Not everything is about you."

"Felicity and Frank, then," he said. "If it's not me and how you can make me even more aroused, it's them and whether they're alive or dead. Two vastly different thoughts in juxtaposition, which disturbs you but doesn't stop you."

"You have no idea," she whispered, fleeing his steady gaze.

"Oh, I think I do. It disturbs you even more that you can't stop, even though I don't seem to be the sort of man to form attachments. You'd be right too. At least not after my wife, anyway. I grab whatever happiness I can in the moment.

Because, you know, happiness doesn't last, people and animals are disposed of daily, and we need to stop making commitments we can't sustain."

"Hmm," said Dayna. "So that's why you study polar bears. Because you have no interest in preserving anything."

Shaun gave a short laugh. "I guess you've got me there." He turned away from her for a moment, then dropped his head down on her belly and buried his face there. She paused and caught her breath, then gently ran her hands through his hair. He turned his head so he could breathe, but he didn't kiss her or make any sexual gesture other than the intimate placement of his head.

"I'm a hypocrite, aren't I?" he whispered.

"Absolutely," she said.

"And you don't respect me."

"I don't know you."

"What would you say if I told you that this, *even all of this*," he said, touching her thigh, "is about regaining some self-respect?"

"I would tell you that I'm very confused. But I'm not innocent, either. I'm not a child who's easily manipulated or has no clear sense of judgment. I came into this with my eyes open. I like being with you, Shaun, even if I do feel guilty about it, too. Not because of your lack of commitment, but because Felicity and Frank are out in the wild, possibly in grave danger, and we're doing nothing to help them. But if you need to confess something to me, I'm ready to listen."

Shaun snuggled his face deeper into her belly, but he didn't respond.

Did she have to force it out of him? "How does sex help you regain self-respect?"

"Not just sex," he said, sitting up as suddenly as he'd dropped down on her. "Sex with you. Sex with someone I respect."

Dayna frowned. "Because of your wife? Because you didn't respect her?"

Shaun released an exasperated sigh. "Yes and no. Oh, you couldn't understand anyway." He crawled on top of her and kissed her thoroughly.

"Stop," she said, tearing her lips from his and holding his face in her palms. "Make me understand."

"I don't know if I . . . You can't imagine . . . They hate so much," he forced out through stiff lips. "I mean, *she* hates so much," he quickly corrected. "I could never hate . . . Felicity, Donna, Tony . . . you. Never." Dayna had never heard so much pain in a man's voice before, not even Evan's when their child had died.

He rolled away from her and sat on the edge of the bed.

"Who are 'they'?" Dayna asked.

He didn't speak.

"I wouldn't blame you for anything 'they' did," she said. "But you have to tell me who they are and what they're trying to do."

"One slip," he said with a mirthless laugh, "and you're all over it. Or maybe it was more than one slip, wasn't it? Is that why . . . you're all over me?"

"Oh . . . my . . . God. Are you really so fragile? Or is it just that men place so much value on sex that any thought that there might be some other motive than that we aren't totally turned on by you makes you deeply offended? Okay, I'll soothe your bruised ego. I did not jump into bed with you to pry information from you. And yes, you did slip up more than once. And I still jumped into bed with you, even though the things you said alarmed me, because I am attracted to you. Satisfied?"

He didn't look at her, but sat hunched over the side of the bed.

"If these people in the cult hate others so much, they won't stop at doing unconscionable things. Sex isn't going to protect us, Shaun."

He laughed again, and then planted his feet firmly on the ground. He grabbed his boxers and yanked them on. Then he pulled on his jeans, without casting her another glance. He buckled his belt, but paused when the sound of several voices floated in from outside. The muscles on his back knotted and he caught his breath, then whipped on his T-shirt.

Before she could pose another question, he swept her clothes from the floor and hissed, "Get dressed," tossing them to her.

She raised an eyebrow, but swiftly began donning her clothes, because she'd never seen him look this frantic before.

"What . . .?" she tried to ask, but he clapped a hand over her mouth. The voices had grown in volume and now sounded like they were right outside the door.

"You're right," he whispered in her ear. "Sex isn't going to do anything. We have to run."

Scanning...

Located: Chapter 42

IS IT BETTER to be alive or dead?

Bob nibbled on an energy bar and stared blankly at the mossy green pond that rippled near his feet. A day had passed and another long lonely night since he'd climbed back down the rope into the sinkhole, the tablet clutched in his hand in so desperate a grip it threatened to crack. He'd stumbled along the boulder-strewn path on auto-pilot, hardly registering the alien environment that would now become familiar.

When he'd reached the pond and the supposedly oxygen-friendly biodome, he'd discarded his mask and tank, fully prepared to test the limits of the new chromosome that had now infiltrated his cells. After all, what would it matter if he died anyway? It might spare him years of soul-crushing pain and loneliness.

But the chromosome and the oxygen-generating plants had proved to be adequate. At least he continued to breathe, although with what efficiency and what long-term effects to his body and brain he had no idea. He still felt weak, and his lungs strained sporadically, shocking him with an occasional sharp lance to the chest. That could be the result of a moderately insufficient intake of air or oxygen, or it could be because his lungs had developed more surface area that his chest had not fully accommodated. Certainly the metabolic pathways described in the publication would mean his cells would have fewer energy-rich molecules to consume, and he'd have to learn to expend less energy and work at a slower pace. Work. Work to survive. But what was the point?

And yet . . . a few hours after he'd collapsed at the side of the pond, he began shaking, engulfed by a frenetic chill, and he'd gotten up and searched through the vast storehouse of supplies for a heater and a power source. Wires dangled beside the windows, and he'd wondered if Lucas's co-conspirators had installed solar panels on the planet's surface. In his search, he'd unearthed rechargeable battery packs and connected them to the wires, surprised to see how quickly they recharged. Once the battery had drawn a decent charge, he'd plugged in the heater and cuddled up close to it. He didn't want to die.

Bob sighed and nibbled the last few crumbs of his energy bar, savoring the sweet flavor.

"I don't want to die because I want to *somehow* get back at you, Lucas. I want to sentence you to the same everlasting torment and isolation."

He had to stop thinking about that damned Judas. He had to concentrate on matters that didn't eat away at his mind.

His thoughts drifted to Rossi, his sexy, shy girlfriend. He visualized her sweet heart-shaped face and imagined the warm, satiny feeling of her skin under his hands. He could picture her smiling, accentuating the dimple in her cheek that he found both charming and erotic. She always smiled when they talked about his dreams of Mars and her dreams of Earth, but not as if she were indulging their fantasies. She truly believed there was hope for both.

Rossi was a travel photographer and a conservationist, a contradiction that she tried to reconcile by demanding wildlife protection funds for every creature she documented in her travels and funds to offset her traveler's footprint. She had no desire to travel off-planet. Yet she had never denied him his dreams. She would have relinquished her comfortable life to join him as a colonist, because she openly admitted she loved him and couldn't imagine life without him. And he couldn't imagine leaving her behind . . . for longer than a few months. Now they'd be separated forever, and he couldn't even say good-bye, because he probably couldn't leave this cave without suffocating.

He tossed the wrapper onto the ground and kicked it away. It slipped into the pond and floated on the murky surface, weaving through golden reeds and emerald lily pads. What appeared to be a piney cluster of mountain crowberry with lavender flowers and a scant amount of indigo berries lay sprawled over a rock near the water. This micro-oasis was all that was Earth-like on the entire planet.

"I'm not going to live in this cave. Do you hear me, Lucas? No, you can't hear me. But I think you're hurting. You couldn't kill me, so that means you have a conscience. Unless I'm just an experiment."

Friend and enemy. Friend and enemy. Impossible!

Well, he had two options. A third, if he wanted to consider just jabbing a knife through his own heart. He could set up camp, make this alien landscape into a quaint little home away from home. Construct a basic chair, a table, and a comfy bed from the materials available to him—mostly plastic and titanium, no doubt. Acquaint himself with the garden and determine if there were any edible sprouts, roots, or fruits. Inventory his supplies to see if he could rig a radio that was powerful enough to contact one of the satellites in orbit around Mars and somehow relay a message to Earth. He could do all that. It would probably take weeks, if not months.

Or . . . he could chase after Lucas. Which would probably be the same as jabbing a knife through his heart. He could breathe within the cave, but it was extremely unlikely that he could do so without a tank and mask outside its protective walls, since the blue-green algae they'd deposited on the surface was not yet particularly pervasive, and he had no idea how little oxygen his body could tolerate, let alone whether the carbon dioxide in the environment had been displaced enough to make the atmosphere less toxic. The two tanks of oxygen he'd found in reserve wouldn't last long—certainly not the length of time it would take to reach the Tempe Terra base on foot. And he had no damned rover. Besides, Lucas and Gita were probably halfway there already, and they would depart on the MADVEC as soon as they reached it. Lucas wouldn't waste any time before liftoff, in case Bob did discover some decent communications equipment and send a message to Gita. The only way Bob could outflank them would be to cross the Mawrth Vallis canyon—a canyon with an erupting aquifer that was discharging water in such massive quantities that the current would likely sweep him away as soon as he waded into it. Even if he did survive that traverse, he would then have to cover miles of open plain that might also be flooding, and eventually cross the Kasei Valles, an even broader canyon with an even deadlier current. Knife through the heart.

The other bases had been established in the south, thousands of miles from his position. He had no hope of reaching them.

Friend and enemy. Friend and enemy.

The wrapper bobbed on the fecund pond. It bobbed and dipped and refused to sink.

"Boat," he said, sitting up. "Suicide," he said, and sank back down. As the heater puffed warm air into his face, he luxuriated in it. Comfy home away from home. Food, shelter, survival.

"I'll be a hermit, Lucas. I'll grow hair down to my navel. Is that what you want? You don't care, though. You don't care that I stuffed your intestines back into your body and stitched you up not once, but twice. You don't care that I sacrificed my own air supply for you and nearly died trying to save you. They told me to kill you, but I couldn't do it. I believed, no matter what designs you had on Mars or what nefarious plans your group had devised, that you still had an ethical core, a thread of decency. I was such an idiot."

But Lucas hadn't participated in the terraforming mission in order to land on Mars and add more supplies and DNA samples to this storehouse. He'd had no desire to explore Mars at all. He had no intention of testing this chromosome on himself, either. He had something else up his sleeve. Bob had nursed suspicions after he'd caught Lucas juggling mission coordinates for the return to Earth, but he couldn't see the sense in sabotaging their mission. It wouldn't get the secessionists any closer to establishing an exclusive colony on Mars. But if Lucas did intend to sabotage the mission, or the *Phoenix* spacecraft, and Bob did nothing to stop it . . . Gita might die. And all their efforts on this mission and the years prior to it would have been for nothing.

Bob glared at the mountain of supplies that would sustain him for years, maybe for a lifetime. But what an empty life it would be. He could never leave the planet, regardless, but he wasn't going to sit here and wallow in self-pity. He was a man of action, and he had a mountain of supplies.

He stood and marched toward the stacks, although he had to stop every ten steps to gasp and fight off a wave of vertigo. He began sorting through the vast stocks of survival staples, shunting them to a pile near the pond, snapping open plastic boxes, ripping the packaging off materials, and listing them on his tablet—the very tablet on which Lucas had typed his earth-shattering message. It came in handy now. The largest packages contained what appeared to be inflatable HAB material. But it was the containers themselves that galvanized him—lightweight and airtight. He opened several boxes of food supplies and eagerly scooped out handfuls of protein bars, freeze-dried vegetable and meat dishes, and other packets high in protein and carbohydrates—things like dried calamari, beef jerky, fried rice, and pasta. Since his metabolism would now rely on glucose more than fat, he reduced the fattier foods and increased the carbohydrates. He examined the two rebreather tanks, which he could possibly reprogram. If he could reduce the oxygen burden and the volume of recycled air, he could conserve more oxygen and extend their life.

But what to do if he actually accomplished this mission impossible? If he beat Lucas to the Tempe Terra HAB and the MADVEC? Lucas was considerably more robust and in better condition than he was, injury or no injury. He would need a weapon. He tromped back down the endless aisle, scanning the shelves, looking for a gun, while feeling a little ridiculous. Of course there was nothing of the sort. This terrorist faction needed weapons on Earth to accomplish their goal, but they probably wouldn't require them here when they arrived. He did discover some multifunctional tools, including some Swiss Army knives, and jammed one into his pocket. But would that be enough to disable the bastard? He'd have to somehow surprise him and aim at a vital organ, or slash his throat. But as he walked deeper into the alcove, he found himself staring at the medical supplies sitting adjacent to the DNA samples—anesthetics, sedatives, narcotics, many in preloaded syringes. Exactly the items that would satisfy his hunger for poetic justice—at least somewhat.

He could jab Lucas in the neck, just as the bastard had done to him, and quickly incapacitate him. Then he'd tie him up and punch his face, crack his ribs, break his legs. Or maybe he'd just keep injecting him until he died. But first he would send Gita back to Earth and take his time repaying Lucas for his betrayal. After all, they had nothing but time. He grabbed a handful of syringes, everything that might do damage in strong enough doses, and jammed them into his utility pocket.

"I'm coming for you, Lucas," he said.

Lucas couldn't sleep. They'd finally stopped traveling when the sun had set, a slowly sinking gossamer orb feathered with mist. Gita had returned to the rover, eaten a hastily prepared meal of rehydrated potatoes, corn, and chicken, spoken not a word to him, and settled into bed.

But her icy behavior wasn't as wounding as his own bleeding conscience. He kept reliving the moment he'd plunged the needle into Bob's neck. The astonished and hurt look in his eyes. He'd done what was necessary. The man was not and never would be his friend. He didn't even share the same ancestral DNA. And he'd been recruited to spy on Lucas. He would have exposed him and the Movement before they could escape Earth and establish their colony. His revelations would destroy them all.

But every time his belly clenched at these thoughts, it aggravated his wound and caused a flash of pain to erupt in his head. Now the strike had dulled, but it still throbbed, and he couldn't close his eyes.

Hours passed. He could hear the gentle sough of Gita's breathing as she drifted along in her dreams. Her dreams were not calm, though, since she often tossed and turned, agitating the rover and smacking against the tinny wall. Her restless sleep seemed even more damning, and it pecked away at his own attempts to slumber.

Maybe he should contact the Movement and let them know of the new complications. That would likely be too risky, but he had to do something to keep his mind occupied. Maybe he could email his brother again. He'd only contacted Shaun once since their arrival, updating his brother on the condition of the planet and his own injuries. But what should he say this time? He couldn't confess. Shaun certainly wouldn't sympathize, and the ISA might read his mail, even if it was marked "private." You never knew. But even that distant, delayed contact with someone he knew and cared for, someone who understood what it meant to be an outsider, might ease his mind. And as they'd proceeded farther north, they'd come within range of the nearest satellite, so he might even get a quick response.

He tapped on his tablet, immediately dousing the bright light and switching it to night mode. He entered the messenger application and began to write.

Hey Shaun,

How you doing? Still enjoying the cold Arctic and the polar bears? I've never understood your fascination with them, but at least they aren't dying out yet like every other creature on Earth. And maybe someday they can make a comeback on Mars.

We've experienced some more setbacks here on the Red Planet. I've not been injured again, but we lost a crewmate after we had an incident that jeopardized our rocket fuel and oxygen tanks. We managed to restock our supplies, but there are only two of us now—Gita, and me. I'm not sure if we'll escape this planet. We're seeking a passage around a very long stretch of river—yes, river—and if we don't find one, well . . .

I just wanted to touch base with you and let you know that you can't change my mind anymore. I've made irreversible decisions and I may make a final one, too. Either way, you probably won't ever see me again. But you are my brother, and I hope you will see this business through to the end. Or at least not get in our way.

Love,
Lucas

He tapped *Send* and set the tablet aside. Now he should try to sleep again. He had to be alert come morning to continue their tedious circumnavigation of the canyon, to prevent the rocket fuel from bouncing on a rock and exploding, to determine the safest and most expeditious route to the MADVEC. His eyes drifted closed, as he felt Gita throw herself around again, in her tedious slumber, giving the rover another vigorous shake. But he couldn't escape the relentless tide of flashbacks. He eventually nodded off, but even his dreams mocked him by repeating the critical scene.

He started awake, still hearing his own words: "You'll be okay, though. I guarantee it."

A chime sounded, emanating from his tablet. He looked at the digital clock in the corner of the screen. Four-forty, Mars time, which was approximately the same as Earth time, except the solar day was extended by 39 minutes here. Yes, enough time had passed for a response from his brother, especially with the rapid laser transmission.

He opened the messenger app, then paused, because the sender wasn't Shaun. The name looked glaringly familiar. Louis Saunders. ISA CAPCOM for their mission.

He opened the message, dread foaming in his gut.

> What kind of setbacks are we really talking about here, Luke? Are you telling us Jolson is dead? And what are the odds you'll make it back to the MADVEC? How long should we give you before we decide to remote-pilot the *Phoenix* back home?

So now there was no doubt they were monitoring his private messages. The tone was brusque, exasperated, and beyond angry.

He could think of all kinds of responses, like "This wasn't my idea, remember?" But he'd still agreed to the excursion, so they wouldn't accept that excuse. Or, "Yes, Jolson is dead, but it was due to his own negligence." Partly true, at least. How about . . . "Look, I know the odds aren't stacked in our favor, but give us at least a month to return to the Tempe Terra base. We have enough oxygen to last us until then." But something in Sanders's words was nibbling at his mind, prompting him to rein in all these excuses and pleas.

He accessed the message and typed in a reply.

> Yes, Bob is dead. Three days. Give us three days and if we're not back by then, call the *Phoenix* home.

He hit *Send* with a definitive tap. But he didn't return the tablet to sleep mode. Instead, he accessed the *Phoenix's* computer with a relay through the satellite. He opened up a cryptographically protected program in the computer system and began uploading instructions. The ISA wouldn't see these instructions, since they were cloaked in code and buried in a seldom monitored drive. At least Bob hadn't noticed his late-night forays into the engine room, or the ISA might be a little more judicious in evaluating system variations. He was pretty sure they were still oblivious, since they hadn't mentioned any concerns in previous transmissions. As it stood, they wouldn't know that he had hijacked their ship until it was too late.

It wasn't until he'd finished uploading the last line of code and switched off the tablet that he noticed that Gita was sitting up on her bunk, watching him.

"What are you doing?" she asked.

"I couldn't sleep. I sent a letter to my brother."

"Did you tell him about Bob?"

"Of course. I can't get him off my mind."

"Neither can I," she said, adding a sniffle. "I've been thinking about what you said, and I suppose you're right. We have to stop wallowing in grief and try to get home. I shouldn't keep blaming you, either. I don't really know what transpired down there in the cave."

"No, you don't," he said, trying to inject some resentment into the phrase, but it still came off sounding hollow.

"The sun's beginning to rise," she remarked. "It's almost five o'clock. Maybe we should have a quick bite of breakfast and get started. I'm exhausted from all the walking yesterday. I'll drive this time while you scout."

"Can I trust you to drive?"

"What do you mean?" She sounded indignant.

"Can I trust you to keep heading toward the MADVEC? Or will you get some crazy idea in your head that you can still recover Bob and turn the rover around?"

She scowled at him. "That would be insane. We'd never escape the planet, then. Never make it back to Earth. And I'd be leaving you to die."

"You've made it pretty clear you don't care about me, just Bob."

"That's not true!"

"But do you care about yourself?"

She stared at him, slack-jawed and uncomprehending.

"Is retrieving Bob, dead or alive, more important to you than your own survival?"

"Lucas, are you telling me he's alive?"

"No, I'm asking you a simple question. If we turn the rover around that means we all die. Do you love Bob's broken body that much?"

She spent several seconds glaring at him before she replied. "No," she said quietly. "I promise I won't turn back. I'm not crazy."

"Good to know," he said. "Why don't you get breakfast ready? I'm going outside to check on the flatbed and fuel before we head out."

"I'm not your maid. Cook your own food," she snapped.

"Fine," he said. "I'll be back in a minute."

He strode to the airlock and shimmied into his jumpsuit in record speed. After strapping on his mask and tank, he sealed the lock and exited the rover.

"Less than a minute," he muttered as he marched up to the hitch assembly. With a brisk yank, he withdrew the pin. Then he strode back to the airlock and jumped inside.

"What did you inspect?" asked Gita, as he opened the inner hatch. "You weren't gone very long."

He ignored her and grabbed a bag of dried nuts and a water pouch, upending the bag into his mouth and crunching down on the meal of convenience. Without another glance at her, he proceeded to the cockpit and slid behind the wheel.

"I'm driving today," she barked, dashing in behind him.

"Not today," he replied, starting the engine. She gaped at him as he cranked the wheel around.

"You're going back," she said, flabbergasted. "After you just grilled me about whether I would."

"I just wanted to see how far you would go. Maybe just to prove to myself that I was willing to go further." The rover lurched around in a semicircle as he guided it with the wheel. "You see, you wouldn't have turned back. Not at this point. Not if it meant your own death. You may be angry and grief-stricken and miserable, but you wouldn't have made the ultimate sacrifice for him."

"How dare you?" she said.

"*Would* you?" he asked, unable to disguise his satisfaction.

"I certainly would if I knew he was alive," she said, through gritted teeth.

"Point taken."

"Why do you feel you need to prove you're better than me?"

"Oh, Gita," he said, shaking his head. "I'm not better than you. I don't in all honesty ever think I can measure up to you. In fact, I'm far worse than you can even imagine. But I'm still going back."

Scanning...

Located: Chapter 43

DAYNA HAD NO sooner whipped on her clothes than Shaun grasped her hand, while at the same time he lassoed his backpack and tugged her toward the open window in their tent-style room. He slid open the screen and boosted Dayna through, just as a steady knocking came at their door. Shaun tossed his pack to her, leaped through the opening, and whisked the screen closed, crouching down and pushing her down beside him as their door burst open.

"Anything?" said a deep, gravelly voice.

"No," replied a woman in a clipped tone. "Although it looks like they left recently. In fact the bed is even warm. *The bastard.*"

"Better check around the back," the first voice commanded. A series of heavy footsteps followed, indicating that several others were exiting the room. And they were accompanied by resounding clicks, as if they were cocking guns.

Shaun looked at Dayna with alarm, then eyed the potential safety of denser brush and grass that was the length of a football field away, across an open area of neatly trimmed flower beds and wooden walkways. He pointed to the porch on which they crouched, the elevated platform that supported the framework and canvas of their room and prevented flooding or the easy access for wildlife to guests of the lodge. Without waiting for a response, he grabbed her hand and leaped off the porch, pulling her with him.

They landed with a mild jolt in a cluster of groomed shrubs and star-petaled flowers, the sharp branches and leaves scratching Dayna's legs and arms. Shaun's hand gripped hers like a metal clamp as he pulled her under the porch, dragging his pack with him. They crept forward on hands and knees, Dayna uncomfortably aware of the possibility that animals were concealed there too, particularly reptiles. As she placed her weight on her left hand, it plunged through a hole in the ground that was loosely covered by twigs and leaves, and she fell flat on her face, crushing her nose and scraping her cheeks. She withdrew her hand and skimmed it over the ground until she found solid support, then managed to raise her head. But as she dusted her face and attempted to rise up farther, a shadow passed over a brightly-lit gap along the side of the platform—an area without bordering shrubs. Shaun instantly shoved the rest of her body tight to the ground.

"Anyone out there?" asked the woman, her shoes tapping on the porch above them.

"Don't see a soul," responded another male voice, a resonant tenor. "It's funny how we came here looking for those students Mbeki has recruited, especially the *!Kung* expert, but we found your ex instead."

"It's not funny," she snapped.

"Well, we all know he can't get enough of the common folk, especially the young ones. But who's this older woman he's snagged? Older chicks aren't really his thing, are they?"

"Shut up!"

"I think she's the one we really want dead," said the gravelly voice. Ice traveled down Dayna's spine, knotting every attached muscle. "The Harvard professor who sent those students to Northern Ontario and to the Everglades. My contact in the RCMP told me she appropriated the bodies."

"So they must know by now, Hondo."

"They know enough. Too much. We still need months, or more likely years, before Mars is prepped for our arrival. If they start yammering about those bodies, someone may connect them to our movement and to missing supplies and rockets and to certain accidents. Eventually they'll begin testing everyone. Our people in GenTech won't be able to bury or alter the results anymore. And if the anti-terrorist units in WEPA or Interpol begin watching us, we won't be able to take the necessary next steps even if Lucas succeeds in his mission."

Lucas? Dayna tumbled the name through her head. Where had she heard it before?

"Well, I guess we need to find her then," said the woman. "And the grad students. But what about Shaun? I'd love to kill him for this, but Lucas won't allow it. You know that. Do you think he told her about us?"

"Not yet, or we would find ourselves already under strict surveillance. But he is so damned soft. He's still trying to protect them and us at the same time. He'll eventually find that he'll have to become the enemy of both."

"He doesn't know everything, or I think he *would* have turned us in. Maybe not Lucas, because I don't think he knows his brother's role, but the rest of us."

Dayna suppressed a gasp. *Lucas.* Of course. He was Shaun's brother, the man who was on a mission to Mars. What did Mars have to do with these people? Was this all about some sort of revolution?

Dayna turned her head to glare at Shaun, or to at least see how he was reacting to the conversation, but instead she found two glittering eyes peering at her from the hole her hand had penetrated. *Don't scream,* she told herself, or she'd expose their location and then she'd be dead for sure. A furry head popped out farther, revealing a ruffled caramel-colored pelt and a twitching knob of a nose, and she recognized it as belonging to one of the many mongooses that had crossed her path. It looked as alarmed as she at their mutual discovery. Shaun touched her arm, and she met his eyes. He signaled to her to stay calm.

Calm? Sure. I've been marked for a hit for God knows what reason by these insane cult members of yours. I'm not going to scream because a mongoose might nip at my nose. But I am going to scream at you if we get out of this alive.

The mongoose didn't nip. It stared at her for an extended period of time like a small furry hypnotist, but it must have determined she wasn't a threat, because it climbed out of the hole, buffing her face with its coarse fur.

"If we find Shaun, we'll hold him," said the gravelly-voiced man, Hondo. "If Lucas goes to prison when he returns—or at least if they hold him for questioning for years—then we'll decide what to do with his brother. But, for now, we can't give Lucas any reason not to complete his task. And I'm sure you don't really want to kill Shaun, Reena."

"Some days I do," she said. "He's never believed in our cause. He acts as if he's ashamed of who he is. And now he's doing this. Trying to dilute his DNA with every woman he meets, even though he knows it's impossible."

"Or at least difficult," said Hondo, with a chuckle.

"I've had enough of his cowardice."

"Well, he can't have gone far. This is an island, after all. Unless they did take a boat into the Okavango. Let's do a thorough search and question the staff a little more intensively. We'll find him."

Their footsteps tramped on the wooden boards above, but eventually faded. Dayna caught Shaun's gaze, but he shook his head, so she remained stationary as a troop of mongooses exited their tunnel and shuffled past, every one brushing her cheek with the length of its body. It would have been hilarious, if she weren't a bundle of anxiety.

"We have to get out of here," he finally whispered.

"No kidding. But how, if they're searching the grounds and watching out for us?"

"Boat," said Shaun. "We head out into the Okavango. It may be dangerous without a guide, but it's also our only hope."

"Shaun! They want to kill me! Are you going to tell me what's going on?"

"Yes, when we get clear. I promise I'll tell you everything. Dayna." He shuffled closer and caressed her cheek. "I won't let them hurt you. Damn it! I didn't even want you to come along. But now you're here and we— It would kill me if they hurt you."

It was unbelievable, but he leaned forward and kissed her, before she could even think to pull away. And then she didn't want to pull away . . . again. She leaned into him and let him tenderly devour her mouth. Finally, she forcefully separated her lips from his, because this was insane.

"You can't stop bullets with sex," she whispered.

"No," he responded with a husky voice. "But you can stop . . . divisions."

She frowned. "What do you—?"

"Later," he said. He stroked her hand, brought it to his lips, then snatched his backpack from the ground and towed her toward the open corner of the porch.

They peered out, scanning the immediate vicinity for their pursuers, and they did spot a man in a khaki jacket and scruffy jeans casually leaning against a nearby tree and lighting a cigarette. Shaun hustled to the adjacent corner and crept out with Dayna into an area of exposed pathways and a few scrub bushes. He pointed to the lagoon, a good thirty feet away. Two *mokoros* were nestled side by side where they'd been hauled onto the grass beside the waterway after an excursion. They were conveniently placed for a potential escape attempt.

Shaun beckoned urgently and dashed toward the boats, keeping Dayna's hand crushed in his own. She could feel yearning and desperation in his grip. They made it through the clearing without the sound of yelling, stampeding, or gunfire. But something else caught her notice, just at the outer limits of her peripheral vision. Yes, there were elephants and antelope, perhaps even hippos out in the channel, plodding through the mud and spraying gouts of water. But rounding the bend in the meandering stream, framed by waving papyrus fronds and a background column of palm trees, was another *mokoro*, and then another.

As they pounced upon the nearest dugout, Shaun immediately began guiding it into the water.

"Shaun," Dayna whispered, her eyes now glued to the horizon. "I think that's Felicity, Frank, and the others."

He paused, and looked, his face frozen in clear dismay.

"No. Not now. We have to warn them," he muttered.

He turned back to his task, beckoning her to help. She ran to the stern while Shaun grasped the bow, and they hefted the lightweight vessel off the ground. In an instant, they were splashing through the shallows and the boat was gliding into the water.

Dayna waved to the approaching dugouts, using a frantic sweeping gesture to signal a retreat, and someone waved back.

"I'm not welcoming you home. Get away. Please. Turn back."

"We'll have to meet them in the channel," said Shaun. "To warn them off."

"Or we'll just wave and smile cheerfully as we await their arrival," said a now familiar gravelly voice.

A fountain of terror gushed up through Dayna as she looked to the side. In a nest of crushed grass and weeds crouched a man with grimy jeans and a sweat-stained white T-shirt wearing an amused smile on his face. A revolver poked through the reeds, pointed directly at her.

"So gullible," said the woman, Reena, from another disguised location.

Shaun released the boat, his face swiftly draining of color. Then he leaped in front of Dayna. "Don't kill her!"

"Oh, you are so pathetic," said Reena, stepping out of her nest, a gun protruding from her hand. Dayna caught her breath. She was the most exquisite woman she'd ever seen. Ringlets of golden hair framed an olive-skinned face beset with uncanny green eyes. Altogether an ethnic blend. Nothing about her physical features added up.

"Keep your anger in check," said Hondo. "We will have them all, if you don't screw this up."

The two *mokoros* drew steadily closer. Yes, they would have them all, and then they would kill them all, except maybe Shaun. What was the point in letting them dictate the situation, since she was already caught? She could scream at her students, run toward them, but would they really understand and turn back in time?

She made a decision—the only decision she could fathom to protect the students she cared about as much as if they were her own kids. She stepped in front of Shaun and within full view of his ex-wife, Reena.

"Say what you will, but he's not pathetic in bed," she said. "In fact, he's the best I've ever had."

Reena's face turned to ash and then to stone. She raised the gun and pulled the trigger.

FELICITY SIGHED AND trailed her fingers in the water, although only where Baruti assured her there were no crocodiles. It was a relief to finally be heading back to the safari lodge, after spending three days chatting with the *!Kung* and sleeping in close proximity to a variety of dangerous animals. Baruti had instructed Kushe and company to move their *werf* to another location, to eliminate the possibility that the miners would discover them, but they grinned as if they were indulging Mr. Obvious.

"You be careful," Kwi had said to Frank upon their departure, giving him a strong-armed handshake that left him shaking his hand afterward.

"I will," Frank had replied. "But I really don't think they even know I exist."

"Keep to the ground, then."

Felicity had burst out laughing at this remark. She loved it that the *!Kung* called Frank a snake. In many ways, she agreed with their assessment.

He'd thrown her a dark look, but she hadn't cared. To them it was a compliment; to her it was nothing but the truth.

As they drew nearer their destination, Felicity was struck by a ripple of melancholy regret. Although she couldn't say she enjoyed this outdoor lifestyle, she would miss sharing close quarters with Baruti. He was still recovering from his illness, so she'd not pushed the boundaries of their relationship yet, but she had snuggled near him at night and often watched him breathe. That he might share DNA with a species that had preexisted *Homo sapiens sapiens* didn't change the way she felt about him. In fact, it made him even more fascinating and exotic, especially since his very existence now seemed woven into her own studies. She wondered if he would share a room with her at the lodge.

"Should we take a few days to unwind at the lodge, before we . . . What are we going to do, anyway?" she asked.

"I need to contact someone," said Baruti. "And I want to see if Professor Lugan has finished her analysis of the skull yet. If these people are what we suspect, that would establish the connection between them and the *!Kung* once and for all. The answers I get will determine what we do next."

"Professor Lugan will probably still be furious with us. What if she didn't run the tests?"

"It's possible," he said, skimming his fingers through the water in front of her and leaving trails for her own digits to explore. "But I think she will be curious. She's a scientist, after all."

"Even if she confirms our suspicions, I'm not sure how it will help us, unless we know what these people are planning. They can't just hijack a plasma-powered spacecraft and leave the planet. They'd first have to get into orbit and reach a space station, and I doubt they'd even get that far with all the security they'd have to clear, and with the number of shuttles they'd need. I think Pedro's idea is way too far-fetched. They must be contemplating something else."

Baruti shifted in the *mokoro* and turned to face her. "You're right. It does seem impossible. We're just speculating because we don't have enough information. I think there's only one way to get that information, and it will be messy. You, Frank, and Pedro should find yourselves a safe haven until I do what must be done."

"Baruti . . . Are you thinking of torturing . . . ?"

"They tried to kill me, Felicity. They may have killed Tony. They've made your acquaintance too, so they won't hesitate to eliminate you, or Shaun Wilson, if they think they've been exposed."

"Shaun! I forgot about him."

"Really?" said Baruti. "I doubt that." His retracted his hand from the water and cast a brooding look over the channel.

"Why do you say that? I may have defended him because I didn't think he was a killer. But I wasn't interested in him in any other way. In fact, he irritated me. He acted as if I wasn't strong enough to do my job."

"Trying not to hear," said Frank, from the hollow of his own *mokoro*, a mere car-length away. "Trying not to barf."

Pedro chuckled, his massive chest rippling beneath his t-shirt.

"I believe you," said Baruti, ignoring Frank. "But he certainly was interested in you. Regardless, we should try to contact him, to ensure he's alive and well and find out if DeLuca was also poisoned. He may have to disappear too, like you and Frank."

"I'm not wealthy," said Felicity. "I don't have the resources to just disappear. Although I'm sure Frank does."

"Ah," said Frank. "A dig. Now I'm supposed to feel guilty because my family has money."

"I didn't say you had to feel guilty," she snapped. "I'm just pointing out the flaw in Baruti's plan. You can just drop off the edge of the planet. I'll have to stay in plain view because I have no other option but to return to Boston. I rely on scholarships. They won't pay for world travel."

"Maybe I can find a place for you to hide," said Baruti. "I'll think about it."

"Frank'll pay for her," said Pedro.

"Bud– dy?" Frank's voice cracked on the word.

"You don't wanna see her dead, even if ya hate her," Pedro said. "We're in this together, tryin' to keep everyone safe and stop the killin'. You're a good man, Frank, even when you don't wanna admit it. You protect people."

Felicity could see the words form on Frank's lips: *Not her.* But he didn't say them. "Fine," he grunted. "I'll pay for her too. We'll all hide together. One big happy family."

Felicity opened her mouth to object. The last thing she needed was to be grateful to her surly rival. But Baruti cut her off.

"Thanks, Frank," he said. "If it becomes too much of a burden, I'll find a way to pay you back."

"I really don't need anyone to look after me," she shot at Baruti.

"Of course you don't," he said, dipping his hand back into the water. "And if all things were equal, as they are among the *!Kung*, you'd never have to ask anyone for a favor or a helping hand. But the world hasn't evolved to their level yet."

Felicity met Frank's eyes. Then they both turned away from each other, in a moment of shame. The *mokoro* rounded a bend in the channel and the curvy northern stretch of the island they sought appeared, bedecked with the raised canvas trappings of the lodge. In the distance, Felicity spotted two figures at the border of the lagoon, hauling what looked like another *mokoro* into the shallows.

Their bodies were still indistinct from this far away. All she could determine was that one was a man and the other a woman. But as they drew closer to the island, their shapes took on color and clarity. One was tall, heavily-muscled, and fair. The other voluptuous and brunette.

"Dr. Lugan," she gasped. "And I think that's Shaun."

"They came after us," said Frank. "I didn't think Dr. Lugan–"

"DeLuca," said Baruti. "Because of DeLuca."

Felicity waved. Dr. Lugan was waving back, a bit frantically. Strange. It was almost as if she was waving them off.

Another woman appeared from the bushes and stood across from the professor, her glossy golden hair reminding Felicity of a Norse goddess. Shaun suddenly leaped between them as if he were a mother bear protecting her cub.

"Something's off," she said. "Besides the fact that Dr. Lugan and Shaun are together. I think—"

Before she could say another word, Dr. Lugan stepped around Shaun, and a few seconds later a shot rang out. Her professor, the one woman who cared for her despite all her foibles and failures, the one person who'd always *believed* in her, collapsed into the shallow water.

"No!" Felicity shrieked, tilting toward Dayna, almost falling into the channel. Baruti grabbed her shoulders and pulled her back.

"Turn this damned boat around," he barked.

He didn't have to say another word. The guides jammed their paddles into the water and swung the *mokoros* around in a half-circle. In a frantic burst of energy, they thrust alternately like pistons at the smooth surface, creating miniature tsunamis. Shots blasted behind them, slapping the water on either side and producing a muffled staccato. Baruti shoved Felicity down in the canoe and drew a gun from his pack. While crouching and aiming haphazardly, he shot repeatedly behind them, the sound like bomb blasts in her ears. Finally, they must have rounded the bend because the shots from both sides died off.

"Dr. . . . Dr. Lugan," she said, hugging herself tightly. "No. Not her."

No one spoke in either boat. Baruti set his gun aside and touched her arm.

An uncontrollable fit of shaking clutched her. She shouldn't be acting so weak again. Why couldn't she be strong like Baruti, who'd defended them and attempted to help Dr. Lugan? Why couldn't she brandish her own gun and make a stand?

She gradually straightened, gradually sat up, but her teeth were chattering. She looked at Frank, the only person who could understand. But would he?

Frank's face was ashen. Frank was holding his head in his hands as if it were too heavy for him to support. Frank, the snide, calculating, remorseless bastard, was crying.

He looked up as if he sensed her scrutiny and met her eyes.

"We killed her," he said in a muffled tone, wiping his nose with his sleeve.

"We led her here, we got her involved in a deadly insurgence, and then we killed her." He paused and swallowed painfully, as if he were eating knives. "You know what we did? We killed the best part of us."

This was the first time Felicity had ever heard Frank tell the unvarnished truth. She slumped back down in the dugout and couldn't suppress the tears.

Scanning...

Located: Chapter 44

BOB GAVE A final yank on the cable that, miracle of miracles, was still attached to the pulley system that bridged the sinkhole. The electric winch—which was fastened to the rear of the rover—was gone, of course. So he'd had to employ his own feeble muscle-power to hoist the container—his makeshift boat—along with survival staples and the last of the oxygen reserves, from the floor of the cave. It had taken the better part of the day, but now he could release the central lock with a remote signal from his tablet and roll the container along the cable to the edge of the hole. The final challenge would be hauling the load over the brim, as it dangled below the level of the opening.

Bob gasped and his muscles quivered as he pulled, nudged, and scrabbled at the container to get it up and over the final hump. When he was positive that the load was resting on solid ground, he collapsed, his back and shoulders burning and his head swimming with fatigue and dizziness. His chest sucked and heaved greedily for air, a thirsty in-drawing of overlapping tissue and skin into the wells of his ribcage, as his body begged for energy that he couldn't supply. He'd increased the oxygen percentage delivered from the tank to allow for his extra exertion, but had been mindful not to spike it too high, which might overwhelm his modified respiratory and metabolic systems. But he'd needed to slacken his pace and rest every fifteen minutes in this entire excruciating exercise, not to mention pausing to snack so frequently he often felt stuffed. It added extra time to his schedule that he couldn't afford.

It was now late afternoon. The sun that pierced the incessant gloom of the omnipresent fog was angled toward the canyon in the west. He had potentially three hours of light remaining in which to descend a treacherous slope into the canyon, reach the near bank, and then cross the newly born river, if he had any hope of catching up to Lucas. He didn't have time to rest. He didn't have the energy to move. Bloody conundrum.

With the least amount of exertion he could manage, he zipped open his backpack and removed a package of trail mix, along with a chocolate bar, and began to gnaw at the nourishment. But it was only half the equation. The other half was oxygen which, due to his altered and downregulated metabolic pathways, he could not supply to his cells in any significant amount. He would have to wait until his body recharged and allowed him to move again.

He wasted an hour in this recovery mode, then finally forced the issue, rising to his feet and loading the boat onto a trolley he'd acquired from beside one of the shelves, which had undoubtedly been employed when Lucas's associates had originally stocked the underground warehouse. Then he began pushing the boat-trolley combination along the muddy, rock-stippled ground. Where the terrain remained level, it was a fairly effortless task, except through the thickest mud. But where it sloped upward, it became a Herculean enterprise. And where the ground tilted downward, he had to grip the handles and plant one foot at a time, to prevent the trolly from careening to the bottom, out of control.

But he made progress. As the sun crept steadily toward the horizon, the canyon expanded into view. It became less a dark, distant etching on a rusty canvas and more of a splotch, then a scoop, then a hollow bowl. A surge of adrenaline coursed through his veins. He would make it, at least to the water's edge. He would master the second leg of this unimaginably brutal challenge. The third leg would be the killer, though. Fighting his way across the channel in the midst of erupting pockets of water and gas, all while navigating a maze of ice floes.

No team at the ISA would ever have signed off on this mission, and he'd had no opportunity to practice with simulators.

He probably wouldn't survive the crossing, but survival wasn't what motivated him, anyway. If it were, he'd have stayed comfortably couched in his den, enjoying the fruits of caveman life and trying to deny the emptiness. But he was determined to survive long enough to face the man who'd robbed him of a happy existence, the man who'd left him with no other option but revenge. He'd never before been so consumed with rage, so reckless, so . . . irrational. The ISA taught their astronauts to set aside emotion—to work the problem. But this problem was beyond the scope of the ISA to solve, even if he could reach them. One could insert additional chromosomes into a cell, but once rooted in the body, he was ninety-nine percent sure they'd be impossible to remove. Lucas hadn't just tinkered with his cells, he'd altered his DNA. There was no antidote, no reversal process to counter the widespread changes in his body. Even if he could someday send a transmission to Earth and place the problem in the hands of genius genetic engineers, he doubted they could devise a solution without access to the original inventors, who would do their best to sabotage any attempts to design a reversal.

He was doomed to live his life here and eventually—or maybe sooner—die here. He might as well make his death worth something. Might as well at least try to prevent the cancer from spreading.

He'd now reached the brim of the canyon—a wide gouge in the planet's surface with steep precipices, interspersed with moderate slopes like the scalloped rim of a pie crust. The trick would be to determine the shallowest slope and initiate a controlled descent. He couldn't afford to tip the contents out of the container or puncture what he carried in any way. His final oxygen tank lay strapped to the bottom, moderately secure, but a bouncing trip downhill might dislodge and rupture it. That would end his excursion, once and for all. Bob rustled straps out of the pack and laced them around the handles of the trolley. A quick scan told him where he could find the least punishing grade, and he pushed his load to the tipping point.

Now to brace for the traction.

It came with violence, like a punctured airlock, and nearly ripped him off his feet. But he slipped and slid and finally established a grip on the ground with the treads of his boots. He muscled the trolley to a near stop, then braced himself and stepped forward again. One step, then another, gradually guiding his load downhill, until he finally reached a level plateau and rested. And then whipped off his mask and vomited every remnant of his latest snack.

"Too much, I know. Too much," he hissed through gasps. He wiped a string of saliva from his lips, then slapped the mask back on. "I'm like a pathetic old man, now."

Rest. He needed to rest.

But the sun shrank deeper into the mist, preparing to dive below the rim of the planet. He couldn't wait. He had to push on.

Bob grappled at the ground, then rose to his feet, teetering and gulping air. He gripped the straps and nudged his trolley toward the next slope again. Knees nearly buckling, he finessed it downward inch by inch, mile by mile. He could hear the gurgling river now, spy the rich cobalt ice floes and sediment-laden waves flowing at a relentless pace. It did little to settle the percolating acid in his stomach. But he had finally caught sight of his initial—if suicidal—destination.

He braced and stepped forward, braced and stepped forward, braced and . . . slid. His feet flew out from under him, and he lost his hold on the straps. They whipped underneath him, dragged him several feet, then tore loose. The trolley and container went flying down the slope, teetering, bouncing, then finally . . . tumbling.

"No," he groaned, as he witnessed the contents flying in all directions.

It couldn't be over. Not yet. Not so soon.

Bob staggered to his feet and raced down the incline, even though his lungs felt near to bursting. He stumbled to a halt at the bottom, mere inches from the eager current, and found the container upside down, but with no obvious puncture wounds. But the oxygen tank . . . He scanned the debris: exploded packages of food and water, along with some intact parcels, a grimy blanket, a first aid kit, but no tank. He backtracked and scrutinized the misty surroundings until . . . there! He spotted it. With his heart in his throat, he rushed toward it and ran his fingers over the cylinder, probing, searching . . .

Dents, but no detectable punctures. Phew! He gathered the tank in his arms as if it were a delicate baby and carried it to his boat.

Bob gasped and wheezed when he reached the vessel. He really should rest. Really.

But if he did, he would have to wait till morning to make the crossing, and that would put him behind schedule. Behind Lucas, who would not wait.

It took several minutes to gather his scattered supplies, those that were still intact. Then another minute or two to set the boat right side up and reacquire his improvised paddle—the lid to a narrow, rectangular container. Not a motor, not properly shaped, probably useless. But all he had to do was apply enough momentum to get the vessel to the other side. It didn't matter if he traveled several miles past a perfectly straight route across. He just had to make it across . . . alive.

If Bob had been a religious man, he would have said a prayer before he pushed off. Instead he said, "I'm going to kill you, Lucas."

Then he jumped into the boat, which was simply a boxy container that had no idea it was a boat. It rocked and nearly capsized right at the outset. He tried to define a center to stabilize the wobbly craft, but it refused to do anything but dance and spin as waves splashed over it—dousing Bob from head to toe—and ice smashed into its thin hull. Bob thrust the paddle into the water and push-guided the boat in a direction he presumed was south, although he was growing increasingly dizzy. But the boat wobbled even more, and tipped, and water rushed over its side before it bounced upright again.

He was bounced around so much that he must have hit his comm unit and turned it on. A crackle and hiss snapped in his ears, but he hadn't the energy to fumble it off again.

"All you have to do is get from one side to the other," he growled at the boat. "Is that so hard?"

A wave slapped him in the face, as if in response.

Then an iceberg, partially submerged and therefore as devious as the one that sank the Titanic, thudded into the hull. And Bob heard a loud crack. A splinter. And a gush.

And so it ends, he thought, looking at the distant bank that he would never reach. He turned back to the one he'd just left, potentially within swimming distance.

He squinted because . . . he saw something.

There, on the bank, glistening in the ethereal glow of twilight. The rover. Or was it a mirage?

As water poured into his boat and swirled around his waist, he even caught sight of an astronaut or two climbing out of the back. And he heard a voice. An irritated one.

"Really, Bob? Did you really think that would work?"

"Lucas," he replied. "You bastard! Did you really think I would give up?"

THEY'D BEEN TRAVELING for the better part of the day without a word.

Gita had refused to scout their pathway, so Lucas had to rely on the lidar images and his own eyesight to avoid any catastrophes of the giant boulder persuasion. They'd been lucky—only one near miss. However, they'd experienced countless stomach-elevating bounces and a few nerve-wracking tilts, but without the worry of losing or damaging the rocket fuel, these only seemed like minor irritations.

Now they were approaching the Vitalis Cave and should veer away from the canyon soon. Gita had spent most of their trek in the crew cabin, offended by the mere sight of Lucas. But she must have sensed their proximity to the cave, or she'd been calculating distance on her tablet, since she'd silently entered the cockpit and just as silently slid into the navigator's seat as soon as the ebony gash in the ground appeared.

A wind had stirred in this sector and cleared the thickest fog with brisk gusts. An unobstructed view of the canyon and the rushing river below filled the windshield.

"Shouldn't you be turning toward the cave now?" Gita finally spoke, her voice scraping on every word.

"Yes," said Lucas. But he didn't turn the wheel. Something mysteriously symmetrical had caught his eye near the riverbank in the canyon.

He stopped the rover, grabbed a pair of binoculars from a slot behind his seat, and tipped them to his eyes.

"Bob's . . . broken body . . . wouldn't be in the Mawrth," she said, her voice cracking in the middle of her sentence.

Lucas adjusted the focus just as the boxy shape pushed into the warring waves. He sighed. Then he placed the rover into gear and scanned the slope, assessing the angle of descent. It would be a steep, treacherous drive whichever pathway he chose, but he had little choice. He swung to the right and began to nose the rover down the slumped canyon wall.

"Are you crazy? Where are you going?"

"Down to the river," he said.

"Why in the world . . . ?" She snatched the binoculars from his hand and swept the terrain back and forth until she paused, and refocused, and paused.

"He is alive," she finally said. "I should have known. How could you leave . . . ? Why would you . . . ? He's going to die out there."

"Not if I can help it," said Lucas.

The "raft" or "craft," or whatever it might be dubbed, was already sweeping toward them as the exuberant current captured it. Lucas ground down on the accelerator, ignoring the rasping sounds as the rover's bumper grazed the gritty earth, and the precarious tilts as bulbous rocks threatened to flip the vehicle over. As the angle diminished and they came to a level plateau, Lucas pushed the vehicle to even greater speed. They reached the riverbank in minutes. Lucas parked the rover a good distance from where Bob's craft had entered the water, to allow for his approach with the current. Accompanied by Gita, Lucas scrambled to suit up and exit through the airlock.

Outside the rover, Lucas scanned the erupting gully until he spotted Bob's craft. Except . . . it was floundering and *sinking*. Dammit!

He sprinted toward the river, but at the same time couldn't help but express his annoyance at this man who irritated him beyond measure but still prevented him from delivering a kill shot.

"Really, Bob? Did you really think that would work?" he snapped.

Bob's answer underscored the man's fury.

"Lucas. You bastard! Did you really think I would give up?"

The craft or container—whatever it was—rapidly became swamped and dramatically sank from sight. Bob splashed about in the strong current and tried to swim, chopping through the bitter waves with bold strokes, but he wasn't getting very far. And he looked weak.

Gita dashed toward the river and *plunged in*, the stupid woman.

Lucas gritted his teeth, pounced on her before she could travel beyond his reach, and tossed her back onto the shore.

"Stay there," he growled. "And follow us with the rover."

Then he dove in, the chill of the water slicing through him like a blade. He surfaced, the mask maintaining a tight seal and at least giving him air, although chunks of ice battering against his face threatened to rip it off. He stroked through the current with determination and drew closer to Bob, who continued to flail at the waves with pathetic arm movements and the odd half-hearted kick. Lucas advanced to within an arm's length of the man. If only Bob would give one strong kick. . . . But he didn't, and he swept past.

Lucas leaped and dove down and somehow grabbed Bob's leg. He grappled upward, groping clothing, and pulled himself onto Bob, momentarily immersing him in the icy flow. Then he flipped him around so that he was facing the bank. Bob continued to kick and flop his arms, but it did nothing to propel them forward. Lucas was already feeling drained, all his energy siphoned away in the deadly cold water. But, by God, it wasn't going to end like this. Not after he'd made the most agonizing decision of his life.

He gathered his remaining strength and pounded the water, kicking with both legs, pumping with one arm while he pushed Bob with the other. They made creeping progress toward the shore, while the current carried them hundreds of feet beyond the rover. Lucas shoved through clusters of ice and the muddy swirls of eroded soil that threatened to tug them underwater or propel them back to the middle of the river. Bob was gasping and muttering, his words ringing in Lucas's ears through their still functioning comm units.

"Why would you even come back? Why bother? What is the point in keeping me alive, you bastard? I don't want to live here alone. I *can't* live here."

"Just . . . keep . . . swimming," said Lucas.

He thrust Bob through the water, tempted to smack his head against a thick jutty of ice.

"Fine," said Bob. And he batted at the waves with his arms, although he seemed to grow more limp and ineffectual by the minute. His breathing rasped through the comm, a grating sound that gnawed at Lucas.

They bobbed up and down as Lucas kicked and stroked, and it seemed that they would never reach that elusive bank, but on the next rotation of his arm he touched something solid and anchored. He clawed at it, lost his grip, but found it again at the subsequent downward stroke. He clutched at dirt, which crumbled into the river rather than providing a purchase for his hand, but eventually he caught hold with Bob still firmly in his grasp.

Pushing, grabbing, thrusting, jamming, he gathered Bob up and hurled him onto solid ground. Then he muscled himself out of the water, collapsing beside the man.

They lay side by side, not moving, not talking.

Gita's voice chimed over the comm. "I'm coming to get you in the rover. I'm getting closer. Hang on."

"C— copy that," said Lucas.

"Is Bob okay?"

Lucas didn't answer. He was still trying to catch his breath. Bob didn't answer. His hoarse puffing and wheezing suggested that he might never catch his breath.

"Lucas? Bob?"

"We're alive," said Lucas. "No more chatter for now."

"'Kay," she responded.

Minutes passed as a breeze fluttered over them, which then became a brazen wind. The chill whittled its way deeper into Lucas's body, sometimes producing a balmy numbness, sometimes cutting like razor blades. Bob was undoubtedly feeling even colder, but he suffered in silence. His breathing hadn't settled yet, either. It worried Lucas.

A crunch of tires announced the rover's approach. Its quiet engine purred, but the sound hardly registered above the whistle of the wind. Lucas turned, although he felt so brittle it felt as though he might flake apart with any significant movement. He sat up, even though every muscle screamed in self-defense. Gita jumped from the airlock door and hurried toward Bob. She performed a cursory examination, then met Lucas's eyes.

"I can't lift him alone," she said.

"I know."

"Are you strong enough to help me?"

"No," he replied. "But I'll try."

He crept to his knees, muttered several curses, then staggered to his feet. His knees began to buckle, so he gripped Gita's shoulder to steady himself. She stood firmly centered like a rock, giving him support but not offering it. When he felt reasonably balanced, he nodded to her and they bent down and grasped Bob under his arms. In one swift motion, they hoisted him to his feet and laced their arms behind his back while Bob shivered and his lungs rattled. Surprisingly, he gripped Lucas's shoulder and tried to shuffle his feet as they trudged toward the airlock.

Gita and Lucas lifted Bob and held him suspended between them as they stepped into the airlock, then slouched as a unit onto the bench with their fellow astronaut propped up by their weary bodies. Gita tilted Bob against Lucas while she stood and activated the seal. Bob's head slumped onto Lucas's shoulder since he had no energy to keep it upright. How bizarre and disturbing. Lucas was sure it was the last thing Bob wanted to do. But he kept him cradled there like a child in need of comfort until Gita released the inner lock and began fumbling with Bob's mask.

"No," said Bob in barely a whisper. He turned his face away.

"Bob, you're safe in the rover now. The airlock is sealed and we have enough oxygen."

"You . . . have . . . too much," said Bob. "Right . . . Lucas?"

Lucas slipped off his own mask, but he didn't respond.

"What are you talking about?" she said. "Do you think he's suffered some brain damage?" she asked Lucas.

"Would have . . . been better," Bob gasped. He struggled to raise his head from Lucas's shoulder, but he couldn't manage it. But he could elevate his hand just enough to let it flop like a flipper against Lucas's chest.

"When I . . . c— c— can breathe, going . . . to beat . . . you . . . death."

"I don't know what happened between the two of you," said Gita, "and I can understand why you're angry, Bob. But we need to focus on your recovery. First we'll remove your wet clothes, and that will be easier if we take off the mask. If you require more oxygen, we'll set up a new tank."

She reached toward the mask again, and Bob couldn't dredge up the energy to bat her away. So Lucas clutched her wrist, arresting her grasp.

"I think Bob has adjusted the oxygen concentration to match his needs," he said. "We'll work around it while we remove his clothes and get him wrapped up in a blanket. I could use a blanket too, and a huge cup of hot chocolate."

"To match his needs? What the hell is going on, Lucas?"

Bob raised a trembling hand again and slammed it down on Lucas's chest, producing a resounding snap.

"Lucas . . . has a story . . . to tell," said Bob. "Before . . . I beat . . . him . . . to death. A story of . . . betrayal. A story of . . . a friend and enemy."

Before Bob could elaborate, he collapsed onto Lucas's lap and passed out. Gita stared at him, completely baffled, then raised her eyes to meet Lucas's with a slowly spreading scowl.

He shrugged, fled her gaze, and said, "It's his tale to tell."

Scanning...

Located: Chapter 45

FLASHES OF MEMORY assaulted Dayna as she lay prone on the grass—or was she lying on a bed? A tug at her arm that wrenched her to the side. An explosion. A spray of blood. Pain that seared through her body like hot needles. Weakness, dim vision. A face that blurred in and out—a pained, perfect masculine face. He had a name, didn't he? But all she could dislodge from her muddled brain was the word "sex." Face equals sex.

Sad that he didn't have a name.

She drifted into sleep or unconsciousness, trying to dredge up a name.

A scorching feeling woke her—hours? days? weeks?—later. A web-like fire at her shoulder that radiated outward and gripped her neck and chest. Her head was throbbing, too. And her throat was raw, crying for moisture, calling for a stream that would never end.

She opened her eyes and the face became her entire world, the extent of her visual field. His breath whispered over her lips and sifted through her hair.

"S—" What was his name? *Don't say "sex."*

"It's okay, Dayna. I'm here. You're going to be okay."

"So the princess awakens," said a sneering voice behind the world of his face. "Stop lying to her, Shaun."

Dayna sighed. At least he had a name. Then she cringed and shivered as the searing sensation traveled through her like a train.

"Sh— Shaun?" she said. "Sh— shot?"

"Yes, sweetheart. But it went straight through your shoulder. Through and through. You'll be okay. It'll take some time to heal, but . . ."

"'Sweetheart.'" The sneering voice again. "But the thing is, *sweetheart*, that you're our prisoner. And if you don't answer our questions to our satisfaction, we'll put another bullet through your heart."

Suddenly she remembered . . . *everything*. She groped with her less painful arm and grabbed Shaun's shirt. "Felicity? Frank?"

"They got away," he whispered, with a certain degree of smug satisfaction. "You're brilliant, and absolutely imbecilic. Let me be the hero next time."

"She wouldn't have shot you," she said.

"I wish everyone would stop talking as if I weren't here. I am listening to every word, *sweetheart*. And yes, I think I would have shot him. I'm still considering it now."

"Did you mean what you said?" asked Shaun, continuing to turn a deaf ear to his ex-wife. "I'm the best you've ever had?"

"There goes that ego again."

"I mean, it wasn't just a ploy, was it?"

"Let it go, Se— Shaun. Don't you realize I'm in awful pain? Do you have any painkillers here?" She shivered, which dug the needles ever deeper. She released his shirt and groaned.

"Yes, we have painkillers," said Reena, thrusting Shaun away from Dayna and stepping in front of him. "But we're not going to give you any until you and Shaun start talking. What are you doing here? What are your students up to? What are they doing with Baruti Mbeki?"

"And why is he still alive?" asked Shaun.

Reena narrowed her eyes, and thrust the gun under his chin.

Dayna gasped and gripped the bed. "Don't shoot him," she pleaded.

"Wow," said Reena. "I actually think she cares about you, Shaun. Now let's not make her suffer anymore. Tell me what you know about Mbeki."

"I don't know anything about him other than that he's a scientist who joined me in Ontario to assess the polar bear situation. But I know that your friend"—he looked beyond Reena to some distant corner of the room—"must have poisoned my friend, Tony DeLuca."

"I can't believe you would actually call him a *friend*." Reena jabbed his chin with the gun.

Dayna tried to move. She had to do something. But any attempts to sit up were met with bursts of agony.

But she needn't have tried. The other man—the one with the gravelly voice—stepped forward and wrenched the gun out of Reena's hand.

"We're not going to kill him. His brother, remember?"

But when Shaun narrowed his eyes, he added, "Unless he makes us kill him, by doing something stupid."

"If you kill me, he will know before he gets back. We chat regularly. And if you kill her, I'll force your hand."

"Yes, no doubt. Now about the chatting." Hondo pointed to where Shaun's tablet was resting on the bedside table. "What do you think he meant by 'irreversible decisions,' if he can't get off-planet?"

"I have no idea. Why did you kill my friend?"

"Answer me first, then I'll answer you."

"Fine. I think he means he's so brainwashed by your perverted ideology that he'll find a way to do whatever you asked him to do, even if he never escapes Mars. He has such blind faith in your cause, and such blind rage at the death of our father, that he won't hesitate to carry out whatever homicidal scheme you have in mind.

"Quid pro quo." Shaun flipped his hand toward Hondo, palm outward.

Hondo acquiesced. "Your friend and Dr. Mbeki stole samples of our genetic material. They were not inclined to accept our explanations of our mining operations and our generous attempts to clone and repopulate extinct species. We hacked into Dr. Mbeki's phone and email and discovered he'd contacted a suspicious character."

"Suspicious character?"

"Someone from WEPA," said Hondo. "I suspect, though, that he isn't a standard government official."

"Does it really surprise you that we have come under surveillance? Did you really think we could stay hidden forever?"

We? Why is Shaun saying "we"? Dayna's pain-befuddled mind tried desperately to follow the conversation. *Didn't he say that he was no longer part of their cult?*

"No, it doesn't surprise me. But it does alarm me, since it seems to be occurring before we can begin our exodus. You know that's what we need to do, Shaun. You know we can't live together in harmony, once they know the truth. We have to grab this opportunity before they can wipe us out like the Romans tried to do."

Romans? Who are *these people?* Then Felicity's discovery rang through Dayna's mind. *Romans who aren't Romans. Phoenicians who aren't Phoenicians.*

"The Romans tried to wipe everyone out, everyone they couldn't rule. We're living in a different age. Your paranoia and old hatreds have lasted longer than those of the Arabs and Israelis. You haven't even given them a chance to understand who we are."

Who we are? Non-extinct PBPP?

Dayna blinked, her vision once again filled with Shaun's face. Then the scientist in her awoke, ticking through the underlying features that formed the man's skeletal foundation: the wide, rounded brow, the fierce, decisive jaw that was a hair longer than most men. Shaun was a reflection of a 70,000 year old specimen. He was so much more than sex to an anthropologist.

"You think they won't instantly label us, and then invent reasons to fear or hate us?"

"From where I'm standing, they wouldn't need to invent anything."

"You know what happened to your father. Maybe you had to see it like Lucas to understand how irrational they are. But you didn't have to witness his murder to realize how destructive they are to the planet, how parasitic and greedy, how predatory. Now they'll do the same things to another planet. They'll resurrect it, and then they'll devour it. And they'll continue this pattern throughout the galaxy, and eventually into the next."

"They aren't all like that. *She* isn't like that," Shaun emphasized, pointing at Dayna.

"*She* is the one who will expose us," growled Hondo. "She would never keep us a secret, because we would earn her a Nobel prize. She is as rapacious as any one of them. Maybe more so."

"May she speak?" asked Dayna. Pain shuddered through her again, but she tried to ignore it.

They all turned toward her, and Reena arched her eyebrows in surprise.

"By all means," said Hondo. "Speak."

She cleared her throat and weighed her words before uttering them. Her response could mean her life or death, and her students' as well.

"I've never wanted a Nobel Prize," she began. "I've only ever fleetingly craved glory and riches. All I ever wanted was to have a child, and when that became impossible I turned to secondary aspirations. My true desire is to understand the people who came before us. I dug in the European bogs and I extracted their tormented bodies; I gazed in wonder and horror at their sunken skulls. I tried everything within my power to get them to speak to me. I had no idea they were standing in front of me all this time. And they were speaking, but I wasn't listening. But I'm listening now. And you don't need to be afraid of me."

For the longest time, no one spoke at all. Then Shaun's face lit up like a resplendent sunbeam breaking through cloud.

"And she isn't even extraordinary," he said. "She's just one of many."

WHEN THEY FINALLY chose an island, deep enough in the Delta to make discovery a remote possibility at best, they crawled out of their *mokoros*, hid them in the bushes, and crept to a central location to set up camp. Baruti suggested a spot with a dense thicket of baobab and mangosteen trees to camouflage their tents. They hastily erected the pop-up nylon shelters, and then they all collapsed, except for the guides, who rustled up food such as dried roots and berries so they wouldn't have to light a fire.

Frank slumped down beside Felicity—the only occasion he had ever sought her out—and cast her tentative glances. He didn't know what he was searching for. Commiseration? Anger? Reflection? Did she feel the same constricting guilt, as if an iron chain were wrapped around her throat? They'd led their professor away from her fairly secure lab to the farthest reaches of the planet, and exposed her to the criminals they were investigating. Did Felicity regret fleeing the scene, even though it was their only option?

Pedro crumpled on the other side of Frank, massaging his bandaged biceps. A bullet had grazed his arm, and Frank had returned a favor. On their lengthy *mokoro* ride through the network of channels, he'd cleansed and bound the wound with diligence and compassion. His belly had ached as he administered the first aid, reminding him of another attack that was etched in his flesh. But even that one hadn't deflated him as much as this latest savagery. To see the woman who'd guided him through several years of study with more consideration than his own parents assaulted, maybe murdered, in front of his eyes?

"You didn't kill her," said Baruti, squatting down by Felicity and wrenching open a container of assorted seeds and nuts. "You can't blame yourself for another man's evil."

"But we drew her here," said Felicity softly. "Frank is right." She sniffled and dipped her head onto Baruti's shoulder.

Another first. The first time she'd ever agreed with Frank. Why did it have to be about this?

"Wilson drew her here, most likely because DeLuca was poisoned and he was desperate to find us, to ensure we hadn't been affected. And your professor would assume an almost parental obligation for both of you, because she had directed you to investigate the bodies in the first place. They took the risks upon themselves. Certainly they knew they were dealing with dangerous people when I explained the miners' shell game and their subsequent massacre of the *!Kung*. If I witnessed everything correctly, I do believe your teacher provoked the attack to protect us, to warn us off."

"We can't just leave her in their hands," said Frank. "What if she's still alive? We fled like cowards."

"We retreated," stated Baruti with subtle force, "so we could live to fight another day. We would be no help to her if we were all shot, too."

"But that may be too late for Dr. Lugan," said Felicity. "I say we go back now. They'll never expect us to do that, so we'll catch them completely unawares. We take whatever guns you and the guides have, and we try to rescue Dr. Lugan and Shaun."

Frank tilted his head as doubts flitted through his mind but, hey, he was actually considering it. "I never pictured you as Bruce Willis or Wyatt Earp," he said to her. "They will expect us to come back eventually, because we have nowhere else to go. We can't survive on the Delta like the *!Kung* because we don't have their knowledge of the local resources and perils. If these miners are really determined to eliminate us as a threat, they'll wait us out. But I don't see that we have many options and, even if it's a long shot, we can't just let them kill her, assuming she's still alive."

Baruti sighed and ate another handful of nuts, then offered some to Felicity, who promptly refused.

"You have to eat. You're no good to anyone if you don't keep up your strength. But what you've suggested, Felicity and Frank, is suicide. You only saw two or three people confronting Dr. Lugan, but these villains always travel in packs. They will have henchmen, or whatever you want to call them, with plenty of firepower. What we should do is wait for the floods that will extend the channels in the Delta farther south and allow us to travel closer to Maun. Once I get there, I can contact . . . the cavalry."

Frank raised his eyebrows.

Baruti answered his unspoken question. "I'm not the only one with suspicions."

"How long will the floods take?" asked Felicity.

"At least another week."

"Too late," said Frank. "While she's bleeding to death, we're going to take a grueling canoe trip through the Delta and call in your elusive cavalry, to give them what? Sketchy suspicions? A witnessed attack and a possible poisoning, plus plenty of *!Kung* fables? But no real facts. No verified plans, heinous or otherwise. Even if they believe every word of our speculative theories, they probably don't give a damn about Dr. Lugan. They'll beef up security at every launch pad, but they won't make more than a cursory search for her and Dr. Wilson, by which time they'll be long dead and buried, no doubt."

"A frontal attack is suicide," said Baruti.

"How 'bout a sideways one?" suggested Pedro. He accepted the dried roots and berries that Dave placed in his hands.

Baruti squinted at him, then shoved the container of snack food at Felicity. "Eat," he demanded. Then he turned to Pedro, his eyebrows arched. "You have my attention."

"Well, you're an expert of sorts in these parts," Pedro said, chewing audibly. "There ain't much left, I know. But what's left could be . . . useful."

"Yes," said Baruti. "Go on."

"Well, the lodge ain't nothin' more than some flimsy tent material and wooden frames decked out to look all fancy. When I'm scouting for some cheesecake at a family reunion, all laid out nice and pretty in the middle of the dining room, I know I ain't got a chance in hell of gettin' a slice when all the old ladies are lined up for first crack. And there's always guards. You know, the uncles and aunts who think a big boy like me don't deserve such a rich dessert, when it comes down to it. They point their middle finger and say, 'Back o' the line.' So I gotta be sneaky, right? To get what I want. And I'm not sayin' I don't sometimes get caught. But other times I might jus' be sneaky enough to pull off a heist."

"What do you do?" asked Felicity.

Frank tried not to smirk. Maybe Pedro wasn't a scientist or a garden variety expert, but he did have some expertise that came in handy when you were fighting off snakes or planning a surprise attack.

"I pull my cousin's hair on the other side of the room, and she thinks my bro did it. They start screamin' and punchin' each other, breakin' things. Lamps and knickknacks, dishes, they all go flyin', sometimes out of nowhere. The old ladies start duckin' for cover; they flock to the kitchen or even out of the house, and sometimes they slip on some cookin' oil that accidentally got spilt. Yeah, I know, it's mean, them being old ladies and all. But sometimes old ladies can be mean, too. And, hey, then the cheesecake is left all by its lonesome, not even half-eaten. And I swoop in like a bat who's been hidin' in the corner and I take it—not just one slice, but the whole damn cake."

"What if an aunt or uncle is still standing guard by the cake, not buying your diversion?" asked Felicity. "What if he or she decides to stomp on it rather than let you have it?"

"Then I'd be no further ahead but no further behind either, since they were goin' to eat the cake anyway. But we can't worry 'bout that before it happens. If we want to hit them sideways, we need to find lamps and dishes and cookin' oil. Since you love that cake so much, you have to be willin' to hurt the old ladies. And if it comes down to it, you gotta be ready to smack that aunt upside the head and maybe stomp on her first. Neither you nor Frank never done somethin' like that before."

Frank swallowed and studied the ground, as the shadows lengthened and the air grew quiet.

"Pedro's right," said Baruti. "You talk a bold streak, but can you really back up your words? This isn't a virtual game. You'll be using real guns with real bullets. When you shoot, you have to shoot to kill. I know I told you that you were the man for the job, Felicity, but this isn't a man's job. It's a soldier's. And it isn't one person that you need to protect yourself from, but several whom you must coldly murder. That's what it is. Calling it anything else would be deluding ourselves. We can justify it, because these men are murderers themselves. But it won't lessen the impact when it comes to pulling the trigger. I know. I had to do it once, and it haunts me to this day. The man was killing children, whipping them to shreds in the blood-diamond days in the Congo. I was just out of graduate school and had begun my career by studying the shy gorilla. I thought that all a biologist needed to be was an observer and recorder. And a dedicated conservationist with an active blog. But speaking softly or loudly for the animals didn't save them. When I came upon that man who attacked a boy, even while surrounded by his dead victims, I knew that nothing I could do would save the boy, unless I became the man I abhorred."

"You're not the same," said Felicity. "You were defending an innocent child."

"A righteous kill," murmured Frank.

"But how many righteous kills does it take, Frank, before they become unrighteous?" There were tears in Baruti's eyes. "I hate these people who murdered my friends. I despise them to the core. Even if I share half their DNA, I will not hesitate to kill them. Deep down, I know they're a danger to us, and so I will cling to that justification, just as I'm sure they feel their actions are justified. But I won't delude myself into thinking that I am a good man. If you do this, you will wallow in guilt for the rest of your days. Make no mistake."

The silence that ensued was unbearably painful. Frank knew that he wasn't a good man. He'd already crossed that line, although nowhere near the extent that Baruti had described. Felicity had her own faults and passions that had always painted her as the quintessential inveigler of academia. But would she be willing to become a killer?

She released a long drawn-out sigh, then she spoke. "And won't we wallow in guilt if we do nothing?"

"We will," said Frank. "But this isn't a catch-22. We were already damned when we discovered their secret. Even if we escape and call in the cavalry, even if we hide in the Himalayas, we'll still have the sword of Damocles hanging over our heads for the rest of our lives. If these people are an ancient species, then even if they didn't procreate as prolifically as our own species did, there still must be a considerable number of them scattered around the globe, hiding in plain sight. If the cavalry kills off this group, that doesn't mean we're safe. And this is Dr. Lugan we're talking about."

Then Pedro sealed the deal.

"I ain't never killed a man, though I ain't a saint, as you might have guessed. This ain't gonna be any easier for me. But I liked that Ms. Lugan. I liked her from the start, even though she kinda didn't trust me, I think. And she ain't done nothin' to nobody. If this is what we gotta do, then I say 'let's get us some cake.'"

Scanning...

Located: Chapter 46

LITTLE REGISTERED ON Bob's awareness, except brief flickers of sensations and scenes. A damp, piercing core-deep chill, gradually replaced by a painful thawing. Throbbing throughout his flesh that momentarily raised the curtain on his mind. Lucas, dammit, hovering over him, hanging a warming solution, a needle biting into his vein. Then sweet oblivion. Feeling adrift.

Another wave of experience. The soft down of a blanket, trapping him on a firm mattress. An ache in his chest, a gurgle in his lungs. Coughing, hacking, sitting up. And Lucas, dammit, supporting his back until the coughing fit subsided. Where was Gita? There, at his side, bringing a warm, soothing drink to his lips. He swallowed and sank back against a fluffy cloud. He chose to float around in its yielding buoyancy rather than rise again to confront that face.

Time passed. Hours or days.

He opened his eyes. Coughed. Looked around.

Of course that face was there, with its probing catlike eyes. Lucas was lounging on his own bunk across the aisle, staring at Bob.

"So?" Bob said.

"So?" said Lucas.

"Did you tell her?"

"No," Gita said, striding in from the cockpit. "He's refused to speak. All he's done is examine your modifications to the original rebreather tank, and make the same adjustments to the one we had to swap for it, once it was empty. The adjustments don't make sense. You shouldn't be alive."

Bob tried to sit up, but his muscles quivered and balked, threatening to topple him. Lucas leaped forward, dammit, and guided him upward with the sturdy support of his overly developed arms.

"Stop helping me," Bob snapped.

"Okay," said Lucas, and dropped him back down on the mattress.

"I'll help you," said Gita. She gripped his arms and tugged him to sitting position, then propped him up with pillows. "Now," she said, sitting beside him. "Are you going to tell me what's going on?"

"Lucas is a bastard," he replied.

"I got that. But what did he do? And how come you require a *lower* concentration of oxygen?"

"Lucas isn't who you think he is," said Bob. "That cave is not a stockpile of supplies for stranded astronauts. That cave is a cryogenic zoo of DNA samples and a cache of vital equipment to begin a colony on Mars. An unsanctioned colony."

Lucas crossed his arms, and grinned, of all things.

Gita frowned and scrutinized Lucas with frigid intensity before she responded. "Go on."

"I was sent to watch Lucas, investigate his activities."

"By whom?" Lucas asked.

"Like I would tell you that," snapped Bob. "He's been on a watch list for some time. Along with a few other astronauts. Astronauts who disappeared on missions, then reappeared. Days unaccounted for. And the ISA suspected there were unsanctioned launches, too. They tracked their departures on satellite, but couldn't determine exactly where the spacecraft were launched from, or track their destinations. But I had no idea this radical group of secessionists were prepping *people* for colonization, too."

"Yet if you really thought about it, it would be logical," said Lucas.

"Gita, you need to contact the ISA right now."

"I still don't understand," she murmured, a grit underlying her soft tone. "How do you prep *people* for Mars, other than with HAB equipment and supplies and appropriate training?"

"Or are you going to finish what you started, Lucas?" asked Bob, ignoring her question since it aroused so much fury. "Are you going to kill us both, before we can warn them?"

"I'm not killing anyone," said Lucas. "Why would I do that after I *rescued* you?"

"Unless . . ." said Gita, still puzzling. "But that wouldn't be a simple matter."

"It wasn't simple, was it, Lucas? They've been working on this for years. I have an extra chromosome now, Gita. I don't need as much oxygen to survive, but I imagine with my altered lung tissue and metabolic system I would be prone to oxygen toxicity if I returned to Earth. Lucas has ensured that I can never leave Mars."

Gita's eyelashes fluttered, her brow contracted, her face grew pale. "That's not— How could you—? I should contact the ISA."

She rose from the bunk, eyeing Lucas with caution and simmering fury. Since he made no move toward her, she turned and strode to the cockpit. Why wasn't Lucas reacting? Why wasn't he barring her path, or tying her up, or shooting her full of extra chromosomes? Instead, he smiled as if with gracious encouragement.

In the cockpit, Gita flipped on the comm unit to send a message, but half-turned toward Lucas to keep a lookout for any interference on his part.

"You're just going to *let* her?" asked Bob.

"Long-range comms are down," said Lucas.

Bob expelled an exasperated sigh. He leaned his head against the pillows, breathing hoarsely into his facemask. Of course, he'd expected no less. "It's no use," he called to Gita. "He sabotaged our comms."

She examined the link, then switched the unit off. Flushed, she crept back into the room, gazing in wide-eyed wonder and wariness at Lucas, as if he were a monster.

"What do we do now?" she asked. "Why did you even come back for Bob, if you know he can't leave the planet?"

"Well," said Lucas. "I figured he'd probably do something stupid, like what we just witnessed, rather than accept his fate and make a nice cozy home in a comfortably oxygenated cave. And something he said on our side trip to the ocean resonated with me, too."

"Something I said?"

"You know, about settling here on the planet."

Bob's heart thumped painfully in his chest. He was finding it difficult to breathe again. "Are you stranding Gita here, too?"

"I really don't see that I have a choice. I could have kept going, Bob. Headed back to the MADVEC, left you here to fend for yourself. If you'd stayed in the cave, you would have been fine. But I guessed that wouldn't sit well with you. And believe it or not, the thought of your death really bothered me."

"Bothered you? Like a nagging itch?"

"Exactly. Or maybe a festering wound. Regardless of the severity of the bother, I made a rather sacrificial choice, if you think about it."

"Yes, you risked your life to plunge into a raging, hypothermia-inducing river to save me. How noble."

"A death-defying superman type of thing."

"But what happens now, Lucas? You toss us both back into the cave. You force me to inject Gita with your genetic cocktail so I will have a companion? So you're not quite so bothered?"

"You did want to live here, if I recall your words."

"Yes, in a colony! Once the planet has settled down from the bombardment of comets and asteroids. In a HAB on the planet's surface, not in a cave."

"Minor details," Lucas countered. "In all honesty, Bob, I've given you an opportunity you never would have had, had you returned to Earth. And I've supplied you with all the tools necessary to survive. Now you'll even have a partner. Oh, maybe not the one you wanted, but she is rather pleasant to look at."

"You bastard!" said Gita, and launched a vigorous kick at Lucas's leg. "To think we put you back together." She slapped him. "To think I actually thought you had a generous heart." She kicked him again, and would have continued kicking him, if he hadn't stood and grabbed her and pinned her to his chest.

Bob fumbled upright to try help her, but Lucas swatted him down, and he hadn't the strength to fight back.

"Sit down!" he said to Gita, and slammed her onto the bunk beside Bob.

"Now," he said. "I'll tell you what you're going to do. You're going to stop wrestling with me, fighting the inevitable, and making this harder than it has to be. You're going to descend into that cave and start setting up a HAB. You've expressed your love for Mars. Now you need to show it."

Bob's eyes strayed away from Lucas, wondering how he could help Gita escape. Then he caught sight of his discarded jumpsuit, crumpled at the bottom of the bed. At the waistline, he spotted a bulge in the pocket—the outline of the syringes he'd jammed in there before he'd vacated the cave. Sedatives, anesthetics, and other enticing drugs. He shifted to the left, edged closer to the end of the bed, and nudged the pocket open. He coughed, emitting a dry, barking sound, and then coughed again, the second time to disguise his fumbling. Now he had a weapon in his hand.

He uncapped the syringe as Lucas droned on.

"There's a wealth of material in that cave. And if you'd taken the time to examine it, maybe you wouldn't have been so eager to leave and embark on your fruitless quest for revenge. I know it makes you angry that I took away your choice in the matter, but this is what you've dreamed of. So it isn't a sentence, it's a gift, as I explained to you before. I—"

Bob marshaled his strength, then dove at Lucas, the syringe aimed at his throat. He nearly made it, too. The needle was an inch from puncturing the bastard's skin. But Lucas grabbed his arm and ripped it out of his hand.

"What's this?" he said, shoving Bob back on the bunk. He whisked the jumpsuit from the bed before Bob could grab another syringe. Lucas withdrew the entire collection, five in all. "Look at this. Valium, morphine, ketamine, propofol." He raised his eyebrows. "And last, but not least, Mars Chromosome 47. Poetic justice, Bob?"

"Let Gita go home," he snapped. Or maybe he should try another tactic. "Please?"

Lucas resumed his dictatorial position on the bunk across from them, fondling the syringes in an oddly affectionate way. He gazed at Bob and Gita each in turn.

"I wish I could rewind the clock, Bob, to a time when you didn't hate me quite so fervently. To a time when Gita didn't look at me as if I were shit she'd like to wipe off her shoes. The lifetime we'll spend together is a long time."

He chose the uncapped syringe and nestled it in his other hand, gripping it as if preparing to inject. His narrowed gaze sought out Gita, causing her to scowl, but she also scattered her glance as if looking for an escape. Bob prepared to throw himself in front of her.

"But you'll have to forgive me at some point."

He raised the needle.

"Because I don't think you can kill me any more than I could kill you."

Then he plunged it . . . into his own neck, and injected the contents.

His pupils expanded; his body immediately slumped to the side. Bob couldn't comprehend what he was seeing. He leaned toward Lucas, wondering if he should pounce or shout or simply witness the effects of a poison he knew only too well. He felt his hopes rise, at least for Gita's escape, even though it was the damnedest thing he'd ever seen.

"Don't let Gita leave," Lucas rasped as his head plunked onto the mattress.

"Why not?" he asked. What could possibly stop her now?

But Lucas was never one without a plan.

"Because she has nowhere to go," he replied. Then he followed up with a statement that slammed Bob's soaring heart back into his chest. "Because . . . I sent the *Phoenix* back home."

Scanning...

Located: Chapter 47

DAYNA WONDERED IF they would all sit around in a circle and chat about the old days, or whether they would simply shoot her and be done with it. They did neither. Shaun propped her up in bed and Hondo offered her codeine to alleviate the pain. At least she hoped it was codeine and not the poison they'd administered to DeLuca.

Hondo dragged a chair across the room, the scraping sound whittling at her eardrums, then plopped it in front of her and sat as near to her as the bed allowed, his knees indenting the mattress. Reena, looking exasperated, retrieved her gun from Hondo, slid it into a holster at her waist, and plunked herself down at the foot of the bed, jiggling the mattress. She raked Dayna with a severe look, scanning from head to toe. Shaun nestled down beside Dayna on the side of the bed, far too close to deter the stirrings he always elicited in her. Damn him for being so attractive and caring, and yet so conflicted and promiscuous.

"You're hungry, aren't you?" said Hondo, tapping her arm.

"Not really," she said. If anything, she was feeling nauseous.

"Yes, you are. Hungry for our story. You've already pieced half of it together. You've examined our DNA."

"I'm not as hungry as you think. It has more to do with passion than appetite. Beginnings inspire me. But, yes, I've looked at your DNA and I can't fathom how you've remained hidden for so long in our modern world. You must have had to give your doctor countless DNA samples, every time you needed even the most insignificant health-care treatment."

"It wasn't difficult at first," said Hondo. "We lived in isolated communities. Since we were so often ostracized in the past, we selectively excluded ourselves from the general population. You see, we have a slow reproductive rate. We can only have one or two children in a lifetime, which made us odd. And we couldn't breed among your people, either. Oh, the odd hybrid would occur, like the mule, a cross between a donkey and a horse. Inevitably sterile. Sterility wasn't accepted well in those days. Plus, our size was often intimidating. Sometimes they called us gods, others titans. Occasionally, they called us demons or angels, or the unholy spawn of angels and men, as in the Book of Giants from the Dead Sea Scrolls. One of the fragments that refers to the angels says 'they defiled and they begot giants and monsters.' In all these references they describe our freakishness, call us preternatural. Eventually, your species became so numerous, they ridiculed us and cast us out. At one time or another, they tried to eradicate us as if we were cockroaches—the irony being that *they* were the pests."

"Consuming all the land they could find, when all we needed were small, scattered plots," snarled Reena.

"So we fled and established new colonies, scattered throughout Asia and Europe. The odd colony even made it to North America, as they crossed the land bridge between Alaska and Siberia. As the Romans and others kept expanding the breadth of their occupation, we even set out for more dangerous territory, virtually uninhabited, like the Canadian North, or the far reaches of the southern continent, and remote islands. We lived among the Phoenicians for a time, and learned how to travel great distances by boat. And wherever we went, we burned our dead. That has been a feature of our funerary rites as far back as our tribal memories can stretch. It began in southern Africa, where it was more convenient and efficient than burial underground, and we continued the practice as we migrated north. So we had to return recently to eliminate any remains from the period of time before we began cremating, in case the bones were discovered."

"So your presence here . . . alarmed Dr. Mbeki?" ventured Dayna, very carefully. How far down that road did she dare to tread?

"Our *actions* alarmed him," said Hondo.

Reena snorted.

"And you know exactly what those actions were. The *!Kung* knew us; the *!Kung* developed fables about us long ago. The *!Kung* hoarded our bones in that distant past, because they're terrified of spirits and they thought our burial rituals would anger the spirits. They possessed the only clear evidence of our existence."

Dayna experienced a ripple of abhorrence, but she tamped it back down. She couldn't show these people that she was a threat, although they weren't stupid. Even if she expressed her outrage, she doubted that it would change her fate.

But she wanted more information, not just for the remote possibility of indicting them, but because she craved it. Despite how despicable their actions, they were another species of *Homo sapiens*. How extraordinary that she was speaking to them face to face, not just analyzing their bones, that they were laying out their history for her.

"But that doesn't explain how you managed to avoid medical tests."

Hondo grinned and tapped her arm again. "At first we had our own doctors. Even our own medical centers. But when GenCorp centralized everything, it became easier. We sent some of our people out into the world, even though we still maintained isolated communities. We sent people like Shaun and his brother, Lucas, to become trained in the sciences, and our specialists have seized most of GenCorp. Any results flagged with our particular genes that aren't filtered through our own medical community are buried, lost, or replaced. We have our own geneticists, as you already know. We've even darkened or lightened our skin, so we appear to have ethnic diversity. We were essentially unknown and unknowable, until a certain Cree girl stumbled onto a bog that contained our ancestors. We'd been searching in that location for some time, because we knew of the lost explorers—a tale handed down through generations that we suspected was true. And as civilization encroached on that site, we worried that they would be discovered before we could . . ."

Dayna raised her eyebrows, but Hondo wasn't about to reveal his agenda. Not yet, anyway.

"We were already installed there as miners. It was easy to poke around, even though Shaun wasn't too impressed with our arrival. We paid for his education; we pulled strings to get him that assignment. But he turned his back on us the first chance he got."

"Because he's soft," said Reena. "Pathetic."

Shaun, who'd been unusually quiet up to this point, stiffened and glared at his ex-wife. "I'm not a killer," he snapped. "I didn't attend assassin training school like you did."

"That isn't what we asked of you," said Hondo, in an icy tone.

"No, you asked me to do a geologist's work, which isn't within the scope of a biologist's training and made no sense. And because it makes no sense, I figure it has to do with your plan to depart the Earth. There's no way your plan will succeed, unless you do something drastic. And drastic, in your line of work, always involves killing innocent people."

"No one is innocent!" roared Hondo. "They've been killing for years." He pointed at Dayna, and she shrank back against Shaun, although she doubted he could protect her from this man. "Decimating the animals and fish. Killing each other. Raping the planet. But then they began by killing us."

"So you want retribution," she said, cautiously.

Hondo paused and moved to tap her arm again, but instead grasped it painfully. "Did you ever have to live in shame?" he asked. "Did you ever have to hide the very essence of your being because, if you let it be known, let the world understand that this is who you are, it would probably mean the end of you and everything you hold dear?"

"No," she said. "But my grandfather did, because he was gay. My aunt did, because she was mentally ill. The world is changing, Hondo. It's becoming more tolerant of differences. And every human has some sort of genetic aberration or other. We are so closely related as species, you can't think that we will turn on you because of a few alternate bases in your DNA. But if you kill people, if you perform reprehensible deeds, we will think you reprehensible."

"Lip service," he sneered, still squeezing her arm.

"Let her go," said Shaun. He reached across her to grab Hondo's hand, but Hondo released her before there could be a battle.

"Always so caring and considerate of everyone but your own people," said Reena.

"Are you 'my people'?" asked Shaun. "Do I have to be associated with you because we share 'a few alternate bases,' as Dayna said? I choose who I am and to whom I extend my love and compassion, and I will never join your bloodthirsty enterprise."

"You don't have to join us, but you can't escape who you are," said Hondo. "You can live with them, make attempts to breed with them, but you can't dilute your DNA. I'm tired of your shame. We will start a new colony, and we won't need to hide any longer. But we can't even attempt it until we're satisfied they won't be hunting us or trying to eradicate us, again. Lucas told you not to stand in our way. If you do, I do believe I'll have to kill you."

"Standing in the way of what? How can you possibly annex a planet that they've spent years and billions of dollars terraforming?"

"By keeping them very, very busy," said Reena. "Preoccupied."

"Reena, that's enough," said Hondo.

"Why? She's not going to live to tell anything. And neither will you, Shaun. Not if you're so determined to protect them."

"Standing in the middle," muttered Dayna. "And in the middle is where you die."

"Excuse me?" asked Hondo.

"Oh, just something a mad old man said," replied Dayna. "Only he wasn't that mad, I think. But if you want a separate colony on Mars, why not petition for it? I would gladly back you up. There are peaceful ways to go about this."

"Are there?" asked Reena, slamming down the words. "They'll just hand Mars over to another species? I doubt that. But, you see, we really don't want to go about this in a peaceful way. We've cowered in the shadows long enough; we've endured your bullying, your dominance, your egotistical insistence that you are the chosen species, your religions that single you out as being more worthy than others. We're tired of it. And we have never forgotten how you tried to kill us off, more than once. Now it's our turn."

Ice worried its way through Dayna's every fiber as the implications of Reena's words took root. Their turn to do what? Did it have global implications, as Baruti had suggested? But that was impossible. They could set off nuclear weapons, but did they possess enough to eradicate every human being? What did they have in mind that would keep every world official very, very busy?

"And I think we should start with you," said Reena, grabbing her gun from her holster and pointing it at Dayna.

But before she could pull the trigger, before Shaun could move to protect Dayna, a crashing, pounding, thunderous commotion sounded from outside the cloth wall. And the canvas-draped corner of the room suddenly collapsed.

Scanning...

Located: Chapter 48

When Lucas awoke, he struggled to breathe, and his chest burned and ached, and his flesh prickled with pins and needles. When he opened his eyes, he noticed the mask hitched to his face, supplying him with a reduced concentration of oxygen. Then he noticed Bob, with an identical mask, watching him from across the aisle of the crew cabin.

"Strange sensations," he murmured, extending his arm and shaking it.

"Do you really want to compare notes?" asked Bob.

"Well, it is one way to begin, as scientists."

"Begin what? The birth of our little colony? You think we can all be friends now, or some kind of dysfunctional family, and eke out a living on the planet as Martians?"

"Something like that. If we can't get along, we will . . . have an unpleasant life here." His chest ached with every attempt to speak, so he took a few moments to breathe and ignore Bob. That was when he noticed Gita perched on the bunk beside Bob, her features compressed in a look of pain.

"Do I have to inject myself too?" she asked, deadpan.

Lucas regarded her, not unkindly, he thought, but she bristled at his scrutiny. "The *Phoenix* will be gone by now. I instructed the ISA to begin remote piloting our spacecraft on the 10th sol of this month and," he looked at his wrist display, "that was two days ago." He paused to catch his breath and absorb the onslaught of intensive cellular growth and alterations in his tissues. He was already feeling frustrated at his body's lack of cooperation with his demands. He forced himself to continue.

"Yes, Gita. If you want to survive, you will have to inject yourself with this remarkable chromosome. You could return to the trailer and use the extra stores of oxygen we liberated from the cave to keep the rover at an Earth-equivalent concentration, but eventually those stores will run out." He gasped and reminded himself to rest between statements. "Even if you returned to the Tempe Terra base . . . and radioed Earth and waited for their potential rescue . . . you wouldn't have enough oxygen to last that long. But if we conserve the remainder, we could use it for . . . brief excursions at a lower concentration as we begin to develop our colony. Eventually we could reconfigure some of the components in the Arabia Terra fuel factory to produce what we would need for longer forays."

"Or we could just kill you," said Bob.

Lucas rolled his eyes. "That doesn't solve Gita's problem. And I'm your best expert . . . on the adaptation chromosome, and the biodome in the cave, and the other resources we have. I'm not saying you can't survive without me, but I will be an asset . . . once you get over your rage. Start looking at this logically. I decided to stay here with you to help you adapt, to suffer the same setbacks and challenges, to explore and redefine Mars. I didn't have to."

"And in the process sentenced Gita to the same fate. You didn't have to do that, either."

"Gita was pining over you and your unfortunate demise. If she'd known you were alive, she wouldn't have left. I've indulged her desire not to abandon you."

"But you could have continued lying to her until you were well on your way back to Earth. Or even beyond that."

"Gita is right here," said Gita. "I can make my own decisions."

"Sorry," said Bob. "But Lucas didn't leave you with any choice; there are no decisions to make. He was so keen on keeping his secret that he made us prisoners here, which is a little easier on his conscience than actually killing us. Then he felt so guilty about that, he decided to share our suffering. Now we're supposed to be grateful, and praise and adore him because he is so noble and sacrificial."

"Let's work the problem," she said, staring right at Lucas and, surprisingly, ignoring Bob. "We have limited oxygen supplies, but limitless oxygen in the cave, am I correct?"

Lucas nodded.

"This chromosome alters the body to adapt to a lower oxygen concentration."

"And lower pressure," said Lucas. "And makes us more tolerant of radiation."

"So we can breathe without masks in the cave indefinitely?" she continued.

"Yes," he replied.

"There are vast supplies of food, water, and even potentially some edible live plants available to us, according to Bob. HAB material, heaters, solar panels, even some genetic engineering constituents and preserved DNA?"

"And a genetic lab, if we want to initiate a few Lazarus experiments," explained Lucas. "We could try to establish the hardiest plant life on the surface, now that the algae has spread so rapidly." It was hard to keep the eagerness from dancing in his voice. These weren't the people he'd dreamed of beginning this colony with, but they were capable of continuing the work of the Movement. Although they were the antithesis of the entire philosophy of the Movement.

"So at least we won't die," she said, "assuming this chromosome doesn't kill us. Has it been tested very long?"

"It's never been tested," said Bob. "It couldn't be tested on humans in a Martian environment, since this is not an environment you can recreate on Earth."

"We tested some mice," said Lucas, "here, in the cave several years ago. The mice survived, and that convinced us we were ready for the next step. But when the ISA amped up the terraforming, it became too risky to begin the human testing stage."

"So there you are," said Bob. "We're guinea pigs. We became expendable, and then you thought why not begin the experimentation with us?"

"No," said Lucas, shortly. "You made it necessary for me to stop you from interfering. And I couldn't kill you. You're right about that. So, yes, we are testing it now, because otherwise you would have shut us down and made it impossible for us to create a proper home. Even so, the planet isn't ready for an exodus from Earth, yet. So we will be true pioneers and explorers. And guinea pigs. But certainly you were a guinea pig when you set foot on the *Phoenix*. Any minor damage to the VASMIR engine, say from a micrometeorite, and we would have become nothing but space debris or vapor. You gladly welcomed that risk."

Bob scowled and adjusted his blankets with brisk strokes of his hands.

"And then, when you suggested we visit the planet and I listed, in no uncertain terms, the many hazards and potentially life-threatening catastrophes that could ensue, you still insisted. And then you chose the one site I'd vetoed. Okay, you had your reasons, but that was imprudent. So I ask you, since you could have died several times over since we embarked on this enterprise, why balk at *this* risk?"

"Really?" said Bob. "You expect me to gladly embrace it?"

Lucas didn't answer, not because he wasn't inclined to, but because he couldn't catch his breath, felt inundated with waves of vertigo and nausea, needed to rest his pounding head. He closed his eyes and concentrated on taking slow, deep breaths.

"I will," said Gita, somewhat shrilly. Lucas flicked his eyes open, then recoiled his head, shocked by a close encounter with her flushed face. "I hate you," she said, "for thinking you and whatever group you're mixed up with have exclusive rights to Mars. You think you're the only ones who will have any regard for this environment? But I tell you that Bob and I will be consummate gardeners. The whole of idea of adapting humans to Mars has been discussed for years, but no one has achieved any workable results, so we continue to try to adapt Mars to our requirements, which is far more costly in time and energy. This," she swept her arms around, encompassing both Bob and Lucas, "is remarkable. You've given us the means to cultivate Mars, to witness, first hand, its blossoming birth, and time, endless time—assuming this chromosome doesn't kill us first—to explore the planet that we've dreamed about for years. I'm furious at you because you didn't ask. But if you'd asked, I'd probably have said yes.

"But with Bob, it's different. You assaulted him—not just physically but by introducing this genetic alteration without his consent. A violation. Then you abandoned him, left him to think he would have to spend the rest of his life in absolute solitude. He won't forgive you for a long time, if ever. And he has a girlfriend back on Earth whom he loves and now can never see again. Maybe he will somehow come to terms with you, in time. Our chances of survival are higher with all of us in on this together. And maybe, eventually, we can send our legendary stories back to Earth, along with the data from meaningful scientific studies. Unless," she said, her voice once again grave, "that isn't allowed? Unless we truly are prisoners?"

Lucas regarded her quietly. How he wished she'd continued to rage at him, as she had earlier, rather than ask questions he couldn't—or at least didn't want to—answer.

"I guess that's answer enough," she said.

Bob harrumphed as if he'd known the answer all along.

"Do you really think a group of colonists can simply annex a planet? They won't get away with it. You should know that. Why not take what they've given us and use it for the benefit of all mankind?" she inquired.

"It isn't that simple," said Lucas, riding out another wave of nausea. "They need this planet." This would never make sense to them without a more detailed explanation. Should he tell them the truth? What harm could it do, since they'd never be able to contact Earth before the chain reaction began?

"We need this planet because we can't live peaceably among you. We're different, and you've perceived it all along, although you couldn't identify the precise incongruities. Our DNA is uncommon. Considering the differences in our genetic makeup, it's quite surprising that Bob's body is accepting the alterations from the chromosome so well, although they only encompass certain genes that we might share. Regardless, it's our genetic and physical differences that are at the root of our problems with other humans. On Earth we are outsiders, although we have managed to remain hidden for thousands of years." He proceeded to explain the history of his people, the near-genocides, the flight from the Romans, the search for a home where they wouldn't be persecuted, even the changes they made to their own appearance to blend in with the modern population.

When he completed his tale, the rover was pregnant with silence. Of course, he hadn't told Bob and Gita what his people really intended to do, other than colonize another world.

Bob got up from his bunk, crouched down beside Lucas, and rested his hand on Lucas's shoulder. At first, he touched him tentatively, as if battling his own reluctance, then his grip grew fierce.

"We are not so different, you and I," he said. "We originated in the Vitalis Cave, developed on the Martian surface, were ricocheted off the planet by an asteroid, wound up in a soup of suitable molecules, and evolved through a long, slow climb. Your branch must be closely related to ours, so close you can barely tell us apart. We are not all rational—you least of all, Luke, or you would have told me your story rather than shove a needle into my jugular. I can't apologize for the transgressions of our ancestors because I didn't commit them. But I do hope we have evolved enough not to keep committing them. You risked your life to save mine. And risked your secret, too, I suppose. Gita and I did the same for you. Maybe it's time to stop bearing old grudges and use that as a foundation for a new tradition. If you'd told me about this before I saved your life, it would have made no difference. You're not another species. You are an astronaut and a friend. I guess it's time to forget the enemy part of the equation."

Lucas felt the warmth in Bob's grip before he hastily released it. And for a minute, he regretted his actions before he'd turned the rover around. Maybe even two minutes.

Scanning...

Located: Chapter 49

FELICITY TENSED, AS the net the *!Kung* had donated nearly pulled free from her hands. But she tightened her grip and tried to remain balanced in the *mokoro* as assorted fish struggled to escape their new prison. Frank held the other corner, while Baruti and Pedro maneuvered the forward section underneath the wriggling mass. Once they'd captured a sizable batch, the guides poled them through the channels until they reached a lagoon in the southeastern corner of the island they were setting up for a chaotic awakening. They released the fish, but strung the net across the lagoon's narrow outlet, to prevent their escape to the greater Okavango.

An about-face and twenty minutes of fervent poling returned them to their cache—two burlap sacks bulging with lamps and dishes and cooking oil, or the Okavango's equivalent. The larger of the two, which bordered on gigantic, insisted on writhing ominously, and Frank insisted on avoiding it. That particular diversion, or weapon, would be lashed to the bottom of Felicity's boat. Oh, joy. And the other, much smaller, but also squirming bag, went into Frank's boat, although he seemed just as reluctant to have that one nestled near his feet.

Baruti explained how easy it would be to trigger a stampede among wild animals, and that doing so would be their first course of action when they approached the lodge. Although there weren't many rooms in the lodge, they had no idea where Hondo and company had taken their friends. So what they needed to do was create as much of a ruckus as necessary to roust the entire group, but not enough of one to endanger the very people they were attempting to rescue. They didn't want to "flatten the cake," as Pedro put it.

"All they need to do is catch our scent," he explained, directing the guides to position their boat behind the elephant herd that he'd spotted earlier near the western flank of the island. "If they think we're sidling up too close, they'll become spooked. When they begin to panic, they'll probably topple the flimsy wooden framework by grazing it with their huge bodies, but they won't batter their way through the middle. They may not be graceful, but they still manage to avoid obvious obstacles."

Their unexpected intrusion into the herd's peaceful pursuits did exactly what Baruti had described. The elephants were drinking and lazily splashing themselves with their dangling trunks, when the cow nearest the *mokoros* trumpeted her alarm. The entire group plodded forward, then trotted, then thundered onto the island, as their anxiety diffused from elephant to elephant. Most of the beasts avoided the higher elevation of the boardwalks and porches around the tents, but a few became so alarmed they leaped up and trod heedlessly on the planks until more became equally venturous. Eventually, they mowed down the wooden framework and canvas walls of the various rooms, but avoided trampling through the heap of the collapsed structures. In this way, the lodge began to topple, one room at a time, like a series of massive dominoes tipped by mud-encrusted bulldozers.

Frank grabbed his burlap sack and Pedro the rifle he'd obtained from Dave. Since Baruti didn't own an arsenal, Frank and Felicity had to go without weapons—at least of the usual variety—until they'd acquired their own. The two men leaped off the *mokoro* as soon as it beached in the swampy mud, ducking down to avoid detection. They'd landed a short distance from the inlet where Dr. Lugan had been attacked, on the northern stretch of the island. A sentry was still posted precisely in that location, although camouflaged in the long grass. Baruti had scouted the island a few hours earlier to identify the guards' positions and determine if there was an area where they could land that was guard-free and provided moderate concealment. That had led them to this stretch of reeds and brush feathered with a copse of leafy mangosteen trees. Frank and Pedro crouched among the reeds and crept forward, heading for their chosen point of attack.

Felicity slipped into the water before the *mokoro* touched solid ground, practically rolling over the side to avoid notice. She skulked among the reeds, assisting Kelong as he guided the vessel to shore. The guide would now have to find cover. He wasn't enthusiastic about joining the battle, but he'd refused to stay behind on one of the islands, as Dave had, while they began their assault. He was probably worried that no one would ever return for him. But as he scurried away, he retained his rifle to protect himself, leaving their small assault team with one less weapon.

Baruti flipped out of the opposite side of the boat and aided Felicity in tugging it into the veil of frizzy papyrus strands and tall stalks that thrived in the mud. He braced himself as he captured the writhing bag within. Felicity dug her arm underneath the flailing bundle on the other end and hefted it, gasping at its enormous weight.

"All right?" Baruti whispered.

She nodded, although her shoulder felt as if it would break or dislocate. Plus the contents of the bag kept struggling and squirming.

"Is this *really* necessary?" she said under her breath.

"I think it's appropriate. Even symbolic," he muttered.

"That doesn't answer my question."

"Symbolic is sometimes necessary."

"Then Frank should be carrying it," she said.

He turned and tilted his head, studying her with undue severity. "You're sometimes a little cruel, aren't you?"

"Only when it comes to Frank," she replied.

They scuffled forward, her knees nearly buckling under her burden. But then she spotted their quarry, highlighted by the carnelian glow of sunset as he balanced on the collapsing boards. Hondo, the African miner she'd met in Northern Ontario, the tall Amazon-like woman she'd seen shoot Dr. Lugan, and the captives themselves. They were fleeing the crumpled shell of a room—*her* former room, to be exact—that was positioned centrally in the compound and directly in their line of sight. Shaun cradled Dr. Lugan in his arms in an intimate and tender way. And Dr. Lugan herself was grimacing and gasping as if in excruciating pain, but she was still very much alive. Relief washed through Felicity like a warm, frothy wave. Then Hondo shouted and gestured at a dozen men who were zigzagging across the compound, scrambling to escape the agitated herd of elephants.

"Get them out of here!" he cried, pointing at the rampaging animals.

As several men headed to the eastern end of the island, following the direction many of the elephants had taken and where Frank and Pedro had sprinted as well, gunfire erupted in a series of crisp pops. Baruti crouched lower to the ground and set the sack down, directing Felicity to do the same. They'd maneuvered into a hollow near the boardwalk—a snug bowl that was well concealed. But the wriggling contents of the sack kept trying to move forward. So Felicity clasped it and held tight, which perturbed it even more.

As Felicity struggled with the sack, Baruti tore his gun from his belt. He cupped his hand, leaned toward her, and whispered in her ear, "You stay here and get ready to release it. I'm going to pick off a few stragglers. And remember . . . once you open that bag, run like hell."

Are you kidding? she wanted to shout, but instead tried to do it with her eyes. But he didn't respond or even look at her anymore. He deserted her and slithered forward through the grass, and the sack sought to slither after him. Baruti wasn't asking her to kill anyone yet. But he'd charged her with an impossible task. Keep the one-hundred-and-fifty-pound python from ripping free of its sack and escaping before it could become another trip wire for the terrorists. Keep it from slipping away prematurely, rendering it useless in their defense.

Unworkable.

Obviously a job for Frank or Pedro.

But, by hell, she was going to do it. She threw her entire weight on the bag and struggled with the gargantuan creature as, no doubt, her rival Frank had once done. But this time she wouldn't need the help of a stranger. Unlike Frank, she would manage the beast on her own.

****

FRANK COULDN'T BELIEVE he was doing this—storming the castle, so to speak. The wriggling bag that dangled from his hand was the most deadly weapon in all of Africa. But it needed to be discharged at close range. And he'd probably only have one shot. Better make it a good one.

After they'd landed on the island's northeastern corner, he and Pedro had circled the perimeter at the easternmost point, near the outdoor restaurant where they'd gathered on the morning they'd embarked on their voyage through the Delta. Men were dispersing from this location like a disturbed hornet's nest, as the elephants tramped across the wooden floor of the restaurant, which began to crack under their weight. The beasts scattered tables and knocked down support beams, collapsing the thatched roof. The waiters and cooks had the sense to evacuate, but some of the terrorists couldn't sort out which direction to go, and a few were trampled.

But one, a robust redhead with a profusion of winged tattoos inked on his neck, aimed directly for Frank and Pedro. He crashed into the bushes, froze when he saw them, then groped for his gun. Pedro fired his rifle before the man managed to aim at them. Tattoo Man dropped to the ground, his eyes registering shock, and then pain, his gaze emptying with his death.

But the shot from the shoreline and the fall of one of their men woke the others to a new reality. This wasn't just an accident of the wilderness, a sudden grip of madness in the animals. This was an attack. And they all automatically pulled out their guns and scanned the brush and trees around them.

This is it, thought Frank. *This is where I die. Let's hope it has more meaning than a snake attack—even though the !Kung seemed to ascribe a great deal of meaning to it.*

Several men sprinted toward them and opened fire. He and Pedro ducked behind nearby palm trees, as Pedro kept shooting, reloading, and shooting. Some men were hit and fell. Pedro was grazed by a bullet. Frank felt another one whistle through his hair.

"We have to get closer to them," said Frank.

"We'll never make it," said Pedro. He shoved another magazine into the rifle. But Frank knew that they had very little extra ammunition. How many more magazines remained until they were spent?

"I need a weapon," said Frank.

"You have one," said Pedro. "Use it, or we'll never see that treasure you bin talkin' 'bout." He sighted down the barrel and sprayed bullets into the advancing army.

Use it? But he was too far away. Then an idea sprouted. "I'm going to circle around behind them. Cover me, and pray they don't pick me off."

Pedro nodded, slapped him fiercely on the arm—an obvious goodbye, if there ever was one—and began to lay down a suppressing fire. The enemy's gunfire ebbed momentarily as the men dove for cover, and Frank dove and rolled and dove to the north. He surfaced beneath the octopus roots of a baobab tree, scooted forward, then crawled toward the sprawled, crumpled structure of the restaurant, creeping up behind the men who were rapidly closing in on Pedro. A few men occasionally scanned behind them, but they didn't detect his slinking approach.

Frank grappled with his burlap sack, fumbled the ties open, then flipped it upside down and retreated in a crouch-run. He ducked behind the baobab roots again, and sent his new snake-sense toward the creature. He almost chuckled at the thought.

The reptile shot forward in a swirl of scales and rage at its capture. It turned back once to look at Frank, considering whether *that one* should be the object of its attack, but it must have caught a whiff of Frank's supernatural charm and turned back toward the terrorists. It struck without warning, digging its fangs into the nearest calf that was presented to it—that of a tall fellow of ample girth. The thin threads of khaki that covered the calf meant nothing to the enraged snake. The man howled, looked down, and began shrieking.

"Black mamba!" he yelled. "I've been bit."

The snake had already released him, but it wasn't satisfied with only one target, and the men were making an irritating racket that must have provoked it even more. It struck again, and another man howled, and then suddenly the blizzard of gunfire stopped, and the gunmen retreated, some backing away as the snake advanced, while sending poorly aimed shots at the small target, some bolting toward the south side of the island where a series of *mokoros* were conveniently parked in the lagoon. They raced into the water, dragging the *mokoros* with them, as Pedro took the opportunity to aim and pick off a few as they ran.

Frank broke cover and snatched up the gun one of the snake-bitten terrorists had dropped as he collapsed on the ground. The neurotoxin was already taking effect, causing the man to twitch and howl in pain. It wouldn't do damage as quickly as a bullet might, but it held a certainty of death. The black mamba continued to pursue the terrorists, and Frank took pains to avoid its path. But he only hesitated for a moment before he opened fire. The convulsing man on the ground was enough evidence that he'd crossed another line. Those men who weren't scrambling for the lagoon or scattering from the oncoming path of the snake returned fire.

Frank dropped to the ground and rolled behind a tree. But he continued to spray bullets at the men, forcing them into the water.

At first the water was smooth as glass, with barely a ripple disturbing the surface. But as the men prepared to leap into the boats, startled expressions appeared on their faces, and then the screams began. They frantically beat at the water, inadvertently tipped their *mokoros*, and floundered and splashed as the water developed a rosy tint. One by one, they sank from view as the surface erupted like a boiling cauldron in a frenzy of feeding tigerfish. Five men stopped at the water's edge, their faces frozen in terror. But Frank and Pedro didn't spare them a moment to consider their options. They pumped bullets into their weapons and mowed them down.

BARUTI SLUNK THROUGH the grass, edging around the nearest room of the lodge—now a hodgepodge of splintered wood and ripped canvas—and doing his best to avoid the snorting, shrieking elephants that had become separated from the herd. He would like to make a beeline for that murderous bastard, Hondo, but the man had ushered his group toward the western tip of the island—away from their booby traps—and he was protected within a circle of his henchmen.

The best course of action would be to eliminate the stragglers first, before he went for the aunt who would stomp on the cake. He ducked under a pyramid of fallen support beams and jutting canvas that would conceal him as the terrorists ran past. The gunfire from the east end of the island had intensified, sounding an endless barrage of snaps and pops that blistered his eardrums.

As long as the firefight continued, he maintained some hope that Frank and Pedro still lived. But what a grueling, unrelenting battle they must be enduring. How long could they hold out? They were only two men. But at least they were two resourceful men, one of whom was linked to the strongest animal spirit in the world—the python. Lank and wiry, Frank presented as a prime example of a snake, although nowhere near as imposing as the gigantic, muscular python. But Baruti didn't think the *!Kung* were wrong. They could see beneath his layers to a quiet power that dwelt within him.

Two men burst from the center of the crumpled lodge, dodging a belligerent elephant who looked familiar to Baruti. The jagged tear in her ear, possibly from a crocodile encounter, placed her as a regular patron of the lodge. Gertrude. She looked miffed at their intrusion and boxed one sprinter on the rear end with her trunk, sending him skidding to the ground.

Baruti thanked her silently for the gift, took aim, and shot the man through the heart. Pain lanced his own heart at his actions, but he didn't stop. Not for a second. He pivoted and fired at the man who followed. Four more men and one woman weaved through the debris, seeking Hondo under the flapping remains of a room, no doubt worried they'd failed their leader. Five. That would be a challenge.

He could drop one, maybe two, but eventually they'd zero in on his hideout and shower it with bullets. The canvas and thatch would do little to protect him. Then he looked at Gertrude. Maybe someone would. But that would mean risking her life, and he was loath to do that when so few beauties like her still remained. It was enough that he'd committed to sacrificing two snakes, or that a stray bullet might have hit one of the elephants already.

Gertrude suddenly looked up, as if something had occurred to her, and trotted in his direction. Now, he didn't possess an animal spirit like Frank, despite the *!Kung's* having suggested that he had a lion in him. He didn't believe he had communicated his need to her in some sort of supernatural telepathy. She wasn't a pet who was drawn to protect him, either, although she'd lived side by side with humans at the lodge and wasn't afraid of them. She was still a wild animal.

But perhaps she didn't like these men. Perhaps she sensed their violence and the danger they presented to her world. So he wasn't exactly surprised when she grasped a beam from the heap beside him and slung it at them. The beam flew through the air and battered into the first four men, upending them, cracking ribs, wrenching the rifles from their hands. The fifth man jumped back and spun his weapon into firing position. He would have emptied the chamber into Gertrude, if Baruti hadn't fired before he could tap the trigger. The bastard spun backward and collapsed.

Gertrude trumpeted, as if in triumph. Then she grabbed another beam and turned toward Baruti.

Baruti met her gaze and said calmly, "Go to it, then. We've killed enough of you, invaded your territory, taken it over, created droughts and floods with our climate-changing toxins so you died in droves. But that wasn't enough. We had to slaughter you for nothing, not even food, just the resplendent ivory of your tusks so we could carve meaningless little keepsakes or sprinkle it into our soups for nonsensical superstitions. I wouldn't blame you. Just try to make it quick."

But she didn't slam the beam into him. She turned and flung it at the moaning woman who was still trying to stagger to her feet, batting her back down to the ground. Then she snorted and bopped Baruti on the shoulder.

Suddenly he remembered where he'd seen her before. It wasn't just outside the lodge. It was several miles away, when she was several sizes smaller. She was standing beside her slaughtered, tuskless mother, surrounded by lions who'd been drawn by the smell of blood. The herd had deserted her when she refused to leave her mother's side, and now she was defenseless.

It was the time Kutera had seen him, furious at the poachers and willing to risk his own life for the motherless calf.

Baruti had scattered the lions, shooting puffs of earth at their feet, making tumultuous noise. He had prodded the bellowing calf to walk through channels and across islands, as he fended off the odd crocodile, too. Eventually, he'd discovered her herd and ushered her into their midst. They'd accepted her back, but maybe she'd always been an outsider, and that's why she lingered around the lodge near people. Hating some, loving others, living a life of confusion, as many do.

But this time she wasn't confused. And she had known him instantly, even though he hadn't recognized her.

"Thanks, darlin'," he said. "I wish I could stay and chat but . . . I'm still hungry for cake, and parsimonious, big-booted aunts."

He darted around her and headed west.

Felicity was already exhausted. The monstrous snake kept rippling beneath her, stretching the fibers of the double-layered bag, gradually migrating from the cover of the hollow toward the glaring spotlight of the boardwalk. She had used every ounce of strength she had to keep it pinned.

The waiting was worse, though. Sounds and smells overwhelmed the air. *Pop, pop, pop.* The constant staccato of gunfire. Cordite biting her nostrils. The trumpeting of elephants and the smashing of beams and boards. And screams like those that were undoubtedly heard on a battlefield in a war. Screams of absolute terror, agony, and slow death.

Could she do what was required of her? Could she not only release the snake without being captured within its coils herself but, in doing so, deliberately kill another human being?

The snake flexed its muscles again, shivering against her body, communicating its misery and unrelenting desire to escape.

"Where are you, Baruti?" she wailed silently.

Her ears captured a nearby shout, and she lifted her head to peer through the gloom. Not Baruti, but *them.* Four human shapes wending their way toward her, aiming to grab the *mokoros* at the adjacent inlet and flee. Two guards trailed the quartet, continually pivoting and firing at an unseen enemy. Then a support beam came hurtling out of the shadows. It struck and upended the two men before they could react.

Felicity blinked, utterly confounded. *What just happened?* Baruti wasn't strong enough to fling beams; even all three men together, her stalwart companions, would have had trouble executing that maneuver. But she didn't have time to ponder the mystery, because Hondo, the woman, Shaun, and Professor Lugan were speeding toward her. Shaun still carried Professor Lugan in his arms as Hondo prodded him from behind with a gun. This was the best-case scenario, although it didn't match the original plan. Baruti had hoped to herd the primary culprits this way, especially if he couldn't get past their henchmen to shoot them, but hopefully after he'd separated them from their victims. With them all grouped together, it would make things more difficult for her. She had to be patient and wait for the right person to set foot on the boardwalk. She had to hope that the snake was somehow more than a symbol, that it had some significance in their story. She had to trust that it wouldn't attack her or Dr. Lugan or Shaun.

The four people approached, tramping over the boards. Hondo wrestled Shaun forward with gritted teeth and poked him deliberately with his gun, while the blonde woman kept pivoting and firing blindly behind her.

"How many, do you think?" the woman sputtered out.

"There must be dozens," the biologist mumbled. "They're getting the better of your men, Hondo."

"Dozens. Or maybe just a few," barked Hondo. "And some very clever animals. Perhaps a biologist who would rather be a spy."

"Baruti can't control the animals," scoffed Shaun. "He must have called in other spies."

"That was an elephant pitching beams at my men. It's an easy task to agitate animals and spark a stampede, but not to put the creatures through trained maneuvers and circus tricks. He has other talents, this Baruti. But he will not win this war. It's not like we are his only enemies."

"You think this is a war?" asked the woman, pausing on the boardwalk to peer into the trees. "This is a rescue mission, plain and simple. I say we just kill the professor and be done with it."

Icicles needled into Felicity's spine. She should release her bundle soon.

"She may still be useful as a hostage," snapped Hondo. "You don't kill the hostage until you are free and clear. Which you didn't really grasp when you shot her and let them escape."

Dr. Lugan moaned and begged Shaun to stop moving. He complied, gun or no gun at his back. He had been striding crisply across the boards, a resilient silhouette in the dull glow of the sinking sun, when he suddenly crouched down and set his burden on the walkway.

Not there! Felicity wanted to shout.

"What the hell do you think you're doing?" yelled Hondo. "Pick her up."

"She can't go any farther."

"So what? You can. Don't force me to . . ."

"What? Shoot me? Shoot her? If you do, your fate is sealed. If you kill her, I will kill myself, and Lucas won't finish what you started."

"Shaun!" the woman shrieked, and pointed her gun at him. "I don't have the same restraint as Hondo. If you don't keep moving, I will finish you."

The ferocity in her eyes was enough to make Felicity cringe, and the words startled her even more. But they moved the biologist to react, and quickly. He reached down and scooped Dr. Lugan up in his arms, eliciting a groan of pain.

But as he straightened, he looked down into Felicity's hollow and met her eyes as she silently struggled with the sack. When he stood, it was with exaggerated sluggishness. He turned and began walking, but stumbled only a few feet farther along, holding up his tormentors again.

Well, it was now or never.

Felicity pulled her knife from the pouch at her waist and slashed the bag open. The snake sprang free and unwound its coils. It turned toward her, even as she backed away as quickly as possible. It advanced and she raised the knife, as the terrorists, drawn by their movements, noticed her and aimed their guns at her.

One gun barked and a bullet slammed into her left arm. She choked back a scream as the pain sizzled through her, but she still kept her right arm raised. She slashed at the snake, nicking its flesh. She didn't want to injure it, just make it retreat. Then she heard a voice—a nasal, irritating, masculine voice—call out.

"This way!" he shouted. She could hear him plain as day, but there was no sign of him.

But the snake spun around as if it were a hound that had caught a sweeter scent. It wound across the grass in sinuous swirls, then ejected itself onto the boardwalk. It slithered ever so determinedly toward Hondo. The terrorist shot at it—one hit, then two—spraying blood and scaly flesh into the air. But the snake didn't retreat. It leaped at him and sank its bone-snapping jaws into his hip—a familiar location that recalled the placement of Frank's wound. Then it coiled itself around him and began to squeeze. Hondo's eyes bulged and his ribs cracked. The woman, her eyes widening in horror, pumped bullet after bullet into the snake, between little gasps of effort. But it didn't release the man. It wouldn't stop squeezing; and it wouldn't die. The woman kept shooting, until she was clicking on an empty chamber.

She stared at Shaun. He smiled so widely that his teeth gleamed in the sputtering sunlight.

But the woman wasn't finished yet. She wrenched a knife from her belt and dashed toward him—toward Dr. Lugan. She gave no thought to the petite girl who'd released the snake. The snake was the only threat in her mind.

Felicity had observed the snake attack, had not run as instructed, had edged forward rather than retreat. The moment the woman exhausted her bullets was the moment she leaped onto the boardwalk behind her. As her enemy shot forward, Felicity did too, and plunged her knife—still wet with snake blood—into the woman's exposed back. Felicity had tears in her eyes, but she pressed the knife deep into the woman's heart. And watched her collapse. And fell to her knees behind her.

That was when Baruti stepped from the shadows, toting his gun. Had he been there all along? If he had, he hadn't come forward. He hadn't prevented her from doing her duty. He hadn't guided her or supported her or removed the most difficult choice from her. As blood spurted onto her hands—hands that still gripped the knife—she knew that he'd held back deliberately. The stains would never wash clean.

"I am the man for the job," she said. And then she began to cry.

Scanning...

Located: Chapter 50

LUCAS SWUNG OVER the cavern mouth, swiftly reeling down the rope into the inky depths of the most revered ground in the solar system, maybe the entire galaxy. The beam from his flashlight reflected off shiny obsidian and the silvery speckles of molybdenum embedded in quartz and other igneous rock formations. Far below, just within the reach of his bobbing light, a view of the cave floor emerged: gouges and scoops of sepia-tinted water, the seemingly placid pools of primordial soup.

Bob had already descended, and then Gita, their rebreather tanks firmly attached to their backs, their masks providing the necessary, if diminished, requirement of oxygen. Both astronauts were dipping specimen containers into the scattered pools.

Lucas couldn't contain his exhilaration at finally getting the opportunity to explore the Vitalis Cave. Six weeks had passed since he'd injected MarsChr47 into his bloodstream. After determining that he and Bob were suffering no adverse effects except a diminished capacity to perform physical tasks, Gita had injected herself a week later. Two weeks after that, they'd retrieved the reserve oxygen and fuel tanks that Lucas had dumped several miles out along the canyon rim and returned them to their new home. Together they had set up a rudimentary camp beside their pond, using the material in the stockpile for necessities and comfort. From within the multitude of boxes they unearthed blankets, several heaters, a miniature stove and microwave oven, and even shelves that they erected as a pantry for their food supplies and water. They'd discovered a container of various rechargeable batteries, which they charged with the solar panels to provide them with power for lighting, cooking, and heating. They'd even rigged a recyclable water system, collecting mist and the water that drained into the cave, along with their own urine, so they wouldn't need to deplete their provisions too rapidly. After distilling the water for use, they adapted one of the heaters to create a hot water tank so they could even occasionally take showers.

But the most important pursuit in their new abode was the continued support and expansion of the plant-pond oxygenation system. They'd combined their own waste with decaying plants and supplementary nitrites to produce more soil to feed the spreading carpet of plants. Animalcules were already active in the process, converting nitrites to nitrogen in the air, while the plants produced oxygen and consumed the carbon dioxide from the atmosphere, reducing its toxicity to human life.

Their next step would be to introduce onto the surface the genetically modified plants that were tolerant of the extremely salty soil on Mars and capable of surviving very low oxygen concentrations. The modified blue-green algae, which was anaerobic, had begun the process of oxygenating the air, exactly as it would have done long ago on Earth. These plants would continue to produce oxygen, but at a higher concentration and an accelerated rate. The team would have to do more extensive surveying of the area to find the richest soil. Theory predicted that nitrate beds should exist in the Chryse Planitia, due to the extreme volcanism in the higher elevations, which could have fixed high concentrations in the soil, then washed and deposited them into the early oceans. If they could locate these deposits, that would be a good place to start the experiment. Also, with the blue-green algae bogs producing peat, and the addition of modified lichen breaking down the rock, they could actively create more soil. The key to the rebirth of Mars would be the diverse and resilient plants in the cave that was now their home.

But the key to the genesis of life on Earth, which began 3.7 billion years ago, was within the adjacent cave—the one they were now exploring.

Lucas touched down on the slippery surface and removed his clip from the rope. He crouched beside the nearest pool and dipped his gloved hand into the gloppy sienna substance, marveling as the liquid slid along his fingers almost as if it were a living creature already.

"Hard to believe life started here," he murmured.

"The dry compounds still exist on the walls," said Gita. "Since they're seeded with molybdenum and boron, they should have precursor molecules in different phases of development. I can't wait to see the evidence on that mass spectrometer Bob found. The hydrogen cyanide and amino acids, the primitive RNA molecules, the ribosome. And look at the walls and floor of this cave, now replete with moisture and beginning life all over again, just as life began on early Earth."

Lucas smiled. "Yes, that will be extraordinary to see," he murmured, reflecting on the origin of life (see Appendix B).

The first explorers of Mars had discovered the precursor molecules in this cave, along with all the necessary ingredients to produce primitive life. They'd even discovered RNA in various stages of development on the walls and floors of the cave, before moisture had intruded, due to the terraforming efforts. So it seemed rather certain that the panspermia hypothesis had been proven—the theory that life had originated on Mars and was transported to Earth on a meteor or asteroid that had first collided with Mars. On Earth, the conditions of abundant water fostered explosive growth, once RNA was already an intact molecule.

"Yes, essentially, we *all* started here," said Bob, looking up from where he was squatting near the cave wall to smile at Lucas. "Life begins in the tiniest packages, and these packages can be altered, as you've already shown us with this chromosome. We incorporated bacteria into our cells as mitochondria; we are linked to the most primitive creatures that exist. Now that we know this, I wish we could all trust each other and stop manufacturing feuds over a few base differences in our DNA."

"I didn't manufacture the feud," said Lucas. "Nor the paranoia. The feud began with the attempted genocide—or speciescide—of my people. And the paranoia grew from observing other feuds and genocides that were perpetrated for less pronounced variations. I know this barbaric behavior doesn't encompass all human beings. But it's present in enough of them to make a small minority nervous. It wouldn't take much to screen for our genetic differences once they are known, and label us with some symbol that will then become divisive, like a star. To erect barbed wire between us, to revert back to a world of slaves and slavers, which some people keep trying to do."

"You honestly don't believe that, do you?" said Gita with uncommon bluster, as she stood and capped her specimen container.

"I honestly believe that starvation and food riots will increase as the human population grows, and the argument will be presented that since there aren't enough resources for all the people on the planet, then certain people should be excluded from receiving provisions. Primitive people. People with more limited DNA. If those particular people are long gone, if they've taken themselves out of harm's way, then the hordes will have to choose another victim."

"But the authorities of the United Nations and the ISA will begin to move people off-planet, too," said Bob. "That's what the terraforming is all about. Do you think they will let you settle here unopposed? Do you think they'll let you annex this planet and the vital territory on it without a counteroffensive?"

"No," said Lucas. He stretched out beside the pool, removed his glove, and dangled his finger into the stew, causing Gita to protest, since he was contaminating the precious medium.

"Sorry," he said, retracting his hand. But he didn't say anything else. What point was there in terrifying and further infuriating the two people who were likely to be his lifelong companions?

"And eventually they'll learn what happened to *us*, too," said Bob. "They're not going to just assume that we've died. They'll search long and hard for us, and they might spot the rover on a satellite revolution."

Lucas looked at Bob, who had lined up six containers at the edge of a rippling pool that was unquestionably being fed by a warming underground source. He'd obviously already taken samples from several unique sites on the walls and floor of the cave before Lucas had fully descended. But something in his eyes gave

Lucas pause—an odd shifty motion that seemed to suggest calculation.

"You can't keep this a secret forever," Bob continued, still dodging Lucas's steady gaze.

Gita cleared her throat. "We're supposed to be on a vacation, guys. And in my view, this is the best vacation spot in the solar system. Let's not start bickering again."

"Are you trying to tell me something, Bob?" asked Lucas.

Bob flexed his shoulders and dipped another jar into the pool in front of him. He said nothing.

"Are you trying to tell me that you've already contacted Earth?"

Bob capped his container and still didn't reply.

"Do you think I didn't realize you were mining the cave for communications equipment? Do you think I didn't notice that you erected a satellite dish near the rim of the canyon, even though you tried to disguise it? When did you send the message? Yesterday? A week ago? It won't make any difference. They're going to be far too occupied on Earth to worry about us for a very long time. Not that they can rescue you, anyway."

"Why?" asked Bob, finally meeting his gaze. "What are your people up to, Lucas? Are they planning to bomb the ISA?"

Lucas smiled, then rummaged through his pack and removed a thermos of coffee. He slipped his mask to the top of his head, sipped at the contents, then replaced the mask. It was his turn to erect a cone of silence.

"Lucas?"

"He's just messing with us, Bob," said Gita. "With all the heightened security measures in recent years, they'd never get a bomb into the agency or onto a launch site."

"Lucas, there is nothing that could stop the ISA from acting on that message. They will investigate your people for terrorist activity. I'm sorry, but you gave me no choice. I can't allow this paranoia to endanger our plan for Mars and the people on Earth." Bob fidgeted with his container, then ripped a thermos from his own bag and began to slurp at it vigorously.

"I'm not surprised," said Lucas. "I expected it, really. You were wounded by my actions, and I was wounded by yours, and so we keep inflicting more wounds. I guess it will never end. We will have very tiresome lives until my people arrive."

"Your people aren't going to arrive," said Bob.

Lucas smiled and sipped his coffee again. What a naive man. But was he seeing correctly? Were the creases in Bob's forehead smoothing and the sparks in his eyes growing?

"It's not what your people are going to do, is it?" said Bob. "It's what they asked *you* to do."

Gita, who'd sent longing glances at her bag, obviously considering a break too, suddenly looked up, confused and wary. Bob gulped his coffee down and slammed the thermos on the slimy rim of the pool. He readjusted his mask, then stood and stomped toward Lucas. Before Lucas could scramble to his feet, Bob had grabbed him by the folds of his jumpsuit and hoisted him into the air, even though it took a tremendous toll on him.

He gasped, then yelled, "*Did you sabotage the* Phoenix*?*"

"Wh— what? Why?" asked Gita. "That would accomplish nothing. A collision will do damage locally, but it won't change anything. They have another ship in space dock. Yes, it will cost them billions, but it will merely delay the program, not end it."

"It was supposed to be an asteroid, wasn't it?" said Bob. "Our Near-Earth Asteroid towing mission. You changed the coordinates deliberately to send it on a collision course with Earth. But the potential for it to do damage is limited, since it's not very big. Even if you'd directed it at ISA headquarters they'd still survive, since their experts are scattered all over the globe. But the towing wasn't going to occur, so you reprogrammed the approach vectors of the *Phoenix*. To where, Lucas?"

Lucas gripped Bob's hands and forcibly removed them from his suit. He looked directly into the man's eyes, their masks nearly touching.

"To think I believed you for a moment when you said we were the same. Where's all the compassion now, brother? As you put it, you *warned* them. You didn't explain our predicament as much as condemn us immediately. I knew that would be your reaction. Not a compromise. Not even a suggestion that we share this planet, or you at least set aside a portion of it for us. No. A warning that we were threatening *your* program, *your* plan. Did you ever consider there are several astronauts and scientists within the ISA that are like me? So it isn't exclusively *your* program or even *your* ISA."

"Lucas, calm down," said Gita. "And release Bob before you hurt him. We can still prevent this. You can send instructions to the ISA on how to disable your tampering before it's too late. I still believe you have some decency in you. Prove me right."

"I have no intention of obeying your orders this time, Gita. But I'm not going to *hurt* Bob," Lucas snapped, easing his grip. "I've accepted that he will always stab me in the back, and I believe he's accepted the same thing about me. Because we will do what is best for our own people, first and foremost."

"What will the collision accomplish?" asked Bob, his eyes still shimmering with rage.

"Nothing," Lucas replied. "Unless the nuclear engine is reconfigured to go critical upon impact. Even so, you won't see a great deal of damage, if it's aimed at an ocean. It will kill a few hundred thousand people, maybe a million, if it's aimed at city. It will temporarily blind the ISA if it's aimed at their headquarters. Or, if it's aimed properly, it will eventually bring about the destruction of the planet."

Bob blinked. "Aimed properly? What location could possibly be so destructive?"

Lucas couldn't keep his triumphant smile contained. "The very thing that's creating a viable planet here," he replied. "A bog."

Scanning...

Located: Chapter 51

FELICITY LET HER eyes drift away from the exhausted group assembled around the conference table. She shifted on the rigid pine chair, eliciting a sharp pain in her arm again. While attempting to remain inconspicuous, she looked down at the mottled flesh and the compressed scar in her mid-forearm. Another to add to the one in her leg and the many in her heart. Every time she recalled the bullet slicing through her, she broke out into a sweat, and then the other memories would pile on. The snake slithering toward her, her stabbing defense, the snake's sudden reversal at the sound of Frank's voice, the attack of an alternative victim, and her final action, a brutal slaying that echoed again and again in her mind.

Frank still denied that he had called out at that vital turning point. Maybe he had done so subconsciously, or maybe he consciously denied it because calling to a snake would be illogical. Maybe there really was something mystical about Frank and snakes after all.

Felicity looked up, beyond the buffed gleam of the mahogany conference table. She looked behind Frank and Pedro, who sat across from her and seemed uncomfortable, as if they were still hearing gunfire. Through long panes of sparkling windows, tall forested mountains jutted from the land, and quaint chalets balanced precariously on the narrow plateaus that peppered the mountains. If she turned her head slightly to the right, she could see a pearly waterfall spraying mist behind Shaun and Dr. Lugan.

Dr. Lugan still carried the deepest aftereffects of the terrorists' attack on her. Her skin appeared wan; her frame was thin and fragile, although apparently her wound was healing well. Her shoulder sported bulky bandages, and her arm was supported in a sling. She sometimes experienced sudden bouts of nausea, and Felicity had discovered her vomiting in the ISA restroom fairly frequently since their arrival. Sometimes she wondered if it was more than just illness, since Shaun had insisted on sharing a room with her when they'd moved into the Swiss village after Dr. Lugan had spent some time in the hospital. He'd obviously shared more than a room before the attack, too. But if everything they'd revealed about Shaun's species was true, what she was thinking was impossible, wasn't it?

She peered at Baruti. Or maybe it wasn't.

Baruti must have noticed her furtive glance. He reached clandestinely under the table and captured her hand. He was perched in his usual spot on the long wooden table, nestled as close to her as he dared. They weren't sharing a room yet, even though she'd offered him many invitations. His excuses were several. She required more time to heal. She should consider how deeply she was willing to go in this relationship, since he wasn't one for casual hookups. There was every possibility that he would eventually contract severe mental illness at some point in his life, like his mother. Would she be able to endure that? And the most decisive argument: He was a hybrid of the two species. He had no idea what that would mean in terms of children, should their relationship extend that far.

Felicity didn't care about any of these considerations. She loved him. It was real, undeniable, and not only sexual. He was the most ruthlessly caring person she'd ever met. Even an elephant couldn't help but agree. It was a contradiction, of course. He'd allowed her to kill, even though he knew it was the most painful thing a person with any conscience could endure. He'd pushed her to be strong, even though he knew it would weaken her with time, since she could never forget. He didn't spare her as others tried to because of her physical limitations.

He was not her rock; he was her partner.

He smiled at her now, a weary tug at his lips revealing a shadow of his own suffering.

And the grilling continued. A shuffling of ideas, reliving the nightmare, as if it would somehow bring the real plot into the light.

Six weeks had passed since they'd rescued Dr. Lugan and Shaun, three weeks since they'd arrived in Switzerland to be debriefed by various members of the ISA. They were required to keep rehashing their experience and discoveries, but it seemed to produce very little illuminating data. Two days ago, another man had whisked in and begun the process all over again, questioning them on matters they'd already discussed ad infinitum.

James Gerard of the World Environmental Protection Agency was stout and portly. He wore a tweed jacket that looked decades out of date. A scruffy salt-and-pepper beard sprang from his chin, perhaps a failed attempt to disguise a series of puckered scars. And he had a sweeping forehead that stayed constantly smooth as if he needn't ponder anything; he just knew. Baruti seemed familiar with him and called him "the cavalry" behind his back. Even Dr. Lugan seemed to recognize him and mistakenly called him Mr. Bond once.

"So," he said, placing his elbows on the table and clasping his hands. "The massacre in Botswana was merely to cover their tracks. Seems like overkill, but I guess they were extremely afraid of eager archaeology students like you, Frank."

Frank gritted his teeth and gave a brisk nod.

"And killing archaeology students would set off louder alarm bells. This action, they thought, could be attributed to poachers."

"I suppose," said Baruti, his grip tightening on Felicity's hand. "I found the *!Kung's* cache of skulls in the Tsodilo Hills. But that's old news since we discovered the bodies in the North. We've run additional tests and, as suspected, they are ancient and belong to this particular species. PBPP, for lack of a better name." When Gerard raised his eyebrows, Baruti added, "Polar Bear Provincial Park, where they were first discovered. Like the *Denisova hominins*, which was named for the cave in Siberia where they were cached. I'm sure Shaun would prefer something more precise or exotic."

"I really don't care about classifications," said Shaun. "I'm human, just like you. Why don't you start by calling the people involved in this plot by their name, the Gilgamesh Movement?"

"Gilgamesh," said Gerard thoughtfully. "As in the epic poem from Mesopotamia? You never mentioned this before. Why not?"

"Because," said Shaun, "everyone was explaining this in terms of species. But I'm getting tired of being grouped in with murderers, and Lucas mentioned that name once."

"Interesting," said Gerard, stroking his beard. "Not an annexation movement or an exodus movement, which they might label the Octavian or Moses Movement. Gilgamesh. An epic poem that might be considered the originatory piece of great-flood mythology."

Dr. Lugan massaged her shoulder and then began fidgeting with the buttons on her blouse. But she spoke up, since who was better qualified to explain?

"The poem—or poems—is actually an assortment of stories etched onto tablets that tell of Gilgamesh's exploits, including disobeying and angering the gods, which results in his best friend's death. Fearing his own death, he searches far and wide for a window into eternal life, which is where we're introduced to Utnapishtim, the equivalent of Noah in the Biblical great-flood story, and one of the few humans who survived and was granted immortality. Utnapishtim recounts a story that is very similar to the account in the Bible, and explains that eternal life was a gift uniquely granted and suggests that Gilgamesh should stop wasting his life seeking for something he cannot hope to receive. But yes, the flood myth may be significant. Baruti thinks these people have some type of global destruction in mind. And they are keeping an ark of Earth's arctic species in Northern Ontario, or at least their genetic equivalent. These people seem to have gifted geneticists in their ranks. Perhaps they are thinking beyond progeny and are tinkering with an immortality gene, or a code that can extend the life of cells, too."

"Hmm," said Pedro. Felicity eyed him carefully, now fully attuned to what he might say. In the beginning, she hadn't bestowed the respect on him that he deserved because he wasn't university-educated. But after their rescue of Dr. Lugan, the success of which had depended on his plan, she often felt like hugging him. And she had done it once while they were waiting for transportation to the hospital, much to his shock. "You deserve all the cake in the world," she'd said. He'd returned the hug without a word, but there were tears in his eyes.

"Ya can't live forever if somebody shoots ya," Pedro continued. "If you've pulled off the biggest heist in the world, knocked off the Louvre and the Crown Jewels, you will have all the cops chasin' you to the ends of the Earth. Or in this case, the solar system. And you'd have to steal a spaceship, or two or three or ten, to get all your folks off the planet. The only way to escape would be to kill all the cops."

"Or to kill everyone," said Frank. "Like in a global flood. A series of well-placed nuclear bombs would bring about an apocalyptic result. World organizations, governments, leaders in countries that are the most important bread baskets. It would create chaos and interrupt food production."

"But what does Lucas have to do with that?" asked Dr. Lugan, twisting a button back and forth. "Your brother, Shaun? He had an important mission. One they wouldn't do anything to jeopardize, even refraining from killing you."

"Whatever his mission was, it's probably moot," said Gerard. "He and his crew never returned on the *Phoenix*. He instructed the ISA to remote-pilot the *Phoenix* back to Earth."

"What *was* his mission?" asked Baruti.

"A comet release on Mars, then an asteroid tow to our moon station," said Gerard. "Nothing that would present too much of a danger to us, although we knew of several unsanctioned excursions to the planet before his mission. I sent," he grimaced, "a good man to investigate him, which is why they landed on the planet. Everything seemed to go wrong once they landed, but nothing that I could attribute to a terrorist action until I received communications from Mars this morning."

Everyone looked startled, and Shaun leaned forward.

"Not from Lucas," he quickly explained. "From my man, Bob Jolson. Apparently, he discovered a stockpile of supplies and even a genetic cryogenic zoo, which wasn't a surprise, considering their objective is to settle there. But what is surprising . . ." He went on to explain how Lucas had assaulted Bob and injected him with an artificial adaptive chromosome. "Unfortunately, none of the astronauts can ever leave the planet now, including Lucas," he said. "So if he had a destructive mission, he can no longer fulfill it."

"At least they're not dead," Shaun murmured. "At least he didn't kill them. I don't think I could stomach it if Lucas had done what the others have."

Felicity shivered. She could still feel the blood pouring off her hands. She had done what Lucas had not. To think she'd been reluctant to handle bog bodies just a few months ago. It felt like years since that first baptism in a seemingly distasteful job, and swimming in a stew of body parts seemed like a heavenly experience now. She no longer had any desire to be Minerva, goddess of war. But could she still tap into the goddess's wisdom?

She'd extracted the body of a young girl from that bog—the first clue. Had Donna been killed because she'd stumbled into the bog and discovered the bodies, as Shaun and Dr. Lugan had disclosed after their conversation with Hondo and Reena? But why leave them there, then? Why not cremate them, as they'd done with the other remains? Maybe . . . they didn't think it was necessary.

"Polar Bear Provincial Park," she said suddenly, interrupting Gerard's questioning.

"Yes?" he said, raising his eyebrows.

She turned to Baruti. "They were mining, right? What were they mining, again?"

"Energy," said Baruti, creases developing in his forehead. "Geothermal energy, although it was probably just to cover up their search for cold-weather species. But it was a legitimate rig."

"They were drilling there because of a possible mantle plume," said Shaun. "Tony mentioned it over and over again in his delirium. But I couldn't understand the significance."

"What would happen if that mantle plume ruptured?" asked Felicity.

Both Shaun and Baruti stiffened and met each other's eyes. "Potentially . . . massive volcanic eruptions." said Shaun. "And earthquakes."

"Couldn't an asteroid do that?" asked Felicity. "Say one that was supposed to be towed to the moon but veered off course and collided with the Earth in that plume region? Wouldn't it incinerate a certain bog where they didn't bother to remove bodies?"

"Would it have global consequences?" asked Dayna, her voice quavery and high-pitched.

"Well, possibly," said Shaun. "Ash clouds could blanket the Earth, and locally it would be disastrous. But we've had eruptions for years all over the planet. It wouldn't be that consequential."

"Or would it, in a bog in the Canadian northland?" asked Baruti. "In a land of permafrost and methane? Wouldn't it release clouds of methane into the air? Wouldn't it set off a runaway greenhouse effect, something we're desperately trying to achieve on Mars but are desperately trying to contain on Earth? That would have global consequences. Weather anomalies. Hurricanes, massive floods, droughts. An even greater rise in sea level. And a mantle plume eruption could affect the mantle convection in the planet too, triggering more earthquakes and volcanic eruptions. It would keep us extremely busy, and it could kill hundreds of thousands, or even millions, depending on how it affects our food supply. If food production and the availability of safe water were disrupted, we could have mass starvation and rampant disease."

"Yes," said Gerard. "I think you're on to something. But they failed when Lucas didn't leave the planet."

"Didn't leave," said Shaun, sifting the words through his lips.

"What are you thinking?" asked Baruti.

Shaun looked directly at Gerard. "*Couldn't* leave or *didn't* leave?"

Gerard frowned and flicked on his tablet. He tapped a message and scanned it quickly. Once he found the determinative paragraph, he looked up and met the biologist's gaze.

"Didn't," he said. "He had the opportunity, but he chose to turn back and deliberately stayed behind with Bob. He chose to join him on the planet and continue the terraforming experiments. He could have potentially returned to the MADVEC; he had a rover, oxygen, and rocket fuel. He didn't do it."

Shaun gripped the table and took several deep, chest-expanding breaths.

"That's a good thing, isn't it?" asked Dr. Lugan, touching his arm. The intimacy seemed odd to Felicity, but Shaun's behavior unnerved her the most. He grated his teeth back and forth, as if he would grind them to dust.

"My brother isn't an evil man, but he is a driven one. He blames you," he spread his arms around the table, "for the death of our father. It was a horrible scene of mob mentality—a Black Friday event—and our father was trampled when all he wanted was to obtain a toy for his son. Lucas witnessed my father's death when he was a boy, and it has left him horribly scarred. He believed all the rhetoric the people in the Movement spouted, the propaganda they spread among our people. He believed there was hope for us elsewhere, on a new planet—a place where random acts of violence and futility wouldn't occur—as if we would be immune from them there, or as if we are without flaws ourselves. I would like to hope that he would abandon his mission and decide to make amends to this Bob Jolson, a man he has personally harmed. I would like to hope this."

"But you don't believe it," said Gerard.

Shaun shook his head.

"But the tow mission was scrapped, without the astronauts to direct it. He couldn't deliver an asteroid to Earth," said Frank.

Then Felicity remembered Gerard's words. "Remote-pilot the *Phoenix* to Earth."

"Would a nuclear-powered spacecraft with a VASIMR rocket engine have the same impact as an asteroid?"

The entire room grew silent, like the calm in the eye of a storm.

Gerard cleared his throat. "No. It doesn't have enough mass. It would only be dangerous if the nuclear engine is reconfigured so that it goes critical upon impact. But we have safeguards against that."

Dr. Lugan glanced at Shaun, her brow suddenly creased with furrows. "Would Lucas have the ability to remove those safeguards?" she asked, turning back to Gerard.

Gerard paused for two seconds, then grabbed his tablet and pulled up a number. He chatted urgently with an administrator at ISA Mission Control. He listened to their response. He talked some more. Eventually he was handed over to the Flight Director. What Felicity could gather from the conversation was that the *Phoenix* was on approach, but it wasn't decelerating at the moon station. At its current heading, it would crash to Earth at a remote location in Northern Ontario.

"On the thin crust above a mantle plume," she whispered.

Baruti squeezed her hand and closed his eyes. She could hear his breathing scatter, as if he couldn't find a rhythm anymore.

"Can't you redirect?" bellowed Gerard.

"Normally, yes," said the Flight Director. "But the computer is not responding to our commands. I think we've been locked out of final approach. I don't understand it. That would only be possible if communications were not operational or had been jammed."

Gerard switched on the screen in the corner of the room and linked it with an ISA satellite view of the approaching spacecraft. It loomed ever larger as it swept into camera range, a massive silver and white object with several rotating modules and an enormous cylinder projecting from the rear. According to the ISA broadcast, it was perfectly angled to penetrate the atmosphere and not skip off into space. As it entered the atmosphere, some sections burned and peeled off like the layers of birch bark that curl and flake away after being ignited. But the rocket-powered engine, within its magnetic shielding, remained intact. That was until it plunged the final mile to Earth and crashed into a mining camp beside a granite bulwark. The explosion pulverized the spongy earth, decimated the bog, melted every frosted acre of land within a twenty-mile radius. Soil and rock spouted into the air, and a view of a gigantic fireball consumed the screen.

But that was only the first explosion. . . .

"We're dead," said Frank. "We're all dead." He sprang to his feet and kicked the table. He kicked and kicked and kicked, eventually splintering the wood. "It's all meaningless. Everything I've ever done, good and bad. This!" He grabbed something out of his pack and slammed it on the table. "This is meaningless!"

Felicity stared without blinking, although at first the object appeared blurred. Gradually her vision cleared and she could discern a bubble-wrapped envelope. She reached across the table and retrieved it, sliding it gently toward her. With fumbling fingers, she tore open the sealed package and unwrapped the carefully cushioned item within. Awash in the flickering light of the explosions and the erupting lava from the screen was a copper scroll. As she carefully unrolled it, elegant etchings that were undoubtedly Aramaic writings were revealed on the ancient metal. She fingered it delicately, tears filming her eyes.

"No, Frank," she said. "It's not meaningless. I know you were thinking of the treasure it might point to, but it is a treasure in and of itself. It's us and you, too," she said to Shaun. "It's our journey. And it isn't over yet. We're going to bury several more of these along the way. And even if our world does come to an end, it should end in an act of kindness and not one of rage and division."

She reached across the table, took Shaun's hand, and placed it gently on the scroll. Then she raised the hand still clutched in her own, the hand of the hybrid who shouldn't even exist, and tenderly laid it on the other end. And one by one, she encouraged everyone in the room to lay claim to the treasure—a symbol of their history, their bitter-sweet existence, the first living molecules that danced in a cave on a faraway planet.

And she said the words they all were loath to say.

"Lucas, I forgive you."

Author's Note

This book involved several years of painstaking research from conception to completion. I wanted to create a novel as intriguing as *Ice Tomb*, but, of course, with more depth than that of a first novel.

The initial inspiration was a bog body that I encountered on a visit to the Canadian Museum of History. It was a traveling exhibit that displayed various bog bodies from Europe, including the Yde girl, a child I will never forget. The exhibit showed her exactly as she was when discovered in Holland, then reproduced the stages of remodeling that determined something like her original appearance. With each successive layer applied to her face, you could see the corpse developing into a real person with a real story. This gruesome but fascinating display has haunted me to this day. For more information, see my blog: A Haunting – The Inspiration for The Furies' Bog.

As the idea grew, so did my realization that this book would require an inordinate amount of research. I began reading genetic studies in the *Annual Review of Genomics and Human Genetics*. As I struggled to understand the material, it became clear that I would have to go back to school. My degree in science was twenty years out of date. So I found some online courses in biology at MIT and set aside five months to study, attend lectures, and increase my knowledge so I could examine genes at the National Center for Biotechnology Information, read and interpret publications on genetics, and develop my own study. I also found it fascinating to use the online resources to examine proteins and enzymes at the molecular level.

I began this novel with the study itself—Human Artificial Chromosome MarsChr47. I decided to incorporate an entire gene sequence, so readers would understand the incredible length of one gene alone. We have 23 pairs of chromosomes—46 in total—approximately 20,000 to 25,000 genes, a count that constantly fluctuates as science advances, and about 3,000,000,000 base pairs—the As, Ts, Cs, and Gs mentioned in the book. I wanted to emphasize how a small mutation in this entire length could alter the function, or trigger the dysfunction, of a protein and upset the balance in our bodies, or even entirely alter the way our bodies work. These mutations can lead to cancer or other diseases, or set us on a new evolutionary path.

The study of genetics was only the beginning. Since this book involved Mars as much as it did Earth, I needed to understand the environment on Mars. That meant poring over books on Mars geology and atmosphere, and investigating the rover missions online. I spent many a day hunched over a tremendous tome called *This is Mars*, a book of images taken by the *Mars Global Surveyor*, *Mars Pathfinder*, and *Mars Express* and transmitted back to Earth. I also examined terraforming theories and spacecraft designs. It was challenging to study this planet, but rewarding as well, since we are step by step preparing to send humans to this beacon of exploration. But the greatest challenge will be to adapt to the environment, alter the environment to adapt to our needs, or change our own genetic makeup to suit the environment. Perhaps we will have to do all three.

Of course, the research didn't end there. I also studied archaeology and new scientific methods in this field. I had to understand theories of evolution and migration patterns. And mythology is always close to my heart. I explored the *!Kung* culture, their traditions, and myths, and I hope my portrayal of them shows my respect and affection for their culture.

As a fiction writer, I took several liberties, but tried to hold true to science as closely as possible while at the same time standing by my vision. As you can tell, the story isn't finished. But neither is our endless quest for understanding our own path in evolution—without dismissing others', I hope—and our continuing need for exploration.

I hope you enjoyed the story. And I hope it will inspire you to look further, to investigate all the marvels of genetics, archaeology, and interplanetary exploration.

Appendix A

Below is the entire DNA sequence of the LIPE gene, including introns that are sequences for micro-RNAs and other non–gene-coding portions.

LIPE Gene

Rectangles indicate exons (gene-coding). Introns are represented by the intervening lines. Numbers indicate the full complement of base pairs in each exon. Arrows denote the direction of the reading frame.

Primary Assembly

First bold text = promoter sequence

Alternating italics and bold = exons: coding for gene

Underlined within exons, with alternate base substitution noted at end of gene sequence = single nucleotide polymorphism: mutation

No alterations = introns: noncoding for gene

CTTCTT GTAAGA GAGTGC TAGGCA CATAGC CTCCTC CTATTC CTAATC CTCCCA
CCAAAG AAAGAG GCACAG AGTTCA TTACTT AGTGGG GGCCAG CTGTGA TCGGCC
AACTGC CAGCTG CCTTAA AAAGGA AGACCA GTGATG CTAGGA TGGAGT GAAACC
CAAGAG GAAGTG CCATCA TGAGGA ATCAAT GAGAGA TCTGTG AAGAGA GAGGGC
TGGGTG GGAGCC CAGAAG GATAGA ACCTGG AAGATC AATATC TCCCGT GAGGGA

AATAAC AATG*GA GCCAGG TTCTAA GTCAGT.GTCTAG GTCAGA CTGGCA ACCTGA ACCACA*
CCAGAG GCCTAT AACCCC GCTAGA GCCTGG GCCAGA AAAGAC ACCCAT AGCCCA GCCAGA
ATCGAA GACTCT GCAGGG ATCCAA TACCCA ACAGAA GCCTGC TTCAAA CCAAAG ACCCCT
CACCCA GCAGGA GACCCC TGCACA ACATGA TGCTGA ATCCCA GAAGGA ACCTAG AGCCCA
ACAAAA ATCTGC TTCACA AGAGGA ATTTCT TGCCCC ACAGAA GCCCGC ACCACA GCAATC
*A*__CCTTA C__*ATCCA AAGGGT GCTGCT CACTCA ACAGGA AGCTGC CTCCCA GCAGGG ACCTGG*
GCTAGG AAAAGA ATCTAT AACTCA ACAGGA GCCAGC ATTGAG ACAAAG ACATGT AGCCCA
GCCAGG GCCTGGG CCAGGA GAGCCA CCTCCA GCTCAA CAAGAA GCTGAA TCAACA CCTGCG
GCCCAG GCTAAA CCTGGA GCCAAA AGGGAG CCATCT GCCCCG ACTGAA TCTACG TCCCAA
GAGACA CCTGAA CAGTCA GACAAG CAAACA ACGCCA GTCCAG GGAGCC AAATCC AAGCAG
GGATCT TTGACA GAGCTG GGATTT CTAACA AAACTT CAGGAA CTATCC ATACAG CGATCA
GCCCTA GAGTGG AAGGCA CTTTCT GAGTGG GTCACA GATTCT GAGTCA GAATCA GATGTG
GGATCA TCTTCA GACACA GATTCT CCAGCC ACGATG GGTGGA ATGGTG GCCCAG GGAGTG
AAGCTA GGCTTC AAAGGA AAATCT GGTTAT AAAGTG ATGTCA GGATAC AGTGGG ACGTCG
*CCACAT GAGAAA ACCAGT GCTCGG AATCAC AGACAC TACCAG GATACA G*GTGAG TGTGAA
TCTGGA GGAATT GAAGCC TCTCAG GGACAG TCATTC ATTTAC TTAAAA AATACT AAAAAC
TTACGG TGTATC AGGTTA GCTCTG GTCATC CTTCAA CAATCC TGAGAT AAAGAT CAACAT
CCCCAT TATTAA AAAAAA AAAAAA AAAAAA AAAAGG CTGGGC GCAGTG GCTCAC ACCTGT
AATCCC AGCACT TTGGGA GGCCGA GGCAGA TGGATT GCTTGA GGCCAG GAGTTC AAGACC
AGCCTA GCCAAG ATGGTG AAACAC CGTCTC TACTAA AAATAC AAAAAT TAGCCA GGCGTG
GTGGCA GGTGCC TGTAAT CCCAGC TACTCG GGAGGC TGAGGC AGAGAA ACACTT GAACCC
GGGAGG CAAAGG TTGCAA TGAGCT GAGATC GTGCCA CTGCAC TCCAGC CTGGGT
GACAGA GTAAGA CTCCAT CTCAAA AAAAGA AAAAAA CAAAGT CTCACT CTGTCG CCCAGG
CTGGGG TGCACT GGTATG ATCATG GCTCAC TGCAGC CTCAAA CTCCTG GGCTCA AGCGAT
CCTCAT ACCTCA GCCTCC GGAGTA GGTGGG ACTACA AGTGCA CCACCA TGCCCC GCTAAT
TTTTAC ATTTTC CGTAGA GACGTG GCCTCG CTATGT TGCCCA GGCTGG TCTCGA ACTCCT
GGCCCC AAGCAA GCCTCC CACCTC AGCTTC CCAAAG TGCTGA GATTAC AGGCAT GAGCCA
CCGAGC ACCTGG CCAACA TCCTCA TTTTAG AAATGA GGACAT CAGGTA GAAAAT AAAGAA
GTAAGG GTTCTT GCACAG GGCCAT GCAGTT AGGAAG TGGCAA AGTCAG GATTTG AAGCCG
GGGTCT TTCTCC CCTGGA CCAGGC TGCCTC CCTATA GAGGAT TTGGGG AAAATC AAATCC
CAGAGT GGGAAG GCACTC TGAGCT AGGGAC CAGGAG ACCAGG AAAGCG GCCCTC
TTGCCA GTGTTC ATTCAT CCATCC ACAGAA ACTGAC TGAGCA CCAGCT CTGGGG TAGACA
CGGGCG TAAGTC CCAGCA ATACAA TACAAA GACGGT ACCTTA CCCTTC TGGAGT TTCCAG

GCAGGC TAGGCA GAACAT TGGGGC ATCAAC AGTCTC TCAGTT TACCAG GTCTGT CCTCTT
CTGCCA GGAAGA TACCTG CTCCCT GCCAGG CTGCCT CCATAG GGGACT CAGTCC AGCCAG
GCGGAA GGGCCT TGCGGG TTGTGT TCTCAG CAAGGA GGAGCC GGGAGA GAGGTG
CGGGAG CCGCCA AGGTCT CAGGCA AGGTCA GGGACT GACGGC AGGAAA GTTGGG
GGAGCA GCATCA GAGGAT AACGGG CCCAAG GCTCTG GGCTCA CCGCAG GCACTC CCTCGC
CTTCTC CGCCTC TTCCCG GGGCCC AGTGCT GCCCCC TGCCTG CTTCAC AGGAGC CCCAGG
AAGCTC CGATCT TCCTTC TCTAGG CTCAAA ACCCCT GCCATG GAGAAG GGGGGA ATACAA
GTTTTA TCTATG GAACTG GAGGTT ACTTGT TGAAGT CCCCTG ATGTGG GGGGAA AAACCA
ACGCAG CCCTAA TCCTGA AGCTGA GGGTAT CTGTGA GGCCCT GGTCCA GAGGGC AGGCAA
TGGCGG CCCCTC CGCCCA GAGGCC AGTCTG TCTTGT CTCTCC CACAGC TGATAA GAGAGT
AACGCG TTTCTC AGCGCC GGGGCT GCTGGG TATGCT TTGAGA GGGAAG GAAGAG
GGGCGG CAGGCA AAGGCA GGGATT GAGGCC TGCTCT CCCCAG TGCTGA GGATAG AAAGCT
GTTTCT CCAGGC CTCCAG AGCACA GTCTCA AGGGAT GCCCGC CCCACA CCACCG CGGCGG
GCGAGG TTGCCT TTCAGG CGGTCC AGAAGC AGTTGG CTGTGT GCGTGT GAGCAA GGCGGT
CCAGAA GCAGTT GGCTGT GTGCGT GTGAGC AAGCCT CGAGCC TCCTCT GTTTCC CGCCAT
TTCTCA AGCATG CGTCGT TCCCTC TACCTC CGCTCT TGGGCC GGCCCG CGGCCT GAAGCT
AGTGCG CAGGCG CCGAGC GTTCTC CTACCA CCATCC CCCACC CTCATT ATCGGG AGCATG
GATTAG GGGGCG GAGACA GAGGGA GAAAGA TCCCCC AGGAAA AGCGCA ATAGGA
GAACTA GGAGAC AGGAGA GGGAAA GCGGGG CTCCCT CCTCCA ACGGCT CTCAGG
CACAGC CACGCC TCCAGC GCTGGC GCCCCG CCTCGT CTTTGA GTTGGC AGAGGA CCTGGC
CCGCCC CCACCC CAGGCA GAGGCT CAGAGG CGCCCC ACTTTC CCCCTT CAAAAG GCGGGC
CGGGCC GCGTGC TAGGGC ATCCCT CCCTGG GAAGGT GAGTGG GATGGC GAGACT GAGCCA
GCACAT GGGAGG CTTCCC AGCACG TGGGAA GATCGG GACTTC CCTGCT GGGGTG CTCCCC
GCGGGG CTCCGC ACTAGT CCTGCC CGAAGG ACGCTT TTCGCC ACCCCC GGGGTT GCCTTT
TTGTTG GCCGCG AGCCCT TTAATG CGCGGT AGGGGG CGGAGC CAGATC TTAAAT TCTGGC
GGTTGG GGGCGG AGCACG GCAGCG GAGGGA GACCAG AATTGG TTAGGG AGCTGG
ACCCAG AGAAGA GCAAGC TCGGGA TTGGGT AATAGG GGGGCC CGACAG TAGTGT
GTAGCG AGGATT GGCCCT CCGGGC AGGGCC TCGCGG CTGGAA TTGGCC CCCGCG GGAGGA
CCGCGG GGAATT GATGGA GTTGGC CGGGGG AACGGA GCCCGC CGAGGC CGCTAT GGCCCC
GGCCTC GAAGAA TGCCAA AGAGGG CTCAAG GAGCCA CGGTCG CCGGCG GTGGCG
AAAAGA CAAGGC CAAAGG TGAGCG CGCGGA GACCGG CAGCAG CCCGGA AGGAAC
CTCGTA CATCCTA CGGGGC AGTGGG GACAGC GTGGAC TGGCCC ACTGCC ACAGGG
AGTTGG GGGGGT CCGCGG ACTGGC CCATTG CCGCTT GCGGGG ACAACG GGATGA TCCATT

GTGAGA AGGGGG TGATGT GACAGC CGAGAG GCCCAC CCTGGC ACAGGG ACTAGC
TGACGC CCGGAT CGGCTT GGGAGC AGAGTC CGGAAT GCGAGC TTCGTG GACCAG GGTTCC
CGCTCG GATTCC GTATTC GCTGTG TGACCA AGGGCA ACGGAT GCCCTC AGTGTT TCCCAC
CTGGGG AATGCT TCAAGC GCCGAT GTTCAG GGCTCC AGCGCT CTTGAG AGGATA AGGGGG
AAGGAG GTTAGC AGGTGT TACTCA AAGAG GAAGTC TAGCGG TGAGTC AAGGAG AGGTAG
GAGGAA GGGGTG CCCATA GTGGAG AGTGCA GCGGGG CCAGTA AAGTTC ATCGCA GTCCCG
GCCTCC CACCCG GCAAGT CAGTCC ATCCAT CCATCC ATTCAT TGTCAG TCAACC CGCTTC
AGCCGG CTCCAC TGGGGC CTAGCC CTGACC CCTACC CTTTCC AGGACA ACGGGC CCTGGC
TTGGCT TCAGAC CTCCAC ACCTGC CTCAGC AAAAGG GAAGGC CTCATT TCTCTA GGGTGT
CACATT ATTTTCA GGTCTC AAAAGG CGGAAC AAAGGC TGACAG ACCAAC AGAAAT
GCTGCA AGCCTC AGGCAG GGGCAG GTCCTC AGTTAC AAGCAT TTATCA ATCAGC ATGGGG
ACCCGT GGGAGG TTCCCA TGCAGG AAGGAA ACTAAC ACCACC CCTCAG CCCCAG GGACCC
CAAACT CATTGC TTCCCC TGCCGT AGAACA CATCAT TAGCCC AGAATA GACCTG GAGTTG
GCTTCA GACACA CGCAGG CTCAGA CAGGCT CAGAGG GCAGAC GGACTG GAGCCC
AAGGGC ACTCGC TGTCAC AGCAAG ACACTG AGCCTC ACACCA GTATAG CATACC CAGAGG
CAGTAC AGACTG TAGTTA AGAAAC GTGGGC GTCGGA GATCCG GTTCCT CAGGCT GGGAGC
TGTGAT GTTCTG GGCAGG AGACTC CCTCTT TCCCTG CCTCAG CTTTCT GAGCTC TAAAAT
GGGTAT GATGAT AGGAGT ACCTCC TTTTGT GAGGTT AGAATG AATGTA GAGCGT TTGGCA
CAGGCA CGCAGC AAACCC TCAGGA GAAGTG AAGGTT ATTGT TACTGT TAGTCC CCACCG
GACGGT GAACAT CCTAAA AGCAGG GCTGTA TCTGCC TTGTTT ACCCTG TATTTC TAGAGC
CTGGTA TGCCAG GCAAAT AGGCAC TCAAAT ATTTAT TGGATT AATAAG TGAAGG AATGTG
TGAACT GTAACA GAGATC ATAATA ATCACG CTTCCC TTAGGG TTGTCA TGAGGA GTCAGA
ATCCAG TTGGGC AGGGCT CCCTGC AAAACG AGCCAT TCACAA AGGCTC ATTCCT GCAAAC
TCCAAG ATTTGC CTGTCA TTTCCT GAAGCC CCGCCC TCGTGC CAGGCT TTAGAT AAATTA
ATCAGA CCTCAC TCCTGC CTCAAG GGCATC TGGGCT GGCTGG AGCAAT CCTCGT CATCAG
TTTCATC TTGCCA GTAACT GGATGA GGCTAG TGTCCT TAGGAT CACCCC ATTTCC CAGATG
ACGACA CTGGGG CTCTGA GGGACC AAGGCC GCCTGG GCTTCC TTACTT GGCCAG TGAGGG
CAAAGA GATGGC TGCCTC AGCCTC CTCGGG GCAGGG AGTTTG TGGACG CACAAC TGCTGT
GGGCCC AAACTT GATTCT GGGCCC AAGAGG TTCCAG TCACAC AGATTC ATTCAG CAGACA
TTCACT GAACAC TGAGCT GTGCCA GGCCTG GGCTGA CAGATT CACAGT TGAGCT GGGGAC
ACAGAT ATTACT CAGATA AGACTA TGATTG TAAACT GTGATA AATACA ACAGAG AAAAAC
ACCCTG GGAAGA TAGAAT TGAGAG GCTTCC CAAGGA GGCAAT ATTGGA CCCAAG ATGGAC
AGGCGT TAAGTG CTGTGC AGGGGG CAGGCA GGGGAA CAGAGA GGACAG TATGGA

GAAAGA CCCGAG GCTTGA GGAAAC ACTGAG TTACAG TGCAGA GGGAGC TCAGCC
AGGGCC AGGAGG AAGAGG AAGAGG AAACAG GGCAGG CAGTTT AAGAGA GGAGGA
TGGTAG CTGGGT ACAGCG GCTCAC ACCTGT AATCCT GGCACT TTGGGA GGCCAA GGTGGG
AGGACC CCTTGA GTCCAG GAGTTT GAGGCC AGCGTG GGCAAC ATAGCG AGACCC CGTCTC
TACCAA AAACAC AAACAT TAGCCG GGCATG GTGGGG TGTACC TGTAGT CCCAGC TACTTG
GGAGGC TGAGGT GGGAGG ATCAAT TGAGCC CAGGAG GTTGAG GCTGCA GTGAGC TGTGAT
CGCACC ACTCTA CTCCAG CCTGGG CAACAA TGAGAC TTTGTC TCAAAA AGAGAG AGAGAG
AGGAGG ATGGTA CCTGGC TTGGGA GGCCAT GTGCAG GATTGG GGGCTT TATCCT GAAAGC
AAGGGA GGGGGT GTTGAA GGGTTG GAAGTG TGTGAA CAGATT TGTGTG CTAAAA AGATCC
TGTGGC TGCTAT GTGGAC AACAAA TCAAAG AGAACA AAATCA GAAATA TATAAA GATCTG
TCATAG TCACCC AGGTAA TGATGC TACCGC CTGGAC CAGGGA GGAGGC AGTGGA GGTGGG
GAGAAG GGCCAG GTTCCA GAGGCC TTTAGT AGGCAT AGTGGG CAGGAC TAGGGG ATGGAT
TGCATG GGAGTT GGGGGG TGGGGA GGTGGC CAGGAT GACATC CTGGGT TCCAGC TTGAGC
AAATGG GGAGAG GTTTGT TCTCAA CACACA CACAGA GACCAA GACACG CACAAG CATGTA
TATCCA TTCATA CATAAA CAAACA CGCCCA CACAAG CTCACA GGCCAA GAGAAA CAGAGA
CACAGA TACATT CACAGG CATACA AACATT CATACC TTCAAA TGTACC AGTGCC GACGGA
CACAGG CCAGGA CACACG CCAGCC ATGACA CATACC TGCAGA GGTACA TATGTA CACGTG
AACCCC AGACAC ACTCAC ACCCGA CCAGAA AGCATA TACTTT GAAGCA CAGACA GAGGGA
GCAGCA CACAGA AACACA GCAGAG ATCAGC AGCTCT GCCCTG GAGCTG CCCCCT GCTGGC
CGTGTG ACCCCG GGGGTT ATGTCA CCTTTC TGTGCC TCAATT TTGTCA TCTGCC AAAAGG
GATGAT AATGGT CTCTCC CTCATA GGTTGT GGGGCA GGCGAC ATGAGT CACTTC ACATAA
AACACA TAAAGA AATCTC ATCACC TCCTTT GAGAAT GAAAAA AAAAAA AAAAAG AAAAGA
AATCCC AGCACT TTGGGA GACCAA GGCAGG AGGATT GCTTGA GCACAG GAGTTC GAGACC
AGTCTA GGCAAC ACAGCT AGACTC GATCCC TATTTT AAATTA AACACA CACACG CACAGA
GAAAGA GACCAG GCACGC AGAGGC TGTTGG TGCAAC GTTTGC TCTTTA TGCACA
CACTCT CGGGGA TCCAGC CACTCA TTGTCC CCACCT GCATCT GATTCC AGGCTT CCTGGC
TTCAGA AGCCTT TGCTTC CTCCCA GGCCCC ACACCT GGCCCT TCCTCC ATCCCC CATCCA
CCCCCA CCCCAC TTCCTT CCCCAC CGCCCT CCTTAC CCCTGC TCAGTC CCCAGG AGTCGG
ATTCAG CTGTCC AGAAAC TCTTCA GGGCAA AGAAAG GTCCAG TGCCCA GTCAGT GGGACA
CCACCC AAAGCC AAATCC CCTCTG CCCTAC CTCTCC CCTAGT CCTTAC CCACGG CCCCAG
TGGGCC TACCCC TGCCCC AGTGCC CTCTGC CAGGGA TTCCTG GCGAGT TGCTGG CAACCT
CAGCAT CCCTTC CTGCCA GCTCCA CCCAGC CCAGTC CTCGGG GAGCCG CCTGGA ACAGGA
CAAAGG GCAGAG CTCTGG AGTCCC TAGGGC CTGGGT CCAGCC CCTTCC CCACTC CTTTGT

GCAGTC ACTTGT TTTGTT GGAAAT GTCCCC TCTCCT CATCTT TTTATT TATTTT ATTTTA
ATTTTT TTGAGA CAGAGT TTCTGT CTTGTT GCCGAG GCTGGA GTGCAA TGGTGT GATCTT
GGCTCA CCGCAA CCTCTG CCTCCC AGGTTC AAGCGA TTCTCC TGCCTC AGCCTC CCGAGT
AGCTGG GACTAC AGGCAC GCGCCA CCATGC CCGGCT AATTTT GTATTT TTAGTA GAGACA
GGGTTT CTCCAT GTTGGC CAGGCT GGTCTC GAACTC CCGATC TCAGGT GATCCA CCGGCC
TCAGCC TCCCAA AGTGGT GGGATT ACAGGT GTGAGC CACGGC GCCCGG CCCCCA CTCCTC
ATCTTA AAAGAT CCCTAC CGGCAT GGATGC TACCAC TTTACC AAGGGG CGGCAG TGCACC
AGGCAC TGTCCA AAGGCT GAATAA AAAAGG CAAAAG TCCCTG CCCTCA GGGAGT TTACAA
TCTAGT GAGGGA ATCAGA GAGCAA ACAATA TAAATT CAGGCA TGTCTC AGAGAT ATTTGG
GGTTCA ATTCCA GACCAC TTGATA AAGTGA GTCACA CAAATT TGTTGG TTTCCC AGTGCA
TAGAAA AGTTAT GTTTAC ACTATC CTGTAG TCTATT AAAGTG TACAAC AGCATA TGTCTA
AAAATA CCATGT ACATAT TTTAAT TTTTTT TTTTCT GTAGAG ACGGAA TCTCAC TATGTT
GCCCAG GCTAGT CTCGAA CTCCTA GCCTCA AGTGAG CCTCCT GCTTTG ACCTCC CAAAGT
GCCAGG ATTACA AGCATG AGCTAC CACGCC TGGCCC CATACT ATGCTA ATGATC ATCTGA
GCCTTC AGCAAA TCCTCA TCTTTT TGCTGG TGGAGG GTCTTG CCCCAG TGGTGG TGGCTG
CTGACT CACGAG GGTGGT GGTTGT AGAAAG TGGCTG TGGCAG TTTCTT AAAATA AGGTAA
CAATGA ACTTTT CTGCTT CGATTC ACTCAC AAAACT GTTCTC TGTAAC ATGTGA TGCTGT
TTGATA GCATTT GGTCCA CAGTAG AACTTT CAAAAT TGGGGT CAGGCC AGGCAC GGTGGC
TCACAC CTATAA TCCCAG CACTTT GGGAGG CCGAGG TGGGCA AATCAC CCAAGG TCAGGA
GTTTGA GGCCAG CCTGGC CAACAT GGTAAA ACCCCG TCTCTA CTAAAA ATACTA AAATTA
ACCAGG CGCGGT GGCAGG CACCTG TAGTCC CAGCTA CTCAGG AGGCTG AGGTAG GAGAAT
CACTTG AACCTG GGAGGC GGAGGT TGCGGT GAGCTG AGATCG CACCAT TGCACT CCAGCC
TGGGCA ACAAGA GCGAAA CTTGTC TCAAAA AAAAAA AAAAAT GGGGGT CAGTCC TGTCAA
AGCCTG CTGGTG CTCTAT CAGCCA AGTCTA TGTCAT AGTCTA AATCCT TTGTTG CCATTG
TTCCTG CTATCA AATGTA TTTCTG TTTTTT TATTTT TTTATT TATTTT TTGTAG AGGGGG
AGGGTC TCACTA TGTTAC CCAGGT TGATCT CAAACT GGCCTC AAGCTA TCTTCC TGCCTT
GGCCTC CCAAAG TGCTGC GATTAT AAGTAT GAGCCA CTGCAC CCAGCC TACAAA ATGTAT
TTCTAA ATGTAT TTCTAT TTTTTA TTATTT AATAAG ACTTAG AGCTGG GCATGG TGGCAC
ATGCCT GTAATC CCAGCT ATTCAA GAGGCT GAGGCA GGATGA TCACTT GAGGTC CAGTGT
TCAAGA CCAGGC TAGGCA ACACAG CCCTGT CTCTTA AAAAAC ACAAAA AATTAG CCAGAT
GCAGTG ACTCTC CCAGCT ACTCAA GAGGCC AAGGCA GGAGGA TCTCTT GAGGCC TGGAAT
TCAAAA CCAGCC TAGGCA ATATAG CAAGAC TCTGTC TCTAAA AACCTG GAAAAA AAAAAA
TGAACC AGGCAT AGTGGT GCCCAT CTGTAG TCCCCA CTACTC AGGAGG CTGAAG TAGGAG

GATCAC TTGAGC CCAGAA GTTCAA GGCTGC AGTGAG GTATGA TCGTGC CACTAC ACTCCA
GCCCAG GTGACA CAGCAA GAATCC ATCTCT AAAACT AAAAAT TTTAAA AATAAG AATAAC
AAATAA TAAGAC TTAAAA GTTGAA ATTGGC CGGGCG CAGTGG CTCACG CCTGTA ATCCCA
GCATTT TGGGAG GCCGAG GCAGGC GAATCA CGAGGT CAGGAG ATCGAG ACCATC CTAGCT
AACATG GTGAAA CCCCGT CTCTAC TAAAAA TACAAA AAATTA GCCAGG TGTGGT GGCGGG
CGCCTG TCGTCCC AGCTAC TCAGGA GGCTGA GGCAGG AGAATG GCGTGA ACCCGG
GAGGCG GAGCTT GCAGTG AGCTGA GATTGC GCCACT GCACTC CAACCT GGGCGA
CAGAGC GAGACT CCGTCT CAAAAA AATATA ATAATA ATAACA AATAAC AAGACT TAAAAG
TCGAAA TTACTC CTTGGC TGGTGG GCTGCA GAACAG ATCATG TGTTAG CGGGCA TGAAAA
CACATT AATCTA CTCCAC CAGGGC CCTTTG GTAACC ACATGC ATTGTC ATTGAG AAATAT
TTTGTT GTTTTC TGTGCA GTCCGT CTCAAC AGTGGG CTTGAA ATATTC AGTAAA CCATGC
TGTAAA CAGACG TGCTGT CATCCA GGCTTT GTTCCA TTTAAG AGCATA GGCAGA GTACAT
TTGGCG TAATCCT GAGGGC CCTAGA ATTTCT GGAATG ATAAAT GAACAC CGGCTT CAACTG
AGTCAC CAGCTG CATTAG CCCCTA ACAAGG GGGTCA GCCTGG CCTTGA AGCTTT GGCGCC
CAGGCA CTGACC TCCCCTC CAGCTA GGAAAG TCCTGG ATGGCA TCTTCTT CCAATA
CCTGGT GGTTTT ATCTAC ACTGAA AATATG TTGCTT AATGTA GCCGTC TTCATC AATGAT
CTTAGC TAGATC TTCTGC ATAACT TGCTGC GGCTCC TCCAGC AGCACT TGCTAC ATCACC
TTGCAC TTTTTT TTTTGA GACAAA GTTTCAC TCTTGT TGCTCA GGCTGG AGTGCA ATGGCA
CGATCT CGGCTC ACTGCA ACCACC GCCTCC CAGGTT CAAGTG ATTCTC CTGCCT CAGCCT
CCCAAG TAGCTG GGATTA CAGGCA TGCGCC ACCACG CCCGGC TTCTTT TTTGTA TTTTAA
GTTGAG ATGGGG TTTCTC CATGTT GGTCA GGCTGG TTTCAA ACTCCC GACCTC AGGTGA
TCCACC TGCCTC AGCCTC CCAAAG TGCTGG GATTAC AATCGT GAGCCA CGATGC CCGGCC
GTCACC CTGCAC TTTTAT GTTACA GAGATG CCTTCT TTCCTT AAATCT CATGAA TCCACC
TCTGCT AGCTTC CAACCT TTTTTC TGCAGC TTCCTC ACCTCT CTCACC CTTCAA AGAATT
GAAGA GGGATA GGGCTT CGCTTG GGATTA GGCTTT GGCTTA AGGAAA TGTGGC TGGTTTG
ACCTTC TATCCA GACCGT TCAGAC TTTCTC CATATC CACAAT AAGCCT AGTTCA CTTTTT
TTTTTT TTTTCC AGACGG AGTCTC ACTCTGT CACCCA GGCTGG AGTGCA GTGGCG
CGATCTC GGCTCA CTACAA GCTCCG CTTCCC AGGTTC ACGCCA TTCTCC TGCCTC AGCCTC
CCTAGT AGCTGG GACTAC AGGCAC CCACCA CCACGC CCGGCT GATTTT TTGTAT TTTTAG
TAGAGC TGGGGT TTCACC GTGTTA GCCAGG ATGGTC CCGATC TCCTGA CTTCGT GATCCG
CCCGCC TCGGCC TCCCAA AGTGCT GGGATT ACAGGC ATGAGC CACCAT GCCCAG CTAAGA
CTGGTT CACTTT CTTATC ATTCAT GTGTTC ACTGGA GTAGCA CTTTTA ATTACT TTCATG
AATTTT TCCTTT GCATTC ACAACT TAGCTA ACTGGC AGAAGA GGCCTA GTTTTT AGCCCG

TTTCAG CACTGG ACATGC CTTCCT CACTAA GCTTAA TCACTT CTGGCT TTTGAT TTAAAA
TGAGAG ACATAA GACTCT TCTTTC ACTTGA ACACTT TGAGGT CATTGT AGGGTT GTTAAT
TGGCCT GATTTC TATTTT ATTTTA TTCTAT TTTTCA TCTCAT TTCATT TATTTG AGACAG
ACTCTC GCTCTA TTTTCC AGGCTG GAGTAC AATGGT GTGATC TTGGCT CACTAC AACCTC
CACCTC CCGGGT TCAAGC GATTCT CCTGCC TCAGCC TCCCGA GTAGCT GGGATT ACAGGC
ACACAC CACCAT GCCCAG CTAATT TTTGTA TTTTTA GTAGAG ATGGGG TTTCAG CATGTT
GGCCAG GCTGGT CTCAAC CTCCTG ACCTCA AGTGAT CCACCT GCCTCA GCCTCC CAAAGT
GCTGGG ATTACA GGCATT AGCCAC CGTGCC CGGCCT CAATAT TGTATG TCTTAG GGAATA
TGGAGG CTCGAG AAGAG AGATGG GGGAAA TGGCTG GTCAGT GGAGCA GTCAGA ACACAC
ACAGCA TTAATC GGTAAA GTTCGC CCTCTT ACGTGG ACATGG TTGGTG GTGCCC CCACTC
ACAATA GTAACA CCAGAG ATCATT GATCAC AGATCA TCATAA CAAATA TAATAA TAATGA
AAAAG TGTGAA ACACTG TGAAAA TTACCA GAATGT GACACA GAGACA CAAAGT GAGCAA
CTGCTG TCAGAA AAATGG TGCCAA CAGACT GGTTTG ACGCAG GGTTGC CACAAA CCTTCA
ATTTGT AAAAAA TGCAGT ATGTGC GAGGCA CAGTGA AGCAAG GTATTC CTGTAG TAAACT
GTATAG TATGCT AGATGG TGACAA GTGCCG CAGAGA AAAATC ACCCAA TACACC ATCTCA
GGAAGG CCAAGT GAGCCC ACAAAG CAAACC ACATGC AGAACA TGCCGG CCATGG
CCCCAC TTATAA ATTATG TCTCCC ACCCTG AGCCAG CAGAAC AGCCAA GTGCAG TTTCCA
GATGAG GAAAAC AGACTC ATCCAG GGTCGC CAGCAA GGGCTT GGGCCA TCTTTC TTTCCT
TTTCTT TTCTTC TTTCCT TTCTTT CTTTCC TTCCTT TCCTTT CTTTCT TTCCTT TCTTTT
CTGACA GAGTCT CGCTTT ATCGCC AGGCTG GAGTAC AGTGGC GTGATC TCAGCT CACTGC
AACCTC TGCCTC CTGGGT TCAAGT GATTCT CCTGTC TCAGCC TCCCAA TAGTGG GGACTA
CAGGCA TCCACC ACCATA CCGCTA ATTTTT GTATTT TTAGTA GAGACG GGGTTT CAGCAT
GTTGGC CAGGAT GGTCTC GATCTC CTGACC TCGTGG CCCACC CACGTC GGCCTC CCAACG
TGCTGG CATTAT AGGCAT GAGCCA CTGTGC CTAGCC CACATC GTCCCA TTTTCA CAGCTG
CAAGCC TAACAC TGCCTC CTGAGG CCTCTG TCTATC CATCTG TCTGCC AGCCCT GGGGAG
GGGCCG TCCTCT CCTGAG CTAACT AGCCCC TCTGCC CTCGCT CTGCTT CTTCAT GCCTTC
CTTCCT GCTTCA TATATC CACTGA GCACCT GCTATG TGCCAG GTCCCA TGATAG GCCCCA
GGGCCA CCTGGG GGATGA CAGTCC GGGACA GAAGAT TCACTT CCAGCC AAGCAA ATGACC
CTGAGG CCTCAG AGCCCC TCAGTC ACACAG GCCCCT TTCAAG GCCCTA ATCTTT TTTGTTT
TGTTTT AAGACA GAGTCT CGCTCT GTCACC CAGGCT GGAGTG CAGTGG CACGAT CTTGGC
TCAGTG CAAGCT CCGCGT CCCAGG TTCACA CCATTC TCCTGC CTCCGC CTCCCG AGTAGC
TGGGAC TACAGG TGCCCA CCACCA TGCCCG GCTAAT TTTTTT GTATTT TTAGTA GAGACG
GGGTTT CACCGT GTTAGC CAGGAT GGTCTT GATCT GCTGAC CTCATG ATCCGC CCGCCT

CGGCCT CCCAAA ATGCTG GGATTA CAGGCG TGAGCC ACCACG CCTGGC CCAAGG CCCTAA
TCTTGT ATTTGT AATTCT GTATTT CTTCTT CCTAAA GGGCCA CACCCC GGTACC TTATAA
GTTTCA TGGCTC CATAAA ACCTAG TCCTGTC CTGGGG GAGATG AACAAA CACGTA AACAAA
TTATAA AGTGTC AAATGG CAGGAT GGAACA GAACTA AATATC ATGGCA GAAAAT AACGGG
GGCGTG CATATC TTAGCT GGGGAG AAGCAA CTGGGG AGTACC TCTTGG AAGTG ACAAGC
TGAGGC CAGACA AGGAAT CTGTGG AATGAC ACGGGT GAATGA CATGGG TGAGGA ATCTCT
CTCTCT GAGCCT CTGTTT CCCTGT GTGAGG TGGGGA TGCCAG TCACAG CAGGGT GGGCTG
AGAGGG GTAAGT GGCAGG TCCAGG TTACCC AGTGTG GTCACA CCACCC AGTAGG ACCGAC
AGGCAG CTCAGG CCCCTA GCTGAG CCTGGC ACTGCC CTTAAT CGGCTT TTGTCC TTCCAG
GAGGGA CAGGCA GGGCTG GCTACC TCCTCTC TCCCCC CAACAG CTGGGG CTGGCT
GTGCCA GGGCCA GACTAG GAGGCG GGAGCT GAGATC ACTGGG CCTTTG GCTCCC TGAGTC
CTCTCT GGGGAC AGAGAG GGCAGC CTGGCT GGGTGA GAGGGG ACGGTT TGTTCA
GGACTG GGGCTA GGACTC CTGGGT CCTAAA GGATGA AGGGGC TGGGGG CCTGGA
CTCCTG GGTCTG AGGGAG GAGGGG CTGTGG GTGTGG ACTCCT GGGTTC TAAGGC AGAGGA
GCCTGT AACAGG ACTACC AGTTGA GCTGAG TCTGGG AGCAGG TGGGGG GCAGAG
CAGGGA GCTGAG CCCTCT ACTCTG TTTACA GCACGT GGTCCT CACTGA TCTTTC TGGGTG
GGAGGT GGCTTG TGCGGC TACACC CTGGGC AGGCCA GCCCCG CCCCCG GGTTTA TTGCCC
CAGGCT GCTACT GGCACA AGCCAC AGACCA GCAGTC CCAGCC CAGGGA AGCTCG GAAGAT
GCCTAG GAGGGG TGAGTG TCCAGC CAGCTG AGAGAC GGGAAT GGCCGC TGCCAG
GCCCCA GGACCT AGAAGG GAAAGG AAATAC CTTCTT CTAGGG GAACAG GCAAGG
TGCTGG GCTTTG GGAGGG AAGTCA CTGGAG CAGATG GTAGCA TTCCAC CAAGGG
CAGCTTG TTCAGG ACCTGG GTGACA GGGCAT CCAAGA AACAGG GCAGCC TGAATG
GCTGGG AAAGGA TATCAG AGGAAA GATCAC TGGGGA CTGGAA AGTGTG GAGATC AGACGT
AGTCCA GGGCAA GTTTTGA GATGTG GCTTCCA GAGTCC TAGCGG GGAGCC CCACAT
AAGTGT GGCTGT GGACCC AGAGAG CTGGGT TTACAA AAGCTC TGCCAC TTGCAG TGCAAC
TTTAAC CTCCTC ACTTAA AACCTG AGCCTC AGTTTC CTCTCC TGTAAA ATGGG GATGCT
GGCAA TAATAG AGATTT GAACCT AGGTGG TGTGGG TCCCGA GGGTTA GCACGC TAAAGC
AGCAAA CACACA GAAAGC TCTCAG CACGGG ACCTGC ACGGAT ATGCTC AAGGTC GACACC
AGTGAT GAGTAT CGCTGT TCCAGG CAGGGG AGCAGG GCCGGC CATGCA ACCCAG GACCAG
TGGACA AGCCTG AAGGCC AGGGGA CCCCAC TGGGGG AGAAGC AAGACT GAGTTT
TGGGGA TCTCACA GAGAAA CAGGGA GGGAAC TGGGAT TTGGAG GGGGTT CCACAG
CCAGAC TTGAAG GATGAG GAATGA CTCTTC AGTGAA GTCTAG AATTGT GAACTC CTGAGT
TCAGGG AGAGCT GCGCTT GGGGA CCAGGG TCCCGA GAGATG GGAATG GGAGG GCTGGG

GCTGAA CTCTCC CAAATG TTGTTG GAGGG GAAGGG CCTATG GGTAGC ACTTGG GGCCTA
AGAAGG AAAGAT GGGATG GGGGAC CCGGAC TCCTGG GTCCTG AGAATG GGGACC
AACTGG AGGTTT AGACTT CTTGGA ATCTAG GAGAAG GAGTCT TGGGCC CCAGGA GAATTC
ATGGAG ACAGGT GACTAG ACTCTT GGGTTC CTGGAA GGAAGA AAGAAG GACCGG
CAGCCT CCTGGA TCACAG GAGAG GTGAA TGAGTT AGGGAA GCAGAG TCGTGT GGGCTC
AGGGAA TGTCCG GATTCA GGAGGC CAGGGC AGCAAG TTTCTG AGTCCC AAAGAG GTGATA
GCAGGG GCTCCT GGGTCC TGAAGA GGAAGG GCTTGG GGCTTG GACTCC TGGGTC
TGAGGG AGGAGG GAGCTG AGGGCC CAAACT CCTGGC TCCCGA GGAGGG ACAAAG
GCACTG GGAACT GGGGCC CCAAAC TTCTGA TTCCCA GAGACA AGAGGG TGACCT CTTATG
TCTAAG GGAGGA GGAACC TGGGGT CCTGGG CCCCTG GAACTG AAAGAA GACAGC
ACTGAG GTTTGA AGGAGG AGTGGG TAAGCT ATGGCC CAGACT CCTGGG CCCCAG CTAAGC
AAGGCT TGATCC AGCCCC ACCTAA CAGGCC TCCCCA CCTGCC CACAG**C CTCAAG GCTCAT**
CCACAA CATGGA CCTGCG CACAAT GACACA GTCGCT GGTGAC TCTGGC GGAGGA
CAACAT AGCCTT CTTCTC GAGCCA GGGTCC TGGGGA AACGGC CCAGCG GCTGTC
AGGCGT TTTTGC CGGTGT ACGGGA GCAGGC GCTGGG GCTGGA GCCGGC CCTGGG
CCGCCT GCTGGG TGTGGC GCACCT CTTTGA CCTGGA CCCAGA GACACC GGCCAA
CGGGTA CCGCAG CCTAGT GCACAC AGCCCG CTGCTG CCTGGC GCACCT CCTGCA
CAAATC CCGCTA TGTGGC CTCCAA CCGCCG CAGCAT CTTCTT CCGCAC CAGCCA
CAACCT GGCCGA GCTGGA GGCCTA CCTGGC TGCCCT CACCCA GCTCCG CGCTCT
GGTCTA CTACGC CCAGCG CCTGCT GGTTAC CAATCG GCCGGG GGTACT CTTCTT
TGAGGG CGACGA GGGGCT CACCGC CGACTT CCTCCG GGAGTA TGTCAC GCTGCA
TAAGGG ATGCTT CTATGG CCGCTG CCTGGG CTTCCA GGTGAG CCCCCT GCCCCG
TGCCCC TCTGGG CCCACA ATGAAG GCACCT GGTGGC CCCTGG CCTGGC CTATAG TATGGT
AAAGTA ACCAGT GGTCAG CATTAT CGGACT CAGCAA ACAGCA GGTACA GAAAGG AGAAGT
TGGCTG GAGCTC AGACAG AGCTGC ACCAGG GGTCTC AAACTC ATGGTC CCTAGG TCATA
TCTGCT AGGTGG TAAGAA ATGCAA CTTGCA GAGCTT TTTTCA CCAGGA TATCCA CTACTC
TCTATT GTCCTA CATGCA AGAGAT GTATTC ACTCTT TGTTAC CTGTCT GGCCCC TGAAGT
CACTTG AGTTTG AGACCC CTCAGG GAGGGA TCTGGA GCCATG TGACCC TATAGT CATTCTG
GCCCTC TCTGGG CCTCCC CGCACC TCAGCC TCCCCC TCCCAC CCCACA TCTCCA GGCTTC
CCTTCA GGCTAG CCTATC CTCAGC AACCCA GCCCAG GCATTC CTGGAA ACCTCC CCTCAC
CAGGGC TGAACC CACAAG TATTGA TCAGCC CAGCTG GGCCAG CCAGCT CCTCCC TGTGTC
CCAGCC GTGACC CTAGAG TCATGA GAAAGA GATCCC GGGGCT GCCCAA ACCAGC ATCCCA
GCCACA ATAGCC AGGCAT CAGGTG CCCTCT GGCCTA CTGGGC GCACAG CCAGGG GCAGGG

CCCAGC TCTGCC TTGGTG CAGGGC AGTCTC CCCTTT AAAATG TCCGTC CCCGGG AGGGCA
GAGGCC TCCCCT GTCTTG GTCACT GCTCCA GCCCAG TGTCTA GCATGC AGTAGG AACTTG
GCCAGT ACAGAG TGAACA GAAGAA CCCGCC AATCCC TTGCCT TGGCCT CCTATG GCTCCA
TTTCCT CTAATC CTGTGT CCCCAT TGTATT TTTTTT TTTTTT TTTTTT TGTATT TTGTTT
AGTAGA GATGGG GTTTCA CCATGT TGGCCA GGCTGG TCTCAA ACTCCT GACCTC AAGTG
ATCCAC CCACCT TGGCCT CCCAAA GTACTG GGTTTA CAGGCA TGAGCC ACTGCA CCTGGA
CCCCAC TGTCTT TCCTTA ACTGCC TGTCTG CTCTGT CAGACG CTGTCT CTCCCT GCCCCC
GTGGTG GCTGGC TGGTCC TATGTC TAGGCC TCAGTC TCCCTCT CTGACT GTCTTT CTGCCT
CAGGTC CCTGTG CCTGGG GGGCTG TCTCTG GCCATC TCCCTG TTCCTG TCTTCC AGCTGC
CTCCTC TCCCCA TCCATC CTCTCT CTGACT TTCAGG AAGTCC CTGCAC CATCCT ACTCCC
CACCTC ACAGCC TACCAG TGGCAC CACCCC GCACTG GGAATG AAATCC AAATTC CTCTGC
CCAGGC CCTATA TGAGCC CCCTTT GCCTCT CCAATG TCACCA CCTGCC CCTCTC CCCACT
GCTCAC TCTGCT CCAGCC ACACTG GCCCCC TGACTG TCGCTA CCCAGG TCAAGC ACCAAG
CATGAG CTCACC TTTTTT TTTTTT TAGAGA CAGAGT CTCGCT CTGTCG CCCAGG CTGGAG
TGCAGT GGTGTG ATCTCC ACTCAC TGCAAC CTCTGC CTCCTG GGTTCA AGCGAT TCTCCT
GCCTCA GCCTCC TATGAG CTCACC TTTAAG CCTTCA TGCTCT CTGTTC CCTGTG CAGGGA
ACACCC TCCCCT CGCTTC AGTCAG ATCTCT CCTCCG AGACCC GCTAAG TAGCCT GACCCC
TAGTCA TCACTG GTGCCC TCTCCA CCTACT GCCTTT TTTTTT TTCCAA ACCATT CGTCAT
TCCTTG TCATGA TACTGC GCGTGG CTTTGC TTATCT GCTGAT CATTTGT TTTCCC TTTGAG
AACATC AGGTCC GTGAA CCAGCC GAGAG CTATGC CCAGCA CACAGT AGGAGC TCATGA
AACGTT TACTGA ATGAAT GTGTCT TCCCCG CACATC CCTGTG CCTCGC TCCTGC CCTGTC
CCCATC CCTCTC TTGAGC GGTGGG TGACGC AGCCGC GTCTCT CCACAG *TTCACG CCTGCC*
ATCCGG CCATTC CTGCAG ACCATC TCCATT GGGCTG GTGTCC TTCGGG GAGCAC TACAAA
*CGCAAC GAGA*CA GGCCTC AGTGAG TCCCAG CCAGGT TCTACT CGCAGC CTACTC TCTTGG
CCCTCC TCCCCA CTCCTG CCCAAG CAGCCT GACCCA CTGGGG CTCCCT GACACC CCTTCT
GACCCC TAGGTG T**GGCCG CCAGCT CTCTCT TCACCA GCGGCC GCTTTG CCATCG**
ACCCCG AGCTGC GTGGGG CTGAGT TTGAGC GGATCA CACAGA ACCTGG ACGTGC
ACTTCT GGAAAG CCTTCT GGAACA TCACCG AGATGG AAGTGC TATCGG TGAGGG
CCTGTT GCAGAT GGGGAC ACTGAG GCCCAG AGACTC ATCTGA GGCCAC AGTAGG TCTCTG
TGGGGC TCCAGG CCCAGG GATGGC ACACAA GGGGA AAGACT GGGGAT CAGAGG GAGAG
GTGAAG GGCACC CCTGCA GGCAGA CCTTCC CTAGCA CCCCTT CTGTCC CCTCCC TCCAG*T*
CTCTGG CCAACA TGGCAT CGGCCA CCGTGA GGGTAA GCCGCC TGCTCA GCCTGC CACCCG
AAGCCT TTGAGA TGCCAC TGACTG CCGACC CCACGC TCACGG TCACCA TCTCAC CCCCAC

TGGCCC ACACAG GCCCTG GGCCCG TCCTCGT CAGGCT CATCTC CTATGA CCTGCG TGAAGG
*ACAG*GT AGGGTT CCAGCC TCAGCC AGGGAC AGGGAC AGAGCC GAGGAG CGTGGG
CAGCCC CCACCT TGGCAT CCCCAT GGAGGG GTGCAG CCCTGG CCAGCT CTCCCC AACCTC
ACACAC CGTCTC CCTCCT CACCCC CAG**GAC AGTGAG GAGCTC AGCAGC CTGATA**
AAGTCC AACGGC CAACGG AGCCTG GAGCTG TGGCCG CGCCCC CAGCAG GCACCC
CGCTCG CGGTCC CTGATA GTGCAC TTCCAC GGCGGT GGCTTT GTGGCC CAGACC
TCCAGA TCCCAC GAGCCC TACCTC AAGAGC TGGGCC CAGGAG CTGGGC GCCCCC
ATCATC TCCATC GACTAC TCCCTG GCCCCT GAGGCC CCCTTC CCCCGT GCGCTG
GAGGAG TGCTTC TTCGCC TACTGC TGGGCC ATCAAG CACTGC GCCCTC CTTGGT
GAGCCT CAGGCC CCCACA GCCACC TGCGCC TGCTCC CATCCC ACCCAG CTTGCT TTAAGC
TCCTCC AGCCTC AGCCTC ACACCC TCTACC TTTCTC TCCCCC CACACC TCCCAG CTCCTG
CTCACC CAGGTC CTGCCC AATCTT CCACCT CAGCCA CTTTAT CCTCTG TCCCCA ACTGTG
GCACCC AGACTC TCCATC TCCTCC ACCTCC ACTTCC CACCCA CCGTCC TGTCTC CCTGGG
CCTCTG TCGTCC CCCTCT GATAGC TCCAGG CCCTGC TCTCCT GTCCTA CCAGCC TCCTGG
CCCACA GTCCAG CTTCTC TGACCT CCCTCT TCGAA GATCAA CATCTT GGGAG GACACT
GAGGCA CAGAGC AGAGTG TGGCCA TGCCCC AGGGCA CAGAGC TTGCAG CCCAGC
CCCTCT GTACTG ACCCTG AACCCT GACCTT CCATTC CCGCCC TCTGAG GCCCCC CTCCTG
CAACAG GCCTGA GCTCAG CTCCCC TTTCCC ACCACC TGCCCT CCCTGC TCCCAA CCTCCA
GCCCCG ACAGAC TTTCCC AGTGCT TCCCTG GGCCTC TCCAGG TCCTGA GTCATC CTGACC
CTCTGT CTACCA CATGAG CCCAAA TCTGTG CCTCAG TCTGCC AGTCTC TAAAAC TGCAGT
CTGCTA GGCCTT GGAGT GCCCCA CACCCC ACCTTG GAGAG CCCAG TTCTCC CAGCTT
GAGTTC CTCCCT GCCCTC CTCCCC AGGCCT CTGCCC CTGCCA GGTTGT CACCAA CCACCC
CTCTCC CAAACC AG*GCTC AACAGG GGAACG AATCTG CCTTGC GGGGG ACAGTG CAGGCG*
GGAACC TCTGCT TCACCG TGGCTC TTCGGG CAGCAG CCTACG GGGTGC GGGTGC CAGATG
GCATCA TGGCAG CCTACC CGGCCA CAATGC TGCAGC CTGCCG CCTCTC CCTCCC GCCTGC
TGAGCC TCATGG ACCCCT TGCTGC CCCTCA GTGTGC TCTCCA AGTGTG TCAGCG CCTATG
*CTG*GTG AGGCCC ACACCC TCAGCA GGGAAA CAGGAC TGCATG GATGTC TGACTC CTGCAG
GGACGG GCTGGG GACCAG GACTCC TGTGAC TGAGGA AGGAGA GGCCAG GCAGAG
GAATCT AAGACT CCTTGTC CCTTTTT TTTCGT GTGTGT GTGTGT GTGTGT GTGTGT GTGTGT
GTGTGT GTGTGA GAGAGA GAGAGA GACAGA CAGACA CAAGGT GTCATG TCGCTC
AGGCTG AGTGCA GTGGCT CAAACA CACCTC ACTGCA GCCTTG ACCTCC CAGGCT GAAGCA
ATCATC CTGCCT CAGCTT CCCAAG TAGCTG GAACTA CAGGCG TGCACC ACCACT ACCACG
CCCAGC TAATTT TTGTGT TTTTCG CTATGT TGCCCA GGCTGG TCTTGA ACTCCT GGGCTC

AAGCCA TCCTCT CGCCTT GGCCTC CCAAAG TACTGG GACTAC AGGCGT GAGCCA CTGCGC CCAGCC TCCTTA TCCCTT TTGAAG CGATTG GATATT CTCGGG TCCCTG GGACCA CAGATG CCTGAA GTTCTG GGCGTT AAAACT GGGCCC AGAAAG GGGAAA ACAACT CAGCTA CCCACA TATATT CTGCAG **GTGCAA AGACGG AGGACC ACTCCA ACTCAG ACCAGA AAGCCC TCGGCA TGATGG GGCTGG TGCGGC GGGACA CAGCCC TGCTCC TCCGAG ACTTCC GCCTGG GTGCCT CCTCAT GGCTCA ACTCCT TCCTGG AGTTAA GTGGGC GCAAGT CCCAGA AGATGT CGGAGC CCATAG CAGGTG AGTGA**TT CACTCCC GTCACAT GCCCAGC CAGGGT GGGCAG GAGGGA CAGCCTA GCACAG CAAAAG TCCCAG GGAAGA TGCTGG GCATGG TGGTTC AGACCT GCAATC CCAGCA CTTTGG GAGGCT GAGGTG GGCAGA TCACTT GAGGT CAGGG GTTCAA GATCAG CCTGGT CAACAT GACGAA ACCCTG TCTCTA GTAAAA GTACAA AAATAT TAGCCA GGTGTG GTGGTG CACACC TGTAAT CCCAGC ACTTTG GGAGGC CAAGGT GGGCAG ATCACT TGAGGT CAGGAG TTCGAG ACCAGC CTGGCC AATATG GCAAA ACCCCT TCTCTA CAAAAA AATAAA TTAGCA GGGTAT GGTGGA GTACAC CTGTAG TCCCAG CTACCA GAGAGG CTGAAG CATGAG AACCGC TTGAAC CTGGGT AGCAGA GGTTGC AGTGAG CCAAGA CTGAGC CTCTGT ACTCCA GCCTGG GTGACA CAGCGA TACCTT GTCTCA AAAAAA AAAATT TAAAAA AAGAGT ACGCTT ACTGGG CTGTGG TGAGGT CTGCCTC CAACCA TTTGGC CAGTAC AATATA TGGCAC CCAGTA GGTGCT ATTAGA AGATGC CAGCAC CCCTGG TGTGTC CATTCT GTTCCA GTGACC CTCTGG GCCACA AAGTAC TTAAGT AGTTAT TCTCAC ATTGTT TTGCAC CTCACC TTCGTA GATTTA TAAAGA CAAGTA AGGCTG GGTGTG GTGGCT TACGCC CATAAT CCCAAC ACTTTG GGAAGC CAAGGC AGGCGG ATCACT TGAGGT CAGGAG TTCAAG ACCAGC TTGGCC AACATA GTGAAA CCCCAT CTCTAT TAAAAA TACAAA AATGGG CCAGGC GCAATG GCTCAT ACCTGT AATCCC AGCACT TTGGGA GGCCGA GGCGGG CAGATC ACGAGG TCAGGA GTTTGA GACCAG CCTGAC CAACAT GGTGA AACCCC ATCCCT ACTAA AAATAC AAAAAT TAGCCG GGCATG GTGGCA TGCATC TGTAAT CCCAGC TACTCA GGAGGC TGAGGC AGGAGA ATCACT TGAACC CAAGAG ACGAGG TTGCAG TGAGCC GAGATC ACGCCA CTGCAC TCAAGC CTGGGT AACAG AGTGAG ACTGTC TCAAAA AAAAAA AAAATA CAAAAA GTAGCT GGACAT GGTGGC ATGCCT GTAATC CCAGCT ACTCAG GAGGCT GTGGCG GGAGAA TTGCTT GAACCC GGGAGG CAGAGG TTACAG TGAGCCG AGATCGC ACCACTG CACTCC AGCCTG GGCAAC AGAGCA AGACTC CATCTC AAAAAA AAAAAA AAAAAG TAAAAA ACTAAA ACTGTA GCATCT TGGCCC TCATGG TAGGCA GTGTGG GTCTGA TAAAAT GAACAG AGCTGA GGCCAA GCTGGG CACGCC AGGTGG GCTGGA AGTGTA TCTTTA GCATCG TTTGGG CACTTG CTTGCC TGGTCA CGTGAA CGGATA AAACTG AAGAAC ACAAAG GAAATG TGGGGA AGCAGA TCCATG TGGCTA CAGGTG CCAGAC CCCTAG AAATGT GATACA

CCCTGG AGACTT GTTAGC TCCCTG TGAACA GAGCCT CCCTTC AAGCCA CTGGGC CTGCTT
ACTATT CAAATC ATTTTG ATCCAT TTACAC CTTGTG GTAAGT GTAATC CCAGCA CTATGG
GAGGCC GAGGCG AGCGGA TCACTT GAGGCC AGGAAT TCGAGA ACAGCC TGGCCA
ACATGG CGAAAC CCCATC TCTGCT AAAAAA AAAACA CAAAAA TTAGCC GGGCAT GGTGGC
ACATGC CTATAG TCCCAG CTACTC AGGAAG CTGAGG CACGAG AATCAC TTGAAC CTGGGA
GGTGGA GGTTGC AGTGAG CCATGT TCTTGC CACTGC ACTCCA GCCTGG GTGACA GAGCGA
GACTTT GTCTCA AAAAAA AAAAAA CAAAAA ACGATA TATTAT GATCCC CAGTGG GTAGCG
GTACCT AATCCC ACATCT TATCCC ACTGAG TCCTGC CACCTA TGAACC AAGGAC TATTTT
CATTTC CTTGAT CTAGAA GAAAAA ATAGGT TCCTAG AGGTAA ACTGCA CCTAAT CTTCCC
AGTCAC ACACAC ACACAC ACACAC ACACAC ACACAC ACACAC ACACAC ACACAC ATCCTT
CACTAG AACACA CTGCCC CACTGC CAAGAC CCCCAC CATGAC CACCTG GGGCAT CTGGAA
CTCCAC CCATCC CCTAGG CAAGAG TCTGGG GAAACA CAGCCT TTCACA GCGCTC CACAGG
CGACTG CCCTTC CCATGG CATTCC CTGCCA GCCACA CACACA ACCAAA CTAACG GAGCCA
GGCCTA TCTGCTC TCCCTC TCTCAG *AGCCGA TGCGCC GCAGTG TGTCTG AAGCAG CACTGG*
CCCAGC CCCAGG GCCCAC TGGGCA CGGATT CCCTCA AGAACC TGACCC TGAGGG ACTTGA
GCCTGA GGGGAA ACTCCG AGACGT CGTCGG ACACCC CCGAGA TGTCGC TGTCAG CTGAGA
CACTTA GCCCCT CCACAC CCTCCG ATGTCA ACTTCT TATTACC ACCTGA GGATGC AGGGGA
*AGAGGC TGAGGC CAAAAA TGAGCT GAGCCC CATGGA CAGAGG CCTGGG C**GTCCG T**GCCGC*
CTTCCC CGAGGG TTTCCA CCCCCG ACGCTC CAGCCA GGGTG CCACAC AGATGC CCCTCT
ACTCCT CACCCA TAGTCA AGAACC CCTTCA TGTCGC CGCTGC TGGCAC CCGACA GCATGC
*TCAAGA GCCTGC CACCTG TGCACA TCGTG*G TGAGCG ACAGAG GGGGCC GGTACA GGTGCA
TTTAGA GAAGAG CAGGGC ACCCGG GGAGGA GGGGGA CCGGGC ACGGGT ACACCT
GGGAAA AAGAGC TCCGGA GTGGGG AGAAAG GGACAG GCGTGT CCCCAG GGGAGA
ACAATG CCCCGA ACGAAC GGGAGG AGGACA AGAGTC AGGGCT GCCTCC GTTTTA CTTTGC
AATTTT GAGTAC CAAGAG ACAGGA TCAGTG GGGCAG CCCCTT GGGCTT GGAGAA TCAAGA
GAAAAA AAAGGT GGGTTT GGCGGG GTGGGG AGGGAG AGGCTG GAGAGA GGCCGG
GGATCG CAGTTA AAGTCA TTCTCCC ATCCTT CCCACA ACTCCC CCCATT CCCTCC ATTCTC
TCCCCA ACTCCT CACCCA CCATGT CTCCTG CCTCCG TCCACT CCGTCT GTATCC GTATTT
CCCGCT CCCTTT GTTCAT CAAACC CCTCCT CGCTCT ACCCGA CCCCGG TCTGTC TGTCCC
CCACCC TCTCTC CACGTC CCTCCC CGCTGT CCCGTA G**GCGTG CGCGCT GGACCC**
CATGCT GGACGA CTCGGT CATGCT CGCGCG GCGACT GCGCAA CCTGGG CCAGCC
GGTGAC GCTGCG CGTGGT GGAGGA CCTGCC GCACGG CTTCCT GACCCT AGCGGC
GCTGTG CCGCGA GACGCG CCAGGC CGCAGA GCTGTG CGTGGA GCGCAT CCGCCT

CGTCCT CACTCC TCCCGC CGGAGC CGGGCC GAGCGG GGAGAC GGGGGC TGCGGG GGTAGA CGGGGG CTGCGG GGGGCG ACACTA AAAGCC TGTTGT TCCCAT CTGCGC CGGCCT CCGTCA TGAATG CCTTCC GGGCCG GGCGGA AGGGGA CGCGGG CTGTGC CTTACT TAAGTC GGGGGT GGCAAG GGGGCG GGGCGG GGGCCC GAAAGC TGAGAC CCTCGC CACGGG GAGGGG GACGCG CACACA CACCGG TCACCG AGACGG CTGGAC CTGCAC GCCACC GCTGCC TTTTGCT GCTGCT GCTGCG GCGACC GCCGCA GGGACG GGGACT GGCCCT CCCTTG CAGGTC GGTTTG GTTTGT TGTAAA TAAAAGT ATTTAA TTAGTT TGGC

The following is the gene-coding sequence that includes exons spliced together in this fashion by RNA transcription. Italicized and bold areas are the sequential exons. The start codon for the gene is atg, as per usual. The promoter in this section is not altered. Underlined sections within the sequences contain the SNPs indicated by brackets. The stop codon is taa.

1 CTTCTTGTAAGAGAGTGCTAGGCACATAGCCTCCTCCTATTCCTAATCCTCCCACCAAAG

61 AAAGAGGCACAGAGTTCATTACTTAGTGGGGGCCAGCTGTGATCGGCCAACTGCCAGCTG

121 CCTTAAAAAGGAAGACCAGTGATGCTAGGATGGAGTGAAACCCAAGAGGAAGTGCCATCA

181 TGAGGAATCAATGAGAGATCTGTGAAGAGAGAGGGCTGGGTGGGAGCCCAGAAGGATAGA

241 ACCTGGAAGATCAATATCTCCCGTGAGGGA AATAACA*ATGGAGCCAGGTTCTAAGTCAGT*

301 *GTCTAGGTCAGACTGGCAACCTGAACCACACCAGAGGCCTATAACCCCGC TAGAGCCTGG*

361 *GCCAGAAAAGACACCCATAGCCCAGCCAGAATCGAAGACTCTGCAGGGATCCAATACCCA*

421 *ACAGAAGCCTGCTTCAAACCAAAGACCCCTCACCCAGCAGGAGACCCCTGCACAACATGA*

481 *TGCTGAATCCCAGAAGGAACCTAGAGCCCAACAAAAATCTGCTTCACAAGAGGAATTTCT*

541 *TGCCCCACAGAAGCCCGCACCACAGCAATCA****CCTT(C)AC****ATCCAAAGGGTGCTGCTCACTCA*

601 *ACAGGAAGCTGCCTCCCAGCAGGGACCTGGGCTAGGAAAAGAATCTATAACTCAACAGGA*

661 *GCCAGCATTGAGACAAAGACATGTAGCCCAGCCAGGGCCTGGGCCAGGAGAGCCACCTCC*

721 *AGCTCAACAAGAAGCTGAATCAACACCTGCGGCCCAGGCTAAACCTGGAGCCAAAAGGGA*

781 *GCCATCTGCCCCGACTGAATCTACGTCCCAAGAGACACCTGAACAGTCAGACAAGCAAAC*

841 *AACGCCAGTCCAGGGAGCCAAATCCAAGCAGGGATCTTTGACAGAGCTGGGATTTCTAAC*

901 *AAAACTTCAGGAACTATCCAACAGCGATCAGCCCTAGAGTGGAAGGCACTTTCTGAGTG*

961 *GGTCACAGATTCTGAGTCAGAATCAGATGTGGGATCATCT TCAGACACAGATTCTCCAGC*

1021 *CACGATGGGTGGAATGGTGGCCCAGGGAGTGAAGCTAGGCTTCAAAGGAAAATCTGGTTA*

1081 *TAAAGTGATGTCAGGATACAGTGGGACGTCGCCACATGAGAAAACCAGTGCTCGGAATCA*

1141 *CAGACACTACCAGGATACAG***CCTCAAGGCTCATCCACAACATGGACCTGCGCACAATGAC**

1201 **ACAGTCGCTGGTGACTCTGGCGGAGGACAACATAGCCTTCTTCTCGAGCCAGGGTCCTGG**

1261 **GGAAACGGCCCAGCGGCTGTCAGGCGTTTTTGCCGGTGTACGGGAGCAGGCGCTGGGGCT**

1321 **GGAGCCGGCCCTGGGCCGCCTGCTGGGTGTGGCGCACCTCTTTGACCTGGACCCAGAGAC**

1381 **ACCGGCCAACGGGTACCGCAGCCTAGTGCACACAGCCCGCTGCTGCCTGGCGCACCTCCT**

1441 **GCACAAATCCCGCTATGTGGCCTCCAACCGCCGCAGCATCTTCTTCCGCACCAGCCACAA**

1501 **CCTGGCCGAGCTGGAGGCCTACCTGGCTGCCCTCACCCAGCTCCGCGCTCTGGTCTACTA**

1561 **CGCCCAGCGCCTGCTGGTTACCAATCGGCCGGGGGTACTCTTCTTTGAGGGCGACGAGGG**

1621 **GCTCACCGCCGACTTCCTCCGGGAGTATGTCACGCTGCATAAGGGATGCT TCTATGGCCG**

1681 **CTGCCTGGGCTTCCAG***TTCACGCCTGCCATCCGGCCATTCCTGCAGACCATCTCCATTGG*

1741 *GCTGGTGTCCTTCGGGGAGCACTACAAACGCAACGAGACA***GGCCTCAGTGTGGCCGCCAG**

1801 **CTCTCTCTTCACCAGCGGCCGCTTTGCCATCGACCCCGAGCTGCGTGGGGCTGAGTTTGA**

1861 **GCGGATCACACAGAACCTGGACGTGCACTTCTGGAAAGCCTTCTGGAACATCACCGAGAT**

1921 **GGAAGTGCTATCG***TCTCTGGCCAACATGGCATCGGCCACC GTGAGGGTAAGCCGCCTGCT*

1981 *CAGCCTGCCACCCGAAGCCTTTGAGATGCCACTGACTGCCGACCCCACGC TCACGGTCAC*

2041 *CATCTCACCCCCACTGGCCCACACAGGCCCTGGGCCCGTCCTCGTCAGGCTCATCTCCTA*

2101 *TGACCTGCGT* ***GAAGGACAG*****GACAGTGAGGAGCTCAGCAGC CTGATAAAGTCCAACGGCCA**

2161 **ACGGAGCCTGGAGCTGTGGCCGCGCCCCCAGCAGGCACCCCGCTCGCGGTCCCTGATAGT**

2221 **GCACTTCCACGGCGGTGGCTTTGTGGCCCAGACCTCCAGATCCCACGAGCCCTACCTCAA**

2281 **GAGCTGGGCCCAGGAGCTGGGCGCCCCCATCATCTCCATCGACTACTCCCTGGCCCCTGA**

2341 **GGCCCCCTTCCCCCGTGCGCTGGAGGAGTGCTTCTTCGCCTACTGCTGGGCCATCAAGCA**

2401 **CTGCGCCCTCCTTG***GCTCAACAGGGGAACGAATCTGCCTTGCGGGGGACAGTGCAGGCGG*

2461 *GAACCTCTGCTTCACCGTGGCTCTTCGGGCAGCAGCCTACGGGGTGCGGGTGCCAGATGG*

2521 *CATCATGGCAGCCTACCCGGCCACAATGCTGCAGCCTGCCGCCTCTCCCTCCCGCCTGCT*

2581 *GAGCCTCATGGACCCCTTGCTGCCCCTCAGTGTGCTCTCCAAGTGTGTCAGCGCCTATGC*

2641 *TG***GTGCAAAGACGGAGGACCACTCCAACTCAGACCAGAAAGCCCTCGGCATGATGGGGCT**

2701 **GGTGCGGCGGGACACAGCCCTGCTCCTCCGAGACTTCCGCCTGGGTGCCTCCTCATGGCT**

2761 **CAACTCCTTCCTGGAGTTAAGTGGGCGCAAGTCCCAGAAGATGTCGGAGCCCATAGCAG***A*

2821 *GCCGATGCGCCGCAGTGTGTCTGAAGCAGCACTGGCCCAGCCCCAGGGCCCACTGGGCAC*

2881 *GGATTCCCTCAAGAACCTGACCCTGAGGGACTTGAGCCTGAGGGGAAACTCCGAGACGTC*

2941 *GTCGGACACCCCCGAGATGTCGCTGTCAGCTGAGACACTTAGCCCCTCCACACCCTCCGA*

3001 *TGTCAACTTCTTATTACCACCTGAGGATGCAGGGGAAGAGGCTGAGGCCAAAAATGAGCT*

3061 *GAGCCCCATGGACAGAGGCCTGGGC* ***GTCC(A)GT*** *GCCGCCTTCCCCGAGGGTTTCCACCCCCG*

3121 *ACGCTCCAGCCAGGGTGCCACACAGATGCCCCTCTACTCCTCACCCATAGTCAAGAACCC*

3181 *CTTCATGTCGCCGCTGCTGGCACCCGACAGCATGCTCAAGAGCCTGCCAC TGTGCACAT*

3241 *CGTG*GCGTGCGCGCTGGACCCCATGCTGGACGACTCGGTCATGCTCGCGCGGCGACTGCG

3301 **CAACCTGGGCCAGCCGGTGACGCTGCGCGTGGTGGAGGACCTGCCGCACGGCTTCCTGAC**

3361 **CCTAGCGGCGCTGTGCCGCGAGACGCGCCAGGCCGCAGAGCTGTGCGTGGAGCGCATCCG**

3421 **CCTCGTCCTCACTCCTCCCGCCGGAGCCGGGCCGAGCGGGGAGACGGGGGCTGCGGGGGT**

3481 **AGACGGGGGCTGCGGGGGGCGACACTAA**AAGCCTGTTGTTCCCATCTGCGCCGGCCTCCG

3541 TCATGAATGCCTTCCGGGCCGGGCGGAAGGGGACGCGGGCTGTGCCTTACTTAAGTCGGG

3601 GGTGGCAAGGGGGCGGGGCGGGGGCCCGAAAGCTGAGACCCTCGCCACGGGGAGGGGGAC

3661 GCGCACACACACCGGTCACCGAGACGGCTGGACCTGCACGCCACCGCTGCCTTTTGCTGC

3721 TGCTGCTGCGGCGACCGCCG CAGGGACGGGGACTGGCCCTCCCTTGCAGGTCGGTTTGGT

3781 TTGTTGTAAATAAAAGTATTTAATTAGTTTGGCAAAAAAAAAAAAAAAA

Missense Mutations

Mutations that code for another amino acid.

Translated codon from mRNA: tac = tyrosine (Y)
Mutation c for t = cac
Translated cac = histidine (H)

Translated codon from mRNA: cgt = arginine (R)
Mutation a for c = agt
Translated agt = serine (S)

Translation

Amino acids coded for lipase

MEPGSKSVSRSDWQPEPHQRPITPLEPGPE KTPIAQPESKTLQGSNTQQKPASNQRPLTQQETPAQHD
*AESQKEPRAQQKSASQEEFLAPQKPAPQQSP*___Y(H)___*IQRVLLTQQEAASQQGPGLGKESITQQEPALRQRH*
VAQPGPGPGEPPPAQQEAESTPAAQAKPGAKREPSAPTESTSQETPEQSDKQTTPVQGAKSKQGSLTELG
FLTKLQELSIQRSALEWKALSEWVTDSESESDVGSSSDTDSPATMGGMVAQGVKLGFKGKSGYKVMSG
*YSGTSPHEKTSARNHRHYQDT***ASRLIHNMDLRTMTQSLVTLAEDNIAFFSSQGPGETAQRLSGVF**
AGVREQALGLEPALGRLLGVAHLFDLDPETPANGYRSLVHTARCCLAHLLHKSRYVASNRRSIFFR
TSHNLAELEAYLAALTQLRALVYYAQRLLVTNRPGVLFFEGDEGLTADFLREYVTLHKGCFYGRCL
GFQ*FTPAIRPFLQTISIGLVSFGEHYKRNETGL***SVAASSLFTSGRFAIDPELRGAEFERITQNLDVHFW**
KAFWNITEMEVLS*SLANMASATVRVSRLLSLPPEAFEMPLTADPTLTVTISPPLAHTGPGPVLVRLISYDL*
*REGQ***DSEELSSLIKSNGQRSLELWPRPQQAPRSRSLIVHFHGGGFVAQTSRSHEPYLKSWAQELG**
APIISIDYSLAPEAPFPRALEECFFAYCWAIKHCALL*GSTGERICLAGDSAGGNLCFTVALRAAAYGVR*
*VPDGIMAAYPATMLQPAASPSRLLSLMDPLLPLSVLSKCVSAYA***GAKTEDHSNSDQKALGMMGLVRD**
TALLLRDFRLGASSWLNSFLELSGRKSQKMSEPIA*EPMRRSVSEAALAQPQGPLGTDSLKNLTLRDL*
*SLRGNSETSSDTPEMSLSAETLSPSTPSDVNFLLPPEDAGEEAEAKNELSPMDRGLGV*___R(S)___*AAFPEGFH*
*PRRSSQGATQMPLYSSPIVKNPFMSPLLAPDSML****KSLPPVHIVACALDPMLDDSVMLARRLRNLGQP***
VTLRVVEDLPHGFLTLA**ALCRETRQAAELCVERIRLVLTPPAGAGPSGETGAAGVDGGCGGRH**

Appendix B

The Initiation of Life

The predominant theory is that RNA came first, before DNA, since the RNA molecules were able to act as enzymes, or catalysts, to the basic reactions required for life. Certain catalytic RNA molecules are known as ribosomes, and they exist as a construction factory for proteins. Eventually, RNA also catalyzed the construction of DNA to encode the formulas for these reactions in genes, and it also transcribed those genes before transporting the code to the ribosomes. But primitive Earth was covered in oceans and had no oxygen to speak of, and RNA breaks down in water. It would require other minerals or elements to stabilize the molecule, namely molybdenum and boron, which were scarce on early Earth but not on Mars.

Basically, the formula for life would go something like this:

methane + ammonia + hydrogen + lightning = brown primordial soup

brown primordial soup = hydrogen cyanide + amino acids

hydrogen cyanide + amino acids + boron (which helps to form and steady five-carbon sugar molecules like rearranged stable ribose, from which the "R" in RNA is derived) + oxygenated molybdenum (the catalyst that rearranges these sugars to make ribose) + soluble phosphorus (the backbone of RNA, DNA, and proteins) = RNA.

Eventually, this process gave rise to single-celled organisms and the basis of all life: the cell.

Glossary

ACREV – Asteroid/Comet Redirect Vehicle, a robotic spacecraft that tows asteroids and comets from distant locations like the Kuiper Belt to more accessible sites in the solar system

EVA – Extravehicular Activity, i.e., a spacewalk

GALRES – Galactic Resources, a mining company that prospects for and excavates mineral and other resources in extraterrestrial locations

HAB – Habitat, a self-contained module for habitation on Mars, the moon, or other extraterrestrial locations

ISA – International Space Agency, a Swiss-based international organization concerned with space travel and planetary exploration

ISPP – In Situ Propellant Plant, a factory for producing rocket fuel (methane) and oxygen from local resources, namely carbon dioxide

MADVEC – Mars Ascent/Descent Vehicle, a spacecraft designed to descend to Mars from orbit and re-achieve orbit from the planet's surface. It docks with the *Phoenix*, and other interplanetary spacecraft too cumbersome or not designed to penetrate the atmosphere.

Bibliography

ALTO, NEAL M.; DIXON, JACK E.; AND NAVARRO, LORENA. (2005) Functions of the *Yersinia* effector proteins in inhibiting host immune responses. *Current Opinion in Microbiology* 8(1): 21–27.

DAYAL, DISHA; MARTIN, SEAN M.; LIMOLI, CHARLES L.; SPITZ, DOUGLAS R. (2008) Hydrogen peroxide mediates the radiation-induced mutator phenotype in mammalian cells. *Biochemical Journal* 413(1): 185–191.

FRIEDMAN, JACOB MD AND KESSLER, GERALD MD. (2015) Metabolism of Fatty Acids and Glucose. *Circulation*. Correspondence.

HOCHACHKA, PETER W. (1998) Mechanism and Evolution of Hypoxia-Tolerance in Humans. *The Journal of Experimental Biology* 201(8): 1243–1254.

ROSA, ANGELO O. AND RAPOPORT, STANLEY I. (2009) Intracellular- and extracellular-derived Ca^{2+} influence phospholipase A_2-mediated fatty acid release from brain phospholipids. *Biochim Biophys Acta* 1791(8): 697–705.

SOMMER, CESAR A.; STADTFELD, MATTHIAS; MURPHY, GEORGE; HOCHEDLINGER, KONRAD; KOTTON, DARRELL N.; MOSTOSLAVSKY, GUSTAVO. (2008) Induced Pluripotent Stem Cell Generation Using a Single Lentiviral Stem Cell Cassette. *Stem Cells* 27(3): 543-549.

UDPA, NITIN; RONEN, ROY; ZHOU, DAN; LIANG, JUNBIN; STOBDAN, TSERLING; APPENZELLER, OTTO; YIN, YE; DU, YUANPING; GUO, LIXIA; CAO, RUI; WANG, YU; JIN, XIN; HUANG, CHEN; JIA, WENLONG; CAO, DANDAN; GUO, GUANGWU; CLAYDON, VICTORIA E.; HAINSWORTH, ROGER; GAMBOA, JORGE L.; ZIBENIGUS, MEHILA; ZENEBE, GUTA; XUE, JIN; LIU, SIQI; FRAZER, KELLY A.; LI, YINGRUI; BAFNA, VINEET; HADDAD, GABRIEL G. (2014) Whole genome sequencing of Ethiopian highlanders reveals conserved hypoxia tolerance genes. *Genome Biology* 15(2): R36.

ZHOU, DAN; HADDAD, GABRIEL G. (2013) Genetic Analysis of Hypoxia Tolerance and Susceptibility in *Drosophila* and Humans. *Annual Review of Genomic and Human Genetics* 14(1): 25-44.

Gene information derived from the National Center for Biotechnology Information, NCBI.

Acknowledgements

A novel of this size and detail is rarely a solitary effort. I would like to thank the following people for their invaluable assistance.

Jeremy Graaskamp, an aerospace engineer, provided technical expertise and opinions regarding space travel, spacecraft development, and the terraforming of Mars. He also guided me in some plot considerations. I'm truly grateful for the time he spent on this novel in his very busy schedule.

Deborah Booth made a number of critical observations regarding character and plot on the original draft, which forced me to focus more deeply on the mystery. I really appreciate her comments.

Rachel Eugster, my wonderful editor, has once again smoothed and tenderized my rough draft, polishing it in her usual insightful way. I both love and hate the red marks, but honestly appreciate how necessary they are.

My amazing daughter, Jessica Jackson, has taken on the challenge of cover design, interior design, and typesetting. Her talent is truly impressive!

To my husband, Brian, and son, Liam, (and Jessica, too) thank you for continuing to support my writing endeavours. You are constantly by my side, even through the darkest moments.

I would like to take a moment to thank MIT for providing online courses that helped me refresh my education in biology and establish a basis for my research into genetic engineering.

My last, but certainly never least, nod is to my readers. Thank you for reading and expressing your opinions. A book is only complete once it's read. I hope you enjoyed the story, and I welcome your input for the next one.

About the Author

Deborah Jackson received a science degree from the University of Ottawa in 1986, graduated from the Winghill Writing School in Ottawa in 2001, and is the author of several science fiction and historical fiction novels. Deborah is a member of the Society of Children's Book Writers and Illustrators and SF Canada. Her novels include *Ice Tomb* and *Sinkhole*, adult science fiction thrillers, the Time Meddlers series for children, ages 9–14 *(Time Meddlers, Time Meddlers Undercover* and *Time Meddlers on the Nile),* and the eerie ghost story, *Mosaic*. Articles about Deborah and reviews of her books have appeared in the *Ottawa Citizen, MORE Magazine, RT BOOKclub Magazine, Canadian Teacher Magazine, SF Site, Neo-opsis Science Fiction Magazine,* and many more.

Thank you for purchasing my book.
Connect with me online:

Website: www.deborahjackson.co
Blog: www.deborahjackson.co/#!blog/c112v
Twitter: twitter.com/DeborahJackson5
Facebook: www.facebook.com/DeborahJacksonFictionandPhotography
Google: plus.google.com/u/0/112408648937674336682/posts

65156425R00289

Made in the USA
Charleston, SC
12 December 2016